THE BOWL IS
ALREADY BROKEN

Mary Kay Zuravleff

BLOOMSBURY

First published in Great Britain 2005
This paperback edition published 2006

Copyright © 2005 by Mary Kay Zuravleff

The moral right of the author has been asserted

Bloomsbury Publishing Plc,
36 Soho Square,
London W1D 3QY

A CIP catalogue record for this book is
available from the British Library

ISBN 0 7475 7936 9
9780747579366

10 9 8 7 6 5 4 3 2 1

Printed in Great Britain by Clays Ltd, St Ives plc

www.bloomsbury.com/marykayzuravleff

For Theo Matthew Zizka and Eliza Lee Zizka,
whom I love to distraction

Part I

All Fall Down

Museum of Asian Art, National Institution of

Science and Art, Washington, D.C.

January 7, 2000, 9:30 a.m.

When the dust settled, there was only dust, and the Chinese bowl rested in pieces at the bottom of the museum steps. Experts had admired the bowl's radiant white exterior as much as the decoration within, an elaborate scene of magpies lighting on plum branches in full flower. Unfortunately, the distinction between interior and exterior grew fainter with each step the vessel bounced. This morning's tumble threw the magpies from their perches and reduced the plum branches to so much mulch, which was too bad, because only thirty minutes earlier, a dozen staff and dignitaries had gathered to welcome the porcelain into the museum's permanent collection.

Promise Whittaker was the ceremony's emcee. She may have been a petite, cartoon-voiced scholar whose home life could be generously described as chaotic, but she was also acting director of the Museum of Asian Art. The spotlight shining upon her seemed more like a searchlight, and she felt about as honored by her title as she did by her pregnancy. She was trying to rise to both occasions. For today's affair, she had stepped bravely into heels, fluffed her hair up above her widow's peak, and lengthened her eyelashes—anything to make more of herself. Being six months pregnant filled her out too, but it also swelled and loosened her vulnerable ankles.

Before she'd left home that morning, Leo had helped her on with her coat. "You look like my second wife," he had said, which she knew was supposed to be flattering but made her wonder if she had overdone the makeup. Then he gave her, his first and only wife, an exaggerated kiss, slipping a hand inside her worn lapel to palm the fruity curve of her breast. Whatever juices that act stirred up agitated the baby, and Leo drew back, transforming his randy gesture into a pointed finger. "Don't forget to hold on to the banister. Those stairs get slick." Pregnancy did that to husbands, made them lascivious one minute and absurdly overprotective the next. Unfortunately, his warning aroused her fears that her feet or her bladder could easily give way beneath her.

Although Promise was forty-three, to the crowd at the bottom of the museum's extravagant central staircase she looked like an eighth-grader playing dress-up. Neither wardrobe nor makeup could mask her turned-up nose or her unshakable faith in the Institution. Many accused her of being naïve, and it was true that her loyalty kept over-shadowing the hard evidence: she'd practically grown up at the museum under the protective wing of R. Joseph Lattimore, the former director.

She showed plenty of skepticism in her field, where she cast a discerning eye on manuscript pages illuminating the poetry of Jalaluddin Rumi. In royal workshops of the sixteenth century, court artists had put together albums of manuscripts and taken them apart, but so had centuries of con artists. Promise was alert to their wiles, suspicious in a way she hadn't expected would be necessary with her employer.

Promise had been acting director of the museum for two queasy months, and she climbed the polished marble steps mindful of her condition. Cecil Hawthorne, Secretary of the Institution, was at her heels, close and wavering as a shadow. He could no longer straighten all the way up, and he trod carefully on his unreliable old-man legs, lest he take the fall that separated the emeritus from the fully retired.

Neither Promise's hormonal tidal wave nor the Secretary's palsied limbs were remarkable in this gathering. Two of Cecil's bosses followed tentatively behind him: the head of the Board of Regents and the chief justice of the United States. In fact, the thin, wide steps might have been slabs of ice the way the procession of twelve minced and clutched.

Here was the ambassador, who'd earlier thrown over his morning coffee for a mug of whiskey to fortify himself before surrendering his bowl to the museum. Next came Arthur Franklin, the curator of Chinese ceramics, who had finessed this exceptional specimen from the ambassador; Arthur's excitement and anxiety, in combination with antidepressants and megavitamins, made him volatile as rocket fuel. Arthur was trailed by the two ancillary directors, Zemzemal Assaad and Talbot Perry, who were in charge of the museum's finances and administration, respectively. Zemzemal had moved some columns left, and some right, to fund this purchase. Talbot, who had essentially been second-in-command to Joseph, had himself expected to take Joseph's place.

Madame Xingfei was also in attendance. The last living link to the Founder, she had to be 110 by now. She represented the museum's Advisory Committee—it was Madame X who'd told Promise that the vote for acting director had not been unanimous. And Min Chen was present too, for she was both Madame X's protégée and the museum's curator of ancient Chinese art. For the sake of the ambassador's bowl and other complicated reasons, Min had raised a great deal of money. Put bluntly, she was pinning her hopes for a son on the auspicious outcome of this event. The last two members of the group were the museum photographer, who was unaccustomed to seeing people in the museum, and the conservator, who usually avoided the stairs because of her foot problems.

And so, even before disaster struck, they were a jittery, fragile corps.

Promise wished she could turn the clock back six months to the days in her basement office, where she'd padded around the stalagmites of books sprouting up from her overlapping Turkish rugs. She loved excavating all the commentaries published on a single manuscript page. To paint the falcon's feathers, had the artist used a brush made from a squirrel's whisker or the chin hairs of a kitten? Is it true that depicting the floor treatments—parquet, enameled tiles, and elaborate carpets, all in a space three inches wide—permanently damaged the artist's eyes? Such efforts could fill an entire afternoon then, back when Joseph was director, she and Leo had only two children, and the museum's future was secure. Her specialty being sixteenth-century paintings devoted to a thirteenth-century Persian poet, she was practiced at turning back time; meanwhile, the crowd let her know that their clock was ticking.

Farther up the central staircase Promise led her entourage, quiet except for Arthur, whose heel taps applauded him on every step. She escorted them up the grand approach to the disappointing summit, for the peak was nothing more than a narrow terrazzo landing. Still, she was glad to have made it this far.

Corridors to the galleries branched off east and west. Directly ahead was a glass wall looking out onto a fountain and lush foliage that was home to two pairs of peacocks. The Founder himself had designed his Asian museum in Washington, D.C., employing an Italianate style popular among captains of industry. He'd sketched a square building, each side a block long, surrounding a central square "open to the sky but closed to visitors." The pink waxy camellias in the courtyard seemed cut from the same cloth as Promise's maternity dress. Lined up against the glass, the four leggy birds gathered to watch the festivities.

"Orioles used to roost there," Cecil Hawthorne said to Promise. "Back when I first came." She assumed that was the era captured in the portrait hanging in his Castle office. In that oil painting, Cecil posed alongside the bicentennial laurel, which had long ago rotted from the inside out. Nearly bald, with his increasingly hunched back and dangling arms, the Secretary now resembled the leafless weeping maple near the Founder's urn. He said, "Once, Joseph brought me a prothonotary warbler that had flown into the glass."

Promise didn't want to talk about Joseph or the bird, presumably dead of a broken neck. She wished she could escape the museum's dank tomb smell, which all the sophisticated electrostatic air cleaning couldn't filter out. She said, "It's been years since we've acquired such a significant piece. This bowl might have ended up in an auction house." She patted Cecil's twig of an arm. "How good of you to help us celebrate."

Cecil patted her in return. "It's probably the last time, dear."

Her own husband had ultimately convinced her that the Castle's plot was graver than the usual budgetary threat. Leo had been waging his campaign of shame up the rungs of the Institution's ladder; it was to his credit that the Secretary, the head of the Board of Regents, and the chief justice had all agreed to attend this ceremony and a subsequent meeting.

From where he stood, Arthur Franklin heard the chirp of Promise's voice and wondered if it reminded the Secretary of a particular species. Viewing the silver wisps stretched across the old man's shiny scalp prompted Arthur to run his fingers through his own hair, wavy temple all the way to his cashmere-covered shoulder. Anyone with hair like Arthur's would keep it long, and he wore fitted suits with an antique sensibilty; today's ensemble might have been updated from one in a daguerreotype. One week in, the year 2000 held great promise for Arthur, if he continued to have a job.

"Aren't you posh," the ambassador said, and the curator bowed slightly in reply. "I presume your vest is Japanese silk."

"Meiji period," Arthur acknowledged. "My tailor bought a bolt from an old geisha kimono supplier, or so his story goes." He pointed the Secretary out so the ambassador wouldn't be disappointed by such little ceremony. "Cecil usually attends only bird-related events. There's the chief justice, and that banker type is a regent, I'm pretty sure."

The ambassador clasped his shaky hands together. Before his wife had left him, he'd come upon her searching their vault for this very bowl. She'd apparently forgotten that they'd loaned the wedding present out, and she was looking to smash it to bits. The ambassador said, "Our bowl will be the first thing visitors see."

My bowl, Arthur wanted to gloat. When they'd started up the staircase, it was all he could do not to fight his way to the front of the line. The reviews his exhibition had been enjoying and the sight of his book, featured in the museum shop next to his author photograph, were soon to be capped by this fine example of Jingdezhen ware. He wished Morty could be here. Maybe then he'd understand the urges to which Arthur had succumbed in pursuit of the porcelain. How else to show that the museum was at the peak of its powers?

A low winter sun shone through the huge plates of courtyard glass, projecting the peacocks' shadows onto the landing, and the beveled edges of the panes bent the white light into prismatic stripes here and there. Peacocks and rainbows—Arthur would not be surprised if a harpist and some winged cherubs showed up next. He'd talked the art handlers into lifting off the glare-proof German-glass vitrine, allowing the bowl to shine forth like a full moon. Its glowing countenance reflected the courtyard sky, a patch of turquoise with spindly clouds. Arthur was in such a reverie that when Talbot Perry cuffed his shoulder, he barely thought about palming his ass.

Chitchat subsided as people turned their attention toward Promise.

She was so short she had to stand on a step stool to rise above the bowl; at six months along, she was so rotund her belly cast a shadow like an eclipse on the porcelain. From atop her perch, she could see the length of the corridors. Maps on placards lined the hallways as if this were a map museum; at the far western end stood a fourteenth-century Japanese temple monster—ten writhing feet of wood—guarding a ficus. She needed to draw the art out of the galleries, sprinkle it through the hallways like bread crumbs to entice the visitors.

Although a peacock and peahen couple scratched at the courtyard window, Promise ignored their antics, directing everyone's gaze from the glass box at her back to the pedestal in front of her. In Arthur's cosmology, to look upon the white bowl was to see the face of God. Nearly three hundred years ago, the bowl had survived trial by fire, once to melt the clear glaze on its moon-white body and then as many trips to the kiln as there were colors painted on the inside. Here was another crucible for it to pass through.

Leo and Talbot had coached her to speak as if the museum were set in perpetuity. Hoping her faith sounded deeper than her voice, she held forth from her pulpit. "My hardworking colleagues, what museums do best is preserve what is valuable. On this day, when we welcome such an important porcelain into our permanent collection, I am deeply honored to be this museum's acting director."

Arthur Franklin felt his customary pang of jealousy. They could not have chosen a less likely acting director than Promise, a fortyish pregnant woman *from Oklahoma*, who was married to a guy who smoked dope and wore socks with sandals. Imagine his surprise when the Advisory Committee let scholarship sway their decision. He consulted his pocket watch, an affectation he shared with the former director.

Gas burned a hot blue flame beneath Promise's sternum, the result of coffee, nerves, and compromised internal organs (the baby was sitting on her bladder, hammering her ribs like an inspired marimba player). When her reflux abated, she couldn't help but smile affectionately at the gathered. She said, "To acquire this work of art, we've depended on your profound friendship, another reminder that we must all stick together."

Was she *trying* to make Arthur feel like a heel? The diamond studs in her lobeless ears winked at him. Used to be, if she had research to do at the Met and he had to court a Park Avenue dowager with a nice set of ginger jars, they would make a day of it. He'd heard she couldn't manage India very well, but she crisscrossed Manhattan as handily as an item on one of her endless lists. They had been on the train together when she told him Joseph had promoted her to chief curator. Then she'd softened the sting by asking him to help her splurge on diamond earrings, and they'd haggled their way, arm in arm, through the diamond district. Those earrings were the nicest thing she owned. She'd bought them, but he took the credit.

Up on her step stool, Promise should have been bragging rather than giving a sermon. Next she'd be quoting her beloved Rumi. If only Joseph were up there on this, Arthur's day of days. With his booming voice and broad swagger, the former director could move crowds—just as he could move furniture and, when absolutely necessary, at least one small tree. R. Joseph Lattimore was sorely missed not because he was a great fund-raiser or administrator but because everyone at the museum had something of a crush on him. Joseph would have elevated Arthur's bowl into a cultural keystone and Arthur into a hero: *Multitudes throng to save any Renaissance painting, and yet Asian civilizations endure because of your singular connoisseurship! Every object you attend to is a relic of a vanishing world.*

Promise was keenly aware she was not Joseph. When they'd needed an interim director, they'd chosen her, a scholar dedicated to the cult of Rumi. She could talk for days about her Sufi, whose mystical writings on love and devotion had set the dervishes whirling and were still turning people inside out. But for purposes of this ceremony, she focused on the ceramic before her. To her discerning eye, this bowl was just the right size for heating half a bag of frozen peas in the microwave. Its asymmetry was hardly an asset (requiring that the mount be built up on the right like an orthopedic shoe), its white glaze seemed ordinary, and the birds on the inside looked like mottled, long-tailed crows. Min Chen, the curator of ancient Chinese art, had told her the interior painting was an entreaty to bear sons. Arthur had a different translation, but he also proclaimed its imperfections intentional and the glaze transcendent.

Promise said, "Arthur Franklin regards this piece of Jingdezhen ware as unparalleled. I believe that, and I salute him. The *Times* deems it priceless, which I don't buy. Ambassador Young donated half the funds necessary to bring this bowl into the museum's permanent collection, and we wholeheartedly thank him. Permit me to crow about my staff's exemplary work as well. I cherish you all; as Jalaluddin Rumi wrote, 'If every tip of every hair on me could speak, I still couldn't say my gratitude.'"

She extended her hand to Arthur, and they struck a pose. In the light of the photographer's flash, Arthur detected hairline fissures on either side of Promise's mouth, stained half-moons beneath eyes crackled with red. They were the same age, and for a moment he wondered if the acting director gig would have aged him so swiftly. As Promise dismounted the step stool, she took hold of his sleeve so that he had to stroke the wool, lush as a pelt, to erase her mark. In so doing, he recalled stroking the plum blossoms inside his bowl, marveling at how the decoration was incised here, raised there. He could run his fingers all over a loan object, but after this ceremony, he'd have to make an appointment in storage for a supervised visit.

Arthur assumed his rightful place before the assembly. His gaze kept returning to the porcelain's fair face, radiant atop its pedestal at the landing's west edge. He said, "Behold the glory of Yongzheng imperial porcelain, crafted circa 1723. How well I remember meeting this piece for the first time. When I perfunctorily turned the bowl over, there was the clearest *yuzhi* mark I'd ever seen. When I held the bowl to the light, the near translucence of its thin walls and snowy glaze was a wonder. I remarked to the ambassador, our generous partial donor, that the piece looked as if it had never been used. He responded to my compliment by lifting a pitcher of water and emptying its entire contents into this vessel—" Arthur paused to let them gasp.

These people have forgotten they're looking at bowls, thought Min Chen, who did not gasp. All her life, she'd been slurping soup from bowls swimming with lotuses and fish and turtles. Like Arthur, she was a Chinese curator, though the bronze and jade pieces she championed came from layers older than topsoil; like Promise, she was pregnant, though not publicly. They were both of them, Promise and Arthur, taking credit the American way. Because Arthur had no concern for progeny, he read the bowl's decoration one way: "May you have joy up to your eyebrows." Superficial well-wishing, like a greeting card from the grocery store. The message, painted in the first half of the Qing dynasty but perhaps intended for her, actually read, "Winter offers the joy of a new life." Plum blossoms were a little too womanly for the hopes she harbored, but then wasn't she a woman? She made herself listen to Arthur as he returned to his story.

"Ambassador Young knew that water would magnify the astonishing details cupped within this porcelain, details we were given the opportunity to appreciate when he loaned it to my 'All Fired Up!' exhibition. Honestly, the condition report may as well be blank, because—ladies and gentlemen—this bowl does not have a scratch on it. This pristine example of *doucai* porcelain transports me to southern China, to an era of unprecedented artistry and innovation.

"In the last year of the Yongzheng reign," Arthur intoned, "an imperial artisan moistened a vat of pale powder, thinned, kneaded, and smoothed it into a lump of clay with no thought for this moment. His successor gave it shape; another rolled out a strip and, using water as glue, attached a foot beneath the bowl. Decorators in turn had their way with it, incising pink blossoms along a twisted branch and daubing glazes like icing to the petals. After each glaze they returned the bowl to the kiln, an inferno stoked until the heat could crumble bones."

Arthur consciously slowed his breathing; honestly, this bowl was capable of making him hyperventilate. Who knew how many were on hand at the bowl's creation? Scholars debated the numbers, the way theologians squabbled over Man's creation out of dust. Did God act alone? Did anyone?

Impatient with Arthur's idolatry, Talbot Perry drummed his long fingers on his folded arms. Maybe if their little mausoleum had fewer drama queens, the Castle would have included them in its future plans. Even Arthur's outfit was too much, his jacket cut like a morning coat. Rewrap his tie into a floppy bow and fan out his ridiculous hair, and Arthur could be meeting Whistler after the ceremony.

Talbot was of two minds about this ceremony. He'd grudgingly come to respect Promise, having long discounted her as Joseph's pet. Still, gusto in general rankled him—curators were supposed to be critical and, above all, cautious. By acquiring this one expensive bowl, Promise intended to show that the Museum of Asian Art was not only a player but also a winner, deserving of its place on the National Mall. Talbot had a more radical plan for getting the Castle's attention, and he was eager to see which way the chips might fall.

Arthur sighed aloud, lifting his palms to heaven in a show of reverence. He said, "There was such specialization among porcelain artists that generations of a single family painted carp exclusively. On our bowl, it is probable that one painter depicted the plum branches, a second the buds, a third the blossoms. Among the bird painters, perhaps the tasks were as distinct as feathers, shafts of feathers, and muscles beneath feathers, all of which can be perceived through the humble magnification of water." Once this bowl entered the museum coffers, it would never know water or dust again—to touch the rim to his lower lip, guzzling noodles until the magpies were visible beneath lunch, would be impossible.

As much as he'd yearned for this moment, Arthur was suffering. His heartache was that of an animal lover at a zoo: While captivity may be necessary, it is not natural. He beckoned for the ambassador to join him at the front and, because he had a crush on him, Talbot. Cecil came too, prompting Promise to follow. The lineup represented the top of the Castle food chain: collector, curator, acting and ancillary directors, and Secretary of the Institution.

Arthur was staging a full-blown curtain call. One second, he was taking a bow on behalf of his bowl; the next, he was working the porcelain free from its mount, going so far as to bend back one of the coated wires that gripped the foot. *I'm overdoing it*—the thought ran across his brain like the crawl on the cable news screen. He might have damaged the mount. At the very least, the piece would have to be cleaned again, making this installation ceremony entirely bogus.

Whether the ambassador interpreted Arthur's antics as an invitation or he wanted to bid a symbolic farewell to his adored, cheating wife, he stepped closer to the porcelain. Its satin sheen was smooth as her forehead after a Botox treatment. *Auf Wiedersehen, mein Liebchen.*

Promise did not like where things were going. Arthur was recklessly waving the bowl around, when he of all people knew they'd staged this event to secure the bowl's permanence. Worse was the ambassador taking custody of the bowl and lifting it to his face. Given the tang of his breath, Promise was determined to reclaim the vessel before his lips touched its glaze. She had to raise up on her toes to grab the sides of the bowl, overlapping his manicured nails with her dishpan hands, then working her fingers over his. Just as she registered that the porcelain was remarkably cool to the touch—like any bowl perhaps but not like any piece of art—the ambassador let go, throwing her off balance. At that moment, it seemed the baby gave her a jolt from inside as well.

Everything was happening at once. Arthur saw his rash gesture degenerate into a game of hot potato. He followed Promise's agile move left, but it turned out she was faking. Outside the frame of his glasses, she twisted right and passed off to Talbot, whose hands had palmed a thousand basketballs. When Talbot returned the bowl to Arthur, all should have been made right. Arthur's fingers knew the piece by heart: his right hand instantly appreciated the thin flared lip of the very top; his left, the thicker and rougher unglazed bottom edge of the foot. But there was movement to the bowl, backspin perhaps, and while he had his hands on the porcelain, he did not have a handle on it. Arthur was the one who had picked up the piece. Technically, he was also the one who dropped it.

The bowl cracked loud against the base of its custom-made pedestal. Still intact, it rolled along its rim to the stair's edge, then bowled itself over. With each step, the break was rendered more irreparable: flakes of glaze chipped off, the foot kicked away from the body. About six treads down, the vessel halved at the initial fissure. Crumbs started mounting up after that.

The mob gasped—to think they'd earlier gasped over water touching the bowl!—and their hands shot up in the air as if the bowl had pulled a gun on them.

A peahen cried out in the courtyard. Witnessing the bowl's chalky disintegration, Promise wanted to cry out too. With this disaster, Joseph's office was destined to become an egg-roll stall, a deep fryer positioned where his desk currently sat. Japanese screens would be stashed to free up storage for foam cups and their clever lids. She hadn't wanted to be acting director, but she hadn't wanted to fail at it either.

Conceivably, there were people who could shrug off such an accident. These things happen, they might say. Pragmatic people far outside the museum world might observe that if Chinese porcelains lasted forever, museums would be unnecessary. Or they could point to the collection, which included hundreds of clay bowls, many from China and most far older. For this crowd, however, there was no other world. Having enjoyed centuries of pampered care, the designated masterpiece crumbled into dustpan fodder within sight of its caretakers, who were similarly cracked or chipped or completely devastated.

Only Arthur Franklin ran to the bottom of the stairs. A lifelong advocate of smoking and inactivity, he would not have predicted he could sprint down those wide, flat steps, his heel taps rat-a-tat-tatting through the vast art temple. He flung himself down the steps the way a widow, crazed with bereavement, might leap into her husband's grave, the way a mother might plunge into rapids after her toddler, even though the dive meant certain death. His act brought women to mind, because what man would so jump after his dish? Without a thought for himself—which for Arthur was as earth-shattering as the act he followed.

Though he arrived prepared to resuscitate, there was no pulse—no body even! Severed from the bowl was the foot, which he had derided as clumsy, although stolid as it was, it remained more intact than the rest of the piece. Rubble smaller than shards—*and shards are pretty small!* He extracted one of the larger chunks, incised and painted and glazed. He might have collapsed in tears as he held the jagged chip, or he might have used it to slice his wrist, falsettos surging around him as in every Beijing Opera finale he had ever seen. What he might have done was preempted by what he did.

Arthur bowed his head over the wafer of porcelain, which he held with the reverence of a first communion. His chestnut hair fell forward, forming a privacy curtain around his upturned palms. All that the delicate vessel had endured was immaterial and had not served to further its existence.

Testifying before the flock, he hadn't even gotten to the bowl's astonishing provenance. Arthur was mortified to think how many people had touched the vessel without harming it when he who loved it best had destroyed it. In his fog, he heard the sound of a stampede rushing down the staircase toward him. He felt a little woozy, either not himself or more completely himself than he'd ever been, as he slipped the souvenir of his beloved bowl into his silken vest pocket.

From Mughal Court to Food Court

Six months earlier—July 6, 1999

Joseph Lattimore's assistant brought in the mail, curtsying for comic effect. "Your correspondence, good sir. Do you wish me to review it?"

Slender, expensively dressed, she was the latest in a parade of young women who invariably left for graduate school just after learning how to submit travel forms; however, their model looks and confidence made them particularly talented at handling potential donors. Joseph brandished his jade letter opener. "On a slow midsummer's day such as this, I shall slice open my own dispatches."

"Very well," she continued in her loyal-subject way. "I assume it's the usual stack of honorary degrees and museum accolades."

He waited for her to leave before straining to reach the far corner of his desk. Better curb the bourbon and crème brûlée, restart his hiking habit. He and his wife had a custom of identifying people by the artist most likely to model their features, and in the body types of art history, he resembled a Breughel peasant, though not as bulbous or stooped—perhaps a George Bellows boxer gone slack.

Joseph was feeling rather low; returning to work after Independence Day was a greater letdown each year. The Mall had started filling with people on Friday, a flood that brought his museum a welcome runoff. Early Sunday morning, folks staked a claim to any turf they could find. Stages abounded, where a Sousa-playing marine band was followed by a rogue Appalachian fiddler. There were families as far as the eye could see, and when it got dark a grand fireworks display. All he'd ever wanted was for these people to come on in to the Art Mahal, as his sons called the museum. Witness Asia's version of Sousa and Appalachia. Open your eyes to treasures beyond compare.

Eighteen years ago, Joseph had inherited this cabinet of curiosities, whose aging curators presented unchanging shows of ill-lit objects. The only other personnel were a janitor, two guards, and three conservators. Although the curators were men of great scholarly renown, their idea of an exhibition was to jam objects into display cases like clowns into a Volkswagen. Upon their eventual retirement, Joseph filled the ranks with gifted recruits. It had been a joy to enlist talent worthy of the Founder's collection. After that, he'd garnered funds to launch entire departments, including Exhibition Design, Publications, and Education. He hired a public affairs wizard, appointed Promise chief curator and Talbot ancillary director, and then brought on Zemzemal as a second ancillary director to commandeer finances. The museum's Advisory Committee, the old guard of Asian art, fretted over every change.

As for the awards he'd been given since he turned sixty, frankly, a little adulation offset the recurrent budget cuts of the last few years. Whether or not times are lean, continuity is important to a museum: you can't properly care for things when you always feel threatened. Walking the hallways had become like walking the streets of Calcutta, where mendicants pleaded for attention and discretionary funds. Little did they know how little there was for them. In acquisitions alone, they'd been reduced to buying belt buckles and jars with missing lids.

His assistant was back in the doorway, her regal posture abandoned. "Hey, you want a muffin? I'm going on break soon."

"No, thank you." Joseph patted his gut.

Poking out from the bundle was a photocopied memo on the Secretary's letterhead, with the picture of the Castle centered at the top. On the original stationery, the raised image was the brownish red of the actual building. He assumed his assistant had reviewed the notice, which was not in an envelope. The first sentence read: "Part of serving our public is recognizing their changing needs." You've written the right man, Joseph thought, for not all of us cater to the visitors. He regularly reminded his staff that Asian art had a message for novice and expert alike.

He checked the date, July 1, 1999, which meant the missive had leisurely traveled from the Castle to his office by interoffice mail. Someone could have walked it over in three minutes. Because of the Fourth, the memo had probably sat for days in the tunnel mail room, halfway between the two buildings. The page was a flimsy photocopy delivered faceup without a cover sheet, and so Joseph expected only minor praise or encouragement. Sailing smoothly along, he was thusly sent over the falls: "Mindful of our audience, we have revisited spatial allocations at the Museum of Asian Art with the goal of maximizing visitor use and comfort levels in the next fiscal year."

Joseph mucked through the infernal memo-speak, moaning with the effort. It read as if cinder blocks of jargon had been slurried and re-poured into this thin slab. The words pressed upon him: "We would be negligent to ignore the lack of food service on the National Mall. To fulfill our responsibilities, the decision has been made to reconfigure the Museum of Asian Art as a food court worthy of our guests."

Kayaking in icy water felt like this. Spearfishing, too, where the goal is to eat anything that doesn't eat you first. But a day in the office had never felt like this, and he couldn't recall why he'd ever courted the sensation. He'd been playing the sheet of paper like a slide trombone, straining with the effort to read without glasses. "Renowned throughout the Institution, the museum shop will be expanded; current management may be asked to stay during the transition period or beyond." At that sentence, he fell back into the arms of his complicated desk chair.

While he did not exactly believe he was invincible, Joseph prided himself on being harder to vince than most. Full grown at sixteen, he'd carved a tulip tree trunk into a canoe for tackling the Columbia River. At seventeen, he'd hiked Sourdough Mountain solo, carrying matches, pemmican, and the pocketknife that was more third thumb to him than tool. His approach to scholarship was similarly rugged. Pakistan, Afghanistan, Turkey, and, of course, India were the backdrops in the family photo albums. His specialty being the Islamic emperors of India's Mughal Empire, he and Emmy had honeymooned on a palace garden dig without running water or wine. In Fatehpur Sikri, Jules and Henry were but five and two when Ravi came along and then Sanjay, a mere fourteen months later. Joseph was writing a book about Akbar's Great Mosque, which Akbar had built in 1570 as thanks for his own two sons.

Joseph had grown accustomed to being lauded—at the very least, to leading. Now he sat openmouthed and gurgling as if he were in a dental chair, the memo lying upon his chest like a lead bib. He gazed out his east window, which was adorned with a mahogany carving in the style of a Mughal mosque. It had been fashioned for his Akbar exhibition, a show that had also inspired the designers to erect the inside of a dome beneath the gallery's ceiling. Afterward, the carving had been installed in his office, and through his filigreed portal, Joseph saw the Castle and the Mall the way he saw everything, with a distinctly Asian perspective.

Summer tourists crowded the periphery of the Haupt Garden like pilgrims along the Ganges. For many, camera and video gear offered more coverage than clothing. There was a family struggling with a stroller on the gravel path. Two lanky young people passed them, and the girl's navel glinted in the sun, perhaps a jeweled or pierced belly button. That was a recent phenomenon, as was the tattoo she had on her lower back. Sparrows bathed in the fountains and the dirt, sprinkling dust and water at the feet of an elderly couple. Swathed in long sleeves and trousers, they read the plaques on every bench and tree.

A summer-camp group of black children headed into African Art, and the two black families he saw were both walking toward that museum. African Americans came to African Art for all kinds of events; they were feisty-proud of their roots. Joseph had expected the same of Asian Americans at his museum, but the visitor count did not support him. His son Sanjay had told him the Asian kids who came to the museum were the ones adopted by white families.

Joseph looked beyond the formal garden and archways to the red stone towers of the Castle: some days, he could discern Cecil's hunched back in the wavy leaded glass of his tower window. Now his gaze traveled from Cecil's turret to his modest proposal, which played out beneath a photocopied impression of that very castle. "The National Gallery and the Museum of Natural History have agreed to accommodate the collection, which will stay together in separate venues. Our advisers maintain that the Founder's will, stipulating the care of these objects in perpetuity, could be honored in another location . . ."

As if trying to breathe on Everest, he could not fill his lungs. Memos like this one should come with their own oxygen tanks. How dare they toss off the Founder's will so casually! The Castle's advisers were not exploiting a loophole; on the contrary, their proposal was pure cheek. The Founder built the museum to house the art but neglected to specify that said art must remain in the aforementioned building. And what the hell did that mean, the collection "will stay together in separate venues"—either it's together or it's separate.

His first reaction was outrage on behalf of the Founder; his second was on behalf of the museum. Presumably, there were surveys, lawyers aplenty, and consultants leading this charge—it angered him to think of their fees compared with the sums recently denied for new banners to replace the wind-slashed, faded ones outside. He'd devoted his adult life to putting the Museum of Asian Art on the map; if the Castle decided they would prefer a dozen fast-food franchises where he had constructed an altar to the magnificence of Asia, really, what could he do? Paddling wouldn't help. A jackknife would not save him; nor would a snakebite kit or a tourniquet for that matter. Rescue gear implies the possibility of rescue.

Joseph picked up the phone, then returned it to its console. His thumbs pushed toward his vest pockets, stroking a roll of flab instead. Just this summer, he'd stopped wearing a vest—with the weight he'd put on, they'd begun to looked like corsets.

Might the memo be a joke? This notion calmed him, although he couldn't imagine who might stage such a sham. His staff did enjoy a good hoax. For his sixtieth birthday, they'd colluded to replace an album in Gallery XV with a birthday cake of the same dimensions. The book was displayed in a case about hip height, open flat to the page illustrating *Emperor Jahangir with Bow and Arrow*. Except that his staff had substituted his face for the emperor's, the sheet cake was a dead ringer for the seventeenth-century painting. Thinking he might get some scholarly insight from such a cunning forgery, he'd asked the designer to explain the frosting technology; alas, the jargon of scanners and computer graphics was beyond him. And so he appreciated the reproduction, down to the pearl necklace and the floral arabesques on his sash, as well as the re-created splotches where, on the original, the opaque watercolor had chipped off to show gold beneath. The proverbial icing on the cake was that they'd substituted his name in the inscription, written in the same *nastaliq* calligraphy as the original, "This is a portrait of R. Joseph Lattimore. May God continue his kingdom forever."

A touching prank that was, not so stroke-inspiring as this. His phone buzzed, and his assistant announced that Arthur Franklin was here to discuss a catalog cover. Sliding open his desk drawer, he laid aside the memo as well as his jade letter opener, which he noted could stab in a pinch—would he really defend his museum with office supplies?

Arthur swept in, ever the dandy in a linen suit the color of butter. Starched stiff, he made July look like March.

"Good to see you," Joseph said genuinely. He came out from behind his massive cherry desk to shake the curator's hand. Here was the most passionate man on his team, so fanatical he could be besotted by a common ginger jar. Aside from an unfortunate misattribution of a Chinese water dropper, Arthur had a decent enough eye.

Arthur said, "I've brought the cover treatments for 'All Fired Up!'"

"But not the Publications Department," Joseph noted wryly, as the curator fanned out his array on the coffee table. Arthur would have one believe he performed all his own stunts.

Joseph was tempted to show Arthur the memo on the chance he would proclaim it a fraud. What a relief to have someone pull this thorn from his fleshy paw! Arthur was arguably their best-connected staff member; he bummed cigarettes off museum guards and shared a beach house with the Portrait Gallery's director. His boyfriend was an undersecretary at the Department of Transportation and often in the *Post* as the highest-ranking gay member of the administration.

Arthur began narrowing the cover possibilities before Joseph had fully registered them. "Allow me," Joseph said, and Arthur backed off. The three remaining mock-ups each featured a loan object. "None of these is in our collection."

"You never know," Arthur said. "Someone like Ralph Kwan sees his cup on the cover of the catalog, maybe he'll write us into his will."

"Don't count on it. Putting a piece on the cover doubles the asking price." Joseph picked up the treatment of Kwan's peony cup, a lush red and yellow flower on a cinnabar-colored background. Its lines might have inspired William Morris or Rossetti.

Arthur jumped the gun. "That's my favorite, too! They laid on the enamels so thickly, they look like real flower petals. I was actually thinking about this one when I named the exhibition 'All Fired Up!' because they had to fire it separately for each layer of color." Though he could hear the panting in his voice, he was powerless to rein himself in. "It dates to around 1650, but the design seems more contemporary—almost Victorian, don't you think?"

Joseph shot him the same expression of reproof that Morty gave him at home. Arthur inwardly defended himself. What was he guilty of exactly—enthusiasm? If you couldn't gush to your partner or the director of your museum, what was the point?

Exchanging that cover for the next, Joseph studied the image of a yellow dish with a long green dragon rearing up like a cobra. He said, "Around 1550, the Jiajing emperor placed an order for twenty-five thousand bowls and fifty thousand dishes decorated with five-clawed dragons. You'd think these would be common as dirt."

The director always dropped some fact to let you know he was as familiar with your field as his own. Smart, intrepid, and the best writer by far, Joseph could take them all on. "Remind me," he said. "Who was assigned green dragons on a yellow background?"

Luckily, Arthur knew. "Concubines of the second and third order. I brought it because Publications said it's worth considering an image associated with Chinese art, like a dragon." He'd stuffed his bitten-down nails into his pockets.

"Did Publications single out any objects that we actually own?" In addition to the dragon dish, Joseph picked up a treatment of Ambassador Young's bowl with birds and plum blossoms. "At least these two aren't blue and white." Every congressman's wife with a willowware saucer had been in to see him about her precious antiques.

"With due respect, they *are* blue and white—see how the motifs are outlined in cobalt oxide?—but they're also 'tea dust' and 'oxblood' and 'mirror black.'" Arthur savored the names French collectors had assigned the colors. "The peony cup is the only one that's not blue and white; *falangcai*, it's called. The motifs are outlined in red enamel, then filled with yellow enamel, turquoise, chartreuse, and black enamels. It's also older and rarer."

"What did Promise say?" Joseph asked, knowing Arthur would have asked her advice.

"She chose something the Founder bought."

"Ah, the Founder." Joseph was glad someone cared about the old guy. Promise thought the Founder practically infallible—perhaps she should take a look at the memo on his desk.

Joseph lifted the image of the bird bowl up under Arthur's nose. "This one," he said. "The peony could be Dutch or English or even American. Besides, Hazel says ducks sell."

"Those are magpies."

"I can see that, Arthur. I am extrapolating."

"The shop manager picks catalog covers?"

Wearily, regretfully, the director said, "You'd be surprised how decisions are made." He used to have the luxury of discounting Hazel's advice. "Kiss of death," she'd warned him about an Islamic cover; the attic was full of his design choices.

Arthur had asked Ambassador Young himself if the museum could borrow the piece, which he loved—but he loved the graphic, lush peony cup a little more. Arthur would have used the bowl's provenance against it, if he could have figured out how to highlight Marlene Dietrich without mentioning Thomas Jefferson. It was surprising that Joseph didn't ask about past owners. Finally, Arthur appealed to the director's love of antiquity. He said, "That bowl merely dates to around 1730. Would you like Sam to shoot a grouping of the three finalists?"

"Too crowded," Joseph said. He slipped his watch from his pants, flipping open the huntsman's cover of a buck in the forest. It was a signal he'd established to end a meeting, and he didn't even register the time. Arthur gathered up his cover choices.

Joseph said, "Speaking of crowded, some of your exhibition cases need to be trimmed—say nine or ten pieces altogether." He wasn't sure if he was testing Arthur's loyalty or kicking the dog.

The curator stared at his boss, whose rallying cry was: Never underestimate the power of an original work of art. Arthur declared, "These are the greatest pieces of Jingdezhen ware ever to be shown together."

"So you've said. But you wouldn't want anyone to view them as bric-a-brac."

"Certainly not. Here's an idea: why not expand the gift shop and fill it with my bric-a-brac?" Arthur kept his voice even, but his hands had escaped. In his peripheral vision he could see them flailing about. "We could sell cappuccino in museum replicas—buy a Big Frothy, take home a ram's-head rhyton from old Assyria—" He wanted both to indulge in and resist the dramatics.

"Let's hope it doesn't come to that," Joseph excused him. He was relieved in a way to have set Arthur off; unfortunately, once he was gone, his hyperbole stayed. Joseph walked behind his desk to retrieve the memo, then paced the strip between couch and desk teasing apart the words in hopes of clearing an escape route. "We foresee one year as a viable transition period, during which time staffing needs will be resolved in accord with Institution policy." He read up one side and down the other, but all he could spot were two typos and the occasional factual error, whose presence rubbed salt in his deepening wound. It was Teddy Roosevelt, not Taft, who had accepted the Founder's gift of "Asian curiosities and books" on behalf of the American public. And the library accounted for one-fifth of their visitors; therefore, tossing the art but keeping the books about the art would not continue to serve "most" of their audience.

Nowhere was Joseph's input requested—this was a rout! Such a pronouncement should be calligraphed on vellum, imprinted with a wax seal or Cecil's signature in pure gold. Those assholes didn't even know how to do Important. Finally, Joseph experienced outrage on his own behalf. Copier paper was an insult, the same medium as the announcement regarding thermostat settings, and it was all he could do not to ball it up and throw it in his recycling bin. If you are coming for my head on a pike, have the courtesy to make a pageant of it.

Four sons, hundreds of eager students, and then a museum: Joseph was practiced at leading an army. He took as his model the tolerant Akbar, the Mughal emperor who had allowed his Hindu, Buddhist, Jain, Christian, and Zoroastrian subjects their religions, skimming the cream of their philosophy and artistic traditions for his own Islamic court. But Akbar also claimed Genghis Khan and Timur as his ancestors, and when people had felt compelled to cross swords with him, he had felt compelled to disembowel them.

Faced with mass extermination, Joseph's staff would not go gently. Wasn't Arthur's hysteria an indication? They would grab mace or shield, match pen against sword, in an endeavor to save what they deemed sacred. Much of the art in the museum portrayed violence too graphic for cable television. Whenever psychologists railed against the glorification of gore, he gave thanks that they didn't look at art. (He and Fatima Hakim, the Islamic curator, could stage an entire exhibition on severed heads and spilled guts.) The history he'd been safeguarding was a grim saga, one predicated on conquest. He would order Cecil doused with toner and burned alive with his own memos!

Joseph reached into his back pocket for a handkerchief and mopped his forehead, slick with sweat. So this was how righteous indignation gave way to bloodshed. For secession to be viable, he would need to raise an army—would that be easier than raising money for an Islamic show after the 1993 World Trade Center bombing? Speaking realistically, theirs was an old, well-heeled clientele who were pretty tapped out.

"Call Talbot," Joseph said to his assistant outside his office door, but before she swiveled in her chair, Talbot Perry materialized.

"Getting hungry?" he asked, noting that the memo Joseph held was from the Castle.

"Fine idea," Joseph said. One of Nathan's lunches would be suitable fare before a battle. "But first come inside. I require your opinion."

A veteran of closed-door sessions, Talbot swung the door forcefully enough to latch it without slamming, evidence of grace coupled with cunning. His exaggerated height and thin face were those of a young Byzantine saint; a thousand years later, the elongated figure populated Persian painting, whose artists had copped the style from Byzantine icons.

Despite his physique, Talbot was a curator of Japanese art. He'd also been a college basketball star, a defensive wonder who'd rarely scored but kept the other team from doing so. Talbot's stomach for dicey personnel issues had inspired Joseph to create the ancillary director position. The enigmatic curator didn't possess the passion for his subject matter that Joseph did for India, which was a disappointment, but that might be the fault of Japanese art.

The director sat behind his desk to hide his heaving chest. Blond hair and glasses aside, Talbot really did look like a clean-shaven young Byzantine—it was the way he bent like a willow, the way he inclined his head. Joseph passed him the offensive memo; while waiting for his reaction, he revisited the calligraphy framed on the opposite wall. Around 1530, Mir Ali had been abducted from his home to be a court scribe in Bukhara, where he'd penned the thick and thin of his sadness.

A long life of exercise bent my body like a harp,
Until the handwriting of this unfortunate one had become
    of such a canon
That all the kings of the world sought me out, whereas
In Bukhara, for means of existence, my liver is steeped in blood
My entrails have been burnt up by sorrow. What am I to do?
How shall I manage?
For I have no way out of this town.
This misfortune has fallen on my head for the beauty of my writing.
Alas! Mastery in calligraphy has become a chain on the feet of this
    demented one.

Joseph had tried to discover how Mir Ali's lamentation had survived. This was an unofficial rant, especially revered for its sincerity. Another scribe might have found the scrap of paper and brushed the great calligrapher's work with crushed lapis, malachite (suspended in a solution of gum arabic and water), and ground gold. Or maybe not. Mir Ali's captors were marauders who showed their good taste by dragging artists home to ink in new lines in royal genealogies. Mir Ali may have written this complaint right under the nose of the sultan, who didn't even read Persian.

Talbot wore frameless glasses that were nearly invisible. He was stealthy like that. Nothing in his expression suggested that he smelled a prank. "So it's come to this?" he finally responded.

Not, I'll get my saber. Or even, How dare they?

His long thumb stroked the paper. "That's rich: they didn't even send you letterhead. You tirelessly champion the original, and the Castle mails you a *photocopy* of its relocation plan."

Talbot seemed to be rubbing it in, which was worse than his nonchalance. Though Joseph had no memory of retrieving the letter opener from his drawer, he was clutching the jade dagger in his hand. "It's disgraceful!" he prompted his deputy.

"Disgraceful!" Talbot showed a little spark. "My mast-rigging pulleys and tea grinders will be in a case with *mannequins* at Natural History." Seeing the power drain from Joseph's florid face made him uneasy. He laid the memo down, and then, on either side of the sheet of paper, he rapped his index fingers on the coffee table's edge like a drumroll. "And the National Gallery won't show anything Asian post-Renaissance—art moved to Europe then."

"Exactly." Joseph wished Talbot would flatten his hand and, with a swift hatchet chop, shatter the table. Talbot was right—the National Gallery cared solely for blockbuster Asia. "They'll want the terra-cotta warriors of Qin; better yet, Iskandar's Gordian knot."

"Iskandar?" Talbot looked puzzled. "Say goodbye to Iskandar—he answers to Alexander the Great in their temple."

Right again. In their own museum, Iskandar was the foreign conqueror who had destroyed Persepolis and Babylon; at the National Gallery, he would be Alexander the Great, pupil of Aristotle, who conquered the East with Zeus's support.

Talbot had taken off his glasses, slowly rotating them until he was peering through the wrong sides of his lenses. His thin lips turned up into a smirk. "Kabobs in the Islamic gallery, I suppose. And falafel. Though it could go the other way if they cast against type. Then it's barbecued pork wafting under Muhammad's nose and cheese steaks near the Jain art."

Joseph had relied on Talbot's imperiousness—so different from his own clear enthusiasm or displeasure—because the staff worked relentlessly for the guy's approval. Emmy attributed the phenomenon to his good looks. Joseph couldn't see handsome; it was like being colorblind. But he could see the deference that Talbot inspired, and he regretted having encouraged it.

Joseph asked him, "Did you read to the end? They would have us reassign the staff."

"Pity," Talbot said. "It would be such a pleasure to fire most of these deadbeats."

Joseph was not the kind of parent to shake his sons down. Emmy had been adamant about respecting them even when the little fools fell victim to self-centeredness or hormones, which was most of a boy's life at home. Sometimes she had needed to walk around the block to resist knocking their heads together. Wrangling over territory or dish duty, launching themselves from the reading chair to the fainting couch: they were rowdy, clumsy tiger cubs scrambling about the den. Quieting them had required an occasional roar; roughhousing had worked, too. How surprised Emmy would be at Joseph's urge to throttle his deputy.

"I'm disappointed," the director said. "I was looking to you for some resistance."

"Maybe after lunch," Talbot said. "As they say, 'An army travels on its stomach.'" He gestured toward the door, buttoning his suit coat with that same long thumb. Joseph had written books on lithe characters like Talbot, their robes and turbans furthering the elastic effect. Perhaps you are how you're built, which would explain the ancillary director's lofty, and frighteningly flexible, demeanor.

"How about this one?" Talbot asked. "What did the Dalai Lama say to the hot dog vendor?" He paused the requisite beat. "'Make me one with everything.'"

Joseph could not have been less amused if Talbot had spat on him. "Really, that's more Lao-tzu; if it's any kind of Buddhist, maybe Zen."

"It's a joke told among the masses."

"It misses the mark." Joseph felt his neck chafe against his collar. He lowered his voice to professorial. "I'll be at lunch shortly. Put in my order if you don't mind. And as you might suspect, ours was a confidential conversation."

Talbot raised his eyes to the ceiling tiles. "Is now and ever shall be," he said.

Joseph crossed his arms at his chest, lest he slap him. What if the remainder of the staff was equally glib? Were they here so they wouldn't have to teach or, for that matter, publish?

In his private lavatory, its smoke sensor replaced by a passable forgery, Joseph puffed a cigar and took a dump. The rest of his day used to be that satisfying. He washed up, gargled a capful of mouthwash. Checking himself in the mirror, he could no longer spot a patch of black hair among the gray, and his fleshy face, except for a few broken blood vessels, was all one color. Used to be that by the Fourth of July he'd have his summer countenance—peeling nose and squinting lines of white radiating out along the tops of his tanned cheeks—but he'd rarely been outside this summer. He whisked the dander from the shoulders of his suit coat. Sometimes Talbot did that. Now he began to wonder if Talbot was unmoved by news of the upheaval because he'd had advance knowledge. Who else's shoulders might the stealthy one be grooming?

As soon as he'd returned to his chair, there was a rapid knock at his office door. Promise Whittaker leaned in, barely head and shoulders above his doorknob. She was wearing her usual thrift-shop attire, especially striking after visits from Arthur and Talbot. Joseph was hardly fashion-conscious, yet whenever he visited the National Gallery, he was impressed by how richly the women dressed.

"Help," Promise said.

"Help yourself," he replied, as he always did. She was fingering the bottom of a photocopied page, and he craned his neck to see if the Castle was at the top. When she approached him—what took Talbot three steps took her twice that—he saw it was copied from an Asian art journal.

Hummingbird-like, Promise was a blur of energy who stuck her nose deeply into the details of her work. Joseph had invited her to accompany him to the museum before she'd completed her doctorate at Penn. Both a quick study and a fast writer, she also shared his interest in showing visitors what she discovered.

"This footnote on Persian headgear seems wrongheaded—" She laughed at her pun. "She suggests that the *taj* or stick coming up out of the turban is ornamental, yet I remember reading that the grooves cut in the *taj* symbolize the twelve Shi'ite imams."

Promise looked up at him expectantly. His face felt flushed, and his hair was wet against his forehead. "Is it hot in here?" he asked preemptively.

"I'm fine." She shrugged inside the cardigan she wore all summer.

"Well, you're right about the grooves, though I haven't the source on me." He pinched and kneaded his earlobe. Emmy had told him there was a pressure point in there, and he was certainly under pressure. He said, "I'm distracted because there's a Castle skirmish going on."

"Good luck." As far as she knew, he always won his skirmishes with the Castle. She said, "'You must ask for what you really want.'"

"What does that mean—is that Rumi?"

"Yes, because I also came bearing good news. We got the NEH grant."

"Nice work," Joseph said, making himself smile. She was generous to say "we" when she deserved the credit; he sincerely hoped there would be a museum for her exhibition. Joseph wanted to throw his tie in the wastebasket, snip his trousers off above the knee, and embark on a sweltering summer hike. Midday temperatures were probably around ninety degrees; with a bottle of water, he could be in shady

Rock Creek Park in twenty minutes. Maybe he could think straight there. Maybe he could breathe. He withdrew his watch, though he didn't even have to open the cover for Promise to head out.

"See you at lunch," she said.

"I'll be there soon," Joseph said. "Talbot's gone ahead."

Actually, Talbot had just stopped by the lunchroom to tell Nathan that Joseph would be late. He didn't really care for the camaraderie of the long table and had taken a carton of yogurt to his office. Could something this big take the director by surprise, he wondered, rapidly losing respect for Joseph. It would be impolitic to go over Joseph's head; besides, in his few meetings with Cecil, Talbot had never felt the presence of authority. At least Joseph had that. Talbot had warned Joseph something was up when the Castle funded both a strategic planning initiative and a visitor survey but wouldn't fund any of the recommendations. That was what they'd done at Natural History before shipping the film collection off-site to make room for more movie theaters and enlarging the gift shop to fill the whole east wing. Joseph seemed to think the Founder's will protected them from intervention.

Joseph hadn't made it out of his office either. He'd settled heavily into his leather club chair, his fingers habitually running over the brass nailheads the way soldiers fondle the bullets in their ammunition sashes. He was facing Mir Ali's calligraphy again: "My liver is steeped in blood. My entrails have been burnt up by sorrow. What am I to do? How shall I manage?" He wanted to rise up and conquer, but the flaw in his battle plan was that he knew himself to be a scholar and not a soldier. A sportsman, even, and he reeled in his phone while he still felt there was a sporting chance.

Joseph punched in the speed-dial code for the Castle. "Cecil, please. This is Joseph Lattimore at the Asian." He looked up to the Secretary's parapet, but he couldn't make him out in the hazy summer light. "Asian curiosities and books"—how dare he quote the Founder against himself! Cecil was a myopic ornithologist, who would look at Asian art if a warbler was nesting on the page. On hold, Joseph scrawled a few notes, determined to paper the Mall with protests.

How far he had fallen, from Mughal Court to food court. "Founder's will" he jotted down; "largest collection of Chinese bronzes in America." His letters wobbled, the writing shaky as an old man's.

More and more, violence seemed the answer, except that he had only ever written about violence.

"Joseph. What a pleasure. How've you been?"

"Rarely worse. I'm reviewing your edict at present. Am I not owed the courtesy of a consultation?"

Cecil cleared his throat. "I must say, I expected your call months ago, when I told you as much over tea. I believe I mentioned that the need for guest services had become crucial."

Joseph cast his mind back to their spring visit. Frankly, he considered tea with the Secretary a quarterly nicety, harboring as much breaking news as a nursing home chat.

Cecil said, "I'd just read an article about bird trade along the Silk Route, and you surprised me, I remember, by saying you and Emmy both wanted to go on a dig in the Taklamakan Desert. What's the name of the language you're studying?"

"Kharosthi," Joseph said, unsettled by Cecil's upper hand memorywise. He said, "I wish you'd spelled the situation out for me. I could have made a case for our museum."

"I'm afraid I made your case, but we're becoming relics ourselves."

Joseph didn't know what to say. Consider this my reliquary.

The Secretary said, "You've been telling me for years you don't have enough money to run the museum properly."

"Jesus, Cecil, it's my *job* to say that. We haven't been running things improperly, if that's what you're getting at."

"Not at all. Everyone knows you could have accomplished more with additional funding."

Joseph swabbed his forehead. "This very day we've received news that the NEH is underwriting our Sufi exhibition, and the Getty's practically onboard." When the phone nearly slipped from his grasp, he clutched the receiver in both hands. "We have one of the largest collections of Asian art in America. The Metropolitan's expanding its Asian galleries—to great fanfare, I might add—and you'd empty ours out?"

"Granted," Cecil said, "you are probably offended by the notion of the National Gallery acquiring that which you've cared for, but we must consider the good of the collection. I'm sure they wouldn't object to your help."

Joseph let his breath out in puffs, the way Emmy had taught him. Breath of fire, she called it, but it felt more like cornered bull. "My help was required before this plot was hatched. The Founder built this museum and filled the galleries himself. He visited quarries to find the stone that would complement temple sculptures from Persepolis and Ur. He brought a ship of Japanese artisans and wood here to construct a teahouse in Gallery Eight." Which brought to mind Mir Ali being carted from his home because of his mastery in calligraphy.

"And now Development and Membership rule the roost," Cecil said. "Neither of us wants to hear that, or that ten million doesn't buy what it used to."

Outside, the golden sun was directly overhead and shade was hard-won. An elderly busload carried an umbrella apiece. In the next cluster, a mother dug through her backpack, pulling out baseball caps for each of her children, while three teenage boys at the garden's west fountain dipped their T-shirts in the water and spread them on their heads. All any of them had to do for relief was step into his commodious museum.

Cecil said, "These days, ten million won't secure you a 'naming opportunity' anywhere except at Modern Art."

"The whole Institution got going with half a million dollars," Joseph countered. Legacy of a generous bastard, he refrained from saying. If the illegitimate rock hound had been recognized by his earl father, there'd be no National Institution of Science and Art. The rejected son had never been to America, which in 1829 was still considered Britain's brash bastard child.

"Half a million," Joseph repeated.

"And from such an acorn a mighty oak has grown." Fatigue weighed Cecil's voice down an octave, reminding Joseph of their age difference. "Nevertheless, we are strapped. To be heard, you'd have to put a billion dollars where your mouth is."

"A billion dollars."

"At least a billion."

Joseph wondered how low he might stoop for a billion dollars. Hollywood Buddhists, bestsellers about Japanese geisha, CD compilations of pop singers reading Rumi's poetry, stars covering themselves with henna tattoos—would that cheapen or publicize their cause? A billion dollars, a billion people, the poorest in the world: empty their pockets, shake out their saris. If every single one of them—infant to guru, rice farmer to snake charmer—could cough up a dollar, Joseph might be able to share their culture with Americans.

"I've got China. I've got India at a billion apiece. Grant me a population count, and we'll outnumber all the museums on the Mall combined."

"Not in visitors, you don't," Cecil said.

"That's nothing new. We've been the least-visited art museum on the Mall ever since a second one was built." He resisted quoting the latest count, assuming Cecil knew that summer tours trooped through to use the facilities. It seemed the Castle saw the dictates of the Founder's will as hurdles. Maybe Joseph could sell off everything and borrow back the good stuff.

"Joseph, my friend, lobby me or don't lobby me—I'm not the problem. Truth is, you can't clip a falcon's wings and expect him to hunt. Development says the people want bathrooms and bagels near the subway, and when they stand atop the Metro escalator, they see your building."

"Which is an art museum."

"To you."

Is now and ever shall be, Joseph thought but did not say. The high standing of the museum world, so patrician and well-mannered, was a myth he had exploited. People assumed that behind these walls, beautiful decisions were arrived at in an intelligent, courteous manner. Let the record show it might as well be mud wrestling.

He said, "You're the one who told me that the number of heartbeats during an average life span is roughly a billion."

Cecil concurred. "The meter for each species, whether hummingbird or vulture, runs out at a billion."

A billion, Joseph's temples hammered, a billion, a billion, a billion. "If I'd put aside a dollar every time my pulse beat, we'd be well on our way."

"I'd be nearly there," Cecil said. His wavering voice suggested a fluttery pulse under papery white skin.

A billion dollars, a billion people, a billion heartbeats. Joseph's heart revved in his chest, and he felt his life span shortening accordingly.

God's Plan

July 6, 1999

Promise sat in museum storage staring at one vexing detail of a manuscript page, a seventeenth-century illumination of a Rumi poem. Was that tiny white bundle a wadded-up cloak? A turban, as suggested in the headgear footnote? (Joseph had acted so strange that she wished she'd brought him in to see the original.) Despite the piles of work waiting at her desk, she could not take her eyes off this spot until she figured out what the miniaturists were up to.

What got to Promise was how the artists managed to use the poet's words as a lantern for their light show. Rumi was born in 1207 in Afghanistan, on the eastern fringe of the Persian Empire; his family fled to Turkey before the armies of Genghis Khan closed in. Rumi inherited his father's position as sheikh in Konya's dervish community; however, in 1244, a wanderer named Shams of Tabriz showed up looking for a teacher. In the heat of Shams, Rumi caught fire. Their inseparable companionship is described as an unending spiritual conversation, an ecstatic connection. Were they lovers in the carnal sense? Did Shams disappear because Rumi's son murdered him? Promise didn't investigate those questions. She sifted through gold-dusted pages covered in all manner of calligraphy and inset with paintings executed in astounding detail. If she stared at the pages too intently, there was always the chance that her head might crack open and a flock of doves fly out.

As a kid in Oklahoma, she'd tried again and again to tunnel through to Asia from her own backyard. What was on the other side of that bright red clay, she wanted to know. She did not believe the whole world was flat. Living in the land that enforced one god, one country, and maybe two opinions, she pursued the most confused border disputes, the most divinities with the most arms, eyes, and outlandish stories. She was especially partial to India. Born of a virgin? Ha! The Buddha came out of his virgin mother's *hip*, and in the pastry case of Hindu confections, there are infinite flavors of divinity, like the decapitated son of a god who was given the head of an elephant, or the blue-skinned cowherd whom ladies find irresistible. President following upon president? Would you believe prime minister following upon queen upon king upon maharaja upon sultan upon avatar of Vishnu? Love of country? How about love of cow and tree and bud and leaf and insect on leaf and flea on insect on leaf? World without end, indeed.

During graduate school, she stopped flinging so much dirt around. She went to India and found she liked the world a little flatter. In fact, she liked libraries and museums. Books, religion, and art blended into the art of religious books, specifically Rumi. To get his drift, Promise learned Arabic, Persian, and passable amounts of Turkish; the tenets of Islam; the arts and political history of Turkey, India, Iran, Iraq, and western China (or, in her father's opinion, "one useless thing after another"). She could hop her way across the river of Rumi on footnotes, but that wasn't the appeal. The appeal was an understanding deep in the body tissue, a universal connectedness that sounded simplistic, if a little goofy, yet was impossible to sustain for ten minutes.

It was misleading to call the miniatures she attended manuscript pages, because they were more often collages pasted back to back and gathered into scrapbooks. A long arabesque had been sliced and glued to fit around a particular verse, or a passage of calligraphy had been pasted into the archway of a palace door already painted by an artist. Because each page had become so valuable, albums were disassembled and double-sided folios split apart. The ten-by-twelve-inch page Promise was studying had been worked loose from both its album and its backing page. She suspected it was fashioned sometime around 1620, probably in Delhi, by artists in the royal workshop of the Mughal emperor Jahangir.

The Founder had amassed a sizable collection of Rumi pages, any one of which could practically send Promise into a seizure. Take this sheet, on which someone had glued the calligrapher's golden inscrip-

tion in diagonal lines along the top and bottom, framing an illustration
of a wedding feast. The passage, which had taken her a month to trans-
late, was from Rumi's *Mathnawi*, his volumes describing everything in
heaven and on earth:

> *Little by little, wean yourself.*
> *This is the gist of what I have to say.*
> *From an embryo, whose nourishment comes in the blood,*
> *move to an infant drinking milk,*
> *to a searcher after wisdom,*
> *to a hunter of more invisible game.*
>
> *Think how it is to have a conversation with an embryo.*
> *You might say, "The world outside is vast and intricate.*
> *There are wheatfields and mountain passes,*
> *and orchards in bloom.*
>
> *At night there are millions of galaxies, and in sunlight*
> *the beauty of friends dancing at a wedding."*
>
> *You ask the embryo why he, or she, stays cooped up*
> *in the dark with eyes closed.*
> > *Listen to the answer.*

There is no "other world."
I only know what I've experienced.
You must be hallucinating.

Having fit the final pieces together, she'd gasped at Rumi's astonishing, timeless message, ingeniously pasted above and below "the
beauty of friends dancing at a wedding." Her flush of joy had made for
a more than usually festive Fourth of July. Despite Lydia and Felix's
whining about heat and crowds, Promise had kept everyone's spirits up
for a picnic on the Mall. At night, there were millions of galaxies and
mosquitoes, too; plus Felix spilled his chocolate protein drink all over
himself and Lydia cried when the fireworks exploded directly overhead, strips of singed paper raining down on them from the bombs
bursting in air. Nonetheless, Promise felt gushes of otherworldly affec-

tion for her five- and nine-year-old, and she still had something left for her husband after they made their way home. Despite Leo's misgivings about her profession, he was happy to reap the benefits of her rapturous breakthroughs.

When she'd finished the translation, she should have moved on. And yet here she was, days later, back at the same page, because something had lodged in her mind's eye. The calligraphy filled three inches of the page's top and bottom. Along the left border were wild animals lightly inked in, perhaps illustrative of Rumi's "more invisible game." In the central wedding scene, ornately dressed guests enjoyed a feast, and dancers circled the newlyweds. What had been haunting her was a tiny white oval on the edge of the feast table, perhaps someone's cast-off turban. This morning, she'd come across the footnote that had sent her reading about Persian headgear and on to Joseph's office. After lunch, she'd had to attend an Accessibility Committee meeting and then answer a dozen phone calls. She hadn't been able to get to her page until the last hour.

There was the puffy speck, the size and shape of a maggot. Facing the lavish spread of food, the nearest person nonetheless rested a hand on the bundle. That wedding guest (male or female, it wasn't clear) was an inch tall, the bundle no larger than a grain of rice. In the midst of preparing her Rumi exhibition, Promise didn't really have time to consider every millimeter of every manuscript page in the show. Yet such efforts had been richly rewarded in the past. She didn't cotton to what the footnotes suggested—maybe that was what Joseph was trying to tell her—so she looked more intently, if that was possible, at the pillowy parcel.

Promise took out a loupe, careful not to rest it on the page, and under magnification she could see something in the white bundle. She blinked, she wiped her eyes, then she buzzed Arthur from the phone in storage.

"Can I borrow your set of magnifying glasses?"

"Where've you been?" Arthur asked. He still hadn't recovered from his morning scuffle with Joseph. Did *she* think his exhibition should be trimmed? Could she help him appeal to Joseph to let him pick his own book cover?

Arthur heard one of the art handlers say, "We have magnifiers." So Promise had been hiding out in storage.

"Never mind," she said. "And don't let Joseph get to you—your show will be grand." She hung up before he could drag her back into his problems. With her loupe, which was 2x, she'd seen a speck; at 5x, folds in the white bundle were visible and the roundish shape within looked to be unpainted paper. At 10x, she could see the face of a baby, his body swaddled in white. Brilliant, they were brilliant to re-create the unseen world in *an illustration*. Even more brilliant to hide an embryo-sized baby in such a poem. Sometimes she felt she could spend her entire career on a single page.

"Look, come look!" She called the art handler over to point out the baby's ears and mouth.

"How could they paint something they couldn't see?" the art handler asked. "That blows my mind."

"Exactly," Promise agreed, happy to share the gist of what Rumi had to say. She'd been in a whirl all weekend; at the same time, some portion of her brain had been fervently working on this detail. She yawned, now that her spin had caught up with her—that and the long list she'd pushed aside to concentrate on this dot. She relinquished the page to the art handler and signed herself out of storage. Obligations shadowed her all the way to her office, where she grabbed a stack of articles she'd already carried home three times. Joseph increasingly relied on her, and she struggled to keep up with his standards.

She'd never make it as a mystic—she had too many errands. Fiercely as she loved her family three, their daily maintenance threatened to consume her, and sure enough, her first step onto the ramshackle porch actually cracked a sagging board. Promise hopped to the side, then leaned over to hug Felix.

He yelled his news into her ear: "Delilah had puppies and we can have one for free!"

She picked up her son, who was still light enough to be carried. Specialists wanted at him to take growth hormone readings or test pituitary levels; thus far, Promise had fended them off. After all, she was tiny, her grandfather was tiny. Some folks were small!

From inside the living room, Lydia was pressing a drawing of a dog against the windowpane. The skittish nine-year-old hadn't been on the porch since the cicadas had begun marching up through the dirt, splitting open their crackly brown skins and leaving them behind on the tree trunks.

Felix put one hand on either side of Promise's face, turning her to him. "Daddy said maybe to a puppy, and now it's God's plan. Can you believe it?"

She suspected the babysitter had introduced him to the notion of God's plan. "Daddy said maybe—I said we'd do some dog research."

"Research," Leo echoed. "That could add a few years to the project."

Despite Leo's collusion on the dog issue, she was glad to see him rather than Althea, the gloomy babysitter. His light woolly hair looked particularly leonine today. When she pointed down at the floorboard to avoid, she saw his inside-out socks puffing up between the woven straps of his fisherman's sandals, though his muscular legs looked fashionable enough in white tennis shorts. Kissing him, she noticed the finger smudges covering his glasses, which meant he'd been reading of atrocities, head down, all day long.

"Hard day?" she asked. His sultry eyelids drooped past sexy to sad.

"Brutal," he concurred. "Felix, let your mom in the door so we can show her the dog bed we're working on."

What the boys had started was more dog fort than bed. Packing peanuts and blister wrap, scissors and knives, jagged flaps of cardboard and strings of duct tape that had gotten away from them littered the entry hall.

"Great, guys," Promise said. "Though you'd have more room on the porch." She knew a project like this was balm for Leo. All day long at Amnesty International, he was something like an emergency-room worker, organizing the first response to news of torture, executions, and "disappearances." At home, the children counted on him to get down on their level and imagine.

"Did you go outside today?" Promise asked. Both kids mumbled a no. Lydia's wheat-colored hair was in a hundred braids that sprouted from the top of her head; at least Althea had been near the children this afternoon.

What this family needs, Promise thought, is professional help: a real babysitter, a carpenter, electrician, plumber, and a housekeeper. Since they couldn't afford any of that, why not a puppy? The one under consideration was half border collie, half fence-jumping terrier; on the other hand, adopting from the neighbors would circumvent a home visit by the animal-rescue people.

Promise and Leo's fixer-upper barely inside the D.C. line had been a compromise between the suburbs and the ungentrified downtown neighborhoods. No matter the project, every estimate was a few thousand dollars; their nonprofit careers allowed for a limited number of budgeted repairs. She would concede that their zip code hiked up the price and that an entire house could be built in Haiti for the cost of refinishing their floors if Leo would put his talk about the working man to work. She'd even mend his "Tax the Rich" T-shirt if he'd wear it to patch and paint the porch.

Felix said, "The puppies can't see yet, but that's okay, because they still drink from their mom. You know, what's to see?"

Promise kept herself from smiling, lest he think she was on the puppy wagon. She unlooped her purse from around her neck and dropped her keys in the key bowl next to a framed clipping from the 1916 Sears, Roebuck catalog advertising their abode. The entry featured a line drawing of the house, which had been built from a kit of lumber, hardware, and "clear instructions." *Delivered to your local depot for a sensible $4,000.*

Felix pointed to the drawing. "Daddy says it's lucky we never fixed our house up."

"For purposes of housebreaking and chewing," Leo said. "That's what I meant."

"We're so lucky," Promise said, visualizing the housebreaking and chewing possibilities. Puppy damage could be the straw that broke the house.

"In most parts of the world, this place would hold three families."

Promise wasn't falling for that.

Lydia said, "Delilah doesn't shed. I want a dog with hair that sheds."

Of course you do. And isn't it cute when they spread the trash all over the kitchen? She'd learned not to respond to everything the kids said; instead, she hugged her daughter. "Speaking of hair, yours looks beautiful like that."

"Can you take it out? The braids scare me—it's like there are snakes on my shoulders."

Promise ran her hands over the tight weaving. "I'm not sure I know how," she said honestly. She picked up a rubber band from the floor and gathered Lydia's braids. "Let's tie them back. Your dad's probably mentioned that puppies are a lot of work. They need to be walked often."

Lydia said, "In Chevy Chase, you can hire people to walk your dog. I read it in the *Post*."

Promise laughed at that. Unlike Leo, she took status with a grain of salt. It amused her that their D.C. address was all cachet, probably because of her Oklahoma roots. Museum colleagues from every world capital talked about her homeland as if she'd been born an orphan with rickets: "Are you aware she's from Oklahoma?" (Of course, her parents' Oklahoma home looked newer each year her father tended it, while she and Leo were barely above parking their car on the lawn and tacking up sheets for curtains. Probably they would if they had a second car or decided they needed curtains.)

Leo said, "We'll walk the puppy together." And to both children, "You'll be happy to know that I'm boiling water." The children ran to the kitchen to bicker about noodle choices. Promise heard Lydia actually speak the sentence "I want lemon-garlic penne with Gorgonzola." Leo was going to make them move out of Chevy Chase. Good old Felix replied, "That stuff smells like farts!"

"Think Parmesan!" she called from the stairs. She changed into shorts and a sleeveless shirt. In the house's only bathroom, she washed her face and hands, then put on a swipe of lipstick—she'd been meaning to do that since 7 a.m. Lifting her hair off her forehead brought to mind her mother saying her widow's peak was a mark of beauty. Then why did they call it a widow's peak? She reached into the medicine cabinet and punched a red pill out of its blister pack because she was congested but also because she still had the shank of the day to get through. Hard as she twisted the water off, the faucet still dripped. There was no air circulating through her bedroom, where two out of the three windows in the bay had long ago been painted shut. It took some doing with the tines of the plug to get the fan to come on.

In 1916, everything needed to build their house had been delivered to the Chevy Chase Depot: thirty thousand numbered pieces accompanied by directions. Two boxcars packed with beams and walls, nails and hinges, electrical wiring and both plumbing and light fixtures, down to a pair of trees. Promise wished she could order up a boxcar of replacement parts and upgrades for the historic mess. It was the perfect house for a childless couple who had each made full partner.

When she tried to fall back on her mystical manuscript discovery, she couldn't rekindle the blaze that had burned through her all weekend. No matter how much attention a Persian manuscript required, a family required more. It wore a body down, with the diarrhea and dioramas, the head lice and book reports of the school year now supplanted by summer's pinkeye and boredom, squabbling and scooter mishaps. Not to mention a relentless three meals a day.

"Lipstick," Leo said suggestively when she showed up in the kitchen.

"Why not?" She grinned. It had been fun to put their gritty, sticky children to bed the other night and then drink margaritas on the porch—nothing like tequila and fireworks to light up a marriage. Leo's woolly hair had smelled like gunpowder, and when she'd pointed that out, he'd led them to the shower, where they'd perched their drinks on the windowsill.

He sidled up behind her tonight as she grated cheese, putting a hand on her curviest spot. "Will we be seeing more fireworks later?"

"I thought you didn't approve of nationalistic displays."

Leo said, "That was before I knew their effect on you." He raised his fist to chant "U-S-A! U-S-A!"

Eager to join in, Felix shook the saltshaker maraca-style, spraying the kitchen floor with crystals. "Salt is for food," Promise said. "Can you put the forks on the table?" Trying to keep the mood light, she threw the forks one by one into the air, until she got a circle of flatware going.

"Mommy!" Felix called in delight.

When all else fails, juggle. It was a skill that had served her well. She caught the forks one, two, three, four, by their handles. Wrapping Felix's hand around them, she aimed him out of the kitchen, saying, "Let's eat in the dining room tonight." Lydia unwittingly kept him on task by whining, "Setting the table is my job. I'm supposed to do it for allowance."

"Mommy asked *me*."

Promise touched the braids that clung to Lydia's scalp, rows and rows hard as beads. "Honey, did you want linguine or bow ties?" she asked, letting Lydia decide for the family. The salt was gritty underfoot, and she looked to the back of the door where the broom was supposed to be clipped. Her peripheral vision caught it leaning against the corner. "Broom," she pointed out to Leo.

"I'll do it!" Felix swept in. Of course, when he tried to wield the long stick, he knocked a box of cereal off the counter, then goosed his sister, who screamed.

"Leo, broom," Promise said, and Leo took over.

Promise got to work turning boiling water into food. Witness the miracle of the noodles and the cheese. Bagged salad for the adults; for the kids, raw carrots, which she bought already peeled and washed, and a bunch of grapes apiece. Two waters, Felix's high-calorie canned drink (the last in the fridge), and Lydia's chocolate milk—ta-da!

She and Leo came together at the sink, where she laid the colander down and he poured the pasta through. Steam fogged his big glasses. She said, "I found a baby in a painting today." She squeezed her thumb and finger together. "A teeny tiny baby."

"You should have brought it home," he said. "We were good with babies."

First a puppy and now a baby. He must have had a harrowing day. Sometimes he just needed to talk about the other end of things, hear that life goes on. When Promise brought the plates into the dining room, she saw the cloth napkins Leo insisted on. Less waste, he contended, because he didn't do the laundry. She reminded the children to wash their hands and portioned out their dinners. As soon as she sat down, she heavily buttered a slice of bread, flipped it over to butter the other side, then handed Felix the fat-laden slice. It was gratifying to see the children dig in. Imagine how much they'd enjoy a real dinner.

She said, "I met with the Accessibility Committee this afternoon. They want 3-D versions of the manuscript pages so blind visitors can feel the whole scene, from rugs and elephants to nose rings and inscriptions. Isn't that absurd?"

Lydia sucked in a long noodle, which slapped at her chin and nose before disappearing. Promise wondered why pasta didn't remind Lydia of snakes. Still chewing, she said, "It would be so cool to see the tiger rugs and all the jewelry and then touch the stuff. You could feel a painting!"

Coming from a child, the idea sounded appealing.

Leo said, "Remember those Cambodian women with hysterical blindness? Maybe running their hands over Cambodian art could help bring them back." Promise was shaking her head no, no, no. "What? Is that too much?" he asked. "Usually, you're leading the charge for hands-on exhibits."

"Usually I am," she agreed. "Felix, eat up, honey." She heard Lydia's enthusiasm and Leo's lovely notion of art's healing powers, but she also heard *More work for me*. She said, "I can't imagine where I'd find someone to fashion 3-D relief versions of Persian miniatures. I'd rather make brownies for everyone attending the exhibition."

"I could do it," Lydia said. "I'll use my own clay. Tell the lady your daughter can do it."

"We're making brownies?" Felix's expression changed to hopeful.

"Why not?" Promise tried to remember if there was a mix in the cupboard, eggs in the fridge. Felix could use the calories. "Clean your plate and we'll make brownies."

Felix unfolded his cloth napkin, which he hadn't needed because he was wearing a shirt. With two hands, he spread the napkin over his dinner plate and wiped up the remaining noodles in their cheesy sauce. "Clean as a whistle!" he announced, holding the plate aloft for inspection.

———

Dinner hour at Joseph and Emmy's home was far less raucous. Joseph draped his suit coat onto the kilim that was itself draped over his grandmother's threadbare chaise, then he fixed a bourbon and branch water, acutely aware of the age and condition of his surroundings. He was a reasonably fit sixty-two years old, the bourbon was a tasty twelve, the trilobites and ammonites embedded in the countertop some 300 million, though they'd been residing in Joseph's house a mere ten. When he set the decanter on the bar, fossils appeared to swim beneath amber waves of drink. A Venetian might have been carving this very decanter from rock crystal during the same era that slave labor laid the brickwork of their Capitol Hill row house.

Emmy pulled up a stool. Joseph's former student, she was merely fifty-one. When he met her, she was Emmy Lou Brandt, a cattleman's girl set down in Philadelphia. In straight jeans, a pearl-snap cowboy shirt, and with a thin braid down the middle of her back, she barely cast a shadow. He learned soon enough not to take that for meekness. Her long-bridged nose and clear eyes were those of a Modigliani subject, as were her arched eyebrows and narrow mouth, which made her look as if she'd swallowed the canary. He hadn't seen her in jeans for years, and she'd cut off her braid when she got sick. Since her surgery, she'd been wearing an Indian pants-tunic outfit every day.

"I would so love a glass of water," she said, as if it would be the most invigorating drink on earth.

Joseph lifted crescents of ice with silver tongs and dropped them in a tumbler of Irish crystal. "We've reached a new low, my dear. That difference between educating the public and pandering to them? You were right all along."

Presumably, Emmy knew she'd been right all along. She closed her eyes as she drank—Joseph imagined her tasting not only the water but also the freezer off-gases tainting their ice cubes. Back in 1967, Emmy Lou was a freshman fresh from five thousand Texas acres—her daddy's cattle ranch was wrapped in its own brand of barbed wire. She'd come to Philadelphia the way other girls went abroad. Joseph sometimes feared that Emmy's love for him was really gratitude, for he was the one who'd introduced her to Buddhism, which she'd taken to like a freshman to dope. They'd married before she graduated. As much a thorn in his side as his confidante, she'd urged him to champion Asia in ways blockbuster exhibitions could not: by repatriating artifacts, for example, or challenging the State Department on its policies toward Tibet, Burma, Cambodia, Kashmir.

Emmy put her water glass on the bar. "Were you fired today?" she asked.

Joseph rubbed his burning eyes with both hands. If she guessed what had happened, he'd be spared from repeating it. "Since when did museums have to turn a profit, let alone justify themselves? The Founder collected unparalleled art from a little-known continent; he paid for a public building and allowed anyone in. I believe that's laudable." Appealing as a second bourbon was, he tried to pace himself. "Open every day except Christmas, free admission—how much more accessible can you get than open every day and free?"

"You can't," she said. Since she'd left the museum, she'd lost interest in the Castle's shenanigans. Her part-time job training docents had been like missionary work to her, so much so that she'd scheduled chemotherapy after work on Friday to be stable enough to lecture the following Wednesday. Maybe they were right to cut the docent program, because as soon as she stepped away, she saw what a small gesture she'd been making. Each session, she taught sacred information to six retirees, who recited it like park rangers. Worse, they felt *better* than the visitors for knowing a few tidbits about Asian religions or art. They weren't devotees, they were show-offs.

She gently asked, "What's going on?"

"It's richer than you predicted. They've targeted us to be the museum every visitor will want to attend, with but a single catch: we have to get rid of the art."

"You're not making any sense." Was he drunk? "That's like saying, We like everything about your house except you—or your furniture."

She didn't seem that surprised, but the set of her mouth was always on the smug side. He said, "So now it's all the people, none of the culture. My assignment is to fire my staff, send our collection to the National Gallery, and make way for cheeseburgers."

She hoped he was exaggerating. "I thought I'd be lost without the museum, but I didn't miss it after I left, a lot like my breast, I guess."

"You're all about detachment," he said, not intending to make light of her cancer.

Her tunic hung straight down, as if her thin shoulders were a clothes hanger. Because she'd always been flat-chested, the cancer had scarcely affected her profile, although he noticed that she was rounding her back and leaning on the right, her bad side.

Elbows up on the bar, Joseph rested his forehead on the meaty parts of his palms. Emmy slid off her stool and wrapped herself around his broad back and gut, which he pulled in. Though strands of hemp from her outfit poked through his shirt and her lavender oil mixed badly with the horse-harness whiskey in his nostrils, he tried to give himself over to her compassion.

She said, "Every muscle in your body is clenched."

As she gingerly moved his head from side to side, his neck bones ground together with the sound of brakes gone past pad to wheel drum. Emmy pressed her fingertips to the bottom of his skull, which hurt exquisitely.

She said, "The trapezius actually starts way up here, at the occipital bone." Then she reached around to the front of his face, placing it like a piano with two fingers of each hand on either side of his nostrils. "Levator labii superioris and zygomaticus minor," she crooned like a magician.

"What do those do?"

"They elevate the upper lip, as in smiling or sneering."

His first genuine smile of the day pushed up against the fingers of his wife, who understood what stressed him most. Pointing to her glass of water, Joseph said, "I could throw that across the room just to watch it shatter."

"Go ahead. The glass is already broken, right?"

"Not to me," he said. Joseph well knew the monk-disciple exchange she was referring to, a lesson that nothing lasts.

Emmy changed the subject. "Have you noticed how every news story has something to do with the new century?"

Joseph nodded. "Including whether 2000 is the beginning of one?"

"Right, Professor," she said. "Today, I realized that the reason it keeps surprising me is because it's still 1989 in my head. I'll hear the door, and before I can register that it's the mailman fiddling with the slot, I'll think the boys are home. I expect them to tear through the living room carrying the cat or squirt guns."

"I know what you mean," he said. He still pictured himself as a young father. "Remember when you'd play your flute, and Henry's tabby would jump on the table to bat at your braid?"

Emmy lifted herself back onto the barstool. "I remember that. Do you?"

Come to think of it, maybe she'd only told him about that. After dinner—when he was home—he usually went to his study to get a little befuddled and tuck into his latest translation. Most of his family memories were from the field; in Washington, he'd given up his family for his work. He'd donated his family life to the Institution, an in-kind contribution they were throwing back in his face. "Why does the public get the last word? The public can't find Bangladesh on a map. Recorded tours buzzing in everyone's ears like mosquitoes, monitors luring them away from the art. You don't go to a museum to watch television!"

"*We* don't," Emmy said. "When I think of what you've endured to put that museum on the map. You've done more than anyone else to spread the word."

Joseph straightened up so he could catch his righteous breath.

Emmy said, "Maybe we should go back to the field. The kids are gone; nothing's holding us here." She'd been resisting the urge to empty out the boys' rooms since Sanjay left for his senior year at Haverford. Instead, she'd started in on her own clutter. At that point, she was halfway through chemo; consequently, the first things to go were dresser boxes stuffed with hair implements. Combs, clips, chopsticks. Christmas, Mother's Day, birthday. It was as if she'd kept her hair long all those years so Joseph and the boys would know what to bring her every holiday.

Joseph traced a fossil on the bar. "You'd go to the desert now?"

"I could leave before dinner," she said. Until tonight, the dig had been a postretirement possibility, a testimony to their marriage that the same godforsaken site suited both their purposes. He had his Kharosthi work; she wanted to travel the path on which Chinese monks, crazy to find the hot spots of the Buddha's life, had knee-walked to India on their pilgrimage for texts and teachers.

When he slumped back down, Joseph looked remarkably like a sack of laundry on a barstool. He said, "When Cecil implied these changes were all for the best, I thought of your daddy having to put down his entire herd. He didn't wait for the government edict on hoof-and-mouth. You told me about how the preacher paid him a visit, and Hank said—"

Emmy interrupted in her father's own voice. "'Preacher, don't you start in about the Lord's mysterious ways, 'cause I'm so pissed I could shit.'"

"Me too." Joseph closed his eyes. "Isn't that what *amen* means? Me too."

———

Halfway between Chevy Chase and Capitol Hill, on a tiny Logan Circle balcony, Arthur was also having a cocktail before dinner. He spread a thick layer of olive tapenade on a sourdough crisp, admiring the flecks of red pepper amid the green. The night was turning out to be less sweltering than usual; occasionally, a breeze lifted the flap of his kimono. After the salty olives and toast, the sweet mojito he sipped tasted especially tropical. He sent crumbs off the table to the birds, who were singing the praises of the gentrified neighborhood.

Morty leaned out the kitchen window. "Relaxed enough?" They'd arrived from work within a few minutes of each other. Arthur had taken a shower, then made himself a drink. He sat with one leg up on the railing, sipping from a sugar-rimmed glass and flashing his bikini shorts at the pigeons. In the meantime, Morty had emptied the dishwasher, brought Arthur the mail, unpacked the groceries he'd bought, rubbed two halibut steaks with spices he'd ground, and started the charcoal.

"This mint is so refreshing," Arthur said. "Remind me to let you taste the next round before I add the rum." He was still recovering from his clash with Joseph, who always made him feel like a scrawny aesthete. The man wore a forty-six suit; his hobby was building stone walls. As if that weren't enough, his clear-thinking scholarship and good manners set the standard for his field. Had there been wilderness in need of settling, Joseph would have been the one to do it. Clear timber by day, notch together a cabin and a legal system, entertain guests by night! "How could Joseph edit an entire case of dragon dishes from the show?"

"Maybe less is more."

"Well, I'm going to fight for that peony cup on the cover."

"You told me."

"Joseph's so intimidating that I sometimes forget: I'm the one who knows porcelain. The decoration on the ambassador's bowl is sloppy, like there were rival gangs in the imperial workshop. One eunuch carved the magpie's claw and the next painted the foot an eighth of an inch off, then in a hissy fit some court painter made a swoop on the feather that wasn't even incised." He heard himself protesting a little too much.

Morty carried a cast-iron pan to the table. Two halibut steaks were studded with red and green peppercorns the same colors as his tapenade. "Don't get carried away," Morty cautioned.

Arthur spit a lime seed over the balcony. "That's what I do best. Which reminds me. I gave a smoke to Officer Jackson this afternoon, and he made some crack about whether there'd be a smoking section in the museum's restaurant. The Eatery, he called it." Arthur took another gulp from his drink. "I'll tell you one thing about that bowl: the white glows like T-shirts in that black-light biker bar."

"Probably lead in the glaze," Morty said. "It ultimately leached out and made them all sterile." On the tiny balcony, it was an effort to get by Arthur without touching him. So many aspects of Arthur's career were beginning to make Morty's skin crawl, like the antique Japanese kimono. One day soon, he expected to come home to find his lover wrapped in clammy silk, sucking on an opium bong and grinding his own lampblack ink to brush poems on a mulberry-paper scroll.

Arthur started to say something about the guards at the Jingdezhen kilns, but the mood was getting dark enough without bringing up eunuchs again. He tried to gauge if Morty was more annoyed than usual—that was how strained things were becoming. And speaking of eunuchs, why did they make the best guards anyway? They were entrusted with both the concubines and the porcelain, but they still had lips. They still had hands. Arthur refused to believe that all their desire had been dashed in the process.

From back in the kitchen, Morty said, "Is this the kind of jumble that sets Joseph off? You're supposed to be choosy."

Arthur had to tilt his chair back to see what was being held against him. The cupboard shelves were chockablock with his acquisitions. Morty held up a Japanese raku teacup, too humble to sport a handle, and a coffee mug in the shape of a muscle shirt.

He knew Morty would have preferred eight thick-lipped mugs of the same color. Dishwasher-safe, microwave-proof, stain- and chip-resistant. When Arthur let his chair back down, only Morty's muscled torso was visible through the open window. He pictured the buzz cut and the beard style Morty had settled on for convenience. While Morty's efficiency may have helped him stay off the booze, his notion of aesthetics serving the traffic flow seemed excessive even for an undersecretary of transportation. If they made it to January, it would be seven years since they'd met, near the end of the fidelity rage brought on by AIDS. The sick were looking for their final caretakers; the well were looking to stay well. In that environment, Morty's addictions had seemed mild compared with those of Arthur's clique, and alcoholism was not contagious.

Arthur said, "My job is to cherish objects. It's not as if I'm attached to every coffee cup."

"Prove it," Morty said. He came out on the balcony waving the muscle-shirt mug. He looked as if he might throw it over the railing.

"I'm an enthusiast," Arthur said; then he concentrated on spreading olive paste on a crisp without it breaking. He offered Morty the appetizer. "You've been lifting like crazy," he said.

"It keeps me sober."

Frankly, Arthur could have used someone a little less sober. He'd said as much to Promise the other day. "Tell me you kept that to yourself," she'd scolded him. In fact, whenever he confided his restlessness to someone, he got the impression that Morty was better liked than he.

"Would you sit down a second?" Arthur patted the seat of the other chair. "Let me know what's new with America's arteries."

"I'm working on a few things by the airport," he said.

"Do tell." Arthur gathered the mail together and stacked the cutting board on top to make room at the mosaic table.

Because it was so rare, Morty succumbed to Arthur's attention. He took a seat on the balcony, where the evening was cooling off and the smoke from the grill kept mosquitoes at bay. Looking at Arthur's long glossy ponytail, his kimono open like any old bathrobe, Morty could pretend he was back in Mendocino with the love of his life.

He said, "University of Maryland sent me an agriculture intern. We've got funding to try tall grasses, maybe even corn, along that stretch where the de-icer and the idling fumes end up."

"How about wheat?" Arthur asked. "With wheat, you'd see amber waves of grain as you landed in our nation's capital."

Morty smiled, pleased that Arthur was following along.

Arthur leaned in close for what Morty thought might be a kiss on the cheek; instead, he picked a crumb from Morty's beard and tossed it to the birds. "Quite a career," Arthur said. "If it isn't pavement, it's fumes. So what do you think of my predicament with Joseph?"

Morty pushed away from the table. Taking the top off the grill, he held his hand over the coals longer than necessary. Arthur's fit in the director's office probably meant he'd be passed over again—remember when Talbot was picked to be ancillary director? "If you care what I think, I say accept Joseph's cover choice, and you don't have a predicament."

"It *is* a decent piece of Yongzheng ware, made from the purest kaolin on earth." He could feel himself falling for it, his tongue getting thick in his mouth as he described its attributes.

"White clay," Morty said, to show he remembered. "White, chalky clay."

"Right." When Arthur smiled, his bleached teeth shone. "In the South, they sell packets of the stuff for people to snack on."

"South China?"

"No, *the* South. Georgia, South Carolina. Next to the Slurpee machines at gas stations. Fried pork rinds, corn nuts, kaolin packets. People crave the stuff."

"Well, *you* can understand that," Morty said, wanting to be craved half as much.

A Heavy Meal

July 20, 1999

Standing alone on the northern landing, Joseph took in the three visitors on the other side of the courtyard. One checked her watch repeatedly. Another held a cell phone to his ear. Perhaps they were exaggerating their busyness because the third visitor was a homeless man in a jacket made of stitched-together ties. The museum's attendance figures consistently surprised Joseph, who believed the landings should be as packed as a Tokyo subway platform. After eighteen years, he still expected the worldly mix that attended the museum's openings to visit during the day. Theirs should be an indoor bazaar with children everywhere, though no chickens or open grills. What more could he do as director?

He had no idea why people stayed away in droves from the Museum of Asian Art. Asia was home to the most riveting, diverse, lively art in the world. Just look at India, really more subuniverse than subcontinent: Hindus, Muslims, Buddhists, Christians, Jains, and Zoroastrians overlaid with Chinese, Mughal, Dutch, and English empires on an indigenous culture. The combinations of those influences would never be exhausted; thus far, they had bred art that ranged from folk painting to the finest calligraphy, watercolor, manuscripts, pottery, and jewelry. He knew museums weren't for everyone, but neither was college, and in his time at the university, his Asian studies seminars had swelled until he'd had to hold court in the packed auditorium.

From his vantage point at the far corner of the landing, Joseph could peer undetected into the staff room, whose windowed wall made up the courtyard's eastern border. He watched Promise and Arthur arrive, joining others at the long table. Fatima Hakim's black chador was instantly recognizable, as was Nathan's chef's hat. Arthur was talking in his animated fashion, but all Joseph could hear was the courtyard fountain, which drew his attention outdoors. Artificial-looking clematis vined around a pergola that was itself crowned by a square of blue sky. Downstairs in the museum archives was the hotel napkin on which the Founder had sketched his building plan, essentially a square box with a courtyard cut out of the center.

"Simple and elegant" was the phrase everyone used for the Founder's plan, and it was true that the Florentine marble in the galleries made a tasteful backdrop for encrusted Indian necklaces or unglazed Japanese teacups. This courtyard, however, was something of a slap in the public's face, since the stairways dead-ended in front of the closed-off garden, essentially bringing one's nose up to the glass. Weary visitors saw a bench and a fountain they could not rest by; they saw people eating in a room that was not on their map. Maybe the Castle was onto something.

He spotted the ever-optimistic peahen beneath the rosebushes, scratching out a nest that the horticulturist would come by later to fill. He hoped Cecil wouldn't deaccession the peacocks to the zoo, or worse, dismiss the drab peahens in favor of a flock of showy males. At twilight, the peahens' cries could rattle your teeth, and their plentiful leavings greased the flagstones. But give a kid a crayon and he drew peacocks, just as his own boys had whenever he showed them some marvel of Mughal architecture. Adults were charmed, too; many a museum review opened with a description of their plumed mascots.

Joseph had enjoyed such a good run here. Proud as he was of the museum, he was also pleased to have maintained his integrity; he'd treated those above and below him with respect, including the assholes. Emmy suggested he go out with fanfare: give everyone on his staff a cash bonus and stage the bash of the century. This from a woman who'd celebrated the end of her cancer ordeal by lighting a candle. He didn't need a party or more awards. Right now, he needed a heavy meal that would sit on his gut, diverting all his juices to digestion.

He abandoned his lookout, passing the museum shop and his office before turning down the eastern corridor. On the left, Galleries XIV, XV, and XVI displayed the collections of Islamic, manuscript, and

South Asian art. Cut into the corridor's right side was the unmarked door to the staff room; when Joseph disappeared into the camouflaged entrance, it looked as if he were walking through a wall.

———

Sitting at one end of the mahogany lunch table, Promise fixated on the color of Arthur's tie, which flickered from yellow to green. She admired how it pulled his ensemble together: maize shirt, chestnut hair, tortoiseshell glasses, and brown suit, slubbed more than most linen (what another person might reject as flawed). *Chartreuse.*

"Something's wrong with Joseph," Arthur said. "He looks like he's off his feed." Promise didn't react to the slang he'd used for her benefit. He knew she couldn't skip a single footnote of an article; yet she regularly ignored him. She acted as if the spoken word evaporated with little consequence. "Are you paying any attention at all?"

"I'm here," she said. Her to-do list was playing in a constant loop in her head. Text for her Rumi project was overdue in many forms, including not only the book and wall labels but also the video script, press packet, and Acoustiguide (for which she was supposed to provide Sufi chants in some digital form she had never heard of, the notion of *digital Sufis* itself was a stumbling block). It was a tribute to Nathan that no matter the workload, no one missed lunch. "Do you think we could get out of here in twenty minutes? As usual, I'm a little overcommitted."

Arthur took his glasses off to clean them. "What do they sing in *Oklahoma*—you're 'just a girl who cain't say no.'"

"Arthur!" Nathan called.

Arthur couldn't help thinking Promise had some sort of organizational disorder, much as he adored her. Add to her workload the confusion that was her life: a nonprofit husband, two kids, a star-crossed babysitter, with talk of throwing in a puppy. "Hey," he greeted Nathan at the lunchroom window.

Nathan said, "Don't tell anyone, but I topped your polenta with shaved Parmesan, and there's bacon under the arugula."

"Will you love me when I'm two hundred pounds?" Arthur asked. He doubted the toque was really necessary.

The chef slowly smiled. "They say the flavor's in the fat."

"So I hear." Arthur returned the smile, unsure how much to put into it. Morty behaved as if Arthur had already begun tomcatting, though he had yet to decide whether he was available or not. He moved over to the condiment counter, where he grabbed two sets of silverware.

"Promise," Nathan called out.

Arthur watched his petite friend walk the length of the room. Curators were supposed to be people of taste. She was wearing an oat-meal-colored cardigan, which had a raised peak between her shoulder blades from the hook on the back of her office door. Her blue plaid skirt would pass muster at a Catholic school, and her freckled complexion cried out for some alpha hydroxy followed by moisturizer that didn't come in gallon jugs.

"What a feast," Promise lauded Nathan, wishing she'd requested a take-out container. Leaving food on one's plate offended the chef; however, taking it home subjected her to Leo's ribbing. "Polenta?" He'd raise one eyebrow. "Eggplant ragout?" Working on behalf of human rights victims could make him insufferable. Even though this perk was funded by its own endowment, the notion of a gourmet lunch for government workers stuck in his craw.

Leo had a point. Nathan's epicurean skills were appropriate for the staff pictured in archival photographs, buxom men intent on devouring the world. One hundred fifty years ago, collecting art was the sublimated form of conquering people, and those men needed a hearty supper to keep up their strength. Committed to well-sauced European dishes, Nathan allowed Asia to influence only his desserts, arguably the continent's weakest course. Despite the recipes people brought for drunken noodles or chicken tikka, he persisted in producing marbled cuts with an abundance of cream sauce. (After all, the Founder had equipped the kitchen with individual silver gravy boats.)

Arthur had set their places, and he relieved Promise of her salad bowl so she could settle in. They both oohed and aahed over the chef's ample repast. Here was an offering worthy of an art museum. Medallions of pork tenderloin were layered upon purple-veined beet greens and polenta the color of sunflowers. He'd zigzagged a trans-lucent eggplant puree across the top. The bright salad held greens you could never find in the store, adorned with a few tightly curled shavings of cheese; snuggled against the side of the bowl was a crusty homemade roll, which blew out a wisp of steam like an elegant smoker.

Arthur raised his eyes from this still life to Promise's pilled sweater. "When you made full curator, you promised to stop shopping in the girls' department."

She waved away his criticism. "This was a hand-me-down. I've had it for years." Though she'd pinned a large cameo to her chest, the coffee spill underneath showed up each time the heavy head pitched forward. "My shoes are new. Leo says for what I paid, I could have fed an Indian family for a month." She extended a strappy sandal, reminding Arthur again how Chinese men would come running at the sight of her tiny feet.

Zemzemal Assaad entered the lunchroom and held the door open for Talbot Perry and Min Chen. Although all three arrived at the same time, it wasn't apparent if they were together, a distinction that mattered to Arthur.

Min had on a pair of navy pants and a Mao jacket. Her entire wardrobe looked like a Red Guard uniform, including the satchel of a purse she carried around all day as if someone might steal it. She claimed the spot next to Promise every way she could: laid her purse on the seat, hung her jacket on the chair back, and spread a napkin out flat where her plate would eventually be. "Promise," she said. It sounded more like "plums" the way she pronounced it. Her English was choppy and difficult to understand. She said, "Sally swims in her clothes at summer camp."

"It happens," Promise assured her. "Sometimes Felix changes into his swimsuit because he needs *dry* clothes." Promise felt Arthur's resentment, keen as sibling rivalry. She and Min were the only mothers on the professional staff, and Min's daughter was Lydia's age. "At least you got Sally into camp. Do you think the girls will be old enough next year for sleepaway? Nothing too rugged, but maybe riding horses and swimming in a lake would beef up Lydia's courage."

Min shook her head. "Douglas will not let Sally go. He supposes disaster everywhere: suspicious bologna, deadly sunburn."

Fathers, ha ha ha. Before they could revert to their mom routine, Arthur broke in. "We were going to talk about the ambassador's bowl."

"We were?" Promise moaned. "We've been talking about it for the last three weeks."

Min was baffled by the friendship between straight-shooting Promise and greedy, sly, sexist Arthur (and it took a lot for Min to flag sexist). All her training taught her to see people's worth in how they could help you: as a gay, white American, Arthur could not benefit her professionally or personally. She envied his maleness, while she knew he envied her Chineseosity. In their field, her ethnicity trumped his gender. Joseph generally deferred to her.

Min looked over the top of her black glasses at Arthur. "The ambassador's bowl has been placed on your book cover even though it's only Yongzheng reign."

"Yes, I'm aware of that," Arthur said. What did she care whether the cover piece was 1730 or a thousand years earlier? Neither date would be old to her. She hung out on the opposite end of the time line, in the Shang dynasty. That was where he wanted her to stay, back in 1700 B.C. To Promise he said, "It's from a period when color exploded. They figured out how to suspend the pigments in a lead-and-silica compound, so the glaze looks like stained glass."

"Talbot," Nathan called from the window.

The chef might as well have said, "Your attention, please," for all the diners followed Talbot's rise and watched him tuck his hair behind his right ear, then give a tug to the bottom of his suit coat as if he were about to walk onstage. Tall, blond, and handsome—everyone's type, Arthur liked to say.

Talbot kept his blond hair long enough to push behind his ears but not long enough to stay there, and his valiant efforts to smooth it past his temple and cheekbone, anchoring it for the slightest minute, mesmerized some and drove others to distraction. Promise thought Talbot's inability to commit to long or short hair, along with the sarcasm he leveled at all targets, was the crux of his personality.

Talbot sat to Arthur's right, an empty seat between them. "You like that Jingdezhen ware—personally, you think it's attractive?"

"You don't?" Arthur asked. Yesterday, he'd waited for the art handler to go on break so he could run his tongue over a dish painted with pomegranates.

"It's colorful," Talbot said, as if that were a crime. "I read that *Ars Orientalis* piece explaining the motifs."

Promise thought Arthur was the only one who had time for *Ars Orientalis*. At break this morning, he'd had been carrying on about the mummies in the Taklamakan Desert—apparently they were created with essentially the same salt scrub touted in *Men's Health*. One of the things she loved about Arthur was that he was equal parts superficial and studious; for someone obsessed with surface preservation, the Institution was a fortuitous place to end up.

Since his colleagues seemed interested, Arthur explained. "Some decorations are symbols—cranes signify longevity because they have long lives—but a lot of them are visual puns. In Chinese, 'vast good fortune' sounds like the phrase 'red bat,' so artists painted red bats on porcelain."

Zemzemal asked, "What's the meaning of the ambassador's bowl?"

"It's a rebus," Arthur answered. "The word for magpie literally translates as 'bird of joy,' and the word for 'plum' is a homonym for eyebrows, so magpies hanging out among plums reads: 'May you have joy up to your eyebrows.'"

Promise said, "I like that. Usually, they wish the recipient a thousand sons."

Joseph came through the swinging door just then and reported in at the serving window.

"I was terrified your pork might cool," the chef said. He always acted as if the director's attendance made his hours spent reducing stock worthwhile.

"Not to worry," Joseph assured him.

The central table was nearly filled, curators seated closest to the kitchen. Design and Publications, Photography, Conservation, and the registrar's staff were at the same long table but farther down. Support staff congregated separately, as did East Asian conservators, who talked among themselves as if they were on a Beijing street corner. Along a back counter, one or two contract employees read as they ate. While Joseph couldn't offer the contractors health insurance, they did get a free lunch.

Joseph enjoyed seeing the room at capacity. As he approached the main table, all of the curators lifted their gaze to him, and their spectacles had the reflective glare of museum cases. He and Promise were the only two scholars who did not wear glasses; the king of primary sources, he joked about their viewing the world through a lens.

Joseph sat down between Zemzemal Assaad and Min Chen, who sprang up to get him silverware and a napkin despite his protests. When Nathan called Joseph's name, Zemzemal insisted on retrieving the director's lunch. Zemzemal wore pleated pants and blousy printed shirts to work, although he was just below Joseph in the hierarchy. The resort wear was in keeping with his gracefulness. He had a way of waiting on everyone without being the least subservient, as if they were guests in his country.

For the staff, the pleasure of eating this meal together was heightened by Joseph's arrival. Unsupervised, they could bicker like siblings, but they were at their best with him.

Min briefed Zemzemal when he set Joseph's lunch on the table. "We have moved on to the finest source of ribs." (It sounded to Zemzemal as if she said "finest sauce of lips.") "In Haiphong, at the former palace, four sisters take turns keeping the fire going overnight. They serve ribs on celadon ware; this enhances the experience."

"Maybe," Promise said, "but the best I ever had came on flimsy paper plates at the Luling City Market, between Houston and San Antonio. The rib smoker's in a glass booth in the middle of an old five-and-dime. You walk into the booth and order by the pound—flies are buzzing all around and the sauce leaks through your plate. They serve white bread on the side."

Jill Ratner, the curator of Near Eastern art, pushed her huge red glasses up over the ridge on her nose. She said, "The Little Pig in Hong Kong. On the way home, I might add, from two months on an Iraqi dig."

Joseph relished their tales as much as his lunch. Because he sopped up juices with his roll, they all did. Today, the plates would go back with only a turnip rosette at most. How he prized these people, who were the opposite of xenophobic. Promise was the exception: she'd always appreciated the art in the museum far more than in situ. As for the rest of the curators, to find the exquisite in the hellhole was a source of pride. It was like archaeology, stumbling on a fragrant noodle soup in the alley of a dusty, rutted street. He wished they were as intrepid back home, where it seemed to him they left their museum offices only for lunch or the library.

Zemzemal, who'd lived all over Central and West Asia, weighed in. "Believe it or not, the best ribs I ever had were in Kathmandu. At least they said they were ribs."

"And they probably said they were beef." This from Fatima Hakim, curator of Islamic art.

Bracelets clanked beneath Fatima's veils as she scooped yogurt into her carmine-colored lips, lips that shunned Nathan's pork. Joseph had always been fascinated by what rustled beneath Fatima's chador, which inspired more fantasies than it quashed. Her prominent cheek-bones and square jaw were nicely framed by the medieval getup. Not every woman could wear a black hood.

"Nias, gang," Talbot announced.

"Oh, please," Promise said. "Were you running cinnamon or something? I'm not sure I know where Nias is."

Talbot said, "Take a right at Sumatra, if you're paddling."

Joseph liked that Promise wasn't in Talbot's thrall. Looking past his deputy's head, Joseph saw an actual tourist family on the north landing, where he'd been standing before lunch. Husband and wife were clearly arguing over how to get to where he was now. The father sucked at a large water jug like a baby bottle; one of their toddlers pressed palms and nose against the plate glass. Joseph didn't realize he was staring until the toddler waved, which caused him to study his plate. He cut into another piece of succulent meat so expertly cooked that it blushed at the center. Any Washington restaurant would be lucky to have Nathan. Where was he to send the rest of his staff, specialized far beyond the general population?

The museum's sole American conservator said, "We're heading over to the National Gallery. Come on, Jill, you can skip the mung bean cakes." She and the Near Eastern curator bussed their dishes with the expertise of art school graduates, giving Joseph hope for the ones with table-waiting skills.

Jill asked Joseph, "Remember the Louvre's offer for us to restore Sargon's winged bull?"

He said, "Our floor couldn't bear the weight."

"The National Gallery *reinforced* the floor of their lab," the conservator reminded him.

It was possible that Joseph had trouble with her name because she tended to be critical. That and the fact that she ate only raw food, which he thought was weird for a scientist.

Her name was Lucy Yarmolinsky, and she had more to say. "They also took the delivery port apart, made it two feet taller."

"Bully for them," Joseph said. "A loan of that ilk can sink a museum."

Then he remembered that his museum was sunk. Vinaigrette and garlic backed up into his throat—how could he have been enjoying lunch under the circumstances? Maybe he'd been too cautious during his reign, unwilling to spend hundreds of thousands to trap Sargon's giant bull. The Founder had stipulated that they were allowed to borrow and show art from other collections, as long as their own pieces stayed in-house at all times. Even Joseph had to admit that a museum that is not allowed to lend or sell an object, *ever*, can seem a little stale. His face felt as hot as if he'd been clearing brush, a satisfying chore he'd welcome about now. Was it a mistake to have respected the Founder's wishes? If he said he was only doing his job, he would sound like every government flunky he'd ever ridiculed. Perhaps if he'd bent more rules, the Castle wouldn't have felt the need to make a clean break from the benefactor.

"Speaking of Sargon," Promise chimed in. "Did you know the Founder bought extispicy models before anyone knew what they were? I saw the collection in storage."

"Was extispicy a prophecy ritual?" Min asked.

Jill sighed. "Yes, from a millennium before Sargon, around 1800 B.C. The priests would sacrifice a sheep and study its guts for omens, then someone would make a clay model so there'd be a record."

"You spend far too much time in storage," Joseph said to Promise. She knew the very entrails of the Founder's original purchase.

"It's so frustrating." Jill shook her fists in the air. "Sargon's winged bull is on the Mall and I still have to stand behind the velvet rope. I have to *visit* it. We've got clay sheep guts if anyone's interested; meanwhile, the National Gallery snags the most famous piece of Near Eastern sculpture in the world."

Arthur said, "The National Gallery may as well be co-opted by Disney, with their Asia Fantasia shows. That place is for people who have never heard of China."

Talbot laid down his fork and knife. "Tell me you wouldn't work for them." Heads nodded around the table.

Arthur brought a nail-bitten hand to his lips. "I didn't say that." For Joseph's benefit, he added, "Not that they've asked."

"Stay on their good side," the director advised.

Arthur would chew on that all afternoon. Somehow his defense of the museum had backfired.

"There, there," Joseph gave him stern comfort. "Have you told the ambassador about your cover?"

"He's delighted," Arthur said.

"Well, maybe he'll let the museum have it," Joseph suggested. "Wouldn't that show you're ready for the big time?"

There, there, indeed. Joseph's backhanded compliment stung, and it might have ruined the day except that it started Arthur thinking about the possibility of actually owning the bowl.

Jill and Lucy still hadn't shoved off. The conservator swept bread crumbs from the table into her hand. "The National Gallery doesn't have a lunchroom like this. I don't eat Nathan's cooking, and I show up every day—this is the only place I can talk about Sargon without the stare of pity."

The crew concurred, offering up examples from their particular fields: "Guanyin," "Hammurabi," "Jami."

"Which reminds me." Arthur saw a chance to redeem himself. "Before closing yesterday, I saw three big white guys in Gallery Three. Beefy guys—one of them had a brand of truck on his cap."

"They had stumbled in?" Min asked, envious that Arthur's galleries were closest to the front entrance. He filled the cases with ceramics, lacquer boxes, and brush rests; meanwhile, Min's important Neolithic jades and Shang dynasty bronzes were on the opposite side of the museum, in Galleries XI and XII near the back door.

Arthur said, "I figured they were waiting for their wives to come out of the shop or the restrooms, but when I got close enough to eavesdrop, one guy says, 'That Yuan dynasty flowerpot is a fine piece of Jun ware.' Turns out he's a collector, and they'd all lived in China. I practically asked them out for a beer."

Promise smiled. "And you thought they didn't know porcelain from stoneware."

Joseph leaned past Min, so he could see Promise. "If you're finished, I'd like to have a word in your office."

Joseph didn't even make a show of clearing his plates before exiting the room. Promise hustled her dishes to the kitchen, where she waved off dessert, and then scurried after Joseph, her new sandals slipping on the terrazzo floor. From years of dogging her big brothers, she'd devised an extra half hop every few steps that nearly caught her up. It sounded like she was dancing alongside him, which struck her as apt: her relationship to Joseph was somewhere between little sister and dance partner.

Though she got to her office seconds after him, Joseph was already straightening a column of slippery monographs on South India. "Your den has all the dangers of an archaeological dig: breakage, cave-ins, dirt."

"It's a filing system of sorts." She pointed to a stack of books in a dozen languages, most with a common word on their spines. "These are devoted to my favorite mystic."

Promise and Joseph sat facing each other, a desk in between them. They had been taking these places for twenty years. Joseph picked up a Lakshmi figurine, absentmindedly fondling her exaggerated hour-glass shape. Thumbing the curve from her extra-wide hips to her extra-tiny waist, he ended up at her breasts, round as two marbles.

Promise said, "Now that I've got kids, I find some of our stuff a little explicit." Joseph put the figurine down, but she was referring to the Mughal Court paintings that were his specialty.

"Never forget"—he spoke without enthusiasm—"violence is history; sex is parable."

"I can gloss the violence," she said and fell into museum-label jargon: "'Paintings of a princely one goring an intruder were propaganda commissioned to glorify the victor and intimidate potential usurpers.' It's the sex that's tricky. The princely one goosing a milkmaid is as real as peas and beans, but our copy talks about her being touched by a god."

Promise's devotion to Joseph was based on his vitality. She expected him to wag his finger provocatively, maybe even wink, as he reminded her of the party line: "Copulation is a metaphor of the union between human and divine." Coeds had thrilled at his affection for the lurid expressiveness in the art—sophistication was not giggling during his slide lectures on voluptuous, coupling deities. And so she was shocked to see the light gone from his eyes. Something was definitely wrong. Joseph seemed deflated. Was it a trick of shadow? Skin bunched atop his cheekbones, sacks of weariness she had never noticed: his face looked to be a portrait in encaustic, lumpen wax with oddly colored streaks.

"Are you well?" she asked.

"I'm overworked. As are you." If he wanted to rebut the Castle memo, he'd have to do more than slash expenses, and he was relying on Promise to know something about the public's "changing needs." He should have suggested they meet in his office, because the plastic lip of her inadequate guest chair was pressing into his fleshy back, forcing him into a slouch. He could not hold his head high, as Emmy had extolled him to do, and he was further stifled by the effects of lunch. This wasn't going the way he'd planned. Facing the projects mounded on Promise's desk, he finally said, "Go easy on yourself, won't you? An interactive video isn't crucial, and you could forgo the color brochure for a photocopied flyer."

She didn't know what to make of his clemency. Joseph had merely trimmed Arthur's show by a few pots; here, he was absolving her out of a job. Did he propose to hit each of them where they lived? It was sort of dear, his being bothered by her workload, except she didn't want to appear overextended.

Although he straightened up, Joseph could not bring himself to tell Promise what he was struggling against. Instead, he fell upon the story Emmy had referred to the other night. "Do you know the one about 'the glass is already broken'?"

Promise wagged her head as if she was trying to hum to a tune. "Sort of. It has to do with appreciating what you've got. No"—she stopped abruptly—"you'd better tell me."

Joseph said, "A great teacher was questioned by his student: 'You say we shouldn't cling to anything, but you have a monastery, disciples, even a beautiful water glass. What gives?'"

Promise leaned forward, concentrating as if she'd be tested on the material.

"The teacher replied, 'You're right, I like this glass.'" Joseph mimed offering a toast. "'It's useful, holding water for me to drink when I'm thirsty, and it is beautiful. Also, it was a gift, which makes it special and reminds me of the friend who gave it to me.'" Then he flipped his hand dismissively. "'But I am not attached to this glass, because it is transitory—one day it will slip from my hand or be knocked over. I accept that; in fact, for me, the glass is already broken.'"

"Yes," Promise said enthusiastically. "All our work here exists in that continuum, doesn't it?" She held up a photocopied page. "Even as I'm attending to this, I know other manuscripts are disintegrating or being taken apart and sold. The fact that this one is out of harm's way is satisfying until I think about the others."

Maybe that was the bigger lesson Emmy had wanted to pass on. At the time, he'd thought she was rubbing it in a little bit, telling him he should have known things fall apart.

"Nevertheless," he said, his voice returning to its usual timbre. "Rather than knock yourself out, treat your book as an exhibition catalog—lavishly illustrated, minimally explicated. You've got four strong books under your belt. Take it from me, they stop counting after four."

She wished he would talk about why he looked so low. The baggy skin, the sloughing off of his specialty—he must be ill. Worrying that she'd misunderstood his parable, she panicked. He might have been alluding to his own transitory nature. Embarrassed by her attachment to him, Promise opened her shallow drawer, wedging her hand in to push stuff out of the way, and came up with a few unmarked sticks of chewing gum. "Gum?" she offered.

Joseph accepted the flat, foiled parcel. Later this afternoon he had an appointment with the head of the Education Department to deliver bad news. "A drastic and regrettable decision." Eliminating the department was part of his counteroffer to the Castle, though he suspected that taking his own museum apart limb by limb was exactly what Cecil and the Board of Regents wanted.

He unwrapped the gum and laid it on his tongue. It was good to feel the stick soften and juice up in his mouth. "Spearmint," he said. There was satisfaction in working something over. For the moment, director and chief curator, professor and pupil, appreciated their communion, chewing the gum that was already losing its flavor.

Not Your Fault

July 26, 1999

Min Chen caught her urine in a clear specimen cup, snapped the lid snug, and recorded her name on the side. She was always surprised at the container's heat—body temperature was nearly as warm as a lingering cup of tea. Yet she herself was freezing. Her fingernails were blue with cold, and her mirror image revealed her lack of faith. She closed her eyes to envision Dr. Fan declaring her pregnant. Wasn't she shivering? Didn't she have a headache? From the onset of carrying Sally, she'd experienced those symptoms, although she opened her eyes to the possibility that anxiety and the overly cooled medical office might be the cause. She turned the hot-water knob on all the way, then held her hands under the spigot until the water became steaming hot. Squinting at the mirror, she tried to picture her shrimp-pink lips and tiny teeth on a boy's face. At forty-one, was a baby boy too much for her to ask?

In the outer room, a nurse stood Min on the scales, then wrapped her arm in the blood-pressure band, which she inflated like a swimming aid. Sometimes Min's blood pressure was so low the nurse had to repeat this step. After these preliminaries, Min gathered her shoes and followed the nurse to the inner room, where Douglas was already waiting. Seeing him holding her purse made her uncomfortable but oddly proud as well. He wouldn't be that attentive if they were still living in Taipei.

Min changed out of her work clothes into the waffled-paper gown, ever bewildered by its sash; this time, the thin strip tore when she tied it around her waist. Douglas had found a pen and a notepad emblazoned with medical advertising, and his hand scribbled across the page like a water bug over a pond.

"I am agitated, too," Min said.

"So sorry," Douglas apologized. He put aside the notepad, which he'd nearly filled with numbers. "They are obsessed with their payment. Out in the waiting room, they spoke to me again."

Min held up a hand to stop him from talking about money. She said, "Let us first hear from Dr. Fan."

She boosted herself onto the examination table, a tan vinyl bench covered by slick white paper, and Douglas sat in a gray chair by her side. Min assumed that the absence of color was a deliberate attempt by Dr. Fan to lower patients' expectations, which she understood, but she did not appreciate the two posters hanging opposite her. The one on the left was an anatomical drawing of a woman, back to the wall, hands splayed flat on either side, and her head turned completely in profile. A woman in that uncomfortable pose would be a woman trapped, flinching from what pursued her.

In her quest for a baby boy, Min was pursued by money concerns and the customs of China. She and Douglas had already gone through their savings and were paying the bill for this in vitro procedure, her second one, with Institution funds. Just as troubling to Min were the Chinese rituals she'd sworn to ignore. While pregnant with Sally, she'd observed only convenient superstitions; eschewing all scissoring, for example, she'd enlisted Douglas to clip coupons and trim her bangs. She'd pulled loose threads rather than cut them, lest her son develop a cleft palate. Always she'd tried to sit with a straight back and not expose herself to vulgar sights or tastes. Douglas had read poetry aloud to her and the baby, even after the second sonographer had predicted a girl.

And so, on the fifth day of the fifth lunar month of 1990, when Min felt birth pains rip across her belly and she indeed delivered a healthy girl, she also tried to deliver herself of unproductive rituals. Chinese orphanages were teeming with baby girls, daughters of women who had followed every wives' tale. She took Sally's unlucky date of birth as another reason to be glad they had emigrated.

"Five sacred mountains," Douglas had said by way of comfort. "The five blessings—may she have them all."

Adrift in her postpartum fog, Min could still list all the blessings: wealth, long life, health and tranquillity, love of virtue, and peaceful death. With such a love of five in Chinese culture, why was the fifth day of the fifth lunar month branded the most pernicious day of the year?

Holding his daughter's tiny hand in his own, the new father had remarked, "Five ugly little fingers."

The dimple in his left cheek deepened, and Min was profoundly relieved to have married such a clever man. She would speak of Sally's beauty aloud when she felt a little braver.

Then he'd teasingly said, "Five poisonous creatures." His mother had sent them charms of lizard, adder, centipede, toad, and scorpion on a baby bracelet, which Min had found clasped around the rod in Sally's closet. In his own defense, Douglas had pointed out how Min had banished some rituals while accepting others as harmless or even sweet.

He was right. She felt especially hypocritical now, in the throes of fertility treatments that rivaled the most peculiar Chinese practices. A shiver ran through her, shaking her by the shoulders. How long did it take Dr. Fan to dip the stick into her urine sample? Min looked with empathy upon the exposed poster woman cringing against the wall. The poster on the right was a straightforward 1999 calendar, just a rectangle of twelve square months, seven columns of days in each. She and Douglas could take their places on Dr. Fan's wall: she was the woman flattened and turned inside out; her husband was a matrix of days, doses, temperatures, menstrual periods, doctor bills.

When Dr. Fan finally entered, Min observed that his pea-pod lips were turned down. She hung her head, seeing just beyond the paper gown to the spider veins scribbled in red ink along her thighs. Her eggs were the same age as her old-woman thighs.

"I'm afraid the desired results have not been produced," Dr. Fan said in English.

"Not your fault." Douglas automatically forgave the doctor.

Maybe not, Min thought, but he is to be paid regardless. With the backs of her thighs adhering to the waxed-papered examination table, she felt a chilly humiliation, as if the doctor were mocking her many times over. She was so deeply disappointed that her fingertips went past cold all the way to numb.

Min was accustomed to being at fault. Not enough eggs to work with, the ones she produced too fragile or for unknown reasons resistant to Douglas's fine, though limited, sperm. Her fervent desire to have a son had started as soon as she'd weaned Sally eight years ago; unfortunately, she could not get pregnant. She wondered if Chinese women, after being scolded about overpopulation for generations, had begun to censor themselves.

Doctor after doctor refused their case. These self-proclaimed "specialists" were uniform in their approach: shoot Min full of hormones, harvest her eggs, have Douglas spume into a cup, mix him and her in a dish, and then identify the most robust possibilities. "That could be a girl, a boy," fertility masters said, "or both."

We already have a girl, Min and Douglas said. Min suspected the doctors would be more sympathetic if they were an American couple; Americans boldly announcing their preference for a boy would be considered savvy consumers. Douglas came up with the idea of finding a Chinese fertility doctor.

Dr. Fan had listened to their request with no sign of disapproval. "You love your daughter like a son," he had said, which they took to be a compliment. "Let me explain procedures." Therein started a volley of esteem between Dr. Fan and Douglas to rival Nixon in Beijing. You, who are most wise. No, you whose advice we humbly seek. No, please, you praise me unjustly. Once the veneration had subsided, Dr. Fan put forth the possibilities for Min not conceiving, beginning with the premature onset of menopause and including fibroids, endometriosis, insufficient body fat, and nerves.

Min had trouble listening. Douglas Chen, Jr., she was thinking. Or perhaps she would name the baby after her personal hero: Will Rogers Chen. Infertility aside, she felt their problems had been solved.

That was before she had been through a colposcopy, biopsy, ultrasound, and two rounds of laparoscopic surgery: eighteen months of invasive procedures and one in vitro attempt that had drained them of their savings. Forty thousand dollars and no baby to show for it, a humbling outcome, except that Dr. Fan wasn't ready to quit. Indeed, he asserted that they'd made some progress. With that slight encouragement, Min had signed on for a second round of hormone therapy, egg-gathering, fertilization, and implantation, subsidizing this medical voyage with her museum travel funds. After all, she didn't need to travel the way some curators did, returning to Japan or Iraq to see a cup or go to a library.

And now she had reached a second dead end. As Dr. Fan listed possible reasons why her implanted embryos had left the womb, she resisted sticking her fingers in her ears. She only wanted to hear if they had another chance.

"Of course, more sperm would mean more opportunity for fertilizing," the doctor was saying. "We see fewer sperm for many reasons. Sperm like warm conditions—they like moist, too—but not hot. That is why runners, whose testes heat up, have low counts."

Here we go, Douglas thought, prepared to finally be singled out as the cause of their failure. He'd allowed Dr. Fan to fixate on Min when he could have come forward, and he vowed to answer all questions the doctor put to him. You couldn't get more bourgeois than running around a circle inside a building during work hours.

But it didn't come to that. Dr. Fan said, "For this reason, we recommend loose briefs or boxer shorts to men." He closed the folder holding Douglas's lab work and returned to Min's thick accordion file, resuming his routine: As a healthy forty-year-old, Douglas has one-third the sperm he should—let's operate on Min. Douglas had expected a specialist to help them have a son and, if not, to extend his professional sympathies as they bowed out the door. Instead, there was always something more that could be done to Min. Though he longed to speak up, he sat by as Min and Dr. Fan egged each other on to distressing procedures.

"I'm sure you're disappointed," Dr. Fan said, "but we could revisit the left ovary. More plaque may have formed. We could enhance your offerings with donor eggs, fertilized, of course, by Douglas's sperm. We could switch from synthetic hormones to harvested hormones."

Surgery, alien eggs, or mood swings.

"Harvested animal hormones?" Douglas asked.

"No," Dr. Fan said, "quite human."

Douglas wasn't sure this was as comforting as Dr. Fan was implying. The synthetic hormones had some disturbing side effects—witness Min's budding American chest—and while baboon hormones might bear their own drawbacks, at least one knew where the baboons had been. It reminded him of those ads in American comic books, the highest childhood contraband. Among the magic and muscle kits were offers for wigs that boasted "genuine human hair." Whose? Worse than scalps, because of the anonymity and the possible ancestral humiliation. Apparently, wigs were not as freakish as he thought, but neither were they ingested.

"These are hormones from a controlled population," Dr. Fan was saying.

Min wanted the doctor to spare the euphemisms. "Prisoners?" she guessed, trying to sound neutral, just as she had when Sally had recently asked, "Why didn't you and Daddy have more kids?" All Min had managed to say to that was, "We try."

Dr. Fan assured her that prisoners were not the source. He said, "Purified gonadotropins are gleaned from the urine of postmenopausal Italian nuns."

All fell silent between the sacred and profane of that information. Nuns peeing. Nuns having periods. Nuns no longer having periods peeing. Nuns no longer having periods selling their pee.

Min had heard Dr. Fan's theories regarding the meeting of sperm and egg: sperm magnetically sensitive to the ovulating pole or pheromone-sniffing sperm. Whenever he got going, she looked for signs that he was duping them. He could just as easily have spoken of yin/yang for vaginal pH, ancestral appeasement for genetic history. But he never did, much to her admiration.

Dr. Fan said, "I should tell you each injection costs five hundred dollars."

"And then?" Douglas asked.

"If newer hormones are efficacious, fertility-enhancing medication and some luck would allow another implantation in four or five months."

Min wondered if postmenopausal Italian nun urine was as scarce as rhinoceros horn, whose crumbled powder was cheaper. "This is what you recommend?" she asked. "You are thinking this approach will be successful?"

"I don't see any other way for pregnancy. Perhaps you have changed your minds." He held up a rubber-gloved hand and waved it around the inner room. "You may desire to take a break from this." His gesture would have seemed more generous if he hadn't then said to Min, "Though each passing month reduces your chances of conception. However you decide, I will honor that."

After he left, Douglas sat up on the table next to Min, warming her in his arms. "We have our Sally," he said.

Sally was a comfort, smart and capable at such a young age. Not only did she read book after book but she was also clever with her hands. Min brought home activities the Education Department devised for schoolchildren, admiring the earnest way Sally followed directions to make a mask or a small folding screen.

Douglas slid off the table to retrieve Min's hanger of clothes. She stepped into her white cotton underwear and handed the paper robe to Douglas, who forced it down the throat of the trash can. Zipping her plain blue skirt, pulling on her blue jacket and unornamented flats, she realized that, for all her talk about leaving China behind, she dressed like a Beijing student. She'd have to get shopping help if she wanted to work at the National Gallery.

They made their way out of the inner room, past the outer room, and through the waiting room. Whenever Douglas had to spend time here, he always sat under the aggravating sign to avoid rereading it: "We do not accept payment from any insurance providers. Charges must be paid in full at time of service." Forget jogging, he thought. You couldn't get more bourgeois than paying for another child.

Min drove on the way back, because Douglas was prone to small accidents. "What did they say to you before we met with Dr. Fan?" she asked.

Douglas had been making calculations in his own notebook, which he tipped toward his wife. "Their records show a balance due of eight thousand eight hundred dollars. I'm afraid they are correct."

"We will pay that."

"They say we will have to settle our balance *and* pay in advance for further treatment." When Min didn't respond, Douglas said, "They apologize for any inconvenience."

Min had to take one hand from the wheel to steady her trembling chin. Was it really possible that she'd have nothing to show for all the surgeries and medications, for the amounts of money she'd never dreamed two people could spend?

The Potomac smelled like sewage on this humid summer day, and overhead a jet bore down so close that its roar was not delayed. They passed the small park along the edge of the airport, where she and Douglas used to come when the quiet in their new life seemed oppressive. They would sit on the pavement directly beneath the jets' final approach, exhilarated by the ground-shaking roar. Had the noise or the fumes affected her fertility? Had the plum wine she'd drunk? Lately, every memory was tinged with self-recrimination.

Beyond Arlington Cemetery, marines jogged across Memorial Bridge in the high-noon heat. Min assumed anyone traveling back and forth like that must be patrolling.

Douglas finally spoke. "Maybe we are too persistent."

Min agreed. "Our determination has not paid off."

She remembered Joseph signing off on her travel and acquisition requests, when he'd said, "Spend it while you can." That remark made more sense after Madame Xingfei said there was talk of making the museum into a food emporium. Though, as always, it was hard to tell if Madame X was prescient or paranoid.

Min had reassigned her travel funds for a baby. Madame X wanted her to spend money from her acquisitions funds on a three-legged bronze urn called a *ding*. Decorated with interlocking dragons and thunder motifs, the *ding* was made in Houma around 1100 B.C. and dug up in 1979 by Beijing archaeologists, who had no means to guard the one thousand tombs they'd discovered. By 1985, every single tomb had been robbed. This urn had surfaced recently in a Hong Kong shop. It might be from Houma, in which case it was worth ten, twenty times the asking price, or it might be a fake.

Madame X had written a letter stating that she'd seen the piece in Macao in 1955, testimony that would allow the dealer to send it on speculation. If the *ding* made it through customs, Min would be complicit in the deception, but the old woman was pressuring Min to acquire this piece before the museum changed hands.

A baby or a pot? A new life or a Bronze Age bronze? Min asked herself these questions as if she were spending a stack of bills on one choice or the other. For risking his life and breaking the law, the peasant who had unearthed the prize probably netted a hundred dollars. It was better for a museum to have the *ding* than for some private collector to squirrel it away, as someone had for the last twenty years. Min would know whether it was stolen or forged as soon as she set her eyes on it.

Douglas intruded on her thoughts. "Slim chances," he quoted Dr. Fan. "Do you think he meant as slim as when we began or possibly slimmer?"

"Slimmer, I think," Min said. Staying hopeful was a challenge; two years ago, their enthusiasm had been tainted by in vitro's 20 percent success rate. She asked her husband, "What do you think Promise would do?"

Douglas gave that some thought, uncomfortable with where their fertility quest was going. "She has been helpful to you before," he said. Min had relayed to him what Arthur and Promise brought up over soup and sandwich, topics never visited by Chinese.

Min had meant the question hypothetically, but she did wish she could consult Promise about her fertility treatments and whether Madame X was altogether there. The whole business of looting China's national treasures was sickening; if the Shanghai or Taipei Museum had the money, they would have bought the bronze. Still, Min was feeling squeamish about her involvement.

Douglas said, "We discuss matters with each other. Did our parents have that?"

"No." Min's parents had to follow orders dictated by extended family on both sides: you will double up with your brother's new relatives; it is your honor to prepare the New Year's feast. Brothers and sisters were their lifetime companions and adversaries, multiplied by whatever families each sibling begat. Mutual silence in that environment would be the greatest of intimacy, a marital conspiracy. Min was more grateful for Douglas than for anything else in her life, including Sally.

She pulled into the taxi zone in front of the museum, giving her husband an affectionate nod before getting out of the car. Douglas scooted over to drive himself to George Washington University, where he would spend a lonely day preparing the fall syllabus for American Tax Theories. When they'd first come from Taiwan, he'd railed against Americans' quick intimacy, along with their disregard for hierarchy and veneration. (Students' excuses proved his prejudices: "Sorry, Dr. C. My shrink says I shouldn't take exams until there's twelve hours of daylight.") Social as magpies, his students expected him to chat, which he resisted until he was mostly left alone. Now, students sent their excuses via e-mail. And there were fewer students than there used to be.

Douglas told himself that running was a prudent use of his excess hours, though he needed to come clean to Min before he competed in the Marine Corps Marathon. He looked forward to throwing himself into the panting throng. In fact, the effort so embodied their conception struggle that he took his low sperm count in stride (he was about two hundred million short). Surely, the confusion and jostling within a full-strength crowd would trip up many contenders at the starting gate. A hundred million seemed more reasonable and modest, two qualities he had been honing his entire life.

Dr. Fan talked about opportunity coupled with competition, as if conception were a free-market phenomenon. And yet, in Taiwan, Min had gotten pregnant unassisted. Douglas now regretted having serenaded her with capitalism. *Strum:* respect is mightily reimbursed in America. *Strum:* you can take all that bowing and scraping to the U.S. bank, as your talent and hard work escalate you to the top. Perhaps because he was the supposed expert, his shock was greater upon their arrival. It was a few months shy of Sally's birth when they moved to Washington; actually, to Virginia, because housing costs were such a surprise. Subsequently, the entire delivery process alarmed him. Douglas was supposed to remind Min to breathe, and in a hospital, surrounded by doctors and nurses, he had to cut the umbilical cord himself. At least Min's labor had been induced, allowing him to defend Sally against her unlucky birthday.

Min had foreseen such opportunities for them in their new country! She viewed Americans as a people set free from drudgery: dishwashers, clothes dryers, automobiles. Douglas was as guilty of this misconception as Min. But this was only because he had never given a thought to how one might accumulate said luxuries. Turns out, you could wash your own dishes or spend the time working for the money to buy a machine that washed them. In addition to buying the machine, someone still had to rinse the plates, arrange them, and put them away, which Douglas believed to be less efficient than just washing and drying them himself. He didn't have good data on this, because in Taiwan he had never been called upon to do dishes.

Min's projections had largely panned out. Associate curator of Chinese art at the National Institution—they may as well have painted her sky red. Her foreignness was treated as an asset, as if the more Chinese she was, the more her aesthetic insights counted. The museum provided her with extra editorial assistance and increased secretarial help. How could she be expected to find her own books in their library? She was Chinese.

Douglas would likewise have been in greater demand if his specialty was Asian trade practices. He hadn't counted on Americans being reluctant to ask a Taiwanese economist about their fiscal outlook. Then there was the workload, if he wanted to advance: one well-received paper secured your reputation for a semester; a book was worth maybe two years. More research, more publications, more children: compared to this, his old life seemed one of great leisure.

———

Try as he might in the last three weeks, Joseph could not conceive of a plan to raise a billion dollars, and so he decided that Cecil had snatched the number out of the air. Next, he presumed that the Castle memo had been lobbed into his office as an opening volley rather than as a grenade; thusly deluded, he swung back with a counterproposal that offered a café along with a drastic budget cut.

Determined to be as patient as necessary, Joseph watched Cecil pick at his scone. The Secretary's fingers showed a dexterity left over from feather plucking. Holding up a tiny currant, he said, "Why you made such an effort mystifies me. I apologize if my instructions were ambiguous." He'd nearly defruited the pastry when it disintegrated, an outcome that seemed to both devastate and amuse him. "And here I had my heart set on a scone."

Was the Secretary daft? Joseph cleared Cecil's crumbs off his papers—the resulting grease spots were the only marks on the document.

"Actually," Cecil said, "this is not just about tightening your belt."

Joseph raised his ridiculous china cup. "That's why the proposal accommodates your food-service request." He recapped the major changes. "No Education Department, I'm sure you noticed that. The archives would be subsumed under the library, and we'd lose half the curatorial assistants. I've tightened our belt so much, it's cut us off at the knees."

Cecil whinnied. "Comical. I hadn't thought of belt-tightening as a tourniquet. I shall miss you, Dr. Lattimore."

The movie villain always spoke a line like that before sending the hero into a tank full of sharks. In fact, Cecil was hunched over his teacup like a villain, and turning sideways revealed his crooked smile. The old man obviously intended to pull the trapdoor lever. "Your 'proposal' is not germane because it presumes the existence of a museum. Frankly, you've made it apparent that you're not up to this transition."

Joseph laid down his rose teacup next to the silver bird-claw sugar tongs, setting them both clattering. Perhaps he was coming across as too conciliatory, he thought, and so he spoke plainly. "A memo doesn't close a museum."

Cecil slowly buttered a bite of pastry, giving it far more attention than he'd lavished on Joseph. Eventually, he spoke in his most patronizing tone. "We're prepared to appoint an interim director for the museum's transition. Perhaps this would be a good time to return to your fieldwork."

"Did you even read my goddamn proposal?" Joseph heard himself say far too loud even for the hard-of-hearing Secretary.

Cecil balked. "I looked it over—thought it showed good thinking in a pinch."

Joseph flinched from Cecil's cruel compliment, which hurt him deeply. He would have responded if he had anything left to concede, but he'd already offered to sacrifice his staff and programs. His ready defeat stunned him. He pushed himself up from the velvet wing-back chair, eager for a glimpse outside the suffocating tower. Resting against the stone sill, he eyed the tourists distorted by the leaded glass. It was more gun turret than window really—weren't Cecil and the Regents picking the visitors off one by one? Children ran onto the garden grass, only to be shooed away by guards. What harm were they causing? he wanted to ask, knowing how cheap a bag of grass seed was and what little skill it took to spread a handful here or there. Obviously, he was out of touch. He took his seat again, leaning forward to encourage the blood flow to his light head. Maybe the audience for his museum was aging faster than he was.

Cecil cleared his throat three, four times, and when he spoke again he sounded more like his old ornithologist self. "Just because I want to see the ivory-billed woodpecker—no matter my determination or qualifications—there's every chance I will fail. Nonetheless, if the species is not extinct, it would be only game of him to show himself to me. Do you see what I'm getting at?"

"No," Joseph answered honestly. Frankly, he couldn't tell if the Secretary was speaking nonsense or if he was merely reminding him that life was not fair.

Cecil brought his rounded shoulders up to his ears in a show of contrition. "When I told you a billion dollars might turn the tide, I'd been misled. The fate of the Asian was already compromised." The Secretary picked up a fresh napkin and placed a miniature sandwich atop it. "Last year, the Conference of Governors was to hold a meeting in the Castle, and one group took the Metro over from Capitol Hill. Naturally, they came up out of the ground in front of your building."

"I hope someone explained our private endowment," Joseph said. He could imagine a bunch of out-of-town politicians taking their talk of fiscal responsibility to illogical conclusions.

"You're on the wrong track," Cecil said. "They objected to your subject matter. Stepping onto the National Mall, the governors were surprised to see—first thing—a billboard for Asia. The arts of Islam, Buddhism, Hinduism: those were the banners hanging that day."

Those were the banners every day, Joseph thought. He'd been proud to highlight the world's religions.

Cecil said, "Sometimes these ideas take on a life of their own. As I understand it, the governors' objections turned into a tussle over patriotism. By the time everyone gathered in the Castle and the vice president asked what he could do for them . . ."

Now Cecil looked upon him with downright pity. The air-conditioning kicked on in the aged building, and a puff of cool air brought old-man smell to Joseph's nose. Trying to settle himself, Joseph concentrated on the *Ramayana*, that epic tale that inspired courage in him. He'd told Rama's adventures over and over to his boys, though he'd never confessed that he identified with the mythic hero. Rama was chosen, anointed—he was an avatar of the god Vishnu—but he also had to think fast and usually resort to running someone through. Joseph remembered the dilemma Rama faced when he learned that his father, the king, had died. Although Rama was in line for the throne, he was serving out an exile imposed by his stepmother, and he was not allowed to return home. When news of his father's death reached him, Rama passed out cold. He was leveled not by grief or weakness, the *Ramayana* explained, but by a surfeit of thoughts: Under the circumstances, what are my duties? What about my people? Would it be braver to serve out my exile or to renounce it?

"Let me get this straight," Joseph said. "With the authority vested in you, you're asking me to resign." He turned from the old man to Cecil's official portrait, which had been painted back when the Secretary had his own unruly teeth and was possessed of a head of hair like a bird's nest. From the corner of his eye, he caught Cecil admiring the man in the painting as well.

The Secretary said, "I have the utmost respect for you, Joseph; nevertheless, you can see my limitations here." He pointed to the tea tray, then rubbed a tarnished spot with the tablecloth. "I can't even manage to get myself a plain scone."

Joseph looked at the pile of currants on Cecil's plate. They were all on their way out, weren't they? If the ruling junta wouldn't grant the Secretary a plain scone, they'd never let Joseph pluck his museum from ruin.

Joseph said, "These are the same nitwits who brought us Ronald Reagan Airport."

"I'm afraid so," the Secretary agreed. "I remember when that vote was pending—every senator and congressman I ran into said he was against it. They all wanted the airport to remain Washington National. And yet the vote was unanimous."

The episode had become something of a Washington parable.

Cecil said, "At parties, legislators explained to me that none of them could go on record as being against the name change. It was a done deal."

Joseph felt the fight go out of him, although not the self-righteousness. He reached for a silly finger sandwich, and sealed off in the Castle tower, he could hear his ground-down molars shredding the stringy watercress. "How long do you think you'll be here?" he asked. There was some satisfaction in knowing he wasn't alone.

"They've already formed a presearch committee for my job," the Secretary admitted.

Joseph recalled what Rama did after coming to—the blue-faced god served out his exile with everyone's sympathies and good wishes for a safe return. He and his wife, Rama reasoned, would live to rule again. Though Joseph had seen hundreds of paintings of this scene, what he was trying to picture was Rama taking a severance package and becoming a consultant.

———

A week after her appointment with Dr. Fan, Min Chen still could not decide if she was willing to put herself and Douglas through another pregnancy attempt. When she'd gone to the Accounting Office to collect the remainder of her travel budget, they'd told her there was a problem and asked her to step into the supervisor's office. Joseph had signed off on her forms, and he surely knew she didn't travel. "Perhaps another time," she'd said and fled the office, whose doors opened into the underground corridors of the Castle. The narrow winding hallways were cluttered with staff wheeling computer carts, hauling loops of cables over their shoulders, and carrying bins of potato salad through passageways tourists never saw. Min was able to walk on the far right, along the stone wall, because low-hanging pipes kept most people to the middle.

Back at her station, Min checked her phone and e-mail messages, relieved that they carried only the usual threats. How the underlings loved to scold. "I'm sorry, so very late," she might say to them, but she had no intention of rushing. Were they not working for her? Her personal concerns overshadowed rewriting label copy or approving images for the shop's calendar.

She reviewed the prescriptions Dr. Fan had written for her, wondering if there was a limit to how far she was willing to go for a son. Her childhood was peppered with fairy tales devoted to the quest. One mother cooked down the family fortune into a golden boy, whom she planned to animate with her fierce love. Another mother, seeking intervention from the moon goddess, spun silk for ten years so she could make a ladder that would reach to the moon. At least that woman had a thousand yards of silk to show for her efforts. Dr. Fan had recommended the next outlandish step; would he ever recommend they stop? Hard as it would be to talk about, she decided to seek her friend's guidance.

"Promise at lunch?" she asked Vanessa.

"Plums?" the curator's assistant guessed. She held up her index finger with its lacquered, slightly curved nail.

Min tried again. "Promise's schedule available?"

"Plum sketch of a label" was what Vanessa heard. Stroking a large hoop earring, she silently manipulated the sounds, trying to make a match. When she did, her puckered lips smoothed into a smile. "Promise's schedule!"

"Her schedule," Min repeated, flustered by this impossible language. She had observed Vanessa talking a dozen different Englishes, from research assistant to girl from the street. Why couldn't she ever understand Min?

Vanessa paged through Promise's calendar. "That woman is booked through doomsday. Arthur was after me, I told him lunch was his best bet. If I ate those meals, I'd be facedown asleep in the afternoon."

Min was getting only a word here and there: Arthur, me, lunch, I, I, I. She concentrated on Vanessa's lips, pink-brown and ridged like two earthworms in rich soil.

Vanessa said, "Promise is in the big house."

On television, "the big house" meant prison. Min stood still, hoping Vanessa would explain herself. Instead, Promise appeared, her arms full of Joseph's notorious color-coded files.

"Hello, Min," she said. "Vanessa, can you do something with these?" She spoke with the voice of a cricket, but Min saw that both her eyes and nose were weeping.

Min followed her into her messy office. When it became evident that what Promise was hunting for was a box of tissues, she offered up her own. "I have many nosewipes." Min hovered nearby, frantic. "You are upset. It is the children."

"No, no, no." Promise waved her off. "They're right as rain. Close the door, please." She lowered her voice to a whisper. "It's Joseph. He just told me he's leaving in two weeks. I thought maybe he was sick, but I never thought he'd fly the coop."

Right as rain, fly the coop—as Min deduced the meaning of Promise's idioms, she also recognized the convergence of a dozen puzzling paths. "Museum is closing," she announced. "Someone makes Joseph leave."

"What?" Promise sniffed loudly. "This is how rumors start. No—what I said was Joseph is quitting. He says he's ready to go back to fieldwork. I told you because you can keep it to yourself."

Min kept everything to herself, though it wouldn't matter in this case: Promise was always the last to know these things. It wasn't true in Promise's field, where she was famous for her daring attributions. She'd once told Min that when she examined a manuscript page, she simply had to know whose hand Rumi was in. At parenting, too, Promise had extensive knowledge. Min had been reduced to the simple-minded women's magazines before she'd befriended Promise, who'd steered her through Gymboree, Ritalin, Girl Scouts. She'd come to ask Promise, What would you do to have another child? Instead, she said, "What happens to us when Joseph leaves?"

"We soldier on, I suppose. I should have guessed when he handed over his *Padshahnama* book for me to finish. Lordy, Lordy! Now I have twice as many fields to plow." Promise picked up a stack of papers, rotated it, and put it on another pile.

Min saw Promise move papers over and back to the same spot. She was obviously frantic about being at the museum without Joseph. Fluttering around the office, she knocked a tower of books into rubble; both women dropped to their knees to rebuild the stack. Min was glad to have something to do, uncomfortable as she was with Promise's affection for the boss.

"You are very productive," Min said. "Much is expected of you because you already do much. 'Want something done? Ask a busy person,' I have heard it said. You are like that. So many books and exhibitions you have performed, Joseph chooses you to carry on his work."

Promise hoped Min would stay the afternoon praising her. There was safety as well as prestige in being Joseph's mentee. She straightened the stack of monographs and got up from her knees to her desk chair. As soon as she'd declared her major, Joseph had helped her secure grants for a trip to India. In the Mughal Court workshops, a cross between prison and salon, many artists had chosen Rumi verses as the basis for their elaborate illuminations. Joseph had urged her to see for herself where they'd ground the malachite chips, brushed rivulets of gold around Rumi's words, which made base instincts holy and linked the profane to the humane. Alas, living in India tarnished the glow for her: too many base instincts. And far too much humanity.

Min stood beside Promise's other chair, on which several more projects were stacked. "Rumi is fortunate to have you as a follower, fortunate as Lydia and Felix are to have you as a mother. You keep many things going—like your juggling."

Promise smiled. She'd given Min a few demonstrations of her talent.

Min pointed to the pictures along Promise's bookshelf. "You have an important job, but also you have a husband, a family." Finally, she was ready to talk about herself, though she put her hand in front of her mouth as she asked Promise, "Do you ever think of another child?"

Here was the opportunity Min had been manufacturing, an opening for colleagues to share a candid exchange of personal information. Min could confess that her yearning for a son was so insatiable that she'd consented to—*paid museum funds for!*—Dr. Fan's increasingly absurd and intrusive procedures.

Promise said, "Do I want another child? I don't even want a dog. Listen, thanks for the pep talk. Maybe I'm not ambitious enough, but I could have stayed in Joseph's shadow for years." She heard the stress in her voice, which sounded like a tape recorder on fast forward. "I feel strange taking on his projects without him."

Min pressed on. "I want another child. No, I only want to have my son."

Promise jerked her head up as if Min had hooked her like a carp in a pond. "You have a son? Older than Sally?"

"No," Min said. She mashed her glasses against her face in frustration. "I want a new boy baby. But we are not able to conceive."

"I'm so sorry." Promise came to Min's side. "Have you talked to someone?"

"Just you."

"I mean a doctor." Promise gave her a full appraisal, seeing how thin her friend was. And Min was at least forty.

"Yes, there is a doctor. He has operated—attending to blockages and cysts—and there are drugs to make all my eggs drop at once." She bit her lip and folded her arms tight in front of her chest. "Our expenses are great." Promise's arm around her shaking shoulder melted what little resolve she had left, and she understood the hazard of confiding and being met by sympathy.

"I'm so sorry it didn't work out," Promise said.

"You have a son, and now Joseph chooses you. You are honored."

"Min, my friend. You should be so honored."

Min bowed her head. That was the highest tribute Promise had ever paid her, diminished somewhat by her misunderstanding. Min wanted to tell her that they were still working on a son. She wanted to admit how they were paying for the procedures, but she was rattled by Promise reaching around with her other arm to envelop her in a hug. Min's arms stayed stiffly folded—hard elbows in front of her breasts— and up close she saw Promise's large green eye and her tiny lobeless ear. Min willed herself to relax her arms apart and down, until she was returning the hug. She clung to Promise for the comfort, despite having her hunches confirmed: those big round eyes might see well enough, but those little ears did not hear all they should.

Hold This Together

August 12, 1999

Emmy greeted Joseph at the door, eager for assistance with yet another distended box. She'd been wearing her ubiquitous roll of tape like a bracelet. "Hold this together for me, will you?" she asked.

"Are we saving anything?" he asked. He squeezed the edges until they met, then he toted the carton to the alley behind their Capitol Hill house. He'd come upon her in the attic last week snapping the wings off model airplanes that he and Jules had once assembled. Seeing the stack of fuselages, he'd had to retreat to his study, where he smoked an entire cigar down to ash.

For Emmy, Joseph's situation put a match to the nest she'd started emptying back when she feared her illness would prevail. At her appointments now, her doctors congratulated themselves on catching her just in time. She was thankful, of course, though she did wonder if they might have caught her a little earlier. In her dreams, they ran back and forth like circus clowns holding a giant net as she plunged head-first toward them. Might they have rescued her before she fell through the pain of cancer, the dread of losing her family, the regret of giving her life over to Joseph and the boys? She'd endured but, oh, the scars.

What elation, then, to clear out the house in good health! Off-loading cartons put her in mind of when she'd thrown over her Bible Belt up-bringing. Back in the Texas Hill Country, where the bluebonnets were so abundant that springtime washed over the fields in an ocean tide, Southern Baptists had staked an early claim to her soul. They commanded her to close her eyes and let God lead, and she could do it out there, where God loomed large. His breath was in the gusts that up-ended compact cars, his light in the stars at night, big and bright. Could it be that Texas was God's Country and the rest No Man's Land? Because at Penn, she couldn't close her eyes to the campus mayhem or the bloodshed in Southeast Asia, which the students went nuts protesting. Wide-eyed, she took to her books, and when she read that it's a world of suffering we inherit, that no violent action comes to good, that mindfulness and compassion are the ultimate goals, she felt she was being given a badly needed heart massage. Emmy found solace in these teachings and in the arms of her art history professor. She wasn't sure which upset her parents more.

In fact, both her husband and philosophy had sustained her. She couldn't say that about any of her possessions, from the family silver to the boys' art projects. Buddhism had given her a community as she and Joseph had traveled through Asia, and it had soothed her when she was a young mother living in Calcutta. Most important, Buddhism acknowledged the fear, like a low-grade fever, accompanying her devotion to her children. She'd served a long apprenticeship dealing with small losses, like pets or soccer games. But thank God for the practice, for now the losses carried a much bigger wallop. Both her parents, her right breast, the museum for her, too. It was in preparation and gratitude for the next phase of their life that Emmy gave away bikes, shin pads, soup tureens, and evening wear. It had been her idea to sell the house. She shed all that she could.

Joseph, meanwhile, was finishing off his museum days in a round-robin of second guessing. Cecil had made two requests: he'd asked Joseph to submit a list of potential directors and to keep his counsel regarding the museum closing. In the end, compliance seemed the only way Joseph might aid the museum. If he refrained from denouncing the Castle, they might choose a successor from his list who might, in turn, take them on. This was his incentive to put together a roster of candidates; it was likewise his incentive to exclude Talbot Perry, whose nonchalance he still felt like a punch to the gut.

Joseph was mindful of each candidate's character and pluck. With Talbot out of the running, there was his other ancillary director, Zemzemal Assaad, who knew the most propitious mix of federal and private funds for each project and was Muslim to boot. As for curators, Arthur Franklin would doubtless love to be asked. Chic and ambitious, he certainly cared about the museum, or at least about his porcelains. There was Dr. Zhao, who was head of the museum's Advisory Committee. He led a Fortune 500 company with offices in Beijing and New York, and he was fiercely protective of the Founder's wishes. Finally, Masami Yamamoto was the youngest and most dynamic member of the Advisory Committee; he was also rich and Japanese. Any one of them might struggle to keep the collection intact, and Joseph's final project had been copying pertinent documents into separate binders for all four, whose needs for information did not entirely overlap.

He was in the middle of collating when Leo Wells swung by.

"Hey, man," Leo greeted him.

"Look at you." Joseph was surprised to see Promise's husband clean-shaven and wearing a nice pin-striped suit. "What brings the human rights crusader to us?" Joseph stood up and extended his hand, but Leo came around for a bear hug. He smelled surprisingly like India, an aura of cumin and hemp.

"I'm in a hearing on the Hill. Senator Cooper requested a break, which I hope he uses to get his facts straight." Leo took a step back and appraised Joseph. "What's your hurry? I can't believe, after how many years, you only gave two weeks' notice."

"Eighteen years." Joseph filled in the blank. "Well, Emmy and I have a dig to catch." He was happy to see Leo, whose irreverence could be a tonic. "Still fighting the good fight?"

"Trying. Listen, I wanted to see you without Promise or Emmy around. I've heard some hair-raising stories about where you're headed. You guys bringing along army escorts?"

"Only three or four guides know how to get to Niya."

"All of whom could be terrorist-related," Leo said. "Every side of the Taklamakan is disputed territory. That calls for a certain amount of paranoia."

Rather than mention the terrors lurking right here, Joseph put a hand to his chest, simultaneously self-mocking and self-aggrandizing. "As Sir Richard Burton said before his Mecca trip, 'What remained for me but to prove, by trial, that what might be perilous to other travelers was safe to me?'"

"I'm serious," Leo said.

"I know you are, and you're good to worry, but we're digging up a fourth-century Buddhist oasis. We're not out for valuables."

Leo refrained from telling him, To terrorists, you are the valuables. What they were digging for was irrelevant; they were Americans and Americans were always the biggest fish to catch. He pulled two cards from his wallet. "Humor me, would you, and pack these. There's one for each of you." Though the laminated cards wouldn't stop a bullet, they had aided a few hostages. Translated into a dozen languages, the Geneva Convention filled one side; the flip side was packed with survival tips along with phone numbers and e-mail addresses. "If you give it a squeeze—see?—there's a razor blade in there, flat matches, some water-purification tablets, and a small reflective blanket. You have to take my word for it, because if you slip the blanket out, you'll never stuff it back inside."

"I thank you," Joseph said. "I'm actually looking forward to a certain amount of adventure. You know, *taklamakan* is Uygur for 'you come in and no way out.'"

"Like roach traps," Leo said. He wondered if Joseph and crew had access to the Defense Department's maps. "How extreme is it?"

"Daytime temperatures hot enough to explode a can of beans; nights so cold, water freezes in thermoses. It rains, on average, once every *ten years*." He became positively frisky detailing the hardships. "Snakes and scorpions the only animal life. Sandstorms the likes of which buried the Niyan king, along with his three daughters and his fortunes, fifteen hundred years ago, after the king fell in love with his youngest daughter."

"I hope Emmy's as tough as you," Leo said. He had to get back to testify on international political prisoners, several from that part of the world. "Good luck, man," he said. "You can't imagine how much Promise is going to miss you."

"She'll be fine," Joseph replied automatically, but he didn't meet Leo's eye as they shook hands. He had a guilty conscience about Promise. Despite the fact that she had published more than Arthur, brought in more grants than Talbot, and was taking over all his projects, Joseph hadn't put her on his list of candidates for director. Frankly, he'd been trying to forget she was here, sincere as cash, as

Emmy used to say. She must have been avoiding him as well, because she'd usually drop by a few times in the course of a week, rapping on the door and letting herself in. "Help," she'd say, armed with a complicated question his own scholarship had overlooked.

Joseph clicked open his pocket watch, deeming it late enough to ditch his candidate packets and go home, although home was not much of a refuge. The wrenching question waiting for him there was: What to keep, what to deaccession? He made the short drive from the museum to the Hill, and sure enough, when he came in the front door, two familiar boxes sat in the entry hall, tagged for pickup. *Court Paintings of Akbar's Reign* wouldn't mean much to shoppers at Goodwill, but a worse thought was how little the book had meant to those in his very field. He'd never needed to retrieve a single copy.

Emmy was stretched out on the living room floor. It spooked him to see her in Indian garb, lying on her mat with her eyes closed like after chemotherapy, the stench of chemicals in the sheets and towels. But she was only sleeping. The turpentine smell was from painters' prep work. In their efforts to erase the house's memory, they'd sanded and filled the pockmarks gouged by balls, sticks, and pucks. Behind the door, they'd skimmed a coat of plaster across the wayward jabs that had radiated from the boys' old dartboard.

"Hello, dear," Emmy said. She rolled over on her side, and the sound of her callused feet against the vinyl mat echoed in the nearly empty room. With that rustle, Joseph's concern shifted to annoyance. Thank God he'd claimed a few things: his grandmother's chaise, still covered in red damask, water spots and all; his father's revolving bookcase, which held the *National Geographic*s Joseph Sr. read after a day at the salmon canning factory; a few books no library would carry. In the end, sentimental value was all that mattered.

He said, "You gave the damn couch away?"

"I did," she admitted. "It was pretty worn." She pointed across the room to three new boxes. "These are incoming, for you. Presents."

Joseph's two weeks' notice hadn't been enough time for the museum crowd to plan a theatrical send-off. He'd thought not having to go to a party was the best parting gift until he opened these cartons in the privacy of his denuded home. A dozen camouflage-printed boxes were filled with thoughtful items suited to his upcoming journey: a multipocketed travel vest, hand-bound field journals, a safari hat, and pens guaranteed to write through sand and excessive heat. The crowning touch was an ultraslim computer designed for fieldwork. "'The solar pack of this machine,'" he read from the label, "'along with its impermeable carrying case, was tested by Shuttle astronauts and gulf war troops. What conditions could be more extreme than space or combat?' What, indeed."

"I like your hat." Emmy stretched her arm out. "Can you believe the space we had? Someone was always stepping on my foot."

"It looks like a gallery now."

"Don't worry. Another family will come and clutter it all up." She let out an exaggerated sigh. "I tell you what—I feel light as a feather."

He was taken aback by how eagerly Emmy had swept away their personal history; nonetheless, he saw the freedom she'd been after. He looked at himself in the mirror over the bar. He liked his hat, too.

Emmy took him by the hand. "Ready for the final round?" she asked, leading him to the third floor. He was surprised none of the boys had ever claimed the cavernous attic as a bedroom. Thus far, they hadn't been much interested in the contents either. Ravi and Sanjay were too young to be nostalgic, and Jules was in Bangkok. It was a relief when Henry took in furniture and selected artifacts. He reclaimed all the snapshots Emmy had discarded—tilted, badly cropped, showing one or another of them bucktoothed or pimpled. If she'd presented him with archival-quality albums, he would have rolled his eyes. Better to let him sift through the midden.

All that was left were the nearly indigenous attic boxes, ones that had never been unpacked in this house. Joseph felt a thrill of suspense breaking the seal of a box marked "1970–80," any memento of their early family days suddenly dear to him. He took the newspaper from around an empty Wild Turkey bottle, which he recognized after all these years. "You kept this?"

She knelt next to him. "I'm in Kathmandu with two little boys and a baby cobra falls on Henry's pillow. Thank God you packed the bourbon."

She was the one who'd rolled Henry out of bed. All Joseph had done was bludgeon the slinky bastard, revered in that territory. "I snuck the carcass out in a pillowcase."

"The places you took us," Emmy said. She dipped into her daddy's low register, more Texas brawl than drawl. "'Señorita, it's going to be hard to keep that dog under the porch.'"

"He thought I'd be unfaithful?"

"No, a traveler, which is worse for a Texas daddy. Well, I don't know if it's worse, but if your son-in-law's a cad, you still get to see your baby girl."

Joseph couldn't wait to see what she'd pull out next. She lifted a tissue-wrapped bundle, a sweater she'd knitted for him that he'd miniaturized in the dryer. Each of the boys had worn it at younger ages. Then, from the magic box, an early ziplock bag. She said, "Here's Ravi's gauze." After Ravi had befriended the charnel man's son in Calcutta, they'd stood by the Ganges swathed in white gauze to watch his cricket chum set fire to the body of a holy man.

Joseph swallowed hard. He kissed her on the top of her hair, which had grown in spiky gray. "Ah, señorita," he said. He assumed she was as moved as he was until she got up off the floor.

"Adios, amigos," she said, emptying the souvenirs into a plastic trash bag. Before she could tie the handles off, he reached in to rescue the cardigan. "It's the size of your handkerchief," Emmy said. "You could practically put it in your pocket."

Joseph mimed stuffing it in his pants, and the gag brought up Leo's laminated cards. "We're supposed to pack these," he said. He showed her how the thin edges parted like lips. "Leo says in case of emergency, squeeze card."

At that moment, Joseph realized that if he wanted his candidate list to be taken seriously, he would have to add Promise. Neglecting to include a woman could provide the Castle with an excuse to disregard his list, and anyway, Promise was an obvious choice: books galore, international exhibitions and symposia, growing esteem in the small Persian/Indian/Islamic field. She could raise money, he'd give her that. But having young children made her current job already a stretch. Also, Leo was a kick as well as a potential embarrassment. He could ruin an opening with talk of the Tamil Tigers or the Taliban.

On his last day at the Museum of Asian Art, Joseph revised the candidate list despite his ambivalence; then he rooted through his drawer until he happened upon a museum notecard. The photograph on the front showed a boy around eleven or twelve standing in a skiff among grimacing, ten-armed goddesses, life-sized statues of dusty clay. It was a scene from the final day of Durga Puja, when villagers headed out on the Ganges with their boats full of Durga statues. Summoned forth to destroy evil, Durga held every divine weapon imaginable, including Vishnu's discus, Shiva's trident, Varuna's conch shell, a garland of snakes, and a thunderbolt. Durga obligingly went on a rampage of destruction to make the world a safer place. Having thanked her for a week, devotees tossed her statues overboard at the festival's end.

Joseph had prepared four candidate binders, replete with attachments and color-coded tabs. For Promise, he bent back the corner of the card that had been foxed by his drawer and, pinning the octopussy arms of the Durgas against his desk, scrawled an obligatory note and sealed it in an envelope. Then he emptied the contents of his top drawer into his trash can and went into his bathroom for a final cigar.

The Shame of a Thousand Mothers

October 14, 1999

Although Leo had been right about Promise missing Joseph when he left, that was nothing compared with how much she missed him two months later. She felt she was making herself sick with extra work and aggravation.

"Since when did you defer to Talbot?" Arthur tried to cheer her up. "You're the chief curator—the curatorial meeting is your territory."

She said, "He made it look like he thinks more of the curators' writing than I do." She looked over her shoulder. "We shouldn't talk about this here, though I'm torn between privacy and this muffin."

Arthur smiled. "When I'm acting director, curators will be allowed to eat at their desks." His reign, with privileges and cash awards, had become a running joke between them.

"When you're acting director, will you muzzle him?" Promise said.

Arthur was sympathetic to a degree, but he'd liked Talbot's suggestion to streamline the label process by going right to copyediting. Publications was always rewriting Arthur's exhibition text, forcing him to endure multiple drafts; they barely lit on Promise's copy. Changing the subject, he said, "When Joseph told me that acquiring the bowl would show I was ready for the big time, maybe he meant acting director."

"The bowl, the bowl, the bowl," Promise chanted.

"It's all I think about," Arthur said, speaking like a man in love. It had been building ever since Joseph had picked the magpie-and-plum bowl out of the lineup. "You know, I lobbied for the peony cup, but now I can see it's better suited to my friends' Arts and Crafts interiors."

"You thought the bowl was too recent," she goaded him.

"Not anymore. It took those potters millennia to acquire the techniques to create this particular bowl. Yet any later or more mainstream, they would not have incised the design. They would have turned it into mass-produced transferware."

It sounded like he'd been putting in more research. "What's the whole provenance?" she asked.

"Sexy," Arthur said. "No gaps that I can tell. It spent a few decades with China's imperial family and then was sent to the court of Louis the Sixteenth, who made a present of it to America's minister to France, the young Thomas Jefferson. At the end of his life, plagued by debt, Jefferson sold it to a collector in Sèvres." This compact vessel had sealed international relations and staved off a former president's financial ruin. "It left France for Germany in the nineteenth century; fifty years later, it traveled back to America in Marlene Dietrich's suitcase."

"That would be a first for us," Promise said, enjoying her muffin and Arthur's company.

"You know what I found this afternoon? Over at the Library of Congress there were snapshots of her boudoir in a movie magazine, and I could see the bowl in two of them! In one photograph, it's next to a silver candelabra on a highly polished table. In the other picture, the same table's covered with empty bottles and highball glasses, and the bowl is mounded with cigarette butts." In that shot, an aging Miss Dietrich looked as if she'd smoked every fag. "Then someone told me to read the latest JFK bio, because it says—get this—when she visited the White House, either JFK bedded her or she bedded him."

"Hardly documentable," Promise said.

"I know, but it brings the bowl full circle. Might they have been humping away in the very room where Jefferson displayed the piece, a *petit cadeau* from King Louis?"

"I dare you to put that in your label copy," Promise said.

————

Whoever had been programming computers—that great tool of the future—hadn't managed to think past 1999, and many feared that taking the step from December 31, 1999, to January 1, 2000, would be like walking off a cliff. Computers brewed the coffee, turned the traffic lights red, and dispensed twenties from cash machines on every corner. What opportunistic bastards might take advantage of power failures or global chaos? The folks at Amnesty International had some idea, which was why nearly all Leo's officemates were at one conference or another, briefing away on the world's biggest menaces.

Leo was alone at the Urgent Action Desk, where daily he dwelled on the most dastardly acts people and their governments visited upon one another. Working at Amnesty International was like fulfilling his childhood dreams of being a fireman and, though he never admitted it, a cop and a priest. Mostly a fireman. Sit around shooting the shit, knowing that when disaster strikes, everyone will scatter, their hearts moving from their sleeves into their mouths. Sometimes the alert was the cat-in-a-tree call, like a dumbshit college kid getting nabbed in a foreign country trying to buy hash. Most other times, it was beyond gruesome.

Human rights being a slow burn of a cause, it was Leo's job to generate letters, faxes, and e-mails to bring up the heat. Lately, he was burning out. Just try to complain after hearing that the Rwandans had raided the refugee camps or that an Afghani woman—a professor!—had been stoned for speaking to a man in the marketplace. So the world's ugliness has grown tiresome? You say your house isn't air-conditioned and the printer's broken again? As his team leader would say: Hard cheese, that.

Promise's apolitical stance wasn't helping. His wife's energy was evenly divided between her work and her family. If she suffered because little was left for her, Leo suffered because she spent nothing on the world. Steeped in punishing politicism, he'd initially found comfort in her neutrality, but after years of fighting the same fight, he wanted to convert her. He needed to know that she was on his side, that he did not look ridiculous in her eyes. He tried to recruit her into the Green Party and, when that didn't work, at least the Democratic Party, a pale version of what he truly considered democratic. She countered that no one had been more critical of Clinton than he, and it went downhill from there, such as when he outright accused her of being a Republican. "Lincoln was a Republican," she'd said, "and Teddy Roosevelt too. There's human rights and conservation." Point, counterpoint.

Neither was professionally helpful to the other, really. Promise's shorthand, to say that Leo worked to free political prisoners, shamed him. Wasn't the D.C. jail full to bursting with political prisoners? Wasn't D.C. itself, when you considered the politics of being poor or mentally ill or uneducated? He actually viewed most of the museum's contents as political prisoners. Even if the Founder hadn't relocated any temples in their entirety, he had bought several frescoes and the walls they came in on. The old connoisseur might have schemed to move Angkor Wat to the Mall had the syphilis not done him in. Promise's colleagues decried looting cultural artifacts—now. As to the Founder, they pointed out how governments themselves willingly sold off artifacts and that much of what endured was thanks to museums. Leo heard this from Promise, because the museum gang kept their distance from him. Mayhem and torture of the pre-Renaissance were more compelling to them or more abstracted than the stories he could tell about Iran and Turkey, China or Kashmir, Cambodia or Indonesia.

To be fair, Promise never discounted his mission—she found it remarkable that he could dissuade a thug with a handful of letters. She likened Amnesty's pressure to the shame of a thousand mothers: We know what you're up to, and we would appreciate it if you'd knock it off.

All these thoughts took place as he brewed himself a triple espresso. Two sugar packets for the bittersweet charge needed to retrieve the morning updates. Someone had off-loaded rolls of fax paper as an in-kind contribution, so the reports as he separated them curled and flopped about, ailing walleyed fish. Albania, Burma, Sri Lanka, Philadelphia. Where is safety? Leo asked himself daily. His roster of prisoners included rabble-rousers and journalists, their curiosity as provocative as poking a stick in a rattler hole. But the poets and latrine-digging volunteers met with equal heartache—did they realize their danger? Finally, there were the random attacks, the scariest and hardest to defend against. What evidence is there of a disappeared daughter? What made two Swedes on holiday in Cairo political targets?

Leo started a stack to forward to writers' unions, who had access to the best letter writers. When the atrocities got to him, he snagged a falafel from a Turkish deli and watched guys play chess around the fountain. In Dupont Circle, his moth-eaten Afghan freedom-fighter coat drew notice only because he wore it over a well-cut suit—he had a weakness for both ends of the clothing spectrum. For his lunchtime stroll, he'd slid on cheap sneakers, crushing the heels down in a

Moroccan slipper effect. Aviator glasses, midlength hair, and no piercings or tattoos all marked him as fiftyish; his age and obvious straightness were noticed more than anything else. Though he could buy falafel from a different Middle Eastern vendor every day, he'd be lucky to find a passable one two miles north in Chevy Chase, where even the bagels had Asiago cheese or pancetta bits. Two miles was all it took not to fit in, he thought, marveling at how many D.C.s the city held. He wished the world were more willing to mix it up a bit. That was the element both his and Promise's work shared.

At least she was true to her nonpartisan beliefs, for Leo had an agenda he was hard-pressed to admit. Deep in his very own heart, the part that cares nothing for the world and only for the self, he had been hoping Promise would quit her job. The kids would be spared the long-suffering Althea. Instead of the mad rush each morning, he pictured Promise squeezing fresh juice for him and the children, maybe more children. Did every man harbor this fantasy, more shameful these days than porn? He'd just been wishing she were more political, when the truth was he wished she were more domestic. Maybe he was the one who needed a change, though neither of them could afford to quit. Their combined salaries barely made one by D.C. standards.

Back in the office, fax paper was scrolled in big loops on the floor. Leo cut off one act of violence from another, filing as he went along. At home, he couldn't keep his clean and dirty clothes separate, but his workaday organizational skills were legendary. Only an efficient crusade had a chance of being effective. And so it took another hour to get to the most sobering account of his day: four rock climbers who had disappeared in Kashmir had been captives of the Al-Faran for ten days.

He pulled files within files until he ran down the Al-Faran, a splinter group devoted to guerrilla war with the "apostate Indian government" in the name of Islam. Funded by Pakistani intelligence, they had a training camp in the mountains of southern Kashmir and their numbers hovered around three hundred, making imprisonment dear as death to them. Leo fingered a path along the Silk Route, trying to remember whether Joseph and Emmy were on the north or south rim of the Taklamakan Desert; both rims were on the opposite side of the world's tallest mountains from Srinagar. On the other hand, never underestimate the nerve of Allah's deputies.

Confidence was Joseph's familiar, and why not? Amid political up-heavals and all manner of cultural unease, hadn't his white, Christian, prosperous American ass remained unskinned? Joseph acted as if he'd been inoculated against harm, which was why Leo loved him, even if his bravado was that of a nineteenth-century conqueror.

Leo's dry throat and skippy pulse spurred memories of his coke-and-speed era. In those days, the rush had cleared his head to write elaborate term papers, but now his fingers kept skipping letters within words as he searched the Internet. He stopped to listen to the BBC on CNN. The Brit had somehow escaped; in fact, he was the source of the story that the Al-Faran were responsible. Bedraggled, eyes jiggling like soft-boiled eggs, the climber recounted his arduous story, ending with his stumbling into an Indian soldier encampment. Within the hour, the Indian soldiers had found the Norwegian, who had not been so fortunate. He'd been decapitated, and the Al-Faran had announced their identity by carving it into his chest.

Leo called his wife, who surprisingly answered her own phone. "Is Joseph at the dig yet? I wasn't sure how long they're spending on the road."

Promise said, "All I know is that he's not here working on these cat-alog entries, and I am. We worker bees are on our own."

He heard her wrestling with a wrapper and then chewing—lately, she was either sick or starving. Because she never wanted to have sex if she was the least bit ill, he'd been feeling sorrier for himself than for her. He said, "There's a bunch of Islamic militants running amok. They want Kashmir ceded to Pakistan but—"

"The Al-Faran?"

"You've heard of them?"

She took a loud slurp of something. "I'm having a snack. I heard they had four hostages, one of whom got picked up by the Indian army last night. The Al-Faran kidnapped these guys outside of Srinagar—Joseph's on the other side of the mountains, in China."

"Yes, I know, but they're called extremists for a reason." He'd been acting as if she specialized in art from Idaho. Her in-box was probably blue with State Department warnings.

"Back on the home front," she said, "have you made any calls for a pink boy's two-wheeler?"

Felix's favorite color was pink, and he did not understand why backpacks and bikes for boys were available in only primary colors. "Not really; maybe after dinner."

"His birthday's in eight days."

"The Internet is open twenty-four/seven to take your money. Do you think Talbot is around?" Of Promise's inner circle, Leo was perhaps the only one who appreciated the way Talbot stockpiled information. Also, his snarky attitude, which Leo enjoyed in contrast to the reverence everyone else paid the museum.

"What do you need with him?" she asked. On her notes from that morning's curatorial meeting, she'd drawn a head with rimless glasses and horns.

"I figured he might have ship-to-shore contact with Joseph. Listen, I'll send out some e-mails and then make bike calls." He wanted to hang up the phone, whose cord was twisted like intestines; it should be technologically impossible to call a toy store on an Amnesty International line. She probably knew he had no intention of making bike inquiries and would say anything at home: the stores were closed; they ran out; no boys' bikes come in pink.

They said their goodbyes, and Leo's gaze settled on the stack of survival cards he kept near his telephone, the ones he'd pressed on Joseph. His contribution had been the succinct advice he'd crafted from hundreds of survival stories: "Should you be an unwilling guest, attempt to humanize yourself to your captors. When possible: (1) feign pain, (2) pack snacks, (3) use a ruse, and (4) get out but don't get lost." Now, the guidance struck him as not only glib but useless: the card was meant to be slipped into a wallet, but wouldn't a wallet be the first thing confiscated?

Pessimistic about his results, Leo nonetheless performed his job. All he could do was send global warning, though probably he wasn't even doing that. Probably his dispatch, broken down into grains of information, was heading out to the vast desert of unread bits collecting in the dunes of cyberspace.

———

"Daddy will say it!" Felix yelled at Leo before he'd removed his key from the dead bolt.

Skidding into the entry hall, the five-year-old had a piece of foil candy wrapper hanging out of his mouth. Imagining the foil touching a filling induced Leo to shudder. He would have rather thought about that bit-in-the-mouth feeling, he would have rather turned back to a desk groaning under crimes against humanity than negotiate Felix's mood. Every day closer to his sixth birthday ratcheted up the tension until he was more high-strung than ever. Leo held out his hands, palms up, and Felix spit the wadded wrapper into them.

"Say you're Christian, Daddy!"

Promise showed up in the entry hall. She had big circles under her eyes. "Say you're late."

"I'm late. Sorry."

"Say you're Christian!" his son demanded.

Standing out of Felix's line of sight, Promise urged him on. Do what he says, her inclined head and tipped-up nose gestured. Do it, and no one gets hurt.

Felix climbed on the arm of the couch; he was infused with the salt-and-lard smell of kids' dough. "Don't ask more questions, Daddy. Just say it."

"Why?"

"That's a question!" Felix howled.

Leo bent over his balled-up boy. He didn't even think of "Why?" as a question. It was an involuntary reflex, natural as breathing to him.

Promise mimed giving Leo the back of her hand. "Althea told him we'd all go to hell if we weren't Christian, and he was hoping you'd save the family."

"That was mighty Christian of her," Leo said, having witnessed religious fervor in all its ripe abundance, today's example being the Norwegian mutilated by the Al-Faran's divine machetes. The only thing more mysterious than faith was the zealots' rage. If these folks so dearly believed in God, why couldn't they leave the smiting to him? Ditto for Althea.

But his little one was genuinely distressed. "You can be Christian if you want," Leo said. He picked up Bow, Felix's beloved stuffed dog, and danced the floppy puppy along the sofa arm. "If you wish, my son, you may believe in the Dog Almighty."

Felix wiped his nose on the shoulder of his shirt. "What is a Christian? Do you have to be brown?"

That his kid had lived this long without indoctrination made Leo either remiss or evolved. "No, buddy. A Christian is anyone"—and he sang—"*red and yellow, black and white,* who follows the teachings of Jesus Christ. His big one is 'Love your neighbor as yourself.' Doesn't that seem like good policy?"

Felix looked out the bay window. Leo followed his gaze, although in his peripheral vision, Promise was charading away. Standing on one foot, she pedaled through the air with the other. She mimed steering the handlebars, and her eyebrows nearly floated off her face with their implied questioning. Leo shrugged and pointed to his watch, letting her make up her own answer.

Felix was pointing too. Singling out the Shandlings' house, where his favorite babysitter lived, he said, "How about this? I'll love that neighbor." Then he gestured to Ricky's house. "But I won't love that one. Is that okay?"

Leo cleared his throat. His first instinct was to take him to the river, wash him down. Everyone on earth is your neighbor. None merits your enmity, even the one who called you "penis head" and attacked you with foam darts on your first day of school. Putting his arms around Felix, he inhaled the salty-dough-and-cheesy breath of his boy child, who had arrived at his own narrow interpretation of God's laws. Love one neighbor, don't love the other. He wanted to be expansive, but cynicism's dark fog clouded his moral compass, and he said, "Why should you be any different from the rest of the world?"

When they sat down to dinner, Leo's irritation intensified. The rice seemed to have canned soup on it, and in the center of the table was a fruit salad of plums and apples.

"I didn't know plums were in season," he said.

"They are in Chile," Promise replied. She had her elbows on the table, and she was leaning on her arm as if she might fall asleep.

"Any Joseph news?" he asked.

"They made it to Niya. Turns out, his GPS is transmitting to someone who called someone who called Talbot. He's known for a while."

"What's GPX?" Felix asked.

"You explain it," Promise said. "I'm too tired."

"It stands for Global Positioning System, this little machine that sends out a signal, which is picked up by satellites and bounced back. Because the satellites' locations are known, the machine can figure out where you are."

"Like a bat," Felix said. "It's echolocation."

Leo was impressed that his five-year-old got it when he barely got it himself. "Nice work, buddy."

Lydia said, "That's from his bat video. He watched it three times today."

Leo turned to Promise, who was nearly facedown on the table. "I thought we agreed that Althea wouldn't just plop them in front of the TV."

"We did," Promise said. "We most certainly agreed on that. He watched it twice while I ran to the store and then started dinner."

"You left them alone while you went to Whole Foods?"

"I was in charge." Lydia sat up tall.

"I went to Safeway," Promise admitted. "Brace yourself—the sauce is canned soup, and the poultry's not free range."

Lydia made a face at her forkful of chicken. "Taste the cruelty," the nine-year-old said.

Leo said, "I think it's important for us to pay for our beliefs." Even to himself, he sounded pedantic. But he felt strongly about this. Going highbrow to justify his badgering, he said, "The reason to live thoughtfully is that every act has political consequences—where to shop for apples, what apples to buy, what soap to buy for washing apples."

Promise roused herself. "Except that you don't buy the apples around here. Or wash them."

"True enough." He didn't want this degenerating to housekeeping. Just because the personal was political to him, the lack of political didn't have to be personal.

Promise said, "You're doing good work, and you're good at it. I can strongly believe both of those things without denouncing Islamic governments or my favorite mascara. As it is, I give more than most to your cause: I give you."

He resisted the urge to ask questions about her mascara. It was sinking in that his pride and fury probably benefited from her containment.

Meanwhile, she was looking longingly at his plate. "You going to eat all your fat?"

"Mom," Lydia said, "that is so gross."

"You can have my fat," Felix volunteered. A scoop of the creamy rice was too heavy for him to lift until he gripped the spoon with both hands. "See how nice I am?" Always eager to please his mother, Felix was also increasingly aware of his birthday's proximity.

"I'll match you bite for bite," Promise said. Everyone but Felix recognized her offer as a trick to make him eat.

Leo was still agitated when he put the kids to bed, only to find the kitchen was the way they'd left it. After he cleaned up, he found Promise in the study, traveling back to Rumi time.

"I'm hiding from the dishes," she said.

"Done," he said.

"And the children."

"In bed."

She smiled at Leo for the first time that night. "So did you get a bike or not?"

"Not yet. We've got time."

She saw how this would play out. He'd never get around to bike research, and then he'd manage to find some gift that would create more work for her while at the same time making him a hero in Felix's eyes. A big chemistry set, perhaps, with materials for making a lava-spewing volcano. Or a robot composed of thousands of tiny pieces that had to be soldered together by hand.

Determined not to nag, she showed him the tooled calfskin cover of her book. "It's a facsimile of the *Padshahnama*, so it's *only* a couple thousand dollars. The original album documents Shahjahan's reign; there are about five pages with Rumi poems on them." She hugged the puffy volume to her chest, but the strong smell of animal hide was sickening. It smelled too much like India, all those open-air tanneries upwind of the markets.

"Joseph's book will be a page-by-page discussion of the album. I was already doing the Rumi before he dumped the rest on me. Here, check out these color plates." She offered Leo a jeweler's loupe so he could appreciate *The Death of Khan Jahan Lodi*. Having killed three gang members, two soldiers were sawing away at the neck of Khan Jahan Lodi, who was obviously still alive. "See how the artist captured a skin tone of lifelessness in the three dead heads?" The warriors each held a head like a bowling bag, hanging on to a shock of hair. "*Look!* There are even flies swarming round, and their tiny bellies are engorged with blood. Those helmets are so detailed that Cecil identified the *plumes* sticking out the front."

This was her usual energy level, not like how she'd been at dinner.

Promise's zeal was the reason Lydia and Felix begged her to read to them. She got just as excited pointing out the dewdrop on the grasshopper on the leaf on the bush as she did showing Leo the sawteeth on the blade at the neck of the victim. Couldn't she see the difference—the bedtime story she was fingering wasn't fiction, it was genocide! "Show a little humanity, woman."

"Oh, come on. Look at that guy's *leg* armor. Each of his knees is capped with gold chased into the shape of a face. And on the same soldier, the artist not only painted embroidered trim on his robe but painted it as an embroidered Koranic inscription. And look at the trajectory of blood spurting from that neck . . ."

Talk about missing the big picture! So enamored of the art, Promise neglected to question its genesis or the bloodshed that had ensured its survival. It was getting to the point where her work seemed nearly immoral to Leo, even as he recognized the lessons that could be learned from such paintings. Considering she'd told him that Khan Jahan Lodi was an Afghan who supported one of India's Mughal emperors but opposed his son, the painting seemed especially relevant. The lesson was the same today as three hundred years ago: infidels will not be tolerated.

She would probably say they were both about promoting tolerance; that was what his better half would say. Appreciating Islamic culture, giving it voice at a quasi-governmental institution, et cetera. Leo denounced that defense. Ethically, she fit the quandary titled "Attila the Hun's cook," which examined whether it was corrupt to take a job making stew for the despot who'd worked up his appetite gutting soldiers and raping their wives and daughters.

She stroked the manuscript's leather cover. "What?"

"Do you ever think about quitting your job? You could devote yourself to us, who dearly appreciate your every talent. Even if we had to downsize, at least you wouldn't be so swamped. No more feuds with Talbot, and you wouldn't have to scramble around every morning, dressing up and running for the Metro, which is due for another fare increase." None of this was spoken. It was only Leo's thoughts dripping their way into his consciousness—such drips would have to form long accretions, stalactites reaching from the clammy chambers of his primitive brain to his throat, tongue, and lips, where, given breath, his caveman desires could be voiced.

Mercifully, she had turned the page to an illuminated spread. She said, "There's something about painting with gold and lapis that still sounds impossible, like breathing chocolate or taking a diamond shower." She looked up at Leo, her cheeks flushed. "You know, they bedecked the heck out of Rumi's hymns, and his pure message shines brighter than anything they can pile on it."

"Like the way a beautiful woman is sometimes less beautiful slathered in makeup?"

"Not really, because they're not making less of Rumi. I was thinking the way a brownie sometimes tastes better without ice cream and fudge sauce."

"That's the same thing."

"I guess," she agreed.

He put his arm around his odd little wife, who led his index finger to yet another particular, so that now he was pointing up details. She said, "You can see the warp and weft of the painted carpet in this one. Whether they had magnification or not, how could they paint details invisible to the naked eye? Like those blood-engorged flies."

"Makes you wonder what they could've done if they hadn't been working at knifepoint."

"They *were* mostly prisoners," she conceded. "In this volume, the poems are so inspirational—and particular—I have this theory that the illuminations are infused with Rumi's mysticism. Nothing publishable, mind you, just my take on their superhuman ability. Though it could be the knifepoint thing; some people do their best work under pressure."

Leo felt pressure building up behind his eyes. "That's your definition of culture? After a rough day of murdering and hoarding, the ruler unwinds with poetry from his imprisoned artisans?"

"Did you mean whoring?" Promise asked. "Or maybe looting. You said hoarding."

"What I meant was, why don't you have a problem with this bloodshed? You're fascinated by a gentle mysticism that's been preserved by Asia's thugs."

She wouldn't even bite, which might have been to her credit. What she was thinking was, Why can't they isolate the gene for strong opinions—whether someone is a cat/dog lover, or more relevant, politically obsessed/apathetic—so you could get a like-minded family? If she admitted that she wasn't crazy about what Asia's thugs were doing these days, she'd be subjected to the dreaded second wind. He felt so strongly about this he'd taken his arm from around her and stood up off the couch. Patting the cushion at her side, she summoned Leo back down to her level. The next page was one of the Rumi pieces; it featured a domestic scene of a prince and princess kneeling on a rug, which was placed over geometric tiles, which were in turn decorated with dainty plants. In this facsimile version, the pages were large color plates. Here and there you could see evidence of the cutting and pasting that had gone into fashioning the original.

Calligraphy spiraled down the pillars and across the connecting arch; Promise pointed out the inscription on the rug the couple sat upon. "He covered their house with Rumi's poem; he built them a house of Rumi." Leo thought he recognized the handwriting reserved for poetry. The Arabic of Koran pages was usually blockier; Arabic used for Persian script resembled his mother's grocery lists, which she wrote in the shorthand of her secretary days.

Promise began reciting what she'd translated of the couple's house: "'Out beyond ideas of wrongdoing and rightdoing, there is a field. I'll meet you there. When the soul lies down in that grass, the world is too full to talk about. Ideas, language, even the phrase *each other* doesn't make any sense.' I swear, whatever you choose at random always manages to speak exactly to your condition."

"Even so"—Leo wasn't touching her—"your neutrality can piss me off."

"Whatever we love about someone ultimately drives us nuts."

"Is that Rumi?" he asked.

"No, it's my mother. Or your mother. Or Rumi's mother. You used to love my neutrality."

"That was before I was cultivating a mob morality."

Promise laid the book on the couch and pivoted sideways to rub two fingers across his temple, which usually served to relax his jaw. Then, scooting into his lap, she kissed him on his closed eyes and on either side of his nose, where his righteous nostrils flared. She leaned back to catch her breath, put off by the garlic and mushroom of tonight's dinner on Leo's skin.

Maybe he should come home pissy more often, Leo thought, happy to have Promise in his lap. She was kissing him like he had bad breath, her little mouth puckered tight. "'Out beyond ideas of wrongdoing and rightdoing,'" he quoted, "there is a bed. I'll meet you there."

In the bathroom, Leo smoked the butt of a joint, its smoke mixing with the steam of his shower as the paper wilted. After showering and brushing, he sloshed some mouthwash around for good measure. "'When the soul lies down in that grass, the world is too full to talk about.'" Her whirling dervish did have a knack.

Promise rubbed his back as he climbed into bed, and when he faced her, she rubbed against his front. "Are you really put out with me?" she asked.

"Yes, but if you put out, I may forgive you. Promise?" He liked to invent ludicrous requests for her, because she'd told him about grade-school misunderstandings linked to her name.

"What is it?" she prepared for his sweet tease, the tickling of foreplay.

"That, come spring, you'll clean me like a mother cat cleans her kittens . . . That if I die, you'll find someone too good for you . . . That you'll call the children every week, even if they're in prison."

And she affirmed, "I Promise."

Are You Busy?

November 1, 1999

Looking deeply into her lap, Promise was trying to discern if the stain on her dress more closely resembled the head of an elephant or the Indian subcontinent, minus the disputed territories.

"Ruminating?" Vanessa asked at the opened door.

Promise raised her chin. "I was," she said, pointing to the Rumi volumes.

Had Vanessa come a moment earlier, she would have found Promise wading among still pools of scholarship looking for a darting flash of wisdom. Clutching her last pen, she'd been aiming all morning to spear a nourishing morsel or, failing that, hook a magic carp who'd clarify a challenging Rumi passage. Deeper she went and deeper still. With one book open inside another inside another—four deep—she'd dipped into a German scholar's interpretation of an American poet's adaptation of the British translator's work, surfacing, disoriented, in a lagoon of the original Persian. She was tired and a little bit cross-eyed.

"Who needs me?" Promise asked, hopeful that Vanessa might one day reply, "No one. I have just come to offer you a hot caramel sundae. Truly you are wise and good." Probably she'd come to tell her that someone had defaced the labels in the Islamic gallery or that Lydia had hyperventilated in science because of a passing reference to snakes.

Promise traced Vanessa's look of shame down to the stain on her outfit.

"Wait until you have two kids, a puppy, and a husband."

Not even then, Vanessa pledged to herself. Dedicated to her own good looks, she wished Promise had spent time on her clothes and makeup. More than most white women, her boss could be transformed by some well-placed smears. Lately she'd begun to look like a mother in a detergent ad, the kind who succumbs to a giant barrette across the bangs. "The Advisory Committee is calling."

"Dr. Zhao told me it was a closed meeting."

Vanessa shrugged. "The buzzard buzzed."

Despite the way Zhao's narrow, hunched shoulders and tilted neck rendered him vulturesque, Promise reminded Vanessa that he was president of the Advisory Committee. She was light-headed, and she tried to remember if she'd eaten lunch. Her desk was mounded with piles marked "URGENT!" Though she'd diligently buried them, general queries from the public kept resurfacing. She also owed replies to visitors, a task that could nearly be covered with three varieties of form letters: "I'm sorry you were offended by the (a) big bare breasts, (b) intercourse (between consenting, multiarmed gods, eager lovers, or men preying on camels), (c) graphic portrayals of bloody mayhem, including severed heads depicted either singly or strung together as necklace or belt." She often wished her specialty was the Korean collection, one celadon vase after another.

Any announcement the Advisory Committee made about the acting director would be met with grumbling. Arthur had been obsessing over the post, which she maintained would be thankless and demanding. Poor consecrated one. A year or more would pass before the search party could line up the usual suspects and put them through the talent, evening dress, and fund-raising competitions. Until the pageant was over, the acting director would be expected to shoulder the burden with no additional compensation and little authority.

She slid her ID into the security doors separating curatorial offices from public spaces and went up the north stairs. Just left of the landing was the museum shop, followed by the director's office, still bearing Joseph's name, in the northeast corner. She should have gone the other way to the conference room at the opposite corner, but she liked to see who was in her galleries. On this fall day, the only audience for manuscripts was a well-dressed elderly couple speaking German to each other. Although there were three people in the South Asian gallery, two were resting on the bench.

Gallery XIII, which was devoted to Buddhist art, was empty. Spanning the west wall, a carved stele chronicled the Buddha's life: he sprang from his mother's hip, was shorn of his hair, found enlightenment under the bodhi tree and protection beneath a cobra's hooded head, lay down to die, and ascended into heaven. To loose these objects from their moorings, the Founder had paid nearly nothing, his supposed goal being "to bring them to the light of civilization." What if you bring such wonders to light, and civilization ignores them? And if you pirate such wonders away from their original settings?

She had rounded the southeast corner and was picking up her pace when Min stepped out of Gallery XI. "Excuse me, please," she whispered.

Startled, Promise moved closer to the curator, who moved backward an equal distance. Maybe it was from growing up in a Beijing apartment and then, in her married life, living in an even more crowded one in Taipei, but Min always preserved a buffer of empty space around her. At the same time, she kept her voice so low that Promise was forever inching toward her as she ebbed away.

"Are you busy?" Min asked.

"They're expecting me down there." She pointed to the puffy leather doors at the end of the hallway.

"You are called. I am not." Min wanted to learn how usual was a summons from the inspector general. She knew enough to distrust the phrase "routine questions," suspecting it had the same connotations here as in Taiwan. She never had returned to the Accounting Office after they'd asked her to see the supervisor. Still, there had been numerous instances of her fears being unjustified, like the day she'd seen a sign-up sheet for staff to "volunteer" their blood.

"I'll call you," Promise said.

"Of course." Min's cheeks reddened into two plums against a porcelain plate. "Give my regards to Madame Xingfei."

"You bet," Promise said. The doors to the conference room, ten feet high and tufted, unlatched when she fed the reader her ID. More so than usual, she felt as if she were entering a sealed tomb. Filled with tarnished grandeur, the room was always a little stuffy. How long had Nathan been keeping that coffee warm? Promise had an eerie feeling of being able to sniff out each and every person in attendance. Zemzemal waved to her above the elderly committee members, and

Talbot stood out as well. Aside from her (and Nathan), they were the only staff members in the room.

The darkly paneled conference room was a cross between a Delhi pub and an Agatha Christie play: velvet settees and club chairs lounged on Tibetan rugs that still smelled vaguely sheepy, and the Founder's trophies gazed down from the wall. An Indian nilgai and a Queen of Sheba gazelle had allowed Promise to identify their species in several manuscripts.

Three committee members, hunched with age, congregated in a huddle. They had been old when she started working at the museum, but these days, the changes among them were as accelerated as her children's. It was as if a plateau extended from twenty to seventy, with the years on either side full of rapid growth or shrinkage, revving up or dwindling down.

"We've been waiting for you, young lady." Mr. Balichakra spoke as if he were her high school principal. He was in a brown tweed suit that may have been dapper in Bombay before Independence.

"Good to see you," Promise said, taking his hand in both of hers. She bowed to Madame X, who was the most senior committee member and a constant reminder that the Founder's wishes could not be circumvented, then she kissed Miss Stranger's cheek. The Founder's last living relative—his brother's third wife's daughter—Miss Stranger was perched on chopstick-thin heels in a lemon-lime chiffon gown, like a secretary in a fifties TV show. Promise was eager to escape from her and Madame X's overabundance of perfume. Maybe when fewer people walked the earth or one had audiences with the empress dowager or maharaja, anointing became a social rite. Promise imagined them dipping into pomades of ambergris and myrrh that Lawrence of Arabia had given them.

She was grateful, then, when Agatha Morada slipped an arm through hers. "You're looking robust, my dear," she said. Dr. Morada had been one of the first women to earn a doctorate in Near Eastern studies, and she'd achieved a degree of fame between World Wars I and II. Having seen the winged bulls excavated from the palace of Persepolis, the Bible-reading public became fixated on locating Noah's ark, the Tower of Babel, Christ's tomb. Even with her strange pinkish hair, Dr. Morada had the air of a celebrity, left over from when newsreels reported on her desert digs. Now, she indulged in enough makeup to fill the wrinkles etched by those digs. Shaky hands were perhaps responsible for the unevenness of her eye and lip liner, as she was beginning to lose her edges.

Masami Yamamoto, the dashing zipper heir, was the only committee member under fifty. The metallic scent that clung to him was as distinct as the tanning lotion Promise recognized as Talbot's nimbus. (Mr. Yamamoto had actually been to Promise's hometown and delighted in the Sooner State's absurd aspects. He got the paradox: you could see for miles because there was nothing to see.) She felt possessed of a weird radar—she could detect Nathan's canapés from across the room. In her nose, the pâté, fish mousses, and imported cheeses were redolent of cat food and dirty underwear. She remembered what Min had recently told her about silkworms, which are so delicate a strong smell can kill them.

Bowing over Miss Stranger, Dr. Zhao plucked a pen from her grasp. Promise heard him say Zemzemal Assaad's name with a measure of disdain. Everyone thought he spurned Assaad for being a Muslim, but Promise knew he disliked accountants. As far as Dr. Zhao was concerned, Assaad was a servant who bound numbers so they would fit some pretty arch.

Dr. Zhao gripped Promise by the elbow and steered her away from a mushroom tidbit. "You must abstain from strange foods, my dear."

Promise interpreted his remark as longevity advice, so she was confused when he also thrust her past Miss Stranger, in her chiffon.

"You must avoid unpleasant colors," he whispered. "Shall we get everyone's attention?"

She prepared herself to be gracious. If they had followed Joseph's lead, they would doubtless be inducting Talbot Perry. As figureheads went, he would make a handsome one. Talbot was the tallest person in the museum as well as one of the few natural blonds.

"Ladies and gentlemen," Dr. Zhao said. "Early last month, I received a letter from the esteemed Joseph Lattimore. Might you lend me your ears?"

Chatter dimmed. Dr. Zhao gestured for Promise to sit in one of the Windsor chairs facing the crowd. Agatha Morada and Estelle Stranger sank into club chairs, expelling wheezes from the thick cushions.

"Word from our Joseph," Mr. Balichakra said. Bemusement settled over the room as they prepared themselves to be charmed and educated. A brain, a heart, courage, and a good eye—these were rare qualities to find in a single museum director.

"'Dear Friends All,'" the letter collected them in his inked embrace. "'As you know, Emmy and I are making our way to the Taklamakan Desert. We began with a Roman holiday; how fortunate that the Silk Route is among all roads purported to lead there. In fact, it was Pliny the Elder who broke the silk story to the West, mistaking the silkworm cocoons for a fuzz that grew on trees. Yet it wasn't until the nineteenth century that a German coined the name Silk Route. In addition to silk, merchants trafficked in glass and ivory, tea and incense, as well as ideas. I'm sure you're all aware that in the first century A.D., as Christianity burned along the fuse between Italy and Israel, Buddhism was leaving India for China along the Silk Route.'"

Zemzemal Assaad was taking notes on his ubiquitous index card. Even a missive from Joseph was a lesson, Promise thought. As Dr. Zhao read, she watched pillars of dust swirl in the hot columns of outdated lighting. Though she was breathing a little easier now, she could have sworn she smelled the sepia ink Joseph favored, an archival brand made from cuttlefish.

"'This letter I post from Samarkand, where a linguist is tutoring me in Kharosthi. Employing some two hundred fifty syllabic symbols, Kharosthi may have developed in northern India under Persian rule, an unpopular theory I intend to promote. I am, alas, finding this venture more challenging than Sanskrit, Hindi, Arabic, or Persian, not to mention French, German, or Italian.'" Dr. Zhao paused to absorb the polite laughter.

Talbot could not believe the way people soaked Joseph up, as if he were the most watery of water. It was just like him to sound humbled by his own achievements. Here, Joseph had managed to list all the languages he knew and still seem modest.

"'Next week we journey east to meet our team at Niya, between Kyrgyzstan and Tibet. Niya was the Buddhist watering hole Xuan Zang immortalized in his seventh-century account. Marco Polo came through six hundred years later, and Sir Aurel Stein made numerous expeditions there, carting home 182 crates of artifacts from a single dig.'"

Talbot hadn't come here for an art history lesson. He eyed Masami Yamamoto, wondering if he was any competition. Fortunately, Dr. Zhao had finished the endless epistle and began introducing Agatha Morada to the only people who knew her.

"Dashiell, please," she said, flapping her arms to lift herself from her seat. Standing at the lectern on stick legs, neck kinked and pink hair tufted above her head, she looked like a crane. Her trembling voice was equal parts Boston Brahmin and Alzheimer's: "This decade has been a prosperous one for the Museum of Asian Art. Renovation, conservation, acquisition, scholarship, exquisite reviews—we've had it all."

The crowd shrugged, acknowledging the mystery of their good press. Despite their visitor count, they enjoyed the praise of awestruck critics all over the world. Dr. Morada continued, "Although Joseph Lattimore has returned to his fieldwork, there is much of him here with us. The Founder's collection deserves fine scholarship but also appreciation by a wide audience. Exhibitions of these artifacts merit displays and writing of the highest quality."

Talbot could not believe what he was hearing—Agatha Morada was paving the way for a Joseph clone. Was the Advisory Committee completely in the dark? Although he knew things that would make her old-lady teeth fall out, he hadn't predicted this outcome.

And Dr. Morada said, "I have been asked to announce the great good news, which I'm privileged to oblige. Ladies and gentlemen, it is the decision of this committee that Promise Whittaker be named acting director of the Museum of Asian Art."

A jolt went through Promise, a shock the likes of which a cattle prod might deliver. She hadn't managed to hire a competent babysitter or keep the basement dry; what made anyone think she could run a museum? Talbot's glare reached her from across the room; then again, Agatha Morada was radiating such admiration that Promise made an effort to sit a little taller.

Promise concentrated on Mr. Yamamoto's kudos. "A connoisseur whose frank charm has persuaded both collector and financier alike to give again and again." Gregarious beyond his nationality, he had a wart on his cheek and an underbite, and Promise occasionally had fantasies about him. "We cover the world," he said in closing, "from Oklahoma to Yokohama." This was a group who appreciated mile span, and they applauded wholeheartedly.

Dr. Zhao said nothing; he merely bowed at the waist toward Promise, who got up from her chair and stood beneath a well-endowed ram the Founder had shot. The air rang with congratulations in the manner of an earlier era. "Good show!" "Well done!"

Though shaky, she was flattered by their recognition. "You can't imagine the honor this is for me," she said, wondering if anyone had ever refused the calling. What ran through her head was: No more wearing knee-high stockings, regardless of skirt length. Nevertheless, she heard herself say, "I'm devoted to this museum—it's been a privilege to study and document the Founder's collection—and I only hope I can live up to the compliment you've paid me."

Frankly, this promotion didn't feel like the pinnacle of her career; it felt more like riding backward in the family station wagon through the Ozarks. Deep breathing was the answer, except that her long inhalations brought in Madame X across the room, a formaldehyde scent topped by a hint of violets, and she plopped unceremoniously into the Windsor's saddle seat. Acting on their own volition, Promise's fingers released the top three buttons of her dress, and the bevy that had circled in to cheer now worried over her.

"You're flushed, my dear," Mr. Yamamoto said. "Are you going to hell?"

"I hope not," she managed to answer, just as she realized that he'd actually asked, "Are you quite well?"

She was on her feet again yet did not remember standing.

Zemzemal extended his hand in assistance, turning his clasp into a congratulatory shake. Although Talbot Perry was directly in front of her, he kept his arms by his sides.

"Such an honor, you know," she mumbled to the group. "Such a surprise."

"We're all stunned," Talbot said, glowering at her over the top of his rimless glasses.

Madame X was frowning, and Mr. Balichakra stepped in front of her, escorting Promise back to Miss Stranger, who said, "My dear, how we cherish you."

Somehow, Promise escaped from the conference room, bowing away as she backed out the big leather doors. She click-clacked so fast through the corridor it sounded like she was riding a horse over the terrazzo. Rounding the bend, she passed the menacing shadow cast by the Japanese temple monster.

"Everything all right, Miss Promise?" Sergeant Becton called from his post outside the Chinese galleries.

"Fine, I'm fine." Joseph's private bathroom—her bathroom—was at the far end of the hallway, and she kept up her galloping pace until she reached his door, mercifully unlocked.

Promise leaned over the toilet, wondering if Joseph had ever used the facilities in this manner. She attributed her nausea to shock, because she didn't usually suffer from a nervous stomach. A cold wave brought goose bumps to her arms; as saliva filled her mouth she remembered being sick on both the first day of school and parents' night. Come to think of it, she'd been puny at Felix's birthday party, too, though she'd blamed the tacos. In each instance, she'd made it to work the next morning. Her time as a mother had retrained her to think of her leave as belonging to the children; throwing up all night was better than getting sick on a Thursday when the curators met.

She only spit into the toilet, nothing more, as blood circulated back into her tingly arms and the nausea subsided. At the sink, she splashed her face with water, then lifted from the rack a real terry towel, an unexpected office perk. Acting director. Could she take it as a compliment?

When Promise left the bathroom, she closed the door behind her. Having been in Joseph's office untold times as a welcome guest, she now felt like a peasant trying to pass as a pandit. "Caste party," Leo would tease whenever staff and dignitaries were invited to the same opening. Promise tried to dismiss the remark, except that truly she felt outclassed.

Twice-born Brahmin are the priest caste. Sudras have one birth only. (Nightly, whilst rounding up chipped plates, she recalled the fate of the lowest class. Of them, the scriptures declared, "They shall eat their food from broken dishes.") All this from Joseph's seminar on the Vedas. There was transcendent beauty in those repetitive volumes. Their incantations and magical spells surfaced mostly in her dreams, where mumblings sound the same as precious secrets.

Promise paced around Joseph's suite, so much more spacious and airy than her underground lair. Show-offy publications lounged on the glass coffee table, and the lacy shadow of his mosque porthole draped across the camelback sofa like an afghan. His walls had been painted deep red and hung with calligraphy. Everyone else had a white base-ment office. When the path she had been circling brought her to the director's huge cherry desk, she gasped to see an envelope with her name written in Joseph's hand. She had the spooky notion that some-one had slipped it in while her back was turned, because it seemed a hard thing to miss.

She reached into the top drawer for Joseph's familiar jade letter opener but came up empty-handed, an unwelcome reminder that he'd packed up and left in a hurry. Turning the sealed envelope over and back, she wondered if the lab of material scientists downstairs, prac-ticed at dating Asian art to its proper era, could determine whether he'd addressed her three months ago or last week. It was definitely his writing—Joseph alone began her name so puffed up, as if she were Pillow or Princess. She was as curious as she was apprehensive about his message, and were there a kettle nearby, she would have steamed the envelope open in case she wanted to feign ignorance of its con-tents. However, having no means of clean access, she clawed the dis-patch open with her bare hands.

Aiming High

November 1, 1999

Had the surge that Promise felt, scrabbling away at the sealed notecard, been of a mythic origin; had she located Joseph's jade letter opener and plunged it through the envelope into the neutral carpet and beyond; had supernatural sponsorship allowed her to stab the earth at Washington, D.C., and aiming high, follow through from mantle to core to mantle on the other side of the globe, she would have ultimately jabbed the left kidney of her former boss. A cool Washington afternoon was a below-zero night in the Taklamakan Desert, where R. Joseph Lattimore was, in fact, weighing the pain in his kidney against the dark, cold trek to the latrine. The overwhelming heat had dissipated with the day's light, until the blackness consumed any radiant warmth. As cold and uninhabited as his environs were, Joseph may as well have been on the dark side of the moon.

Humbled, prepared to confess his discomfort if he could locate a listener with a helicopter, he longed for his flannel sheets and down quilt. Just getting here had been an ordeal. Like a child, he'd gotten *airsick* on the flight from Samarkand to Kashgar: gusts from the Pamir mountains buffeted them from the south until overcome by winds coming off the Tian mountains. That should have been an indication that he wasn't up for this trip. From Kashgar, they went to Hotan, a three-hundred-mile drive that had taken Aurel Stein a month to traverse on horseback, camels carrying everything from gear to ice for drinking water to Dash, his fox terrier. That was 1900; Joseph's caravan made the trip in ten hours, sneaking out of Kashgar before the blistering sun arose, which is to say in paralyzingly cold darkness. The Jeep's heater blew hot sand through the car vents; when the driver thawed out, the air grew ripe as a stable. By then, the sun was up, dimmed by airborne dunes that seemed to form and re-form as quickly as ocean waves.

Counting the driver, there were seven of them packed in the Jeep. Emmy pointed out different sand colors as if they were on a family vacation. Powdered granite from the Karakoram, or Black Mountains, formed curvy black stripes separating yellow dunes from orange-red flats. She wondered aloud whether the variety of blowing sands had inspired Tibetan monks to construct their intricate sand mandalas and then scatter them to the wind. There was interest in the front seat, where the two Japanese men had just come off a monk documentary. Sharing the backseat with Joseph and Emmy were two Australians, an art historian and a scientist, both of whom specialized in the mummies of the Taklamakan. Divorced from his daily routine, the scientist was apprehensive that he'd forget to take his heart medication, and Emmy volunteered to remind him. No one complained about the grit between their molars or scraping the backs of their throats, and so Joseph didn't mention it. While daylight held out, Emmy continued to be charmed by the white tornadoes of dust dancing on the horizon, where Joseph kept his gaze in hopes of staving off carsickness. Trying to remind himself of his past rugged treks only made him nostalgic. Better to watch the sand funnels, the widest ones actually kicking up shrubs, but most like stretched-out springs. Tilting and then righting themselves, many spun themselves straight. "Like strands of silk!" Emmy marveled. The last ten miles were so bumpy that when Kanraku, one of the cameramen, lifted his sunglasses out of the glove compartment, the screws had vibrated out of both temples.

Joseph blew and blew his nose, but he couldn't get all the sand out. Within twenty-four hours, he developed a sinus condition, and Emmy left him in the hotel room as she browsed the markets with the Japanese. They had a week in Hotan waiting for the caravan to coalesce. Once the pounding behind his eyes subsided, he joined the group for a dinner of Chinese dumplings with fat mutton, only to be felled by something intestinal. Certain that his system would right itself, he ran through his supply of antibiotics before they left for Niya. Even so, he had to endure a camel trek to the site while suffering from the runs.

Surrounded by futuristic travel gear, he and Emmy were sleeping in a yurt. The round hut was essentially rugs on a bamboo frame. A pop-up tent would have been both more portable and efficient; however, the caravan could ill afford to carry equipment with only one purpose. Rugs peeled off the outside served as extra blankets, tables, or shade. Stuffy and hot during the day, the yurt cooled down too quickly, so that sleeping in it was like being outside minus the view. The camel men slept in makeshift graves near the fire. After dinner, when the temperature was already minus ten degrees Celsius, they would dig shallow holes the length of their bodies and shovel embers from the cooking fire into them. A thin layer of sand and a sleeping mat kept them toasty through the night, or so they said. Joseph declined their offer to prepare a bed of coals for him. What he yearned for was his four-poster in his Capitol Hill home, which had been sold out from under him.

Courage, there! Joseph steered himself away from self-pity. He was autonomous, resilient, with education enough for ten men. He was also remotely related to Sir Richard Burton, whose African discoveries paled only in comparison to his Persian translations. But lineage was wan solace in the desert cold.

A thin stream of sand came through the yurt at a spot near his head. How had Burton managed to survive the Congo? Pre-sunscreen, or for that matter, pre-antibiotics, how had he withstood the threat not only of vipers and malaria, cannibals and leprosy, but also of sunburn on the tender strip of neck between hat and collar?

No one would have suspected Joseph of having such a tender strip of neck. Cumulatively, he had spent some two decades in and around India, a region renowned for health and hygiene mishaps. But he had always been warm. And younger. He had always been younger then. In the context of Indian festivals, who missed restaurants or theater? Skinny girls danced to music they shook out of their legs, anklets of bells and tin balls, while the villagers ate mangoes on sticks in the jasmine-scented night air. Enveloped by hand-spun, hand-dyed, and hand-loomed blankets, who missed flannel sheets? The fantastic muddle that was Indian life had invigorated Joseph. He would have retired in India had the crush of museum administration not led him to yearn for isolation.

"Your teeth are chattering," Emmy said right out loud when a whisper would have sufficed. It startled him to hear her announce his condition. "Should we zip our bags together?"

"No, darling, I'll be fine." An involuntary shudder jarred his hips and knees. He couldn't bear the thought of being uncovered for a moment, even for Emmy's musky warmth. Muscular, vegetarian, with some smartly placed fat deposits, she was the model of a well-insulated person. But he couldn't risk letting any hard-won heat escape his shiny cocoon.

Centuries after its renown as an oasis had evaporated, Niya was due for rediscovery. Fernand Grenard and Dutreuil de Rhins came relatively close in the early 1890s while making maps for France (that expedition ended tragically when de Rhins was killed by nomads in Tibet). Sven Hedin got closer on his treks in 1895 through the Taklamakan, which he called "this second Sodom." It was Sir Aurel Stein who found his way to Niya in 1901 and wrote vividly of the remoteness. "There is no road, and travelers in coming and going have only to look for the deserted bones of man and beast as their guide."

And yet centuries of looters had managed to make the trek, sifting the shifting sands for the possibly mythical king's golden camel. Such pillagers would not stoop to collecting everyday detritus; when Joseph could stoop, he found plenty. Actually, if Joseph were to complain, the diarrhea was more trouble than his searing gut cramps, which at least induced a cold sweat. He uncovered a wealth of coins, pottery shards, horns and vertebrae and unhinged jaws, a mirror handle. Cigarette cheroots that could as easily have been dropped by Stein as by one of their present camel men. Trekking back and forth to the latrine took so much time and energy that, instead of registering every fragment on the grid record, he reburied quite a few.

Never before had Joseph so coveted ease. His own children had survived with minor scrapes—if a broken collarbone and hepatitis, both cured, could be counted as minor—and Ravi had recently announced plans to join the Peace Corps. As kids, the boys loved dal as much as bologna, and the tiffin wallah delivering tinned lunches by bicycle was their equivalent of the pizza truck. They'd witnessed bad habits, too, like Indian teens drinking arrack until they passed out, and this had come in handy back in Washington—the boys seemed to keep an anthropologist's perspective on the antics of their rich private school chums. Joseph was proud of the job he'd done, showing them that an American could be more flexible than conventional wisdom had it.

But desert winds cover and uncover with equal indifference. They swept over Joseph's affability right away, leaving his reputation for elegant adaptability as another mote in his eye. And what the blowing sands exposed was a view he'd never considered. His research had taken place entirely amid throngs of respectful folks. Although his children had been exposed to uncommon filth and germs, they'd had recourse to medical attention, the best in a large radius around their site. They'd always had mail and phone service, albeit sporadic. Journalists, diplomats, scholars, and villagers had reached out to Joseph's family with a generosity that would not have been shown to an American professor in the Italian countryside. He had set himself up as the hip American with first university and later Institution connections who was ready to come among the people and be showered with attention, not to mention bejeweled artifacts. Had his colleagues seen him this way all along?

The landscape he and Emmy now inhabited was devoid of hospitality—as Stein had written, "pregnant with death and solitude." Niya's ruins had been freeze-dried in a climate that had brought civilization to its knees and was bringing him to ruin as well. The beasts snorted and brayed in a tight circle; guides occasionally yelled back in response. Aside from the wind, there was simply nothing to make a noise—no hawks, grasshoppers, or wisps of dried grass to be rattled. Not even mosquitoes or flies. Not even vultures. If the wind could work itself beneath a saddle blanket edge, you'd hear it flap; wind through a grommet rose and fell like a siren.

Their caravan was twenty people in all and as many animals. A Japanese television crew, two Buddhist monks, Chinese, Australian, and American scholars, three desert guides, and five camel men. With thanks to prior monks, the group had spied their destination—there was a tall limestone stupa that had withstood lacerating sandstorms and temperatures so severe they'd sent the Niya River underground. Imagine excavating a river! Different experts had their hopes set on different milestones. All Joseph cared about were the documents: sacred texts, memos, grocery lists written in one of the earliest Indo-European tongues.

In the 1890s, Grenard and de Rhins had acquired a birch-bark manuscript written in Kharosthi, which proved to be a recension of a sacred Buddhist text, the *Dharmapada*. Joseph believed that the flourishing of the Silk Route was recorded in Kharosthi beneath his feet, and he fantasized that the Japanese crew would capture him discovering the find of his career.

Meanwhile, health anxieties interrupted every synapse like a busybody on an old party line. He had been thinking about the porcelain traffic along the Silk Route until his diarrhea butted in to remind him that kaolin, the white chalk mined for porcelain, was also the main ingredient in Kaopectate. Hoping to take his mind off his infirmities, he cast his thoughts further back to the Persian incense that was also traded along this route. Christ's birthday presents of frankincense and myrrh may have been carried along here too, but that thought led him to Emperor Nero, who was said to have burned an entire year's harvest of frankincense at his wife's cremation.

Thinking had always been his salve of choice, and so when his gastrointestinal distress would not abate, he became aware of the possibility that his constitution might betray him. Having the runs on a caravan was a delicate business. The crew resented his needing so much water. (Lately they'd been distracted by news of some rock climbers taken captive near Srinagar. At least that was what he thought they'd said—after the news ricocheted about in Uygur, Chinese, Japanese, Turkish, and English, who knew how much of the original story was left?)

Yesterday, he'd reached under his shirt for a scratch, only to discover he'd developed a rash on his chest. Nothing too dramatic, but the welts were multiplying, maybe even forming a crust. And he'd thought museum life was stressful. Freezing cold, aching to piss, itchy, Joseph reaffirmed that asceticism was not the same as self-mortification. What was it Talbot had said? "It would be such a pleasure to fire most of these deadbeats." He remembered his last days at the museum, when a bunch of scholars in the desert had seemed the ideal antidote.

All those years mocking rich collectors had brought him to this. Not penniless, no; he was too patrician for that. Even as Emmy had been casting off material goods without a backward glance, he had stashed some assets. They had, however, liquidated the bulk of their possessions, and returning to their old life would require crawling back over a few burned bridges. At that moment, he welcomed the notion of crawling right up to a burning bridge and thawing his backside. Closing his eyes, he tried to summon forth the roasted tuber soup Nathan served in the staff room, ladled from the Founder's own tureen. Instead, he kept coming back to his private bathroom, until finally, he had to go to the latrine.

He already had all his clothes on except his coat and boots. Silently, Emmy helped him out of his sleeping bag; once he was ready to make the great trek, she handed him their motion-charged, magnetic-battery flashlight, which he shook up to get going. The wind nearly knocked him back into the yurt, and he closed his mouth a second too late to protect his gums from the bitter blast. The latrine was 120 steps north-northeast from their yurt; he took a reading from the illuminated compass in the base of his flashlight and began counting, wishing he'd tied his boots rather than slipped them on partly unlaced. Cold sand flooded his feet. He thought he heard low singing, moaning that must have been the wind. It came and went, coarse microtonal keening in a viscera-shaking key. He saw the trucks ahead, which served as a welcome windblock on the familiar path to the latrine. On the other side, however, there was a party happening. All of the camel men and two guides were circled around a fire. At first Joseph was alarmed by the blaze itself—were they burning poplars from the fourth century?—until he saw their feast. They were grilling fragrant kabobs nearly a yard long and bearing what looked to be most of the caravan's meat ration. They stopped singing when he approached.

Forty years as an art historian had honed Joseph's reflexes to automatically classify their instruments: here we have the makings of a *mukam* ensemble with a *tanbur,* the long-necked lute; an *aijet*, a two-stringed fiddle with a long neck and a gourd-shaped body; and several sizes of hand drums, called *daff*. The names came into his head effortlessly, as if he were standing on the stage at the museum, explicating the group's culture to an appreciative audience. When the music stopped, one camel man looked up from the pot of jam he'd been eating by the handful. His companions pointed at him and laughed. There was no alcohol on the trip, so they weren't liquored up, but they must have been drunk on the sheer quantity of food they'd liberated.

Their dark eyes squinted and looked sideways, the universally recognized expression of pranksters caught jam-handed. Later, Joseph wasn't sure if it was his tenure as a museum administrator or as a parent that had enabled him to do what he did, namely, flail and castigate until the head guide came running out of the desert to scream at them in their own language. Joseph didn't understand a word of Uygur, but the yelling sounded rather halfhearted. Was this mischief or was it malice, he wondered, fearful that the crew might tear through the rations and leave them stranded in the desert. Then the head guide gave the jam eater a mighty slap, which was more convincing than the tone of his rebuke. Musicians scattered, while Joseph assisted in rounding the food up into their locked chests. The nighttime cold would keep the cooked kabobs until the morning, but no longer. Once the head guide had closed the locks and left, Joseph took a piss right on their fire. Frankly, he was nervous about being jumped in the latrine.

"Are you all right?" Emmy asked when he returned. He'd been gone longer than usual, and he was breathing hard. She propped herself up on one elbow. "I heard yelling."

"Frat party," Joseph said, describing the scene he'd come upon. As he told her about the musicians and their purloined kabobs, he felt better than he had in weeks. Perhaps he was more suited to administration than he'd given himself credit for. He should have anticipated that a harsh desert dig would require a difficult transition, but he imagined he'd turned a corner now. If nothing else, his run-in with the crew had gotten his blood flowing, allowing him to move his fingers and toes without needly pain.

Listening to his story, Emmy worried that his actions would enhance the resentment radiating toward them. Her efforts to blend in had been as unwelcome as Joseph's imperious attitude. Though she'd learned who each guide was, they were clearly offended if she called them by name.

Joseph drifted off to sleep, and Emmy was relieved to see him slumber, even if his teeth continued to rattle. Because he'd never been seriously ill, she couldn't read the signs of dehydration, possibly dysentery, certainly despair. She knew him to be uncomfortable, but she could not imagine him in danger. In fact, she refused to imagine it, as the last thirty years of her life had been devoted to him and the boys. She did not regret her roles as wife and mother, but having sustained herself on two yoga classes a week and maybe ten minutes of daily meditation ("Mom, do squirrels carry rabies?" "Was the front door expensive?"), she was ready for the next phase.

Her friends had gone the way of personal trainers and conservation-minded cruises, but Emmy was more selfish than that. She wanted to go almond-eyed with inner wisdom. In that quest, she'd been keenly anticipating her desert trek, knowing the children might have to wrestle with its resemblance to abandonment. Let them. Such struggle could well lead the team to nurse and referee itself.

Emmy didn't care if the caravan came away with nothing, for she had come to pay tribute to a Buddhism separate from its artifacts. The museum world's appropriation of her religion had led her, like the Niya River, to flow underground. Dealers and scholars bickered over the rubies dangling from Siddhartha's ears or the thickness in gold of his *ushnisha*, and their greed emboldened looters. The very statuary that had once calmed her now infuriated her, as she witnessed the international trafficking in sacred bric-a-brac.

Out here, preservation was a double-edged sword, for the desert both eroded and sustained. In their first week, she had already helped uncover an intact spinning wheel, its spool bulging with flax in spite of the fact that Niya had been uninhabitable for a millennium. Someone could ostensibly restart the continuum as soon as the wheel was brushed off. It was like the cartoon Ravi had sent her after her breast surgery: "Good news, Mrs. Radowitz! Except for the cancer, you're in remarkable shape." What she had survived to come here. Others spared death would have chosen an Umbrian vacation in a lemon orchard or maybe donated a larger than usual chunk to charity.

———

"Time to start the day's digging."

Emmy was talking to him again. Considerably weathered, her golden skin looked like dried fruit, and her gray hair stood up on her head like iron filings.

"Joseph, honey. They're finishing up breakfast."

"Your hair's gray." He was slowly catching up to the present.

Emmy said, "It was gray before, but I used henna."

He knew she wasn't an apparition; however, talking to his wife meant he'd made it through the night, a development not entirely welcome. As cold as it had been last night, that was how hot it would be by noon. Air temperature, 100 degrees; on the sand itself, 140. He thought of the party he'd broken up last night, the men wearing thin-soled boots and, at most, a kind of bathrobe in that biting wind. During the day, the barefoot guides did not even bother with floppy hats. Joseph remembered when a T-shirt and a pair of dungarees used to be the sum of his expeditionary ensemble (and the dog tag ID he wore to humor his mother). That was because there was something to work with, whether he was following the Columbia River or trekking through Olympic

Forest. He'd come home brown as beef jerky, teeth daily brushed with a frayed sassafras twig, hair and clothes rinsed in the water of glaciers.

How might a man know his limit before overextending himself? Joseph understood that this was one trip more than he should have taken. All night he had shivered and rocked. His rash had spread across his ribs, and his neck and wrists were still blistered by lotion-resistant burns. Sixty years of confidence and bravado done in by an ill-planned excursion across Asia's phantom limb.

Joseph had succumbed to the hype of mail-order catalogs, which had him welcoming a sun that kept others away. In his linen pants that held a crease, he'd slide tablets from the sand like bread from an oven, all the while enjoying the comfort of socks whose fibers wicked moisture away from his feet. He'd donate his surplus water to the deserving camels, stay up long after his exhausted guides to record journal accounts, and review the work of his peers. As it turned out, he couldn't even muster the resourcefulness to check his e-mails.

It was as if he had so identified with his nifty gear that he had forgotten his own physical limitations. He was the man who, fearing the pain of a pebble beneath his unprotected arch, could no longer step barefoot outside his front door to retrieve *The Washington Post*. His teeth were too sensitive for him to drink ice water anymore. What was he doing in No Man's Land, a place so arid that the winds mummified and preserved victims whose knees buckled in the light of day?

On the way to breakfast, he passed the sorting tent, where the Hellenist from Hopkins was reassembling the mummy that would guarantee her tenure. Her splash in academia—Caucasian-featured mummies wearing tartan plaids—struck him as old news. Sir Aurel Stein had found as much when he came through Niya in 1906 (though Stein had also unearthed a large collection of Kharosthi). "Culture," for Stein, meant evidence of European footsteps. On the cusp of a new millennium, what constituted culture was again up for interpretation. Did culture mean trade? Religion? Water? Each looked in his biased direction; meanwhile, it all ended up in the triage of the sorting tent. You could tell a lot about a person by the way he sorted.

"I wish there were a shady spot for you," Emmy said. "A day or two out of the sun would bring you back."

She wasn't offering to sit out with him. "That's not necessary," he said. "We'll have our delicious, what is this, amaranth? And then it's off to the salt mines."

Before long, he was a regular bulldozer of antiquity. Inside the doorway where Emmy had been working, a spinning wheel poked above the sand. He dug near the base, farther into the dwelling. With the sand as fluid as water, digging resembled swimming; grains flowing back into each depression made for slow progress. Six inches under, the sand was studded with curios the size of Cracker Jack prizes. A bronze arrowhead, ceramic chips (one bearing what would eventually be called a swastika), a piece of an incense burner: such was the residue of previous lives.

A long bone lay near the fragment of incense burner. Make that two bones, probably human thigh bones judging from their length and thickness. There were many reasons apart from a grave for two thigh bones to be in the sand. He wasn't really in the mood for human remains, and he actually pushed one of the bones back into the ground, which wouldn't give way. Brushing aside an inch of sand, he saw why. There was a skull to complete the trio—a skull and crossbones— which seemed like a warning sent directly to him. Spooked and dehydrated to the point of lunacy, he was glad it wasn't a mummified body, the sight of which might have sent him screaming across the dunes.

Emmy was down by the stupa sifting sand, out of earshot, and so he breathed in a chestful of baked air. He was a rational man. Neither hysterical nor easily frightened. A man trusted to set policy. His wits told him this, as his mind sang, "Down by the stupa, sifting sand."

"Desert dementia" they call the syndrome whereby the only two drivers within miles of each other manage to have a head-on collision. The strangest thing about it is that the dementia has to affect both drivers to result in a hood-to-hood crash. Concentrate, man! He focused on the human remains, hot as plates fresh out of the dishwasher. Of course, now he was looking not for heat but for relief from it. A bandanna-full of cool water, wrung out over his face, would help. What good is a full canteen to a dying man? His crusty lips had cracked so deeply that it hurt when he licked them. He looked out on the yellow dunes. "All looks yellow to the jaundiced eye," some poet said. Aware that he was being watched, he flung his hat to the ground, out of respect as much as discomfort. That was when he opened his canteen, splashing water over his face and hair.

"Dr. Lattimore!" the cameraman screamed. "Water for drinking!" Kanraku swung his lens up to record Joseph's glistening countenance.

As if he were on a bike race, the tall Japanese man wore tight nylon shorts and a tank top, which clung to his muscular build. Joseph stood perfectly still while the lens scanned the bones in his lap, dappled with tinned water. Staring, he saw the bones soak up the splash, and he looked to Kanraku for evidence that anything had happened.

"Is the camera off?" Joseph asked.

Kanraku's scrub-brush hair shook in time with his finger-pointing. "You know better than that!" he scolded. Unless he said, "You no better than that!"

While any number of contrite replies would have sufficed, Joseph simply said, "Maybe, maybe not." Then he dropped his booty and scurried away like a sidewinder into his snake hole of a tent. Failing to record the locations of artifacts and changing the locations of artifacts were worse crimes than spilling water. Chances were good that he'd be shipped off one way or another, in either death or dishonor.

In his opinion, the water he'd poured upon himself was not wasted. The droplets had refreshed his skin before evaporating, heat leaching the moisture away so quickly that he smelled like a freshly pressed shirt. He unscrewed the cap of the canteen and drank, swishing the water to wash the brine from the roof of his mouth. More and more, he understood that the transformation of Lot's wife into a pillar of salt was something short of miraculous.

He began to wonder at what point the skull and crossbones had entered the sand. Could that grouping have occurred naturally, the largest bones in the body congregating in one spot? It might have been one looter's warning to another. Maybe the bones had been recycled as a percussion instrument, two drumsticks and a drum. Going over such possibilities made Joseph realize that, whatever he was suffering from, it wasn't dementia.

Four weeks down and four to go. He reminded himself that he'd already seen pieces enough to ponder when he was ensconced in an air-conditioned facility under cool, artificial light. He meant to stick his thumb back into the sand and pull out the very plum he sought, artifacts important enough to turn some heads in Washington. He recognized that this would be less of a success if he happened to perish. But except for a quivering vision of his impending death, he told himself, things were going moderately well.

Expect Great Joy

November 1, 1999

Promise gripped the envelope from Joseph until it puckered with her distress. Everything mailed from India looked like that: over-handled, textured like the seersucker that originated in those parts. In what might qualify as her first out-of-body experience, she watched herself rip into the envelope that bore her name. Her name but not her name, for it seemed she was opening someone else's mail. This was duality such as she had known only through myth. Whatever she read inside that envelope could not then go unread. Deduction worked rat fast in her head, quicker than her ten scrabbling fingers: the envelope had no pockets of weight, as might be the case for an enclosed key; the ink was ballpoint blue rather than Joseph's cuttlefish brown; the card was from one of their exhibitions, as opposed to stationery procured in Istanbul.

She slipped the card out and saw it was a photograph from Durga Puja, probably as celebrated in Varanasi. On the last day, villagers bid Durga farewell and dump statues of her into the river, the water bloated with women rather than the reverse. An involuntary spasm crossed Promise's shoulders, a shiver of memory from her Indian trips. Unfolding the card, she saw two lines of Joseph's formal penmanship against the eggshell stock.

"Promise, You are a talented, bright woman. Help yourself. Joseph."

She flipped the card over, then checked the floor around her feet; neither a postscript nor a scrap of paper had fluttered to the ground.

She'd expected a treasure map of sorts, a diagram showing where the saber of power might be buried. Thus far, the only attraction to her new duties was in learning such things as why an Asian museum held chamber music concerts.

Unenlightened, she returned to her basement office, where Vanessa squealed with the news. "Do we get a raise? I could *dress* myself."

Promise was glad someone was excited. She said, "They haven't shown me the fine print."

"I can keep a secret, if it's still in the can. You know, at African Art they spent a year and a half getting a director. Has Zhao put together a search committee?"

Promise had no idea and gave Vanessa permission to spread the word just as Arthur arrived.

"Come in and sing her praises. Make your wishes known." Vanessa prepared the congregation to give glory in the highest. "She's the one, chosen above all."

Actually, Vanessa and Arthur looked to be chosen above all. Beautiful, braided Vanessa, her purple suit snug in every good way. And Arthur, whose style extended from his vintage tortoiseshell glasses to his red leather boots. The fountain pen she'd always coveted showed its lapis head, gold clip hugging Arthur's camel-hair jacket. But then, aware that his luster had not attracted the Advisory Committee, she felt the hot tongue of gloating lick her ego.

"I know all about it," Arthur said without expression.

"How?" Promise asked. "It just happened."

Vanessa excused herself. This would probably still be news to the support staff.

"Elementary, my dear. Nathan blabbed." Did it look fishy to anyone else that Joseph had handed the baton to the other Indian specialist, his former student at that? It was also irritating that, Joseph aside, the museum had gone from a haven for older gay men to a women's arena before he'd become an older gay man. He said, "If it couldn't be me, I'm glad it's you," and he sort of meant it.

"Thank you," Promise said.

"Expect great joy at home. Can I buy you a drink?"

She closed her eyes. "All day long, I've been on the verge of barfing."

He said, "Surely there's a Persian word for that. Directors don't barf."

"Acting director," she corrected him. "You know what I did when Agatha Morada pointed her shaky finger at me? I *swooned*. Everyone smelled like mothballs and incense."

How Arthur longed to have been in that room, filled with the perfumed fag hags of the Founder. "Don't fall apart before the fun starts."

She took a step back. "Have you been smoking?"

"The guards," he lied. He'd picked up the habit again, mostly because he liked having to step outside for break, soaking up sun and gossip. Many a scoop started with the security staff.

Promise hefted her briefcase, groaned, then let the satchel drop to the floor. When she reached for her coat, Arthur scooped up the khaki rag and gallantly assisted her.

"Did they mention my exhibition?" he had to ask.

"Well, Talbot Perry said you were a dish. Does that count?"

Arthur was tempted to point out that Joseph's humor stopped short of teasing. All he had wanted was to have come up. Well, that wasn't entirely true. All he wanted was everything. Barring that, they could at least have praised his name and his latest project.

———

Plodding to the Metro, Promise pledged to start taking megadoses of vitamins. Or Dexedrine. She was going to need a serious infusion of energy to be acting director. And how about a new coat? Swaybacked and spent, having lost most of her buttons, she held her trench coat closed at her throat. A bright, humid autumn had turned dank since daylight saving time had ended, and without the chipper tourists, Washington was bleak and insular. Although it was not yet four-thirty, floodlights shone on the flags circling the Washington Monument. Their fluttering shadows rippled across the white obelisk, making it both night and day outside, the way darkness appears in a movie.

She could relate to that effect, being in the dark and the light herself. Wait until Leo hears this, she thought with dread and excitement. She'd figured out that what Leo had against leadership was the raising up of one person over another, especially himself. He had a high opinion of himself. As for Promise, she appreciated the kind of leadership that allowed her to do her work.

The packed train was muggy, and the orange decor gave a sallow cast to the white people, most of whom stared zombie-straight ahead.

Clear plastic panels perpendicular to the side doors helped separate riders from entrance and exit traffic. The panels and doors bounced reflections back and forth, superimposing commuters or shifting their body parts out of context. Promise spied a thin arm ringed with bracelets and holding a familiar book, and it took her two stops to trace the apparition. A teenager in an aisle seat was reading a volume of Rumi. Seven hundred years after his death he'd made it onto the *Times* bestseller list. Promise was still surprised enough to point. "Rumi," she said to the girl, who flashed her a peace sign.

At Metro Center, the train coughed and then inhaled another load of people, pollen up a giant nose. Promise flowed into the stream heading for the Red Line train, and she tucked herself in the corner near the door so she wouldn't have to stand nose to armpit in the aisle. Amid the reflections, she spotted an immense rump in a similar trench coat. Eating down Felix's supply of Halloween candy had done a number on her own hip region; unfortunately, her relief at seeing a wider trailer lasted only until the Woodley Park stop, where she nearly said "Excuse me" to her own butt. She scanned the crowd, imagining they'd been making jokes at her expanse.

Maybe it was all the candy, but lately she'd been ravenous and petulant—her very metabolism seemed to be changing. As thrilling as being crowned acting director was the prospect of an early bedtime. She had a notion of what her thickening waist and squeamishness might indicate: the looseness of joints, a sleepy weepiness that anemia alone could not justify. She nearly recognized her own symptoms, but they were in a code she did not wish to crack.

Two trains, a bus ride, and a short walk later—forty-five minutes after leaving work—Promise swung open the unlocked door of her dark house. She would have to remind Althea once again about safety. You'd think that someone whose sister was paralyzed in a drive-by shooting would see the need for security, though Promise could also imagine that random violence would make a dead bolt seem futile.

She listened for the loose change of the puppy's tags and the scrape of his toenails. Instead of a bike, Leo had brought Felix a puppy for his birthday. Every night, Flipper slid toward her as if someone had bowled him down the entry hall; his nails left long parallel scratches on the wood's finish. She bent her knees, but Flip was not in earshot. She saw a glow from the kitchen and smelled the smell of cooking without any food, the not entirely odorless aura of burning gas. Sure enough, blue flames sat atop two stove burners like miniature crowns. Promise lunged at the dials, grateful for the sound of arguing upstairs, shrill voices that let her know the children had been neither nabbed nor gassed.

When she extinguished the blue blazes, the downstairs was dark. Considering how early night fell, she figured the children had been upstairs watching television since the moment they came home from school.

"You early," a voice said, and Promise froze until she could identify the source. Of course it was Althea, but that tenth of a second of terror—a voice in the recesses of her unlocked home—gave her a start. Coming home was always like this; she had to drop her museum self on the porch and jump into motherhood the way a firefighter slid into boots and gear. She especially resented it today, when she craved a moment of triumph with her family.

Althea was folded into the corner, her emaciated frame and gray-black skin more shadow than person.

"The burners were on," Promise pointed out, trying to steel herself for contention.

"It's cold in here," Althea said. "Something not working right."

Overhead, a loud thump sounded, followed by a yell. This was not the first time Promise was torn between attending to her children and trying to squeeze a story out of Althea.

"What's going on up there?"

"They fighting," Althea said.

In her most authoritative tone, Promise said, "I count on you for adult supervision."

Who was wearier? The babysitter, a decade younger than Promise, let go a heavy sigh. "I don't like to be around when they clawing and fussing."

It was hard to argue with that. "You need to make sure they don't hurt each other."

"They have till quarter to for making peace. I gave them that."

Promise had seen pictures of Althea taken before tragedy befell her husband and sister. She had been on the fat side of robust, but that much grief slims one down. Now her joints were larger than her Tinkertoy arms and legs. While Althea ran her hands over her nearly shaved head, Promise surveyed the appliance clocks, each of which promoted a different version of the time. Depending on whether she believed the oven, microwave, countertop radio, or coffeemaker, it was somewhere between 5:12 and 5:35.

"Got to let them work it out," Althea said. "You're awful over-protective."

Promise yawned, which surprised both of them. At the moment, the thought of walking up a steep incline and facing whatever spat Lydia and Felix were having was more appealing than going one-on-one with Althea. "Please don't turn the burners on for heat."

"It's cold in here," Althea repeated. "Your thermostat's busted."

"Why don't we call it a night?" Promise said.

Althea left without saying goodbye to the children, even though she knew Promise was keeping score. She was tired of Miss Priss judging her—the woman spent more time reading about kids than being with them. And wasn't she looking like last Sunday's plate of eggs?

A whining from the basement set Promise to worrying that the washing machine was about to go. A unanimous decree declaring her potentate should have given her an adrenaline surge like no other, but she was all in. Another woman would have fired Althea and tripped upstairs to share news of her freshest success with her cherubs, no doubt engaged in some harmless roughhousing. The steps were so worn that each one sank in the center; Promise profoundly appreciated the slight cradle they provided.

Upon reaching the summit, she could see the immediate problem in that Lydia was sitting on Felix's head.

"Stupid, stupid, stupid, stupid squirrel," Lydia hissed.

"Lydia Morgan! Get off your brother."

From the looks of Felix's face, she had been on top of him for some time, perhaps with all of her weight. Each of the children took one of Promise's arms and tried to tear her apart. It wasn't much of a contest: Lydia had thirty pounds on her brother and a hale grip.

"Felix bit me," she whined. "I'm going to have a scar that never goes away."

"She squished my head, Mommy. She blew a stinker on me."

Promise smelled that gas in the air, too, but there was also a fresh bite on Lydia's cheek of just Felix's circumference and spotty toothiness. She had a morbid thought of the entire household being identi-fied by Felix's dental records, so regularly did he bite. Several pieces of furniture bore his imprint, as did book covers and picture frames she discovered when tidying up.

Both children hung from Promise as if she held the scales of jus-tice. Felix could tell he was losing in the balance, so he went right for the capital offense. "Lydia used the S word."

Promise asked, "Has anyone seen Flip?"

Lydia was especially thrown that her mother would change the sub-ject before declaring who was most at fault. Which was more egre-gious, Felix biting her or her sitting on his head and swearing? Usually their mother weighed their transgressions and tossed off a judgment in a matter of seconds. It was a process that gave Lydia a thrill—the sus-pense, the decision of less than/greater than/equal to, the excitement of either being wronged or being bad, all taking place within her mother's wingspan. She was torn between begging for the call and her concern for the puppy.

"Flippy," she called out, anxiety constricting the volume in her cry. "Where is he, Mommy?"

Promise's first thought was that Althea's stove-top heater had gassed him, and her second thought was to be ashamed of her first. A lethal mix of manic breeds, Flipper had nothing in his genetic makeup to curb his appetites. If someone had left the door open, their impulsive, spirited puppy might well have run out onto the street to see how tires tasted.

With the children quieted by fright, the rhythmic din rose again from the basement. The washing machine had probably rocked itself up the stairs by now and was coming to seek its revenge on the family of filth.

Lydia clenched her fists. "Flipper!" she hollered loud enough to rat-tle the closet door.

As the whining downstairs became a yelp, what had seemed to be appliance revealed itself to be dog, thus holding out the hope that the puppy recognized his name. "I think he's in the basement," Promise said.

The children looked at her with the sure knowledge she was right. She was eerie that way. A gouge in the rocking chair and she guessed that a tool of Felix's had not quite accidentally done the damage. Purple marker on the living room wall could have been from a number of pens in the house, but Mommy somehow knew that Lydia deserved the blame.

The children raced down the steps. Felix took a sock-slick spill onto the second landing, then bounced right back up. Promise was sure that had hurt more than anything Lydia might have done to him.

By the time Promise got all the way to the basement door, Flipper had been freed. He launched himself at each of the kids, allowing them to welcome him back into their fold. Then he commenced to speed around, running one side and then the other of his bearded muzzle along the Oriental rug. Next pass, he switched sides. "Zipping," their vet called this habit dogs had of wiping scent from themselves. If Promise didn't stop him, Flipper would have a fat lip, but when she reached out, he shocked her with the static electricity he'd built up revving along the dry carpet.

The puppy was circling with such speed that Promise smelled him before she saw what he was spreading round the house. It was offal, and many varieties at that. His blaze was as dark as the rest of his face, his bushy tail clumpy. Because she was in her work clothes and silk did not cotton well to puppy leavings, she opened the back door and threw a rubber caricature of Clinton onto the deck. Flipper lunged at the effigy, oblivious to the swinging door grabbing for a bit of tail.

Promise switched on the basement light to see that, trapped belowdecks, the puppy had apparently lived a week in a few short hours. He had chewed his way into a sack of cow manure Leo was going to use any month now; in no certain sequence, he had also vomited, pooped, peed, rolled in all of the above, scratched a sizable welt in the door, and chewed the bottom step. And this was just what she could see.

It took all of Promise's reserves not to rend her clothes and, forswearing allegiance to the Whittaker-Wells clan, pluck a key from the key bowl to unlock a neighbor's door and join another family. Lydia and Felix sensed the end of her forbearance, but being children, they saw only that they were dirty and not the hours of cleanup Flipper's sprint would require.

What order should restoring order take? Promise began arranging the matrix of considerations: Flipper needed a bath, so did the kids, the carpets, and the basement; dinner had to be served before terminal crankiness set in. She pushed the kids up to the kitchen table, which was in a drafty spot but out of touching range for any more damage, and poured two bowls of the sugariest cereal she could find.

Thus was Leo greeted when he came in from work, his children unsupervised and sitting in the cold, eating what looked to be candy bars in milk sauce. He would have to remind Promise how he felt about the groceries: if you didn't vote with your wallet, those sugar pushers would never get the message. His concerns overrode his dogma as he came closer. Felix sat as if nailed to his seat, and both children smelled like shit. Now he was worried.

"You guys all right?" he asked. "Is Mom home?"

Lydia sniffled, her chin quivering. "Mommy's mad at us."

Leo squatted down, arms outstretched, and the children screeched their chairs away from the table to rush him. Though they stank, he held them close. Where the hell was Promise? He consoled them in a low voice aimed at the floor, hopeful that she hadn't heard he was home. He was counting on her to rush downstairs and save them all.

Promise was trying to get going, God help her, but her clothes proved complicated as armor. Panty hose, half-slip, belt. She let her dress fall in a heap—it was stained anyway. What next? The question floated into her murky brain the way type appeared in the bottom of Lydia's Magic 8 Ball, and she immediately tried to unthink it, knowing that the mischievous gods, their eternal lives abundant with spare time, lie in wait for such questions. Sure enough, when she opened the door of her closet, the crystal knob came off in her hand. She deserved that, she thought, and tossed it onto the bed, where she should have been. Never before had she been jealous of a doorknob. She fished leggings and a sweatshirt from the clothes hamper, gagging a little at the funky fleece. Really, what was going on, that she was capable of smelling around corners?

The answer to her questions had been gathering such momentum that when it hit her, it knocked her on her ass. She was pregnant. Promise fell back onto her bed, and the doorknob rolled down to nestle against her. When she tried to recall the date of her last period, she had no access to a mental calendar. That was a consequence of her profession: she regularly spent a morning in the spring of 1260, investigating Rumi's conversation with Shams of Tabriz, and an afternoon describing an exhibition scheduled for 2005. No wonder she was dis-oriented.

Pregnancy has its own timetable, notorious for its selfishness and lack of subtlety. Like a five-hundred-pound gorilla, pregnancy sits any-where it wants, clearing months away with a hairy paw, plopping down in your most delicate chair—mind if I sit here?—oblivious to the deli-cately lathed legs snapping under its weight. Just get through the mo-ment, she coached herself. Don't think about the nausea so bad you couldn't brush your teeth for gagging, the leg cramps that made you yell out in the middle of the night. Exhaustion that had you sleeping under your desk. And now, your fabulous new job! Don't. Think. About. It. Step into your socks one foot at a time and return to your bickering, shit-caked children.

Down in the kitchen, kitchen so low, everyone was either talking or barking. Promise hung her head over and heard Felix's razor-sharp voice recount his chain of events. "Lydia was flattening me on my face, and Mommy didn't even make her go to her room or anything—"

"He *bit* me, Daddy," Lydia interrupted.

"But Flipper lost hisself, but we gots him to bark, so, actually, he smeared gunk on the red chair." Felix pointed to the back door. "Mommy put him out."

"Mommy!" Lydia said, as if she hadn't seen her all day.

And then Leo caught sight of his wife. Surely this was more than the work of a dirty dog. "Hi, dear," he said.

Promise spread out her arms. Behold, she thought, the acting di-rector of the Museum of Asian Art. And she's not alone! "Where should we start?" she asked. The chaos prevented her from sharing her news, though she had no intention of telling anyone, not even Leo, about her pregnancy until it had been confirmed.

Leo set to work scraping the rugs, then spraying muddy streaks with the remains of different carpet cleaners. Two were foam to be mopped into the pile, one came with a scrub apparatus. He planned to let them all soak in and vacuum the crust in the morning. Because it was his cow manure that had been stacked in the basement since spring, he took it upon himself to tackle that mess as well. It wasn't bad, though he knew Promise would have done it differently. With a push broom, he swept everything to the big drain in the center of the

cement floor. What was too chunky to pass through the sieve, he shoveled into a plastic bag, then he poured down a generous glugging of
bleach. If he were an architect of family homes, he'd incorporate a
drain in every room.

Promise, meanwhile, had taken Flipper and the children to the
bathroom. That doorknob also came off in her hand. The radiators
were going constantly now, desiccating the matchsticks or whatever it
was that held those huge crystal balls on their stripped bolts. They
needed to invest in two or three humidifiers, which depressed her not
so much for the expense as for more cords along the floor and the additional filling/emptying/sanitizing tasks that would be hers. These
days, carrying water from the well and beating clothes upon the rocks
seemed comparable to her chores.

She thought about Emmy, Joseph's wife, who'd raised four boys in
challenging climes. How could she cop some of that grace?

It was hard to get Flipper wet. The water beaded up and ran right
off him, rivulets careening every which way to avoid touching the dried
clumps on his fur. Promise emptied a half bottle of baby shampoo
working up a lather. Then once soaked, he quickly exhausted the supply of dog towels available for drying his many layers. The children
talked to him reassuringly, actually helping. They were old enough now
to push a stroller, bring in groceries. She let them rub his fur with the
damp towels as she decontaminated the tub.

"Run and be free," she said to the drippy dog when she opened the
bathroom door, Felix and Lydia cheering his release into the wild. He
stood on the other side of the threshold and looked back at them; then
he gave one tremendous shake of his body, from muzzle to tail, which
sent a wide arc of droplets along either side of the hallway. Promise
doubted she would be lucky enough to have those dry clear.

"Leo!" she yelled. "Flipper's on the way!" The puppy stared at her in
a moment of confusion over whether he was in trouble or not, and then
he bounded like a drunken bunny down the hallway.

Promise stood the children together in the shower for a rinse before
filling the tub. They had not bathed together in a year or more, and
Felix naked compared with Lydia was an alarming sight. His taut skin
clung jealously to his skeleton, allowing neither fat nor sinew to muscle in. He simply could not gain weight. Bathtime revealed what the

physicians saw: his thighs had no folds of fat near his crotch nor his knees any dimples, and when he turned his back to Promise, his butt was a flat, droopy W. Cream for his cereal, she added to the perpetual grocery list she kept mentally. Salami and fat mayonnaise. Avocados and egg custard. Butter on everything!

Once the children were scrubbed, swaddled, and on their way downstairs, she leaned out to look at Felix's clock—it seemed impossible that the train was only between the eight and the nine. Because she'd pulled off the bathroom doorknob, she couldn't close the door against intruders, let alone lock it, and so she lamely pushed the step stool against the door before ransacking the medicine cabinet. The last time she'd bothered to clear out the expired unguents and prescriptions, she had been dangling a half-empty box over the trash when she felt Leo's hand on her wrist. She pulled her head out of the cabinet to see what he wanted with the flattened, water-spotted carton. A lone pregnancy stick rattled around inside, the one that had remained after its twin registered positive for her Felix pregnancy.

"Don't throw that out," he'd said. "It's probably still good."

"Good for what?" she'd asked, and they'd exchanged one of those complicated married people looks.

She found the box, marked "Best before June 1999." So it was now officially expired. "Clear Sign" bragged the brand name; the side of the box showed the bright pink line that would appear in the indicator window if it detected pregnancy hormones. She rotated the container as if it were an artifact. "Be confident about your plans!" "Get results the first day of a missed menstrual period!" "Test any time of day!"

Promise peed on the stick and watched as no clear sign was revealed in the indicator window. Eventually, a faint pink line showed up alongside an even fainter, thinner one and a dot. The lines were straight, the dot was round, which implied she was getting some kind of sign. She divined that her sentencing had been postponed, although the stick might have been more prescient than the copywriters knew. The longer she stared at the lines and the dot, the nearer they resembled Persian calligraphy written in *nastaliq*, also known as the "bride of scripts." Maybe if she studied her pregnancy test intently enough, she could read the sign in the window. Maybe it was a message from parasite to host, a poem from the embryo within.

———

The entire family gathered downstairs in the living room. The children, their wet hair striped by a comb, were in their pajamas, and they scooted up to the coffee table for cocoa and graham crackers, so far the only dinner Promise and Leo had partaken of. All around them on the Persian rug, puffs of carpet cleaner sprouted like toadstools.

"Is this the general panoply?" Leo asked, gesturing to include the kids, Flipper, and the soiled house. "Or are there further lamentations?"

As soon as he and Promise had mastered spelling at the speed of dictation, Lydia had learned to read. For private conversations, Leo aimed his vocabulary over their heads, while Promise stuck with the tried and true.

"Althea," Promise chose her words carefully, "eft-lay in an it-snay."

"At Queenie?"

"Yes." Promise smiled at his name for her.

"And domestic personnel aside," Leo guessed, "your institution has unduly taxed you?"

"Refills?" Promise asked, so they could meet in the kitchen.

"The flames were up to here." Promise held her hand well above the burner. "I've explained the thermostat. She's not stupid."

"Don't underestimate her," Leo said. "She may have been *trying* to burn the house down."

"I don't think she's up to this, Leo. Have you seen her lately? She looks sicker and sicker."

Leo thought Promise looked pretty sick herself. "Face it," he said, "neither of us is man enough to fire her. Did something happen at the museum?"

"The museum." Promise wiped her brow. "Boy, howdy." She straightened up, attempting to look more successor than victim. Congratulate me! Pity me! Whichever she desired, her family was good at neither. "Guess who was made acting director."

"Talbot?" he asked, but that was wrong. "Arthur?"

"Me," Promise said, remembering Vanessa's words. "I'm the one. Chosen above all."

As he recoiled, the gloating she'd felt with Arthur resurfaced, warming her nearly enough to compensate for her husband's chilly dismay. Up in the bathroom, she'd sworn herself to secrecy, but she realized how mutable that decision was. If he'd cheered her promotion, she would have told him she was pregnant.

He said, "They've got their hooks in you now. Didn't I say you were their best choice?"

"You did indeed." More annoying than his taking the credit was the implication that she was a slab of meat in the tiger's cage. She said, "We're going to need better help."

Leo hoped she was referring to Althea. Before he could ask for details, Felix erupted with his evening fit. "I'll get him," Leo volunteered.

Promise watched him leave; in a city of tight asses, Leo had the loosest walk around.

She held the children's mugs by the cups rather than the handles, instinctively testing that they were not too hot to touch, and returned just in time to shoo Flipper away from a carpet-cleaner mushroom. What did he know of his true food? These days, you weren't to give a dog a bone; instead, you gave him a bone-shaped cookie.

"I'm still hungry," Felix howled. "My head's wet." His lip shook with the nightly injustice of the earliest bedtime.

"You're practically asleep, buddy," Leo said.

Sometimes Felix could make them hold on for another while, though he went to bed puffy and raw with his efforts. "I take a sleep with Mommy," he declared, sounding more like a three-year-old than a six-year-old. He bulldozed stacks of mail, sending a mug of cocoa to the edge of the coffee table. He willed the cup to break into a bunch of pieces, yet he was unexpectedly relieved when his father saved it.

"Easy, there," Leo said in a grown-up tone that made Felix mad again. "You take a sleep with Mommy every night!"

"It's my privilege as the daddy. Let's get you to your room."

Flattening his hands together, Felix swiped at the air. "I'll slice you up. In half and in pieces."

Lydia covered her ears with a sofa pillow. "Daddy, make him stop." She was torn between wanting to ball up like an armadillo and wanting to punch her brother. Felix didn't know as much about the world as she did, like the fact that saying things out loud could make them happen.

"I'm hungry," Felix started over. Then he ran in place and announced, "I got a second wind!"

Ah, the dreaded second wind. Behind him, Promise whispered "Felixity," so that he had to stop thrashing to hear. She held his shoulders and walked him backward to her, wrapping her arms straitjacket fashion across his too-evident rib cage. "Honey, I'm going to sleep too, because I'm all poohed out. If I juggle for you, will you take a sleep in your own bed?"

Felix considered this with gravity. His mother had not juggled for some time. "In my room? With my things?"

It was like negotiating with a terrorist. "Yes," she said wearily. "Go pick out three."

Felix scrambled upstairs to find three items suitable for throwing—the moment of silence Promise had hoped for was only half that. "Ready, set, go, Mommy!" he yelled down.

Flipper ran the full staircase up and back down, accompanying each family member to Felix's tiny room, which looked even smaller when the whole crew was packed in. Maybe children were like goldfish, Promise thought, growing only big enough to fill their pond. She winced at Felix's selections, betting against his tears that she could convince him of the unjuggleable nature of a construction-paper collage, but he readily capitulated, substituting a rubber ball. The two remaining objects posed opposing complications. His stuffed dog, Bow, was loopy with age; the third item, a die-cast dump truck some three inches long, was much denser and would have to be thrown farther afield to stay in orbit.

"The dump truck is going to be tricky," she warned.

"That's not a dump truck," he corrected her. "That's a back loader. How many times do I have to tell you?"

"The back loader is going to be tricky," she said.

Felix exhaled in exasperation, but he also settled in to watch the act. He was on Leo's left, sitting on his shirttail; Flipper was at Leo's immediate right, with Lydia just beyond the dog. Promise planted her feet hip width apart and flung the ball up first. Trying to still her mind, she looked for habit to take over. She had learned to juggle before she had learned to drive, and the automatic nature of the task—balance, judgment, a steady throwing arm, and coordination to spare—came back with the first toss. Flipper yapped at the flying toys until Leo pulled the damp puppy close against his hip.

Leo saw his wife's face within the blurry frame of motion. Her eyes did not dart about; they were focused on neither the flying objects nor her family. Gifted with the peripheral vision of a goddess, she stared straight ahead as her many arms twirled the attributes of motherhood.

She'd put on a few pounds this fall. The extra weight softened her pointy little chin; her hair had ample cheek to fall against. He liked that, not that he could tell her. Weight gain, he knew, was best left unremarked upon. But it made her less fragile, more voluptuous and matronly. The heft of her breasts was apparent even under the sweatshirt, and it reminded him of when she was pregnant. She had not appreciated his lascivious attentions then; how could she when she'd suffered such discomfort? Maybe if she were just getting plump, she would welcome him kneading her fleshy hip or kissing the folds of her tummy. He had been hoping to hear talk of a sabbatical rather than a promotion; selfishly, he wondered how much less there'd be for him.

Promise sensed the extra flab in her arms from the first let-go. "The Great Pyramid," she announced, letting the truck fly and then Bow. The toys shaped a triangle in the air. Still magic, that an object would hover at eye level long enough for her to catch and throw, throw and catch.

Until familiarity replaced awareness, she registered how exaggerated her stance seemed. Hip width was not what it used to be. Likewise, her reach was more constrained than she remembered, and there was added thrust to her tosses. "Ring Around the Rosy," she said, changing her pattern to throw with the right hand, catch and pass with the left. Ball, truck, dog circled like a lariat an arm's length away. Each object was independent of and dependent on her, thrown in a pattern she determined. What else was new?

"Counterclockwise," she said, reversing the objects' orbit. Arms spread open like a book, she considered her two sides: she was forty-three, knocked up, for the moment the head of an art museum. Her son was probably in for some medical attention, her daughter was easily spooked, and the care they received from Althea had been deteriorating for some time. Her husband still smoked dope, and a wolverine in a puppy suit was splintering their home. That was her recto; her verso was crawling through miniature windows into the splendors of another century. Calligraphic loops of rapturous verse, illuminated with pulverized jewels, the artists depicted luxuries unimaginable to us now. She didn't know what she'd do if she had to turn this page.

The spectators of her juggling feats, speechless at first, began talking among themselves. Even as she lost her family's regard, Promise marveled at how quickly the amazing becomes commonplace. About two minutes. Flipper wriggled free from Leo's slackening grip to leap joyously, twisting and floppy as Bow. She wished Felix had left an apple or cookie on his dresser, so she could show off, taking a bite of an apple before hurling it into the fray. It saddened her to lose the spotlight to a rubbery amateur who could chase his tail for a laugh.

Must she drop the ball to avoid having more and more expected of her? Dip it in kerosene, set it afire. Pedal a unicycle, on a high wire. She had it now, the rhythm of jump rope, of clapping games, of marching. Directed by her expert light touch, the toys moved themselves. More satisfying than making it through dinner without anyone spilling. Her hips dropped subtly, lengthening her spine. Whatever juggling endorphins existed kicked in, and she gave herself over to the toss and snag.

Foreign Fabled Country

That same evening

In light of the evening's wackiness, Promise never did mention her promotion to the children. And she certainly didn't mention her pregnancy. After juggling, she took a bow for the second time that day, and Felix dutifully climbed under his covers, much to everyone's surprise.

Lydia, contrite about the puppy havoc, was easy to get to bed. Cold weather held special charm for her, with her flouncy flannel nightgowns and lamb's-wool slippers soft as pets. She avoided going outdoors and yet would read about the most spiteful wilderness. She requested stories from her mother's childhood in the windswept land of Oklahoma, that foreign fabled country.

Promise was looking for her daughter's brush on her dresser. In the process, she uncovered scraggly pigeon feathers as well as doll parts she didn't recognize. A scavenger full of trauma and wonder, Lydia could mythologize from nothing. Grosser were the small collections of gum wads and scabs, both of which Promise hoped had been her daughter's.

Next to a jelly jar labeled "poyzin" nestled a cluster of snakes, purple and pink clay cylinders no bigger than earthworms. "Are these new?" Promise asked.

"Althea and I made them. She's helping me."

Promise unscrewed the lid to the pissy smell of vinegar and immediately resealed it, leaving the jar on the dresser. She stifled a gag— from all the splashy baths she had given that night, water had soaked through her fleece to rest against chill-bump skin, but she was over-heated, too. As far as Promise knew, Lydia had never had a run-in with a snake, and yet her phobia made her world writhe. A garden hose, Felix's belt on the floor of his room, a dangling thread touching her skin—*snake!* Promise's psyche obviously worked a different way. Terrified of getting pregnant or losing Rumi to her work duties, she'd ignored every clue. She backed up against the bed until it caught her behind the knees, and she lay down.

Lydia curled up next to her, nose to nose and nearly knees to knees. At nine, she was practically her mother's height, which only meant that Promise was the height of most nine-year-olds.

"Althea says snakes are just big worms, but that didn't help. Because you know Felix has all those flash cards of snakes unsnapping their jaws to eat a baby deer or a bird's egg." Lydia placed her palms to-gether, hinged at the wrist, then fanned them apart like a snake's hun-gry mouth. Snaking her arms along the gingham quilt, she made her way to her mother's chin, which she pressed between her makeshift snake jaws. Promise knew she was trying hard to be playful. "Althea says that if you're afraid of something, it owns you. Mommy, I don't want to be owned by snakes."

"Oh, sweetheart, that's not what she means. When you're scared of something, then that thing has power over you. Remember the haunted house at school? You guys were screaming because they pretended pickled onions were eyeballs. Those eyeballs had the power to make you scream." Just the word *pickled* brought that vinegar smell back.

"Then Felix ate one."

"That's right. Good old Felix popped one in his mouth and said, 'Eyeballs taste like onions,' and next thing you know, you were all cracking up."

"But snakes are snakes."

"Althea doesn't want you jumping at every twig." Lydia's quilt smelled like Flipper and bubble gum. Holding her daughter's hand, Promise gently pushed the cuticles back with the meaty part of her thumb. "One cold rainy day the Buddha was trying to meditate on the shores of a lake, but he couldn't concentrate, what with the rain sting-ing his skin and the cold dripping all the way down his back. Just then, the serpent of the lake climbed out and wrapped himself around the

Buddha to keep him warm, and he stretched up and fanned out his hood so the Buddha would stay dry—"

"Don't tell me about the Buddha." Lydia wriggled out from her mother's hand sandwich and faced the wall. She didn't really want to be left alone; she wanted her mother to come after her.

Promise scratched Lydia's back in a sideways eight, big infinities. "When I lived in Delhi, I passed the snake charmer each morning on my way to the library. Things hadn't really got started yet. He had his cobra basket and dried-pumpkin drum, but first he'd make himself a cup of tea. If his tea was too hot, he'd work on his turban, winding it 'round and 'round, like a bandage, like a snake, until he had a pillow head—"

"Don't talk about India," Lydia said. "Cobras spit venom into people's eyes!" But when Promise put a pillow on her daughter's head, she turned around laughing.

"I'm trying to think of unscary snake stories," Promise said.

"Talk about Oklahoma," Lydia requested.

That was an unfortunate pairing, because snakes were to Oklahoma what Bibles were to motel rooms. At the Rattlesnake Roundup, for example, cowboys tossed venomous sidewinders around with snake hooks. A typical stall sold fangy snake heads floating in paperweights, entire snakes looped within clear toilet seats, or grilled snake sandwiches.

Lydia sat up, closing her eyes in concentration. Promise followed suit until the coconut scent of some girlie product unmoored her, and she had to open her eyes to confirm that the bed was not a boat in rough water.

"I see a sod house," Lydia said, channeling Oklahoma. "There's a palomino nearby nuzzling her colt. A girl in a calico bonnet is flying a kite she made out of butcher paper—it's polka-dotted because of the meat spots on the paper." She sat cross-legged on the bed, her open posture and closed eyes resembling the flat-chested, girlish sculptures of the Buddha as a young prince.

Promise drank in her sweet girl. Unblemished by chicken pox because there was now a vaccine, unscarred by her first bike crash because a plastic surgeon was on call at Sibley Hospital for just such chin lacerations, she was peach precious. Her lashes fanned out on her cheeks like fringe. Wheat-colored hair fell beneath her shoulders; golden down ran along her cheeks and swirled at each temple into a slight cowlick on either side. Sensing her mother's stare, she opened her eyes: the whites so white, the gray lustrous as stones in a river. Then she lay down again on the narrow bed that had belonged not only to her mother but also to her grandmother, and Promise wondered what false past she had invented for her own family.

At this point in Promise's life, it was something of a fallacy to pose as an Oklahoman. She had lived in Washington for a decade, and before that in Philadelphia for both college and a double dose of graduate school. Her Oklahoma was chicken-fried steak smothered in white pepper gravy, fried okra and inch-thick Texas toast on the side, shades of brown covering a scratched white platter at Anne's Cafe on Route 66. The sky outside the plate-glass window was like an enormous forehead, the way it drew your eyes up, up, up in disbelief. And it was sky blue, crisscrossed by thin jet trails that the wind gradually blurred into fluffy cat tails and finally into puffs of vertebrae along the spines of lounging giants—

"Mommy." Lydia shook her mother awake. "You're on my covers."

Promise obediently picked herself up off Lydia's quilt, and she kissed her daughter's sueded cheek. "I'll dream you a story, honey," she said. "I'm sleeping right now." And it did feel like sleepwalking, this routine that was not so much unpleasant as relentless. She pulled the bedroom door until it stuck in its lopsided frame, then stepped down the hallway, whose floorboards, having long ago lost their finish, could push a splinter into an unprotected foot. Left at the water stain from last winter's ice damage, and alongside the rattling windows of her wind-shaken bedroom. She wished she could face a direction that was not suffering from her inattention.

None of the repairs they'd managed thus far were visible: wiring ripped out and rethreaded through most of the house, horizontal pipes entirely replaced, a modern furnace installed, and a whole new roof shingled on. Her neighbors imported Carrara marble for kitchen counters and built Japanese teahouses in the backyard; they commissioned garden tiles painted with indigenous plants and fossils. Meanwhile, she and Leo taped plastic sheeting around the children's windows, blow-drying it taut to shrink-wrap them for the winter.

She was determined to reach her bed and allow sleep, to paraphrase Rumi, to wash herself of herself, like melting snow. She planned on being unconscious before Leo discovered her whereabouts. Though she would later wake up damp and twisted, she could not muster the effort required to peel off her leggings or heft the sweatshirt over her heavy, heavy head. She'd finally arrived at the end of her yearlong day.

When she awoke to the clattering of plates, she had no idea if she'd slept one hour or eight. Leo was sailing down the hallway wearing the clothes she'd last seen him in. Lit from behind by the wall sconce, he emanated an aura of bright dust. His excessively long feet turned out, and he held no tension in his hips or shoulders. No other man had a walk so lax. Just as she recognized that his rounded prow was a tray, Promise began to smell the eggs and toast. She could sniff cumin as well, which meant he had cooked rather than reheated. "To eat is to eat cumin," he would say, reciting some Hindi proverb of his own invention.

Leo unhinged the legs of the tray on either side of her lap, then he went around the side of the bed to switch on his bedside lamp, whose light threw spooky shadows across the wall of masks. After Promise had bought him a few superhero masks as a credit to his Amnesty work, friends picked up on the notion. Spirits and animals, there were crude wooden carvings from all over the Third World, peppered with a few plastic Halloween characters.

Leo pulled a tissue from a box on the floor. "Here, sweetheart." She realized her nose had been running for weeks, yet another pregnancy clue that she'd missed. How stupid she felt and, now, how guilty for keeping the news to herself. Slack-jawed or leering, the masks bore down upon her. She made a note to tell Leo's friends that he'd started collecting money.

"How is this going to work?" she asked. "As it is, we're on the brink."

Sweet, untrammeled Leo, the goof who criticized her shopping habits, the sage who saw the pulsing ego behind most Washington problems. It wasn't that he'd balked at marriage or home ownership or fatherhood. What was it exactly? A lack of drive, maybe; put positively, a talent for not participating, despite his work rescuing political victims. While she loaded herself down with museum tasks and school assignments, Leo remained notoriously unburdened. Houdini, she'd once read, knew ways to free himself with grace rather than force—the same rang true of her husband. When necessary, he relaxed all his defenses, allowing the chains that shackled and tormented others to fall to the ground in a heap.

"Was Joseph acting director before he was director?" Leo asked.

"No," she said. "He ascended directly into heaven." The egg aroma was like the presence of another person in the room. She had to have a word with those eggs—she had to devour them. They were salty and spicy and so steamy hot that she panted to keep from burning the roof of her mouth. "So far," she said, puffing out steam like a dragon, "the brightest spot is that Talbot will be reporting to me."

"You didn't believe Joseph would endorse you," Leo reminded her.

"You were right." Promise again let him transform her glory into his. She might have pointed that out, except that butter had saturated the toast so it was ideally compromised between crunchy and soggy. In her experience, this texture was only reached accidentally. She ate without ceasing, hoping Leo wouldn't ask her for a bite.

He brushed a blob from her pointed chin. "Congratulations, hon. They couldn't have made a better choice." Except for Talbot or Arthur or maybe Fatwa, whatever the Muslim curator's name was: those three wanted to rule the earth, and none had a family.

"Thank you." She wiped her nose on her sweatshirt, a trick learned from Felix.

Wolfing down the eggs, a drip of snot hanging off her nose, Promise looked like a child. Leo remembered how tiny she'd been—waist like a wrist, he used to say—when they'd met at a grad-school party. "My third eye sees something in you" was how he had introduced himself.

"Tell me more," she'd replied, "but only if your third eye is above your waist."

"It is now," he'd bragged, the two of them drunk and he a little coked up. He didn't know how substantial she was until months later, when he proofed her doctoral thesis.

He asked her now, "What does your Rumi say about leading?" Mystics notoriously championed humility, especially for women.

"Follow, follow, follow," she acquiesced, "but there's also: 'No more muffled drums! Uncover the drumheads! No more timid peeking around. Either you see the Beloved, or you lose your head!'"

"I'm right here, don't lose your head."

While it was India that had drawn them together, their separate sojourns could not have been more different. Promise might as well have been at the British Museum the way she fortified herself against India: iodine drops in her food, boiled water even for washing her face. Leo ate and drank everything there, feeling he'd escaped the petri dish for a genuine, thriving culture. Not everything agreed with him. Worms were not uncommon; once he almost died of malaria. His friends—a mix of Indian, Sri Lankan, Australian, and Californian—left him at a Theosophist clinic in Madras. Promise had ventured no farther south than Varanasi, whereas his India was Calcutta and below.

Promise laid the tray on Leo's side of the bed. "There's more," she said, certain that he'd be gleeful about the possibility of pregnancy.

"No, that's all," he said and took the tray. "Do you want more?"

"Not really," she answered, deciding to leave it at that. She said, "I've been waiting for this moment all day long." And without another word, without even brushing her teeth, she was openmouthed and shut-eyed. You'd have thought she hadn't a care in the world.

Leo cursed Joseph and that decrepit committee for hanging this honor around their necks. It wasn't that Promise took such good care of everything. Still, she was the designated worrier, gathering estimates on water seepage when it looked as if they might lose an entire wall, keeping obligations in her head, such as car inspections, teacher conferences, and the children's doctor appointments. Her promotion at the Art Mahal would require another step away from him and the children. Lately, she'd already been tired when she hadn't been sick. As acting director, she'd have to attend events at night and go on the collectors' circuit. She'd be traveling the globe to hypnotize the rich, charming the money from their pockets, the whatnots from their shelves. Leo saw a future with himself further diminished.

Returning to the kitchen, he slid the empty breakfast tray back into the cupboard, where he spotted a wad of foil nesting in the cupcake tin. Eureka! He vaguely remembered squirreling away a bud back there. From the roll in the drawer, he ripped off a small sheet of foil, which he wrapped around a plastic pen. Then he slid the pen out and flared the end of his aluminum reed. Rubber gloves for the dishes, matches for his makeshift pipe, and he was ready to clean up.

A deep drag on the tinsel pipe rendered the sink bubbles beauteous. Ten years older than Promise, enough to make a difference in their music and politics, Leo had often wanted to speak up for his habit. Personally, he felt it was a better choice than the after-work martini. Conventional wisdom maintained that dope forced drive out breath by breath, but Leo gave the curbing of voracious zeal a positive spin. In a time of limited resources, it was good for more people to want less.

He had spent most college evenings picking at the artifice of so-called government, all while lighting a fresh Colombian with the butt of the last one and dropping domestic acid into Turkish espresso on the nights he wasn't popping amphetamines. Illuminated and suspicious, heightened and speedy, he believed he was his truest self then. And in India, a country perfectly suited to getting things not only into but also out of your system. Fatherhood had dampened his enthusiasm for illegal substances, just as for anarchy. Dampened but not drenched. He still smoked a couple times a week. That and his aviator glasses were just about the only relics of his college life.

Scrubbing dishes, he registered anew the disparity between time spent eating versus cooking or cleaning up. He relit the pipe, spluttering the match in the dishwater, to take a hit of the stale yet resinous dope. Flipper had been curled into a damp heap since his basement reign of terror, and he'd already recharged enough to perform a toenail-tapping dance on the kitchen's tile floor. He yapped louder than the smoke alarm, which Leo had been trying to evade.

"Don't flip out, my flipping pup," he said, amused to be finishing up the dishes so he could walk a dog. Chores aside, this family life was a trip like no other.

The leash didn't feel right in his hands, and it was a block or two before he realized he was still wearing the rubber gloves. The left proved an easy scoop for the dog's leavings but a tricky container; he gingerly peeled it off and threw it into a neighbor's trash can. He was preoccupied by his wife's advancement. Women of his time made their headway into a profession and then rooted themselves like tenacious dandelions. Or was it women of his place? His Amnesty International co-workers were communist Buddhists, earth mothers with a little grizzly-bear mother thrown in (just mention Pol Pot or Milosevic). In his office, ambition was not a necessary evil—it was the only evil. Was his wife's education for the sole purpose of self-promotion? The master's wasn't enough, the doctorate, curator, chief curator. She must have wanted this badly and he had never known.

More Than a Makeover Could Mask

November 2, 1999

In the early morning light, the museum seemed as frail and exposed as Promise. She no sooner noticed the withering pansies outside the front entrance than she chided herself for their condition. Yesterday, she could not have said what flowers struggled to bloom along the heavily trafficked path from the Metro—now she felt it her duty to spade the plot. She who revered the Founder wasn't crazy about his erecting an Italianate building to house Asian art; the choice meant different things today than it had in his time. Perhaps she'd drag some temple Devis outside, where passersby could marvel at how the stone-cutters had managed to impart beguiling as well as ferocious aspects. Better yet, she could install a ten-foot stone Shiva and let the Hindu community swath him in festival garb so silky bright it would reflect all over that tarnished façade.

Ah, that tarnished façade, more than a makeover could mask. She'd spent time on her own makeover this morning, not only because it was her first day as acting director but also because she suddenly saw pregnancy in her pimply chin and the mottled spots on her forehead and cheeks. Her hair seemed to have grown an inch overnight. She blended "camouflage cream" under her eyes and sprayed "lacquerizing drops" onto her hair.

She'd likened her beauty effects to museum conservation, but this museum needed more than conservation. What had seemed an austere shrine now struck her as a doddering fixer-upper in dire need of caulk and repointing. One hundred years of mediocre drainage had wept onto the granite blocks, staining the gray in the most concentrated areas to a black that might even be mildew. Had they tried bleach on that bad spot near the entrance? Her curatorial eye cataloged the shabby stair railing mottled with rust, mortar lost from between gap-toothed blocks, majestic bronze doors whose pocked lower halves looked like the side of a station wagon pelted by grocery carts.

She was one to talk, showing the effects of too many grocery carts herself. Her dress seemed to be shrinking with each step. Was there any possibility she wasn't pregnant? Was there any possibility she wouldn't go through with it? Those were her rationalizations for not telling her very own husband, those and having to suffer his delight.

In the long-sleeved sheath that was tight as sausage casing, her arms would barely bend to slip off her coat. When she looked down at security's sign-in sheet, her stomach pooched out unbecomingly.

"Good morning, Miss Promise," the senior guard greeted her. "Congratulations, ma'am."

"Thank you, Officer Jackson." Her face heated up with his praise. "Has news spread already?"

"I don't know about that," he said. "When are you due?"

"Eight-thirty," Promise said sharply. She strode up the grand staircase to the main hallway, as much as a five-foot-tall woman in a tight, calf-length dress can stride, and took a left. Past the museum shop was the director's luxe corner office, which she walked past before doubling back. In his early years, Joseph used to stroll through all the galleries most mornings. Curators found notes taped to their doors citing map inaccuracies or questions of ambiguous wording in their labels. The man had cared about everything.

Promise hoped some of his authority might rub off on her as she entered the director's office. Framed manuscript pages lined the east wall, and she stopped in front of a sheet of Persian calligraphy, whose ascenders and curls were distinctive of the royal workshop at Bukhara, circa 1500. She thought of that damned pregnancy test, with its calligraphic code; what else could peeing on a stick reveal? She'd never scrutinized this Persian sheet so closely, because he'd hung it facing him. In all her meetings with him, she'd viewed and reviewed a pale slice of Korean, which she didn't know from a laundry list. Now, she stared at the Persian calligraphy until her scholar's memory matched it up with the upper-right-hand side of a page from a museum monograph.

She searched Joseph's bookshelves for the tan spine of the monograph she remembered: moderately hefty, quite tall. Pacing the master's office, pulling out books at will, Promise suspected she'd been born once to Joseph's two or more lives, just as she knew herself to be more of a foot soldier than a mouthpiece of the human race. She detected no residual wisdom or reserves of experience that preceded the time logged in her body.

She could, however, conjure up the stinky paper of the monograph she was searching for, as well as the corduroy dirndl skirt she was wearing when she'd held it on her lap however many years ago. She matched the thickness of pages she recalled holding between her thumb and forefinger, panning perhaps a dozen rectos before she hit gold. The accuracy of her recollections always unnerved her a little.

Bitter and unroyal though its message was, the sheet was something of a masterpiece. The calligrapher was none other than Mir Ali, whose strokes Promise knew because of his Rumi transcriptions. He'd been an art hostage, taken from his home to serve another's court. Lamenting his talent, he'd written that "this misfortune has fallen on my head for the beauty of my writing. Alas! Mastery in calligraphy has become a chain on the feet of this demented one."

Promise wondered if the ruler could read Persian, in which case he might have found the plaintive poem quite moving. I made him sing that song. Perhaps the sultan identified with the artist doomed by his own success: a warrior has more to prove, at higher cost, than a calligrapher. Mir Ali resented huddling over a low table in bad light, but the sultan would be lucky to live so long as to have arthritis. The ruler's own sons were known to have plotted his assassination, and he had to ride across Central Asia slaughtering folks just to keep up his reputation.

And so Promise dealt out all the possible interpretations. She might well miss the obvious in her own life, but she had a talent for looking at a page of calligraphy. She could see greed for appetite or for insecurity; she recognized political motives as well as delusion when it came to motivation.

Never underestimate the power of the original, Joseph used to say, which was her gospel as well. In so many instances, she had only known of things twice removed or in imitation. Even most of the Indians in Oklahoma had been marched there from somewhere else. Original art was hard to come by in her part of the world, unless the Cowboy Hall of Fame counted. Dinner theater and truckload sales of oil paintings tapped a vein of culture that had already thinned to capillaries in Arkansas and Missouri. Her mother had done an admirable job of tracking down a symphony or a wayward ballet troupe. But by and large, living in Oklahoma was akin to a novelization of a TV movie.

When Promise had come to Washington on a high school trip, her classmates had teased her about actually listening to their guides. They toured the Capitol. They toured Ford's Theatre and the house across the street where Lincoln rested his bloody head on the pillow and died. They spent two whole days at the National Institution of Science and Art, home of *the* Hope Diamond, *the* Wright Flyer, *the* portrait of George Washington copied for the dollar bill!

Now she was overwhelmed by the real, not to mention responsible for the real. There should be some satisfaction, possibly jubilation, in being selected for such abundance. She tried to put aside Mir Ali's lament in favor of the poet's rally, "No more muffled drums! No more timid peeking around."

———

Downstairs in the curatorial ghetto, Arthur was also struggling with Promise's promotion. He was so much more presentable, for one thing. And she was practically a knickknack, which he believed worked in her favor—her scholarship seemed all the smarter for her size. She was talented and candid, traits that made her his best friend. But director?

Another B_6 and two Saint-John's-wort tablets. He'd have to see if the vitamin store sold anything for ranting. His was just the kind of intensity he would have welcomed in a director, but apparently he had it backward. You were supposed to be attached to the people who came to see the objects and detached from the objects themselves. He coached himself about impersonating the dispassionate scholar. Once an object won him over, his writings took on a delirious quality, sarcastically skewering those who'd undervalued the piece. God help the scholar who called a wave a flame or misidentified a magnolia as a tree peony.

He had to be careful. Two years had passed since he had mistaken a bad forgery for the skills of a humble master, because a crudely made water dropper had moved him. Promise would not have fallen for that. "Raving," Joseph had scolded him when the forgery came to light, "is for dealers." His posture was supposed to be that of the skeptical connoisseur. He was so absorbed in his thoughts that he didn't notice Talbot standing in his doorway.

"Arthur," he said, neither greeting nor question.

"Talbot, how are you doing?"

"Well, now that I'm ancillary director to an acting director, I'm not so sure." He picked up a rhinoceros-horn brush rest from Arthur's credenza, pretending to toss it toward a backboard, but he stopped when Arthur seized up. "Pretty valuable?" Talbot asked.

"Bought it myself." Then because that sounded so juvenile, Arthur added, "Had to get an extra paper route."

"She's *your* friend, right? You're always together at lunch."

Arthur was torn between embracing and belittling Promise. Talbot's looks were wasted on a straight man. Tanned in November, he was tall enough to be out of mere mortal range but not so tall as to be freakish, and he had a cheek scar that looked to be from a duel, though it was probably from a rebound scuffle. When Talbot settled into the guest chair, Arthur admired how the shoulders of his Italian suit jutted past his actual shoulders. Interesting, to exaggerate one of your most prominent qualities.

"So," Talbot said, fishing for information, "why do you think she was promoted?"

Arthur wanted to give him something so badly. He considered ratting on Promise's dog (who'd chewed through the hand-tooled cover of a thousand-dollar library book)—would that be ridiculous? He hesitated beyond the opening Talbot had given him.

"I should have gone into the Navy," Talbot said. "You know, I don't really care about art much, not like you."

"That would explain your meteoric rise." Arthur tried to picture him with a crew cut, shorn of that blond bob that so intrigued. He said, "Acting director isn't director. Maybe they're just letting her fill in while they find a real director."

"Could be," Talbot agreed. On the wall a photograph of a red and yellow flowery cup was tacked up. "That's Chinese?" he asked, and Arthur nodded. Talbot said, "This museum wouldn't have a Japanese *screen* if it weren't for Matthew Perry sailing into Edo Bay. I can see him blowharding diplomacy with the U.S. Navy at his back."

Arthur said, "Matthew Perry—I never realized you were that branch of Perry."

"Direct line," Talbot said. "There's a Sadahide print in our collection that I've been looking at all my life. The most telling detail is Perry pointing to the dotted line of the treaty with the tip of his bayonet. Cooperate or else!"

Arthur recognized a philosophy when he heard one. He plunged right into his own reason for being here. "In eighth grade, this kid showed up from Guangzhou, and we picked on him until he ended up in the hospital with aggravated asthma. To teach us a lesson, Mrs. Bogdanovich devoted the rest of the term to China: Where do you think paper was invented? Gunpowder? Noodles? You'd just raise your hand and answer, 'China, China, China,' and you'd be right. I traded my baseball trophy for his inkstick and grinding stone, and he showed me a half dozen Chinese characters." And how to kiss, he would have told someone else.

Talbot didn't appear to be listening, but he wasn't drumming his fingers on his thigh either. "That's not what I was looking for."

"You started it."

Talbot had counted on Arthur knowing if Promise had clout he wasn't aware of. He said, "It'll be interesting to see how your friend looks with her hairnet on, supervising the sushi vendors. I guess I just wanted to commiserate."

"And she is a friend of mine." Arthur didn't get the hairnet remark, but at least he showed the strength of character not to deny her.

Talbot pushed up out of the chair. "We'll see . . ." And he evanesced, nothing but a bitter vapor trailing down the hall.

Arthur had read that looking at beautiful people literally widens one's eyes. Pupils dilate in their presence, allowing an excess of light in, which in turn endows the beautiful with a nimbus. This had been a problem when Talbot Perry first arrived as curator of Japanese art. The sight of his bounding basketball-player gait made Arthur agog with lust, and when his long fingers crushed a memo before deftly flicking it into the trash, Arthur's mouth went dry. It didn't take long for knowledge to quell instinct. As he spent time with Talbot, first as a curator and then as a morale-lowering, snide administrator, Arthur was able to rein his pupils in.

The opposite was true for the objects under Arthur's care, whether locked away in vaults or sitting pretty on his credenza. Here, for example, was the seventeenth-century brush rest Talbot had palmed. Unassuming, lumpy, the brown piece steadily rose in Arthur's estimation. Begin to imagine, for instance, a three-ton rhinoceros run through for this trinket. Abhor the killing but admire the decision to keep the bulk of the horn as ornament rather than grind it into aphrodisiac powder. Someone had shaped the bone into the five sacred mountains, employing grooves inherent in the horn as rivulets running down the mountain peaks.

As Arthur grew to venerate each item in the collection, he recognized himself becoming wide-eyed in their presence. He could barely focus sometimes, such was his awe.

It was in this state that he answered the phone. "Arthur Franklin."

"Arthur, this is Ambassador Young. I trust you are taking good care of our bowl."

That the ambassador would call the piece "our bowl" deeply touched the curator. Reluctantly exercising his manners, he said, "I am only its caretaker, Ambassador."

"Perhaps. But as good as you've been to me—Hold on."

He set the phone down, and Arthur heard ice in a glass and the bup-bup-bup of something poured from a bottle. It was nine in the morning. "I've been thinking about our conversations. How you said the market is strong for ceramics this year, and that our magpies might be highly prized."

It was like a dream, hearing the ambassador's proposition. Pay him half what the bowl was worth, and he would deed over the other half. An offer made while drinking breakfast was probably a gift meant to get the ambassador out of some kind of jam, but Arthur did not give a shit. He heard exactly what he wanted to hear.

———

From the inner sanctum of the director's office, Promise greeted him. "Good morning, Dr. Franklin."

"You don't waste a minute, do you?" he asked. If she weren't acting director, he would have remarked on her undersized dress, though he did notice that she'd found time for a bit of makeup. Her lack of vanity shamed him; to think how belatedly he'd hoisted her flag in Talbot's presence. She more than anyone was the one he wanted to tell his news.

Arthur's tie reflected up into the shiny black flecks of his glasses. Promise said, "Want to eat here?"

"It's veal wrapped in phyllo pastry and sauced. He's got lychee nuts for our special treat."

Promise felt a power surge at the thought of ordering Nathan to make lentil salad, curried eggplant, shrimp and lemongrass soup . . .

"Are you listening?" Arthur waved a hand. "This is big news."

"I was pondering lunch," Promise confessed.

"He's willing to donate half the bowl, but in my opinion, his estimate is already half price."

"What's half of priceless?"

"Exactly," he answered, mistaking her remark for sincere. He was still waiting for her to congratulate him. "It may be the most beautiful porcelain I've ever seen."

"I remember when you were listing all the flaws of said piece. Now you're going to buy it. Why do you want my opinion?"

Arthur narrowed his eyes behind his glasses. "Everyone cares what the director thinks."

Oh, yes, director. That would be the person whose approval was needed to spend the museum's money. She'd been dwelling on the terrifying side of power, forgetting there could be privileges. She stood and stretched her arms in the air, reaching as far as her dress would allow.

"Jesus," Arthur said. "Am I that tiresome?"

"We keep having the same conversation," she said, suffused by an unusual freedom not to censor her thoughts. The puffy leather couch drew her to the center of the room. When Joseph had been the inquisitor, that couch had been the hot seat. Under the new circumstances, she surrendered to its puff. Sitting against the armrest, she stretched her legs across the cushions.

From his inside jacket pocket, Arthur pulled out a flannel cloth to buff the lenses and frames of his gleaming glasses. He was put off by her pose on the couch, as slovenly as when she was pregnant. "I'm trying to bring some fresh blood in here. You act as if the museum were a casket for us to exhume."

Rumi had titled one of his poetry collections *In It What's in It*, and that was how Promise viewed the collection. She said, "The Founder owned an entire shipping fleet. He could buy and transport anything he desired. Aren't you curious about the collection he amassed?"

"Asia was the exotica of his time," Arthur said. "Like the young boys he 'mentored.' Besides, he got bargains all over: a handful of coins bought a carved elephant tusk."

"Even so, he might have bought junk. Junkfuls of junk. People talk about the age of connoisseurship, or they credit his eye, but it seems to me he's Mister Love-at-First-Sight. He could afford the whole world, and he chose pretty well. For example: why have you chosen this bowl?"

"I'm an expert," he said, cockiness returning.

She and Arthur had contended with this bone for years. He argued that she served the museum best when she could look beyond its front door. Usually, he managed to sound collegial about it, but today he was leaning in, growling with criticism. She said, "At the end of the twentieth century, I'm studying the Founder's nineteenth-century collection of sixteenth-century stuff. That triple perspective gives me a rush."

"When it doesn't bring on a migraine."

"I know. I alternate between holding a microscope up to a telescope and a telescope up to a microscope."

Arthur was exasperated. "I don't even know what you're talking about."

She took her feet off the couch and sat up authoritatively. "You've got hundreds of porcelains that you could research and publish, and all you care about is getting more."

Maybe it's because I'm not getting any, he refrained from saying. Any interest she might show in his sex life would be feigned. "Not just *more*, particularly exquisite pieces that complement our cache. There was a twenty-year window early in the eighteenth century when everything clicked. Thin, white porcelain bodies covered with the brightest enamels."

He spoke about ceramics the way straight men described women on the beach. Promise said, "'All Fired Up!' opens next month. I would hate to see you thrown by one high-priced lovely." She had often coached him to stay motivated through the entire exhibition process. "What does Morty think?"

"Morty thinks I should be a shoe salesman. The perfect career for a fetishist."

Having indulged Arthur as friends will, Promise began to understand the impatience Joseph had voiced to her. Amazing how quickly the good of the Institution was supplanting her usual sympathy. "What order of magnitude are we talking about?"

"Our half would be six hundred thousand, if you buy Sotheby's estimate." Everyone knew Sotheby's lowballed.

"What was it worth before we showcased it?" She saw Arthur's sheepish look and knew that Joseph had been right. Everyone wants the cover girl.

"The *yuzhi* mark on the bottom is one of the clearest I've seen."

"'Made by imperial command,'" she said, to show she was following along. The light coming from behind his head revealed a pierced hole in his earlobe, an abandoned opportunity for adornment.

He said, "There's a possibility that the hardwood stand they're using is the original, which means the piece was made for decoration. And the magpie's claws!" He clasped his hands together in front of his chest. "The painter had no regard for the incised marks; he brushed each claw just where he wanted it."

"Says you," Promise remarked, remembering when he'd downgraded the piece for the same reason.

"That's one of the things about this piece. Some of the stuff I fall for bores me after a while. Remember that leys jar in my last exhibition? I spent hours looking for a flaw—never found one. Now it looks factory-made to me, uninteresting. This bowl is complicated."

Arthur was rationalizing the way her kids did in toy stores. *And it's big so we won't lose it, and it's small so it won't get in the way, and it's soft so it won't break anything, and it's hard so it won't get broken.* The big difference, of course, being that even the grandest toy came in under one point two million.

He sensed her matronizing tone. He didn't have to take this from her, except that now he did. Thus far, Asian art scholars were most impressed with the museum's ancient Chinese bronze collection. They went nuts for the abstracted dragons and monster faces; Min devoted entire articles to the patinas. Arthur remained unimpressed, and his take on Chinese painting was the same: to the press, he said "subtle and esoteric"; to Promise he called it boring. But porcelain! The notion of dirt, water, and heat fusing as porcelain was on a par with primordial ooze becoming flesh, not to mention transubstantiation. Each to his own miracle. As far as he was concerned, ceramics served the best masters: beauty, ritual, dinner.

She said, "Could we raise that kind of money for one bowl? I don't know, Arthur . . ."

"You can see every feather on the magpie's back!"

He sat right up on the arm of the sofa, closing in as if she had not yet recognized him. To Promise's nostrils, he smelled like something charred. Not cigarettes, not the copier. She asked him, "Did you have burnt toast for breakfast?"

Arthur got to his feet, resuming his distance. "Begging the director's pardon," he said, bowing to the far corner of the couch, where her thickening ankles were propped up.

Her ankles confirmed what her toast remark and posture gave away. Had she really expected to keep this from him? After all, he had been subjected to her last two pregnancies, when her smelling feats had made her something of a queasy bloodhound. Having just been questioned about his need for more porcelain, he should ask her what she needed with more babies. It occurred to him that Talbot had come to his office for news of this magnitude.

Promise hadn't meant to be rude. "You could smell like worse things than toast."

"Listen," he said. "I can't make lunch today. The guys in Photo are showing me their new slide scanner. They have some interactive samples, too."

A knock at the door saved him from concocting as many stories as were necessary to weasel out of their plans. Min stood there, baggier and more submissive than usual.

She said, "I hear you are due congratulations."

Arthur's mouth fell open with a cluck. By the time the two women turned to him, he'd realized Min was talking about Promise's promotion. "Take her to lunch, won't you? She's looking for a date."

Promise said, "If you're so anxious to get out of your commitments, leave us your credit card and we'll go out."

Min could never tell if they were teasing or torturing each other.

Arthur said, "I'll gladly trade you my credit card for some lovely Jingdezhen ware." He spoke to Min in Mandarin: "Ambassador Young says he'll gift us half of that magpie-and-plum-blossom bowl. All we need is six hundred."

In English, Min said, "'When you go half and half on a horse, never buy the half that eats.'"

Promise laughed her chirpy snicker. "Is that Will Rogers?"

Brilliant. Arthur would have attributed her quotation to Lao-tzu, but cunning Min had been brushing up on Oklahoma lore. He spoke again in Mandarin. "Some important people have owned this bowl; it's easily worth two million."

She'd heard about the provenance—a bankrupt early president who'd lately been in the news for taking a slave as his courtesan and a movie star who was liked by boys who liked boys. "The bowl's worth what the Ambassador will take for it," she said.

Arthur pretended she wasn't insulting him. In English he said, "Can you put in a good word for me?" On his way out the door, he tried to smile at her without any visible wiliness.

"I'm sorry I didn't call you," Promise said. "The day got away from me."

In her constricting dress, Promise reminded Min of a snake after mealtime. Extra weight stuck out like stuffed pockets at her hips, but then Min could also look fat with only five extra pounds. Such was the plight of the short. But Promise's coloring seemed different, too; the skin around her eyes was dark, as was the center of her face. "You are sick?"

"No." Promise reacted instinctively. "Well, yesterday, I practically fainted."

"Such a shock," Min said. "I would buy you a special lunch, but I bet all my money on Talbot." The best thing about Min's teasing was its rarity. "You were quite the dark horse."

"The darkest," Promise agreed. She relaxed, relieved not to feel defensive or competitive. Although she enjoyed having friends who were so completely her opposite, she had to stay on her toes with Arthur. "What did you need?" Promise asked.

"Nothing," Min said. "It was my fault. I have solved the problem myself."

"Then let me ask you something. Twice during the meeting, Dr. Zhao steered me away from something. You know how courtly he is, but this was different. He was adamant."

Maybe Zhao bullied them into choosing you, Min was thinking as she worked up a suitable excuse. Once he had forced Promise upon the committee, it would have been best to avoid all dissenters for a while.

"The first time," Promise explained, "we were walking by Nathan's table, and he told me the food was dangerous. Then, Miss Stranger was there in one of her Jell-O outfits, and he literally put himself between us. 'You must avoid unpleasant colors.'"

Min's head filled with a high buzzing, as if an attendant had struck the temple gong too close to her ear. She understood now that the darkened pattern on Promise's face was the pregnancy mask; her extra weight and ill health were not mysterious but to be expected. Apparently everyone knew if Dr. Zhao was already practicing Confucian prenatal care on her.

Min heated up with mortification, her familiar companion. Dr. Fan incessantly talked to her about maximizing her harvest, and in the last few years, he had punched and scraped her most private parts. Having endured one internal plumbing procedure after another, she had seen her chances for pregnancy dwindle down from an optimistic 20 percent. Hormone shots made her weepy and cross, puffy and penniless. Meanwhile, Promise and Leo had a shot of tequila together (that was how Promise had told her Felix had been conceived) and *ying!* Promise was pregnant.

"What's he trying to tell me?" Promise asked.

"It is a tribute," Min said. Sitting erect (arranged among the seat and pillows just so), eluding garish or melancholy colors, listening to the recitation of edifying classics, abstaining from curious foods: such practices would ensure Promise's baby a fortuitous start. "Because you are the leader, he wants only auspicious things surrounding you."

"That's lovely," Promise said. "Times like this, it's nice to be surrounded by traditions. I used to think of all those complicated rituals as a web that snared its believers, sort of a 'pray or be prey' thing." She whinnied at her pun. "But I can see that it's more like a shawl. It won't protect in a downpour or even in cold—still, there's comfort there."

Usually, Min agreed away. "Yes, yes, yes," she'd say in her own high voice, sounding something like a prairie dog yipping to his friends. Usually, but not now. Min's lips were bunched together, a paper bag clenched closed. My fault, Promise thought, regretting her goofy interpretation of Min's sacred ground.

Promise said, "I didn't exactly faint. It was like someone just stopped the clock for thirty seconds or so." She was hoping that Min would look friendlier. "I already have a plateful of duties."

Min wanted to feed Promise a plateful of octopus eyes in carp bladder sauce. Plenty familiar with her own petty nature, she had never felt such injustice. The L'Enfant Hotel was a short walk for her and two Metro stops from Douglas; there were liquor and lingerie stores in the train station. She would call for reservations and, come lunchtime, cast herself upon Douglas.

"I have a meeting," Min said. "You must excuse me." She bowed her head. "My editor says my text needs more work, and the Design Department is displeased."

Promise knew mock shame when she saw it, but she wished Min luck and sent her on her way. This was not the reception she'd anticipated. She would have thought that good friends, each in his or her little boat, would rise in the harbor when Queenie's ship came in; instead, they were paddling full tilt away from her. And worse than that, they were pissy. Was it Promise's problem that Min barely wrote in English? That Arthur wanted every bright stone he could carry in his beak? While she had never expected to be crowned, she was prepared to argue that a good choice had been made.

Promise reevaluated the card Joseph had left, thus far the only thing on her desk. In the picture, the Ganges was the color of tarnished silver, and dusty red statues surrounded the boy, who looked dead-on at the camera, his black eyes set into skin the shade of smudged newsprint. Even amid this dingy palette, the Indian profusion of color burst forth: a tangerine sash, wrapped twice around the boy's waist, held up turquoise shorts.

Joseph's scant greeting sounded as if someone had been holding a gun to his head. "Help yourself." She tried to match the message to its medium, being too visually schooled not to credit his choice of images. The photograph was taken on the tenth day of Durga Puja, when the Ganges becomes a river of low-riding skiffs. Consort of Shiva, worshiped by Hindus, the ferocious Durga was mother of all mothers. Each boat, weighted down by life-sized statues whose wayward arms pointed in feuding directions, seemed host to a mutinous crew. At the sound of the conch, it was women overboard! Voluptuous, fragile, porous mother with feet of clay, we salute you. When the goddesses are pitched off, how the boats do rock, cradles on the water.

Like so much in India, here was a curious mix of veneration and indignity. Certainly she identified with the fiercely loving mother, grimace and all. One more baby might very well pitch her overboard. Not that Joseph could have known that. Joseph liked to say you were fluent in another culture once you could be teased by it, and she did feel provoked by his reference to a holiday that culminated in tossing powerful mothers off the boat.

Talbot walked in on Promise's close reading. "All moved in?" he asked.

"Hardly." Quickly, she swung her feet off the couch.

"Is that from Joseph?" His long fingers stretched toward her card, prompting Promise to pick it up without seeming to snatch it away.

"It's just a welcome note," she said. Talbot smelled like a dandruff shampoo Leo once used. He'd also smeared on some kind of balm, whose camphor overtones hinted at an old injury.

"I thought you might have some questions." He'd expected to find her gnashing her teeth about the museum closing. Jealousy aside, he wanted to read Joseph's message—his description of the museum's fate would no doubt sound like an honor he had ducked. "Joseph had concerns that the next year would be difficult. He confided in me."

"Noted," Promise said. "Once I get settled, I expect to do the same."

How much steelier she was than he'd thought. Maybe she'd known as long as he had—maybe Joseph had told her even more! That irked him as much as her being named acting director.

"Anything else?" she asked Talbot.

"Do let me know if I can help," he said and, whether in mock or due respect, backed out.

His obsequiousness backed her breakfast up into her throat, which was becoming a familiar sensation. She returned to the ergonomic desk chair and dialed the complicated sequence of numbers to get out of the building, the Institution, the government, the city. As her first executive action, she was calling her mother. Peg would no doubt be in the kitchen; her father, at his garage workbench or working on the yard. She answered on the first ring.

"Hi, it's Promise."

"Yes?" her mother said, rather coldly.

"How are you?"

"Fine." Skeptical she was, or busy. "This is my Promise?" she asked, as if there were several per square mile.

"Yes, Mom. Are you all right?"

"You sound different," she said. "How are you, sweetheart? Are the children all right—you know, it's just after ten o'clock your time."

"We're all fine. I called to tell you some news." Tears unexpectedly filled her eyes. Her mother would like nothing more than to hear about a new grandchild. "You remember, the director's been gone since August; well, they chose me to be acting director until they name his replacement."

"That's Promise?" she heard her father in the background. "What's wrong?"

Promise routinely phoned Istanbul and Islamabad from work, yet calling Oklahoma midday always incited panic.

"She gets to pick the next director," Peg said.

"No, Mom, I'm acting director." And then she heard her father wrestle the phone away.

"Are you calling on the government's dime?" Jack asked. If she were paying the bill, he would have to hang up within the next minute; however, if the government were ultimately paying, he would also have to hang up.

"It's an outside line," she said, hoping he wouldn't ask what that meant.

Promise imagined her mother swiping red dust from the windowsill knickknacks. She could picture each object because Peg's exhibition on the marble shelf above the sink never changed: there was a tin canister of baking powder circa 1950, a squat cobalt jar long emptied of its salve, a dark amber bottle shaped like a fish, and various tall shot glasses for rooting houseplant sprigs. Uncountable times Promise had watched her mother tuck the phone between cheek and shoulder as she dusted, the long springy phone cord like a jump rope across the kitchen.

Her mother was back. "Did Lydia get the mouse I sent?"

"I'm on the hall extension," Jack interrupted. "You get a raise? Or do they just save money until they get a real director?"

Promise answered her mother. "She loves that cotton ball mouse."

"Take a hint from your sister," Jack advised. "She'd say, 'I'm not carrying the pooper-scooper for nothing.'"

"I might get to delegate that duty." Honor's salary as a Vegas croupier now made her quotable. For years, Jack had believed she was studying psychology out in Las Vegas, when in reality she had been dancing naked for drunks.

Promise was distracted by Joseph's computer, which had reverted to screen saver mode. A slow exhibition filled the screen: highlights of the permanent collection. The fluid images showed each object from several angles, occasionally zooming in on a telling detail.

"Promise?" Jack was raising his voice. "You're not listening."

"What did you say?" she asked, confident he had just been lecturing. A Near Eastern ewer, practically animated, rotated before her.

Jack said, "I hope you pay more attention to your board than you do on the phone."

"Actually, I do," Promise confessed.

"Who'd want to run a museum?" he asked, justifying her inattention.

"Congratulations, honey," Peg said. "Leo must be so proud of you."

She heard Jack hang up. "Supposedly. Though I'm worried that I'm in over my head. And Felix. Oh, Mom, Felix. Yesterday he ate the grapes out of his lunch and nothing else."

"He needs more than that," Peg agreed. "I don't know if you're interested, but that collector in Bartlesville is building a museum for his Japanese things. I clipped the article for you somewhere."

"Send it over," Promise said. As a kid, she'd thought life expectancy meant what was expected from you. She had an interest in art, so her life expectancy was to be an art teacher in Ponca City. It was easier to exceed your life expectancy in Oklahoma than in Washington or New York, and yet to move away was a disappointment. Whereas another parent might brag about a child living in London after a bout in Tokyo, an Oklahoma mother invariably said, "Maybe after this, she'll get to come home."

Promise told her mother how the committee had passed up both ancillary directors to appoint her. She told her about Arthur's magpie bowl resting on its imperial-stamped bottom and how he wanted it the way Felix wanted another skateboard. Then she asked, "Mom, do you think I'm up to all this?" She wished she had the guts to tell her everything she was up to.

"Sweetheart, the biggest wigs in the business chose you—you're cheerful and smart as a whip. Listen, pick a long weekend for me to come up and watch your two magpies. You and Leo could get away— would you like that?"

"Thanks, Mom. That sounds nice. I've got to go now. Love you." She was in a rush to hang up so she could lay her dizzy head on her folded arms. The funk of illness was in the crook of her elbows, the rolls of her midriff. Oh, for a looser dress or at least a less absorbent one: she smelled the way the kitchen sponge did after spending the night in the sink.

Way out west, Peg was staring at her kitchen knickknacks, each relic a souvenir. The amber bottle was her first big lie, when she had snuck the cod-liver oil out of her own mother's kitchen, pouring it into the okra patch before burying the evidence. The bottle was so well-hidden it hadn't resurfaced for five or six years, five years without okra and two without her mother. The baking powder in the silver tin, its red logo the head of an Indian in a magnificent headdress, had raised the first cake she ever baked Jack; really, her sister had baked it and enough other goods to convince Jack that Peg was the homemaker he bragged he would wed. And there was the jar of burn salve she had gone through when, sloppy drunk on a Sunday morning and determined to make pancakes, Jack had rested his hand on the griddle. Peg kept it as a memento of the day he swore off drinking. They were lucky that after several car wrecks and some scary spanking of the boys, he had burned himself but only burned himself. She kept the squat blue jar as a reminder along with a few shot glasses. He knew and she knew why they were there.

Peg hadn't wanted to volunteer any of the stories behind the souvenirs, except maybe the baking soda tin, but she would have answered questions if Promise had ever asked. She worried that her daughter was too trusting and too insulated for her new appointment—it was just like her sweet girl to see an added yoke as a necklace. Those extra duties might be too much, Peg should have said; or, you might not be suited to bossing. God knows, she and Leo couldn't even make that rickety, overpriced home livable.

Sometimes you want someone to pry so there's the chance to say, I never told you before, but your father used to drink like a thirsty hound. She hoped that away from home Promise was more suspicious of the ready explanation. Just because some potter wrote on the bottom of a vase "Made under the emperor's nose" didn't make it so.

———

Min had stationed herself like a Red Army guard outside Promise's private bathroom door. With her combination backpack-purse and her jacket that may have been her coat, it was hard to tell if she was coming or going.

"Min!" Promise gasped when she opened the door. A mere half hour ago, she'd been making excuses to get away. In the natural light of Joseph's office, her complexion was the color of bad teeth.

"You are my friend."

"Of course," Promise said with more impatience than she'd intended. The smell from the bathroom wafted out into the office, and it seemed that Min took in a whiff.

Min said, "You remember my reaction when they asked me for fingerprints."

"Don't forget the blood drive," Promise reminded her. Apparently, *voluntary* and *involuntary* meant the same thing in China, like *flammable* and *inflammable*. She gestured toward the sofa, but Min refused to sit.

"There are times when I think something serious is only usual business. You have been patient with me then, and I am grateful." Her loyalty was at war with her jealousy. Pulling the sleeves of her jacket all the way over her hands, she practically crawled back into her uniform. She had cultivated only one friend, now the acting director. "I will get to the point," Min said. "Let us tell each other our secrets. I have two."

Min squinted up like a prune, either to keep her glasses from falling off her face or to see, and the fierceness behind the effort made her ugly. The only secret Promise was harboring was her pregnancy, which was more surprise than secret, more accident than surprise. But she hadn't told her *mother* she was pregnant. "What would you like me to know?"

"A *ding* has come to my attention, a bronze urn. The bronze dates to late Shang dynasty, but the object is newer. As I understand the inscription, warriors captured Shang dynasty loot, then melted it down to make their own vessel. They date it to around 1000 B.C."

"The *ding* is a secret because it's expensive?" Arthur must have told Min that she was pulling in the purse strings. That man could spread news faster than a pig spreads mud.

"No," Min said. "It is not that expensive."

"Oh, I get it: unknown provenance. It's not like we haven't seen that before."

"The provenance is known," Min said. "It is stolen."

"If you go back far enough, what isn't?"

Min's specialty was the Shang dynasty, when tribes began to record history on oracle bones. *Late* Shang dynasty was around 1200 B.C., and Promise imagined that Min was overwrought about a sin at least that ancient. "Let me guess." She played along. "Back in 1000 B.C., one nomadic tribe swiped it from another." She took another swipe at Min's story. "Is the British Museum deaccessioning again?"

Min narrowed her eyes into oblivion. "On the dig, the best pieces are found and then—blink!—unfound. They often end up in a collector's house unless a museum intervenes. When I was at Taipei Museum, a curator might offer a 'reward' to find a rumored piece, like a finder's fee. This *ding* should be in a museum."

Promise had been trying like hell to give the curator the benefit of the doubt. She'd been trying so hard she hadn't recognized Min's confession. Raising herself as upstanding as she could, she said, "We couldn't buy something that had been recently stolen."

Min said, "That is my first secret. Madame Xingfei and I discussed this. She has written a letter saying she saw it in Macao in 1955. We have a dealer who will provide us with a bill of sale."

Promise's mouth was so dry, she began coughing and had to go into the bathroom, where she cupped her hands under the sink to drink like a child. Then she returned to face Min. "We can neither accept this work nor display it."

"I am careful. There is nothing on paper about this transaction."

"Careful? Is that what you said, careful?" Because she may have said "colorful" or "cared for." Maybe the whole thing was a crazy misunderstanding they would someday laugh about. Remember that time I thought you had spirited a national treasure out of China? Here I was, imagining you'd paid a thief to hack a *ding* out of an archaeological site, when you were really telling me—what?

Min softened a bit, as if she too saw the potential in clearing this up. She stretched her mouth, exaggerating each sound. "Yes, I am careful. You know the saying: 'Don't tie your shoes in the watermelon patch.'"

"Let me guess: Will Rogers."

Actually, it was an ancient Chinese saying, but Min let the Oklahoma cowboy have the credit. She said, "I like him for how foreign he is." Will Rogers was 100 percent American, with his ability to love the country, hate its rulers. His simple name was nearly unpronounceable, and he was irreverent, another word she dared not try to say. He was magnanimous and wry; Min had wanted to live in a country where people could get away with that.

She explained, "If someone sees you bent over in the watermelon patch and a melon is missing, you are the first suspect. Madame X has taken me under her wing to teach me the right way to do this."

"Good Lord, Min. You're telling me she's done this before. There's no right way to do this."

"Your turn. Say your secret out loud to me."

This gravy of a job was going lumpy. Min stood her ground directly in front of Promise, who refused to be trapped. She touched Min on the elbow, surprised that she actually had to push with a fair amount of force to get to her luxurious couch, where she sat and rubbed her eyes until she remembered she was wearing makeup. She swiped an index finger beneath each eye from center to edge, then transferred waxy liner and gluey mascara from her smudged fingers onto a tissue. Joseph had a red lacquered tissue holder there on his coffee table.

Min stood silently, appalled that Promise would groom herself in front of her.

"Our provenance rules are pretty strict." Promise spoke with caution, trying to avoid placing blame. "I appreciate your worry that important pieces are being stolen, but we compound the problem if we participate in the stealing."

"That is the way your Founder bought a collection."

"Jesus, Min! Is that how Madame X remembers it?" Promise considered herself in the service of the Founder, almost like a nun. Exasperated, she looked directly through Min's glasses into her eyes, hoping to transmit to her the magnitude of her potential transgression. She and Min had shared so much, and Promise had always assumed they shared the same set of museum values. But Min's magnified stare showed no remorse.

That was because Min felt no remorse. She was as exasperated as Promise, whose haughtiness seemed especially disingenuous. The Founder would not recognize himself in her mirror. For one thing, Promise seemed to believe his ridiculous, lofty accounts of traveling from monastery to souk enlightening "Asia's simple peoples." Adamant that they knew what they were selling, determined to give a fair price—the Founder concocted those entries long after the crates had safely arrived in America. Min would hate for Talbot to be right about Promise. He was always hinting that her little-girl voice was indicative of her little-girl knowledge. Min said, "Madame X is aware of how museum operates."

Promise tried to run her fingers through her hair, but she'd put too much spray on and it weighed on her like a hard hat. She said, "Madame Xingfei holds a place of honor here, but she must recognize that the Institution sets the pace for the herd." Trying to be frank meant falling back on her Oklahoma roots. "We've got cash money for things that come on the legitimate market. Maybe we could even use some of our funds to help the Chinese keep things in their own watermelon patch."

Min said, "Your turn to tell a secret."

"No," Promise said. "I'm not having a pissing match now."

This time Min became the gong that Promise, with the strength of two, struck squarely between the eyes. "Pissing match?" she asked, puzzling over the words. She brought her backpack round to her front and rummaged through the pockets. "Wait. I'm having a pissing match now."

Min brandished what looked to be a thermometer: a white wand, plastic-sleeve-encased, with a rectangle at one tip. Slowly, the way she did everything these days, Promise put together the phrase with the implement. Min held it practically under her nose, so she could clearly see that it was a pregnancy test, a urine stick. A pissing match, as it were. Min had dropped her defensive stance, and in a conciliatory tone, she asked, "Is this what you're looking for?"

For a woman under the weather, Promise's pounce was quick as a monkey's. She behaved without thinking—she hadn't even realized her need for confirmation until she'd snatched the wand from Min's hand, scampered into the bathroom, and flipped the door closed, jamming the push-button lock with her thumb. So much for keeping her own counsel. Hoping to invalidate everything she already knew, she wet the stick and laid it on the counter, where, before she'd even righted her panty hose, it blushed a bright jelly-bean pink.

"No," she moaned aloud. If there had been space in the bathroom, she might have pulled a Felix and rolled on the floor or broken something, as the children said, accidentally on purpose.

"Goddammit to hell," she muttered, and then her rising fury bounced off the cosmos and came flying back full tilt toward smug Min, who not only knew about Promise's condition but had come to rub her nose in it. Hadn't Arthur been saying for years that she was devious? To think she'd defended Min as strongly as she'd defended Arthur to Min. Months ago, Min had revealed she couldn't have more children—why did she happen to have a pregnancy test at the ready? One minute, Promise was trying to explain that their museum was not in a position to steal pieces for its collections, and the next, Min whips out evidence that Promise has been keeping things back. "So what?" Promise yelled. She turned the doorknob, and there was Min, practically with her ear to the door.

Shame colored Min's face. "You're mistaking me. I did not make myself clear."

Promise said, "Which part did I mistake—the fact that you're trafficking in Chinese artifacts? Your assertion that this is business as usual? Or did I misconstrue your demand to know my personal business?"

"Yes," Min said.

"Oh, stop it," Promise said, sick to death of her foreigner act and angry as all get out at the messenger who'd brought her confirmation of her pregnancy. She bowed at the waist. "'So sorry, not aware of your ways.' What happened to the meek, respectful Min who is so loath to offend? I swear, if you were on fire, you couldn't even ask for water."

Promise was on a roll until she realized that the pointer she brandished to emphasize privacy and lawfulness was none other than Min's pissing match. Battery-powered, the wand could not have flared a brighter pink.

"Plums," Min said, "I am on fire. Please help put me out."

Hit by a Train

November 2, 1999

Sitting on an examination table in the Takoma Park women's clinic, Promise turned away from the buttery yellow wall and its pictures of nursing mothers. The place was a motherhood shrine, with a mobile of pregnant angels twirling above the gingham rocking chair in the corner and a bulletin board of snapshots featuring newborns, some so fresh their umbilical cords were still attached. Promise concentrated on Mahalia's inky black face. A tiny emerald pierced the flair of the midwife's nose.

"Thank you for fitting me in," Promise said.

Mahalia smiled lovingly. "You're quite welcome," she said in her unusual accent, Ghanaian or maybe Long Island. She said, "A cycle as spotty as yours, you could be well into your second trimester. A sonogram will tell us more. Believe it or not, it's time to decide whether you want amnio."

How about whether I want another child—is now the time to think about that? The tips of Promise's ears began to tingle, a sure sign that she was going under, and she had to lie back on the table. She regretted that neither she nor Leo had been fixed after Felix. She squeezed her eyes shut, and it was Min she pictured, specifically the hatred flattening her face as Promise waved around the pregnancy wand. Promise had made it worse with the cruel things she'd said. "I'm on fire," Min had told her, "put me out," and then she'd spilled her second secret: she'd spent thousands of the museum's dollars on fertility treatments! Technically, just a little over ten thousand, Min had explained, because she'd never claimed the second installment from Accounting. Even so, the inspector general had requested she submit her records for audit and investigation. Min must know how serious this was; frankly, Promise had been too offended by Min's behavior to acknowledge her suffering. You wanted a child so you stole money—how do you justify that?

"Don't you cry," Mahalia said gently, and she pulled a tissue from a box decorated with glued and painted macaroni, obviously some nursery school project. People complained about the sterile atmosphere of doctors' offices. She could have used a little sterility right now. The midwife slid her hand under Promise's like a spatula beneath a cookie. With her other hand, she smoothed back Promise's hair. "Inhale through your nose. Exhale." Rose oil was Mahalia's scent, equal parts cloying and grandmotherly.

Promise did what the midwife said, grateful to be ordered around; however, the long inhalations only breathed life into the emotions she'd been trying to snuff out. "I don't want another baby," she confessed. "I don't want to run the museum." Simply put, she wanted what she had but no more.

Mahalia held a tissue to the side of Promise's face, where gravity channeled the tears. "You take a few minutes and then we'll go over your plans. Inhale through your nose." She squeezed Promise's hand, then slipped out, gently pulling the door shut behind her.

Promise brought her elbows in tight and clasped her arms, rocking herself side to side like a baby, like a lost soul. The waxed paper beneath her crackled as she swayed. Her tears were compounded by guilt at her own ingratitude. If anyone cared, she would tell them how much she loved Lydia and Felix, so lucky to have two such radiant souls to raise, a girl and a boy just like in every dollhouse. She would tell them how rewarding her years at the museum had been, a delightful mix of scholarship and entertainment. Beauty at her fingertips, collegiality in the lunchroom, an in-house mentor. She mourned the end of that era. She cried as she breathed, not the churning, heaving cries that wreck a person. This was a release, anxiety seeping out tear by tear. Be like melting snow, the poet advised, and wash yourself of yourself.

Mahalia would be back soon to talk about Promise's plans, as if, on top of doing everything for everyone, she was supposed to plan, too. She had actively planned against pregnancy, and look what happened. Career-wise, her plan was to sit in beautiful surroundings (that she didn't have to dust or insure) and write about any number of fascinating minutiae. But did the universe respect that plan? She breathed through her nose. Her exhalation was a snort. She had planned on contemplating the Founder's trove from a comfortable office chair, returning home to cuddle a child on either side of her, enjoying a few private moments with her iconoclast Leo.

She breathed through her nose. If only Min had kept her blasted secrets to herself, Promise wouldn't be an accessory to theft and embezzlement. Leo would argue that she was fooling herself: with or without Min, she was complicit. He was freshly offended with each story of inhumanity in Asia, from 2500 B.C. to the present. According to him, every artifact that left its home country was a steal, no matter the price.

She breathed through her nose. Why hadn't she had babies at fifteen, when she'd had all the time in the world? She stared up at the poster taped to the ceiling, a tiger nursing two cubs while a third sat on the mama tiger's neck. Round, fluffy heads, half circles for ears, big cartoon eyes—the tiger cubs were adorable. Possibility flickered its tiny starlight. Could she allow herself a moment of joy at the thought of a new baby?

There was a tapping on the door, and Mahalia came back in. Weakly, Promise said, "You think everyone's pregnant."

"Everyone with your symptoms. I'm sorry I rushed right in with the details."

Printed across the bottom of the poster was the message "Extinct is forever." So clever of them to ally baby-making with the continuation of a rare and beautiful animal. In fact, wasn't overpopulation a major blame for their endangered status?

Mahalia lifted Promise's gown, giving them both a good look at her belly, a small paunch without the jiggle of fat. Squeezing clear gel onto her fingertips, the midwife rubbed a thin chilly layer across her patient's middle. When she rolled transducer against the conductive film, the amplifier picked up marine sounds within, all static and splash. Faint drumbeats from a great distance—one-TWO, one-TWO—grew nearer as she locked in on her target. The baby train was chugging away at 150 lub-dubs per minute. No wonder I feel run-down, Promise thought—I've been hit by a train.

Mahalia held her palm up as if cupping a ball. "It's already the size of a grapefruit. The good news is that you seem healthy, a healthy pregnant woman."

———

At home, Leo tried to fill Promise in on the status of the Al-Faran story. "Have you heard from Joseph?" he asked. "Makes me think I should get out of this business—I feel a knot in my stomach every time I check the fax machine. It didn't use to scare me like it does."

"You really think he's in danger?" Promise asked. "He's in the middle of nowhere." She tried to picture her mentor in the Taklamakan Desert, sporting the survival regalia everyone had bought for him. Would he really wear that hat with the solar-powered fans or the water bladder with a three-foot straw? She could readily imagine slender, inconspicuous Emmy adapting to the extreme conditions, but she wasn't so sure about Joseph.

Because the children kept traipsing through, Promise talked about Min. She was trying hard to mimic their usual evening exchange, except that she dropped the saltshaker into the pan of water, then sliced her finger cutting up a tomato. The juice burned the cut even as her blood flushed it out.

"You're a nervous wreck," Leo said. He slid open the junk drawer for a bandage, which he wrapped around her finger.

Lydia said, "What sits on the bottom of the ocean and shakes? A nervous wreck."

Leo laughed for her benefit; it hit too close to home for Promise to appreciate. Looking out the kitchen window, she saw that although the streetlights had come on, it was still fairly light, and she asked Lydia, "Do you think you and Felix could walk the dog up and down our street before dinner? Not all the way around the block, just up and down."

"Really?" Lydia was delighted. "Do we have to clean up after him?"

"I'm afraid so," Promise said. "You can do it." She picked up one of the plastic newspaper bags they kept in a wad under the sink and reminded Lydia how to slip her hand in, using the bag as a glove. "Then

you bring the sleeve around and tie it in a knot. Put your jackets on."
She saw Leo's eyebrow shoot up in a high arch. She'd never sent the
kids out in the dark by themselves before.

"Felix!" Lydia yelled, happy to boss him around. "Get your coat."

As soon as they were alone in the kitchen, Promise walked up to
her husband. If he'd been wearing his suit jacket, she might have
grabbed him by the lapels and shaken him. "I'm pregnant," she said. "I
saw Mahalia today."

Leo's close vision was starting to go, and Promise was standing just
where things got blurry. "Jesus Christ. I can't believe it." He had assumed she was just getting plump. He took a step back so he could see
her face, which was stretched down in the deep frown she got when
she was trying not to cry. "No," he said, thinking she'd misinterpreted
his distance as distress, then he pulled her into his out-of-focus field to
kiss her. "Sweetie, that's fantastic. A baby!" He scooped his bride up off
the floor and let out a yee-haw.

"Keep your voice down." She grabbed the edge of a kitchen chair
until her feet were back on the ground. His reaction to this news was
markedly different from his response to her promotion.

"Oh, Queenie. This explains why you've been so wiped out. How
far along are you?"

"Thirteen weeks," she mumbled, embarrassed at having been so
oblivious. "Maybe seventeen. Mahalia's sending me for a more com-
prehensive sonogram."

A soft grin spread across Leo's face, giving him the self-satisfied
glow of a yogi. Leo loved babies. While another woman might have relaxed into his joy, Promise felt herself absorbing the stress he released.
His palm on her belly, a tender, proprietary gesture, made her bristle.
"It's only the size of grapefruit," she said, and she stretched the truth a
bit. "It might not even be viable."

"Shh," Leo said. "Don't say that."

To make matters worse, as soon as the children threw open the front
door, he yelled, "Lydia! Felix! We're going to have a baby!" The three of
them hooted and yipped all through dinner, and afterward, Leo took a
pencil to the doorframe hatched with their heights, where he scratched
a line about four inches up from the floor. "Our little Ruby Red," he told
the kids, while the giant grapefruit basket made a sour face.

"You'll have to pick up after yourselves," Promise said. "A baby could choke on a Buildy Tile. Flipper might not be a good baby dog." A baby might put Mommy over the edge.

Felix said, "I'll feed it and clean up after it—honest engine!" He wanted to dance with her, but she would neither swing nor clap. "Why is your mouth so frowny?" he asked.

"I'm not frowny." Promise relaxed her face. "See?" I'm devastated. And that asshole father of yours jumped the gun.

She said as much once the children were in bed. "I only told *you*." She was sitting on the living room couch, whose plush purple upholstery had weathered to crusty prune.

"How long have you known?" he asked. "I don't mind if you keep secrets from your Asian cabal but not us." It pissed him off that she had to process everything before she let him in on it. "I'll bet Joseph out in the Taklamakan Desert knows. I'll bet Arthur knows!"

"Arthur figured it out," she said. "So did Min." She really said that, she was that mean, though not mean enough to say that if he'd been paying attention, he could have been the first. He could have known before she did.

"And another thing," Leo said, as if he were the one who had initiated the complaint. "When Felix notices you're not thrilled, don't gaslight him. Tell him, 'I'm shocked. I'm scared. Babies are a big responsibility.' Something that doesn't mess with his head."

Was Leo so proud of himself that he couldn't acknowledge ambivalence? She asked, "How would Felix feel, to hear that some babies are not welcome?"

"I don't know, but he recognized you were upset. Spin the news any which way; you can't control everyone's emotions."

"I was sparing his feelings." Of the two of them, Leo was the one with the flair for spin. Because she was in no mood to spare her husband's feelings, she said, "I don't hear you crowing about your pot smoking."

"That is an unrelated argument." He dropped the preachiness from his voice. "Someday they'll ask me about my proclivities, at which point we'll see if you can cite me for hypocrisy. The way Lydia is, she'd turn me in to the first cop who lectures them about drugs."

Promise relished the thought of their earnest, literal daughter offering Leo up to the authorities.

Leo said, "You know, Min's case may not be as bad as you think."

"Which part?" Promise asked. She covered her mouth to mask a long burp. All day long, her stomach had been churning over Min's crimes.

"The travel fund. Did she ask her insurance to see if in vitro is covered? You know how secretive Douglas and Min are—maybe they're embarrassed to fill out the forms."

How could Leo be so sympathetic toward Min and not toward her? Promise said, "She wasn't too embarrassed to take the museum's money."

"I guess," Leo said. "Still, it's interesting what some families will do to have a kid."

"Is that supposed to make me happier?" she snapped. "I can't believe you told the children. If I'd issued a press release, it would have said: She is pregnant, but she may or may not have a baby."

"All sorts of things can happen. That's not something to hide from them either." He meant miscarriage or worse, genetic testing detecting a land mine. In his cosmos, these were the last fears left. Her being unwilling hadn't even occurred to him. "I understand," he said, misunderstanding more completely than a stranger would.

What you understand would fit on the head of a pin. Marriage being what it is, she pressed her point. "We have a family and barely a roof over our head."

Leo threw his fluffy head back, reeling at her remark, and there was satisfaction in that. "We live in one of the richest fucking zip codes in America."

"Oh, you take everything to its extreme," she said.

"Implying that we're destitute is pretty extreme. Most of the world doesn't have a pot to piss in. Not to mention that they're sick, too."

A ripple stirred just beneath her ribs, faint as that of a minnow. Although nearly imperceptible, the movement registered in both her long- and short-term memories, and she realized she'd been feeling such flutters all week. Now she matched them to her earlier pregnancies, when she couldn't wait to feel the quickening of a life inside her. She said to Leo, "The truth is, I'm starting to come around. But can't you acknowledge what a setback this is? I need a newborn like I need a hole in the head."

"That's probably what your mother said when she got pregnant with Honor, and your father was drinking, and Tom needed leg braces."

"My father doesn't drink," Promise said, puzzled.

"Sweetheart." Leo got up from his chair to sit next to her on the couch. "We're going to have a baby. In this gloomy, hostile world, what could be more subversive and more hopeful?"

Dancing 'Round Delirium

November 26, 1999

Joseph had struck it rich. Here was a corner, wood, with three squat legs, and what appeared to be mail stacked atop a flat bench, as ordinary and timeless a find as might be in the foyer of his Capitol Hill home. Five tablets, two with unbroken seals indicating they'd never been opened, perhaps never sent! He had found them without infrared detectors or computer projections. A doorway, a spinning wheel, the entry hall, the mail. Other diggers had found more immediate thrills—coinage and carnage scraps—but nothing as intact as what he was pulling out of the ground.

Unless he was hallucinating.

Sandwiched together, bound with twine and sealed with clay, the tablets themselves were wooden, further proof that the place hadn't always been only sand. Evidence of such intact order might suggest that the townspeople had evacuated in a hurry, which was how Joseph wanted to leave.

You go into the desert hoping to find a stack of documents, and by God, you unearth a stack of documents! Leave it to you to make archaeology seem so simple. Forget the satellite position wizardry and thermographic imaging of sites—you are a divining rod for artifacts.

Still dancing 'round delirium, Joseph coached himself against smugness. Digs always sneak in a curse, though he felt some protection from evil spirits because he wasn't looking for gold or even sacred objects. How much mojo could be tied to a wooden receipt for donkeys?

Dealing with monochromatic writing on wood also exempted him from the heartbreaking paradox of discovering versus destroying. More than once, having exposed an early example of polychrome statuary, he had watched the object age hundreds of years in an hour, the very paint he'd hypothesized peeling away in chips and curls when the statue hit twentieth-century air. It was like falling victim to a genie: here's your painted statue, master; next time, you might want to specify that the paint stay on for all to see.

Joseph was supposed to signal if his brush felt resistance in place of the relentless, crystalline sand grains. The crew wore pagers so they could be on hand to videotape rediscovery. Not walkie-talkies but actually pagers; if someone was too far away for a tap on the shoulder, the signaling beamed an alert skyward, where it bounced off a satellite and returned to earth, specifically to the fanny pack of the dig master. Joseph had neglected to transmit a message before hauling his loot to shade.

Emmy had unexpectedly made her way over to him. "You've found tablets," she said. "It's just what you wanted."

He'd been so ill he hadn't focused on her for days. Now that he did, he heard the disappointment in her voice. Her lilt had wilted to a monotone. There were stripes of sand in the creases of her blouse, asymmetric from her slouch.

She said, "I've decided digging in someone's latrine is not walking in his footsteps. When Xuan Zang came through here, he stood on a bridge over the river, contemplating the poplars."

Eerily enough, the bridge was there, as was the poplar forest. The wind had stripped the trees of their bark and their branches. The tall, pointed trunks stuck up like a bed of nails. Joseph put down his tablets and held his wife in his arms. It felt good to comfort her for a change.

"I don't know about you," she said, "but I don't have to stay until the bitter end."

"Where to next?" Joseph asked.

Emmy laughed. "Well, that's up for grabs, I guess."

Then she was gone, and the fact that she'd essentially given voice to the thoughts in his head made him wonder whether they'd actually shared that exchange.

Alone with his tablets, he was genuinely curious to see what he'd nabbed. Joseph didn't know which notion was more poignant, reading unsent or never-opened mail. He couldn't discern that until he could study them in a better climate; for now, he would read only those missives whose seals were broken. Although he had disregarded some of the most important rules of the dig, he couldn't bring himself to break a two-thousand-year-old seal. He examined a pair of tablets, the size and thickness of a sandwich, pressed together and rewrapped with a twine that remained remarkably pliable. A slug of clay clung to the twine, but only the edge of the seal impression was visible. The portability and brevity of the planks pointed away from Buddhist texts; these were most probably interkingdom memos or perhaps personal accounts.

Was he hoping for the sacred or the mundane? A letter to those left behind? Joseph's Kharosthi was limited by his memory as well as his ability to absorb things. It was as if, at sixty-two, his mind were a full sponge. With the slightest jiggle, the last drops taken in were the first to dribble out. A cursory look at the wooden tiles revealed the repetition of several characters. "Camel" was decipherable, and "prisoner." He saw hatch marks and doodles, which might be language, or hatch marks and doodles.

Sir Aurel Stein had discovered as much at the turn of the century. From a rubbish heap at Niya, he'd pulled leather scraps of familiar Buddhist texts written in a new old script. Some of Stein's contemporaries posited that Kharosthi came all the way from Europe; however, their deductions stank with the piss of the Empire. Could Joseph put himself forth as free from colonial influence? There was the rub of his era: Stein and associates knew not their own prejudices, whereas critics presumed Joseph a prisoner of his. The conundrum set his gut cramping; if it wasn't for dehydration, he would have had the trots.

Then he recognized a string of symbols as the phrase "petition for arrest," and he imagined he was reading the entire message fluently. A surge ran through him such as Moses might have felt previewing the commandments. He seemed to be the source of the heat waves undulating in front of his very eyes; he was the burning bush on fire with the Word.

Five tablets left behind in a ruined empire. Joseph, their unintended, did not possess the skills to decode them, bringing to mind the five missives he had left behind for potential directors of the museum. By now someone had been chosen to disperse the collection. The heat on the dunes was quivery as a movie flashback, except the absence of scenery meant that the waves radiated as pure energy across the porcelain-white sky and sand, as if he were sitting on the surface of the sun.

That seemed par for the course in this last phase of his life. As a nature boy, he'd sought out extreme adventures. Initially, the adrenaline rush of being nearly dashed by falling rocks or rapids was the point. Transcendence came in the passage from surviving to adapting. No voice-overs, insipid anthropomorphic remarks, or glorifications of nature. Only the real thing. It satisfied him as nothing before sex had. Was the pursuit worth it anymore? After all, he wasn't searching for the mouth of the Nile. He was merely looking for the origin of a dead language, and anyone who cared could have talked him out of that.

Hypnotized by the dancing air, he registered the caravan galloping toward him. The heat squiggles were a scrim across his vision. Horses, mules, and camels were clanking with gear. Into focus came a half dozen men, thoroughly robed, one in blue jeans. "My good fellows"— the sentence formed in his head—"no one gallops in the desert." Coming for to carry me home. He wondered if they spoke Uygur, or Hindi, or Arabic. He wondered why each had an AK-47.

The fattest one slid off an intensely matted camel; his heavy boots hitting the sand stirred up a cloud. A yellow puff rose around him and was whisked off by the constant wind. The man screamed and pointed his rifle at Joseph, who let the wooden tablets fall and raised his hands to show he was unarmed. Because of their remote location and his ill health, Joseph was less engaged than he knew he should be. He wondered, for example, if such a shiny, well-oiled gun attracted more sand or if the sand was easily wiped away. Seven languages at his disposal, and this raving, gun-toting fellow spoke an eighth. Joseph identified his paper-bag-style hat as Afghan, but it might have been Pakistani. The one in blue jeans had a grenade hanging from each belt loop. Joseph followed the fat one's mimed instructions to put his hands on his head, but the gang was obviously not won over by his efforts. He wondered what had brought them here at a gallop. He wondered why the mummified member of the gang—gauze wrapped around his or her body from foot to head, a rifle holster and ammunition belt strapped at the hip—was aiming the butt of a rifle at his temple. And then he wondered why, in the middle of a sunny day here in the Taklamakan Desert, it had grown so completely dark.

Cooped Up in the Dark

December 2, 1999

Promise eventually stopped having so much trouble keeping her food down and her head up. Not only that, her first month as acting director went far better than she'd expected. Exhibition deadlines and previously scheduled meetings provided momentum from Joseph's reign to hers. It was gratifying to learn how much daily business she'd always managed; chief curator should have been on Zemzemal's and Talbot's level all along. For the first time, she wondered if Joseph had been holding her back.

As in juggling, Promise found a rhythm for keeping her responsibilities in orbit. She balanced an awkward Taiwan-China issue and handled the sadness and urgency of Hazel, the shop manager, suffering a stroke before the busy Thanksgiving weekend. Occasionally she'd focus on Min's transgressions, only to toss them back up in the air. Likewise for the Castle's inattention—Cecil had yet to provide her with a projected budget or a plan to search for a director. Joseph had regularly complained about the Secretary's heavy hand, but she couldn't even get the Secretary to wave at her.

More surprising than not dropping the ball at work was not balking at her pregnancy. Bitterness overtook her from time to time, as did icy fear. Ultimately, the amazing somersaulting baby inured Promise to her condition. This baby, who they knew was a boy, started each morning with a workout in his drum of a gym, and throughout the day, he'd bone up on his kickboxing routine. Despite the dangers of bonding with the unborn, they'd taken to calling him Edgar. Maybe they should have picked a less forceful name, she thought, whenever the "great spear-man" gave her a poke. In the meantime, test results trickled in. Protein levels, amniocentesis, and glucose readings all seemed designed to confound joy with risk, yet her results kept repeating the message: normal, low-risk pregnancy, just like billions of other women.

Once panic subsided, Promise was won over by the sonogram, whose magic turns a person inside out. Leo nattered on about sound waves bombarding the fetus, but it was the instrument of her conversion, and she longed for a tableside model. Because the appliance world had yet to catch on to the clock-radio-sonogram idea, Promise was back in Mahalia's office this morning. She watched the on-screen show the way she had watched the astronauts as a kid. A naked little voyager with visible bones and organs was tethered to the mother ship, balled neatly in a tuck and roll (fetal position!). Floating about, he managed to show his beating heart to the camera; his backbone, too. What more would he need to survive?

When Mahalia and the sonographer left the room for a moment, Promise babbled to the screen. To see inside a body inside your body is bound to bring out the mystics: "'The world outside is vast and intricate,'" she quoted to her homunculus. "'There are wheatfields and mountain passes, and orchards in bloom . . .' Why do you stay cooped up in the dark with your eyes closed?"

"That's beautiful," Mahalia said, slipping back to Promise's side. "But don't give him any ideas. He needs to stay cooped up four more months."

Promise sneezed, then touched a tissue to her raw nose. She said, "My allergies are so much worse. Am I imagining that?"

"No," Mahalia said. "Pregnancy enhances them, but your nausea should be abating a little."

Promise realized she'd brushed her teeth without incident this morning.

Mahalia smiled. "Between now and the end of March, you'll double the volume of blood in your body. Remember that feeling?"

"Oh, yes. With Lydia, I worked on two books at once."

"Invincible," Mahalia said. "One of my patients said she took up mountain climbing in her fifth month, in between naps. You deserve a month like that."

Mahalia kissed her on her cheek, one of the fringe benefits of seeing a midwife. "Start going to Christmas parties," she said. "Have a glass of wine if you wish."

She didn't know which was more appealing, Mahalia's permission to have a drink or the notion of invincibility. Her next appointment was a walk-through of Arthur's porcelain show, due to open in two weeks. Today was also the monthly curatorial meeting, where Talbot was scheduled to give a presentation on his upcoming Japanese exhibition. Promise could use a dose of invincibility. Her day made mountain-climbing look like a walk in the park.

———

Once she had peeled off her coat and sweater, Promise reported directly to the staff room. Fennel seeds filled a saucer next to a bowl of crystallized ginger, luminous as beach glass. Bean-curd sweets that someone had brought back from Japan drew as little notice as a carton of stale donuts might in another office. Promise could smell the cups of anise tea Fatima had left steeping on the counter.

The shrouded curator rustled back in, spike heels visible under her chador. For some reason, Fatima's getup inspired Promise to be cheeky, and she said, "Two cups?" She knew damn well whom the other cup was for.

Fatima said, "Zemzemal would go without if I didn't bring him his tea."

Even Min speculated that Zemzemal might know what was under Fatima's robe. Promise said, "That licorice smell always reminds me of the Easter Bunny."

"I did not realize you were Catholic."

"I'm not. Is the Easter Bunny Catholic? He might be from the Church of the Five-and-Dime."

Fatima said, "It is my faith I have to talk to you about. We do not eat pork, and yet pork is served here, sometimes twice each week. There are lunches I must attend. Many times there is no choice—that is the offense."

Nathan also served shellfish, steak, an occasional quail, and veal. Promise did not oversee the menu, relinquishing each diner to his or her own god. She asked, "Is it a problem that he serves pork at all or just that he serves it to you?"

Fatima weighed her response. "I may enter an establishment serving pork, as long as I do not partake. But he is a fine chef, and I am hungry at lunchtime."

"No confessions, please." Promise didn't want it to be her fault that Fatima had savored a forbidden loin. "What if there was always yogurt?"

"Are you talking about Nathan?" Sam and Lucy, the conservator, had come in for their morning mix. No coffee shop in the city could accommodate the idiosyncrasies of this pack, whose peculiar talents had taken them to the most unpronounceable places on earth: Ailinglapalap, Dalan Dzadagad, Kyzyl Kum, Tiruchchirappalli.

The conservator emptied a stream of salt into a tall glass, followed by glops of yogurt and a can of mango juice. "I don't do cooked food, and Nathan acts like that is more offensive than his putting it in the fire. Even when he has spinach or peas, they end up sautéed in butter."

"It wouldn't be that difficult," Sam offered. "I'll eat anything as long as it's fruit."

"Because?" Promise asked.

"Fruit drops its harvest. Everything else is plucked or cut or *killed*. If Nathan had enough fruit, we'd be okay."

Lucy said, "Well, I need some greens, too."

"Oh, no greens," Sam said.

The conservator had a pale orange mustache from her concoction. Promise was more sympathetic to Sam than to Lucy, who surely could see the hypocrisy in condemning the heating of food she was going to devour. Next, she would want it prepared so she could swallow without biting or chewing. "You're free to put whatever you want in the kitchen refrigerator."

"But lunch is provided," Lucy said. "You guys don't pay for your steak and creamed corn."

If Joseph had been here, he would have performed that trick wherein he had thought through your concerns a shade better than you had. "Sam," he might have said, "you grew up in Iowa. Your people are omnivores." Or "Nathan's offerings are in line with his personal beliefs, and as the Buddha teaches, one needs to accept all gifts sincerely given."

When Joseph said stuff like that, he'd stand next to you, his big dog paw resting on your shoulder and his voice vibrating in your ribs. He might as well be reading your mind. Listen, you and I both know, don't we, so cut the crap.

Anyone else would come across as mocking. Promise said, "Why don't you three organize a Staff Room Committee? I'm due at the 'All Fired Up!' walk-through."

"Yikes!" Sam said. "We're supposed to be there, too."

"You have ten minutes," she said to Sam and Lucy. "I'm meeting with Arthur first."

She headed out of the staff room, past the South Asian and ancient China galleries, down the back stairs, and into storage. She slid her ID through the door's card reader, signing herself in on the other side. The cushiony floor and thick walls gave the room a padded cell ambience. Arthur was in the ceramic area, and though she couldn't see his face, she saw him press the back of his hand to the glaze, as one might touch a feverish infant's cheek. Embarrassed at having caught him in such a lovesick posture, she stomped along on the sound-absorbing carpet, sniffling and humming to let him know she'd arrived.

Arthur heard the approach of a beast come to wrestle his prize from him. Phlegm and heavy steps, tuneless marauding. He straightened up and looked through his glasses at the well-fired glaze.

"Could you please keep your hands to yourself?" Promise teased, though as in all teasing, her opinion shone through. It was unseemly the way he pawed the million-dollar soup bucket.

Arthur's eyes were glassy. He wasn't crying, though he looked to be on the verge of it. He said, "If we raise a few more dollars, this piece is ours forever. So why do I feel like I'm giving something up? From here on out, people can view it only through the distortion of glass."

"Oh, Arthur," she said. For this exhibition, he had three of the four north galleries all to himself, half the space devoted to Chinese art in the entire museum. Publications had busted their chops fashioning a beautiful book from his sloppy, scant text. "You've gotten everything you wanted."

"I'm having a rough time," Arthur whined.

"Let's go see the show." Her refusal to comfort him could have been the crux of their friendship troubles. As they headed up the stairs in silence, she could tell he was slowing himself down to her compromised pace. Why couldn't she bring herself to accommodate him a little? Walk-

ing along the landing, Promise caught a glimpse of frost-tinged courtyard pansies glinting in the sun. Pansies used to be feeble, but now
they were hardy, she thought, mentally updating her perception. She
and Arthur entered Gallery I, where a black-and-white photomural of
the Jingdezhen kilns covered the opening wall. The name of the show
was written in large white letters outlined in bright red, easily readable
on top of the photomural.

"It's nice to see an exhibition on schedule," she said, making an
effort.

"Is that a backhanded compliment?" he asked.

Promise only smiled at her old friend.

Inside the gallery was an empty vitrine. "That was built for the ambassador's bowl," Arthur explained. "Obviously, it will be situated at the
top of the main stairway." Promise turned from the empty glass box to
his first exhibition case, which featured five objects. Four were solid-
color ceramics—a white stem bowl, a shorter red stem bowl, and two
school bus–yellow dishes. The fifth was a tall, strangely shaped ewer
covered with every Buddhist emblem ever devised. Its ornate decoration resembled cloisonné, and its spout was the shape of a mythical
boarlike creature. The company of the crazy ewer enhanced the bowls'
and dishes' lucidity. The white stem bowl looked especially pure.
Slightly deeper and stockier than a champagne glass, it had a thin
flared lip and thin parallel grooves cut into the stem. But wait, there's
more! Promise leaned close enough to fog the case with her breath.
The bowl was lightly carved with elaborate motifs of its own: floral
sprays and lotus blossoms as well as the Eight Auspicious Symbols of
Buddhism. None of this would be visible in a photograph. Was it modesty or arrogance to hide such ornament? Maybe it was neither; perhaps the veiled beauty was about privacy or awareness or heaven. In
any case, the white bowl led Promise back to the red and the yellow
pieces, whose translucent glazes were apparently ornament enough.
Look and then look again: this was exactly what an exhibition was supposed to inspire.

"This is lovely," she said with obvious admiration.

"I thank you." Arthur accepted her praise.

Wall labels were taped into position for the screen printers, who
would have a generous week in the galleries. There would be plenty of

time for the lighting specialists as well; Arthur's show would be noted for the lack of overtime required.

He pointed up at a ladder. "The lighting guys are eager to try out a new filament spotlight. The hype is that it lights without glare."

Promise pondered that innovation. Is glare reflected light? She asked, "Can you have light without glare?"

"We'll see," Arthur said.

Like spiders, members of the Design staff kept crawling out of corners, behind walls, out on ledges. They shouted questions to each other and stuck paper tabs all over the galleries. These tiny flags were color-coded to mark things like silk-screening glitches or dings in the wall paint. When Promise discovered a transposed left/right reference in a label and Arthur noted puckers in the silk wrappings beneath two different groups of vases, they flagged those, too.

Promise objected to the height of several text panels. "Check the disability codes," she reminded the silk screener.

One of the designers came out from inside a partition, startling Promise. "Sorry," she apologized. "I just wanted to tell you Jahangir would be a good name for a boy."

Promise laughed. "Maybe if we moved to Agra."

A lighting guy up on a cherry picker called down, "What about Akbar. Or Humayan?"

Sam started singing, complete with hand motions in front of his telephoto lens: "Someone's crying, Lord—Humayan. Someone's laughing, Lord—Humayan." He swung his camera up in Promise's direction, then feigned shock at the sight of her belly, magnified. But when he took the camera away, he had a look of inspiration on his face. "You know what I'd love to photograph? A pregnancy exhibition. Fertility and creation myths with those lusty Indian statues and whatnot. That would be a gas."

Promise felt a wave of adoration for her talented colleagues, who not only knew their Mughal emperors but, more important, regularly brought off these museum productions. A year ago, she'd seen the exhibition plans on paper, in which tiny photographs of the objects were glued into drawings of cases. Before he left, Joseph had approved Design's six-foot-long model, where a maquette of every ceramic stood in place. People moved the stiff little vases and bowls around like children playing house. Wall color, typeface, floor plans, floor plants:

dozens of people had worked on the best way to showcase Arthur's mania for color and adornment.

Approaching another grouping, Promise picked up Lucy's and Min's reflections in the freestanding case. Where the reflections originated took a minute to figure out, just like on the Metro.

"I caught up to you," Min announced. "I'm the second-opinion curator for 'All Fired Up!'" Her accent made it sound like "All Fried Up."

"Did you hear the first opinion?" Arthur asked.

"I don't have to," Min said. "This exhibition is first-rate."

Promise sighed, relieved to be spared their bickering. Arthur did have an excellent eye. As for the magpie bowl that the ambassador was "partially donating," they had thus far collected half of what he was asking. Arthur had assumed they'd be sandbagged with money—dollar, yen, or yuan—and when that hadn't happened, he vowed to get a few pledges himself.

Min was to thank for most of the funds. Patrons literally pressed money into her palm, and their enthusiasm raised her own opinion of Arthur's bowl, even as she objected to a three-hundred-year-old bowl garnering such attention. By that criterion, Douglas reasoned, the contributors should fall all over themselves to purchase her bronze *ding*, ten times older than the bowl at nearly a tenth of the price. But he was an economist with an inelastic set of value functions. Where to plug in pretty colors, flashy dresser who sleeps with men, smooth talker? Eventually, Min took people's interest as an auspicious opportunity. If not for her, she rationalized, the museum might have had to pay for another development person, who would take a percentage as her due.

Arthur said, "I appreciate the fund-raising you've been doing."

Min hugged her purse to her chest. She said, "I tell potential donors there would be such shame if this porcelain returned to China."

Promise was hopeful that Min could feel shame.

If Min wanted to play on nationalism, that was fine with Arthur. Occasionally, the notion of ulterior motives would float into his vision, but he was experienced at blinking them away. What he focused on instead was: Finally, I am getting the attention I deserve.

"There is more to come," Min boasted uncharacteristically. Though she felt flushed, her fingertips were icy cold and her toes were cold in her thin-soled flats; she bunched and flattened them in the hope of working the blood around. She was scheduled to see Dr. Fan later in the day to start a new procedure.

As they burrowed into the exhibition, more people joined the entourage, and department heads began their status reports. Invitations for the opening had been mailed four weeks earlier. Preliminary catalogs and two hundred posters had reached New York from the Italian printer; after clearing customs, they'd be air-shipped to the museum shop. The rest of the print run was coming by boat. Ads had been placed in D.C. and New York papers, train stations, and bus stops in neighborhoods deemed "arty."

Sam said to Arthur, "You're going to complain to me that the photos are bland." He shrugged. "Don't think we didn't try. Your favorites aren't always the most photogenic."

"They weren't made to be photogenic," Arthur said. "To register in a snapshot, every piece of information has to be visible and high contrast in the same frame. That's not art, that's advertising."

The photographer laughed as if Arthur were joking. He said, "Next porcelain show, you might want to think a little more graphically. A grouping of those solid-color bowls could have the eye appeal of Shaker design, or we could zoom way in on a dragon or a crane, some detail that says 'Asian.'"

And Morty accused *him* of being superficial. Arthur was downright spiritual compared with these hucksters. How to explain the dignity of porcelain as a medium? Paper and silk absorb pigment, diffusing each stroke; however, colors painted onto porcelain are sealed between thin coatings of glass. Transparent glazes impart radiance to the colors, a glow overpowered by Sam's crude flash. "I'm supposed to select pieces based on how well they photograph? Ceramics demand to be turned and studied in time with differing rays of light."

"Then I've got a question for you," Promise said, surprised to have reached the end of the exhibition before the final room she'd seen in the model. "The press kit promises a hands-on area, and there was one in the model. Where did that end up?"

Arthur said, "It ended up looking like tables at a yard sale."

The head of Design nodded in agreement. "You don't want a visitor walking away with a shard, but when we tethered the pieces to a backdrop, it looked tacky, not to mention distrustful."

Promise's legs throbbed, and she wished Arthur had thought to put a bench in this room. She said to him, "Surely you can find a way for people to handle some porcelain."

Lucy rubbed her fingers together. "Ceramic is so tactile. It has that surprising heft and cool temperature."

"Really, we could use a little hands-on," Sam said. "You guys always want pictures of happy kids in the gallery—and I try to explain that there *are* no kids in the galleries."

"Arthur." Promise spoke gently, certain he felt ganged up on. "I know we're not a petting zoo, but we're not a vault, either." She cupped her palms and called to the skinny guy at the top of the ladder, "I'm not sure we're finalized for lighting." He came down a step closer to her head.

"You're all doing an exceptional job," she addressed them. "But at this late date, I still want a shard area." She could tell Arthur was seething; nevertheless, she said, "I'm confident you'll find a way for people to *feel* incised and bisque and translucent."

"We've got two weeks," he reminded her.

"Let them fall in love the way you did," Promise said. "Let them slobber all over it."

———

Fatima Hakim hesitated before choosing her spot for the curatorial meeting. The heavy, claw-footed furniture had been pushed against the walls, and folding chairs were brought in so that everyone could fit around the conference room table. Because Talbot was giving an exhibition preview, today's meeting would not be limited to curators. Promise sat between Zemzemal and Vanessa, who was wearing a tight-fitting red cashmere dress; several chairs away, Arthur was next to Talbot rather than Promise. Interesting. Min also sat apart from Promise, with the public affairs woman and the head of the docents.

Fatima breathed in deeply. These women had pale skin and hair flat as a horse's mane. They had no scent. Except for her and Vanessa, they dressed as if in a hospital rather than a palace of art, making her wonder if she should wear less fragrance and makeup, or more. Vanessa changed her hair from one fashionable style to the next, and Chanel clung to her, feminine as her carmine dress. Faced with being next to Min or Talbot, Fatima gravitated toward Talbot.

"Have a seat," Promise said.

When Fatima reached up to unbutton her purdah, columns of bracelets set off a muffled jangle like an alarm clock under a pillow. Promise watched her draw her veil aside to drink from her mug. She had darkly painted lips, outlined and filled in with the kinds of sable brushes that stroked the manuscripts of her homeland. Bracelets cuffed both her wrists, and she wore rings even on her rings. Her hands belonged in the window of a jewelry store.

Fatima leaned forward, speaking past Talbot to Arthur. "My friend spotted you in Georgetown the other day, driving a dented blue sedan."

Arthur flicked his hair over his shoulder. He drove an oversized clunker, which hinted that his entire life wasn't as shiny as his museum façade. Perhaps that was Fatima's point.

"Who's your 'friend'?" Arthur asked.

Promise found it droll that both Fatima and Arthur seemed to be using *friend* as a euphemism, which was very Persian as well as gay. She volunteered, "Rumi called Shams of Tabriz 'the friend.'"

"I do not mean to give offense," Fatima said, "but many clerics have spoken against your Rumi."

Arthur said, "No offense, Fatima, but many clerics have spoken against museums."

Promise wasn't offended. It was something of a curatorial trait to be equal parts tolerant and judgmental. She wondered what a Muslim of Fatima's intensity was doing around the icons, though she'd forgotten where the curator was from: Yemen? Qatar? Promise could have predicted that Rumi would set Fatima off. In fact, looking around the table, she knew what set most of these people off. This crew was practically in her bloodstream. Maybe that qualified her to be their leader after all. She sipped her water to muffle a yawn. Anticipating Talbot's slide show in the dark conference room, she was worried about paying attention: Nathan's delicious lunch was making her sleepy.

Coincidentally, Zemzemal was just then introducing food into the group's conversation. "A sure sign of autumn in Iran was the beet seller on the corner."

"Persians roast beets," Fatima said. The way she exaggerated *Persians* elicited a purring cat as well as a ripe pear.

"Like chestnuts in New York?" Jill asked.

"Yes," Zemzemal said. "Steamed beets wrapped in foil, drizzled with honey butter. We'd beg for them, though I understand that children here will not eat beets."

"Beets are vile," Talbot pronounced, and sure enough, people piped up to agree with him. Hate beets. Never touch them.

Talbot looked at Promise over the top of his glasses, acknowledging the influence he still wielded. She had yet to mention the Castle memo to him; as far as he knew, she hadn't made one move toward executing Cecil's orders. Such restraint had initially brought her up in his estimation, but he was beginning to think her secrecy was actually ignorance. "Parsnips are good," he said, almost flirtatiously, and the flock flapped their lips in agreement. So sweet, parsnips. Better than carrots and easy to prepare.

"Since you have our attention, Dr. Perry," Promise said, "why don't you begin? I've asked Talbot to give us a slide preview of 'A Japanese Port,' slated to open in June 2000."

Arthur protested. "We usually start with curatorial business."

Talbot looked Arthur up and down. "I am all business," he said and flipped on the slide projector's noisy fan. If she could pretend his exhibition was going forward, so could he.

Fatima Hakim was so grateful for Talbot Perry. She parted her chador, allowing him a glimpse of her leg, ankle to garter, but he missed the privilege because he was giving Arthur the eye, bravely staring down the homosexual. She appreciated Talbot's bitter aftertaste, untempered with the feminine care the others gave each phrase. Men were not supposed to be veiled; the Prophet had given them that. While she flaunted the power in being shrouded, it sickened her to see men act that way, as if they were transvestites. Men could speak close to your face, make unrelenting eye contact, allow their jackets to part and reveal the bulge that hung outside their bodies. Everything about them should be that obvious.

Talbot had switched the room lights off and the slide projectors on, lighting up two rectangles on the wall. He said, "Dr. Whittaker has asked me to provide you with an overview of 'A Japanese Port.'" A pen he pulled from inside his jacket extended into a pointer; with the whirring fan and the bricks of light, he might have been leading a military briefing.

"In 1853, Matthew Perry led a fleet of Navy ships into Edo Bay.

At the time, Japan traded with only one European nation, the Netherlands. In fact, *rangaku*, or 'Dutch learning,' became the euphemism for anything Western, including oil painting, linear perspective, or Western medicine. When Perry demanded docking rights, Japan complied; however, they constructed a separate port for the foreigners. They built Yokohama, a brand-new city, eventually negotiating . . ."

Promise was just about to nod off when Talbot clicked to his first image. The *oban* triptych, three prints squeezed into one slide, depicted rows of buildings with a strip of water below and geometric cloud cover above. The city's orderly layout looked like a board game, while the style—thick black outlines filled with primary colors—resembled a coloring book. She smiled in the dark; surely Talbot saw things differently.

He stepped to the left of the slide, subsuming himself in a nimbus of light. To Fatima he was the embodiment of the Word, pure flame coming out of his head like the Prophet.

"This lurid depiction of Yokohama, dated 1859, is basically a tourist poster. By 1872, artists based woodblocks on sketches made from hot-air balloons. In that interim, the new city had already burned down and been rebuilt, and telegraph and railroad service stretched to Tokyo."

Talbot's choices were heavy on the military, recording every possible view of the massive steamships. Promise preferred the prints that portrayed the waves of Western influence pounding their shores. Artists struggled to capture Western noses, wavy hair, trousers. Many copied the previous printmaker's version, and their fanciful works became a visual game of gossip.

Talbot clicked through a dozen images, stopping on a diptych of a boat split open and drawn as if the artist were looking through X-ray glasses. He said, "That odd cutaway view is a Japanese perspective they call *fukinuki yatai*, literally 'blown-away roof.'"

Promise stared at the innermost chamber of the ship, where an American dinner party was taking place. Men in top hats and women in hoopskirts held their stemmed glasses high in a toast. Urns of fresh flowers surrounded the table, which was laden with cakes on footed stands. The scene struck her as a sonogram of sorts, revealing for the Japanese the life behind those swollen, scary hulls. The *Amerikajin* may have strange customs, but they are more civilized than a runaway imagination might fear. Promise's deep breath turned into a yawn she could not retract; her jaw popped loudly when she opened her mouth.

"I can see I've said enough," Talbot concluded.

"It's fascinating," the Near Eastern curator said. "Rather than demonizing the foreigners, they tried to get it right."

"Obviously," he said. "Still, Westerners were stranger than they could fathom."

"I hope you'll point that out in your didactic material," Promise said.

But it all seemed obvious to him, including the notion that visiting an Asian art museum should be something of a foreign experience. "That visitor survey Joseph commissioned said people spend an *average* of seven seconds in front of an object label." He laid the remote down, freeing up his hands for his hair. "That's hardly long enough to read the ID, let alone what the woodblock depicts, how woodblocks were made, or what religion the artist observed."

What a brat, Promise thought. Her consolation was that in her new position she could simply reject his label copy until he complied with her.

Min spoke up. "The average viewer can admire the prints as you've shown them." She was anxious to get this meeting over with. She had twenty-nine thousand dollars stuffed into her purse, and it was worrying her sick. In an hour, she would be handing it over to Dr. Fan's smug receptionist, enough cash to cover their debt as well as a down payment on another in vitro procedure.

The head of Public Affairs said, "Maybe you could show the stages of making a woodblock print—I saw this once in a children's museum. The artists printed one color at a time, making sure to get the registration right with each pass, and then they carved a little more from the block, to add details with each new color. Did you know they end up destroying the woodblock in the process?"

"Yes," all the curators except Promise answered in unison.

Just because printmaking techniques were a given for curators didn't mean that her idea was beneath them. Promise too thought Talbot had left out some essential information. She said, "Truly, the prints are beautiful, and while that may be reason enough for an exhibition, that's not your reason. Why not tell us your reason?"

Talbot hadn't mentioned that Perry's first visit to Japan was a standoff. The admiral vowed to return in a year, and when his broad black ships sailed back in 1854, the treaty he negotiated ended the shogun's national seclusion policy, which had been in force since 1639. Aside from genealogy, no amount of didactic material could capture the thrill Talbot felt at forcing an entire culture to jump two centuries in two decades. Trade with us. Consume or be consumed! Get going already! He said, "They're important works."

"Obviously," Promise said, "when you know the story. But we have no feel for what Japanese life was like before Perry landed."

"Take a look," Talbot challenged. "I respect our visitors enough not to spell everything out."

Oh, he was smooth, implying that he had a higher opinion of the museum's guests than she did. She'd already fought this battle once today, with Arthur in the morning walk-through, and so she was more aggravated than she might have been. She sat up with a stiff back, hoping he could not see beneath the table to her feet swinging just above the ground. Then again, he could be as tall as the Washington Monument; she outranked him.

"Dr. Perry," she said, "Joseph Lattimore has retired and, should you need to seek his opinion, is currently in the Taklamakan Desert, where legend has it that the sands preserve what none may visit." She gave him the mother's glare, the most powerful arrow in her quiver, but he was looking at the door. Everyone was. A slight man in white painter's pants, a white camp shirt, and a paper cap had let himself in. He gave them a perfunctory wave and a bow, then took a measuring tape to the wall where Talbot had been showing slides. He was an elderly Chinese man wearing the costume of a soda jerk. Promise couldn't read the red and yellow logo on his paper hat from across the room, but she could see that it was written in the Chinese menu typeface they'd long ago outlawed in publications or labels.

The gentleman paid no attention to them as he rolled his tape out, duckwalking along the perimeter of the room. He sucked in the long noodle of tape to make calculations on a pocket abacus and then on a long thin pad.

The soft clicks of the abacus reminded Min of her early married life, Douglas tapping away at his classwork on the kitchen table. She figured the man must be nearly her father's age, despite his waiter boy outfit.

"I don't mean to disturb," he said in textbook English. "But since I have your attention, does anyone here know where we're meant to store our inventory?"

Promise read his cap—Wok On.

"You're in the Museum of Asian Art," Vanessa addressed him. "May we help you?"

"I realize I am early, but I want everything to be well planned." He locked eyes with Min and resorted to Mandarin. "What kind of food are you offering?"

"I am a curator of ancient Chinese bronze and jades," she answered in English. "If you are a vendor of some kind, you may be looking for the Air and Space Museum or perhaps the Museum of Natural History."

He unrolled a blueprint, which Min and Arthur set upon like hungry dogs. Through Arthur's bent arms, Promise could see the schematic of the conference room, occupied in the old man's drawing by tables, chairs, and a lunch counter embellished with the logo WOK ON. It was the same logo that was on the man's paper hat. Above the counter was a pagoda-like frame flanked by Fu dogs in outline. The architect had drawn an arrow to the mouths of the ceremonial dogs and written in all-cap architectural printing: "TRASH CANS—20 GALLON CAPACITY."

In his peripheral vision, Talbot caught Promise's expression: she was pressing her fingertips into her forehead and her lips were pursed, as if she'd sucked up something so cold that she'd been instantaneously struck by an eye-stabbing headache. Now he was certain she'd been left in the dark. Neither Cecil, Joseph, nor the Advisory Committee had told her what was coming, if the Advisory Committee even knew.

"Jesus Christ," Arthur said. "This says 'Projected Date July 1, 2000.'"

"So I am not actually too early," the man said. "I do, however, apologize for any intrusion."

Promise swooped in before anyone else could see the scroll. "May I have this? Thank you." She confiscated the drawings the way she would take a bag of gummy candy away from Felix. Then she rolled up the schematics to disguise the fact that her hands had begun to shake. "This is a private meeting," she said. "You may wait in the hallway until we're finished or you may schedule an appointment. I'll return your drawings later. Vanessa, would you please show this gentleman to the reception area?"

"Certainly," Vanessa said.

The man in white bowed once more. "May I say that hours of enjoyment I have spent here, especially contemplating the scrolls of Wang Meng and Shitao. When I learned of this opportunity—"

"Now's not the time," Vanessa interrupted him, sensing that his every word did further damage. There was silence as she escorted the gentleman out.

Promise stuck her finger in one end of the scroll and tightened the drawings from poster to telescope to cane, narrowing in on the situation as well. When Joseph up and quit, Min had alluded to the museum closing; after Promise's appointment, Talbot had offered to answer any questions she might have about the future. Before taking her seat at the head of the conference table, she nearly bopped Min and Talbot on their inscrutable heads with the rolled-up blueprints. Unlike when her countless pregnancy symptoms had leveled her, this realization infused her with adrenaline. If the conference room was being given over to Wok On, no doubt a hard rain was going to fall. She didn't need to know the extent of the deluge to commit herself to protecting the museum, temple of her soul. Lines of Rumi entered her head: "When the ocean surges, don't let me just hear it. Let it splash inside my chest!"

Here was the strength the midwife had promised. The fetal tsunami she had once so dreaded began to buoy her up. She looked upon her staff, who knew that, for her, an object didn't exist until a visitor was looking at it. All the scholarship she did in her little basement office was to promote understanding and appreciation. She'd always felt she'd internalized her audience; that went double now that she was pregnant, triple as acting director. As for the Museum of Asian Art, the artifacts in their care were generated by the most populous continent on the earth: its people made art, they made babies, they made love, they made war.

"Creativity in all its forms is our passion," she said. "While it may be a disservice to let the objects we steward gather dust, preserving is not the same as hiding or hoarding. The Founder could have erected a giant mausoleum to bury his fetishes with him. But he left money for *public* galleries, a courtyard, an auditorium." Dolphinlike, the baby breached and dove, rocking her in her chair.

Promise steadied herself, palms flat on the conference table. "Go ahead," she resumed. "Electron-microscope the glaze on a piece of porcelain, reassemble Yokohama's original cartography. But do so knowing that your efforts can never be the last word, as long as these objects outlive you. Study whatever minutia floats your boat, and then *move over* and let someone else appreciate the hell out of this art."

What her midwife had called a growth spurt took on a whole new meaning to Promise. She was a little finch of a woman who'd been content under Joseph's wing—it was no wonder people had left her out of the loop. How they gaped, openmouthed, and how she fed them. "Find a metaphor you can work with, friends. One that has people in it, like sending a chain letter along or perhaps paying off some karmic debt. At the least, mentor a new generation of connoisseurs with your super-human educations. Because, believe you me," she said, resorting to Oklahoma syntax, "the unwashed masses will be welcome here. We're going to run shuttles over the Sousa Bridge to kids who live in D.C. but have never been to a museum. There will be Japanese women drumming on our front steps, karate demonstrations in the courtyard, and I'll teach sand painting myself if I can't find a willing monk." Vanessa's tape recorder disgorged its cassette with a mechanical burp, but Promise kept going.

"Where you have found transcendence you must pull others up through the gaps in the clouds. The beauty and variety of expression that have become your day job could save a child's life, such power there is in original works of art. Wonder and craft and history and riches beyond compare have been bestowed upon you, ordinary citizens, that you may fight their battles and keep their faith."

"Yes!" Zemzemal concurred, at the same time that Jill said, "Amen!"

Promise was so parched she had to stroke the roof of her mouth with her tongue to make some spit, and she thought of cowboys in the desert sucking on pebbles to keep their juices flowing. They were all out in the desert, weren't they? Everyone was talking and asking questions and expressing indignation, but there was only one person she wanted to address.

"Talbot," she said, "I'd like a meeting with you in my office." Obediently he stood, gathering his scant papers in a practiced scoop. He opened the door and held it for Promise, who led the way to the director's suite.

Do You Mind?

Two minutes later

Talbot wasn't aware Promise could move so fast. Every few steps she incorporated a peculiar hop that on the basketball court would have been traveling. She'd handled herself well in the curatorial meeting, waylaid by the Wok On man. Talbot usually took exception to her pro-visitor spiels, because she treated the curators as glorified storytellers, or worse, babysitters.

He said, "Nice call to arms. Very inspirational."

"I meant every word," she said. Talbot shoved the heavy door closed without slamming it, as if he knew its precise weight. After curatorial meetings, she usually went to Arthur's office, where they interpreted the nuances of everyone's remarks, especially Talbot's.

Her adrenaline was subsiding, replaced by deep umbrage. She was the acting director, for God's sake. How could she be unaware of such a scheme? Her legs quivered beneath her, which wasn't as creepy as the feeling within—the baby was completely still, and she tried to jostle him without Talbot noticing. Now was not the time for sleeping. Even some side-to-side movement was better than heavy stillness. She sat on the couch with the confiscated drawings. Talbot cleared the coffee table, stacking the fanned-out magazines into his palms like a deck of cards. From the credenza behind her, Promise chose Joseph's second book to anchor the top corner of the drawings, then she hefted a bronze statue of Ganesha as well. The elephant-headed deity flattened the drawings' curled lower edges.

"Ah, Ganesha—remover of obstacles," she said.

Talbot said, "He makes a good paperweight." Tacit in his remark was that Joseph's book served the same purpose.

The topmost drawing committed every cultural offense the museum fought against. Promise pointed to each feature, sputtering. There were the Fu-dog garbage cans as well as a space for a scrolling electronic sign that, in the drawings, read, "Confucius say . . ." Worst was the counter designated for "Takee Outee." Maybe these were an architect's idea of humor.

She lifted Ganesha, and Talbot swung back the large sheet to the second page, which depicted the entire first floor. Every single gallery, the conference room, and the staff room were stamped with logos. Promise assumed she was witnessing the spread of corporate sponsorship; after all, an exterminating company had affixed its name to Natural History's insect display, and the zoo pandas were brought to you by a film company. Naming the galleries for businesses would be shock enough. But then she saw it was far worse.

"My God, it's not just the conference room! Gallery Fourteen says New Delhi Deli, and it looks like Gallery Thirteen is Kabob Hut." It seemed prophetic that her day had started with a discussion of what food should be offered in the staff room.

Talbot smoothed a hunk of blond hair back. "This is news to you."

"This better be news to you, buddy, or you're going on the spitfire."

Talbot splayed his thin, flat hand across his chest. "Pardon me?"

His composure stoked her rancor. She said, "If you knew about these plans, you deserve a skewer through you lengthwise and a slow flame-roasting."

They stared at each other, and then Talbot said, "I'd like to see you try that."

The idea was as ludicrous as the situation they were in. That notion, along with the twinned relief and pain of Edgar giving her a swift kick, made Promise laugh. She sounded like a toy bird, her computer-chip chirp of a laugh powered by the flip of a switch. "I am such a jackass," she said. "I actually imagined they had chosen me: Acting Director of the Museum of Asian Art."

Talbot stood up and walked over to Joseph's desk. "I thought you had nerves of steel."

She should have gotten used to the fact that Talbot would always have inside information. She'd completely used up her wherewithal, and, unstrapping her shoes, she put her swollen feet on the coffee table next to the drawings.

"Do you mind?" he asked.

He was lucky she didn't take off her bra, which was digging into her wing flaps. Then she realized that he was asking her permission to open the desk. "Not at all," she said. "See if there's anything in there for us."

"Like strychnine tablets?"

Promise sighed. "Like gum, is what I was thinking. And would you please get me some water?"

Talbot had located what he was looking for among Joseph's coded files. He presented her with the Secretary's notice. "I hope you'll let me help you."

Thus, Promise finally read the memo, her dry mouth agape all the way to the end. *"Our advisers maintain that the Founder's will, stipulating the care of these objects in perpetuity, could be honored in another location."* When she finished, Talbot was there with her mug of water. She said, "Oh, I don't think so, Mister Secretary. When we wanted to put in another ladies' room, we couldn't break the Founder's will."

"The last I heard, Cecil had asked Joseph for his strategy in shutting down the museum."

"Jesus," Promise said angrily, and it sounded like a sneeze. "Why didn't you show me this a month ago? We were here first: the Founder built the first art museum on the Mall."

"And the closest to the Metro and the least visited. You're in shock, just like Joseph was."

"I am not in shock." Promise shook her finger at Talbot. "I was in shock when my dog ate the library's facsimile of the *Padshahnama*. This is exactly where the Castle's been heading."

He sat himself on the arm of the couch, a little too chummy except that he had just brought water at her command. He said, "You should have seen Joseph. He asked me if any of the ceremonial swords could hold an edge. But he couldn't fight it."

Promise fingered the crappy photocopy. "How hard did the guy try? Everyone loves Joseph. But this memo is dated July first, and he left a month later. He called this place his life's work, then he gets one lousy memo and runs—*wee, wee, wee, wee, wee*—all the way to the Taklamakan Desert."

"Cecil said he'd need a billion dollars to be taken seriously."

"Hooey! It cost less than that to go to the moon."

"'Hooey?'" Talbot's head hung over the couch like a reading lamp. "Is that a regionalism?"

Though she had to look up to do it, Promise stared him down. "Whom do we tell and when?"

"Welcome to the world of administration," he said. "Every meeting I've ever attended could be summarized into those questions."

"Does everybody else know what's going on?"

"I doubt it. These are the first drawings I've seen. The Castle must be taking care of things, preparing to pink-slip us all in a few months."

Promise felt a trickle of sympathy for Joseph, who was never able to get rid of people. He had once told her, "I hire staff; Talbot fires them." She understood that hiring to firing circumscribed many other Talbot tasks, like clipping wings, picking nits, and feathering nests. The thought of a billion dollars was incomprehensible to Promise, who'd balked at the bowl's price tag. Raising a billion dollars would be like buying a thousand million-dollar bowls.

Anger aside, she needed Talbot's help. "Let's assume Arthur and Min saw only the first drawing—that's bad enough. Call the general counsel, for starters. Then see what the ombudsman has to say."

"I will," Talbot said. "What about Arthur's exhibition and his bowl?"

"Full steam ahead," Promise said, without much steam. "More money is more money. Buying that piece will show we can drum up funds 'to fulfill our responsibilities' and be 'worthy of our guests.'"

Talbot said, "Cecil's got a hundred cannons at his command—he's here to tear the walled city down and let the crowds in."

Promise looked at the underside of Talbot's chin, which had been split open some time ago. He was talking about Cecil the way he'd been talking about the U.S. Navy invading Japan. She said, "Are you suggesting we go along with this? I'd like to point out that whenever I tried to let a few of the crowds in, you had a fit."

"That was different." As far as he was concerned, she'd been pushing the museum in the same direction as Cecil, with her hands-on galleries and children's activities. At least with the Castle's plan, his collection wouldn't be here when the sticky-fingered masses arrived. "Joseph said you were a purist like him, yet you fell for everything. If Education said video, you agreed. Acoustiguides, children's books, mood music—the whole lot."

He made it sound like she was a circus promoter, junking up the galleries with sideshows. "Sit down here," she insisted, and when he followed her order, they were nearly at eye level. "What the hell are we going to do?"

He found himself wanting to be on her team despite his disagreements with her.

"I'm always looking for a way in," she said. "I want accessible shows with intellectual underpinnings. You have to admit, not everybody knows what to make of a Japanese woodblock."

"The woodblock is the way in," he explained. "Seriously, everything else is a distraction. Long texts on the walls, earphones tethered to a tape deck, computer screens flashing. The more you tell, the less they look."

"True enough," Promise concurred. "But we should tell the visitors what we tell each other at the lunch table. There's incest and forgeries right up until it's time to write exhibition copy." She'd never been able to discuss the weather with Talbot, yet here they were airing their personal philosophies. She'd rested the memo on her belly, and it seemed that Edgar was using the sheet of paper for target practice, knocking it back into her hands. "We don't have time for a label discussion! You act as if you'd rather send the Japanese collection away than fight—why are you in Cecil's corner?"

Because the pregnant, gay, robed, and Chinese scholars in the other corner don't stand a chance. But she had him on several counts. First, if he'd been named acting director, he would have been dismantling the museum, and second, he didn't really want the Japanese collection sent away. He slouched over, elbows on his knees, revealing the beginnings of a bald spot at the top of his head.

Promise spoke to him in a whispery voice that came out like a threat. "Every hundred years or so, you have to change sides. You're not an officer in the U.S. Navy with a hundred cannons at your disposal; you're Japan and you're being invaded. So build a new port! Prepare to be boarded!"

Talbot sat up at attention as she pushed herself off the couch. She swayed side to side now as she walked over to the phone and buzzed Vanessa. "Could you get Zemzemal over here, please?" She hung up. "That's the best part of the job so far." She pretended to buzz. "Get me Spider-Man!"

"You're going to need them all," Talbot said. "Spider-Man's just a freelance photographer. At least Batman's rich. You should see the Japanese superheroes—they're all warrior priests."

That was when she thought of her personal superhero, the man who fought for human rights with a pen rather than a sword, who rallied support with letters, phone calls, direct mail, and a goodly amount of shame. Rich he was not, but he knew modern Asia better than any of them.

Zemzemal slipped in, seating himself on the far side of Talbot. "Wok On?" he guessed.

"We're in deep trouble here," Promise said. She pushed the drawings, then the memo his way. "Check out the date."

A wide frown pulled his cheeks down his leathery face. "What an insult," he said. "Joseph was right to walk out in protest."

Whether he'd walked out in protest or abandoned them was up for debate. Promise said, "Talbot, let's start thinking about who might help us."

"I'll see who we've got in Congress. You want movie stars?"

"You have some?" Promise asked. His shrug was neither yes nor no. The two men sat on the couch, awaiting her orders. She stroked her belly, whose stretching triggered a powerful itch. "I have to change gears," she said. "I'm worried about the curator whose Vietnamese weaving show might be canceled. But . . . this," she spoke slowly, "this . . . is . . . an . . . outrage. The thing is, my husband keeps a daily watch on Asia's friends and enemies, and he knows who will go to bat for a worthy cause."

Talbot took off his glasses, gave them a complete rotation, then replaced them. "Are you telling us your first act under siege will be hiring your husband?"

"May I?" she asked Zemzemal.

"With private funds, you may do anything you like," he said.

"I might," she said to Talbot. "Don't forget to call the general counsel. Then make me a list of people I should call—we're just doing research at this point. Zemzemal, may I ask you to see what private funds are available?"

"You may."

"Thank you," she said and dismissed them.

Sitting behind Joseph's fortress, she reread the memo from the top. Her pulse beat with a double ferocity; in pregnancy, she could feel the blood travel on its circuitous route. She was thankful that Edgar was up and about, so she didn't have to rouse him. She dialed Leo.

"Hey," he said. "You got my messages?"

"Not yet. You won't believe what happened in the curatorial meeting—"

"Bad, huh? Here, too."

We'll get to you, Promise thought, picking up her story again. "This old waiter came into the conference room and started taking measurements for a Chinese lunch counter that's scheduled to open next summer."

"No shit. Listen, honey—"

"None at all. I grabbed his floor plans, and it turns out the Castle is selling us down the river. The drawings show an entire floor of restaurants."

"What?" Leo stretched the word out; he was clearly astonished. "So that's why Joseph left."

"They're splitting the collection up between Natural History and the National Gallery."

"Oh, man. Unbelievable."

It sounded like he was high, which she knew wasn't the case. He was stupefied, and he spoke with more of a sense of wonder than of anger. "They fucked him. He was their Brahmin leader, their poster child, and they fucked him up the ass. Is this news to Talbot?"

"Apparently not," Promise said. She thought about how Talbot and Zemzemal had been sitting on either end of the couch like obedient lapdogs. "I asked Zemzemal if we could get some Urgent Action help," she said, purposely phrasing it in the jargon of Leo's job, which he'd been bemoaning for months. "Basically, he says private money buys anything we want, and I want you and your superhero powers."

"At the museum? I can't do that now."

She said, "You're all about civilization. After the looting and the whoring, isn't making art a worthy cause? And you don't have to be a government employee the way Zemzemal will set it up." She wasn't asking him to save them, just to lend his muscle to her cause. "If you're worried about nepotism, half the Institution is married to the other half."

"That's not it," he said. "If Joseph couldn't handle this, I don't see why you should be expected to." His voice was trailing off. "I wonder if those cocksuckers have heard."

"Heard what?" She could barely hear *him*.

"I've been calling you all afternoon." Although he'd left her message upon message, he was reluctant to form the actual words.

Promise was pressing the phone hard against her ear as well as gripping the bottom of the mouthpiece. By cocksuckers, she assumed he meant Cecil and company in the Castle, but because Leo was prone to ranting rather than silence, fear percolated through her. Whatever had him spooked wasn't about the children, because he'd wondered if the cocksuckers had heard. And it wasn't about his job, because the cocksuckers wouldn't care about that, either. That led Promise and her powers of deduction to the intersection of Asia, the cocksuckers, and Leo. "Oh my God," she yelped. "Joseph!"

"He's alive," he said. "And Emmy's all right; she's somewhere local, though I haven't pinpointed her yet. Most of them are all right." Now the words were tumbling out pell-mell.

Promise felt as if her lungs were the bellows of an accordion that Edgar had squeezed shut. She wished Leo were here with her so she could hold on to him.

"The Al-Faran made their way to the dig," Leo was saying, "and they took six hostages, and one of them is definitely Joseph. Everyone went to Hotan, the entire caravan, but then the Al-Faran kept going west into the mountains. They want to exchange the hostages for their own people in Indian and Pakistani jails."

She had just been sitting on Joseph's very couch, criticizing him for taking the easy way out, when he had more gumption in his little finger than she possessed in her entire body. Who knew what struggles he'd endured on their behalf? Now he was in grave danger, maybe dead. As much as it hurt to breathe, she forced her lungs to gather enough air so she could moan.

"Honey, are you all right?" Leo asked.

"No." She massaged the bottom of her rib cage. "When did this happen?"

"The day after Thanksgiving—he's been theirs for a week. Emmy and the other Americans went from Hotan to the custody of the Indian government, then to ours. She was flown to Walter Reed on the thirtieth. Do you know anything about a convent—someone from the State Department mentioned a convent."

"In Olney," she said. "There's a Buddhist convent. Emmy went on retreats there."

"That makes sense, because the same guy heard she'd gone straight up Georgia Avenue not that far from the hospital. Christ, this makes me mad!"

At last Leo was beginning to sound like himself, and his rage was an odd comfort, even a source of fuel. She would be needing a steady supply of anger.

He said, "You're five months pregnant, and they blindsided you with this shit. You should quit."

"No," she protested. Someone would have to fight, and it might as well be them.

"Do you want me to come get you?"

"Yes," she said. "But I want you to stay here. It's selfish, but that's what I want. You know how thin you'll be stretched at the office—you'll only get to work on Joseph's case an hour or two a day. Can't we join forces here, martial support for both Joseph and the museum?"

Leo's boss had already reminded him that he had assignments other than Joseph's. Amnesty people often had to put aside the files of friends, especially long-shot files, to attend to abuses in other lands. Besides nepotism, there were probably a dozen laws against his working at the museum, using the government's electricity and phone lines to generate letters on Joseph's behalf. The State Department wouldn't approve of someone in another government office playing detective. And what could he do to reverse a bureaucracy's decision against its own art museum? If he had his way, he'd argue for the Museum of Asian Art to send its contents back where they came from. He heard Promise's panting breath, and he pictured her heart-shaped lips pleading for his help. He said, "I'll come, but I can't promise."

"I Promise," she said. "Stay and I'll promise you anything you want."

"Promise me you won't go into a convent," he said. "Promise me no drug testing," and he hung up, presumably to come to her side.

————

"Oh my," Vanessa exclaimed when Promise opened the door of the director's office. Her boss's eyes were bloodshot, and she had the imprint of a phone on the side of her puffy face.

Promise wasn't prepared to tell Vanessa what had been going on behind that door. She said, "I need a dozen boxes and you in my downstairs office." While Leo was making his way to her and the boys were gathering intelligence, she planned to clear the deck. "Bring anything that will help us organize."

Rather than taking the north steps to the lower level and passing the staff offices, she headed down the east hallway, where there'd be less chance of running into anyone. She worried she wasn't walking a particularly straight line. In her old office, she went right to a stash of granola bars, resisting the pull of each pile on her desk. Edgar ricocheting inside her was a reminder that she'd have to direct the heavy lifting. She coached herself not to get consumed by the little picture, where she usually spent all her energy.

The first thing she archived was her to-do list, three pages of duties. What a rush to scrap the whole thing, even if she hadn't had the satisfaction of checking off each item. Rumi could wait—there would be Rumi scholars as long as there were Asian art museums. The task at hand was more than research and writing; it was riding the siren-wailing red truck, wielding the electric paddles and cattle prods! She'd always considered her scholarship significant; however, in the new hostile light, she also saw the preciousness of what she'd been doing.

Vanessa rolled in a dolly, full as a shopping basket at an office supply store. "I've got file boxes here. I've got archival-quality manuscript boxes that have never shown up in the curatorial closets. And I've got tabs, labels, stickums—everything but glitter!"

"Time to separate the wheat from the chaff," Promise quoted her mother's Bible talk.

Vanessa said, in slow deep southern cadence, "The very sheep from the goats. Boll weevil from the woolly cotton; voracious termite from the unblemished wood; ungrateful, devil-possessed, son of a bitch from blessed obedient child."

Promise laid down her light load. "Amen! That your mama?"

"Yes ma'am, yes ma'am," Vanessa said, making Promise wonder how all of them had made it from wherever they started to here in this building. Oklahoma to India, Mississippi to the National Institution of Science and Art—these were heady journeys. And then there was the beyond, which she couldn't bear to think about, the trail from the Institution to the Taklamakan Desert and into the hands of zealots.

"She was raising us to be the new prophets," Vanessa said. Removing a flat piece of cardboard from the cart, she deftly ripped flaps along perforated edges, folded them in, back out, and pushed a rectangle through to construct a sound box.

Promise admired Vanessa's prestidigitation. "The new prophets. Were you tempted?"

"Don't get me started on temptation."

What Promise had meant was, had she been tempted to follow her mother's dream?

Breaking the pillar of Rumi books in half, Vanessa boxed the entire set, then folded another piece of cardboard for the lid. "There's room in the attic," she said to Promise, and she labeled each end of the box: "Whittaker/Rumi," adding "Attic" in huge letters, which she circled. She did the same with the stack devoted to South India. Either she was familiar with Promise's stacks or she was an organizational genius, deducing the shared subject matter in a glance. Promise would have thought Vanessa's dress too elegant for work like this, but the fact that it clung to her meant that there was nothing to step on or catch. The top of Promise's desk was now visible, and her office grew larger. Vanessa transformed a sheet of cardboard into a hanging file cabinet; then she stood stacks of pages up, smacked the edges on the desk to align them, and slipped them into folders. In small, even handwriting, she filled out labels and slid them into holders, which in turn fit into slits at the tops of the file folders.

Promise wondered when she'd see her Rumi again.

Vanessa stretched out her arms and rolled her head around. "There was no future for my mama—that's why I think she couldn't stop preaching at us. She reminded us every day what she'd been through, how she'd prepared us."

"Is she still in Mississippi?"

Vanessa gave Promise a hard stare. "Mama died two years ago this spring."

Promise flushed with embarrassment. She counted backward to spring 1998—she'd been frantic over her *Mathnawi* exhibition, and her new assistant had disappeared for a "family emergency." Promise had thought her guilty of a euphemism at the time. "I'm sorry," she said, putting her hands beneath the baby, like a sack of groceries, in a cheap ploy for forgiveness.

Vanessa resumed packing. "Mama was something. She'd go on about Moses and Mohammed until one of my brothers pointed out Moses and Mohammed were both orphans."

Promise had never thought about that before. "That would explain their commands to honor thy father and mother," she said. "At least Moses and Mohammed stayed married. The mystics all left their families behind to do their work. No children in the house of the Buddha."

"Even your man?"

"Rumi always had a male companion. But the family he did have he essentially abandoned."

Promise would not be abandoning her family, and so she would have to take a leave of absence from mysticism. Jalaluddin Rumi may have taught the dervishes to whirl in ecstasy, but could he run a museum?

Miracle

December 2, 1999

Emmy Lattimore awoke near the edge of her narrow nun's cot, cocooned in sheets. The sun had fallen through the sky since she'd lain down for a nap, and the call to afternoon meditation was seeping under her warped plywood door. Because her recent trauma bled all over her dreams, Emmy had heard the low chanting as the moaning of wounded men. But she wasn't under an awning in the Taklamakan Desert, sewing up Joseph's split head with dental floss. Ministering to her drooling, bleeding husband had come to be a comforting dream, for if she wasn't in the desert, she wasn't with him. The worst dreams were the ones she spent wandering, heartbroken, rather than being delivered back outside the tent, where she'd played nurse to both sides, tackle box in hand. Yili, their bashful Uygur guide, had herded the women into the sorting tent, barely sheltering them from the brawl going on outside. Beneath her remaining breast, her heart thumped more and more forcefully until someone outside the tent crackled off a round of machine-gun fire and she felt a tingling pain all the way down her arm. Here was the time to detach, she thought, or being in the moment might very well kill her.

Once, at the kitchen table of her Capitol Hill home, the Dalai Lama had told her that nonviolence did not mean sitting on your ass. To the Free Tibet faction he'd addressed that evening, he had spoken more poetically, the message basically being that pacifists are not passive.

Joseph had been mercifully unconscious as she'd unspooled her shirt, the gauze ripping more easily than paper. She was scared out of her wits, and tearing up her clothes rekindled a strong memory of the birth class she and Joseph had taken before Jules was born. Emmy was only twenty-one then, and though she wasn't just off the ranch, she'd found most of the information in the class downright shocking. With a terrifying lack of affect, their instructor detailed all the procedures doctors imposed on their patients. When it came time for the teacher's anti-episiotomy rant, she illustrated the perineum's elasticity by mightily tugging a sheet between both hands to show the give in the fabric. Then she cut a few inches into the sheet and pulled on either side of the cut, which split the thin fabric apart. What had scared Emmy the most was the dissonance between the potential gore of delivery and the miracle of birth, a dissonance that never resolved itself.

She'd made it through pregnancy and delivery four times, which turned out to be a form of basic training. In the course of the boys' lives, she'd found the strength to face broken bones, chipped teeth, gashes, burns, and blood; frightening, but repaired remarkably quickly, thank God. The questions in those cases were: Will he lose the tooth? Will he be able to play lacrosse? Will it leave a scar?

The injuries her frisky boys had racked up were nothing compared with the beating visited upon Joseph. She nearly fell to pieces there at his side, the metallic smell of his blood strong as she leaned over his head. She'd poured bleachy canteen water over his wounds and begun mumbling the prayer. Stitches in his head were as prayer beads. She wound her shirt around and around him for his dressing. She wasn't trying to shame anyone, just perform her task without collapsing, but she could feel them one by one averting their gazes. That was when she tucked a little surprise into the wrap around Joseph's uninjured thigh, a lagniappe, as her Cajun friends would say.

She'd had to go passive at that point, to abandon Joseph to those desert thugs; she didn't protest when well-meaning authorities escorted her to her present life. Of course, she'd been in a daze as they evacuated her and the rest of the camp. It was like rewinding a tape, taking the animals and trucks out of the desert to head west to Hotan. Quite a few times the Uygur guides had even turned their backs to the wind, walking backward alongside the animals.

Emmy had made her way back to America in a truck bed, on the hump of a camel, and astride a donkey, in a diplomat's rounded Ambassador, a jet, a prop plane, and a blue State Department sedan. Yesterday, when they discharged her from Walter Reed, she simply stepped out to the cab stand and caught a ride. About ten miles north of D.C., the convent was off New Hampshire Avenue with all the fringe religions.

Ravi and Sanjay had volunteered to help her find a house, but she couldn't live in a house without Joseph. Henry had offered to give her his very bed, which was sweet. She'd chosen the convent rather than Henry's or a city apartment, but she might as well be in a penthouse for the guilt she felt. She'd imagined desert life would be more stripped down than it was; however, the sand, heat, and cold had required a fair amount of equipment. She appreciated the asceticism they practiced in the convent, where a hot bath could seem as silly as scented soaps pressed into the shape of flowers. Out her window she saw the Ukrainian Orthodox church, its onion dome somehow constructed of wood planks; if she'd had a second window, she might have seen the Cambodian temple, the Pentecostal missionary outpost, or the Armenian mosque.

Emmy hadn't found what she was looking for in the Taklamakan. As harsh as the desert's natural elements was her realization that the Silk Route was devoted to commerce. Of course she'd known that on some level, because trade had carved out the path. And of course, it made sense that monks would prefer to knee-walk on a merchant's highway, considering the desert was known as the Sea of Death. Still, the nature of the trade itself—bartering, trafficking, haggling, smuggling—didn't fit her beatified version. It turned out that going to the Silk Route for Buddhist guidance was like going to Times Square to learn the true meaning of Christmas. And so the challenge for the devout might be to keep your faith in a commercial atmosphere.

Safe in the Olney convent, she was tempted to tune out the world, and she would have except for the hope that she could somehow help Joseph. "You're all about detachment," he used to remark, a misapprehension she was desperate to correct. Buddhists don't detach from the people they love; they're not resigned from life.

There was the possibility that Joseph might already be free and word hadn't reached her, like the delay of starlight reaching earth. There was the possibility that he was dead. If she lay down and died— cancer survivors, she'd learned, couldn't avoid thinking this—she'd never see her beloved boys again, meet their lovers, their children. Unless she returned as the baby staring with inexplicable love at Henry, who would probably have kids first. Maybe she'd return as one of their pets and bask in their care for a dozen years the way she hoped they had enjoyed hers.

In her spasms of sleep, she'd been dreaming about children; more accurately, a child abandoned in the desert. The boy had one leg, but that wasn't what he was dying of. He was bound and gagged and cold and irredeemably broken. Though trauma had affected her memory, she was positive the boy had not been among Joseph's abductors. He was so slight, hollow. She saw flags flapping in the distance, their primary colors inked with prayers meant to be sent out on the wind. What else? Each time she shuddered awake, she tried to recapture the flavor of her dream. Bitter? Buttery? She remembered the smell of fires stoked with camel dung, but sometimes mold brought that smell to mind, too. She tried to match up the images with her past, with her religion, with her family. It was no use because this boy had nothing to do with her; she'd never met him, never seen him before. Yet it was important that she dream him, for little did she know, she was dreaming the dream that would bring Joseph home.

———

Min had made it to Dr. Fan's waiting room and was hanging on to her purse so tightly that the strap made a welt along her shoulder. Twenty-nine thousand dollars was heavy, even in hundreds. Each time the door opened, she both wished and didn't wish for Douglas to walk in. Either he trusted her too much to pry, or he didn't want to know how she'd come up with this absurd amount of cash. Her head was spinning from her efforts to sort auspicious opportunity from ethical breach. When she'd agreed to help Arthur, she'd never expected such a response to his bowl; she gave him a little more credit as a result (to think of the hours she'd spent importuning these patrons for ancient bronzes). In the end, she'd skimmed less than 10 percent from all she'd garnered, less than what the museum would have paid a fund-raiser.

She rubbed her hands together, trying to kindle some warmth. The old waiter in the conference room confirmed what Madame X had been telling her, but if the museum was closing, why hadn't Promise made a sound? And why had she given that impassioned speech about their audience if the art was on its way out? Min signed her name stiffly on the appointment sheet, then leaned close to speak under the glass window of the receptionist's desk.

"I am prepared to settle my account," she said, masking embarrassment with scorn.

"Of course, Mrs. Chen," the receptionist said and gave a nervous laugh.

"Dr. Chen," Min said, acting far braver than she felt.

"Dr. Chen," the receptionist agreed. She hit some characters on the keyboard, consulting her screen and nodding her head. "I understand you have an outstanding balance."

"Eight thousand eight hundred dollars," Min said. "And today we are beginning another procedure." She began emptying her purse as the receptionist's owl eyes grow rounder. The woman craned her neck and searched the office for backup. Min realized how it looked, unloading brick after brick of money as if she'd robbed a bank, but they were the ones who'd demanded ransom. Although her purse eased up on her shoulder, she still sensed its burden. She bit her quivering lip, shoving the rest of the money at the receptionist so she could quickly go to the restroom and empty her bladder.

"We'll account for this as soon as we can," the receptionist was saying. "No one's ever paid in cash before."

Min practically lunged for the bathroom, where she performed the urine-sample drill as she had countless times before: pee in cup, label sample, leave on counter by sink. Because it was just a baseline urine test and because she'd unloaded all her cash, she had no reason to be so jumpy. That was what she told herself, but her hands couldn't keep the squat, wide-mouthed cup in position between her legs. When she washed up, she had to towel off the outside of the sample cup, too. Then she stepped into the outer room for weight and blood pressure. Both numbers were slightly higher than usual. When the nurse escorted her to the inner room, Douglas was waiting for her there.

"What's wrong?" he asked.

Min sat down close to him. She sensed a change in the room, though she couldn't pinpoint what it was. She was gulping air like a fish. "I just paid them twenty-nine thousand dollars. We can start over today."

The amount silenced them both. While Min had doubted Douglas would ask where she'd gotten the money, she was a little disappointed in him. She looked to where the inside-out woman still stood against the wall next to the calendar that would soon expire. Water was running, but when Min turned toward the sink, she saw that a miniature fountain now gurgled in the corner. This pretense of humanizing the inner room profoundly saddened Min, who believed stuffed animals and photographs of plump babies would be less insulting. She hoped the fountain was a decorating tip imposed on Dr. Fan.

Douglas stuck a finger in the fountain and shook water droplets onto the paper-covered examination table. "I expected fake," he said. He wiped his hand against his pants. "Sally's class watched movies all day yesterday. Two full videos because the teacher was sick or tired."

"And no homework. I had her write a report demonstrating that she'd paid attention."

Douglas mimicked their daughter, "There is no homework."

Min laughed at his imitation, so rare for him to make fun of Sally. "Her report was good after she rewrote it."

He said, "In Taiwan, she would know a thousand characters by now. Multiplication tables, too. How can they sit watching a movie when this teacher hasn't even said how to divide one number into another?"

"You have taught her," Min complimented him. "She is lucky to have a father like you." He was probably a better father here than he would have been in Taiwan, where less was expected of fathers. Their conversation calmed her. She said, "An old waiter wandered into the curatorial meeting to take measurements for a lunch counter."

Douglas stared at his wife, whose cheeks were flushed in two small circles. He'd defended the Castle against Madame X's predictions.

Min shrugged. "He looked like your uncle Yat, though his nose was not so flared, and he had the adding beads you used to use. There he was, calculating with his beads—tip, tip, shhh. In Taiwan, I went to sleep with those clicks and woke up to them as well. My dreams made stories out of sliding, tapping noises."

Those years were the clearest in Douglas's memory. They lived with his parents as they raced each other for a doctorate. Plain bowls of rice at breakfast and lunch, because they didn't want to be any more of a burden than they already were. Each month, he presented his mother with their rent—his entire teaching fellowship, Min's translation work. She literally snatched it from his hand, saying, "So little money for so much schooling." It was the happiest time of his life, when he and Min were two brains in one body.

Min smoothed her paper gown. If Douglas was shocked about the museum's future, he wasn't showing it. She said, "In Mandarin, he asked me what kind of restaurant I had. So familiar, he talked to me as if we'd known each other back home."

"Are you thinking more and more about Taipei, too?"

Actually, when she'd said home, she'd meant Beijing. She spotted the lighter in Douglas's shirt pocket and wished for a cigarette—was Douglas smoking again?—then the thought of smoking turned her stomach. She said, "My thoughts are everywhere, like spilled peanuts. Even though he is a complete stranger to me, I wanted to *visit* with him. Imagine feeling such warmth toward this stranger, an old man in a waiter costume who may mean the end of my job. Meanwhile, I can barely speak to my most helpful friend. She gave a speech to inspire our loyalty, and I almost cried with shame, realizing how I have wished for her failure."

"The nuns inspire your shame." Douglas teased her a bit, because he was at a loss. "Whenever I think about nuns helping you get pregnant, I get turned around. Reminds me of the things missionaries wanted us to repeat and to believe. Virgins pee so you can conceive. It must be confusing in your blood."

That was exactly how she felt: confusing in her blood. Angry and then mad about feeling angry. Cynical toward Promise's supposed innocence, then swayed by her friend's obligation toward the museum. Just before Min had left for her doctor's appointment, her assistant wanted to know if she was having trouble retrieving her phone messages. Apparently, the inspector general's office was now calling the Secretary's office. A meeting with them was inevitable.

Min was creasing her robe's edge in a fan fold when Dr. Fan burst in the room. He held the pregnancy wand (the pissing match) aloft, but for all the noise his entrance made—the hangers on the back of the door were still clanging together—he spoke in a hush. "This is a miracle like I have never seen." His smooth face wrinkled up with smiling. "Needless to say, you have saved five hundred dollars for your injection today. You are pregnant, Min Chen." He bowed deeply to the mother-to-be.

Douglas couldn't tell whether Dr. Fan was astonished or self-conscious at being shown up. Douglas himself indulged in a rare burst of pride. It was as if he had fixed his computer with a paper clip, for after all the lasers and sonograms and hormone shots, he—crafty and superior husband—had impregnated Min with nothing more than the tools at hand.

Hot tears ran from Min's eyes, tears that had been heating up for years. She gathered thin, one-ply tissues from the cardboard tissue box (even that a billboard for some fertility drug) and plastered them against her face, but the tears kept coming. A teacup of tears, like the crying doll she had played with as a child. She would fill the bulb of water in Weeping Wu Wu's head, and then squeeze it between her palms to make the doll weep. It had been a pleasing show of force at a time in her life when nothing was under her control. Now she squeezed her own face between her hands, and a teardrop plopped onto the waxed paper of the examination table. Her husband stood up, presumably to hug her, but she crossed her arms in front of her, hugging herself with all her might. He kissed the top of her head.

The men congratulated each other as if they were Ping-Pong partners and she was the winning ball slammed over the net. They had beaten the odds! They had won the competition!

Douglas's smile subsided, and his right hand covered his mouth, a signal to Min that he was wary of what he might say. From joy, he cycled back to skepticism. "Maybe the test has uncovered a hormone surge in her urine?"

"These are baby hormones," Dr. Fan said, his eyebrows high above his glasses. "Nun hormones are estrogen; the synthetic we had been administering was stilbestrol. What happened here is, despite blockages and scar tissue, acidity and low count, sperm got through. Once embryo starts developing, placenta secretes hormone—chorionic gonadotropin—that is present in urine."

Douglas dropped his hand.

Dr. Fan said, "Determined sperm somehow scaled the egg, like a climber on top of Everest. Your sperm must be very hearty."

Min appreciated Fan linking the fertilizing of her egg with scaling Mount Everest, even if it was propaganda. China's historical accounts begin around the third century B.C., with the first emperor, Qin Shi Huangdi, shooting out soldiers to overcome competing kingdoms, which proved fragile as eggs. Qin's workers built the Great Wall some seven meters thick and more than two thousand kilometers long, thus keeping nomads—those determined sperm with horses and axes—on the other side. Such were the tales of China's history. And yet, according to the artifacts Min studied, people reproduced the way crickets jump. Not a quest. Not a summit surmounted against all odds. Just life.

Perhaps men needed to speak like generals, for Fan had carried on like this before. How in normal circumstances, three hundred million sperm shoot out of a cannon into a wall of tissue. He'd said, "The impact alone disorients a goodly number," and he'd spoken of the Great March the sperm must make out of the narrow central passage, where more are lost along the blind curve to the cervical tunnel. That may be; however, she'd allowed herself to be turned inside out, like the woman on the poster, and painted with a map. Hadn't Fan dug a tunnel through her so that every one of Douglas's sperm could slide straight to her egg-filled womb?

All this she thought along with a thousand other thoughts. They might well be homeless because of Dr. Fan's services; jailed, even. Hormones had compromised her energy and mood for years now, and Douglas had suffered an insult to his manhood. She'd pinned her hopes on Dr. Fan for years. Getting pregnant without him angered her, as if he'd been a waste.

"Congratulations," Dr. Fan said yet again. He was fiddling with a thin plastic gadget, in which one flat circle rested on top of another. Dr. Fan spun the top disk around until he'd somehow aligned them. "The twenty-fifth of July is your due date, according to my calculations."

They'd been paying for this primitive level of calculations? Min wrapped her arms around herself again. The welcome news did not guarantee she would be cradling a son when the leaves began to brown. "When can you determine sex?" She searched for her husband's gaze, but the fluorescent lights reflecting off his thick glasses made his eyes unavailable.

Dr. Fan said, "This is a miracle like I've never seen. Because I had no hand in this pregnancy, I cannot be responsible for its sex."

Already he is making excuses, Min thought.

He said, "To detect mother carrying boy, you can rely on CVS at twelve weeks or amnio at sixteen. It is my hope that you can be thrilled with a sister or brother for your prized daughter." Taking a pen from a cup, he wrote on a pad of paper. Pen, cup, and paper were all emblazoned with the name of a drug Min had ingested. "Now we start you on vitamins—have you been taking vitamins?"

"Yes," Douglas answered for her.

Min stared at a speculum hanging on a hook like a can opener. She and Douglas had been in agreement since the beginning of this quest for a son, although they had not come this close before. If the baby was a girl, they would try some more. Hadn't they already shown their mettle? Whatever obstacle had plugged her womb had been cleared. There was a Virginia doctor she'd read about who had just figured out how to separate boy from girl embryos, though his success rate was not 100 percent.

Dr. Fan ripped pages from the pad. "More vitamins; two kinds to try. Unless there is a problem, which I do not expect, you should return for an exam in four weeks, when we will be able to detect a heartbeat." He was talking quickly and with little rising or falling tones, the way the docents did, trying to fit two thousand years of Chinese art into five minutes. "The receptionist will impart a prenatal schedule and the list of what to avoid."

They had only ever talked about getting pregnant. Now, Min wondered if Dr. Fan would tell her to avoid pineapple and open fire, to prevent miscarriages. Would he steer her away from glue, so the baby wouldn't have birthmarks? But he started with the American list, warning her not to handle cat litter and to stay away from secondhand smoke. "Raw meat and raw fish," he said, "have been off-limits to pregnant women for some time. As for cooked fish, I suggest you avoid fish caught late in life." That sounded Chinese until he explained that those fish, usually tuna or salmon, harbored a higher concentration of mercury. His exuberant grin looked slightly stupid, not like the expression of the intelligent, unsmiling man who'd been urging them on, and Min was relieved to see him go.

"Dr. Fan says we have performed a miracle." Douglas rested his hand on the shoulder of Min's paper gown, which puffed up a little as it absorbed his perspiration. "I imagine Sally would probably enjoy a sister or a brother."

Soon Min's very belly would puff up with the sperm she'd absorbed. Unless, unless, unless. She lingered in the state that Douglas had so precisely described, confused in her blood.

He said, "We have tried so much. I think it might not be wise to reject this, our only success."

She dressed silently, not acknowledging her husband's remarks. Conserving her movements, she attempted to get her gown off and her skirt on without jumping off the examination table to the floor. Now that a baby was in place, she intended to move slowly and smoothly through her routine. Douglas saw what she was doing and went along with it, sliding her shoes on for her and then helping her to ground level, where she had to pull her underwear and panty hose up to her waist.

Douglas reported to the billing office on the way out. "My wife will not require another procedure now, because she is pregnant already. Therefore, the advance she administered is unnecessary."

"Congratulations, Dr. Chen," she said genuinely. "However, the entire balance of your bill, with today's visit and pregnancy test, comes to $9,210."

Douglas cavalierly leaned on the window. "Then I shall ask you to remit $19,790, please."

On the empty scroll in her head, Min didn't know what to brush. *Boys care only for themselves; girls care for their mothers*—that was her first thought, because she'd been brainwashed to appease superstition. But this was happening in America, where you were permitted to voice your wishes. And so she rolled past her first impulse to unmarked territory and allowed herself to ink out her true feelings: *To bear a son is to see heaven*.

Off the Record

December 16, 1999

L eo came to the museum, and he stayed. Almost too readily, Amnesty International granted him an extended leave from the Urgent Action Desk to sit at Promise's desk in her old basement office. This was his second week, and so far, the lunches alone were worth changing jobs for. He took back everything he'd ever said against the lunches. As for life at home, Promise had finally confronted Althea, demanding the level of care they all knew she was capable of. In response, Althea quit. No more struggles, but no more babysitting either. Although there were openings in the after-school program, Felix's teacher expressed her strong opinion that six-year-olds should not be at school all day and Promise agreed, of course, because she was unavailable for child care. She acted as if Leo's new schedule was a lucky coincidence: Zemzemal had come up with enough salary for a thirty-hour week, and—bingo!—the kids needed their dad.

When he picked the kids up today, he was newly amazed at the school's army of women: moms, teachers, babysitters, even the principal. The attention he was afforded made him feel like he was stepping up to the plate. Halfway home he bought them candy, further ensuring his popularity; once Lydia finished her homework, they all tore into a round of upstairs-downstairs, a modified game of fetch invented to wear the puppy out. The kids were stationed in their bedrooms, armed with dog treats, and Leo was in front of the TV. When Flipper finally collapsed on his dog pillow, the kids huddled with Leo on the couch to finish watching a gulf war documentary. "It's dark out," Felix announced, looking beyond the rolling credits, and Leo had to scramble to get them to Arthur's opening only twenty minutes late. Fortunately, Lydia knew how to tie her own sari.

Promise had decided to let the opening go on as scheduled. "It's like a wedding," she'd said. "We'd have to pay for the whole thing if we canceled." She'd clapped her hands to her face, mashing her cheeks in despair. "Maybe it's more of a wake." Leo had comforted her, and as the museum's "strategic planning researcher," he'd praised her shrewd strategy for bringing the Asian art dignitaries together on one stage. They'd had to request beefed-up security, because more governmental types than usual were expected.

The children stayed close to Leo as he checked their coats and escorted them up to the Chinese galleries. They were initially cowed by the grandeur of the event, but Leo knew their shyness would soon wear off. The place was mobbed, the gallery as colorful as the guests. Admiring the spectacle allowed Leo to feel more a part of his own family. Shimmering silk draped the tables and the front staircase banisters, uncut bolts of cloth evoking lavish bazaars. Vases and bowls were filled with lotus blossoms and magnolias and peonies in every stage, so that limp brown petals drooped next to promising buds. And the assembled! Brocaded, embroidered, appliquéd, quilted, mirrored—elaborate, multinational apparel sidled up to tux or black dress, as visitors sampled dumplings from plain white plates. Leo had sampled those dumplings himself earlier, as well as the dipping sauces Nathan had cooked up. For presentation purposes, the chef had squirted flavors over the white platters in tribute to the porcelains on display: blueberry blue, parsley-and-coriander green, and the jeweled reds and yellows of roasted peppers. "All Fired Up!" indeed.

Leo recognized two congressmen and a former CIA director talking to the Indian ambassador, who made a point of waving to Leo across the mob. Talbot was clearly visible because of his height and shiny blond head. He had a ring of people around him, while Arthur attracted his own groupies. Separate from both curators was a cluster of Taiwanese men, their nationality revealed in their clip-on bow ties and rubber-soled shoes. They stood near a better-dressed Chinese entourage of either diplomats or collectors. Min darted between them like a runner stranded between bases. Leo sympathized with her divided loyalties as well as with the ethical cloud she'd come under. He was wrestling his own demons: He was not an agent of Amnesty International, the State Department, or the Castle, yet he was working on behalf of them all, whether they approved or not.

Leo couldn't help thinking how his ex-colleagues would scorn this spread. If this were an Amnesty event, petitions on clipboards would be circulating, sometimes at cross-purposes, and you'd be lucky to get one glass of bad wine. He used to believe that Amnesty's grim reality was more sincere than this frippery, and yet he'd come to feel protective of the precious world preserved within the museum's walls. What was the point of working for human rights unless someone somewhere was gathering to celebrate the beauty wrought by human hands?

That was certainly his wife's stance. Leo gave Promise credit for her devotion. He also counseled her against full disclosure of the Castle memo. The museum staff was already agonizing over Joseph; let them think the commercialization of the conference room was the extent of the Castle's interference. Because her training was in sixteenth-century texts, she read the Castle memo as a historical account of the museum's demise. His training was in the fickle ways of Washington and terrorists, so he read the situation differently. "We're out to mess with their heads," he'd told her. "If we hit our mark, the Castle will issue a new memo pledging its continued support."

Sensing that her family was near made Promise more comfortable, for she had a hard time spinning the world Leo's way without him. Their museum crusade seemed more counterintuitive than subversive to her. It was like the notion of clear-cutting timber in national parks to minimize forest fires or, for that matter, couples having babies to keep their marriages together.

A platform had been set up outside Gallery V at the western end of the northern corridor. Promise was standing on the makeshift stage, looking down the length of the corridor, when she realized that the pretty teenager following Leo was their nine-year-old daughter. Behind Lydia, Felix careened through the crowd like a drunk. There were very few children at the opening, and it occurred to Promise that they could have hired a babysitter. But then she would have missed seeing Lydia in her red sari, trimmed in golden strands that might have been harvested from her very own hairbrush. Promise could hardly believe she'd birthed such a vision. One of motherhood's marvels was that the wonder of this creation increased with each year.

Leo's wave caught her attention; she followed his line of sight to the Indian ambassador, who'd already volunteered to be of service. Noted. She was courting people the Castle would find hard to refuse, but these mini-dates required great balance. Talking about challenges ahead without actually saying "food court" was tricky and required as much skill as her guests offering to help with no guarantee of commitment.

While people tore through Nathan's cuisine, Promise found the dumplings unappealing. Lately she'd been craving strawberries and watermelon, hamburgers and potato salad—U.S.A.! U.S.A.! Sometimes she thought it was a consequence of getting pregnant on the Fourth of July.

"My dear," Senator Houlihan extended his liver-spotted hand, and she was tempted to grab on for dear life. The senator was on the Board of Regents, which was not why Promise knew him. Before her time, he'd been the U.S. ambassador to India, where his wife had become a specialist on Mughal gardens. They'd often dined at Joseph and Emmy's house. "Since we're alone," he said wryly, "I'll confess. I fought their proposal, but I was outgunned."

Up on the platform, Promise was at the senator's level. "Is it set in stone?" she asked.

"Nothing ever is in this town. I don't have to tell you how Washington works."

"Maybe you do."

"Change the dynamics, as they say, to make the status quo more venerable. Go get yourself the right guardians—too hot or holy for them."

His pink and white head practically glowed with his message, precisely the one Leo had been trying to project. She finally understood. In Oklahoma, going back on a decision was a show of weakness, a desperate attempt to save your hide; whereas Washington was unabashedly about hide saving. Equivocation demonstrated how reasonable you were; it proved you were listening to the people, representing their interest.

"You're a gem," Promise said to the senator, who was obviously surprised when the pregnant acting director gave his hand a big smooch.

Promise aimed toward Leo and the children, who were swimming through the jammed hallway to her. If the guests would all raise their arms, please, she could walk across the sea of palms to her family. Alas, she pushed her big belly along.

She thanked the directors of African Art and American History for coming—she hadn't attended their openings lately. "We have to stick together," African Art said. American History agreed. "Just be glad your museum's too new to be 'renovated,'" he said. "They've been 'renovating' American Art for six years. I heard rumors they were going to run out the budget and send the collection on the road." African Art said, "Rumor has it, you've got troubles of your own." Pretending not to have heard, Promise gave a smiling nod and merged into the next group over, where she paid her respects to the illustrious Agatha Morada, thus far the only member of the Advisory Committee she'd seen.

Leo was several clumps away, surrounded by people clamoring for the Joseph update. He didn't want to dwell on Joseph's chances of surviving captivity, and so he deflected attention to Lydia, who was not afraid of fawning adults. Felix had a dumpling in each claw; from the boy's once-white shirt, Leo could see he'd eaten something with peanut sauce and what looked to be raspberries.

"Should I put cases in my museum?" Lydia asked. "I've already got some labels." She was making a museum diorama for a school project on her future career.

"I'm all fired up!" Felix yelled, apparently thinking the exhibition's title was intended as the mood of the night. "Aren't you all fired up, Daddy?"

Leo let him bounce around. Along with guards, there were waiters and curators who by necessity were far more attentive. All the art was behind bulletproof glass—was bulletproof necessarily childproof?

Though Leo wanted to get to Promise, Senator Cooper alone at the bar provided a rare opportunity. They had often tussled over human rights. "Good evening, Senator. Leo Wells, formerly of Amnesty International. I've testified before your committee."

"Mr. Wells," the senator said, eyes on the bartender. "Ice water, please." He was still looking the bartender's way when he said, "I imagine you're working on Joseph Lattimore's behalf."

"Not at Amnesty," Leo said. "I'm monitoring that, but my wife, Promise Whittaker, is currently the acting director of this museum."

He thought he detected an involuntary flinch from the senator, whose relations to China might be complicated by the Castle's plans. Leo said, "I'm currently doing strategic planning for the museum."

Senator Cooper turned to face him. "Isn't that a conflict of interest?"

"No, sir. It's nepotism." They smiled at each other, tacitly acknowledging that the senator was married to his legislative affairs director, his third wife. Leo said, "The Castle is talking about making drastic changes to this museum. Are you familiar with any of them?"

The senator shrugged. "My colleagues rightfully accuse me of knowing more about defense than about basket-weaving."

Leo thought strident hawks like Cooper should want to keep the museum afloat—here were the prizes of our enemies' history—but he wasn't about to suggest that defense merge with basket-weaving. He said, "You spoke up when they tried to close the zoo annex out in Virginia. Your opposition carried a lot of weight."

The senator was practiced at deflecting requests. "We were relieved that was a success," he said, tipping his glass to Leo and turning on his heel.

"Merely doing my job," Leo said and then more loudly to his back, "Good to see you, sir."

Leo saw Talbot stop to shake the senator's hand, then clap him on the shoulder. In this case, Senator Cooper turned to watch Talbot walk away, master of the well-timed exit.

"Another admirer," Leo said.

"Just smoothing feathers," Talbot said with a measure of respect. Frankly, he envied Leo his dedication to a cause. On behalf of Promise and Joseph, and maybe the museum, the man would readily jump down a senator's throat.

"What have you got?" Leo asked.

"Senator Houlihan leveled with me about his losing efforts. China and Taiwan were actually mingling, thanks to Arthur, and Senator Kellogg has a Chinese companion who looks like she's World Bank. We're lousy with Hill types, which is unusual."

"Solidarity? Guilt?" Leo asked. "We need all the attention we can get—this place is dying on the vine. If they know the Castle plan, they're either here to help or they're hypocritical pigs."

"Could be a Joseph fest. In his memory, they eat our dumplings."

"A tribute, you think?" Leo took that under consideration. "I wonder how these guys would respond to Cecil wielding a sledgehammer rather than a memo."

"If Cecil could lift a sledgehammer," Talbot remarked.

"What if someone guillotined a bodhisattva or crippled one of your Tang dynasty horses? That's how it was at Amnesty, only worse, because the victims were people."

Talbot deftly slipped Leo's wineglass from out of his hand to a waiter's tray. "The glass is already empty," he said, then he took a full goblet for each of them.

Promise had been repeating her own version of the monk's lesson, "the bowl is already broken," as inspiration to preserve this bowl, this museum. To Talbot, Leo mocked their mission. "I'm no Buddhist," he said, "but the sound of one bowl breaking might turn some heads." Talbot's eyes widened at his impertinence.

Meanwhile, Miss Stranger, step-niece to the Founder, was fussing over Lydia. Her dress drooped with the weight of its beads, and her hair was flipped up on either side like the handles on a vase she was standing near. "You tied your own sari? Delightful. Have you been to India, my dear?"

"They have snakes there," Lydia said.

"Magnificent snakes. Thick as your arm." She looked at the child's slight wrists. "Well, thick as your father's. I tell you, I've never felt so regal as when Uncle took us to Agra. We were carried about in a palanquin, and the elephants all wore makeup and earrings. There was a boy hired to wave a fly whisk; no insect would so much as light upon us."

"The glories of colonial days," Leo remarked. He'd lost sight of Felix.

"Shameful, isn't it? The way Uncle stood out in his white linen suit, white felt hat, and white pigskin bucks, he may as well have been wearing a bridal gown. That's strictly off the record, of course."

Leo wondered if troubling subcontinent news reached Miss Stranger. At Amnesty, he'd responded to bride burning, Muslim baiting, rumors of nuclear testing, and girls sold to the circus.

Miss Stranger adjusted the ice-cube-sized emerald that rested at the base of her fleshy neck. "Poor, poor Joseph. Is there any word?"

"Not yet," Leo said just as Zemzemal and Morty converged on them from opposite sides.

"If you'll pardon us," Zemzemal said, escorting Miss Stranger from the pack.

"Is it something I said?" Morty asked. "Or is it your cummerbund?"

Leo opened his jacket. "That's a Hindi word—*kamarband*." He showed off his Gujarati waist wrap, studded with mirrors and clashing embroidery. "I only do formal on my own terms."

"You only do everything on your own terms," Morty complimented him. "Have you seen the object of Arthur's desire yet?"

"The bowl—sure. Don't forget, I work here now, too."

Morty mimed slapping his forehead. "I assumed that was just part of Arthur's conspiracy theories. He also told me Emmy might be here."

"Nearly true," Leo said. "Promise extended a special invitation, which she declined."

"I'll bet she's inconsolable."

Leo finished off his glass of wine. "Actually, she's eerily calm. They sold their house before the trip, and so she's living at a Buddhist convent out in Olney. She'll sign a letter I write, but she won't spearhead any lobbying or arm-twisting."

"Change your vocabulary, pal," Morty said. "Spearhead, arm-twisting—the woman's Buddhist." They both caught sight of Arthur taking a bow to a cluster of grandes dames. Morty said, "Tonight, his preparations were practically geishalike, what with the hair and that Thai silk tux. Why would you make a garment out of a fabric that is ruined by water?"

"To show you can," Leo answered. Promise and Arthur rarely brought them together because their commonest ground was derision of the museum and its cast. Pointing Talbot's way, Leo said, "For years, I've been told what a weasel that one is. I must say, I like his style."

"Not you too?" Morty moaned. "I have to listen to Arthur obsessing over his sexual orientation."

Leo said, "I assumed he was gay."

"Great news," Morty said. He scratched his beard, which was like a nest around his mouth.

Promise arrived and accepted a kiss from Leo.

"Congratulations." Morty pointed at her belly. "I haven't seen you lately."

"God knows what Arthur's been telling you," she said, a little rudely. Fortunately, Felix returned just then to suck up all the attention.

Promise snagged a cocktail napkin from a passing tray and swabbed her son's face.

The six-year-old quoted a Chinese proverb Promise had fed him to get him past his mashed potatoes: "You cannot fast for fear of choking." Food on Felix's face, shirt, and hands made him look like a pie-eating contestant. They should go to an opening every night around dinnertime. He stuck his tongue way out. "That's Tibetan for 'Hello,'" he said. "Sam taught me that."

"Remind me to fire Sam," Promise said.

"Then you stick your tongue out, Mom, so I know you're not a monster. Monsters can turn into Moms even, Sam says, except they can't hide their forked tongues."

"Leo, would you please be in charge?"

Leo laughed. "He's at home here. How much trouble could he get into?"

"About a billion dollars' worth. Honestly, I'm supposed to be in acting director mode." Better to pull rank than whack her husband over the head. She wasn't being particularly gentle with Felix, who said, "Stick your tongue out, Mommy."

"Not now, honey," Promise said. You might find out I'm a monster. "Leo!" she hissed, though she'd have preferred yelling: Get your shit together! We've got work to do here!

"Shouldn't you be in the limelight?" he asked.

"Yes!" Her voice was so high it was nearly inaudible. As Promise assessed how to return to the stage, Fatima, Zemzemal, and Miss Stranger joined their clump. In her shiny black chador, Fatima looked like the angel of death; Felix and Lydia wisely stayed the hell away from her.

"You want me to cut you a path?" Morty offered.

"Very much so," Promise confessed, and she linked her arm through his.

Fatima spoke to Leo through heavily painted lips. "Have you succeeded in contacting Joseph?"

"No, but I've been talking to Emmy." She had looked right through Leo with the narrow eyes of a cat. "When she feels stronger, I imagine she'll join the fight."

"Emmy is not really a fighter." Fatima was the second to drive home that point.

Leo proudly watched the crowd defer to his waddling wife. At the periphery of the elevated platform, a muscular black woman crawled on her belly like a Navy SEAL, fitting plugs into floor outlets. When she stood, she telescoped two poles of lights up a dozen feet, and the mob blinked back the brightness. Promise introduced herself and gave the floor over to Arthur, who faked faking modesty. In the lights, his tux had a pearly luster that made it look about five shades of black. His hair shone, and his bright teeth were movie-star straight.

Arthur thanked them one and all before going technical, as in "The porcelain masterpieces in 'All Fired Up!' were all fashioned in Jingdezhen, home of the purest white clay in the world. In the eleventh century, Emperor Jingde had artisans stamp their porcelains with his reign mark. Five hundred years later, Jingdezhen factories were producing one hundred thousand pieces each year for the court, where a single place setting required twenty-seven pieces of porcelain . . ."

Leo couldn't help but wonder why all these people had come. Was it a show of support or the chance to get dressed up? Free food? Did they really love ceramics this much?

". . . during the Yongzheng reign in the early eighteenth century, potters saw their bright white porcelains as blank canvases to paint and glaze and incise. While experimenting with new pigments, they discovered how to fire a piece more than once at different temperatures. This technique blew their color combinations wide open and inspired the title of my exhibition."

Everyone at the museum had done a laudable job, but Leo frankly doubted that an elegant opening and a strong exhibition would make any difference to those bent on a food court. He'd learned at Amnesty to tackle injustice one person at a time. People shook their heads in disgust and helplessness at reports of inhumane treatment far away; what moved those people to action was hearing individual horror stories. One devoted nun raped and shot in Guatemala; two Egyptian women stoned; a Burmese writer shot and his infant son burned.

Arthur was going on about the extremely humane treatment he'd like to give the ambassador's bowl, if only the people of the world would give him enough cash. He offered the juicy story of its provenance as a special gift to those at the opening.

Leo imagined someone elbowing the vitrine as a besotted Arthur looked helplessly on. That would get everyone's attention. He hypocritically applauded through the thank-yous and further introductions, that great circle jerk of art-world fanfare. Though he'd come to admire, he was getting more cynical by the minute. When Felix tugged on his pant leg, Leo obligingly lifted his son onto his shoulders. The ensuing head rush, after several glasses of wine, made him concentrate on his balance—as people clapped and cameras flashed like fireflies, the man with the boy on his back was sorting things out. He knew it wasn't appropriate for Arthur to ridicule the emperor's obscene wealth or Thomas Jefferson's need to sell off this bowl so he could keep his plantation in slaves. Or mistresses. Felix had been leaning on Leo's scalp; when the boy tipped back to clap for his mother, Leo had to hold on to his legs, so he whistled for his wife as she returned to center stage. Although she was elevated, people stretched their necks like geese to see her.

"Every joy we share these days," she was saying, "is mitigated by our concern for Joseph Lattimore, whose absence is a hole in our hearts. I am relieved to be able to tell you that his wife, Emmy, is safe and well in the care of a Buddhist community."

Those fucking Buddhists, Leo thought. What are we if not the sum of our attachments? He would go to hell and back to retrieve his wife, that miniature scholar of miniatures. This was the reason he shouldn't drink, he thought, because alcohol made him maudlin.

"Arthur Franklin has organized a magnificent display of porcelain from a region where artists have been making ceramics for two thousand years. This exhibition is uniquely at home here in the Museum of Asian Art, which was built to house the prime examples of Asia's artistic production. Our permanent collection includes ceramics spanning *seven thousand* years. Long before Thomas Jefferson—before *reading* and *writing*—Asian artists were carving jades and gilding silver vessels on display in other galleries of this museum. Don't forget, Asia is home to half the planet's population, and the art of that continent is a vast helping of the world's creative harvest."

The crowd concentrated on Promise, who was determined to fix the museum's importance in their individual cosmos. "As part of the National Institution of Science and Art, this Museum of Asian Art allows us to celebrate some of the earliest expressions of beauty and to follow that continuum to the present. And the best part is, everyone is welcome to enjoy the exhibitions and programs we stage. This is your museum, and if it means as much to you as it does to us, we need you to help spread the word. Tell your friends, tell your family, tell your congressmen that the Museum of Asian Art would love to see them."

Leo's grin was a beacon that reached Promise on her perch. She looked upon a friendly child-man divinity, Felix's clothes stained bright, Leo's mane a pillow for the boy's head. Now they were clapping for her with all four of their hands. Leo extended an arm to Lydia, and Promise half expected him to lift their daughter to the top of the human tower. Maybe they could become a family of acrobats: Watch the juggling mother toss and catch! See the human tower grow to astonishing heights as family members are stacked one on top of the other! This was the language her heart spoke while her mouth said, "I thank each and every one of you for coming. Enjoy the evening."

———————

The revelers stayed after the food was gone, the sign of a successful opening. Promise had never worked so hard in her life. Except for going to the bathroom, she'd been standing for three hours. She'd forgotten to wear her maternity support hose, and Edgar was weighing her down so much she felt she could practically dribble him along in front of her with her feet. Why didn't they make helium-filled maternity underwear or get going on antigravity boots? Just when she thought she might have to get down on the floor, Talbot materialized with a seat.

"Bless you," she said, wondering where he'd gotten the folding chair, let alone how long he'd been toting it around. Her dress was long enough that she could open her legs and let Edgar share the seat.

"I'm glad I found you," he said. "Just before the opening, Zemzemal got permission to apply my exhibition funds to the bowl for the time being."

She looked to either side, but of course, Talbot had already made sure the coast was clear. "How could that be legal?" she asked.

Talbot shrugged. "He told me he got the go-ahead."

Talbot's exhibition funds belonged to the museum, so why did his offer seem so selfless? Considering their balkanized world and Talbot's personality, his teamwork caught her by surprise. She also realized she'd come to desire that little magpie bowl as much as Arthur did. In the worst-case scenario, they'd acquire the ceramic just to hand it over to the National Gallery; however, she saw it as symbolic of the best-case scenario. Promise wiped a tear away.

Talbot knelt next to her chair. "Take it easy," he said, showing a concern that made her even more emotional. His expression was masked by his hair, which he pushed back to reveal his narrowed teasing grin. "It's just a bowl."

As soon as Talbot stood up, straightening those impossibly long legs, the crowd swelled again, bearing him away from her.

In fact, he was swept into an isolated tide pool with Arthur's partner. "Drink?" Talbot asked.

"No, thank you," Morty said. "I'm off the stuff." His paranoia ran through the likelihood that Talbot was taunting him or that Arthur wasn't so proud of his recovery as to mention it. Morty said, "I hear you're collecting military woodblocks these days."

"Arthur talks about my work?" Talbot practically batted his eyes. "Where is the man of the hour?"

"Good question."

Talbot said, "You know, the Japanese will never tell you no, even when that's what they mean. If that doesn't do me in, their humility act will."

Morty imagined Talbot was hard to say no to. "Listen, I just read this article about Japanese basket makers who've reached the pinnacles of their careers. They're all a hundred years old and national treasures, but they don't retire, per se, because that would be presumptuous. Did you see the article?"

Talbot gave him a nod that was neither yes nor no.

"Well, they say they're working on 'the basket that can never be finished.' Basically, to weave the next step, it's necessary to open up and undo the last one." He felt like Scheherazade, weaving a tale to keep Talbot at bay. "Potential customers are told, 'As soon as I finish this basket I will attend to you.' This allows them to turn down another fishing creel while perfecting their technique for the rest of their lives. Each time they unwind the old, they continually remake it with new skills. That way, their mistakes are not there to torment them in the form of inferior work."

"Interesting." Talbot was looking out over his head. "I don't do crafts. Will you excuse me?"

"Of course," Morty said. He'd given it his best shot; now he stood alone, his shoulder against the plate glass of the courtyard. He had a knack for viewing a scene from two vantage points. Whereas some people use one eye for distance and the other for close reading, he was able to see both the trees and the forest. He could see Talbot's head sailing through the ocean, as well as the sunburst cuff links that Cecil wore, flashing in the light as the Secretary ducked away from museum types. Likewise, snippets of conversation reached him from near and far: "National Gallery won't know what to do with this collection.". . ."Fast food, if you can believe it. Falafels where we're standing.". . ."Poor Joseph? Poor Promise." He saw Leo stalking the former head of the CIA, and he saw the reddening bulb of the ambassador's nose, one elbow bender recognizing another. He knew from experience that the ambassador was lit up as much by Arthur's flattery as by liquor. Arthur's adulation mixed best with alcohol, he'd found after going sober.

Morty saw all this; he also spotted the opposing cameras mounted on the ceiling and aimed at the reception area. He thought about how fast-forwarding through the security tapes would show a time-elapsed version of human traffic. Would he be the only person interested in that? One could see shifting clumps of people behaving like cultured amoebas. Stuck in a circumscribed space, folks ganged up, divided, split, and regrouped, sometimes accepting a straggler or a couple and sometimes refusing to let them in.

The curator of Near Eastern art interrupted his reverie. "Morty, right? I'm Jill Ratner. I read the *Post* profile on you. You make the Department of Transportation seem glamorous."

"You're just saying that because I talked about Persepolis."

"Maybe," she concurred. "Have you ever been there?"

"Regrettably, I've only seen pictures."

She shook her head in commiseration. "It's a must-see for anyone keen on road-building."

Morty wondered if that sentence had ever been uttered before.

"We're talking 550 B.C.," she said. "The artisans in Persepolis wrote these cuneiform memos expounding on the features of a kingly road. Any path intended for royal travel should be 'majestic and imposing' and possessed of 'radiant splendor.'" She blushed a blotchy blush as she quoted their elevated language.

"Don't get embarrassed," he said. "That's what's missing from today's federal projects."

"I'm not getting embarrassed. I'm getting drunk. All day long, it's China this and India or Japan that. Let's hear it for the Cradle of Civilization!"

He raised his ginger ale on high. "On this California road I designed, we planted a eucalyptus grove in a steep bend that had spooked drivers. Got that off a Mesopotamian road crew."

Jill said, "I thought Arthur was the visionary. What a team you guys are."

Morty stared at Jill's cheek moles and bit the inside of his cheek. Then he said, "I don't think I've had enough to drink. Will you excuse me?"

Head down, Morty practically butted into Arthur, who was holding two glasses of champagne. "Toast me," he bubbled over.

You're already toasted, Morty thought, but he took the glass. "To you," he said. "To you and you and you."

Arthur clanked glasses with him. "You're going to have to do better than that. Do you know what just happened? We came up with enough money to buy the ambassador's bowl." Having already drained his glass, he traded his empty flute for Morty's full one. "Talbot said he'd asked Zemzemal if he could divert some of his 'Japanese Port' budget to cover the purchase. He just got the nod."

Morty said, "Maybe we should be toasting Talbot."

"To Talbot," Arthur obliged, then he did a swanky little dance step. "Tonight, I'm going to party like it's 1999." He took full notice of Morty. "What's wrong?"

Visionary that he was, Morty came up with something. "Unfortunately, there's a markup tomorrow in the Senate. I should probably be getting back to the office tonight."

Arthur reared up like a circus horse. "You're going to work? Burst my bubble, why don't you?" He gave Morty back another empty champagne glass, as if Morty were his maid.

A silver-trayed waiter off-loaded the flutes from Morty, who gave Arthur's shoulder a squeeze. "Congratulations on a beautiful show. I'll see you at home."

What could he say—he wasn't good at sharing. He'd always been that way, back when the rest of their tribe could be with two strangers a night. Eventually, his monogamous past made him a rather hot property, like a virgin in a whorehouse. For Morty, abstinence harbored its own kind of desire. He wanted one person whole, up one side and down the other, all to himself.

Near the central staircase, Morty saw the blessed bowl, internally spotlit, in its low-glare German glass vitrine. There was the asymmetry Arthur talked about. Without squatting low enough so the rim was eye level, he saw how someone approaching a white bowl would be surprised by the polychrome interior decoration. He didn't want to linger, but he did take the time to see where the painting didn't quite register with the incising, a trait that bewitched his lover. It couldn't be carelessness, but why would the artists care to do that? This was his first glimpse of the actual object, which was certainly more luminous than its transparency. For this, Morty realized, Arthur would do just about anyone, and masterpiece or not, Morty was sorely tempted to give the chosen vessel a great heave-ho over the banister.

———

Arthur was king, Morty had left, and Talbot was by his side, practically leaning on him. Ain't life funny? As recently as two months ago, Arthur would have gone on record as loathing Talbot Perry, despite the fact that he was both powerful and cute. Being passed over for acting director had put them on a more equal footing, except for Arthur's Promise advantage. And now Talbot had volunteered his exhibition funds so that Arthur might buy his current favorite bowl in the world.

Arthur must have given twenty tours of "All Fired Up!" To talk endlessly about porcelains took him to an ecstatic state that reminded him of Promise's whirling dervishes, or the eighties club scene. The museum had never looked more beautiful to him, and Arthur wished they could keep the silk wrappings and over-the-top flowers all exhibition long. People reluctantly filed out of the galleries, guards gently shooing them along.

"I think I had one dumpling," Arthur said regretfully.

"There's a new bar in Chinatown," Talbot proposed. "Their signature drink is a sake martini."

"Why not?" Arthur agreed. He thought it would be entertaining to see Talbot off duty.

Arthur appreciated how easy Talbot's long arms made hailing a cab, and he enjoyed ducking into the backseat knowing Fatima was still standing on Independence Avenue. "Good night," he called out, rubbing it in. The cabbie made a U-turn and headed to Chinatown, just a few blocks away.

Talbot ordered them drinks but kept telling the waiter they needed time to decide on food. Arthur didn't need time—he would have eaten the menu given half a chance. He missed Morty's sober company then, and when Talbot told of Japanese basket weavers who tear out and redo their work rather than take on boring commissions, his thoughts returned to Morty, who loved paradoxes like that. "You'd better feed me," Arthur said drunkenly. He was out of practice.

Talbot remembered he had a porterhouse in his refrigerator.

"That would be the refrigerator at your home?" Arthur asked.

"My hovel," Talbot answered. "My Venus flytrap."

What the hell did that mean? Talbot's hovel turned out to be in Market Square, just a skip and a jump from Chinatown. The entry hall of his condominium led into a large living room, where an enormous Italian leather couch faced a floor-to-ceiling window looking out on the Old Post Office. Near the couch was a gray felt chair and a low-slung coffee table set with a vase that held a single stalk of bamboo. Such austerity might have been evidence that Talbot had just moved in. However, the apartment was free of cardboard boxes, and Japanese prints were well hung on the high white walls. Across the living room, a long metal stairway like a fire escape led presumably to the bedroom. Arthur couldn't decide if Talbot's ascetic look was stylish or noncommittal. Once seated, Arthur never left the couch for the remainder of the evening except to take a leak.

As to the porterhouse in the refrigerator, that must have been an expression, because they ended up having food delivered. It was more like hotel room service than getting takeout, the dinner Talbot ordered of New York strip steaks and mashed potatoes, Merlot and Scotch. After eating so many of Morty's rapini and fish dinners, fiber-rich lentils alongside grilled slices of eggplant, Arthur perversely enjoyed cutting into the thick sirloin, which had been generously salted and finished with a scoop of sage butter, distinct from the garlic butter puddling in the mashed potatoes. It wasn't so different from lunch, really, making him wonder if Nathan and Talbot had ever gotten together. Arthur pushed Nathan out of his thoughts, then he did the heavy lifting and pushed Morty over. Seven years together and Morty couldn't handle an opening—fuck him.

The rich meal and bottles of wine loosened not only ties but also tongues, which led to a sloppy bout of kissing. Rare beef and roasted garlic made for some strong flavors between the two of them. Even as he hardened up, Arthur was just disembodied enough to be thinking, So this is the way he goes. He wondered if Talbot knew how the staff obsessed about his orientation. For Arthur, it was a turn-on to be unlocking one of the great mysteries of the workday. There was pleasure too in being desired by someone he had disliked. Some twist of power to be the adored—I didn't even fancy you, so work against that! Win me over. Let's see what you can do for me. Of course, Talbot had already done more than Arthur could have hoped: he'd made the bowl buying possible and Arthur lusty with thanks.

But if Arthur was prepared to stop talking, Talbot wasn't. "I never trust the Chinese," he said. "They pretend they don't speak English, but the ones I meet—curators and those Taiwanese collectors, you know the type—they understand every word you say. And they always manage to get what they want, am I right?"

Arthur's jacket and shirt were off at this point, tuxedo studs tossed on the coffee table like spent bullets. Talbot had stopped licking his nipple, for God's sake, to make his pronouncement. Were they now going to have a discussion of ethnic stereotypes? Arthur's own opinion was that there was a craftiness the Chinese showed; Lord knows, he'd often accused them of misunderstanding to their own advantage. But he'd said that only to Morty. It was Arthur's experience that those remarks always come back to bite you on the ass, so he took a different tack.

"Your precious woodblocks," he teased Talbot. "You know how those first showed up in America, don't you? The Japanese used to wrap them around Chinese ceramics they exported. Your prints are the nineteenth-century equivalent of packing peanuts."

"Peanuts that are now worth more than the ceramics." Talbot kissed him full-court press and that was the end of that particular discussion. Arthur never even got his cummerbund unhooked from around his waist.

The next morning, Morty was counting on one hand the number of times Arthur had gone out tomcatting in their seven years together. Technically, Arthur hadn't been out all night, but it seemed even more despicable to Morty that he'd returned to their flannel sheets, balling his Thai silk tux up at the foot of the bed.

When his partner finally came to breakfast, Morty apologized first. "I'm sorry I ducked out of your opening. We should have celebrated." He'd practiced it aloud, and it sounded overrehearsed. Arthur neither accepted the apology nor reciprocated. Morty had rolled a napkin into a ring, unwrapped sweet butter onto a china plate, and found the pumpkin spread they'd bought from the Inn at Little Washington.

"Water and toast for me," Arthur said.

His right cheek was raw with whisker burn. Looking into Arthur's road map eyes, Morty said, "I can't wait to see the reviews."

"'Elegant and refined'—I could write their pieces with my left hand."

"You're left-handed," Morty said.

"That's sort of my point. They probably think they could curate, too. But I'll tell you what they couldn't do." Arthur was in high prince mode, working hard not to sound ashamed of himself. He'd already decided that Morty was as guilty as he was, which Morty had confirmed by apologizing. Grandly, he pushed butter and pumpkin spread away. "I was nudging the ambassador ever closer to the precipice, and then when Talbot suggested a donation ceremony, he leapt off the cliff. Promise agreed to it—we're on for the seventh."

"But it's already installed. What's to change?"

"Not much," Arthur admitted. "'Loan of' becomes 'Partial gift of.' They'll lift the vitrine off, and Talbot suggested the ambassador might want to say a few words. I told him about that bat jar we saw in New York; now, that would be something to have."

"You're insatiable," Morty said, resigned. He wanted to blurt out, "I heard the collection was heading to the National Gallery. I heard the museum might be sectioned off into restaurants." With the calm veneer of one prepared to walk away, he asked, "Where'd you go after the opening?"

"Here and there," Arthur said. He didn't want to ruin Morty's affable mood. He hadn't felt this comfortable with his partner in months.

"Here's something you'll appreciate," Arthur said. "Apparently, Japanese basket makers at the end of their lives start in on a basket where each step is going back to rip out and redo the last step. They tell people who want to commission the usual stuff, 'As soon as I'm done with the basket that can't be finished, I'll get to yours.' This is retirement for them. But they're working, see, and they're perfecting their technique. Also, they don't have to look at their mistakes."

Couldn't he smell Morty all over that idea? Talbot had not even bothered to roll in shit, to brush the tracks away with a dead tree branch. That asshole was making fun of both Arthur and Morty without Arthur even knowing it. Talbot had buggered his boyfriend, wooing him with his future ex's own cleverness.

Arthur kissed the tips of his sticky fingers and touched them to Morty's face of fur. "I'm not certain it's true," he said. "But don't you think it's clever?"

No Vaccine

December 16, 1999

We were ambushed by hostile tribesmen. They fell upon us and shot our esteemed leader in the stomach.

Was that what his bandages were from? Stomach, hand, head, Joseph was wrapped in coarse linen or cotton stiffened by his own secretions. As if he were in eastern Egypt or southern Mississippi, some steamy delta land, except that he was beginning to recognize the feel of altitude-thinned air, its dryness irritating the lining of his nose. (Was he bound in hemp? The nomad's fiber, they called it; Asians harvested it before pollination to attain a smoother texture, though this felt like sandpaper on a sunburn. Apart from the bloodstains, the material looked like the shirts Emmy wore.) Maybe he was desiccated from death, in which case he was in some half-assed embalming outfit. Death would explain the stench. But then he wouldn't be thinking, would he, having had his brains extruded through his nose. Blow your brains out—for a moment he thought he'd stumbled upon the origin of that phrase. But "blow your brains out" was from guns, wasn't it? Guns triggered associations with hostile tribesmen—he was reasonably sure he'd met with some. Had they shot him in the head and stomach?

Really, he did not seem suited to retirement, for he was always waking up thinking himself dead. To go from no thoughts to such a torrent spooked him. His whiskery cheeks felt like a stranger's face, and his tongue worried a prominent hole where a tooth had been.

Three years our expedition struggled through the Taklamakan Desert and the Kunlun Mountains. We happened upon artifacts along the way or they were awarded us—a few we bought for paltry sums. Later I would have to answer to charges that we provoked the red lamas, which mortified me anew. The Khamba nomads attacked us, shooting de Rhins and trampling our field notes and instruments of measurement beneath the feet of their wild horses. Once they dispersed, I fashioned a litter for de Rhins's wounded body, but the savages returned to drag the boat of sticks away and throw him into the river to drown.

This wasn't about him, was it? He hadn't died or been thrown in a river, though he might have been dragged, or drugged. Whose narrative was this in his head if not his?

Joseph could picture the antiquated binding of a memoir, an explorer's account through Central Asia. Was it Burton's report? Aurel Stein's? No, it was someone who came between, and it had been translated from the French. He was working on the author's name, even as he remembered that there was a Kharosthi link and one to the Rolling Stones. *Wild horses couldn't drag me away.* That refrain came up first, then the memory of reading Fernand Grenard's memoirs coincidental to listening to the Stones, a truly private joke.

Grenard and Dutreuil de Rhins had been sent by the French government to map western China and Tibet; they'd been searching for the source of the Mekong River when de Rhins was killed. Somewhere along the way, they'd acquired a Kharosthi manuscript that had survived their expedition. Very well, Joseph thought, wondering between what folds of gray matter his own tale was tucked.

How like the large intestine was a brain, yards of undigested matter snaked about and stuffed in the skull. That had been the opinion of Emmy's yoga teacher, who'd placed a premium on colonic health. After enjoying a chlorophyll cocktail in her studio, the room scattered with marigold petals and burning cones of sandalwood, she would have the group take a cleansing breath and then massage their internal organs with a deep side stretch. He imagined pressing his nose into the base of Emmy's scalp, smelling the moldy incense and her castile soap.

Unfortunately, a deep inhalation brought with it the smells of his own shit, animals, and rancid cooking grease. The circumstances of his descent began coming to him across a vast distance, just as he had seen the riders unflinchingly crossing the dunes. *No one gallops in the desert,* he'd thought at the time, and even when he'd registered their determined anonymity and their weapons, what had seemed oddest was their rush. They'd been in a great hurry, and he was in the way of their target. Unless *he* was their target. Was it too egotistical to assume they'd been looking for him? You don't just run across someone in the Taklamakan Desert. They knew who he was. More likely, they decided by looking at him that he was their enemy; before introductions, before even threats, one of them had raised a rifle to his American face.

Wick away sweat with a space-age material durable as steel, breathable as cotton, and cover it all up with a boot made famous in the Great War, when troops were as likely to cross sand as swamp. You can't beat our Desert Fox boots, especially with a lifetime guarantee against any sort of wear!

Gone were his rubberized leather boots as well as his socks of polypropylene glycol (or was that the sunscreen composition?). His travel vest had been ripped of its storage capacity so that only the stitched outlines of pockets remained. The name of each well-chosen accessory floated up in his head, like a bobber on a fishing line, and it was Extreme Outfitter and Off the Trail catalog copy that led him back—hand over hand along a fishing line of associations—to his circumstances. He inched his leg over the edge of his straw mat and struck his bare heel against the dirt-brown floor. It was dirt. How was that for the king of primary sources? The entrance of the yurt had a makeshift gate of crosshatched bamboo, a clue that he was not free to leave.

At this time Multafit Khan was assigned to attack the town of Dharur and its market area. He and his comrades went to the edge of the ditch and fired musket shots to clear out the people of the town who had taken their possessions and families into the ditch to be clear of the cannons and gunfire. Then they entered the ditch nimbly and began to plunder and take prisoners.

He had no idea where he was or what had occurred after he'd taken a blow to the head; however, he could recall passages from the sixteenth-century *Padshahnama* album. Details of the accompanying illustration came to him, inch-tall warriors scaling the fort's outer wall on a ladder whose wood grain was detectable. That was the concentration he'd given Mughal battles at the expense of the splinter culture holding him hostage. His right hand throbbed, stretching the skin with each pulse. Would that he lived to face an audience in the plush seats of the museum auditorium, he would bear his testimony: Art is no vaccine against danger.

He remembered the onset of darkness and the cool of him pissing on himself, which at the time was evidence of his raging fever. Spare Emmy! had been his last coherent thought, he now remembered, though a fat lot of help that had been to her.

Gingerly Joseph rolled to his right side, then pushed down with his unwrapped hand. Now his jaw ached as well. Slowly he raised himself to his elbow. There was another person in the darkened yurt with him. Across the earthen-floor room, a Japanese man slept openmouthed on a straw mat, his regular breathing at odds with his broken teeth and S-shaped nose, both swollen and flat. Joseph's nose had held its own against the butt of a rifle—did it require more force or less to break a recessed Japanese nose than an American beak?

Joseph unspooled his head using one hand, orbiting only his arm around his motionless face, neck, and torso. Breathing was painful enough. In the dim light he could not judge the age of the bloodstains on his dressings. He suspended disbelief as he felt himself up, expecting ooze or scab until he realized that what he touched at his hairline were sutures, neat X's in a long row. Emergency room runs with the boys had taught him that children's stitches last a week. How long did adults take to heal up a head wound? The thought sent a shiver through him, which in turn brought a cough. That single short exhalation stabbed so sharply he felt they'd bound a blade into his side. Then he knew that his midsection was wrapped because at least one rib was broken. Through the wrapping, he felt his ribs with alarming individuation.

His pant legs were slashed open. The fabric parted to reveal a horrific bruise up his right leg. Although his left thigh was wrapped in gauze, that was one of the few places on his body that did not throb. Touching it didn't hurt either. The dirty blue bandage was actually slip-stitched closed, the end neatly tucked under. He stroked the underside of his thigh, trying to determine what had been dressed, and he felt beneath the bandage a pliable rectangle covering the spot where he had an amoeba-shaped mole, which Emmy had monitored for changes. The rectangle was around credit-card size and possibly that thin. Had they assumed his mole was some lesion that might infect them? Because it did not cause him pain, he let it be.

"You have fought bravely," Rama said, "and it is too bad that I must kill you. But right now you are wearied from combat, and it would not be just for us to fight. Go home, salve your wounds, and get a good night's sleep. Tomorrow, once you are fit and well rested, come back for your death."

Had he been given a death sentence instead of death? He'd had many nights' sleep, but he wouldn't have described himself as well-rested. Joseph looked over at the pummeled face of his yurt mate, his black thatched hair gone spiky with grease. Either startled by a bad dream or possessed of the freakish awareness that someone was staring, the sleeper opened his eyes. Each man stared into the other's face, each grateful not to have the other's wounds.

The falling away of the blanket revealed bodybuilder arms bursting from a ragged T-shirt. "Richland Stateside University," Joseph read; he recognized the name as a Japanese invention of American college wear. With those arms and that rippling build, he must have been a tougher capture than Joseph. The accusatory look in his black eyes was familiar. "Kanraku!" Joseph exclaimed, recognizing the documentary maker.

"You know me," the man replied, skepticism draining from his eyes like tears. Perhaps they were tears from the relief at being called by name. He wiped his misshapen nose on his shirt. "You know you?"

You yourself are the ultimate reality, but you are not what you seem.

Kanraku's question threw him back to the Upanishads. Here he was, R. Joseph Lattimore—scholar of Indian art and architecture; cataloger of civilizations that could no longer speak for themselves; past director of the Museum of Asian Art; author of enough books and articles to be himself considered the Source. How he'd gotten here, where his wife was (whether she was even alive), he did not know. But he knew his Upanishads, his *Ramayana,* his *Padshahnama,* not to mention Grenard's Central Asian memoirs and catalogs of camping gear. In the midst of raw experience, he could only conjure up other people's words, other people's battles.

You know you? Kanraku had asked him.

"I know my name," he answered, treating himself with the utmost diplomacy.

"You were digging as I filmed," Kanraku said. "When the men on horses came in, they struck you first and brought you to the main encampment tied like a hog, arms and legs to a pole. They divided up everything into three: men, women, and equipment. All the equipment and some men they took. Women and other men went with two guides."

"Was Emmy with them—could you see? Was she hurt?" Every pounding heartbeat agitated his injured ribs.

"She was not hurt." Kanraku didn't really want to tell him about Emmy. "She was with the women and guides; they went to Hotan, I think. We headed south, then west over mountains."

Joseph recognized the rugs on the yurt as tribal weavings in red, black, and off-white. Camel hair and wool, with all the funk that accompanied camels and sheep. "I didn't fight," he said. "Why am I so beat up?"

"In camp, every protest from the crew prompted them to hit you. Your hair bled, you woke up to scream—people moved fast to cooperate." He smiled to show broken teeth. "I'm afraid I might be the cause of your ribs. They only had six men; we had eight."

"I hope you aren't counting me among your troops. I've been nothing but deadweight. I only remember looking at the butt of an AK-47. Have you any idea what the date is?"

Kanraku consulted his nonexistent watch. "Sixteenth or seventeenth of December. Still plenty of time to plan New Year's Eve party. What shall we do for the dawn of a new millennium?"

The dawn of a new millennium was just another day in this troubled land, which had been keeping a calendar as long as it had been keeping a grudge. Joseph had written a different script for New Year's 2000. He and Emmy sailing on the Bosporus, champagne white-capping in their flutes. *We'll take a cup of kindness yet, for Auld Lang Syne.*

"Emmy must have been terrified," he said. "You're not just talking about the women—you actually saw Emmy?"

"Tall American older lady, Buddhist heavy-duty." Kanraku humored him, though of course he knew Emmy. Only Joseph didn't know everyone. "She went into the largest tent."

Until she'd separated herself from the pack. Once the head cracking had subsided—once the chosen had been gagged with leather belts, their arms pulled behind their backs and tethered with a twine that cut into skin—Kanraku had seen Emmy come out of the tent. Through the slits in his swollen eyelids, he watched her tote the first-aid tackle box up to the man with the grenades hanging on his belt. Kanraku recalled how she'd bowed before him, offering the open tin of bandages and salves. Her actions were fearless but also frightening. She showed the grenade bearer a pill, then beat her palm against her heart. Walking up to the American scientist, she simply unfastened his leather gag and fed him the pill. The eyes showing between the grenade bearer's mask and hat disbelieved what they saw. Emmy held up the pill bottle as if to ask, who will be responsible for giving this man his medication? There was no urgency or pleading in her manner; she just held the bottle like a torch. Leading with his machete, the grenade bearer walked his long boots over and sliced the tethers of the scientist, who was released to the safe tent. She'd saved his life by suggesting he was higher maintenance than they were prepared for. Now there were six captors, six captives.

She set to work on the entire group, swabbing wounds with no distinction between friend or enemy. They lined up like children outside the nurse's office: terrorist, horseman, scholar, filmmaker, and so on. One proffered his gashed shoulder, another pointed to a dislocated finger, which she yanked back into place with a pop. Beneath Kanraku's eye socket, she arranged three butterfly bandages in an arc to pull his split skin together.

Joseph, who could not join the lineup, was understood to be last.

Emmy emptied out her shallow tin and refilled it with canteen water when his time came. All were silent as she washed him, clipped his hair close, scraped a path relatively clean with a razor blade, then threaded a needle with dental floss. Sitting among pieces of his shorn hair, she lit a match and held the needle in its flame. Joseph did not awaken even as she sewed his gashed head closed. Kanraku was five feet away, so he could see the tremor in her hands. It was possible that his vision was shaky or that he was shivering, such was the pain from his shattered nose, an injury beyond her care. He kept his lips clamped shut, lest any air hit the exposed nerves of his broken front teeth.

She pulled the thread through the skin at Joseph's skull as if she were hemming pants. Her lips were moving in what Kanraku assumed to be prayer. The man with the grenades said something to her; in response, she pointed to Joseph's cut. "You did this," she said in English. Kanraku expected the man to hit her, but it was as if she'd stopped time to minister to all of them. Having finished her sewing, she slipped off her long gauzy tunic. Kanraku could see each vertebra along her back, even through her white sports bra. She cut into the gauze, then she laid down the scissors, picked up the garment in both hands, and expertly ripped a long peel of bandage from the shirt off her back. When she spread her arms wide, Kanraku saw that her breasts were lopsided and that she was scarred under her right arm. Though she did not flinch from their collective gaze, she fumbled to get her now-shortened shirt back on.

Emmy wound the bandages around Joseph's head, ribs, and thigh. She swaddled him in her very shirt. Everyone somehow understood that when she was done with Joseph, they'd be separated, and she took an unusually long time. She went so far as to stitch the bandage around his thigh. Even Kanraku grew impatient, so anxious was he about what was coming next. Finally, she ran out of things to do. She methodically replaced scissors, sponge, and unused bandages in the tackle box compartments, scooping up a lock of his hair into the chest as she did it. Her grace was mesmerizing. "You are responsible for him," she said. "He is in your care." Kanraku could not tell to whom she was talking—him? Their attackers didn't speak English, but she spoke in English nonetheless. He remembered what she'd said, but he kept it to himself, because it sounded as if she'd given up hope. To her mummified husband—to all of them really—she'd said in English, "Let us cross the sea of suffering, until we reach paradise together." Then she stepped back, presenting the terrorists with a tidily gift-wrapped hostage.

Bowled Over

January 7, 2000

Buoyed by pillows—under her head, her stomach, her right knee—Promise wished the aquarium sensations in her belly would subside. Even when she got comfortable, she had only about forty-five minutes before a limb went numb, and time between bathroom visits was short and getting shorter.

Leo saw the quilt moving above Promise's sloshing belly. "Settle down, Edgar. Give your geriatric parents a break." He was unabashedly excited about this bonus child. He believed their lives were overabundant with strategy and constraint. They should give themselves up to chance more often, stop pretending all the decisions were theirs to make. Another child at their age made them appear reckless, even if the diaphragm had only slipped a quarter inch or whatever might have happened to spawn this happy mistake. "My dear, you are the perfect example of why those Buddhists have it wrong."

"Because the Buddha left his wife and kids to seek enlightenment?" She was particularly sensitive to that detail right now.

Leo said, "I meant the Four Noble Truths. You know, birth is sorrow, separation from the pleasant is sorrow. Sorrow arises from the craving for sensual pleasure or power. All that." Leo maintained that birth was joy and that separation from the pleasant brought with it the sweet anticipation of fantasy and reunion. Not only that, he avidly craved sensual pleasure and power for the disenfranchised. Assuming Promise had peeled the quilt back as an invitation, he threw a leg over her haunch. Lately, he'd been tortured by her flagging energy when his own was at full staff. He said, "Life reveals itself in passion and desire. The rest is your day job."

"Next time I see the Dalai Lama at my day job, I'll point out the fallacies of his system. Please, your knee." She tried not to sound as irritable as she felt.

He swung his leg back. It seemed to Leo that His Holiness possessed a strong desire or two, like a desire to go home and to get the Chinese the hell out of Tibet.

Promise said, "So Buddhists are anesthetized. Shall we raise this one a Hindu?" As if they were raising their children as anything at all. Many of their friends, having little faith in a god, had made gods of their children. She ticked off Leo's opinions of the world's religions: "Let's see, Taoists are too passive and Confucians are hierarchical. How about a little Theosophist? Sikh? Methodist?"

"Rhythm Methodist," he said, pressing himself along her back.

He parted her sweaty thighs to find a resting place for his penis, which touched a nerve. Promise was trapped between the pillows and him. There was such a fine line between cozy and caught, and she was looking to be nowhere near that line, craving as she did a buffer zone around her tight, itchy belly. Maybe her midwife would tell her to refrain from sex until the baby came, though Leo would probably use that as an excuse to lick chocolate off her belly. She'd felt nearly this tetchy the last two pregnancies, the crowning touch this time being the museum.

Leo was out to relieve her pressure, and he wondered how she could be so voluptuous and so disinterested. Those heavy, veined breasts bugging out in disbelief and that cauldron of a belly moved him in ways both tender and lewd. He wanted to rest between those mammaries, straddle that fertile crescent. He wanted to reach up inside her and tickle that baby under the chin.

Promise tossed and flopped about until Leo backed off. "Tonight?" he asked.

"Honey, I've got a long day ahead of me." She was already making excuses for later. "I've had two conversations with the ambassador, and I swear he's been drunk both times."

Leo lay on his back, the sheet tented above him. "The French always slur their words."

"Ambassador *Young*?" Promise snapped. "He's from Akron, maybe Pittsburgh. You thought he was French?"

"Eyes on the prize here," Leo said. She'd been second-guessing the bowl ceremony all week. Ever since the millennium had come and gone without incident, she was convinced that this would be another anticlimax. Leo had always thought the plan a little esoteric, an opinion he regretted expressing to Talbot. He wasn't worried about his remarks getting back to Promise—Talbot was nothing if not discreet—he was worried about the big guy's recent zeal. Lately, he was as eager as a hit man to do Leo's bidding.

Having taken a deep breath or two, Promise was more resigned than panicky. "So we add an outrageously expensive porcelain to the curio cabinet. What does that show?"

"That you're a player," Leo said. "We've already gotten mileage out of it." Generally, he'd been courting outspoken politicians in addition to pious religious types, among them victims of hate crimes. And so he'd been pleasantly surprised to see that giving Arthur's bowl a home was attracting some press. Leo came around to her side of the bed to help her up, which led to a supportive hug and then his lifting the back of her nightgown to fondle her warm, fleshy cheeks.

A cold draft chilled Promise's backside, and she retreated to the bathroom. After her shower, she blew some height into her hair. If she wore the highest pumps she could safely navigate, she might be eye level with the Chinese bowl. Anything above that depended on her hair. She had to get a good squint on to see herself clearly. This pregnancy, she'd gone past swollen gums and ankles to *swollen eyes*, fuzzing up her crisp vision. She brushed her teeth gingerly to avoid bleeding gums. Then she applied waterproof makeup, a recent purchase because pregnancy made her so weepy.

She should have splurged on another upscale maternity dress rather than relying on one rosy frock. She was in full flower now. Her face had bloomed, and she had a second chin. She looked down at her low-hanging breasts and melon-round belly—sprayed gold, she could be the statue in the Laughing Buddha Steakhouse back in Oklahoma City. She'd have to remember to tell Arthur about that anomaly, a few blocks past the Jesus Is Lord Pawn Shop. These days, she had to save up material for her former friend.

"You're wearing your pretty dress," Lydia greeted her from the breakfast table.

Felix pushed out his lower lip. "I can't see the baby good when you wear that one."

"That's the point, honey. They make special dresses to hide big tummies."

"Is the baby a secret?" he whispered. "I'm not good at secrets."

"Don't we know it," Leo said. He'd put on his gray cashmere jacket and a starched shirt for his museum day.

"You look nice," Promise said. Felix was keeping time on the top of his head with a fork until Promise caught his sticky hand. "Forks are for eating," she said. She brought him a new fork and a wet paper towel.

Before preparing her own breakfast, she lifted the wet plastic wrap and banana peels from the sink. A defrosted waffle box slumped on the counter next to an unwrapped stick of butter—God forbid anyone should put it in the butter dish. A line of coffee, like gunpowder, trailed from the grinder to the coffeemaker. It might be a new century, but nothing had changed. Cereal cartons opened their boxtops to the morning; the milk carton let go its chill in a cold sweat.

Why don't cereal makers use resealable pouches? The answer—*so the cereal will go stale!*—had only recently dawned on her. Truth is, built-in obsolescence was an inconceivable option to someone trafficking in the old. Bowls that don't break after a few hundred years are, by default, the valuable ones.

When Flipper snagged the remains of a toaster waffle from Lydia's plate, Promise didn't bother to discipline him. If he was dainty enough to clean the plates without getting his paws in the butter or leaving syrup rivulets, she would accept the help.

"Mommy," Lydia said, "I'm almost finished with our museum."

"I'll let you borrow my sharpest glass," Felix horned in. "And I gots Flipper's baby fang."

Leo said, "You have glass, buddy?"

"Okay, okay, so what?" he ranted. "It's suckers I smashed. But they look like glass." Promise poured herself coffee, prompting Felix to lunge toward her. "Mommy! Babies can't have coffee!" This from a six-year-old. She figured anything that could be done to lower Edgar's birth weight should be considered medicinal, but she surrendered her mug to Leo and held out her arms to Felix. When he pressed his syruped lips to her belly, she was glad her dress was patterned.

Lydia said, "Wait till you see what I've made."

"You've been working hard," Promise said. The way Lydia had been going through modeling clay, her miniatures might someday be a museum collection itself, like the impressions Agatha Morada had amassed. On her digs of yore, Agatha had taken imprints of every Sumerian rolling seal she had found; these carved, bead-sized cylinders were made for scribes to roll over their clay tablets, part signature and part sealing wax. Soon, Dr. Morada began pushing anything she pulled from the ground into clay, a reburial of sorts that yielded a three-dimensional set of object negatives. The museum had impressions of chariot finials, pendants, oil lamps. Initially scholars had been allowed to use them as molds for study replicas, but now the impressions were objects in and of themselves.

Leo was lacing up his tall boots, as if going to combat. He said, "Last week, Felix said he thought Penisbreath would be a better name than Edgar."

"Daddy!" Lydia was shocked. "You're grossing me out the door."

"I was talking to your mother. I'll take them to school—do you want to drive or Metro?"

"Cab."

"Okay, I'll drive them and bring the car to work. Now, go forth and bowl them over."

"No pressure, please." But she was thinking, Why not be hopeful? Although the opening hadn't earned them as much mileage as she'd wanted, she was genuinely happy that Arthur's obsession had panned out. Good show, friend. If there were a place for extremism in the pursuit of art, it might as well be in a museum.

Talbot had volunteered to come in early to oversee security and find a spot for the flowers Miss Stranger had delivered each morning. Today's arrangement, featuring sprays of ginger the size of baseball bats, was his height, and he stashed it near the umbrella nook. He stood at the top of the stairs to survey the arena, one elbow resting on the bowl's vitrine, which he knew was not alarmed. To establish the placement for

Promise's step stool and the microphone, he blocked out the action like a play under the basket. Then he supervised the art handlers, who restrained from their usual corniness as they raised the vitrine above the gleaming bowl and loaded it on their storage cart. Sam accompanied them, carrying his shotgun-sized camera; footsteps and a squeaking cart wheel were the only sounds as they rolled the glass cube down the terrazzo hallway to the elevator.

Arthur was right about the bowl's decoration: bird musculature was communicated in the subtlest brushstroke. And those plum branches belonged on a tree! Regardless, neither the surrounding exhibition nor the purchase of the bowl had evoked a response from the Castle, seemingly content to run out the clock. Each cadre of supporters they assembled eventually reverted to mush, and Leo was convinced that someone needed to force the Castle's hand. Talbot himself could hardly knock indecisiveness, seeing as how he couldn't even choose a sexual preference. Thus far, he enjoyed the power that came with sex more than the particularities of men or women.

Today's ceremony would mark the first time Talbot had stood for anything other than himself. Though he sensed an unspoken alliance with Leo, he was acting alone. It wasn't that he'd interpreted Leo's rants as a call for volunteers; of all people, Talbot recognized sarcasm. But they were nearly out of time and had yet to generate any outrage outside their own circle. He thought, If Arthur invites me up there, I will play my part.

All gathered for the ceremony, which was unremarkable until Arthur's ardor got the better of him. The security camera trained on the case captured footage of a rosy, jiggling moon eclipsing the view, rising evidence of Promise's belly. However, Talbot was on the other side of Promise, and he saw the play unfold better than a well-executed pick-and-roll. Not only did Arthur bring them all up, he practically guaranteed an accident by working the bowl free from its wire mount. Holding the vessel aloft made for an easy steal by the ambassador. But scrappy Promise went after it, and sooner than a referee would have called for a jump bowl, she wrenched it free. Talbot watched her make the choice between himself and Arthur, flickering back and forth as she took the measure of their skills and her trust. When she chose Talbot, he pressed his palm against the slick, rounded side and imperceptibly jerked counterclockwise, putting a little English on the Chinese porcelain before handing it off to Arthur.

Why don't you play up your gratitude, really give it to them, he'd suggested the night of Arthur's party. This was after topping off Arthur's acquisition fund, sending Morty packing, and pouring all the red wine in his apartment into their two cups. Wouldn't it be great to raise that vitrine cover, just for the ceremony? Nothing between them and the white glaze. Blind them with it. Arthur had responded by raising Talbot's tuxedo shirt, reeling back at the sight of his abs. They were pretty comfortable there on the black leather couch, and they had been kissing, both of them clearly more excited than they'd been in a while. Arthur tasted like salt and pepper from the well-seasoned steak they'd shared. Talbot set his rimless glasses aside and, gripping the temples of Arthur's horn-rims, eased his off. He laid Arthur's glasses on the coffee table side by side with his. You could bring the ambassador up for a round of applause, maybe Cecil. Show him some respect. As seen through Talbot's nearsightedness, Arthur's hair was like an aura. I should do that. I would love to show them I'm ready for the big time. There was more kissing until Arthur bent over Talbot. I should take a bow with it, like this. He unzipped Talbot's pants. I should run my tongue around that beautiful bowl, lick the delicate rim like this. And like this. All around like this. Yes, you should, yes, Talbot said. Just like that but harder. Yes. Even harder. Bring them to their knees.

Part II

Here Come the Plagues

January 7, 2000

Promise's list of worst possible outcomes hadn't included this. She'd chiefly worried that she might stumble or that their acquisition triumph would be met with silence. Immediately after Arthur lost his grip, the courtyard peahen let loose her complaint. Perhaps the bird was lamenting the stand of legs blocking her window view. In any event, her high-pitched squall might have come from Promise's own throat. Less than a second later, the rounded lip of the bowl met the corner of its own pedestal, sounding a clear chime that was the ring of finest porcelain. Then one thud followed another.

Years of motherhood had trained Promise to delay her reflexes in certain situations, and she initially appeased the panic triggered by breaking glass and a tumble off a stone ledge by recognizing that it was only breaking glass and not the fleshy thump of a child rolling down the marble stairs.

It was Arthur rushing past her that reset her alarm.

The exaggerated tails of his coat flapped behind him as he performed his surreal tap dance down the stairs. There was a sense that the whole thing was choreographed. After Arthur gamboled his way to the bottom, coming to rest on one knee, the supporting cast followed in the stop-and-go manner of a movie musical, rushing to witness the crash's aftermath, only to pull themselves up short and avert their eyes. Splayed hands melodramatically covered mouths or even faces. Curiosity prompted them to stampede; dread and manners reined them in. Finally, Arthur stood up and hightailed it out of there, exiting stage left. The sound of his heel taps receded another half story to the carpeted lower level, where he might have been seeking asylum in his office or going all the way out the back door to Independence Avenue. The company eventually made their way to ground level, unavoidably grinding ceramic chips beneath their feet. The nimblest of the group jumped off the last step to avoid walking on shards that had collected there.

Having led them to the top, Promise now brought up the rear. Even in her shock, she knew to take the stairs carefully. Her ankles ached with the effort of balancing on her high shoes, and her hot cheeks pounded from temple to jaw. She felt like a sore thumb, throbbing and red. Nevertheless, she held fast to her physical discomfort, for she knew great sadness was coming. It was almost as if the disaster were still impending, and it had fallen to her to evacuate the building. *You could be next! For the love of God, run for your life!*

There wasn't time to think what Joseph, Rumi, or her mother—Promise's personal trinity—might do. Her instincts told her that saying anything would trivialize what they'd witnessed. Those who'd hoofed lightly down the stairs stood still and heavy as cows, and so she herded them along, pairing off dignitaries with staff members. In a shaky voice, she asked Min to make Madame Xingfei comfortable. Min ushered Madame X toward the half flight of stairs on the right, her flowery, preservative scent marking their trail. Promise asked Zemzemal to see to the ambassador.

People silently obliged to lead or be led. The conservator volunteered to retrieve a dustbin and brush from the lab.

"Thank you, Lucy," Promise said, though ten gallons of gasoline and a match would finish the job. She saw the pity in Cecil's rheumy eyes. *Old man, can you appreciate what we were trying to do?* She said, "I'm sure you'll agree that our meeting will have to be postponed. Talbot, would you escort the Secretary and chief justice back through Security?"

Judging by how quickly they dispersed, they wanted out of there as badly as she wanted them out. Now they were down to three; two, when the head of the Regents joined Talbot's clique. "That will do," Promise said to Sam, who was snapping away in documentary mode. "Go ask Lucy if she needs any help." And then it was just Promise, who unfortunately had to climb back up the stairs to reach her office.

Lucy returned to sweep systematically from landing to ground floor. It would never be known on which step the magpies were shaken from the plum branch, bisecting the good wishes of the bowl. Along the way, she spied many pieces that would add up to "May you have joy" but nothing of the blossoms that spread the sentiment "up to your eyebrows." Sam was back, too, ostensibly scouting for crumbs. He'd jogged down behind Arthur but hadn't been quick enough to photograph the curator pocketing the chunk of flowering plum. Because it wasn't confirmed on film, he doubted what he'd seen.

Promise made it to her office, past Vanessa and through the doorway, sloughing off her ridiculous shoes before falling sideways onto the leather sofa. Sorrow and confusion overtook her, what Rumi described when he wrote "I'm crying, my tears tell me that much." Knees bent, arms around her bowl of a belly, she rocked with angry sobs. She cried for the bowl, ruined by their attention; she cried for the museum, which she'd tried her damnedest to serve. Bitter tears washed her mouth with the soapy moisturizer she wore.

From her spot on the couch, Promise saw the sun glare off an icy patch that caught a child unaware. He recovered from his spill and went at the spot again, this time sliding down the sidewalk. Promise huffed unevenly from her crying jag until the image of Joseph, captive and suffering under the desert sun, sent her into hiccuping sobs. Add Joseph and Emmy to her unfairness list, along with Arthur, whose diva act had scotched their best chance. She'd told Arthur what was at stake, though she hadn't hammered the point home. She hadn't specifically declared that the fate of the museum rested on his shoulders, because she hadn't wanted him to *crack under the pressure*.

Promise's sinuses were congested from so much crying, as if a sponge had expanded to fill her face. She was unbelievably thirsty, and her lips were parched. Simply lifting her head brought on a pounding that forced her to curl up again. Like an armadillo, she thought, like the bugs they used to call roly-polies. She heard the click of her door behind her but did not dare to swivel around.

"Oh my God!" Leo rushed for her. "What happened?"

He knelt at her side, trying to determine whether she was in pain. When he felt her wet sleeve, he ran his hand along the skirt of her dress. The instant he'd crossed the museum's threshold, Sergeant Becton had told him he'd better find his wife. "I'll sign you in, just go to her"—a clear signal from a man who was a stickler for the rules. Leo saw no evidence of blood or the gush of fluid that would result from her water breaking. He concentrated on her face: tears glistened on her eyelashes, and wet strips of black hair framed her rosy cheeks. Aside from her bloodshot eyes, she had the dewy beauty of a nymph. "My Queenie," he said with all the tenderness in the world. "What happened out there?"

"Oh, Leo," Promise whined, and she began crying again.

He embraced her as best he could. Promise moved so he could sit next to her.

"Arthur dropped it," she said. Perhaps her tear-filled eyes magnified the twitch of recognition Leo betrayed.

"Shit!" he said convincingly, though he felt a weightless drop inside. He dreaded hearing the rest of the story.

"The stupid idiot bent the mount wires, he *bent* them so he could take the bowl off the pedestal." She asked him, "Have you seen Talbot?"

Leo's pupils contracted as if hit by a bright light. Too quickly, he answered, "No."

She meant had he seen Talbot on his way to her office. Had he heard, if not the whole story, a rumble of it coming down the hallway. "He and I were standing there with Arthur. That squirrel brought half the crowd up, including Cecil. He's so *stupid*. He's a stupid moron." She'd resorted to calling him all the names forbidden to her children.

"He lost his grip," Leo suggested hopefully.

"He *dropped* it. I got it away from the ambassador, who was lit up like Christmas, and I handed it over to Talbot, who laid it right in Arthur's hands. Then Arthur *woop, woop, woop*—" She reenacted his two-handed fumble, inconceivable to someone who could juggle six objects at a time.

If thoughts were hands, Leo had slapped that bowl off its pedestal a half dozen times; that said, he was not the least bit culpable in any plot of Talbot's. He should never have mouthed off to the guy, whose sarcastic nature seemed the opposite of impressionable, and he especially regretted any bravado he might have displayed telling his Amnesty stories. If he came clean to Promise and copped to his impolitic remarks, she'd no doubt shake it off, convinced as she was that Arthur was entirely to blame.

He hugged his wife close, and she rested her weepy face against his spongy jacket. All he said was "Get ready for some major attention."

———

Fifteen minutes later, Promise was allegedly composing a statement on Joseph's computer, where her meager sentences filled only a few lines of his oversized screen. Leo had reoriented her, adjusted her moral compass such that she was to welcome the fury coming their way. Here was that backward logic Leo excelled at, and Promise was glad to be interrupted by Vanessa, despite having given her explicit instructions to take messages and turn back visitors.

"Miss Downey, the school nurse, is on line four."

Promise pushed away from the desk so hard the chair rolled to the wall behind her. "What's wrong?" She hadn't yet gauged how sensitive Miss Downey's phone finger was—last year's nurse called when there was blood, vomiting, fever, or head lice.

"I don't think it's an emergency, but she says Lydia wants to go home."

Promise's heart missed a beat, then fell all over itself trying to make up for it. Just when you think you've hit bottom, you realize there is no bottom: her downy-cheeked girl was in pain. When she'd been looking over the ledge, hadn't maternal instincts kicked in before anything else? She'd always fretted about those stairs, as merciless on bone as on bone china. Her first thought had been: At least it's not the children. She slid open the drawer where she'd stowed the phone so as not to watch all the lines blinking with alarm.

Promise hefted the console onto the desk, unkinking its thick gray umbilicus. Then she punched the last button. "Hello, Miss Downey."

"Good morning, Mrs. Wells. Your Lydia is in my office. There's no injury or temperature. She's a little upset, is all. I think you might need to come get her."

Some poor kid was howling, and from what Promise could make out of the nurse's message, she thought she might join in. A child is upset, and you call her parents to take her home? You're a nurse, woman. Give the girl a glass of juice or let her skip P.E. (was it Friday? Lydia always had a stomachache on Friday). Promise tried to remember if Lydia's phobias had ever landed her in the nurse's office before. She could not drop everything and drive across town to school—was there someone who might understand that? If, God forbid, her daughter had split something open or passed out, fine; but as to the news that Lydia was "upset," Promise wanted to scream, *I'm a little upset myself!*

Promise raised her voice over the commotion. "I'm in the midst of a crisis right this minute. I'm on a deadline." She was allegedly crafting a statement bragging about how many objects they hadn't destroyed and emphasizing the incredible expense and worth of the irreparable bowl.

"Hold on, please." Miss Downey set the phone down.

She had no choice but to wait. What did it matter, really? She wasn't getting anywhere on the computer, which had reverted to showing off the permanent collection. A Hokusai scroll of Mount Fuji filled the screen, the composition sliced diagonally by a tree branch in the foreground. Hokusai had bent the branch like an elbow in the center of the image, and he'd brushed a boy resting in the crook of the tree, taking a moment to play his flute. Suspended in that silence, Promise relived the horrible moment when the bowl seemed to twirl from Talbot's hands into and out of Arthur's. She'd be reverting to this scene the rest of her life, her personal screen saver, replaying it like the Zapruder footage of Kennedy's assassination. She wished she could watch the action in slow motion, freeze a frame or zoom in on a detail.

"Honey, your mother's busy," she heard Miss Downey say.

Promise recognized the surge of agony in response, finally realizing that Miss Downey had been speaking in code. "Upset" was a ludicrous understatement for what Lydia was. "Lydia, baby." Promise tried to be heard, but her voice cracked. "It's Mommy."

"Mommy!" came the chilling cry, pitched right at Promise's gut. "My pants are full of snakes!"

"It's all right, baby." How long had Lydia been hysterical? While Promise had been rocking herself on the couch, blubbery with sorrow, her daughter had likely been doing the same. Was Lydia's class preparing for a trip to the zoo's reptile house? Had some jerky boy taunted her with a bag of jelly worms? Promise reflexively prepared to run to her daughter's side when she realized she couldn't leave her own snake pit. "Miss Downey, are you there?" she yelled.

There was a tussle on the other end, then Miss Downey spoke in her unearthly calm. "Yes, Mrs. Wells."

"My husband will be there soon. Tell my Lydia her daddy is coming.

Goodbye." She had to get off the phone so she could send Leo to the rescue.

Calling her old office only got her Leo's voice mail, so she returned to where she'd flung her shoes; in the end, she had to kneel with her stomach under the glass coffee table and her nose practically resting on top. The tabletop reflected her face—it was something of a boost to see that, after all she'd put them through, her makeup and hair had endured. As she stepped into her shoes, a glance at her watch informed her it was only ten o'clock. Unaware that life as they knew it was over, the museum was opening to the public for the day.

Outside Promise's door, Vanessa played the phone like a concert pianist. Promise took a page from Leo's book and flashed ersatz sign language her way. She waved her keys in the air, pointed to her watch; she tilted her palm teeter-totter fashion, then held it up flat: I have to go, but I'll be right back, I think. Stay put. Answer for me as best you can.

Fortunately, there was no one in the short span between the director's office and the staff room, where Leo and Nathan were huddled over a mound of used muffin wrappers. Cheeks bulging, Leo gazed upon the chef with awe. "No shit? You buy this batter by the bucket?"

Promise stood frozen by the coffee machine, disbelieving not only that Leo could be eating at a time like this but also his sheer hypocrisy. Before he was on the payroll, he frequently razzed her about the food at work. Maybe, maybe his insouciance was for Nathan's benefit, and he'd been holding court in the staff room to keep up an air of normalcy. "Leo," she said.

He practically spit coffee across the table. "Jesus! I didn't see you."

She was usually the jumpy one. "Lydia needs you at school."

"Is she sick?" he said, as Nathan slipped through the swinging door into the kitchen. "You want a muffin?"

His behavior was surreal, though now that he mentioned it, of course she wanted one. "She's upset. What are you doing in here?"

He said, "She hates P.E. on Fridays; the last time we were at the fountain, she told me she'd wished for a broken leg."

Two weeks ago, he wouldn't have known Lydia's schedule. "I know she hates P.E.," Promise credited him begrudgingly. "This is more than that. She's in the nurse's office, screaming about snakes in her pants."

Leo jumped up. "I'm on it." His eyes had the jittery back-and-forth he got after too much coffee or, if muffins were the culprit, sugar. "You stay. You're needed here. I don't suppose you're ready to go to the press."

"What do you think?" she asked rhetorically. She should have released the memo to them back when she still held the high ground. Now, Leo wanted her somehow to play up the bowl, but in all her years at the museum, she'd never heard anyone discuss broken objects. Was it possible that nothing had broken until her watch? "What a disaster."

"You can't blame yourself," Leo said. "Accidents happen."

"That's what we say when Felix spills his milk! This was a million-dollar Chinese porcelain, and I'm in charge." A swift kick from Edgar was the least she deserved. "Did you brief Talbot?"

"I didn't get the chance," Leo said. In fact, he'd been gearing up for a confab with the bowl breaker: he'd had two muffins and three mugs of coffee. "Let's keep our perspective. The museum is fully indemnified—have Zemzemal get your insurance stuff in order. I'd bet these things really do happen all the time: every single thing you guys have is fragile and priceless. Want me to walk you back to your office?"

"I can manage," she said, though she might have been lying. "Call me when you get Lydia."

"Will do," he said and kissed her on the cheek. Either for her benefit or for Lydia's, he put a little speed in his mosey.

Promise knew she should be on the other side of that door, too, and yet she bit off a mouthful of muffin. She definitely had to get out of here before the staff came through for break. Just two more minutes, she told herself, as if she were huddled beneath her comforter before facing the day. Nathan kindly stayed in the kitchen, so she didn't have to make conversation. Maybe in the time it took Leo to get to school, Lydia would recover. Children were resilient that way; like drunks, they could go from bawling to bemused in an instant. She knew Leo wasn't looking forward to going it alone; picturing the two of them on their respective front lines gave her some needed courage. Any second, she was going to get over herself and salvage their cause. But first, something clicked, the way it did when she was puzzling over a Sufi manuscript. Might Lydia's fear of snakes in her pants have something to do with her pants? The possibility that she could save her daughter propelled her back across the hall.

"You're back." Vanessa was obviously surprised. She waved a stack of message slips over her head, moving the muscles of her lean torso beneath her snug dress. The poor woman had gotten even skinnier since they'd moved to the director's wing.

Promise said, "You're more than I deserve."

She'd evidently had a challenging morning, palm to forehead, because her stiff bangs were flattened straight up. "Remember that when you write my law school recommendations."

"Did Arthur call?" Promise asked.

"Nothing from Arthur."

Promise plopped down in the supportive desk chair. Setting the pink slips aside, she punched the nurse's number on the phone. "Miss Downey," she said. "This is Promise Whittaker—Mrs. Wells. How's Lydia doing? Is she still with you?"

"Yes, ma'am. And Miss Thomas has just brought Felix in. Seems he was fidgety, itching himself until there are little bumps everywhere. Might you have a flea infestation at your home?"

"Fleas?" Promise asked. "Not that I know of." Lordy, Lordy, here come the plagues: snakes tormenting her firstborn, vermin swarming round her boy. She willed herself not to burst into tears. "My husband is on his way, but may I speak with Lydia?"

"Yes, ma'am." The nurse summoned Lydia to the phone.

"Mommy, Flipper gave Felix fleas," Lydia said. Her tattle-telling sounded confident enough.

"Do you have any bites? You sound better," Promise commented.

"I'm not," Lydia whimpered. "The snakes are still on my legs. They're all down my thighs."

"Honey, I have an idea. Are you wearing your velvet pants?"

"Yes, Mommy. And they're crawling inside!"

The low-slung bell bottoms were Lydia's favorite pants, because they looked like the ones on a popular big-headed slutty doll. She'd slide them back on as soon as they were out of the dryer, after Promise pulled straggly threads from their inside seams. That was a courtesy Leo wouldn't have thought of, folding the laundry last night. "Lydia, Lydia, Lydia," she chanted. "You know how we have to trim those pants after they go through the wash? You're just unraveling, my sweet." Weren't they all?

"It's like snakes are moving around," Lydia yipped.

"Sweetie, it's okay. The strings move when your legs do. It must feel weird."

"Oh, Mommy, it does." She sounded unbelievably grateful for her mother's sympathy.

"Let me talk to the nurse, honey." When the phone was transferred, Promise said, "I know what's scaring her, and I wonder if you can help her slip her pants off—the seams are the problem. Maybe you have some scissors you could—"

"I'm sorry, Mrs. Wells," the nurse cut her off. "I'm not allowed to touch the children in an intimate way. You or your husband will have to do that."

"You have my permission!" Promise begged, angry at the bureaucracies of the world.

"I'm sorry. I may not remove her clothes." But then Miss Downey said to Lydia, "Let's put up this screen around you, so you can talk to your mama with some privacy. Mrs. Wells, maybe you can guide her through it."

"Thank you," Promise said. "Lydia, sweetie, step out of your pants."

"Mommy, they'll bite me!"

"Lydia, listen." She tried to sound nonchalant rather than stern. "Remember what Althea said, about your fears owning you. I know for a fact that there are no snakes in there." Radiate calm, she told herself, though episodes like this made her fearful for Lydia's future. All she had to do was get her to drop her trousers. Imagining herself stroking Lydia's hair, she said, "I'm right here."

"No you're not," Lydia said matter-of-factly. "You're at your desk."

"Honey, pretend we're at home in your room. Just pull them down—quick—and jump out. Miss Downey could clip the seams for you, or if she doesn't have scissors, turn them inside out until Daddy gets there."

On the other end of the phone, there was a single high screech, and then Lydia shouted, "You're right! Ewww, it's all dangly. What a mess."

Promise laughed with relief. What she wouldn't give for someone to pull down her pants and show her that her fears were groundless. "You're a mess," she said. "But you're my mess. Okay, Daddy's on his way. Be nice to your brother. I love you."

Lydia said, "Love you more."

Not possible, Promise thought, hanging up the phone. She'd been clenching every muscle in her body, partly, she realized, because she had to use the bathroom.

Afterward, she tried a few stretches standing behind her desk. When she lifted each shoulder blade, there was a pop; the bones in her neck crunched like gravel underfoot. She was too old to be having another baby; not only that, there hadn't been a second available for exercise. With the other two, she'd signed up for prenatal yoga, nature strolls, massages, whatever she could find. Arms straight out, she folded over to the right, bending at what used to be her waist. A grunt took her down so her fingertip touched the top of her thigh.

"Did you lose something?" Talbot asked from the doorway.

Vanessa was behind him. "I'm sorry," she said. "I told him you weren't seeing anyone."

"It's all right." Promise sat down. "Will you buzz us with any important calls?" She was grateful for the help.

Talbot closed the door. He seemed a bit jaunty, if that was possible under the circumstances. "What a morning, huh? I'm sorry that had to happen."

"Don't say that!" Promise turned to look over her left shoulder, then her right. Talbot followed her gaze, but she was only stretching. She said, "I can't stop hearing that first crack. It smelled awful up there—that cleaner they use, the fresh paint—and the ambassador."

"He was tanked," Talbot agreed. "Where's Leo?"

"He had to pick up the children. Have you heard from Arthur?"

"Not a word."

"What the hell was he thinking? He wouldn't have taken the bowl off the mount if Joseph had been up there."

Talbot reached across the desk to hand her a thick orderly file. "It doesn't have to be Arthur's fault—curators handle objects all the time. This is why we have insurance."

Though he was just stating a fact, his remark brought tears to her eyes. She set the file down so she could pull tissues from the nearby box and commence to blowing her nose, wiping her eyes, blowing her nose again.

"Sorry," Talbot said.

"No, you're right. It would be more comforting if insurance could replace it, I mean if another one . . . actually . . . existed." She was breaking up again; she doubted she'd ever get through a day now without weeping.

The phone buzzed. Seeing as how Promise was indisposed, Talbot reached his long arm over the desk to push the intercom button.

"Senator Kellogg," Vanessa announced.

"Thank you," Talbot said.

Promise pressed her palms against her eye sockets in an effort to suck it up. "Institution Oversight Committee, right?" she said shakily.

"Allow me." He didn't even have to compose himself before picking up the phone. "Senator, you're good to call. Yes, it was quite a shock." He was silent for a spell, presumably taking their lumps. He tilted his head the way their puppy did when puzzled, then his thin lips curled into a beatific grin and he said, "You've never broken a bowl?"

Promise was flabbergasted. Evidently, the senator was as well, because Talbot said, "With all due respect, sir, I'm not being glib. You have every right to be outraged by this freak accident." He had yet to take a seat, and though the cord was long enough, he leaned slightly toward the phone. He looked like a blond Byzantine saint in a suit on the phone to St. Peter, an effect that was enhanced when he held up a long index finger. He said, "This is exactly why we have insurance. Of course. Of course not, Senator, nothing can bring it back." Then the saint perched on the edge of the desk and, making a duckbill out of his hand, signed "blah, blah, blah."

He was an accomplished actor. That was what the conversation sounded like, acting, yet it was oddly more satisfying than sincerity. Talbot masterfully allowed the senator to vent without once apologizing for the museum's screwup. From where she sat, Promise was now eye level with his suit coat pocket, which she noticed was still basted shut. If the suit had been Leo's, she would have assumed he didn't know you had to snip the pockets open or, if he did know, he was too lazy to do it. But it seemed just like Talbot to keep his outside pockets not only empty but also sewn up.

"A hearing is an interesting idea, Senator . . . I agree, sir, and I hope you'll say that to the *Times* or *Post*, recognizing the difference between our loss and the Taliban threatening to destroy the Bamiyan Buddhas. We just wish we had your muscle when it came to safeguarding the world's cultural treasures. Joseph considered it his life's work—have you any news for us on his situation? Well, I know it's your highest priority. We thank you, sir."

When he hung up, Promise applauded his performance. Although she hadn't heard the senator's side of the conversation, it seemed that Talbot had managed two things at once. He'd made it clear that the museum was blameless even as he stoked the senator's wrath. Also, he'd somehow implicated the senator in Joseph's capture. "Were you provoking him?"

"A little bit. His outrage makes our bigger point for us: the Museum of Asian Art exists to take exquisite care of bowls like that."

Promise massaged her taut belly until Talbot averted his eyes. She said, "But you did something else there. You turned our ineptitude into deep concern for things that break."

Talbot said, "Leo coached me. He knows just how to play this game."

A tingle of suspicion shot through her, though that might have been Edgar pinching a nerve. "When did you two talk?" Talbot stayed hidden behind his hair, until Promise unknowingly gave him an out. "Did he call you on his cell phone?" She could just see Leo ranting to Talbot all the way to school.

Talbot ignored her questions. He said, "Basically, Leo thinks we should talk about the tragedy of losing a masterpiece, then take it up a notch to the global stage. Get people going about cultural devastation and intolerance. One could even make the point that cutting our funding is cultural genocide of a sort."

The spin was too much for Promise. Leo's words were having the same effect on her that Arthur complained about when she quoted Rumi—namely, they were turning her brain to noodles. Hadn't she politicized the museum's plight in order to get Leo to join up? Wasn't every decision in the Castle budget the result of someone yanking the chain of the person above him? Leo had essentially given her the same instructions for the statement she was drafting. But she hadn't followed her husband's strategy to its obvious conclusion. The rhetoric rankled her until it occurred to her that language wasn't the problem. The part that scrambled her brain was: what if breaking the bowl could save the museum?

Stronger Than Dirt

December 17, 1999

When the rogues came over the mountain, they knocked Joseph senseless, then trussed him as they would a boar. Lashing his arms and legs to a tent pole, two men carried him into camp. The other desert rats rounded everyone and his wallet up. Joseph's body swung like a punching bag, which they battered at any sign of resistance from the crew. Thus spoke Kanraku, Joseph's cell mate, the keeper of his history. It annoyed Joseph to be beholden to someone else for his own damn story. Joseph was surprised at Kanraku's world-class English; they'd exchanged only a sentence or two on the dig.

"They were on the lookout for someone," Kanraku said. "They argued about who to take. You and me—we are winners." He stiffened his neck and smiled, as if for a passport picture.

Joseph smiled back, which hurt. Everything hurt; breathing especially ached. His head and right hand throbbed out of sync. "You put up a fight," he noted respectfully. The cameraman had a barrel chest and the thighs of a football player.

"Not for long. One mule carried a huge mound of guns and bullet belts hanging like noodles. Your Emmy was sent with the women in the sorting tent."

Archaeological finds of every type had been brought to the sorting tent until it was equal parts morgue, puzzle station, and sandbox. Ah, the sorting tent: rock from pottery, sheep femur from goat, hostage from detainee.

"Some of our guides were sent off to the tent, too," Kanraku told him, "but not Yili and Maimaiti. I saw them give those two guns, and Yili handed over truck keys."

Joseph did not know Yili from Maimaiti, but he knew they were both in the group he'd busted for making off with the caravan's kabob ration. None of the Uygur guides spoke any of his languages.

Kanraku said, "I think they would have taken all the trucks, but only one of them could drive. I pretended not to know—how does one manage steering wheel? What is this key for?"

Joseph remembered scoffing at Leo's paranoia. That was rich, having his wounded memory recall his bad judgment. Leo had issued him laminated survival cards of some kind, and Emmy had reissued his to him after fishing it out of the bedroom trash. "You never know what might save your life," she'd said. He'd thrown it away again, this time in the green tea leavings of the kitchen trash. If he had to know the Geneva Convention in Arabic, the jig was up.

Now that the jig was presumably up, he had to think otherwise. Joseph said, "Our guides are the ones Harvard hires. They're the only ones with permission to take people past Hotan."

"Perhaps they are branching out." There was Kanraku's wry humor again. "I think they assume our languages will not match. Sumiyuki is with that Maxwell, Roger with Wu Ling."

"Roger and Wu Ling both speak Chinese." Joseph readily remembered that fact, but coming up with anything else required pulling thread after thread in his woolly head. He recalled that the big hill which served as their backdrop—the one that was always there despite the changing dunes—was known as Mazhatage, which was the Uygur word for "tomb."

He concentrated on his colleagues. Three of the four American men on the expedition were hostages. Maxwell was the bone expert who could determine the ethnicity of a mummy's shoulder socket. Once, Niya had been an urban mixing bowl, where Indian, Chinese, Persian, and Macedonian people mingled more freely than in any of their respective homelands. According to Maxwell, a person's occupation stained down to the bone. He claimed he could identify the types of repetitive motion and injuries suffered by a Macedonian soldier, a nomadic Bedouin horseman, or an undernourished Indian holy man.

For Joseph, unraveling this strand brought along a tangled clump of memories. Sumiyuki was Kanraku's colleague; Roger was a Han dynasty scholar who'd sought Joseph's opinion on Chinese coins and bronze arrowheads; he couldn't remember Wu Ling's specialty.

Kanraku said, "They had the people ride on animals; gear traveled in truck. Last time I saw the others was when your hand got cut."

"Have I been eating?" Joseph felt he'd been in suspended animation.

"Now and then."

He fingered the scar on his scalp and wondered what he looked like with a left part. Pivoting around a fist on the floor, he lifted himself to kneeling, which doubled his vision. He hadn't been aware this many degrees existed between sitting and standing. His bandages were all that was holding him together, like the wallpaper on their old kitchen walls.

"Get your breath," Kanraku said. "Three weeks you've been drifting in and out."

He wouldn't have been surprised if it had been forty days. Wasn't that the legendary number for desert wandering? In his nomadic life—the digs and conferences, sabbaticals and symposia—he and Emmy had never been separated this long. Oh, Emmy, my dear, all that bluster and huzzah! Pangs of longing amplified his hunger and his body aches. They'd collaborated on this fantasy, a trek back in time to where a pious civilization was driven out by the elements. She would witness Buddhism ascending, radiating, its principles encased in sculptural nuggets that, set into the Silk Route's current, flowed west and east. He'd handle a type of writing whose linguistic branch had yet to be traced to any particular trunk. Stars above them, sand below, they'd be stripped to an essence few couples desired, let alone could endure. Meanwhile, they'd plot artifacts on a gridded overlay, illuminating Niya's long reign as a cosmopolitan oasis. At least they'd dragged each other into the desert, so he didn't have guilt hollowing out his chest.

He yearned for Emmy, but as to the dig, good riddance. Now, thirsty camels kept up their atonal lowing, and their house of rugs was probably thirty degrees cooler than outside. He and Kanraku had a plastic bucket, but he could hear what sounded like a toilet flush nearby. In some ways, it was as if the dig were the hostage situation and this his respite: a whack on the head and weeks of bed rest.

He wouldn't mind returning to his life as museum director and reveling in its pettiness. Wall color swatches of "putty" versus "rattan," peacock chow and peacock poop, discussions over whether the museum guard should pack a loaded gun. He'd proclaimed those decisions a waste of his time; however, when Cecil had raised the stakes, he'd left in a huff. What on earth would he fight for if not his museum? Maybe if they'd threatened him with bodily harm, he'd have done more.

"You were badly injured." Kanraku's voice had the plangency of an oboe. "There must be great strength in you."

"Stronger than dirt," he repeated the refrain of an old commercial.

"They don't know what to do with us," Kanraku said. "They pretended to give us vitamin pills with breakfast—act out big muscles—but I palmed mine. Whatever they were, they sent you high as a seagull. When you did drift in, you didn't make sense. Then the other day they brought my cameras in and woke you up. Yili tried to shave you—you remember?"

He squinted his eyes with the effort. All he could come up with were teenage adventures when he'd scared the crap out of himself. In Glacier Park, he'd been careless with his knife and sliced off the tip of his little finger; another time, unexpected white water splintered his broad canoe and pelted him against rocks. Once he nearly didn't return home because poison sumac puffed his eyes so completely he could not see his way off a mountain. "Not really," he said. Poor Kanraku, to have been conscious for all he had mercifully slept through. Unwrapping his right hand revealed the flap of a bad cut. It hurt to flex his fingers.

"You went crazy nuts," Kanraku said. "Maybe you were afraid Yili would slit your throat—he cut your hand by accident. You don't remember the blood?"

"No, not really. A little." His palm was sliced as if for lunch meat. Unreliable as his memory was, he still missed it. Henry, his gentlest child, was always mistaking foolhardiness for courage. He didn't seem to understand bravery, a confusion Joseph inadvertently fed with the endless stories of Rama he told the boys. You cannot fly, Joseph had to remind Henry over and over, no matter how much gumption you've got. He sank back into thoughts about boys and courage and stories they are raised on or tell themselves. He felt far older than his sixty-two years: ossified and feeble.

A crooked little man entered the yurt carrying two undersized bowls. Joseph did not recognize his strange gait as being from their crew. He walked crablike, stepping high and sideways with his left leg, then dragging his right foot to meet his left. Each step created a small splash of liquid over the sides. The sawed-off edge of the bowls' rims as well as their perverse luminosity gave Joseph reason to believe they might once have been human skulls.

In imitation of their previous contents, each bowl contained one gray dumpling in wan broth. The bent man asked Joseph, "You are okay?" His grooved brown skin and sparse hair gave him the look of a talking coconut. A life lived too close to both the sun and the earth had compressed him and hardened his shell, yet he had reddish brown eyebrows like Roman arches above his slate-colored eyes. There was in his features something of every conqueror who had claimed Central Asia: from Greece, Alexander—those eyes, that thin, planed bridge of nose—China's eponymous ruler Qin (fanned out cheekbones), followed by the gangster big-toothed mouth of Genghis and Timur, and finally the refined chin of Babur.

"I've rarely been better," Joseph answered, not looking away. "One or more of my ribs appear to be broken, and while my scalp has healed, I find my hand is badly wounded." He held up his palm.

"You are okay." The man spoke with some relief, apparently understanding only Joseph's intonation.

Joseph pulled at his vest, shorn of its usefulness. "Might I have other clothes? I'm afraid this wardrobe is shot."

A frown closed down the man's entire face. "No one shot yet," he said.

Cold sweat trickled from Joseph's armpit. To show trust and gratitude, he tasted the food, a barley dumpling in a broth of tea with salt and butter. This was the diet of Tibetan monks—whose crossfire had they been caught in?

Kanraku slurped his meal with apparent relish, while Joseph gagged repeatedly on the oily, doughy fare. Such hunger in his belly and they'd given him a stone. Hoping to detain the emissary, he spoke bits of English, Tibetan, Persian, Hindi, and Arabic. The little man spoke Urdu.

Joseph said the only thing he knew in that language: "Crows everywhere are equally black." At least that was what he thought he said.

His captor nodded excitedly. "Yili!" he yelled "Yili!"

A scrawny man entered, and this one Joseph recognized. Yili greeted Coconut Head; together they escorted Joseph from his yurt into sunshine so bright he couldn't see anything at first. While his legs were weak, they didn't hurt, not even the wrapped one. He felt a sneeze coming on; luckily, he was able to suppress it. A sneeze might very well have killed him. When they entered the yurt next door, there was Joseph's laptop sitting next to his fax, handheld scanner, and tape backup, as well as disks of the *Oxford English Dictionary*, site maps, and the complete writings of Burton and Stein. In the end, his efforts to access the world's most sophisticated data would have been better spent packing a crowbar.

Coconut Head unsheathed his dagger: it was a steel blade damascened in wavy patterns—unusual for a landlocked culture—with carving in niello near the hilt. Joseph inventoried its qualities even as the guard brought it to his chest. He was thinking about the Founder's collection, much of it frankly ill-gotten, though they hadn't inherited anything that had been run through the donor. Never underestimate the power of an original work of art.

Yili handed Joseph a newspaper, the *International Herald Tribune* from the twelfth of December. Is this today's paper? Joseph wanted to ask. He read the headline, "Y2K Preparations Intensify" and thought that might have been a Parisian transposition of the mountain known as K2, but then he remembered the end of the millennium was coming.

Yili grabbed Joseph's hand, which he lifted and posed so that Joseph held the front page up, face out, even with his head. "Hold here," Yili commanded, and a camera flashed. When the bright light hit Joseph's eyes, his bowels loosened with fear. Keep it together, man! A photo of a hostage holding a newspaper was proof he was still alive.

"Stand still!" Yili yelled, as someone else took shot after shot.

Joseph focused on the mouth of the yurt, where he could still make out the terrain of rock and sand despite his vision being spotted from the aftereffects of the flash. As the dots faded, he saw a yak skinnier than most greyhounds looking in at him. Outside, all that grew was either thorny or gnarled.

"Who cares if we kill you?" Yili asked. "President, vice president announce no deal!"

Joseph shrugged, helpless to explain his worthlessness. From his previous post, he'd enjoyed pulling strings, though Emmy had maintained that he was tied to too many people. He'd seen it more as tugging on the thick braided rope that summons a manservant—You rang, sir?—and believed in working the system without taking undue advantage of his position. That was, of course, before Washington had cut him off, a point nearly reenacted by Coconut Head pushing his sword against the threads of Joseph's vest. A single thrust would do him in.

"The U.S. will care if hostages are killed," Joseph said, speaking through the dust in his throat. "They may negotiate if you release us."

Yili vehemently shook his head. "You people are known for your lies," he said. "Killed or freed—if you weren't here, your soldiers or India's would hunt us down."

This was what he'd call a lose-lose situation: Yili's men neither wanted him nor wanted to get rid of him. Maybe Joseph did know someone who would listen to them; he'd been in and around India, with some measure of respect, his entire adult life. "Please," he said with the utmost deference, "what is it you want?"

He was looking directly into Yili's eyes, and so he didn't see the other guy come up beside him. Joseph heard the man's angry roar, and then he recognized his felted hat as the one on the guide he'd caught with his hand in the jam jar that night on the dig. The man had his own weapon, a knife with a club handle, which he raised overhead as he spit in Joseph's face.

Yili screamed at the man, and Coconut Head backed off to let Yili and the maniac pull Joseph one way and then the other. But the zealot on the right was a strong motherfucker; worse, he swung his big knife at Yili as readily as at Joseph. Yili let go, despite Joseph trying to cling to him. Everyone had been yelling, the maniac the loudest, until he pinned Joseph's right hand on the stool, like a chicken on a cutting board. Joseph cried out with the pain of his sliced palm opened flat, then his voice gave way. In horrified silence, Joseph watched the deep brown arm bring the knife down toward his thumb, registering what a blade of that size would do. In midswing, the man pushed forward with his fist so that instead of slicing Joseph's thumb, he came down upon it with the bone handle of his weapon, hammering Joseph's nail.

At first there was no pain and then there was quite a lot.

Just what he needed, Joseph thought, more injuries and less hope. He was back in his yurt with Kanraku, who'd given him the pill cadged from when they'd first arrived. Though his suffering receded, Joseph grew weepy with the futility of their plight.

"What purpose did that serve?" He cradled his terrifically swollen thumb, not bothering to wipe the snot dripping from his nose.

"They're disappointed, no doubt, that we're not more important to our countries," Kanraku said. "We will wait them out."

Joseph had no experience being patient, let alone helpless. Kanraku's care embarrassed him, and he whined like a baby. "They'll take me apart piece by piece before they'll get the U.S.'s attention. That was only revenge."

Kanraku said, "Revenge is all they have; it's how they fight for their cause. Our job is to endure."

"I'm pitiful," Joseph moaned. "I haven't even been awake through most of this. How have you kept your wits?"

"There are films in my head," the filmmaker replied. "I watch behind my eyes, as on a screen: rewind, play the scene again in different motion."

So that is how Joseph came to know the movies of Steve McQueen. Quiet renegade of *Bullitt*, chasing murderous mobsters through San Francisco's hairpin streets; tenacious Captain Virgil Hilts in *The Great Escape*, enduring bouts of solitary confinement with his baseball and mitt; another prisoner in solitary confinement in *Papillon*, a blue butterfly tattooed on his chest, trying to get himself and Dustin Hoffman off Devil's Island. Desperate for tales of men with nerve, Joseph was a good audience. Kanraku really knew his Steve McQueen. A suave burglar in *The Thomas Crown Affair* stealing museum treasures and a plain bank robber in *The Getaway*, who gets to have Ali MacGraw as long as he can run them both to safety.

For his part, Joseph led Kanraku through the *Ramayana*, taking it from the top. "Rama, avatar of Vishnu, oldest son of King Dasaratha, was brought to earth with the help of a hermit." More familiar than the Gettysburg Address was the *Ramayana*; to begin it was to fit the key in the ignition and grind the starter in hopes of catching his spark. "In

Ayodhya, King Dasaratha lured a devout hermit out with animal sacrifices, dancing girls, the works. And then the king begged the hermit to bring children into his life." Joseph pictured a palm leaf watercolor, circa 800, from the museum's collection. Tiny dappled dots depicted the bounteous feast, while in the field beyond grazed an ox, a bell (with clapper!) hung on its neck. Jewels pierced the dancing girls' noses, and henna tattoos covered their hands—all this on a leaf two inches high and ten inches wide. "Smoke from the sacrifices reached the gods, and Vishnu chose to come to earth as the king's son, Rama."

"I've heard of Rama," Kanraku said. "There are films of this."

And paintings and books and buildings of marble carved with the entire epic. Where they'd lived in Varanasi, before their two youngest were born, a blind man led a group of Brahmins chanting verses in harmonized antiphony every day from sunrise to noon.

Joseph told the story with a free hand, figuring that embellishing was as good a mental exercise as remembering. "The king was granted four sons. Rama was his favorite, and the younger brother Lakshman was Rama's constant companion. These two were sent to assist a holy man who'd been plagued by the demon Taraka and her daughter, Maricha. Taraka was a widow whose anguish was so great that sages, with their emotional control and concentration, provoked her to hysterical grief. One sage declared that her appearance should reflect her torment, and Taraka's skin bunched up and turned envy's color: moldy, lichen green. Her child, Maricha, became an ugly giant. The demons were determined to crush the skull of Rama's holy friend and feed on his brains. Pure and dedicated Rama let fly his arrows, puncturing Taraka's eyes, which killed her. Then he hit Maricha's enlarged heart, that easy target, and she died as well."

Thus they beefed up their courage and their faith.

When Joseph used to entertain his boys, he'd assign one demon unsavory traits of the school principal and another attributes of their despised piano teacher. Just as his boys had, Kanraku listened openmouthed, though Kanraku's shattered nose forced him to do everything openmouthed. Joseph strung together Hindi and Sanskrit episodes, hard at work on his personal archaeological dig.

Coconut Head came in with the evening barley ball in a hemi-skull. A boy perhaps around ten, maybe an undernourished twelve, accompanied him. The boy walked on a crutch, having lost a leg below the knee, though he easily carried out the bucket that they relieved themselves in. He was back so quickly he must have emptied it just outside their hut. When Coconut Head gave him his soup, Joseph tried to look ailing, lest any convalescence on his part inspire them to more torture. He hoped he was worth more alive than dead.

He said to Kanraku, "This is Tibetan monk food. Have I told you this already? Barley balls and yak's milk."

"The first five days they did not feed us, but Yili comes in with his hand deep in a Fritos bag. This ball tasted good when it came." Happiness flickered over his wide face. "Once they roasted lamb. We got the hooves to chew on and some chickpeas. I ate your share." What little light came through the flap at the door was fading. "Go back to your story."

"Once the holy man was safe, he asked Rama and Lakshman to go with him to Videha, where the king was celebrating an important sacrifice. The lord Shiva had given the king a huge and heavy bow—it sat in a cast-iron box that required one hundred strong men to pull on an eight-wheeled chariot." Now that Joseph thought of it, this episode preceded the last one he'd told. Not that Kanraku would know the difference. "The king's daughter Sita was coming of age, and she was plagued by suitors. The king declared that Sita would marry the man who could heft the ancient bow and string it. Like all men who spied Sita, Rama fell in love with her; however, Sita fell in love with Rama as well. Rama was pure of heart and strong. He lifted the ancient bow effortlessly from its cast-iron box, and with a few strands of Sita's glossy hair, strung the bow and then drew it so hard it snapped in half."

In Joseph's home version of the *Ramayana*, Sita bore a striking resemblance to Emmy, which the boys thought coincidental. She played folk songs on her flute—"Just like Mom!" they'd yell—wove her hair into three braids and braided those. She rose early before her family to do her yoga—"Just like Mom!" The point then was to lull them to sleep with a tale both strange and familiar.

Now, the retrieving and sifting helped awaken him. Eventually, he thought to ask his roommate what had happened to his thigh. It was elaborately wrapped, the edge of the bandage neatly turned under and slip-stitched closed.

Kanraku said, "That binding was never investigated. Probably it did not ooze, and so they left it be."

Joseph realized how much strength he'd lost when he could not rip out the simple basting stitch. The thread was like dental floss. Finally, he managed with his left hand to find the angle where it would rip through the gauze. His strength surged a bit when he peeled the stiff outer layers away to reveal the pale crinkly blue of Emmy's shirt. Precious souvenir, reminiscent of the ash-flecked gauze the entire family covered themselves in when they watched corpses burn from the banks of the Ganges. Layer after layer he unspooled with no evidence of injury. Was this extra bandage a simple gift, something of herself? Was it perhaps a weapon with which to strangle his keepers? No blood stained the blue gauze; there was no pus and no pain.

Kanraku came over to his mat—his funk was that of the elephant house during the Washington summer. "Sit between me and the door," Joseph said, to block the view if someone came in. It was beneath the penultimate layer that he found Emmy's shrewd gift, the survival card Leo had given her that she had so wisely packed. What sleight of hand she must have exercised, palming the card and binding it to him with her very shirt.

He read the succinct advice in the dim light: *Should you be an unwilling guest, attempt to humanize yourself to your captors. When possible: (1) feign pain, (2) pack snacks, (3) use a ruse, and (4) get out but don't get lost.* It struck him as brilliant, an entire plan Leo had crafted in two sentences. All these years, Joseph had been making fun of the wrong people. Now, he memorized the edicts and then looked for a place to stash the card. An actual intact pocket was waiting on the inside of his vest, the lone survivor of the sixteen slashed compartments. Joseph quickly rewrapped his thigh, happy to be wearing a rope, a sieve, if need be, a turban.

"Our 'Get out of Jail Free card' has arrived," he said. "We're busting out, my friend."

Feign pain—he looked forward to healing enough to follow that edict. *Pack snacks*—he could always eat less barley ball, but where to hide the reserves? *Get out but don't get lost*. Time was, he'd known a dozen ways to orient himself. How could he get out and try a few?

What Joseph gained in strength he gained in cunning, and soon enough Kanraku could not tell how exaggerated his physical complaints were. He seemed to have a blush to him, yet he held his side, moaning, and he stank up the yurt something fierce. "I worried about you for so long," Kanraku said, gasping for breath. "Now I'm worried about me."

In truth, Joseph had eaten a soap sliver their guard had left. *Use a ruse.* When Coconut Head had brought in dinner, the guard balked at the smell as well. Joseph performed an admirable dance of defecation—the smell, the mess—and was allowed to relieve himself outside. Each time he spent longer and longer away. Often, he did have the runs, as those barley balls were hell to digest, but near where he'd been latrining, he hid a morsel of food. *Pack snacks.* Even if it was only two chickpeas and a bit of barley ball, even if he'd never see them again. By pulling this stunt at different times of the day, he noted the sun's path.

He saw red mountains, Jeeps and trucks parked pell-mell, and a yurt with smoke coming out a chimney. He sucked up the smells of a charcoal brazier, cumin, and mint, intending to hold that breath forever; however, when he entered his yurt, stink forced the air from his lungs.

Each time the guards came in, he asked after family and camels. Though he'd always disdained charades, there he was, performing the foreigner's hand game. Brrr—isn't it cold? You look tired; sleep well. Occasionally the boy on the crutch would come in. He'd lost his leg to a land mine—had Kanraku told Joseph that or had he just assumed it? Joseph would try to tell him about his sons: four boys! Big and strong they are! I dream of seeing them again! Joseph pretended not to understand that the boy despised him. *Attempt to humanize yourself to your captors.*

Kanraku had an endless supply of Steve McQueen plots. He was Nevada Smith out to avenge his parents' murder, chasing outlaws atop parallel speeding trains; a race-car driver in *Le Mans*; a paid gunslinger in *The Magnificent Seven*, the Hollywood version of Kurosawa's *Seven Samurai*.

Joseph picked up where he'd left off. "Rama and Sita returned to Ayodhya after they were married; that's when his stepmother tricked the king into exiling Rama for fourteen years. Because he could not leave his brother's side, Lakshman followed Rama and Sita into exile, and they were stalked by a vile-smelling hag who begged the princes to marry her. Their refusal sent her running to her brother—evil Ravana, enemy of Vishnu—who transformed his monstrous self into a nimble golden deer that Rama and Lakshman tried to capture. It was then, when Sita had been left alone in the camp, that Ravana swooped in to kidnap Rama's cherished and virtuous wife. But Vishnu saw Ravana's shenanigans and made plans for tomorrow night."

The next day was extremely clear, and Joseph went farther than he'd ever dared to relieve himself. His ribs and hand still thrummed, but his legs were steady. Climbing over a cliff that couldn't be seen from their yurt, he encountered a pile of rocks, one for each time a Buddhist had passed this spot. Then he glimpsed a village cluster that might take pity on Kanraku and himself: prayer flags were strung from a stake in the ground to a pole in the top of a hut, like the flapping strings of plastic that once decorated used car lots. I'll take a lightly used Lexus, Joseph thought. Leather interior please, with a hot shower in the back and my wife at the wheel. There was no telling how far away the village was; desert visibility was either zero or infinite.

That night, he sped through the rest of his tale. "Don't rush," Kanraku said, wanting him to elaborate on the escapades of Hanuman, the monkey general, and Jambhavan, king of the bears, who bravely fought with Rama and Lakshman. When Rama was wounded, Hanuman bounded north and tore off a chunk of the Himalayas in hopes there would be a curative herb somewhere in the lump. "Sure enough, he was healed"—Joseph tried again to wrap it up—"and he returned the top of the mountain Everest, what Tibetans call Chomolungma, Goddess Mother of the World." He saw Kanraku's black eyes looking back at him in the darkness.

Kanraku asked, "What became of Sita? Did Rama get her back?"

"All the demons joined forces to attack. But Rama, brave and cunning and strong, had been given an arrow by Lord Brahma for just such an occasion. Holding his breath, seeing the shaft to its aim, he killed Ravana with a single dart. Because he was pure, because his exile was unjust, because he loved his wife. Good night, friend."

A few hours after the last fires had died down, Joseph gently rocked Kanraku awake. The brawny brick of a man rose, tied on his boots, and was ready. After all, wasn't the epic over? Hadn't all that was brave and right won out?

No guard stood outside their door; they knew that. But they didn't know who might be staking out the camp's periphery at night. Wrapped around each fist, Joseph had the ribbon of Emmy's shirt, which he practiced pulling taut as piano wire. While camping in the wilderness, he'd broken the necks of turtles and rabbits and possum. All his life he had fished, piercing the cheek of his prey with a barbed hook. He'd written monographs on bejeweled eye gougers, displayed machetes crafted to cleave a skull. He'd had Talbot fire an employee rather than send the man to detox. He'd denied worthwhile monetary requests solely on the basis of personality and approved outlandish outpourings of museum funds on the same basis. He'd preferred one of his sons above the others. But he had never killed a man.

Stars shone in the bowl over their heads, and Joseph was grateful for the half dozen Islamic celestial globes he'd written about for an exhibition. In fact, the stars were as silver inlaid in a brass globe, so bright did they shine above him and Kanraku. He let the Little Bear's tail guide him in the blackness past the trucks, around the goat pen and satellite dish, onto the rutted path he'd taken so many times. He was grateful for that path and wondered how long people had scuttled through this mountain pass on these stones.

Joseph counted sixty steps from the beginning of the path so they could reach under a boulder for the pills he'd hidden. The pills might be worth something along the way. On the windless side of the boulder slept the one-legged boy, whom Joseph saw but Kanraku evidently did not. His crutch lay camouflaged against the path, and Kanraku tripped over it onto the boy, who yipped in fear. The man stood up with the crutch in his hand. Pinning the boy down with one foot on his stomach, Kanraku gave a menacing growl.

Who would send a child out to the edge of civilization? Had the boy drawn the short straw that night, or did his disability consign him the lowest rank? He lifted his skinny arms at the same time that Kanraku swung the crutch like a baseball bat. Joseph was slow to register what was happening until he heard the unmistakable crack of the child's stick arm and saw the extra bend due to broken bones. The boy began moaning like a creaky door plagued by shifting winds.

Kanraku had been conscious when the boy's kin had captured them, splintering ribs and noses at will. Joseph had been spared that. However, Kanraku had not experienced the daily challenges of parenting, in which against all odds you try to deliver a child to adulthood with the fewest possible scars. The boy's eyes were dilated in shock as Joseph put one of their pills on the child's tongue and wrapped his mouth closed with gauze. Whether in spasm or defense, the boy tried to kick with his only leg, and Kanraku jumped on his shin. "Stop it," Joseph hissed and shoved Kanraku's hugely muscular arm to get him off the boy. Joseph tied the child's hands together. "Give me that," he said to Kanraku, who handed over the crutch. Joseph propped it against the boy's back, and then he wove the rest of Emmy's shirt through the crutch and around front to the boy's arms, until he'd encircled the wounded child.

The boy had a small goatskin bladder of water on him; he had dried fruit and bread but no weapon. Someone would undoubtedly come for him in the morning. Joseph wished he had something to give to the kid, crippled by all that we claim to civilize us: religion, government, family. Even if he did have an offering, like his wedding ring or a wooden plate from Niya, what good would it do? A hairbreadth from hysteria, Joseph kissed the child warrior on the top of his black-thatched head. Now the boy's eyes were closed, and Joseph convinced himself the child was visiting the semiconscious state he'd just returned from. Joseph counted sixty more steps from the boulder, where he dug into the earth for a piece of bread, just as stale as it had been when he got it two days ago, then one hundred steps to the pile of rocks, where he'd stashed two barley balls and eight chickpeas.

In silence, he and Kanraku walked thirty minutes, maybe an hour. There were no decisions to make as they edged along the rut of a downhill path, and there was nothing to see in the dark. For fear of land mines, they walked the path as if it were a tightrope. The temperature was far milder than in the desert, perhaps as high as forty degrees, but lacerating winds sliced them up. Stabbing pains traveled up and down Joseph's spine until the pain itself finally sparked a thought. Joseph put his hand on Kanraku's shoulder to stop. He fished out his blessed little card and squeezed the ends. Behold, a magic trick I just learned! He slid the silver square out, careful not to lose the three flat matches or the water-purification tablets. Kanraku was excited. Joseph was excited, because he'd forgotten he was carrying a razor blade. *A razor blade!* That seemed to multiply their chances astronomically. He unfolded the reflective square—it opened to a sleeping-bag-sized rectangle. Giving Kanraku one end to hold, he pulled the piece taut with his left hand so that with the razor blade between the first two fingers of his right hand he could slice it into two squares. In the middle of each square, he cut a gash, then he handed Kanraku one square and slipped the other over his head. "Poncho," he whispered.

"Poncho," Kanraku whispered back, grinning his snaggle-toothed smile.

Joseph replaced the razor blade in his magic card, the card in his vest. Two minutes tops, and he might have just saved their lives. The blanket blocked the cold wind—perhaps the shield would stop bullets. As long as it was dark, their reflective surface mirrored blackness. Pinpricks of light shone on Kanraku's back. Joseph smelled a dung-fueled fire, but the way the wind was blowing, he didn't know if the smell came from behind or in front of them.

Their pace was slow. Sedentary for so long, badly nourished, they plodded along the path, stumbling where it got steep. Kanraku hadn't mastered mouth-breathing yet, and while Joseph worried that the thin, dusty air would dry him out, he could hear his companion spit into the dirt every few minutes. There seemed to be mounds of sand in the distance; luckily, their way was one of dust and rocks, else the path might have been covered over. One footstep wide, this narrow furrow they traveled might be part of the very Silk Route.

Already the bowl of stars was lifting. The light was welcome, because they might have wasted all their energy trying to find the village in darkness. He pictured them dead twenty feet from the flapping flags, the way farmers could lose their way going from the barn to their home during a blizzard.

Now Joseph was in front, and he looked over his shoulder at Kanraku, whose poncho had gone from black to an orange blaze. It reminded him of chaste Sita walking through fire for her Rama. Then he happened to look beyond—they'd traveled such a short distance, an effect enhanced by the visibility here at the top of the world—and saw a speck tracing their path. He pointed it out to Kanraku, recognizing Coconut Head by his rhythm: just a step to the left and then a twist to the right. While Joseph watched, the man quit the path for a more direct approach over a rocky dune.

"He's so slow," Kanraku said, his voice wheezy as a mule's. "We might get there first."

Snapped and ragged inside him, Joseph's ribs were tearing him apart. Kanraku caught whatever breath he could in his smashed nostrils.

Joseph was sure the man had passed the boy sentinel, whom they'd broken and gagged.

Kanraku said, "He's on foot. We couldn't risk taking the mules, but why would they send a gimp, on foot, after us?"

"Maybe we're not worth the mule."

They were mesmerized by the approaching speck, which crab-walked over a stone outcropping. Forging his own way, Coconut Head left himself open to getting lost or blown up, if anyone had bothered to booby-trap these parts. Even in his desperation to make better time, Joseph was determined to avoid shortcuts, though the path was narrow and the sands worked hard to erase it.

Joseph took the lead with his own unsteady walk, doubtful that he and Kanraku could reach help in time. He visualized Emmy high atop a far dune standing between him and the sunrise. Rosy-fingered dawn wrapped her in a healthy glow; the winds that had brutalized him play-fully lifted up her skirt. His eyes encircled her waist and traveled up to her breasts—they were a pair again and larger than life. Joseph's juiced-up fantasy, equal parts Emmy, Parvati, and Miss America, got him over the next ridge, where he waited for Kanraku. His friend's face bore a grimace of pain or oxygen deprivation; beyond, Joseph saw Coconut Head still coming at them, closing the damn gap. Joseph reached out his good hand to Kanraku; they stood together for a mo-ment facing their rival.

"Stubborn motherfucker," Kanraku said.

"It's more handicap-accessible than it looks," Joseph replied.

And then—as if the sand were a blanket that someone pulled taut—the speck was thrown high into the pinkening sky. Dust spread out like a firecracker, long triangles of red dirt plumed through the air. In the fraction of a second before the sound kicked in, Joseph recog-nized that he was seeing a man being blown apart. The mine's blast shook the earth beneath them.

Joseph ran—*ran!* Kanraku, too. They bounded, it seemed, like Hanuman the monkey general spanning mountains in a step, like enchanted deer, like free men, placing each foot squarely on the blessed, blessed path. Their ponchos shone forth, silver shields, stars moving along a scraggly field of red. Ultimately the path widened, and they walked side by side, each with one arm slung around the other's shoulder in an effort to hold his friend up, and they didn't stop until the prayer flags, tongues of a dispossessed people, lapped at the sweat and tears of their brows.

Take No Blame

January 7, 2000

Promise was trapped in a loop of logic. Her job as acting director was to safeguard the collection, and yet Talbot (channeling Leo) was suggesting that today's mishap might advance the museum's cause. To break more objects? No, to preserve them. She dreaded the Castle citing their carelessness as further evidence against them and couldn't get off the track where a reckless act led to punishment, reparations, and an apology. Maybe that was the difference between being a mother and a museum administrator.

She tried rising above both roles to that of a mystic, as in "The bowl is already broken." For weeks, she'd been repeating that as a pithy reminder of a material world without museum care. When Joseph told her of the exchange between monk and disciple, she should have quizzed him about his interpretation. Now that the bowl *was* already broken, she heard a lesson on ephemerality or even an unlikely nudge to enjoy things while you had the chance.

Talbot pointed to the phone messages in Promise's hand. "How do you want to proceed?"

His nails were better manicured than hers. She said, "The way I proceed with everything. Let's make a list."

Talbot lifted the wing-back chair overhead to bring it alongside the huge desk. Once, she would have interpreted that as an attempt to intimidate her, but today she saw how natural the gesture was. If she and Arthur were on better terms, she could have shared this observation, that not all of Talbot's moves were premeditated.

Talbot took the yellow pad from her desk and pulled a pen out of his inside coat pocket. She appreciated that he was prepared to do her bidding. By pushing her belly to the left, she could curl her legs up under her. "You know, I'm not quite ready to crow about the accident."

Talbot said, "Remember when that kid carved his initials into the Gudea statue? And one of the East Asian conservators ripped a patch off *Waves at Matsushima*—"

Promise covered her eyes, as if it were happening in front of her.

He said, "Those are just the ones we know of." He moved an inch of blond hair behind his ear. "In all likelihood, something like this has occurred before."

She'd heard rumors of how the museum used to operate. In the old days—maybe even during Joseph's tenure—there would have been gentlemen's agreements to keep such an episode under wraps. "We might say we're being honest by admitting what happened."

"Right." Talbot was twirling his pen with his long fingers, end over end like a miniature baton across the back of his hand. Once it had gone over his pinkie, he managed to lever it against his thumb and bring it back across the top of his knuckles. "And *we* didn't drop the piece. We're rightfully furious—it's sickening! Leo says we should try to light a fire under anyone we can think of. If everyone gets angry, we might not only stay in business but also get more money."

That was a little too calculating for her. Faceup on the stack of messages was a call from the American Association of Museums. "AAM," she said, and he wrote it down. "The next one is from the American Restaurant Alliance. There's our dilemma in a nutshell." Then she was struck by an executive decision. "On second thought, I don't have anything to say to the Restaurant Alliance." She wadded up the pink square.

Like a dog retrieving a stick, Talbot scooped it off the desk and sank it in her trash can.

Promise pointed at the can. "Do you still play basketball?"

"We're playing now," he said. "Basketball is really a mind game, strategy and reflexes. You have to know all kinds of defense as well as when to break for the hoop."

Promise divvied up the messages she cared to respond to, assigning herself the Asia Society and the Metropolitan, National Public Radio, Dr. Zhao, and Senator Houlihan, whom she was actually eager to talk to. Talbot got the AAM as well as the Frick, two congressmen, and the

National Zoo. The phone buzzer sounded, and Promise punched the speakerphone button. "It's the inspector general," Vanessa announced.

"Mine." Promise claimed the call as if it were a rebound.

"Take no blame," Talbot reminded her.

"This is the acting director."

"Hello, Dr. Whittaker. I am with the inspector general's office. We conduct audits and investigations into Institution operations. Is this a good time for us to talk?"

Already Promise was stymied. Was this a good time for a talk?

"Dr. Whittaker?"

"Well, it's a hectic day for us." Talbot put up his fists, pulled in his neck, and shadowboxed a bit. She assumed this was her cue to take the offense. "I appreciate your call," she said, though she doubted she sounded convincing. "Of course, we'd welcome your help in our internal investigation. We're heartsick about the loss."

Talbot flattened both hands over his left lapel and mouthed the word *no*. She wasn't supposed to be heartsick or guilty, unless she could implicate the caller as well.

"I apologize for not seeking you out sooner," the inspector said. "American Art takes up most of my time: you know, donor improprieties, plagiarism charges, lawsuits against their director. They're constantly in the papers."

That was news to her. May our disaster be as easily overlooked, she hoped. She was trying to remember the difference between the inspector general and the general counsel.

"I've been assigned to the case of Dr. Min Chen," the man said. "I understand you're the acting director and you've not signed off on any of her requests, but in the last fiscal year, Dr. Chen has requested her full allotment of travel funds, and I don't see that she's traveled farther than New York."

Promise squirmed out from her pretzel posture to a full upright position, and Edgar bounced himself in her lap. She'd been meaning to look into Min's infractions ever since their confrontation outside Promise's bathroom. But challenged with the survival of the museum, Promise had lost sight of Min. Inhale and exhale, Mahalia had coached her. Take no blame, Talbot had instructed. She gripped the arm of Joseph's chair, gathering her courage not to give a straight answer. All she could think to say was "I am Dr. Chen's supervisor."

Talbot splayed his big hand on Promise's desk. With his other hand, he mimed cutting off his head. We are dead, she nodded in agreement, but then he mimed hanging up the phone. She said, "I'll look into that from our end." In one breathless rush, she headed the inspector general off. "We'll schedule a time when we can all three meet. Either Dr. Chen or I will give you a call within the week. Thank you again." And she hung up.

"That was something else, wasn't it?" Talbot asked.

"Yes, sir," Promise agreed. "I shouldn't discuss this with you."

"But?"

"So I won't."

Talbot pushed his hair back and squared his shoulders. "You're not like Joseph. He couldn't keep a secret."

"From you, you mean," she said, acknowledging what their places had been and what they were now. On that note, she excused herself. With Talbot sitting just outside the door, the director's bathroom didn't seem very private.

When she emerged, Talbot said, "Joseph would go in there for a half hour with one of his cheroots. He used to smoke one cigar a day."

"That's not possible. There's a big fat smoke alarm in there."

"Fake," Talbot announced.

"Are you serious? It blinks." She walked back into the bathroom and there it was, plain as the way to church: an alarm casing with the blank wall visible behind. She was sick of these false fronts, especially since she fell for them so readily. Her scholarly pride was all tied up in her ability to look and search and see what few had bothered with. Meanwhile, she'd been missing everything beyond her desk. She sat down opposite Talbot. "Does everyone think I'm gullible?"

He diplomatically shrugged his impossibly wide shoulders. "You're smart about Mughal art. Where were we?"

"About to go from defense to offense," she said, and she buzzed Vanessa. "Will you bring in those carousels?"

"Sure." Vanessa came through the door with two round trays of business cards, which she held up in her muscled arms like barbells. "Here's our inheritance from the last regime."

"I know these wheels well," Talbot said, recognizing Joseph's stash of phone numbers.

Promise began flipping through the cards. "Let's see. Managing editor at *Arts and Antiquities*, Parvin Proctor at the MacArthur Foundation, head of the National Endowment for the Arts, the vice president's chief of staff . . ."

Thus they buckled down. Talbot had a good memory for favors they were owed, and he showed a talent for the multilevel, flowchart list that Promise loved to assemble and tear through. What she brought to the bargaining table was huge collegial respect and almost no political experience, which is to say few enemies. Promise did a fine job on the phone with the Metropolitan's director; however, she broke down speaking to three different curators at the Asia Society. Not only did they know her entire staff but they were afraid for their own future, worried that their small weary board might ship their collection one mile north to the Met. Promise once again composed herself; in the meantime, Talbot made a masterful call to the Japanese Embassy suggesting no fewer than four high-profile ways they could make a stand. Then Promise had the idea to get in touch with a conservator she knew at the National Gallery, who volunteered a recent mishap involving a shrunken kimono that had to be downgraded to the study collection.

"You're a natural," Talbot complimented her.

The gush of warmth she felt toward Talbot was so intense that, had she been a few months further along, she would have feared her water had broken. It was the first time she'd ever found him attractive, not because he agreed with her but because she was finally appreciating his talents. Whenever one or the other happened upon a choice phrase, Promise typed it into the computer. At one point, Vanessa brought them lunch from Nathan, and Promise felt comfortable enough to take food off Talbot's plate.

After she'd eaten the last of the monkfish, Promise checked in with Leo. "Are you managing all right?"

"We're getting set to flea-bomb the house," he said. "It may not work because the usual flea stuff isn't recommended if you're pregnant. Flipper's getting dipped at the pet store groomer, and I'm taking the kids out to a movie."

"Wow" was all Promise could say. Impressed as she was with his efficiency, it was almost as if he were atoning for something.

"How are you holding up?" he asked.

"Better than expected," Promise said. "Talbot and I have drafted three letters: a 'heads-up' to send to museum directors and our staff, 'look what they're trying to do to us' to the press, and 'ours is a sacred mission' for our overseers."

"Talbot, huh?" He sounded suspicious, or maybe a little jealous. "E-mail your letters here, and I'll take printouts with me. You know how those movies are."

Boring and loud, she knew, having been to her share. But if Leo could edit press releases while animated space aliens made fart jokes, he was the superhero for her. "Call me when you get back home," she said. "My plan is to send some of each out today."

"Good idea. Love you," Leo said.

"Love you more." Promise saved what she had on screen ("saved," she called the document, enjoying the conundrum that resulted, "saved as saved," as worthy of a Rumi title), then highlighted the file name and e-mailed it to Leo.

The shadow from the mosque carving in Joseph's window traveled along the back of the sofa as she and Talbot worked. Senator Houlihan gave them pointers and some deft language. He also knew a *Times* reporter who had interned for him before doing graduate work in Asian studies with his wife, as well as several sympathetic *Post* connections. Promise passed the names on to Vanessa, who located them within their organizations. She prepared courier packets for the letters. Zemzemal uncovered useful statistics, which they happily incorporated, and when Leo called with changes, Promise took nearly all of them. She stopped short of accusing the Castle either of cultural genocide or of selling the Mall to the highest bidder.

At five, museum closing time, Sergeant Becton rang. Promise thanked him for checking in. "He says snow is coming and we'd better get our packages out on the front desk before it's drifted over." It was a running Washington joke that people were afraid of snow. Vanessa had called around for backup; Promise and Talbot were tweaking the third letter as Vanessa and company were printing and stuffing the first two. By six, they'd prepared thirty packets for delivery. Talbot took them out to the front desk.

Retrieving the most recent stack of phone messages from Vanessa, Promise was seized by a hard, pinching pain in her lower back. She shut her eyes tight.

"You go home and go to bed," Vanessa said. "Promise me you'll leave right after I do."

"I Promise," she managed as she sank into the couch.

She was woken by a rattle at the door, someone fiddling with the knob even though it wasn't closed. "Sergeant?" Promise called. It was dark outside the windows, with a few floodlights aimed up into the garden's Japanese magnolias. Joseph's office was dim as well, because he didn't have overhead lights—he thought them unnatural and architecturally inappropriate. "Talbot?" Promise said, when whoever was at the door remained outside.

She was tired enough to be a little spooked—most everyone had a story of unwanted intruders after closing time—so when the visitor turned out to be Arthur Franklin standing in the doorway, she gave a little scream. Hardly the homeless man she'd imagined, he looked just as elegant as he had at the installation ceremony. He wasn't red in the face or even crumpled.

"I'm sorry. I didn't mean to scare you. I'm really sorry."

Frankly, it was a little offensive for him to look so fresh. "Oh, Arthur," she said, numb with confusion. She'd cried herself out hours ago, and it wasn't her style to yell. When he moved in front of her, she saw a telltale mustard stain on the front of his dandified jacket. An ice-cream wrapper stuck out of his coat pocket, along with a brochure. Had he wandered the Mall all day, eating hot dogs and Nutty Buddies? Had he been riding the carousel and taking in 3-D movies over at Air and Space while everyone else cleaned up after him? "Arthur, Arthur, Arthur."

"I have such a sparse imagination that I couldn't think of a place to go. Have I ruined everything?"

Talbot came in behind him, with an expression on his face Promise had never seen. His sneer was gone—his nose was long and unwrinkled—but there was a swagger there, too, a twinkle. "Not everything," he said.

She glanced at her watch; it was nearly seven. The evening of the same day? That seemed impossible. "I don't know," she said to Arthur. "We're trying to talk about this without a great deal of blame, but I'm still sore. There's a reason we keep things under glass. You put us all in jeopardy."

"I know, I know. Can you believe I took it off the mount?" He held his arms out to hug her.

"Honestly, you should be rending your garments and offering to walk barefoot on the shards. At least you could have shown up stinking drunk." Her right leg had a terrific cramp, and she had to massage it before she could unspool herself from the couch. She was starving. "I have to go home." Arthur had frozen in place reaching out to her, but she was too irritated for even a perfunctory hug.

Talbot brushed off his shoulders, then he lightly cuffed him. "Chin up, Butterfingers. Let me buy you a cup of coffee."

His arms sank to his sides. "I don't drink coffee."

"Then let me buy you a martini."

Lit Up

January 7, 2000

T he boys insisted Promise take a cab home despite her feeble protests. A cold wind had kicked up, and snow was already swirling in the floodlights outside the museum. Talbot stuck his long thumb into traffic to effortlessly pull out a taxi. Arthur pressed a twenty into her palm, because he knew she never had a dime on her. Their chumminess was a mild shock, and their eagerness to get her out the door worried her on Morty's behalf. She was exhausted, however, and grateful for the uncrowded trip home.

The cabbie's radio squawked with Turkish and Arabic voices; somehow, he managed to push buttons and talk back. Of course, he was Asian—eventually, wouldn't everyone be part Asian? He made record time getting her home, where the crape myrtle was still lit up in gaudy holiday bulbs. "Nice house," he said in unaccented English, another surprise. Still another to see her house from inside the cab. Darkness hid its dishabille, from the peeling paint to the Christmas tree discarded on the curb to the chaos within. For all the cabbie knew, she lived in a charming Arts and Crafts cottage in one of D.C.'s loveliest neighborhoods.

From inside the entry hall, Promise flipped the porch light off and stood in darkness. "I'm home," she called out. Nothing, not even Flipper's nails trying to get a purchase on the wood floor. A cough-drop smell burned her nose, and after that was something more pleasant, the brine and nutmeg of Leo's crab bisque. She flicked the switch on

the living room sconce, stepping into a loop of accordioned hose tethered to its host appliance. Someone had come through, piling toys into
the corners, and vacuumed the living room.

The top of the television had been cleared of all but a tall silver can,
reminiscent of her father's latest bowling trophy on their family room
TV. Illustrated with a mixed-breed dog sporting a bandanna, the can
was labeled "All-Natural Flea Bomb." It tickled her to think of a meeting where they chose that name, having been part of so many museum
labeling discussions. Could they really, for example, call that Near
Eastern object a "shaft-hole butt head"? She snorted, remembering
that; she was a tad giddy after the day she'd had.

She heard the loose muffler of their Ford backing into a parking
place as she walked into the kitchen, where her clean-house fantasy
ended. All the cabinet doors were flung apart, and everything in the
cabinets and refrigerator had been emptied onto the table or counter.
More than everything: there were piles of crab legs and shells alongside the milk jug, butter, and box of cornstarch, the spice bottles, tall
crab steamer, and crusted whisks, the onion skins, garlic skins, and
carrot peelings. These last husks were mounded on the counter above
the trash can; with one sweep of the hand she pushed them in the actual trash.

The dishwasher looked as if it had been loaded by a blind person
with a backhoe. Rather than reorganize the contents, she rinsed out a
glass under the faucet, then filled it up, actually hesitating for a second
before drinking from it. Living in Chevy Chase had obviously affected
her—in this neighborhood, drinking tap water was practically an
abomination. Most kitchens had special filters or receptacles fitted
with clear barrels of spring water delivered to the house. Promise
drank down two glasses, consigning herself to a night of padding to the
bathroom. She was drawn to a large covered stewpot on the stove's
back burner, despite nearly losing a shoe to a sticky patch of linoleum.
When she lifted the lid, her mouth watered with the salty, slightly rank
aroma of the creamy soup.

"Mommy! Mommy's home!" Felix and Lydia ran from the front door
toward her. "We made you dinner! We cooked crabs with Daddy! It's
starting to snow!" Felix grabbed her dress and dragged her to the pile of
crab shells. "Daddy let me use the mallet. He said I was a big help."

There was a thin cap of snow on their hatless heads. They'd just come from retrieving Flipper, who was fluffy where he'd been matted. A ruff of fur wreathed his head, interfering with his aerodynamic style. The dog made a few halfhearted leaps before collapsing on his pillow, exhausted from a pet shop day of beauty.

Leo looked dog-tired as well, but he seemed proud of himself, too. After he'd left school with the children, he'd taken them to a seafood market in Bethesda, where they bought a half bushel of live crabs. In the course of the afternoon, they'd steamed and picked crabs, consulted with the pediatrician and the vet, taken Flipper for a makeover, vacuumed and flea-bombed the house, seen a movie, and made bisque using the rest of the crabs. Also, Leo had put his stamp on the three statements that Promise and Talbot had crafted.

"I don't know how you do it," Promise said.

The thing was, he hadn't thought he could. When he'd entered the school's main hallway, plastered with cheery motivational posters and the wobbly drawings of grade-school kids, he'd had to force himself to push back the double doors on the other side of the principal's office. Promise was the one who talked Lydia down from the ledges. He heard the distinctive hiccup of Lydia having cried too long. "Daddy!" she yelled, as if his coming were the pleasantest of surprises. And there was Felix's teacher and Felix, too. "Daddy—it's my daddy!"

Lydia's eyes looked like she'd been swimming in a hotel pool, and she had a glistening line of snot along the top of each cheek. Here was a remake of what he'd gone through with Promise earlier. The nurse's office smelled like rubbing alcohol and the rubbery adhesive of bandages; he'd wanted to marinate in the quick healing that children excelled at.

It turned out that Lydia was fine—Mommy had figured out the problem and phoned it in. Miss Downey offered her some sweatpants from the lost and found box, but Lydia claimed the velvet monsters were her favorite. Strings fell in an uneven fringe down the seams of her inside-out pants.

Then Miss Downey showed Leo the tiny welts around Felix's waist and wrists. "Fleas don't infest people," she said. "But they bite."

"I'll look into it. Thank you so much," he said. "I'll call the pediatrician when we get home. And the vet." He would have said anything necessary to get his children out that door. Hand in hand, they walked to their family car, where they buckled into their usual spots, increasing the odds but not guaranteeing that they would arrive safely at their home, if it was still standing, which they did and it was. Leo kept waiting for the children to ask why Promise hadn't come, but they never did.

Now, he helped Promise set the table for dinner. "We make quite a team," he said.

As a family, they broke a column of Ritz crackers together, and they ate comforting bowls of bisque. Promise thought it curious that steaming live crabs, whose spidery clawed legs reached up under the pot lid, didn't creep Lydia out (she wondered if Leo had pointed out her culinary bravery or if he was as oblivious as Lydia seemed). Promise was enormously grateful that they were well and together. Occasionally, the baby swam a lap in her belly and visibly pushed off, already prompting wonder and delight in his siblings. The phone did not ring once, and because Flipper had chewed through the answering machine cord, there were no lingering messages. Now, the flealess puppy lay under the table, resting his chin on Promise's foot. Felix lifted his sweatshirt to scratch around his waist, covered with welts, but Promise was imperturbable. *You're so cute when you scratch your flea bites!*

Lydia held up her Ritz. "Hey, I just thought up a joke. What does this cracker have in common with the soup can?"

"They're round!" Felix shouted with pride. This was kindergarten stuff.

"In common for a joke," Lydia said. "Give up? They're both crab bisque kits—crab biscuits! Get it?"

"That's very clever," Leo praised her.

She and her brother often made up jokes, but this was the first one her dad had genuinely appreciated. Loving the way the night was about her, Lydia tried to keep it spinning. "You know what I've decided? I'm going to show you my museum." Using her hand to place the words on an imaginary sign, she said, "Special Sneak Preview! Today Only!" Then she ran to her room to get her creation.

Promise exchanged glances with Leo. There was no telling what a museum conceived by her pack-rat daughter might contain. Maybe collecting was instinctive: bottle caps, bubble-gum cards, rusty nails.

Maybe she had her grandmother's knack for making the flotsam of daily life pretty.

Leo said to Promise, "It will be interesting to read the *Post* over the weekend."

"I wish I'd taken out an ad on the museum's behalf that simply said, 'I'm sorry.'"

"I know," Leo said. "I'm sorry, too."

Lydia walked slowly into the kitchen bearing her creation, the Whittaker-Wells Gallery. She'd discarded the lid of a cowboy-boot box, and on all four sides of the white box she'd outlined rectangles in black for that blocks-of-marble look. To top off her museum, she'd fashioned a flap of gray felt for a roof, a marvel of fourth-grade design. A few things rattled around as she walked toward them.

Felix was impressed. "It looks exactly like an art house."

Promise cleared a spot on the table where Lydia could set down her box.

"Thank you," Lydia said. "And ladies and gentlemen, thank you for coming to opening day at the Whittaker-Wells Gallery. Please close your eyes while we make last-minute adjustments." The crowd obeyed, allowing her to right a small clay-and-toothpick cactus that had fallen over and reattach a few exhibits on their mounts. She wasn't quite finished with the project, but she couldn't wait another day to see her mother's reaction. She covered the box with the felt flap. Then she said, "Without further ado, welcome, welcome, welcome." And she drew back the gray felt roof for her family.

Inside the front entrance was a lone earring Promise recognized as her mother's. Promise could never imagine her mother wearing such a heavy earring; maybe she'd only worn it once because she'd lost its mate even before Promise's time. Lydia had polished the ornate leaves so their bright silver set off the ovals of sky-blue turquoise. The object was, as they said in the business, prominently displayed, in a plastic box with a magnifying top. Felix usually kept bug carcasses in that box; Promise would have liked to have seen Lydia negotiate that loan. On either side of this treasure, Lydia had anchored a frond inside one of Felix's baby-sized yogurt containers, so the earring looked to be flanked by lush palms. She'd drawn with blue marker on the white yogurt containers, arriving at a convincing facsimile of blue-and-white ware.

Farther down the front hallway, two wishbones were stood up as sculptures suggestive of an ancient civilization but for the glitter nail polish coating them. Lydia said, "The small one's from our Thanksgiving turkey, and that one's Christmas. I saved them." Promise appreciated the self-control she'd exercised not pulling them apart with wishes. On the walls, Lydia had hung free postcards culled from neighborhood restaurants. Mixed in among the ads for movies and vodka were those of an escort service. Busty women in almost nothing contorted themselves to fit in their postcard cages. Was this what the Parvati statues looked like to Lydia, curvy and lewd?

In the center of the shoe box the nine-year-old had placed a gathering of spheres: a fist-sized rubber-band ball, marbles, and some luminous stones from a craft kit. The sweetness of that exhibit sat butt up against an empty spool with an undoubtedly real bullet on top, which made Promise gasp and look away. Disturbing as that was, it was nothing compared with what she turned toward, two crack vials resting in a cotton-lined ring box. Promise wouldn't have known what they were except that a recent *Journal of Material Culture* had written up a collector of them—a person collected crack vials. She should have been looking on the playground with her daughter rather than looking at a magazine, but there you go. What if Lydia had picked up a used condom or pricked herself on a hypodermic needle? Instead of a spent bullet, might she have found a weapon that had been tossed? What Felix's flea bites couldn't erode, Lydia's museum had. Promise had been through such a long day, surely they'd forgive her if she just dissolved in tears.

Leo said, "Honey, where'd you get these things?"

"Why is Mommy crying?"

Fear constricted Promise's throat, as she hoped against hope that, in sifting through urban detritus, her little girl had not exposed herself to danger. She hugged Lydia with all her might.

"You don't like it," Lydia announced.

"I am beside myself with like." How to express her fierce love? This was the kernel of parenting, this mixture of worry and affection that was simultaneously the biggest burden and the most wondrous gift Promise had ever shouldered. "Oh, my sweet little crow."

Lydia looked from one parent to the other. Had she taken something she shouldn't have? On the prowl since Thanksgiving, she no longer remembered where she'd found each object. They weren't supposed to go to the babysitter's house, but Althea used to take them there all the time to play with her kids. There was a lot to see in that neighborhood. At first, Lydia's plan was to record each find, but that hadn't worked because she didn't always know where she was. Locally, she'd rejected attractive rocks from Mrs. Samsky's garden as too available, scouring their alley for rare items. Rare was valuable. She'd learned that from the pitted pots and basket shreds at her mother's museum—often, beauty had little to do with how an object was prized. That was what she had been thinking as she'd made the Whittaker-Wells Gallery, which she'd worked on all during the Christmas break and then after school, when she could get Felix to stop bothering her. She'd built it for school but really for her mother, hoping she would like it so much she'd find a place for it at the Institution. Her mother was crying, and her father was shaking his head. Looking at her museum in a box, Lydia now saw a shoe box of babyish wastebasket stuff.

She shouldn't have shown them her gallery on a day when they'd had to come to school and claim her from the nurse's office (she'd heard Miss Downey say, "Lydia couldn't utter 'boo' to a goose"). She tried to squirm free from her mother's hug. Lydia had a vague memory of Felix coming home from the hospital, but she was surprised she didn't remember her mother puffed up, her boobies sticking out like a shelf.

"Maybe you should go back to work," Lydia said.

"Oh, sweetie." Her mother let go and hung her head like Flipper did when he was scolded, which should have satisfied Lydia. Fishing a wadded-up tissue out of her pocket, she dabbed her face. Lydia was grossed out by the spectacle of her mother overflowing, tears falling into her soup. You'd think she'd need to come up for air, like a whale. But then she did and Lydia remembered the kindness her mother had shown her when she herself was overflowing, sure that snakes were slithering up and down her thighs. Everyone else had tried to talk her out of it or, worse, pretend they believed her. She was ashamed to be acting like a brat, and she threaded herself through her mother, whose hot whisper, "How did I get such a sweet burrito?" warmed her ear.

Promise volunteered for kitchen duty while Leo escorted Felix to the bath. Lydia brought her museum up to her room. Though Promise practically had to unload the dishwasher to rearrange the contents, she fit in all the plates and glasses from the sink and their dinner. She ran hot water with soap in the sink, reaching for Leo's big rubber gloves, but there was only one from a pair. Disturbing details of her day resurfaced as dirty pans bobbed to the top of the water. The dread of Lydia poking around inner-city paraphernalia, the convoluted logic of their bowl response. Promise was careful groping around in the dishwater, lest she slice her hand on a paring knife.

I am doing the best I can, she told her reflection in the window. When she returned to the kitchen table, Flipper scratched at her thigh until she stroked him, something the trainer had explicitly told her not to do. Petting on demand would only encourage him to paw everyone. She petted him anyway, appreciating the directness, the lack of ulterior motive, in the puppy's request. He licked cracker crumbs from her dress. Smart, wonderful dog, whose sharklike teeth had macerated the answering machine. "Good puppy," she said, and his ears folded back as if she'd blown him away with praise.

Talbot had said she was trusting, but she knew herself to be a critical thinker if she saw a reason to suspect face value. Admittedly, Promise had shut out much in focusing on her profession—was that naïve? Being named acting director had opened her viewfinder wide and made her responsible for this previously unseen vista. She was exhausted and wired, not unlike when the morning started; in fact, she went backward through her day, as if this time around it might add up to two days, maybe more. Although it wasn't that late, she could hear Lydia saying good night to Leo. "Good night, sweetie," she called out from downstairs.

By the time Leo sat next to her at the kitchen table, Promise had worked herself into a second dinner. Leo's flat feet slapped the floor behind her. "There's chicken panang in the fridge," he said and put his hands on her shoulders.

"I've got chunky peanut butter." Then she jiggled the milk carton, listening for any slosh.

He sat down. "I bought another milk."

"Milk would be nice," she said, more as a perverse test to see if he'd get up.

He did get up, but when he walked toward the refrigerator, the dog yelped. "Felix—I mean Flipper! Buddy, you moved right under my foot."

Promise stopped chewing to absorb this lesson: man steps on dog, and dog is at fault. That was his gut reaction. He handed her a glass of milk, which he'd poured in the mottled, handblown tumbler that was her favorite. Even so.

She said, "Talbot and I spent the day following your instructions: 'Isn't it terrible that porcelain breaks when you drop it? There should be a place that takes care of art, don't you think?'"

"Look, I was hired for that."

She'd taken a peanut-butter bite, so she had to put her finger in the air to hold that thought. "To drum up support," she finally managed to say. She regretted hiring him and, for this self-pitying second, marrying him. He did not treasure art. He had a skewed sense of responsibility. He was a man who could not apologize for stepping on a dog. "All this doublespeak makes me cross. That bowl wouldn't have broken if we hadn't had to fight our own institution. Why didn't we make the case that keeping the museum open is the right thing to do?"

Her moral ground struck Leo as funny. "It's the right thing to do even if there's no one in the galleries? Even if the art is being mishandled and staff members are embezzling money? Even if space is at a premium?"

"Yes," she said. She could tell he was more amused than judgmental. Or maybe he appreciated her singleness of purpose.

He pushed his chair away from the table so he could come over and kiss her on the neck, a big wet smooch. "What a day for you. The children are all abed, and my baby's feeling blue. Come to the porch in winter."

She pretended not to recognize the poem he was referring to. "Come outside so you can smoke?"

"There's a nice moon out," he said. "And your mother's coming soon. Help is on the way."

He touched her belly, which she thought by now everyone knew she hated.

He said, "'There is light and wine, and sweethearts in the pomegranate flowers. If you do not come, these do not matter. If you do come, these do not matter.'"

Because she was exhausted, because he was the father of her children, whom she surely could not raise alone, because he quoted Rumi to her and held her by the hand, she followed him. He stepped over her puddle of a coat in the entry hall. "Wait," he said and let her go. Having delivered her milk outside, he returned to bundle her in her wrap, practically carrying her to the porch. "It's coming down."

They sat together on the squeaky glider, whose metal seat chilled her all the way through her rubbery maternity underwear. Leo lifted the lid of the little potbellied grill he'd brought in from the yard. He'd removed the cooking grid and stoked fatwood into the round pot, whose low-slung belly nearly met the bubbled paint of the porch floor. Evidently he'd been using the grill as a portable fireplace. Leo wadded up a section of the *Post*, which was stacked right next to the grill. "What? Did you need Thursday's paper for something?"

She said, "These days, I need the paper for the plastic bags." Just the size for cleaning up after Flipper, they were delivered to her door— really, it seemed worth it. She considered Leo's setup: rickety porch, stack of newspaper, hot metal fireplace. All he needed was an oily rag. "Your mother lets you do this?"

He added the newspaper to the kettle, then struck a match against his zipper to light the wad. Inside the house, the phone began ringing. "Shh." He put his index finger to her mouth. "There's my mother now."

On the fourth or fifth ring, Promise remembered anew that Flipper had ruined the answering machine, and she tried to get out from her coat.

"Too late, baby," Leo said. Then he struck another match and lit a joint. He was thinking about his own long strange journey. Still looking for the opportunity to confess the incendiary remarks he'd made to Talbot—could he remember his exact words?—he took a few long drags.

Cylindrical as Camels, his joints were the results of years of devoted practice. He still rolled them with the cigarette machine he'd bought at thirteen, and Promise wondered how much his mother had known. She couldn't say that his vice had been a secret or that drug use had sidelined him—would that it had affected his fertility! She essentially objected to his habit's being illegal and exposing them to risk; for one thing, dope was harder to come by for people their age, living where they did. She blamed Leo anew for the crack vials and, while she was at it, the bullet Lydia had handled. Wasn't violence in D.C. directly related to drugs?

"Do you know what those little tubes are?" Promise asked.

"The crack vials?" Leo said. "I'm afraid so. I wonder if her teacher will recognize them." He blew smoke up high above her head, so she couldn't even smell it.

"I'm terrified you're going to be picked up buying it. Doesn't that worry you?"

"No," he said. "You should have said something. These days, I get it from my doctor, but in all our years together, I've never bought any on the street."

"Dr. Hambleton?" No wonder Leo was so good about checkups. Put it on the list as yet another thing she'd never suspected.

"You're looking at me like you want a hit," Leo said.

She did—how irrational was that? She too had felt they'd made a good team today, and she wanted to revive that team spirit. She needed them to be on the same side. "Do you think it's worse than a glass of wine? I mean, for me. Mahalia said I should feel free to have a glass of wine now and then."

"On the list of things that are bad for you, I've always maintained that it's comparatively harmless. Shall we ask the drug czar down the street?"

Mentioning their neighbor was a clue that Leo was more careful than he let on. The fire heated her up fast, and she lowered the coat away from her face and neck. Get used to it, she thought, for as soon as this baby came, she'd be prone to hot flashes—could you go through menopause while breast feeding?

Leo hummed an old Kinks tune; he'd been humming it since she met him. He held the joint out to her. "No pressure, but it helps some people handle nausea."

"That's right," she said, needing to know he didn't think she was poisoning their child. "I've been nauseated."

"Downright punky. Aah, the eternal flame has gone out." He lit another match, and she put her lips around the joint. The tip glowed taillight red, then turned black.

"You have to breathe in," he reminded her.

A spray of sparks flew up from the flames. Startled, she inadvertently tossed the joint into the fire.

Leo laughed, a deep throaty laugh. "Why didn't you just ask me to put it out?"

"It was an accident," she protested, unless it was accidentally on purpose. That was how mixed up she was. Leo pointed to the grill at their feet, where another flare shot out. There was a spit and sizzle like maracas, a syncopated cha-cha-cha. It smelled like a rock concert on their porch.

"Reminds me of India," Leo said. "Should I fish it out before the neighbors all show up, wanting some?" He looked around halfheartedly for tongs. Then he tried to fashion two pieces of fatwood into chopsticks, but he gave up when they caught fire. "When I was in Madras, this one nurse basically kept me alive." He loosened his head on his neck, letting it wobble, and switched on his Indian accent. "This malaria, sir, is not your destiny. That I am certain of."

He pronounced the disease *myladia*, as if addressing a princess.

He said, "I tried to imagine what my destiny might be. Monogamous, parent of soon to be three, homeowner in Whitebreadsville, federal employee—"

"Hey, that's my destiny."

He pulled her closer to him. "It's a little tamer than I would have predicted," he said. "More challenging; more abstemious. But whenever I come out here for a smoke, I see it, that this is what I was meant for."

Promise was stunned. Anxiety evacuated her body as powerfully as if she had thrown up. The absence made her euphoric. Was it love or secondhand smoke? She was a giantess watching a tiny fireworks display set off in the amphitheater of a pint-sized Weber. She unclenched her hand and held it up, where the fire's glow imparted a red surround. Cold air hit her teeth all the way back to her sensitive molars; still, she was helpless to suppress her big grin. Leo's declaration led her out of the low-ceilinged halls of guilt and worry into openness, the same place Rumi took her. A shiver ran through her, a chill that rattled her teeth. She was stoned on intimacy.

"You're freezing," Leo said. "Let's go inside."

In the living room, they huddled in front of the television, on the corduroy couch whose wales were more crusty than soft. A beer commercial tickled her, and then one of those obtuse drug commercials showed an ecstatic, daisy-bedecked woman twirling around as a voice-over intimated glorious rebirth in pill form. Ask your doctor about enjoying spring; ask your doctor about welcoming the morning. Ask your doctor for some dope, Promise thought. The woman's whirling looked like the *sema* dance of the Sufis. Meanwhile, the voice-over was relating occurrences of severe cramping, migraines, or occasionally, stomach hemorrhaging or death.

"Take it from Rumi," Promise said. "'Either you see the Beloved, or you lose your head!'"

"Nothing in between?" Leo asked. Then a tire ad working the safety angle came on, and he squeezed Promise close.

"Babies." She pointed.

"You've got to love them."

Tubby, multicolored infants sat atop tires traveling on a cushion of air. They'd found the most beautiful babies to advertise their tires, unless there was baby makeup. The babies zoomed off the screen, going for the ride of their lives.

"Bye, babies," Promise said, sorry to see their folds of fat replaced by the lean and muscular weather reporter. She found the remote and flipped the set off before the woman began talking about the snow they could see for themselves. You would have thought they lived in hell for all the coverage flurries got in this town. Where Promise hailed from, people knew that weather happens, and she wondered how different D.C. would be if tornadoes came tearing through every fall and spring. She thought about what she had weathered today, and she was touched again by Leo's declaration that he was living his destiny.

It was unlike Leo to profess anything so religious. Sitting together in the dark, his hand on her swollen breast, was much more his style. Did she believe she had a destiny? What about someone like Joseph, was he destined to be tortured by extremists in the desert? People always talked about the museum's mission. Did the museum have a destiny? Leo was kissing her neck again, he knew she liked that, but she pulled away from him suddenly.

She had a wild look, as if her big dilated eyes had let in a different quality of light, and Leo figured she was on to him. He wondered how long it would be before he absolved himself for his big mouth, Talbot, and that damn bowl.

She said, "What if Cecil, or whoever's behind this, thought of us as a kind of threat? I mean, if we can throw one bowl down the stairs, why can't we throw all of them?"

Leo pinched his thumb and forefinger together, then opened them up. "Oops," he said.

She followed the imaginary object from his hand down to its crash on the couch. It was easy to follow, because he whistled a descending scale and then made the sound of a crash.

He said, "There's always the Jersey approach."

"What do you know from Jersey?"

He spoke in a gangster voice: "That's a nice museum you've got. It'd be a shame if something happened to it."

She clapped her hand over her mouth at his audacity. After so many years of marriage, you tend to doubt what your spouse is capable of.

"Promise?" Leo asked.

"What is it?"

"That when push comes to shove, you'll push . . . That whatever happens at the museum, you'll know I was on your side."

"I Promise," she said, taking him by the hand and leading him up-stairs.

They brushed their teeth side by side, old married couple style. Though he could see her clearly in the sink above the mirror, when she turned her face to him, she was a little hard for him to delineate with his deteriorating close vision. He followed her into the bedroom, where she quickly took her clothes off, leaving them on the floor so she could climb under the quilt. Leo's penis was like a diving board in his pants. It had been two weeks since they'd had sex, and he was going to have to hold himself back from devouring his hugely pregnant, curva-ceous wife. She couldn't lie on her back anymore, and she wasn't com-fortable on her knees. That left plenty. He threw his clothes on top of hers, stepped out of his underwear, and climbed in on her side, leaving his glasses on her nightstand. There were a bunch of extra pillows in the bed, which she would use at night under her belly, between her knees, at her lower back. He pulled them out one by one and put them on the other side of her, then he lifted the quilt to admire her round-ness, barely affected by gravity. They didn't say a word.

Promise wanted to give Leo a taste of the connection she felt for him, which for Leo meant sex. Unfortunately, the baby within her con-founded lust and seemed to suck up most of her juices. The relief in not being able to take pregnancy-related classes this time around was that there was always some nutcase who effused about never having felt healthier or more wanton than when she was pregnant. Promise brought Rumi into her head, "The tambourine begs, *Touch my skin so I can be myself.* Let me feel you enter each limb bone by bone."

Leo kissed one of her breasts, around and around the nipple, then he licked the nipple and listened for her high moan, the sound the slipping fan belt had made in his first car. Maybe they'd discover new spots of pleasure on her body, engorged or mashed together. He guessed at a few, but she moved him away. He could tell she was doing this for him—he knew she was uncomfortable all the time now—and he loved her for making this effort. Soon enough, she rolled over to show him the world in her plummy ass, bigger and better than ever; then she parted her legs. When she guided him into her, he thought his heart would explode.

Snow

January 8, 2000

Promise awoke hot and unsettled from a night of fragmented sleep, and sore from having sex, however brief it had been. She shook the clock with disbelief that it was after nine. Felix bounded out of bed by six on Saturdays, and even if Leo was the one who got up with the kids, it was hard to sleep through the din of breakfast, cartoons, and Flipper action. Too bad her extra hours hadn't been more restful. There was the bowl, of course, a continuous loop of it endlessly falling. A million pieces—do I hear a billion? Who will give me a billion? In one version, Talbot spiked the porcelain through a hoop Arthur made with his arms. But Joseph was there too, poor man. Things hadn't gone so well for him in her dreams.

Joseph's jailers taunted him with museum jargon, which they interpreted literally. Citing *cut backs*, his captors sliced him across the shoulder blades. One traced a dotted line across his chest with a machete drawn from a gold hilt enameled in green. *Meet your deadline*, he taunted. A wizened old Uygur threw his last drops of canteen water in Joseph's face—your *final draft*, the ruffian pointed out. Promise noted the canteen was ceramic, she recognized it from Gallery XVI. The crux of the dream was whether to use or avert her eyes. How could she appreciate the Islamic decoration of a canteen in the hands of Joseph's tormentor? Then came the gore of the *exhibition run-through*, where they plunged daggers into his chest and she admired the incising work of the blade. It was horrific to watch herself cataloging the weapons responsible for Joseph's trauma.

Soothed somewhat to be awake in her own bed, she bristled at the thought of Joseph facing such mayhem. Equally troubling was her dream double, dispassionately appreciating the artistry of the blade at Joseph's heart. This calculating effect—*hmm, what's this worth to us?*—seemed to be the cost of bringing the museum and Joseph onto the front page.

Sweltering, she slid out of bed and pulled on a thin nightgown, then Leo's chenille robe, which barely made it around her belly. Edgar, that water baby, fluttered his feet near her pelvis, on the underside of the globe she carried with her every heavy step. She pulled the curtain back to see enough snow for actual drifts in their tiny front yard. What do you know? Despite the hype, it was still a surprise, because the forecasters so often called it wrong.

The undisturbed cars were lined up against the curb like cupcakes on a bakery shelf. Promise let the curtain drop and shuffled to the bathroom favoring her crampy right leg. The floor was ice cold on her feet, which was so refreshing she laid her hands on the sink to feel that cold as well.

Downstairs, the kitchen table wore the crusty, sticky remains of a family breakfast; however, there was no family in sight. She thought of a line from one of Felix's books, something about how the quiet was so quiet that quiet filled the air. She put clean dishes away and then cleared the table to trash can and dishwasher. At the sink, the sponge grew sodden with water until her fingers squeezed it dry and weightless again. Such was life.

Things intensified when she scooped her oatmeal from box to bowl and added water. This mass-produced vessel might become an object of veneration in a mere two hundred years. She pushed the button that sent microwaves through the oat flakes and water molecules, fluffing up the porridge with a zap, the way a jinn might make food in an Arabian Night tale.

She followed a train of thought for an entire two minutes. How much did Arthur really know about his bowl? She'd just read about the curators at the Tenement Museum guessing the use of a ledge high up in each apartment's kitchen. Citing the influx of Italians and Irish to the Lower East Side, they had deduced that the niche displayed a religious statue until an old lady who'd grown up next door explained it was a shelf for the gas meter. Granted, sometimes it took generations to dig past a person's reputation. In her lifetime, JFK had gone from charismatic president, Navy hero, and civil rights visionary to drug-popping womanizer with mob connections. When the timer rang, she marveled at how far her thoughts had taken her. She dressed her cereal, thrilled to see the brown sugar melt before she added milk. Usually, her oatmeal was cold beige lumps by the time she'd attended to the demands in the kitchen.

Through the back window, she saw Leo holding Felix in front of him as a human shield against Lydia's snowballs, which Flipper went head over heels trying to catch. Promise tapped her nails on the windowpane, and everyone waved. It was a miracle they'd all found boots, snow pants, mittens, hats without her. Leo had actually snagged her coat, which ended high above his waist and exposed a good three inches of bare arm between sleeve and glove. He was wearing her skin; surrounded by his chenille robe, she was wearing his.

She considered her well-appointed oatmeal in its bowl, a utilitarian piece with attractive, fairly generic yellow wavy stripes and no sentimental value. If it broke, big damn deal. On some level, that was how she'd felt about Arthur's brouhaha. Things break. Would she have felt the same way about an album leaf of the same vintage, say if it were shredded or burned? She was glad she didn't have to find out. A bowl was not a life; on the other hand, a bowl like Arthur's was the art that life makes, and we preserve it mindful of that, even worshipful of that.

Without leaving her chair, she was able to find paper and a working pen: a sheet of Amnesty International notepaper folded up in Leo's bathrobe pocket and a pen that had nearly fallen through the radiator behind her. Her list-making reflex took over. Dog-proof answering machine, milk, dishwasher detergent, oatmeal. She drew a line down the middle of the page, leaving those concerns on the left; the right side was for an inventory of people who could come to their aid.

Senator Houlihan had told her to get opposition that was too hot or holy for the Castle to ignore. She jotted down the names of a few writers and artists who shared an abiding love for Asia. What did she know about hot or holy? Whoever had seen the Museum of Asian Art and thought, Good place for a food court—that person needed to be converted. Whose outrage would get people to take notice? Who attracted crowds? Who looked good on camera? The Dalai Lama, Mother Teresa, and Lady Di. Even though the nun and princess were unavailable, she wrote their names down to get her list-making juices flowing. It sounded like the beginning of a joke: The Dalai Lama, Mother Teresa, and Lady Di walk into a museum . . .

A big wet snowball slapped against the window, oozing down the pane like spit. Promise waved at her family on the other side of the glass. She waved with a Lady Di swivel, and in a British accent all her own, she addressed her loyal subjects, "Brilliant, then. Don't even think of coming in; I've locked all the entrances."

The phone rang, and she picked it up with her royal hand.

"Promise, sweetie, it's your mother."

"My mother, Peg? That mother?" Disappointed that Promise and family hadn't come for Christmas, Peg had volunteered to visit. Leo was especially looking forward to her meat loaf as well as help with the children.

Peg said, "I wanted to make sure you have my flight information."

"I've got it all by another phone. How are you?"

"We're fine. I'm coming in six days; we can talk then."

Promise ignored her plea for frugality. "Mom, remember that bowl I told you about? Arthur's bowl?"

"The million-dollar one."

"It broke. In front of God and everybody. Rolled right down the big old stairway yesterday morning."

"Do you have insurance?"

Enough with the insurance bit! she wanted to yell, but Peg wouldn't know the comfort of that had worn thin. "It's irreplaceable," she said instead.

"Of course it is, honey. Are the children all right? How are you feeling with the baby?" Peg wished her daughter would move back to Oklahoma. Three-bedroom houses with big yards were going for less than a hundred thousand. She would probably have a good chance of teaching world religions at the Nazarene College, or maybe she could give Indian cooking lessons. If Leo really cared about the environment and human rights, people were always trying to clean up the Canadian River.

Peg was alone in her thoughts for a moment because Promise had retreated to hers. The repetition of the insurance line coupled with her mother's asking about the baby awakened something dormant in Promise's memory. Min had told her that she'd undergone a dozen different tests, several followed up by surgeries, before she could even attempt an in vitro procedure. If Promise remembered correctly, Min had confessed to spending forty thousand of their own money before looting the Institution's coffers. Surely her tests and surgery would be covered, if not all her in vitro costs. Promise recalled the night she'd told Leo she was pregnant and they'd also talked about Min. Leo had suggested Min and Douglas might be too timid to submit a claim. She remembered all this now, though she hadn't given it a thought for two months. What if there was enough reimbursement in their procedures to refill Min's travel funds?

"Is something up?" Peg asked.

"No, Mom," she answered. "Nothing's wrong with the baby. Let's see: Lydia's seeing snakes everywhere, and Felix—" She didn't know what to say about Felix, who lived on air and chocolate and attracted fleas. "Felix is a case."

"Oh, my Promise, you're too sheltered. You need to get out in the world."

This coming from a retired homemaker in Oklahoma City. "What does that mean?"

"Talk to other mothers, sweetheart. Kids climb a mountain one day and are afraid of their socks the next. Did you know that a child's will is so strong he can hold his breath until he passes out? An adult can't do that."

"Lordy, Lordy—I can't wait till you get here."

"How did the bowl fall?" Peg asked.

"Arthur dropped it. He wasn't even supposed to pick it up, but he couldn't keep his hands off."

"Well, I'm sure he has to answer to himself now," Peg said. "Honey, your father's breathing down my neck. Either he needs to use the phone or he just wants me off."

"Love you."

"Love you more." Peg hung up so fast, she almost cut herself off.

"Everyone has to answer to himself"—how many times had Promise heard her mother say that? More than "People should share their ice cream before it melts." Even more than "To everything there is a season." Peg's notions of privacy and personal responsibility could be more extreme than Leo's; however, her aphorisms had an edge to them. Promise's skin got prickly just thinking about how she aimed her sayings your way, letting you know she was on to you. Some people think more of poets than of God, or there are those who smoke their marijuana, but at the end of the day, everyone has to answer to himself.

Promise looked out at the live oak, its brown shriveled leaves still hanging on to the branches. Tenacious or deluded, who was to say? The trunk was pocked with white circles because the children were making snowballs and handing them off to Leo, who pelted the tree. Felix kicked up a snow shower that he and Flipper ran through. Hats were off, and the children's hair was plastered down, a signal to start up the hot chocolate. Big, fat flakes were still falling, weighing down the wires and bending the tree limbs, with their curled leaves, closer and closer to the ground. It wouldn't be long before something snapped, all the more reason to admire the view from her kitchen window.

———

Individual snowcaps mounded each slat of the American white picket fence at Douglas and Min's house in Vienna, Virginia. Inside the living room, Sally lay on her stomach, feet kicking her rump, ingesting another Nancy Drew book. Her father had the local news on, which bugged her. Usually he watched his channels, and she could hear the nasal swishing sounds of Chinese without being distracted. She was reading a version in which Nancy's blue roadster had become a Mustang convertible, which she drove in the middle of the night to the criminal's lair. Sally had finished all of the original series and was now skipping around the second and third updates of them. Nancy's hair and skirt changed; she went from sixteen to eighteen and picked up Ned, the boyfriend; Bess and George met her at the mall instead of the soda shop. It was like the many versions of "Li Chi Slays the Serpent," one of the stories her mother tailored to the goings-on in Sally's own life. They didn't change Nancy Drew's personality. She was always polite as any Chinese kid, but her nerve and independence were wholly American, as American as the brick colonials that both Nancy and Sally lived in.

Sally looked up from her book to locate her mother. She liked it best when her parents were on the couch and she was on the floor reading, a neat triangle.

In his peripheral vision, Douglas caught the flick of his daughter's hair, like a glossy horse tail, swishing across her back. "Do you want to go to the kitchen?" he asked.

"I'm fine, Daddy," she said. Her father was pretty anxious about things; her mother was not very satisfied either—she'd pick on Sally's posture or her lack of homework—but Sally didn't take their moods personally. Chinese people were serious. The newscasters on the Chinese news stations faced forward and delivered their stories without smiling. On the other channels, the people cracked up through the news, giggling from the headlines to the weather. She thought of her parents as dignified, substantive, and a little nutty. Her mother, for example, could flip from pride to shame in her Chinese heritage, and her father did the same with American stuff, like the Wal-Mart outside their subdivision. Its endless variety amused or irritated him, depending on how long it had taken him to find his green shampoo or what he saw in people's carts. Something like a hot dog maker, a machine that only warmed up hot dogs, really got under his skin.

Sally felt she soothed them somehow, just by turning the pages of her book.

Her father said, "She might be in the bedroom."

"I think she's in the kitchen. It's okay, Dad." Sally looked from her father to the snow falling outside and then at the television screen, where the Washington reporter tossed a snowball directly at the camera.

Douglas wondered if the Metro was functioning and if he could slip out to the university's indoor running track. The Marine Corps Marathon was two months away. He concentrated on the storm coverage, which was dedicated to cars sliding into each other. Such a graceful, slow-motion release of friction until cars touched, then both gave way in a horrible crumpling of steel. Sport-utility vehicles resembled tanks but behaved like overinflated paper bags. Television cameras couldn't get enough of it. "The driver reports that he could not stop . . ." "Apparently, the Toyota crossed the center line . . ." "When the paramedics could not get through, witnesses say, the child could not be saved . . ." People were asked to stay put, and yet on every channel, a news crew had braved it to another accident scene. Bundled-up correspondents pointed leather gloves at flashing lights and steaming wrecks. "Reporting live," "Reporting live," "Reporting live," they bragged.

Min came into the living room with a tray of tea and butter crackers. "This is news, that snow makes road icy?" Both Sally and Douglas relaxed. It was an unspoken rule that if they were all home, they were all together.

"Big story," Douglas said. "Some drive too fast; some are careless."

Sally hadn't seen how trivial the stories were until her parents pointed it out. She said, "This is news, that one car hitting another causes damage?" Her parents tilted their heads appreciatively. She couldn't imagine what was news in Taiwan.

Min had poured their tea into American mugs so she only had to fill them once. She was trying to distance herself from choosing the right cups, reading the tea leaves one way or another.

She'd discounted Arthur's bowl for any number of reasons—its newness, glitzy provenance, inflated price—but she'd also put her egg in that basket. She might as well, she'd reasoned, seeing as how everyone else had. She'd raised an overabundance of money for the porcelain so she could clear her name. She'd also interpreted the good wishes painted on the piece as a sign that "winter would offer the joy of a new life." She read "boy" for "joy." Now that the vessel was broken, it seemed the most precious bowl in the world. Should that surprise her, that something she'd deemed paltry was so precious? Her Sally had already taught her that lesson. She rubbed her hand over her own tiny bowl of a belly, uncertain what message this calamity had for her.

She should have known better than to put her future in Arthur's hands. Was a broken bowl the sign of miscarriage? She'd had some spotting of blood, which Dr. Fan assured her many pregnant women experienced. Arthur wouldn't know about the custom of breaking the rice bowl at someone's funeral. She was so afraid of losing the baby that she felt herself going over to the "boy/girl, just so it's healthy" camp. That seemed a sign in itself.

"Who is this Nancy Drew?" she asked Sally. "You have so many books by her. Is she famous?"

"She's a character, Mommy. She figures stuff out; sometimes I can get the mystery before she does."

Douglas turned off the television. "So clever," he spoke in English.

"She's amazing." Sally thought he was talking about her heroine. "And she can fix a car or gallop bareback on a horse."

"Modest *and* smart," Douglas pointed out in Mandarin. "Remind me why our hearts are set on a boy."

"You've forgotten?" Min asked. She loved her daughter, frankly more than she had expected to, and she knew Sally's worth would only increase with a boy in the house.

Meanwhile, Douglas had been revisiting the givens in their life, including the premise of his being a Chinese economist whose specialty was the American market. He had left China because he'd wanted more and he believed that more was available in America. More children, more choices, more money, more success. If they really wanted to show the folks back home, they should go back to China and sweep up a few girl orphans to live with them.

Min knelt on the carpet with Sally's cup of tea. She saw the surprised look in her daughter's dark eyes when she stroked her black hair. A brother, she wanted to tell her, you're going to have a baby brother! She was looking at Sally but talking to Douglas. "Nancy Drew," she said, then reverted to Mandarin, "solves crimes and rides horses and fixes car. That makes good reading because she's a girl. Capable as girls are, it's always a surprise to have a girl hero. No girl presidents, even in this country that is so high-minded; no girl priests."

"Some girl priests," Douglas said.

"What are you guys talking about?" Sally asked. "What about Nancy Drew?"

"It could hurt your eyes, reading here," Min said. She rocked back off her knees and turned on another light in the living room, then handed Douglas his *Economist* from the top of the reading stack. Beneath the magazine was the pregnancy book they'd consulted daily when Min was expecting Sally. Douglas pushed his glasses against the bridge of his nose to make sure he'd seen correctly.

"That book is for *expecting*," he pointed out in Mandarin. He got up off his chair and came to her on the couch. He didn't want to return to Dr. Fan's laboratory. More directly than he'd ever spoken to his wife, he said, "Girl or boy, I would like us to be expecting."

Min was so turned around right now, she couldn't tell if keeping a baby girl would be a step forward or a step backward. Snow swirled outside the front window, reminding her of all the eggs they'd culti-vated from her and stored in the deep freeze. No matter how many they'd implanted, tiny frozen eggs had dropped right out of her uterus like ice cubes from a tray. Then she and Douglas had gone ahead to make a baby with their own spark, no strangers handling their progeny. What if the baby were a girl: was her heart cold enough to freeze out a child?

Sally closed her book. "What's going on, guys? What's up?" She climbed on the couch but couldn't get between them. Whatever was happening, she needed to be included, and so she reclined across them: her legs were pitched like a tent on the end cushion as she sat on her mother's lap and rested the back of her neck on her father's thigh. He fit a couch pillow under her head for support. She was wor-ried her mother would ask her to sit like a civilized girl; instead, she rubbed Sally's flannel pajamas at her kneecap. If they were a TV or movie kind of family, they might have burst into song. But they were a book family, a painting family, and didn't have to show off. Sally loved having both her parents to herself; she hoped the snow would keep them together in the house all weekend long. Maybe her mother would make dumplings, she thought, yawning as both her parents settled into their magazines, holding them inches above her prone body. From where she lay, she could see over the magazines out the window, where flakes fell from the clouds like down from a feather pillow.

———

Up in Talbot's Market Square loft, Arthur stretched under the sheets, rubbing his foot up and down Talbot's leg. "Is this why you didn't go military?"

"Is what why?"

Arthur pulled back the top sheet to show him what he'd apparently forgotten, that he was in bed with a man.

"There's plenty of this in the military, so I'm told."

So he was one of those. Make you feel stupid if you refer to sex you've had together. Their time in bed aside, Arthur didn't like it here. You had to climb a metal ladder to the bedroom, which had a railing along one side to prevent you from stepping off a ledge should you get up to take a piss in the middle of the night. Arthur saw the snow falling past the oversized porthole, but he couldn't see down to the street. "I just got it! You live on a ship. All you need is a water bed."

"They sleep in cots."

Arthur said, "I think they're called bunks. You want top or bottom?"

Talbot sat up. "Thanks. I'll keep what I've got."

Turning away, he managed to step into his boxers, barely flashing his ass. Talbot's evasiveness was tearing Arthur up. He longed to dwell on the great ceremony they'd envisioned. It wasn't Talbot's fault that Arthur had gone overboard, but at least he could show some sympathy. Of course, the person Arthur should be waking up next to was Morty, who might have predicted this would happen.

Talbot was wishing he'd left Arthur at the bar. When the AWOL curator had turned up in Promise's office, Talbot had practically high-fived him—brilliant execution! Two drinks later, as Arthur wallowed away, it annoyed Talbot to hear him take credit for the drop, almost as much as it repelled him to be with someone so susceptible, a pushover, as it were. The last time they'd messed around, Arthur had shown the self-respect not to be so eager. When Talbot had tried to get him off the topic, Arthur couldn't even stand to hear what good might come of it, stuck in his nostalgia for the bowl that got away.

"How about a shower?" Arthur asked.

"I'm fine," Talbot said curtly.

Arthur wanted them to head for the steamy locker room, where men freely stroked each other's butts and spoke crudely but sincerely. Everything Talbot had told him to forget about had returned in the morning light, and now Arthur felt slutty on top of depressed. He'd lost his beautiful porcelain treasure; he'd thrown it over, just as he'd probably done with Morty, and he could use a little soul-soothing compassion and some more sex to take his mind off things.

Arthur put on his glasses to see Talbot standing at his dresser. It was heavy American, probably from Philadelphia, no doubt a family legacy. Arthur wondered how they had lifted the ton of maple up into the loft. Talbot's smooth back was certainly nothing like Morty's hairy expanse, though their shoulders were equally wide. Talbot pulled on a thick black T-shirt that managed to look French and then took a pair of professionally laundered button-fly Levi's from a hanger in his well-organized closet.

"You look great. Whose shirt is that?"

"Mine," Talbot said.

Arthur didn't even explain that he meant who was the designer.
"May I take a shower?"

"Go ahead. You want coffee when you come out?"

"Sure."

Arthur stepped out of the bed buck naked, exposing himself in a
last-ditch effort to drum up some interest, but Talbot would not look
his way. Sobered up, he looked around the bathroom, where the only
nongeneric decoration was the Japanese-print shower curtain and a
small woodcut of—what else?—a clipper ship. Soap, shampoo, condi-
tioner were all high-end but not specific. Did Talbot have to hide even
in the bathroom? Where was the tan-preserving shower gel for closet-
case athletes with a bit of a bald spot? Arthur had a spasm of panic at
the thought of his pants over the bedroom chair, pants with a chip of
Jingdezhen porcelain in the front pocket that may well have fallen out
or would fall out if Talbot riffled through them just now. Jesus, he
scolded himself, if that's what you think, why the hell did you go to bed
with him?

Arthur knew that what they were having wasn't a relationship. He
leaned against the side of the shower stall, cold tile raising goose
bumps on his upper arms. He needed to get out of here and go home,
if he still had a home. He jerked off and finished up, wrapping an ad-
mirably substantial bath towel round himself. In the medicine cabinet
he found the source of Talbot's beachy smell, and he cadged a Xanax.
There was also a small box of tampons—did that make Talbot more
fascinating or less?

He thought of reaching into that family dresser for some clean underwear. He got as far as opening the drawer, which squealed. Instead,
he put on yesterday's clothes, looking like the skank he was. He left his
vest unbuttoned. Down the cold ladder, where a misstep could ruin
your morning, into the shipshape kitchen he went. He folded his coat
over a chair at the kitchen counter. Two cups were wedged in an egg-
carton-like tray for four. Talbot had filled the remaining wells with
three kinds of sugars, stirrers, and napkins.

Talbot had almost picked up a *Post* too but couldn't risk Arthur
searching for mention of himself. Later, he'd see if there was any cov-

erage; maybe check in with the Whittaker-Wellses. He was eager to get a nod from Leo, had frankly expected as much at some point yesterday. He said, "I didn't know if you took milk or not, so I got one with and one without."

There must have been a coffee shop in the building, because Talbot didn't look as if he'd braved the snow. Arthur scanned the kitchen. The refrigerator door wasn't flapping with snapshots or even nice postcards. The marble counters were bare. Even Morty, who hated clutter, had coffee equipment, including a hand grinder for beans and a double-globed brewing contraption that could have come from a laboratory. "You didn't have to go out. Allow me to make us breakfast."

"There's nothing really to make. I don't cook here."

What kind of person doesn't own a toaster, Arthur wondered. "You have another apartment for cooking. One at the marina, perhaps?"

"What is with you and boats?" Talbot asked.

Arthur reached into his pants pocket and felt the sharp edge of his chip, which he wouldn't mind dusting for fingerprints. Xanax on an empty stomach had been a mistake. If it relaxed his inhibitions, he was pretty sure he'd start bawling like a baby.

Neither he nor Talbot had claimed a cup of coffee. Milk or no milk, Arthur thought, Talbot could not reveal his tastes. In wedging the black coffee out of the holder, Arthur dislodged the lid, burning himself on the wrist and splashing his silk vest. "Shit!" he spit out.

"Do you want ice—I do have that." Talbot swung open the freezer, where a few pints of high-end ice cream lived alone, the equivalent of tampons in the medicine cabinet.

No, I want you to kiss my humiliation away. Stick your tongue down my throat, then throw me on your Italian couch and ravage me. Make me a fucking omelet and tell me, please, what to do with this huge shard in my pocket. Arthur stared at Talbot's cheekbones, barely visible under a scrim of blond hair. "I don't need ice," he said. He was hungry, and he yearned for companionship, two needs Talbot could not meet. Arthur gathered up his coat from the back of the chair. "I think I'll head home."

He hoped it would be snowing on his and Morty's balcony.

Box of Crumbs

January 10, 2000

Even with the snow clogging up the city, Lucy Yarmolinsky got to the museum by seven Monday morning. She turned on the space heater beneath her desk. She washed her hands with the special conservator's soap, dried them, and put on her lint-free gloves. She didn't drink coffee or tea; couldn't sharpen her wits at the risk of the boost wearing off. In her work, she had to maintain the same concentration all the day long. This was also the reason she ate only uncooked food, though people gave her grief over how unscientific that was. Once her feet were warm, she shut off the heater. She'd been doing her exercises lately, so her feet weren't bothering her much.

She was the only American on the conservation staff. Sometimes she was self-conscious about being a tall redhead among six small-boned Japanese men who ignored her. Other times, she appreciated the anonymity. Her job was to stay behind the scenes.

Porcelain is called "china" because it originated there around 200 B.C. As early as the fifteenth century, Chinese artisans learned how to remove dark contaminants from kaolin clay and eliminate blue or gray tints from their clear glaze. Adding china stone to the kaolin intensified the brightness; the result is a sparkling white that European porcelain never attained.

Making porcelain is something like making bread. Recipes abound, which potters adjusted for plasticity or color. There were molds they packed their sticky loaves into, or they shaped them by hand. China stone, however, so affected the clay's flexibility that artisans carved shapes down from the wheel-thrown form or employed molds. Incising, outlining, coloring in, underglazing, and overglazing were done on distinct layers, hence there were many opportunities to ruin a work in progress. The asymmetry of MAA1999.127 had been evidence that its exceedingly thin shape came off the wheel as is.

She reviewed her knowledge as a way of psyching herself up; you had to have some nerve before taking on a million-dollar object. In this case, no amount of motivation or reverence could change the fact that she was faced with a box of crumbs.

Lucy had been standing right there with the rest of them when Arthur Franklin fumbled it. She would have guessed it would be painful to watch an object self-destruct, and so she was surprised to feel a rare second of release, of blamelessness. She was briefly liberated from the conservator's pledge: Do no further damage. The only way to further damage that bowl was to put it in the blender. Next came satisfaction, because whatever repair she was faced with, she found herself asking, "How did this happen?" Of course, having witnessed this accident, she knew how it happened. Then came the regret that this once-in-a-lifetime opportunity was a porcelain bowl, because broken porcelain doesn't reveal much. It was a shame it wasn't lacquer.

Because the piece was initially on loan and then considered for purchase, the object folder was mostly provenance and condition report, and as Arthur had told the gathered, the condition report was nearly empty. Provenance didn't matter so much then, except to know that the piece had been intact—neither chipped nor cracked—when they got it. She did like to know whose hands an object had been through. The grime on a bronze Shiva might be from temple ghee burned at its base or from Park Avenue candle wax. Each culture had different dirt. And different ways of cleaning, too. Obviously, you need a different cleaner to eradicate lemon Pledge versus incense residue. Some effects she erased, others she enhanced: she might take off layers of beeswax but rub again with tea leaves.

She brought pieces back closer to the past, flip-flopping time in her hands. People were always likening her work to assembling a puzzle, which she found insulting. Did they say that to surgeons? The way you reattached that artery, restored the blood flow, threaded a catheter, sutured and stitched—you must love puzzles. She thought of her work as safeguarding the objects' integrity, though in this case she'd first have to reconstruct the object.

After she weighed her box of crumbs, she looked up the weight recorded in the folder. In comparison, she came up short by a sizable chunk. Considering how she'd swept the path of destruction, she'd expected to have picked up a few grams in dust or even as much as the weight of a wayward button. Based on the thinness of the object and the density of this particular kaolin/china-stone mix, she calculated that if all that weight were in one spot, she was missing a chunk about six centimeters wide. There were a few other pieces of that magnitude from the foot; everything else was below a centimeter. Her thoroughness had extended from the top step to a wide radius around the last bounce. Had people published papers on how far chips bounce? There were folks who, under the auspices of testing tensile strength, hardness of materials, or softness of floor coverings, dropped things off platforms at various heights. Art handlers liked that kind of research.

Soon enough the other conservators came in, smelling of fish and cigarette smoke, and they all greeted one another. The boys, as she thought of them, chattered among themselves in Japanese and some Chinese. They had the bad manners from their Chinese apprenticeships, slurping and burping and blowing their noses into the trash can from on high. Their responsibility was anything flat—screens and scrolls, drawings and albums, lately even photographs—and they worked flat, bent over at the waist, for hours at a time. Because museum funds were so dear, she alone handled the rest: sculpture, ceramics, religious statuary, furniture, baskets, musical instruments. She had a huge backlog, which she tried to think of as job security. The bowl had been bumped, as it were, to the front of the line.

Lucy began sorting the biggest shards according to position. The largest chunk of the bowl was an unglazed part of the foot. Wouldn't you know it? Nothing remained with the straight, thin edge of the bowl's lip. Lucy flexed each of her feet and did five ankle rolls apiece. Aah, the unglazed, clunky foot. Army doctors had broken her ankles and reset them when she was three; otherwise, they predicted that little Lucy would never walk right. What could her parents do? As a three-year-old, she did walk funny, and these conscripted doctors were

the experts in her parents' life. She'd had another three or four surgeries after that, in Vietnam, California, Washington; each subsequent
surgeon would shake his head disapprovingly at his predecessor's approach. It was the same disapproval one generation of conservators visited on another. Maybe her doctors had been miracle workers, because
she walked great. She hiked and she ran. But still, her feet hurt. Maybe
she would have outgrown her problems or exercised them away.

Her phone rang, and she slipped off her gloves. On the line was an
insurance man. "I understand you have fragments, nothing more.
Would you say it's a complete loss?"

As a person who worked with whatever she was given, she couldn't
say. She lightly sifted the contents from side to side. "Well, I'm paid to
reassemble the fragments, so to me it's a livelihood."

The insurance man sighed. "It wasn't a philosophical question."

But it was. She asked, "Is it a complete loss if I manage to get it
back together? With this kind of rehabilitation, it would only be suitable for museum living—"

"Think of it as a 'ninety-five Acura that met a telephone pole, head-
on, at full speed. Bumpers shattered, headlights exploded."

"Windshield?" she led him on.

"Busted out," the insurance guy said, with some enthusiasm.
"Crackly lines like a bullet hit it, then all the pieces fall on the front
seat, so now it's not even safe to sit there."

"I'm not following," the conservator said. "I don't know anything
about cars."

————

Promise and Leo had yet to leave for work. The kids had already been
outside this morning, soaking through one change of clothes. Although
there wasn't enough snow to cancel school, there was more than
enough to snarl the commute. Public transportation would be carrying
a sweaty, impatient mob. Promise was lucky to find a medium-weight
maternity dress with a drawstring waist in her closet. When she
checked to see if Felix was getting dressed, he was standing in his underwear holding a nine-volt battery to his tongue.

"Did you take that from the smoke detector?"

"No, my yellow car had it."

"Good," she said foolishly. "I mean, batteries aren't for licking."

He laid his little tongue right back on the terminals, then jerked as if he'd been shocked. "You can tell it's good if it buzzes you."

She felt his forehead, checked the thermostat on the way to Lydia's room. "Who's sick?"

"Is that a trick question?" Lydia said. "Are we all staying home today?"

"Not me. I've got to face the music."

"What does that mean?"

Put my hand in the fire, get raked over the coals . . . "Go to work," Promise said.

Leo handed her a plate of toast when she came downstairs. "Hey, we're all over the editorial page," he said, and he brought the paper closer to her as she flung jelly around, savaging the bread. "Take it easy. We can drop the kids off and then go down together."

"If I leave now?" She could see Flipper in the backyard leaping up and down as if on a pogo stick. Overhead, the children's elephant steps clumped, and then Lydia slid down the banister with a whoop that shook a blob of jam from Promise's toast to her shelf of a belly.

Leo wiped it up with his finger. "You'll just sit in traffic. Metro will be a mob scene."

"True enough," she said, and she looked fearfully at the *Post*. Both the conservative and the liberal columnists had embraced the museum controversy. "You Want Fries with That Painting?" read the headline across one; halfway down the page was "Institution Adapts to Visitors' Needs." Scanning the articles, she saw an abundance of quotations from the Castle memo. Handing over the primary source had been Leo's idea.

"No one from the Castle would comment," he said.

Promise sighed. "Well, I'm glad I'm not the only one the Castle isn't talking to."

"Daddy," Felix asked innocently. "Will you make me waffles and bacon? Mommy said I should eat and eat and eat."

"Yesterday I said that," Promise called from the kitchen. "Sunday."

"Mom?" Lydia said. "Mom? Mom? Mom?"

"I'm right here, honey."

"I made up a new joke. What do your bowl and a gymnast have in common?"

"What?"

"They're both Chinese tumblers!" Lydia giggled with pleasure.

Promise stared at her nine-year-old. "When did you get so clever?" She missed her firstborn, who had complicated her life with so much joy and responsibility. She wished she could take her out for a fancy tea or walk with her in the botanic garden or just brush her long hair. Surely, she could make time to brush Lydia's hair. Lydia was taking her museum, complete with bullet and crack vials, into school. "I'll carry it," Promise volunteered. "I'll hold it in the front seat."

"What if the baby kicks?"

"Put it with us in the back!" Felix demanded, which helped Promise's cause.

She held Lydia's gallery up as Leo drove. An entire museum she kept in her hands, suspended in air above the bumps and potholes. To Lydia's credit, nothing seemed to be rattling around beneath the felt roof of the Whittaker-Wells Gallery; nevertheless, its director kibitzed from the backseat. "Don't drop it!" Lydia yelled. "Is anything loose?"

Promise led the children into school and returned to the car, immediately lowering the heat. On the Pacifica station, the DJ seethed about the government encouraging black women to abort their babies. The paranoia of the radio station, where the tip of the left wing touched the tip of the right, was making Promise queasy, as was the overheated car. She watched people funnel into the Van Ness Metro escalator before Leo's rocket thrusters kicked in and the scenery flew by. Leo changed lanes constantly, anticipating which taxi would pull over for the waving pedestrian and who might suddenly turn left. He never used his horn, rarely his turn signal; in the time it would take to tap on the horn, he'd jump over two lanes and back. Promise counted Leo's driving as another of his superhero traits.

Leo said, "You never asked Min if insurance covered anything?"

"I got waylaid," Promise admitted. "What galls me is how she just appropriated that money—she's so cavalier about it."

"To you," Leo said. "That doesn't mean she's not in agony."

Promise thought of all the phone conversations she'd had since the bowl dropped in which she'd struggled to mask her inner turmoil. Past the zoo, they turned left, snaking under the vaulted bridge and into Rock Creek Park. She said, "The Castle hasn't said a blessed thing, not to me or the press. If they're really going to close us in July, folks need fair warning."

"Has anyone looked into severance?" Leo asked. "Let's hope it comes with benefits, because those people are going to be out of work for a while."

Promise clucked her tongue at him. "Talbot used to say stuff like that."

Leo said, "Remember when you had to review two hundred résumés for an Ancient Near Eastern curator? The other hundred and ninety-nine of them are still out there."

Well, all right. There was some truth to that. It was a narrow swath of the world she specialized in. Because it was half of her whole world, she sometimes forgot.

Leo felt around under his seat for the CD case. Negotiating the twisting parkway, he manipulated the case's zipper and the soft plastic flaps, then slid his choice into the player. Low and unadorned, a voice began lamenting that the plague was coming. Leo said, "He's playing the big Amnesty event. Did you know he's a monk now?"

Promise tried to find the singer's spiritual side—how could someone be so dark and hopeful in the same breath? The notion that everything is connected could be scary; it was the source not only of mysticism but also of conspiracy theories. They were off the parkway driving along the Tidal Basin, spotty with ice. Now the singer was proclaiming "There's a blaze of light in every word" as he sang about a cold and broken Hallelujah. That was what an illuminated manuscript was, brother, the blaze of light in every word. A left turn off Independence Avenue and Leo pulled into their parking spot. Promise smiled bravely at her husband, who was both more and less than she needed. She hadn't had enough breakfast, and she was feeling shaky.

"You okay?" Leo asked, as they signed in with the guards. He held the double doors open and followed her up to the back of the courtyard. "Call me if you need me," he said. "Or just call."

"You'll be where, in the staff room?"

"Initially. There are muffins what need to be et." Then he took her hand. "I hope your Min theory bears out."

"*Your* Min theory," she said.

"Ours," Leo settled it.

With the sun reflecting off the snow, the courtyard was a shining white square. Promise was still holding Leo's hand; now she put her other hand on the other side. "Hand sandwich," she said, grateful for his presence. He smiled his crooked-tooth grin, then kissed her top hand and left her there in a blaze of light. The camellias had been laid low by the snow, which came all the way up to the lip of the fountain. She searched for the peacocks, vaguely recalling them wintering at a farm in Virginia last year. The peacock minder hadn't told her they should be moved; she couldn't bear it if one of them froze to death because of her inattention.

In fact, over at the zoo the animals were starting to die off two by two. Investigations revealed plenty of human error as well as the toll of limited staff, crumbling facilities, and no cash. They'd lost two giraffes, two zebras, an orangutan, and a lion; most recently, an exterminator hired on the cheap had poisoned the two little red pandas rather than the rats in their enclosure. At Promise's museum, they'd broken one bowl.

High-pitched screeches mewled down the east corridor, more cat than peacock. She passed her office and walked to the front of the courtyard, where she located two birds at rest, a peahen leaning against her mate. They weren't squawking with lust or being harassed by an intruder. The other pair was out of sight, though a mallard had found its way to the fountain. When the squealing resumed, Promise followed the noise into her office suite. Vanessa, at her post like the trouper that she was, said, "Arthur and Min are going at it in there."

Promise cocked her head. They were yelling in Mandarin. Rapid-fire and loud, they really sounded like cats squaring off, and she swung open the door to see them spitting mad. Of the two of them, Arthur looked more Chinese. He was wearing his rounded shoulder overcoat, a style that would have easily slipped over an emperor's embroidered robe, had the emperor required a tan raincoat. His hair was in a straggly ponytail, and he hadn't shaved lately, revealing a starter beard in that ridiculous effete Fu Manchu pattern.

Of the idioms Promise knew, she recognized the words "stupid egg" and the expression "head in the water," which Min repeated about four times.

"You care nothing for this museum," Min was yelling. "Pretty bowls with flowers on them—pretty bowls to play with. You should work in a tea shop, in a flower store!"

"For the tenth time, I fucked up!"

"That doesn't help—Americans think 'sorry' lets them off the hook. 'Sorry' is what careless rabbit boy says."

"Breaking something is not a criminal offense. At least I'm not living off my travel funds. At least I'm not trafficking in stolen goods."

Min put a hand below her stomach and backed up to the nearest desk; then she looked guiltily at Promise, who may not have understood the accusations but understood the posture of pregnancy.

Min took her hand from her stomach so she could shake it at Arthur. "How honorable is it to bed someone for his exhibition budget?"

"Whoa," Arthur said, in whatever language one uses to stop a runaway horse. "Whoa," he said again, then sank into the leather sofa. Vanessa, Promise, and Min were all staring down at him when he said quietly, in English, "Talbot pledged that money before I poked him."

"Oh, Arthur," Promise said, remembering how Talbot's face had gone slack when Arthur showed up last Friday. It was no wonder she hadn't looked up from her manuscripts all these years, for this was getting too complicated and too sad. Were they all broken to bits? Could they be of any use to one another? Maybe they were like tesserae, cracked and gleaming, which could be arranged into an impressive mosaic. Probably not. Anyway, who wanted to be cemented in place with these folks?

"Are you two together?" Promise asked. No, Min and Arthur agreed on that.

Vanessa said, "Min was waiting when I got here at eight-thirty."

"Arthur, be a gentleman, won't you?" Promise asked rhetorically.

He hung his head in defeat. Even though his hair was pulled back, there was a hump along the part on one side. "God forbid anyone should attend to the wounded," he sulked. "I'll just go smoke another pack."

Vanessa followed him out. Before the door clicked shut, Min started speaking. "I am sorry to behave so badly, with Arthur. You must think ill of me."

Promise headed for the comfort of the leather couch, reconsidered, and sat behind the imposing desk. Frankly, she didn't know what she thought of Min.

Min stood with her arms at her sides, as if she were facing a tribunal. "The inspector general wishes to audit my travel budget, despite the fact that Joseph approved all my requests."

"Let's leave Joseph out of this," Promise said.

"I would never want to bring disgrace to the museum, and so I have come to reimburse some of those funds." Min reached into the pocket of her blue wool coat, unfurling a check that she handed to Promise. Made out to the museum, the check was for $19,790, which was technically more than she'd absconded with.

Promise rolled her eyes. "Where on God's green earth did you get this?"

"It is from well-wishers."

"You raised money for Arthur's bowl and took a cut," Promise said, aware of Min's surprise. "But the good news is you're pregnant, right? Congratulations."

"Pregnancy may not be viable," Min said.

That was what Promise had said while she adjusted to being pregnant, but Min had admitted this was what she wanted. No, Promise recalled, as yet another piece fell into place, what Min had said was that she wanted a son. "You're pregnant if it's a boy?"

Min backed into the chair. "I'm pregnant either way." She moaned with the nasal twang of the first trimester.

You're in for the long haul, Promise wanted to tell her. She deposited the check into Joseph's desk drawer. "We'll figure out who gets a refund later. You may want to tell the inspector general you're expecting; he might go easy on you."

"People use babies for that?"

"Yes, they do," Promise said. "That strikes you as unethical?" She was getting more perplexed by the minute. The fact that she had missed her own symptoms for so many weeks but immediately spotted Min's seemed indicative of the topsy-turvy world she now inhabited, as was her judgment of Min's desire for a boy. Hadn't she had fleeting thoughts about abortion, knowing that this pregnancy was not what she'd wanted? In a perfect world, she and Min could go to the staff room and tear through a couple of muffins, share their worries and symptoms along with the excitement she'd begun to feel about her own baby.

Promise said, "You told me you'd gone through all your savings paying off your Dr. Fan. Is he a traditional doctor?"

"No," Min said. "He's a specialist."

"A Western specialist? What I mean is, and this may be too personal, but did you pay for routine medical care yourself? Without insurance help?"

"He requires that," Min said, and she quoted the humiliating sign posted next to the receptionist.

"No," Promise said. A tiny light glimmered at the end of the tunnel, though the tunnel might still have dungeon cells enough for all of them. "That sign means their office won't be bothered to submit your paperwork. You know how much work that is, and with specialists, some things are covered and some aren't. Doctors want their money up-front, but that doesn't mean you couldn't get reimbursed for some of it."

Min sank back into the chair, whose brass nailheads framed her wide round face.

"This is why we have insurance," Promise said, remembering how just the other day Talbot had comforted her with the same words. "Do you still have all your receipts?"

The two women looked at each other. "My husband is Douglas," Min said, and a smile flattened out her lips. "We have spreadsheets and calendars, canceled checks and files of test results."

"Of course." At such a tense moment, it was a relief to smile at Douglas's habits. They were two intelligent people, Douglas and Min. Intelligent and desperate. Promise said, "I'll take your check to the Development Office. You get Douglas cracking." She wagged her finger to make a point. "The museum's money must never be considered your bank account. Understood?"

"Yes," Min said solemnly. She put her hand on her heart as if taking an oath.

Promise had to assume Min's sincerity. "Who knows whether any of us will have a job in six months," she said candidly. "If you return your travel funds, maybe you can throw yourself at their mercy. I'm not convinced you were not aware of the impropriety."

Min wanted to understand Promise, but she got lost in all the *nots*. When Promise said, "I'm not convinced you were not aware"—was that the same as "I am convinced you were aware"? Min should have given her friend credit for her deductive powers and knowledge of the American health system; she should have confided in her long ago. She slid forward until her feet touched the floor again.

"Don't go yet," Promise said. "I haven't forgotten your *ding*." Though she'd barely talked to Min in the last month, she was determined to cover her whole rap sheet. "I'm sending you to China."

Min stood stonily still. "You are deporting me."

"That's not my department. As acting director of the museum, I'm sending you there to return the *ding*." Struck by another idea, Promise let loose her tinkly laugh. "We'll use your travel budget, shall we?" She rolled her chair away from the formidable desk. "My mother has an expression: Everyone has to answer to himself."

"Each to his own?" Min guessed.

"No, nothing like that. More like, always let your conscience be your guide."

Min was sitting on the edge of her chair, and she leaned over to pick up her purse from the floor. When she sat up again, she seemed to have figured something out. "The cricket," she said. "In *Pinocchio*, that is the cricket's motto."

"Very good," Promise nodded. The world according to Walt Disney.

"I could mail the piece back."

"No," Promise insisted. "I want you, as a representative of the Museum of Asian Art, to make a public stand against archaeological looting."

"But I am just doing what the Founder did."

Promise didn't experience her usual defensiveness toward the Founder. "Who knows?" she said. "Maybe it wasn't wrong when he did it. It's a different world we live in. Our kids might view meat eating the way we see anti-Semitism or racism. Everyone in America thinks the early presidents were such human rights giants, but they gave the vote only to white men. They owned slaves, maybe even slept with them." She was getting off track here.

"I'm not asking you to judge the Founder or even to right his wrongs. But at the end of the day, I have to answer to myself, and I say we can't accept a stolen object. Your returning it and bringing awareness to their cause is the cost of my support. I'll help you plead your various cases."

Min seemed to be taking the measure of her net, which was admittedly full of holes. Promise did not actually have the authority to absolve or punish her on the Institution's behalf. The curator had broken any number of laws and could very well be fired, prosecuted, *jailed* for all they knew. Still, Promise gave her word that, if Min followed through, she would try to convince the inspector general he had bigger fish to fry.

Min said, "Giving the *ding* to the Chinese as a stand against looting doesn't make sense to me; however, I will willingly do as you ask. I am glad you are my friend."

Promise didn't feel too friendly toward Min, but then she suspected Min wasn't being that sincere either. Maybe when all was said and done, they could try again. Maybe they could take infant massage classes together, provided Min was having her infant. They shook hands, leaning across Joseph's big desk.

Min left quietly, showing little emotion. While Promise believed she was doing the right thing, she could see how some might misinterpret the message of sending Min on a slow boat to China. She visited her bathroom, and this time the smoke alarm looked nothing like the real thing. When she was done, she walked out to the reception area.

"No sign of Arthur," Vanessa said. "You want me to ring him?"

"No thanks," she said. Having endured her meeting with Min, she felt lighter than usual. How she might judiciously deal with Arthur wasn't as clear to her. Should there be retribution for his carelessness? A letter in his personnel file? Put a lien on his salary until he paid the deductible? She had no idea. Down the hallway, she peaked into Talbot's office, which was empty, and then continued on to the staff room. Surprisingly, neither Talbot nor Leo was there, so she headed to her old office. Rounding the corner of the south landing, she saw the snowy, slushy street scene out the back entrance. A tiny thrill tickled her, subtle as a feather against her cheek, to think she'd be giving birth in the spring.

She took the stairs to the lower level, into the hive of museum activity. The staff was working at full capacity to power the magnificent display up on the main floor, high over their heads. Korean, French, Japanese, Arabic—Promise heard the buzz of all these languages as she walked by the mailboxes and the hallway outside the library. She missed being among the worker bees, who greeted her warmly, knowing she was a worker bee at heart.

She liked hearing Leo's voice coming out of her old office. Talbot's conspiratorial chuckle was coming from there as well; once, that would have made her turn on her heel, but today it hastened her step. What a team, she was thinking, as their voices came into range.

". . . stirring up trouble," she heard Leo say. "I should kick your ass down the stairs."

Talbot chimed in. "Let's hear it for no fault, no deductible."

Staying close to the outside wall, she took one baby step, giving her an angle into the room where she'd spent her best years. Rocking the desk chair, Leo was agitated—angry or happy, she couldn't really tell. Talbot sat with his back to the door. He was perched on her folding guest chair like a grasshopper on a blade of grass. His knees and elbows stuck out absurdly, and she almost entered laughing, but she hung back, rebuffed by their bragging tone.

"Seriously," Leo said, and she couldn't follow his lowered voice, except to hear the words "incredibly irresponsible."

"Catastrophic accident," Talbot piped up, "and I'm left with an exhibition budget." He leaned forward to pick up the lacquer saucer she kept on her desk. What Promise had overheard was already discomfiting; however, it was seeing him spin the disk on his finger that enlightened her. He pushed the saucer up off his fingertip, then extended his hand beneath, like a safety net, so it plopped down into his palm. Next he set it whirling on his left index finger.

Promise entered the room as he was performing this stunt; because he was facing away from the door, he didn't see her arrival. Having spent much of his career with his back to the basket, however, Talbot was practiced at reading facial expressions. He saw Leo's pupils contract, blasted by the spotlight that blanched any humor from his smile. Startled, Talbot lost his spin on the saucer, but he did not fumble it.

Her stomach practically grazing Talbot's ear, Promise swatted the lacquer disk out of his hands, sending it clattering onto the desk. She said, "I hope you have insurance on that."

Talbot turned away from her belly. He turned so fast, he created his own breeze, and she smelled his tanning lotion. Promise looked toward Leo, but he was shading his eyes with his hand. Gravity gave Promise a painful tug, and she pushed both palms against the small of her back for some much-needed support.

"Tell me this, boys," she demanded. "Did the bowl fall or was it pushed?"

"Arthur dropped it," Talbot said, like a tattling child.

She relived that nanosecond where she had rejected Arthur in favor of Talbot. Arthur had picked the bowl off its secure mount, and she knew how unstable he was. Once she'd reclaimed the porcelain from the ambassador, she'd handed it off to Talbot. "I trusted you," she said to him. "I chose you."

Leo seemed to have swallowed hot coals. So this was guilt. He picked up his mug of coffee, though he could have used something larger to hide behind. Talbot and Promise both glared, instinctively, for curators were not allowed to have beverages at their desks.

Promise wished she were carrying a horsewhip. She remembered when she and Leo were sitting on the sofa the night after the bowl fell: he'd held up his hand, thumb and forefinger pinched together, pretending to drop objects one by one down the stairs. Her back ached just below her waist, and if she coughed or sneezed, she was sure to wet her pants.

"Leo had nothing to do with it," Talbot said, essentially fingering him.

Leo drank from his mug, attempting to douse the burning embers that had fallen through to his stomach.

For the time being, Promise concentrated on Talbot. "You broke Arthur's heart. How did you get him to take it out of the vitrine? And invite you up there?"

Talbot said, "I suggested it in bed."

"Honest to God." Leo pinched his eyebrows together. "Don't say another thing." Now Leo felt guilt on Morty's behalf—frankly, more than he'd felt for either Arthur or the damn bowl. Husband and wife looked at Talbot, whose entire reputation rested on his discretion. All of a sudden, he couldn't get enough of confessing.

Promise was as distraught by the intricacy of the situation as by who did what and why. She missed her clear notion of right and wrong, a Manichaean view that had become laughable. So Talbot had taken the bowl from Arthur—well, from her—and he'd spun it around, basically ensuring that Arthur wouldn't be able to hold on to it. Maybe later it would matter that Leo was nowhere near the action, because right now it seemed that he'd imparted his spin to Talbot, who'd visited it upon the bowl.

"Leo had nothing to do with it," Talbot repeated.

"Shut the fuck up, already!" Leo insisted.

Promise turned her back on Leo and Talbot to give her office door a slam, closing the three of them in together. Then she faced them, boiling over with hurt and rage. "Stop acting like smug frat boys—this is not a basketball game! You two are so far out of line that I should throw you both out *and* turn myself in." She could hear what scant weight her little-girl voice carried, yet Leo and Talbot cringed from her anger. "You two, with your chickenshit behavior, have disregarded the mission of this institution, not to mention my position or my commitment. Goddammit, Leo, I've had to listen to you for twenty years spouting off about how to live thoughtfully and the political consequences of getting a haircut, for God's sake. What about the political consequences of something like this? And what about the personal ones, did you think about that?" She flashed back to his talk of destiny—wife and kids and a government job—of those three, he'd be lucky if he got to visit the kids on weekends.

Promise hung her head, surprised, always surprised, to see the heft of Edgar under her dress. Talk about irresponsible, she thought. Her office didn't have another chair, let alone a hospital bed she could lower herself into. "I cannot believe either of you could be so callous."

Leo spoke to his wife, talking as if Talbot were their problem child. "I'm at fault here. I told him more than once that I didn't think the bowl ceremony would make a difference."

"You said that to me," Promise reminded him.

"Yes, but what I didn't say to you was that it was worth more to the cause dead than alive."

Promise gasped, and her belly rose up with her constricted breath. Lordy, Lordy, was there no end to his betrayal? He may as well have grabbed her around the neck and choked her. "Is that how you feel about Joseph?" she squeaked out.

"Absolutely not. Never," Leo said. How best to repent? He wasn't sure if he should defend himself or submit to her. "I'm ashamed that I ever spouted off like that. You know how I talk, but he doesn't."

"I do now," Talbot said, the sarcastic tone back in his voice. He couldn't help it; whenever he felt cornered, that smirk returned. The very day Joseph had shown him the Castle memo, no doubt expecting a grand gesture from him, he was flip.

Leo pushed his mug toward Promise, then took it back. Empty. He slid open the deep file drawer of her desk and brought out a sleek silver thermos. Talbot and Promise waited for him to turn the cap and refill the oversized mug, a two-finger-hole number from a Vermont potter. It was like a commercial pause in a heated drama, Leo pouring hot coffee for his wife, and the effort was more convincing than anything he'd said so far.

"Honestly, Promise." Leo spoke with utmost tenderness. "Look what I'm up to here, pressing everyone I can think of on Joseph's behalf. A bowl is not worth what a person is—I've never made that mistake. I'm deeply sorry about this."

It wasn't lost on her that he'd never been deeply sorry in nearly two decades of marriage. The truth was, Promise had put the same onus on the bowl that they had; however, her plan had called for its worship. Worship the cow, sacrifice the cow—they were not two sides of the same coin because of the dead cow in the second approach. Frankly, the bowl wasn't worth what they'd had to pay for it. Arthur had driven up the price by putting it on the catalog cover; she suspected he'd driven up the price more by blabbing from Paris to New York. When it was still an accident, she'd already begun to think that they'd raised the porcelain up so far beyond its station that its topple was inevitable.

The phone on her desk began ringing; the button on the far right blinked. Neither man reached for it or even appeared to hear the bell. Ringing phones were almost ambient noise at this point—her dreams had a sound track of ringing phones—but she'd run out of things to say to these scofflaws, so rising on her toes, she hoisted herself up to sit on the desk and lifted the receiver.

"This is Promise Whittaker."

"Promise" was all the voice at the other end had to say. A low voice that uttered her name with the recognition of everything that had transpired. Distance and danger and disappointment. Relief, affection, hope. This time, she gasped so hard that Leo leapt up and came around the bend. Promise laid a hand over her belly, where the baby wriggled around like a cat caught in a burlap bag.

The man's voice dipped lower still. "I understand you've been promoted."

"Joseph," she said. At the sound of Promise speaking the man's name, Leo grabbed both her shoulders. Promise asked, "Where on earth are you?"

There was only ragged breath on the other end. Little did Promise know she'd asked a problematic question of physics and metaphysics. Part of him was in the Naval Hospital in Bethesda, not so very far from the Museum of Asian Art. His wife was massaging his feet; his vital signs were registering on the many monitors around his bed.

Emmy looked at him with grave concern, and he held on as best he could. She had thinned, though she had never been thick. Glossy. Diaphanous. Her eyes were more slanted than ever, making her all the more resemble a Modigliani portrait. When he'd seen himself in the mirror this morning, he still looked like a Bellows subject, but now he was the guy on the ropes; he was no longer one of the barrel-chested townsfolk of a Breughel painting but rather one of the crooked, emaciated peasants with the weird medieval or Dutch wrappings around his waist, head, and arm.

All he'd officially lost was his right thumb, though he certainly felt it with a stabbing phantom pain. Other parts of him were scattered across several continents. He'd mislaid the concept of the here and now, for example, and whatever part of him thrived on unfamiliarity, that part had disintegrated. Emmy, morphine, blankets: he wasn't sure which he was more grateful for.

"I'm right here," Joseph finally answered. "But what is it your Rumi says? 'Whoever brought me here will have to take me home.'"

Your Tax Dollars at Work

January 14, 2000

Although art historians had already written hundreds of pages per page in every extant Persian manuscript, the illuminations retained a great deal of mystery. When she was working on a manuscript, Promise's goal was to deduce the blend of politics, talent, and religion elemental to these folios, the way a chef breaks a cupcake down to a recipe. It's remarkable to discover all the ingredients in the right proportions; likewise, Promise had learned to withstand the confusion, even appreciate the unknowable, while going about her business as an art historian. Now came the week when she applied that knack to her current situation.

For one thing, she stopped obsessing over why Cecil or his bosses hadn't contacted her. They hadn't. She'd never found out if there was more to the museum plot than fiscal and crowd concerns. Then word came down that Cecil had resigned, which may or may not have been related to their circumstances. Either way, the museum was in peril. And she hadn't determined what consequences Leo, Arthur, or Talbot deserved, considering Arthur had dropped the bowl that had been spun by Talbot, who had been influenced by Leo. The bowl was already broken.

She did give thanks that Joseph had escaped from his captors, because as much as everyone had wanted to help him, he'd saved himself. On Wednesday, Promise had visited him at the Naval Hospital, where Joseph was facing a long recovery. Three of his boys were there, sending him into a panic on Emmy's behalf. He assumed they were gathered because of her breast cancer, and he was especially attentive to Henry. "See how well your mother looks? She's going to be fine."

Then Joseph asked Emmy why someone had brought him the museum's pocket watch, not recognizing the familiar orb with the hunting scene on the back as his. He knew it but he didn't know it, just as he kept being shocked to learn, staring directly at his bandaged hand, that his thumb was gone, *gone!* That Uygur lunatic had clubbed it with the machete rather than slice it—he repeated that part of the story several times. There was no way for Joseph to remember surgeons amputating his thumb, casualty of gangrene, because he'd been under anesthetic at the time. He kept thanking Leo for some card he'd written and asking if the museum was still standing. Promise couldn't fathom the shock of his reentry.

All week, Promise attended to her list of potential supporters. She'd learned to ask for specific favors: Could you write a letter to the *Post* for publication? Might you spend a day lobbying on the Hill with your most devout members? Would you bring a busload of visitors once a week, beginning this week? Washington was a city where no one would commit until others had committed, and so she and Leo and Talbot had to circle back through their contacts to report enthusiasm at any link in the phone chain. With news of the bowl, the potential museum reconfiguration, Joseph's escape, and the Secretary's resignation, the media had a four-course meal on a platter.

Whatever Leo's culpability, his contrition knew no bounds, and Promise let him work it off. He spent much of his office time in the guise of an art detective. Turned out, there were people willing to talk anonymously about disasters at their institutions. One bad day at the Metropolitan, a second-century Roman marble statue simply crumbled—poof!—and a telephoto lens broke a celadon vase in a photo shoot. Leo seemed to be readying an implicate-others addendum to his take-no-blame strategy. He learned of Korans stolen from an important Dublin collection, paintings slashed when registrars cut into cartons, ten-thousand-year-old beads that scattered like buckshot down a corridor, under sofas, into the cuffs of the pants of people walking out the door. Eventually a plan evolved that absolved the caretakers, nay, beatified them. With all this damage *in museums*, the argument went, what would we do without them?

Promise had never known how many ways a piece of art could be ruined. It reminded her of the myriad of things that could go wrong in a pregnancy, disturbances you dared not think about if you planned to survive nine challenging months. She talked about the fragility of the collections on National Public Radio; in an interview with the *Times*, she lamented the loss of objects that never made it that far. For example, she recounted what a Koran folio had endured before being given sanctuary at their museum. The scribe who had penned the folio was tortured for including the *shadow* of the veiled Prophet, whose painted likeness was considered idolatry; after the scribe put an opaque wash over the shadow, his patron executed him. Stolen back and forth by every successful marauder, the folio was separated recto from verso and sold on the black market, traded for weapons, and miraculously reunited. The verso had been donated by a Persian bookseller who had fled the revolution; the recto was a gift of Ross Perot.

Lucy was waiting outside her office when Promise returned from another interview. "After you," Promise said, noticing as she followed that the conservator had a toddler's gait. She motioned to the couch. "Have a seat. Are you handling the remains of the day?"

Lucy guffawed, and Promise reminded herself to be more reverent. The spin she'd been putting on the museum's role was making her loopy. "I'm glad the bowl is in your hands now."

Lucy put out her empty palms. "All I've got is a box of crumbs, and I'm wondering where to start."

Promise asked, "What do you usually do?"

"Usually, I clean a piece, undo any harmful earlier work, maybe apply something new from the world of adhesives or coatings. This piece is beyond conservation. I'm sorry it's so damaged."

"Me too." Promise appreciated her condolences.

Lucy said, "Porcelain restorers use a contrasting material for repair—gold lacquer is popular among Asian collectors—and there's a whole body of writing on the aesthetics of cracks."

Promise recalled the ox bones that ancient Chinese people heated in fires and then handed off to the prognosticators. In the same vein, she'd seen X-rays of mummies and bog people, in which scientists read this fracture and that bone-deep scar as evidence of their lifestyles. Show us your wounds, so we can appreciate what you've been through. She said, "I'm trying to picture cracked porcelain in our collection, but I can't come up with any."

Lucy's smile broadened. "There are precious few. The Founder liked things intact. He gave his broken stuff to Natural History."

Promise was always impressed with people who read up on the Founder. "You're the expert. What do you recommend?"

Lucy bit her lip in concentration, working it over as if it were lunch. "This piece is shot. Still, what have we got that belonged to a Chinese emperor, Louis the Sixteenth, Thomas Jefferson, and Marlene Dietrich?"

I don't know, she would have said to Lydia, what have we got that belonged to . . . ?

Lucy went on, "I could make a cast from the impression in its storage case. Then we'd have a soft polymer body to fit the shards into, or onto, depending on whether Arthur wants people to see the white exterior or the decorated interior."

Listening to this earnest, thorough young woman, Promise heard echoes of herself arriving at the museum.

"One more thing I've discovered, which could prove a serious problem. There's about fifty grams missing. If it's all together, a chunk the size of a small sand dollar."

"Turned up missing," Promise said. "Have you heard that expression? My aunt used to say something 'turned up missing.'"

"That doesn't make any sense," Lucy protested. "I don't know if it's being surrounded by Japanese and Chinese speakers all day, but I'm beginning to understand less English. When the insurance rep called me, I couldn't answer a single one of his questions."

"That's because broken doesn't mean worthless to us," Promise said. "However, broken might be lighter. Is it possible that the bowl weighed more than the sum of its crumbs? Is the Sunday *Times* the same weight if it's put through a shredder?"

Lucy tilted her head slightly to the right and ran her thumb over each eyebrow. She crossed her eyes again; unsettling as that was, Promise was fascinated by the woman's lack of self-consciousness. She was apparently engaging herself in a lengthy discussion.

———

Every time Arthur sought her out, Promise was occupied. He couldn't wait in her antechamber, chatting with Vanessa and thumbing through magazines until she called him in. What he needed was a running start down the hallway so he could burst through her door to make his pro nouncements: *I've slept with Talbot a few times—a huge mistake and not necessarily your business except that I may have traded sexual favors for his exhibition budget.* Morty's done with me—*I'm devastated even though I deserved it and didn't expect to be so affected.* To top it all, I made off with a chunk of the bowl—*now, what do we do about that?*

He couldn't stand the thought of bumping into Promise in the staff room, so he kept going out for a smoke instead of a snack. "Rough break," "Goddamn," various guards and art handlers consoled him throughout the week. Arthur was mortified to be the target of their sympathy. He'd meant to be the target of envy.

"Sorry, man," the lighting assistant said. "Motherfucking cold, huh?"

That it was and uniformly gray. Though a narrow band of sidewalk had been shoveled on Monday, heavy walls on either side of the path had caved in and refrozen a few times since. Arthur stepped carefully.

"Spare a cigarette?" the lighting guy asked.

Arthur shook one out for each of them, then lit both with his silver Deco lighter. He took the smoke into his lungs as if it might fire up his pilot light.

The lighting guy said, "They say Cecil's been canned—figure you knew that."

Arthur most certainly did not know that. Was that his fault? Like a nervous schoolboy, he'd bit his nails to bleeding, ripped his cuticles. In the same vein, he smoked the cigarette down to the filter, lit another, did the same. Need a fag? was how the pickup line went back in the seventies, long before he'd met Morty. When he came back inside, he had a slight buzz. Not only hadn't he smoked this much in years, he hadn't spent this much time outside in years. He signed the security log, and Officer Jackson gave him a nod.

"It was bad," the security guard said into the phone. "Never been devastation like that. Gruesome."

Got that right, Arthur thought.

"His wife couldn't help looking back, which got her killed, but he found a cave for himself and his two daughters. They're safe, see?— but the girls are worried they'll never be with a man, so they get him drunk enough where he'll get them pregnant."

That wasn't about the bowl, the Castle, or even television, Arthur realized, recognizing the biblical story of Lot fleeing Sodom. He moved on, though even in his crushed state, he was a little surprised when someone wasn't talking about the broken ceramic. Morty had often tried to point out that it wasn't all about him. Why did he always think it was?

The conservator, who was standing in the doorway of the director's office, was thanking Promise. Arthur actually ducked behind a palm while she passed. God knows what they'd shared. When the gateway was clear, he trotted past Vanessa and pulled the door closed behind him.

"Arthur," Promise said. "How are you coming along?" She didn't really have time for him right now. She had calls to make, she'd told Emmy she'd visit Joseph this afternoon, and her mother was landing at National around six.

"I'm not 'coming along,'" Arthur said. Anger and humiliation welled up in him. "I see you and Talbot and *Leo* giving interviews left and right. I'm so petty that when I'm not mad at you for bragging about the broken bowl, I'm mad that you're taking credit for my clumsiness."

"That's petty," Promise agreed.

How could he ask her forgiveness when she was mocking him? "I'm not 'coming along,'" he repeated. "I prostituted myself for that bowl, and the sad thing is, like any sex offender, I'd do it again tomorrow."

"Don't," Promise implored.

"I'm bored by substance. I don't have a particularly good eye. I'm greedy and easily turned around."

"Good Lord, Arthur." Promise shook her head. "It sounds like you've hit rock bottom."

"No," he said, wishing he could hand her the chunk of bowl he'd taken.

Last night, when he'd said to Morty, "You'll never guess what I did," and then shown him the shard, anger had blotched Morty's cheeks the way it used to when he drank. Morty's nostrils opened wide as he pushed up his sleeve, cocked back his arm, and aimed for Arthur's jaw. Arthur had it coming, but that didn't mean he didn't take cover. Elbows tucked against his body, he held the porcelain fragment up with both hands, or really both thumbs and index fingers, because it was a shard, a cluster of plum blossoms flowering in front of his eyes. Rather than stealing a slice of magpies, symbols of happiness, he'd made off with the plum flower branch that translated as "up to your eyebrows." We are all certainly up to our eyebrows, he thought, cringing behind his scrap. Just as Morty swerved to avoid smashing the jagged circle into his pretty face, Arthur squeezed his eyes shut and willed himself to become a punching bag. He must have inhaled deeply in his effort to go limp, because he smelled the gin that Morty used to drink by the tumblerful. Then he heard a grinding crack he recognized from the chiropractor's office. Morty's midswing correction had thrown him badly off balance, and Arthur opened his eyes to see his partner crumple to the floor like laundry.

"Oh, you asshole," Morty moaned. "When I sober up, this is going to hurt like hell."

"I am so, so sorry. Are you all right? Let's get you to the couch."

Morty bellowed, "Don't touch me!" Like a hulking crab, he moved along the floor, coming to rest on the strip of Chinese rug between couch and coffee table. Arthur handed him pillows, which he accepted. He put two under his knees and one beneath his head. His beard fanned out on his chest. "I expected you to come clean about Talbot. Did you break off a souvenir from him, too?"

"That was a mistake," Arthur admitted, pocketing his shard.

"Can I just say that the way you feel about that fucking bowl is how I have felt about you."

"Do you still?" Arthur asked. "No, don't answer that. I'll get the painkillers." He ran to the bathroom, overwhelmed by Morty's declaration and the pain he'd caused. When he looked in the medicine cabinet's mirror, as he inevitably did, he was no picture of Dorian Gray. He was a forty-plus man with overly long hair and effete glasses. His chin was becoming a shiny knob. In a few more years, with added paunch and receding hair, he could play Benjamin Franklin at Williamsburg.

Arthur brought water and a bouquet of pill bottles to his partner of seven years. Kneeling by Morty's side, he read the labels. "Vioxx, Vicodin, Percocet, Darvocet, Valium, and Xanax."

"Percocet goes best with gin," Morty said.

Arthur cradled Morty's head, then he gently stretched him back out. Waves of love and remorse wracked him. Here was this loyal, friendly, imaginative man whom he'd driven back to drink. Leaning over, Arthur kissed him on the lips. He said, "What do we need here? Counseling? A big wedding?"

Morty didn't kiss back. "After you help us to our reliable bed, we need you to pack your bags."

The drugs kicked in soon enough, allowing Morty to maneuver into bed without Arthur's help. Neither did Arthur pack—Morty wouldn't notice if he left or not at this point. Arthur did take his dented Buick out for a drive, traveling the snowy streets around the monuments: Lincoln sitting, Jefferson orating, Washington honored as the biggest white shaft in town. From Independence Avenue he doubled back between the East and West wings of the National Gallery to Pennsylvania Avenue toward Georgetown, where his and Morty's first apartment had overlooked the C & O Canal, a few blocks from the Potomac. Beyond Wisconsin Avenue, he pulled over in a fit of nostalgia and self-pity. Harsh as the wind was, it was downright bitter out on Key Bridge, his sight obscured as much by his blowing hair as by his stinging eyes. For all he knew, the river could be frozen, in which case it might not accept his offering. But then he saw whitecaps through the bleary sap in his eyes, and he reached into his pocket to throw the shard off the bridge, regretting it even as he let it fly.

Now the bowl can never be put back together, he should be telling Promise, who had come out from her desk and was stroking his pitching arm. He had the presence of mind not to comment on the clashing shades of red in her dress and tights.

"You all right?" she asked.

He saw the concern in her forehead, bunched up beneath her widow's peak. He said, "Let me tell you about rock bottom."

———

Stopping by the museum shop on her way out the door, Promise bought a book of poems devoted to healing. I'll take a dozen, she nearly requested. Arthur's story was still rattling her—she'd listened to him divulge any number of indiscretions without absolving him, though she'd been kinder about his thieving and infidelity knowing he'd been set up. Why did he have to be so damned inclined?

As Promise waited through the shop clerk's protracted gift wrapping, she thought about Emmy ministering to Joseph in the desert. Emmy had itemized the wounds visited on Joseph's already emaciated body. She said she hadn't even known about his fierce rash until she was wrapping his ribs in gauze for his captors to take him away. "I felt I was preparing his shroud," she'd told Promise.

Along with the book, Promise stuffed recent museum calendars into the bag as well as the new general brochure, which might jump-start Joseph's memory. That gave her the good idea of stopping by the staff room, and Nathan was only too happy to tender an assortment of scones for Joseph. Let the hero worshiping begin, she thought, glad for his return. She ran into Leo as she was going out, and they reviewed the afternoon plan. She was going to the hospital, he was about to head home; she'd meet her mother's plane at six and bring her back in a taxi.

Promise stepped cautiously down the front stairs, which would forevermore be a crime scene to her. They might as well wrap the banister with yellow tape. Joseph, she thought, could use the same treatment. It was a mercifully short walk from the museum to the Metro escalator. Of course their building was in demand, she thought, wondering if the decision was as simple as location, location, location.

The train wasn't crowded this time of day, and the path from the NIH station to the Naval Hospital was well shoveled.. She checked in at the visitors' desk; having set her parcels down, however, she wasn't sure she could lift them.

A young man in uniform materialized as if his orders were to read visitors' minds. "You could use some assistance." He scooped her bundles under one arm, offering her his other.

She'd never been too comfortable with the military side of Washington. "I can probably manage."

He said, "That's what I'm here for, to give assistance."

"Well, if it's your job," she said, wishing she could hand over the baby for him to carry.

"Your tax dollars at work," he said.

Same to you, she thought, referring to the scones and the brochures he'd taken off her hands. For that matter, the same was true for the museum and Joseph and her—your tax dollars at work—though who was beholden to whom was a point of contention. She appreciated that the young Navy guy was not confused. She could tell he was holding himself back to travel at her pace.

"Joseph Lattimore's been through the wringer," the young man said.

"He escaped an Al-Faran camp, found his way out of some serious mountains—we're talking land mines everywhere—and got his buddy out, too."

Promise should have known that Joseph could make a name for himself in the five days he'd spent here. "He's amazing," she agreed.

"Yeah, well, he's just about dead." The young man spoke so bluntly that Promise hoped it was a figure of speech.

She took leave of her escort outside Joseph's room. A slim, bent woman opened the door, and Promise's eyes had to adjust again to Emmy, because her mental image had reverted to the Emmy of yore: part cowgirl, part folksinger. She who had handled so much with grace was now shorn and frail as a camp survivor. Joseph had fared far worse.

"Promise," he said, his voice giving her a chill as it had on the phone. "You haven't come to dump the *Padshahnama* on me, I hope. I've twice run away from that project."

Promise was happy he remembered his book. She knew that he'd been questioned by any number of government officials and that his short-term recall was pretty damaged; for instance, he didn't remember that she'd already visited him. Joseph's robustness was an integral part of his personality; without it, he looked as lost as he did ill. They'd wrapped the top half of his head in the manner of a bicycle helmet, his right hand like a club. Because his skin had taken such a beating from the elements, his beard hadn't been shaved. There were quite a few tubes going into his left arm. Emmy's lavender scent mixed with those of illness, urine and night sweats, stale air and soiled dressings.

"His response is slower than expected," Emmy said tactfully, then launched into a list of what ailed him. "His hand, along with altitude adjustment, hypothermia, malnourishment, sunburn." Then her eyes traveled up and down Promise with true concern. "What about you? How are you holding up?"

"Can't complain," Promise said, which was so absurd they shared a roll of the eyes. Emmy held her hand about six inches from Promise's stomach, her lovely way of acknowledging Promise's girth without touching her or remarking on it. Promise said, "I'm not due till the end of March."

Emmy smoothed Joseph's sheet across his chest. "The boys came and went—well, Jules couldn't get here of course." She sighed over her faraway son. "Joseph thinks he imagined talking to the president, but he really did. And the Dalai Lama called by cell phone."

"That's like God calling," Promise said, amazed at His Holiness's grasp of current events as well as his use of current technology.

"Ladies," Joseph said. "May I ask you something?" He lowered his voice, which was already a whisper. "I haven't heard from Talbot. Does that surprise you?"

Promise said, "I'll send him over."

"Now, that sounds like a director," Joseph said, a measure of respect in his quavery voice.

Seeing her mentor in his current struggle, Promise forgave him for leaving her so vulnerable and ill-informed. Chest hairs poked up from the boatneck opening of his threadbare hospital robe, an antiquated hint of his previous hearty incarnation. His head was turbaned in bandages, and his mind was likewise under wraps. What have they done to you? Promise both wanted and didn't want to know. She said, "I'm not the director you were." Looking up at Emmy, she asked, "Has he heard about the bowl?" and Emmy nodded. "Arthur had the opportunity to acquire the piece, and I admit, I thought a strong opening and an important acquisition could make a difference. That must sound naïve to you."

Joseph said, "I picked it for the cover the day I got that goddamn memo. That piece was worth maybe two hundred grand before Arthur got his hands on it." He tilted his big wobbly head back to look up at Emmy, fear and pain in his eyes.

"You're going to be fine," Emmy assured him.

Promise said, "I brought you some of Nathan's scones, and when you're in the mood for it, some poetry." She reached for the box, thinking that the baking powder and butter smell alone could bring a dead man back.

Emmy said, "He can't eat solids yet."

"Pack snacks," Joseph spoke. "That's from Leo's card. I chanted his advice across the mountaintop: 'Feign pain, pack snacks, use a ruse.'"

He'd thanked Leo for his card before, and Promise had assumed he was confused. But she recognized the language from Leo's handy pocket hostage card. "Is that all of it?" she asked.

"No, that's the setup," Joseph said, obviously grateful to remember something so clearly. He started over again, as if he knew them only as a litany. "Feign pain. Pack snacks. Use a ruse. Get out but don't get lost." That seemed to strike him as funny; he chuckled for a little while. Then he grimaced, and his teeth began to chatter.

Emmy pulled the bedspread up to his chin. At his side, she felt along the tube until she located a button. "Hurting?"

"Throbbing," he said. "Don't push for more quite yet. Unless they let cats in here, I'm hallucinating a bit."

"The morphine mixes him up," Emmy said.

"That's what I want from you," he said to Promise. "I want you to get out but don't get lost."

Promise thought she knew what he was saying. "I'm almost gone, but you have to do something for me. Whose idea was it to turn the museum into a food court? You left, Cecil's resigned, Dr. Zhao's not talking."

"You're asking a lot," Joseph said. "I barely know my name or that breed of cat—is that a Maine coon?"

Promise scanned the room, hoping there was a magazine or a calendar featuring a cat. She didn't see a cat.

"Joseph, I'm right here, right by your side." Emmy got him to tune in to her voice. "They needed a place for visitors to eat, didn't they? Or was it all about money?" To Promise, she said, "He's wiped out."

His eyes darted around the room, a little crazy but also alert. "No, not money. It has something to do with the airport, I think. They changed the airport's name."

"Yes, they did," Emmy coaxed him on. "It's Reagan National Airport now. Or Reagan Washington National. But Promise is asking about your museum."

He held up his good hand and made quote signs. "'National' and 'Asian.' They couldn't see both words in the same institution."

To Promise, Emmy confided, "I always assumed it was about money."

Hallucinating or not, he was on a roll. "The governors started it, and they sucked the vice president in. Not patriotic, they decreed, for visitors to set foot on the National Mall and be faced with an Asian museum, a place that gave equal time to Muslim and pagan religions. What do the Persians say, 'The art of our enemy is our enemy'?"

Promise said, "'The enemy of my enemy is my friend.'"

"That's the difference, I suppose, between Persians and politicians."

Emmy moistened a washcloth with a bottle of water and dabbed at his flaking lips.

"I'm flabbergasted," Promise said. "How do you fight an argument like that?"

Emmy said, "That's not an argument, is it? Paranoia, maybe. Nationalism gone awry."

"I didn't fight," Joseph said. "The Castle decided it was time I did some long-awaited research, in the desert, with my darling wife by my side."

"He'd done enough," Emmy defended him. "And then the desert, well . . ."

The two women looked down at Joseph, sunburned within an inch of his life, robbed of his right thumb, trimmed of forty pounds or more. He *had* fought, Promise thought, or he wouldn't be here.

"Let's not talk about the desert, shall we?" Joseph said, his jaw clenched against the pain.

When the tendons in his neck fanned out flat, Emmy gave the button on his morphine-feeding tube a merciful squeeze.

A Thousand Mothers

January 14, 2000

Leo was grateful the sun was finally shining on the playground. They hadn't let the kids out for recess since they'd come back from Christmas, because the temperature was below thirty-two degrees. Felix ran by, chasing a line of kids; with his foggy breath, he was pretending to be a dragon. Leo's goal was to have Felix let off enough steam to be docile but not exhausted for the walk home. Flipper was tied up at the fence, lunging at sticks kids fed him; when the puppy walked to school and back, he didn't get into trouble. Leo believed a lack of exercise was also at the root of Felix's scant appetite.

A mother from Lydia's class came up to him, dripping with sympathy. "Edalaine told me that Lydia was very upset in class last week. She said she was crying."

"She's fine now," Leo said. As if to prove his point, Lydia ran to the bars near them, yelling "Watch me, Daddy!" and then skinned the cat.

"She gets worked up about snakes," he said.

Edalaine's mother nodded knowingly. "Mine's that way about dogs." She drifted off to a group of women who had plenty to talk about.

He watched a mother help a toddler down the slide; she sat the kid upright, aimed him straight, and then ran to catch him at the bottom. There was a mother holding a baby on one hip and scanning the far end of the playground where the kids were swinging; meanwhile, she talked, reached into her purse, got a pen, paper, and jotted down a note, which she handed to another mother. There were a few dads— he gave them the companionable nod or shrug—as well as circles of babysitters grouped by age or language: young au pairs in short coats that occasionally rode up to expose a tattoo on the small of the back; experienced Central American, Philippine, and African nannies. A circle of women spoke rapid-fire Vietnamese; the embassy housed everyone in the apartments across the street from the school.

When Leo checked back Lydia's way, he saw a mother breaking apart two flailing boys, extracting an apology from one. Mothers hugged each other. He saw a mother weeping, though she may have been a grandmother. He saw a mother buttonholing Lydia's teacher, one passing out flyers, several picking up wayward trash. A scrawny boy plowed over a toddler, and a woman scooped up the toddler while blocking the boy's escape. Leo could see the look in her eyes, a disapproval so powerful that the boy turned away as if slapped. Promise had perfected that look, along with all the mothers on the playground.

And now that his own family was in a bind, who was coming to save them? Promise's mother. He thought that was funny, and he regretted that there was no one here he could share it with. Leo had been packing a cell phone for a few months, but he usually forgot to carry it, charge it up, or turn it on. Today was the rare trifecta—he had the damn thing with enough juice to use—and he punched in Promise's number.

Promise was leaving the hospital when Leo called. Before she even spoke, she could hear the yips and chaos of the blacktop. If Leo had been calling from home, she would have assumed he couldn't find something. But the playground call was undoubtedly trouble: a broken arm, chipped front teeth. Promise instinctively bent her knees, prepared to spring into action. "Is something wrong?"

"We're fine," Leo said. "Why wouldn't we be?"

"Speak up. I can barely hear you."

Leo said, "I'm struck, that's all. Standing here at the playground, one of millions in America teeming with children and their mothers. I'm watching mothers organize and make peace, and heal, and network."

"Yes," she said. "Yes, yes, yes." She thought of the card Joseph had left her, the boy standing amid dozens of clay goddesses in a small boat. We are all, she thought, in the same boat. She said to Leo, "You are new to the Mother Planet."

"Peg shows up . . . troubleshooting, and then there's the next generation . . ."

She lost a chunk of each phrase to the background noise. That, and it was hard to believe he was spouting essentially her philosophy. Mothers carry ten times their weight? No shit.

"Listen," she interrupted him. "I'm just leaving the hospital. Joseph is in and out, but he came up with something. We're a patriotism casualty." She told Leo about the banners that had so deeply offended the Conference of Governors and how they'd been sacrificed as a consequence. Screaming into the cell phone, getting dirty looks from people on their way to the Metro, she'd never felt more Washingtonian.

". . . worse than I . . . ignorant . . . believe it?" was all that came through.

"You're fading," she yelled. "I'm losing you."

"No, not that," she heard him say. "We'll talk at home."

She had a long subway ride to the airport and was glad to be going against traffic so she got a seat. At every stop, she looked across at the jostling commuters leaving downtown. She wondered how many of them would be offended by an exhibition of Hindu art. They didn't have to come bow down, for heaven's sake, but would it hurt them to learn a thing or two about another way of life? Many Hindus believed that the Buddha, like Rama, was an avatar of Vishnu. Some believed Jesus was. There were Buddhists and Muslims who thought Jesus appeared in Kashmir before ascending into heaven, just as Mormons believed he came to America. To each his own paradise.

Waiting for her mother's plane, Promise called Talbot with news about the Conference of Governors.

"How convenient," he said. "That could help the cause, given that the alleged patriotic scuffle took place."

Promise wasn't sure she'd heard correctly. "Alleged?"

"Well, Joseph never mentioned it to me. And he hasn't called since he got back. You know, I was his right-hand man."

Promise was extremely disappointed. She was tempted to point out that Joseph's right hand was now *maimed*—did he think he could possibly rally? Because she knew shame was not an incentive, she simply said, "Joseph asked for you today."

She had to buy a piece of chocolate cheesecake to turn her mood around before Peg arrived; fortunately, the new improved airport offered that with a brownie chaser. When they announced the plane had landed, she ran to the bathroom to make sure her face wasn't smeared with chocolate.

————

Promise had forgotten how much luggage her mother always toted, and she gave the cab driver a large tip to take her suitcases up to the front porch. "Watch the second step," she cautioned both Peg and the driver. The last thing she needed was for one of them to break a hip.

Lydia and Felix were all over Peg as soon as they got in the door. "Gran-Gran, we got a dog!" "Why didn't Grandpa come? Do you still have your canary?"

She kissed them both, grabbing Felix around the ribs. "I'm here to fatten you up," she said, and Promise tried not to feel defensive. Peg said, "I have missed y'all more than my teeth."

"Gran-Gran's here, Gran-Gran's here," Felix yelled.

"Off the couch, sweetie," Promise reminded him. He leapt across the cushions and onto the armrest, launching himself into the air.

Peg tossed a pillow from the rocking chair to the ground, which he understood to be his landing pad. "Again!" he screamed after he hit the target.

"Don't you want to know what I packed?" Peg diverted him.

She took off a winter coat, a suit jacket, and a heavy sweater, handing each one over to Leo as she emptied her pockets of snacks. ("Pack snacks," Promise thought.) "They keep those planes so chilly," Peg said. "And my friend Leta-Adele warned me they can't spare a blessed peanut."

Promise saw the beginnings of frailty in her mother. There was a bowing to her back, and her breasts were even with her waist. Though Promise had never grown as tall as Peg, they were the same height now, partly because her mother had finally abandoned the high tease of hair she'd been wearing since 1965. A circle on Peg's cheek, shiny pink skin showing amid her weathered olive complexion, looked to be a mole recently removed.

Peg laid both hands on Lydia, who let go of the suitcase. "I'm going to teach you how to crochet. I brought yarn and needles and a blanket I can't seem to finish. Do you know how wonderful it feels to finish something?"

"What'd you bring me?" Felix sat on her foot, clutching her thigh.

Peg unbuckled the men's belt she'd wrapped around her largest piece of luggage and flipped open the locks. From deep inside the large bag, she pulled out a full-sized hammer, its red shank spattered in paint. One of its iron claws was broken into a spike, the way it had been since Promise was a child. No wonder she'd always been slightly afraid of hammers. Promise figured her dad had finally bought himself a new hammer, and Peg had made off with this one.

Peg laid it in Felix's hand, which literally fell to the floor with the hammer's weight. She said, "This was your grandpa's, but he thought you might need it. We heard you like to pound."

Felix hoisted the tool up baseball-bat style, and it almost brought him over backward. "It's real!" he squealed. "Mom won't even let me have a plastic one. Thank you, Gran-Gran."

From behind Felix, Peg lifted the hammerhead and helped bring it down, in slow motion, in front of him. "It's a heavy one, so we always have to use it together. Can we make that deal? I'll keep it with my things, and when we want to use it, we'll use it together. I'll probably let you swing it, because Gran-Gran gets tired."

"Okay."

Thus she took the used gift she had brought for him out of his hands before he could play with it, and she put it away, and verily, he did not cry. Promise watched in wonderment as she worked the children over. They purred, "Yes, Gran-Gran. Thank you, Gran-Gran."

Promise cooked a dinner of scrambled eggs, cinnamon toast, and bacon, making the children even giddier with the novelty of breakfast at night. Afterward, Lydia and Felix dragged Peg up to see their rooms. Leo took the dog out, and Promise sat down at the kitchen table, straining to hear her mother's extra-slow reading voice from upstairs.

"Cup of coffee?" Promise asked her after the kids were in bed.

"Don't mind if I do," she said. Her enormous suitcase was still on the floor of the entry hall, and she pulled a jar of instant coffee from it.

"Instant?" Promise said. Her mother was known to appreciate a good cup of coffee.

"Decaf. I should just buy brown drops for hot water." Peg set the jar on the counter, then sat at the kitchen table. Dangling from a long beaded chain were a pair of reading glasses, which she slipped on to scan the newspaper headlines. She'd always been a voracious reader. "So whatever became of that Althea?"

Promise was surprised. She hadn't given Althea a thought since she left. "She wasn't up to the job, Mom."

"I don't doubt it, but it would be a shame to lose touch. She needed you more than you needed her."

Promise felt bad for how that had ended—it was weird to have the point person in your children's life disappear. "We needed reliable child care," she said in her defense.

Back from his stroll, Leo unhooked the leash from Flipper's collar. "Who are we talking about?"

"Althea," Promise said. "I couldn't save her."

"She was snakebit, honey," Peg said. "Her husband gone, single mom to her kids and her sister's too, her health going south."

Leo slapped his leg. "You got more of her story than we did."

"I called from time to time," she admitted. "Not to check on the kids, but to visit with her. A woman wants to know who's taking care of her grandkids."

"You're amazing," Leo said. "How's Jack? Any more liver stuff?"

Promise looked back and forth from Leo to Peg, as if this were a Ping-Pong game. Hey, she might have yelled if she had any spark left. Hey, let me in!

"He's better—the latest tests were normal." Peg took her cup to the sink, rinsed it out, put it in the dishwasher. "I should be getting to bed. What time does school start in the morning?"

"Tomorrow's Saturday, Mom," Promise reminded her.

"I know, honey. I meant on Monday." She left the kitchen, but she was back in a minute with a stack of brown cowboy fabric. "Would you like curtains for the baby's room out of this? It's a little brown, but it was on sale."

There were cattle brands and lariats, bandannaed cowboys riding pinto ponies, and campfires scattered across the brown background. Promise adored the material, which looked like every pair of pajamas her brothers had ever worn. "I can't believe you brought fabric. Mom, I don't own a sewing machine."

Peg was as shocked by that as Promise was by her suitcase contents. "I packed curtain rods, too," Peg said. "You don't have a sewing machine—how do you sew?"

"I don't," Promise said.

"She doesn't iron either," Leo volunteered. "Fortunately, she's good in bed."

"Leo!" They both turned on him, and he grinned.

Peg asked, "Is that community center still down the street—they had three or four nice machines last time I was here. Curtains are just a straight stitch; they shouldn't mind."

Promise scooted her chair back so she could come around and give her mother a hug. "You are a piece of work," she said.

"Oh, no." Peg kissed Promise on the lips. "I just know a hundred ways to make do."

Leo volunteered to take Peg's things upstairs; however, they could tell by his grunts that he was starting with the big suitcase.

"Leave the big one," Peg called out. To Promise she said, "There are no clothes in that one."

"What on earth did you bring?"

"Supplies," she said. "Projects for the kids. If I'd known you didn't have a sewing machine, I'd have packed that, too. Good night, sweetheart. Thanks for having me."

They gave each other another hug and a kiss before Peg went upstairs to the guest room, soon to be Edgar's room. Promise filled the dishwasher and started it, wiped off the table, locked the doors, and turned off the lights.

"That woman has the energy of ten," Promise said to Leo in bed. She was on her right side, her back to him.

"Here's what I love," he said, cozying up against her. "We write Althea off and Peg's still in touch. That's what I was trying to tell you today."

"Your visit to the Mother Planet."

"Stay with me, here. Don't make fun." He really felt he was onto something. "You've been telling me for years that museums are past their conquering phases. Now they're about caretaking and educating."

"That's what Arthur says, actually. It's his explanation for all the women on staff."

"And it makes some sense," Leo said. "We've been trying to show the importance of museums, but the opponents Joseph fingered don't object to museums. They're offended that we're not promoting American values."

"So you want mothers to save the museum?"

"The people who want to help us can get reelected standing up for mothers, as opposed to Asia. Those guys save face even as we shame the rest into not doing the wrong thing."

What he was saying was the intersection of their two essences. If he could be so swayed by the power of her people, could she let him use them for political means?

Leo kept going. "Museums are devoted to beauty and human creation—who taught you to appreciate that? Your mother."

"Stop it," Promise said. "My mother taught me a hundred ways to make do. Much as I admire her, the farthest she wanted my ambitions to take me was Tulsa." She welcomed Leo's enthusiasm, but he was making a common mistake. "Last fall they had a million moms on the Mall marching against guns—did it make any difference? And when those Senate wives banded together to put warning labels on music, you made fun of them."

"That was different," Leo said. "Or it was different at the time."

"No," she said more emphatically, because she'd figured out what was bothering her. He'd spent a few days on the playground watching mothers in action, and he'd found more for them to do. "Leave the mothers out of this. We're busy, dammit!" She thought about her desire to tunnel through to Asia—where had that come from? "As far as my art appreciation goes, Joseph encouraged that more than my mother."

Leo was quiet, which she took as capitulation. The streetlight glow outside their bedroom illuminated a few of the masks on the far wall. Could Green Hornet, assisted by Kato's formidable karate chop, defeat narrow-minded nationalism? What about Plastic Man—did his stretching superpowers work to expand consciousness? She said, "I've always thought it was amazing that the museum sits between the Castle and the Department of Agriculture—can we make something of that? Because those weird juxtapositions are what I find most admirable about Washington."

Leo wrapped his feet around hers, forgetting that pregnancy had toasted her toes. He said, "I've always been amazed that the Middle East embassies are all in the same neighborhood."

She concurred. "We live in this town of a thousand symbols, whether we like it or not." Reaching from behind her, Leo stroked her stomach, and the light pressure actually felt good on her tautly stretched skin. "I've told you about my spring break trip to D.C.," she said.

He traced the letters *DC* on her belly. "A primary source fanatic even then."

She said, "At American Art, I will never forget, there was *The Peaceable Kingdom*, which had been our family Christmas card, then upstairs they had those Cornell boxes and an altar this black custodial worker had made out of scrap wood and lightbulbs and tinfoil—they'd found it in a garage after he died, along with gospels he'd written. He'd invented his own language."

As always, Leo thought, she gave Joseph too much credit. If he hadn't encouraged her to become an art historian, the next professor would have.

Promise turned onto her left side to face Leo. There was a reason her midwife called this the rotisserie part of the pregnancy: getting comfortable required constant turning. Just then, Edgar pushed hard against Promise with his heel or hand. "Yikes," she squeaked, and Leo rubbed the knob of baby that stuck out. He gave it a push, and the bump receded, only to pop up in another spot. This time when Leo gently mashed down, the baby pushed back.

"We're playing, here," Leo said. "Does that hurt you?"

"Sort of, but it's funny." Now that they faced each other, she could smell the smoke on his hair, and she wondered where he smoked when Peg was here. She was making connections and revving like she was a little stoned herself. This could have been Peg's gift; her visit took a load off Promise. Even the fact that Peg had packed curtain fabric relieved Promise, who hadn't given one thought to curtains in the baby's room. Now she didn't have to think of everything.

In her bowl of a belly, the baby settled down, and Leo put his ear against her stomach. "All's quiet," he reported, then lifted his head. "Hey, no one cares if the jewels or dinosaur bones at Natural History were found in America—how come natural history is universal?"

"The biggest, the oldest, the most carats," Promise said. "There it is again."

Leo scrutinized her stomach before realizing she was talking about Washington.

She said, "I'm telling you, everything in this town is symbolic of something." She moved a pillow down by her feet so it was between her knees and patted around until she found another one, which she wedged under her belly. She said, "Now that Joseph told us who's behind this, we can challenge their notion of what the National Mall is."

Leo said, "We might get farther trying to change the subway exit."

She thought of that ride up the escalator, the white Capitol dome straight ahead, the Castle slowly rising into the foreground. Once the escalator brought you up to ground level, the Museum of Asian Art was seated at your right hand, along with the Department of Agriculture. Natural History and American History were on your left, and the Washington Monument had your back. It was a heady presentation, astounding for its concentration. Many a time she'd had to resist the urge to spin all the way around, throw her hat in the air, and let out an Oklahoma holler.

"If you ask me," she said, "the National Mall should both feed people's expectations and confound them. You know, blow their minds a little. A beautiful diamond and a cockroach the size of your hand. The Stars and Stripes and a sculpture made out of ten thousand coffee cups."

"Blow their minds," Leo echoed, "and remind them they're not alone in the world."

"Now you're talking," she said.

"Dammit, we should be *rewarded* for housing Buddhist, Hindu, and Muslim together. Who could bring that message home?"

Promise considered who might best represent tolerance and the perils of nationalism. Well, Joseph was a candidate, having been mugged by Kashmiri nationalists while on an art history mission. She thought back to the snowstorm, when her quest for important names had degenerated into a joke: Mother Teresa, Lady Di, and the Dalai Lama go into a museum. And then, like a vision, she saw the Dalai Lama, friend and mentor of Emmy Lattimore, giver of good tidings by cell phone, standing beatifically on the white museum steps in his resplendent saffron robes.

"Lordy, Lordy!" Promise exclaimed and grabbed for Leo, intending to plant a big celebratory kiss on his forehead. In her excitement, she forgot her burgeoning size, and tipping his head down, she ended up stuffing him face-first into her breasts.

Leo came up for air wearing his dopey grin. "Whatever you're planning," he said, "count me in."

What Did the Dalai Lama Say
to the Hot Dog Vendor?

January 15, 2000

S truggling to get into her pants the next morning, Promise re-assessed her strategy—last night's inspired plan now seemed as ill-fitting as her jeans. The very idea of staging a Dalai Lama shindig was presumptuous, not to mention pretentious. Leo disagreed, or he would have if he were still in bed. Promise was forced to argue his side for him. Hadn't they been going increasingly high-profile to dissuade the Castle from moving ahead? Yes, but. In their care of sacred artifacts, didn't they serve religious communities, especially those under threat? Yes, but.

Downstairs, Promise's mother had the coffee going. "No law against smelling it," Peg said. She'd already fed the children, who were watching cartoons in the basement. "Leo took the dog out," she said, and she took the front section of the paper into the living room, giving Promise a rare moment's peace in her own kitchen.

Sitting quietly with her toast and coffee, Promise stewed as she ate. She'd been building a case for the museum to assuage what she'd as-sumed were budgetary concerns. Stop fussing, she meant to convey, you can afford this. She'd instructed everyone to play up the opening and the bowl ceremony, because those events celebrated aspects of museum work. Neither had worked as planned, but then Joseph's rev-elation added insult to injury. Rather than "We can't afford you," the Castle was actually saying, "You're not welcome here." Of course, Leo was energized by the political twist: just as he'd suspected, a conspir-acy was afoot!

Justifying the museum's existence was further than Promise had expected to go. She'd never claimed her scholarship was essential to civilization. Her life's work was leading people up to the rabbit hole she'd discovered. Silence the din in your head, grow small, concentrate, and you too could slide down this passage, into light. She imagined herself unveiling Rumi's spirituality the way he wrote of revealing the physical world to an embryo: "The world outside is vast and intricate. There are wheatfields and mountain passes, and orchards in bloom. At night there are millions of galaxies, and in sunlight the beauty of friends dancing at a wedding."

Probably she was tormenting herself over nothing, considering the unlikelihood that the Dalai Lama would be available. Still, she owed it to the museum to exhaust every possibility, and so she retreated to her bedroom to call Emmy. Her stomach was jumpy with butterflies or Edgar, she couldn't tell which. What was she afraid of exactly? Overreaching. Selfishness. She wanted to waylay the Dalai Lama, interrupt his sacred, ambassadorial schedule, to help keep their doors open. It was like asking for the moon just to light your own shed.

Promise had decided against rehearsing her pitch, because she wanted to honor Emmy with the depth of her sincerity. She'd already dialed the Naval Hospital when she heard the Mom chant begin. Lydia's voice reached under the bedroom door: "Mom. Mom. Mom? Mom?" Hoping to avoid detection, Promise whispered to the operator, "Joseph Lattimore's room, please."

"Hello?" Emmy picked up.

Promise should have made this call from the car, because now Felix had joined in the search for her. They'd recruited Peg as well, so in addition to "Mom. Mom. Mom? Mom?" there was "Promise? Promise, honey?"

Promise asked how Joseph was doing, and Emmy said, "He's really coming around."

"I called," Promise said, "well, of course, I called. What I mean is I have a huge favor to ask." She took as deep a breath as Edgar would allow. ("Mom. Mom?" "Promise, honey?") Her family was closing in on her. She'd wanted to be spontaneous with Emmy, but now she was too rattled to wing it. "We can't really tell if we're making progress. I mean, the editorials are in our favor, and our visitor count is up—" She abandoned that played-out stream for another creek bed. "We need to go really high-profile here—thin the atmosphere just enough to make the Castle choke on their plans."

"I'm not following you," Emmy said, worry in her voice.

Joseph's baritone rumbled in the background, and Emmy explained, "It's Promise, dear, going mystical on me." Then she genuinely asked, "How can I help you?"

Before Promise could answer, Felix flung open the bedroom door. "Mom!" he yelled. His green eyes lit up. "I found Mom!"

Promise stretched her arm out like a traffic cop—halt!—and Felix stopped so fast that Lydia ran into him. Peg was following behind them; when she saw Promise's expression, she said, "Oh, my. Let's get a move on," and wisely escorted them out.

"Jeez," Felix remarked as the door was closing. "I thought she liked children."

"I'm sorry," Promise spoke into the phone.

Emmy sympathized. "What you're up against," she said.

Promise hoisted herself up onto her tall bed, then toppled over on her right side, phone to her other ear. This was Emmy she was talking to, the least judgmental person she knew. You could say anything to her as long as you didn't impugn Joseph. When Promise let down her guard, her voice lowered too. "Last night I had a clear picture, a vision really, of you and the Dalai Lama on the Mall side of the museum. He was in saffron; you were in lavender. Waves of people lapped at your feet." Back in her bed, where she'd conceived this idea, she began warming to it again. Details of what she'd glimpsed became distinct. "Everyone was reaching up and swaying in unison—their fingers looked like seaweed in the ocean. The crowd, the support was so intense that it turned the tide against our opponents." She masked a burp. "I mean, I know. He's probably booked years in advance, and I'm sure he commands—and deserves—a large donation for his causes."

"So would I ask him to come next week for free?" Emmy said, and she laughed.

"You got it." Promise lightly rocked in place. She didn't have to apologize any further.

"Well," Emmy conceded, "the museum has given him a platform before. He scheduled his meetings at the Asian because of Joseph and, quite honestly, because of Nathan's cooking." There was a long pause. "You think our crusade is worthy of his attention?"

"Yes, I do," Promise said, and then, "No, I don't. That's exactly what I'm struggling with." She was relieved to voice her doubts. "It's a stretch. I keep asking myself, is the museum *essential*? It's more essential than fast food, but for all my talk of bringing art to the masses, I don't want the museum to be cod-liver oil."

"Or cola," Emmy said.

"Right," Promise agreed. She saw a museum of Asian art as an acquired taste, sips available to all, though she couldn't think what beverage that might be. Ginger beer? Pomegranate juice?

"He gave me his cell phone number," Emmy said. "He must expect me to call sometime."

"Oh, thank you, thank you. I had to ask, even if it doesn't pan out."

"You never know," Emmy said. "But I have a favor to ask as well."

Promise clenched one hand into a fist. Please make it something I can say yes to.

"Your visits are a tether. I know—with the children, on a weekend—it's a lot, but Joseph needs to tell his story about a thousand times or it may well kill him. He's eager to see Leo, too."

"We'll come right after lunch," Promise volunteered.

Emmy's request was barely an imposition. The children were delighted to be in the care of their grandmother, who actually preferred entertaining them without Promise and Leo around. She maintained that everyone behaved better that way. Meanwhile, she got Lydia and Felix to make their own lunches and clean up after themselves, the motivation being a project from her mysterious suitcase, which when you came right down to it, was filled with scraps. Children apparently know magic when they see it, and they shared Peg's satisfaction at transforming balls of yarn into a doll blanket, spools and a rubber band into a car.

On the drive out to Bethesda, Promise prepared Leo for the desiccated, feeble Joseph, and so it was a pleasant surprise to find him sitting up in bed, free from tubes, and his face clean-shaven though badly chafed. His head and thumbless hand were still dramatically overwrapped, distended to a degree that would have been silly if it weren't so sad.

Emmy had traded in her gauze pants and matching tunic for Asian import garb: quilted batik jacket, coarsely woven black pants, and beaded tennis shoes. Promise figured she was making an effort to cheer Joseph, but she might just have been out of clothes. "Convent gift shop," Emmy said. "They do pretty well." Pointing to her jacket, pants, and shoes, she said, "Indonesia, India, Thailand."

Leo handed her a bag of groceries. "We brought a few things."

Emmy unpacked each item as if she and Joseph were still stranded in the desert. "Fresh juice, Joseph"—she held up the jug—"and clementines. Oh, boy, vegetarian sushi." Finished with the food, she took Promise's hand. "He was away from his phone. I left a message."

The butterflies in Promise's stomach started flapping around, agitated. And if he called back? And if he said yes? His Holiness had only been at the museum for exclusive audiences, and their auditorium held five hundred. The last time he'd spoken at the National Cathedral, seven thousand people showed up. And another thing. If folks objected to the museum promoting Asia's religions, was the Dalai Lama their best advocate? Promise wished she'd chewed her lunch more thoroughly, because it felt like an entire sandwich was lodged behind her sternum.

While Promise quietly made herself sick, Joseph sang Leo's praises. He kept quoting from the laminated Amnesty International card, which he'd practically ingested in the desert. When swallowing made him wince, he said, "Feign pain." He lifted a cracker in salute. "Pack snacks."

Leo shrugged off Joseph's tributes. "I would have been useless in your yurt."

"Nonsense," Joseph said, crediting Leo and Emmy with giving him the courage to escape. The helmet of bandages atop his unusually gaunt cheeks gave him a snake-charmer look as he spoke of the card's magic. "More than courage—a razor blade, a *poncho*!"

Energized, Joseph regaled them with his and Kanraku's story. He told them about swallowing soap, tucking away food and medication, and trying to humanize himself to his captors; then he moved on to Kanraku's strength and bravery. Pummeled until his nose and teeth were broken, the filmmaker had fought their captors practically alone. Kanraku had tended to Joseph in his semiconscious state, and he'd endured captivity's devastating boredom by reviewing Steve McQueen's oeuvre in all its intricacies. Thank goodness, he was safe at home in Kyoto.

Joseph related his story with a measured calm, even as he made his way up to the Uygur camel man whom he'd caught stealing food and who had dealt his thumb its deadly blow. He told them how he'd condensed the *Ramayana*, wrapping up the epic on the night he and Kanraku broke away. But when he got to the part about the boy on crutches, he started fading.

"Maybe that's for another day." Emmy tried to let him off the hook.

"No," he insisted, though he was clearly uncomfortable. "Probably a land mine got his one leg, but who knows? They put him on sentry duty, this malnourished, disabled *kid*."

Joseph's voice broke, and Leo understood that they were just getting to the part he most needed to tell. From his years at Amnesty, Leo knew the drill. A man like Joseph, still delirious at being alive, would initially downplay his ordeal. Forced himself to eat soap, walked across the Sea of Death in the dark despite his many injuries—had to be done. Inevitably, the narrator would reach a certain spot and loop back, sometimes recap the entire story once more with feeling. Victims would repeat details of the landscape along with accounts of their endurable pain or torture until they broke through the scar tissue. Then the howling would commence, and Leo would brace himself for the inexplicable cruelty, either the random or the pointed violence. What had Leo suffered? Nothing. But what he'd heard could put you in your grave.

"You had to get out," Leo encouraged him. "I'm glad you made it."

"Well, me too," Joseph said. "Then here comes the crippled guard after us. Coconut Head, we called him, because his head looked like a coconut. If your prisoners got away, wouldn't you send a guy on a mule?"

"A guy on a mule would have caught you," Leo said. Once negotiations went sour, the Al-Faran were better off having their escapees perish in the desert than having to kill or feed them.

"We could see the prayer flags of the camp we were aiming at, but Coconut Head was forging a shortcut. We were standing up on a dune, practically making eye contact, when he was blown apart by a land mine."

Promise gasped involuntarily.

"Sorry," Joseph said. "Wouldn't want to give you nightmares."

"I'm all right," she said. She thought she should urge him toward the warm, dry hospital room. "How did you get rescued?"

"Oh, a guy from Detroit, a Lutheran World Federation worker, was in the camp. He had contact with Hotan. What was he doing there, Emmy?"

"Health care, as I understand."

"Nutrition-related," Joseph said, eager to return to the desert. "My conscience can handle Coconut Head's death, that wasn't really my doing."

"Kanraku had been tortured," Leo said. "The boy might have been armed."

"His arm was shattered. This little stick of a kid. And I tied him up." He looked at Emmy. "You saw him in your dream—he didn't make it through the shock." Almost to himself, he said, "I should have carried him."

"You had to get out," Leo repeated. "If you'd carried him, you'd both be gone."

Emmy laid her head on his chest in the semblance of a hug, then she raised herself up and dabbed at his eyes with a tissue.

"That kid was doomed before he met us," Joseph said. "But he was alive. It kills me that we left him there."

His voice was thick as spit, and Promise was eager to get out the door so the suffering man could nap. Sure enough, he was exhausted, and in the next tick of the clock, his bravado dissolved. "Leo," he sobbed through blubbery tears. "I owe you my life."

"You don't owe me a thing, man." Leo reached out to give Joseph's good hand a soul shake.

When Joseph let go, it was to attend to the tube coming out of his arm, the hose with the morphine delivery system. His features had already softened in anticipation of comfort.

Emmy walked them to the door. "Thank you," she said. "It must be hard on you both to see him so compromised."

"Compromised," Promise echoed, struck by how well that described his condition.

Leo said, "We'll come back tomorrow." He'd been hoping to clear his own conscience this afternoon. He was afraid that if Talbot ever did show up, he'd elaborate on Arthur's clumsiness in such a way as to implicate Leo. "That's some guilt he's carrying, about the boy."

"He's a father," Emmy said, as if that explained it.

Leo and Promise held hands as they walked through the hospital's polished hallways, which were as sparsely filled as the museum corridors. A few men in uniform walked briskly past, and a patient shuffled along, wheeling his fluids on a stand behind him.

"You were great in there," she said. "Lordy, you must have heard it all."

He squeezed her hand in response. Around a corner, they came upon a seating cluster where a woman and three children slumped. The family resemblance included chunky legs and round, wide faces. Suddenly, the teenage daughter folded up as if punched in the stomach, and a sibling came over to console her. Unlike the museum, Promise thought, here it was the people who needed saving.

Promise had to stop at a drinking fountain, the pesky feeling like a tickle in her throat that her scholarly career was an extravagance. Measured against survival, any career would be. Joseph's descriptions of the desert vegetation, the sky at night, the nomads' clothing and rugs were familiar to her from the miniatures she studied. And though his story had shaken her up, it had also provided her with a curious insight. The gory battles preserved in manuscripts, each indignity recorded in detail, were accepted as a matter of record, history and bragging rights got down on paper. Just maybe, she thought, some were lamentations, regrets of sacrifices or feuds with bloody consequences. Rather than commanding the scribe to glorify their ruthlessness, perhaps a ruler occasionally enlisted one to take his confession. It was worth looking into.

———

Peg was in the kitchen having coffee with Althea when Promise and Leo walked in. "I wanted to touch base," Peg said.

Although Althea was friendly enough, she looked more sickly than ever. Promise wished she were happier to see her, but feeling as she did, Althea's presence just brought up memories of substandard child care. Case in point: where were Lydia and Felix? And where were Althea's own kids on a Saturday afternoon?

"The kids are working in the basement," Peg said. "Flipper's out in the yard."

Althea held up an apron printed all over with giant apples. She said, "Look what Mrs. Whittaker thought to sew for me."

Promise resisted making a remark about turning on the oven for more than warmth. Worn out as she was, she didn't want to sit down for a chat with Peg and Althea. She and Peg had each been fighting the good fight, yet her mother seemed oddly more effective. Why was that—an apron was not going to cure what ailed Althea. Peg was more informed than Promise on current events, she was a promiscuous volunteer, she was involved in other people's lives. If someone's house burned down, Peg was out there gathering mattresses, canned goods, sweat suits for the children. In light of her mother's hands-on approach, Promise's talents seemed narrow and narrowly prized. There was that scratch in her throat again, which she'd felt at the hospital, and she filled a glass with tap water. "Would you excuse me?" she said.

"Keep in touch, Althea. It's good to see you." Leo followed Promise upstairs.

He encouraged her to take an afternoon nap, which she'd been meaning to do since November. She awoke to the smell of dinner circa 1970: the stale smell of oil used for deep frying, pepper, milk thickened with flour and fat, and the yeasty tang of baked rolls. They all sat down to an early dinner of chicken-fried steak with white gravy and mashed potatoes, green beans, and chocolate pudding pie. Promise purred as she ate.

"Does she know Althea was here?" Lydia asked her grandmother at one point, as if Promise weren't in the room.

"Yes, sweetheart. It's all right," Peg said.

Neither of the kids said much about it, which was strange considering Althea had watched them for a full year.

Felix said, "Wait until you see what we're up to. You won't believe your eyes."

Promise closed her eyes and then opened them in exaggerated amazement. "I can't believe it," she said. "Like that?"

"Again!" Felix said, and they went around the table practicing their astonishment.

Leo took the dog out as the women cleaned up. The children went directly to the basement to hammer away, though it wasn't long before Felix screamed. Promise and Peg ran downstairs to see him caressing the broken-clawed hammer. A wooden plaque on the floor bristled with nails.

Felix said, "I forgot to keep my eyes open, Gran-Gran, and I missed big time." He brought his plaque to Promise, who kissed his thumb. He said, "This is going to be a mushroom." He'd stenciled a toadstool on the square and had pounded nails more or less along the outline.

"I can't believe my eyes," Promise obliged.

"Here's a finished product," Peg said, showing her a wooden square with nails of many lengths poking out to make a garden, their flat heads tipped in different colors.

"Look, Mommy." Lydia held up her plank, where she'd sketched a horse. "Grandpa *made* this square out of *wood*. When it's my turn, I'll put nails in my drawing, then I'll paint the tops with nail polish—get it, *nail* polish?"

When Althea had been taking care of the children, they would jump up and down at Promise's return. However, all the bread Promise baked and birdhouses she painted with them were in her dreams. Their grandmother satiated them in a way Promise envied.

"You're running a craft sweatshop," she teased her mother, who said, "Those who make fun don't get a snow cone."

Felix yelled into Promise's ear, "She brought flavors! And she gots a whole stack of those little paper cones. We're going to use *snow*."

There was a literalness to Peg one didn't find in Washington, an unexpected example of the primary source.

Peg shrugged. "It's much easier being a grandmother than a mother."

Promise loved her for that remark. "Let me make you some brown water," she offered, slowly pushing herself up from the cold cement floor. Opening the basement door to the kitchen, she braced herself for Flipper's ecstatic greeting—*You're back! I'm back! I thought we'd never see each other again!* She was coming to depend on his enthusiasm. When the water boiled, she decided to make them a pot of herbal tea. Her mother had rearranged the cabinets: Promise found the honey with the baking supplies, set inside a paper muffin wrapper. She tugged with more force than was necessary, realizing as she pulled that it wasn't stuck to the shelf. She took a step back to regain her balance.

"I wiped the jar down," her mother said. "You don't mind that Althea was here, do you?"

"A little," Promise admitted. "I didn't mean to be rude, though." Having gone over family news already, they moved out in concentric circles to cousins, her parents' neighborhood and church friends, Promise's school friends and their parents. Peg wove household hints into stories she told.

"Mrs. Wilcox—her awful cat finally died, I think it was twenty-five—she's a widow now, and her son's moved back in with her. She tells your father that spraying the car bumper with cooking spray will keep dead bugs from sticking. Next day at dawn, he's out there coating the whole grille with the stuff." The sound of hammering was getting steadier, which meant either Felix was improving or it was Lydia's turn. Then Peg leaned forward and lowered her voice. "I have to agree with you, honey. Felix needs help of some sort."

Promise didn't want her suspicions confirmed, even though there was some satisfaction in knowing her child. "You said I just needed to see more children."

"Well, I've seen a lot of children, and he needs help. Could be a hormone problem that makes him so short, or maybe he has allergies. Your grandfather was allergic to wheat."

For the first time, she registered Felix's complaint that milk made him gag. Before she could begin feeling guilty about that, her mother blindsided her.

"I was also thinking about your job," Peg said. "Maybe the museum has run its course. Have you ever considered that?"

"Run its course?" Promise asked, incredulous.

Peg folded her hands primly on the table and pushed back her shoulders, the posture she adopted when she had a lesson to impart. "People get all riled up about how few pandas or family farms are left, but to everything there is a season. The dinosaurs lasted a long time, then they became extinct. Horse and buggies, vinyl records. Nothing lasts forever."

Her mother's logic was screwy, confounding environmental destruction and progress. (In all her years in Washington, Promise had never heard anyone concede that the panda might be expendable.) *Run its course*—that's how people talked about the flu.

"Just think about it," Peg said. "The world was smaller when your museum was established, and America really felt we knew best. Maybe you could arrange the return of your collections to the original countries, set an example."

She couldn't dismiss Peg out of hand. After all, wasn't Promise sending Min to China with the stolen *ding* to set an example, albeit a tiny gesture of the kind her mother was proposing? Peg was certainly a problem solver, as willing to go after grass stains as the Institution. Because Promise didn't know how to respond to her mother's opinion, she pushed back from the table to show Peg the baby's shenanigans. She lifted her blouse up above her belly.

"He's a Mexican jumping bean," Peg said.

Lydia called for Gran-Gran from the basement, and Peg took a last gulp of her tea. "I didn't mean to overstep my bounds. It's just something to think about." She carried her cup and saucer to the sink, where she had them washed before Promise could tell her not to. Peg turned the basement doorknob and paused on the first step. "You know, I could stay longer if you need me."

"Thanks, Mom." Promise held on to both sides of her big jumping bean. She lifted her heels up, stretching out her toes, then pushed her heels flat against the oak floor. Her back was having some kind of spasm, and a vein in her left calf throbbed. That was nothing compared with the electrical storm in her head. *Maybe the museum has run its course.* Perhaps her mother was giving her a way out or, just the opposite, provoking her. Well-meaning mothers often harden a child's resolve.

Peg's suggestion shouldn't have been surprising. Promise might have left Oklahoma behind, but she'd been hardwired in the flatland, where folks appreciated individuality and loathed pretension. It was an outlook Promise had roughly paraphrased as "You may not be much, but you're something else." Now she saw that the Oklahoma attitude was as elevated as the impenetrable Upanishads, whose teachings boiled down to "You yourself are the ultimate reality, but you are not what you seem."

Dinner had been so comforting that Promise hadn't stopped after one piece of chicken-fried steak; now her gusto yielded a fierce case of heartburn. Quickly, before anyone could talk her out of it, she went upstairs, where she shook some chalky antacid tablets from the economy-sized barrel, then changed into her nightgown. She'd slept late this morning and had an afternoon nap. Probably she should call Talbot and tell him of her Dalai Lama idea. She should take a look at the *Post*, where the museum was getting national, local, and arts coverage. She should walk down both flights of stairs to watch her children drive nails into wooden boards. She went to bed.

Clarity often comes out of confusion, not to mention five uninterrupted hours of sleep. Waking in the night with a full bladder, Promise padded to the bathroom, then carefully walked down the stairs for another glass of water. Such a small personal cycle, that of voiding and filling, but it satisfied her needs as well as her baby's. Some would call it a wash—pour a glass of water down the toilet and eliminate the middlewoman, they might suggest. The reason it wasn't a wash was that the cycle did not exist independent of the vessel. That was as profound as she was prepared to get at one-thirty in the morning.

Back in bed, she lay awake. She appreciated the originality of her mother's opinion. Peg was a free agent who cared more for giving advice than about whether people followed it. Good thing, because it was the acting director's opinion that the museum had not run its course. Go with your gut was also an Oklahoma approach, Promise thought, and she stood by her first impulse. "Creativity in all its forms is our passion." That was what she'd said to her staff the day the Wok On man had interrupted their exhibition meeting. After Vanessa had taped and transcribed Promise's unscripted call to arms, she'd amended her personal screen saver. Promise got a charge out of seeing her quotation scrolling across her assistant's computer: "Believe you me, the unwashed masses will be welcome here."

———

Sunday morning, Leo spread the *Post* on their bed, where Lydia and Felix were sprawled as well. "Check it out." He pointed at the Arts section, and read to them: "'The Castle would replace thirteenth-century Korans with laminated menus; they would have the staff serve up burgers rather than Buddhism. No match in stature to these six men, the petite acting director begs to differ.'" He turned the paper around, so Felix and Lydia could see the picture of Promise standing in the gallery.

"Mommy rules!" Felix jumped on the bed until Leo brought him down with a pillow.

"Listen up: 'Promise Whittaker points out a page of Chinese calligraphy and a Hindu manuscript, each touting a version of the Golden Rule, though she is just as quick to point up differences among cultures.' Here's Mom talking, gang: 'We showcase the creative expressions that stem from a variety of religious beliefs. If you ask me, the National Mall is an inspired location for us.'" Leo inched forward on his stomach so he could kiss Promise. "Nice quote, Queenie."

Downstairs, Peg was starting a batch of pancakes, pouring the batter inside cookie cutter shapes she'd brought with her: rabbit, butterfly, and duck. When Leo showed her the article in the paper, she said to Promise, "That's a nice picture of you, honey," and returned to the griddle. Promise was worried that her mother was working too hard, though she was enormously grateful for the help. Her family had never eaten this well. "It's nice to be appreciated," Peg said.

The kids were bickering over who would get what shape of pancake, as Peg assured them she had plenty of batter. Promise thought she heard the phone ring and picked up the receiver, half expecting there to be a dial tone. But it was Emmy.

She said, "Kundun called us back. He says let's do it!"

The thrill in Emmy's voice told Promise the news was good; it just took her a second to recall who Kundun was. The Dalai Lama had more names than God. "Wow" was all she could say. "I'm in shock."

"He says the sooner the better—January's a slow month for him."

Promise had moved out of the kitchen onto the basement steps with the phone, closing the door behind her. Now she sat on the steps with the lights off, elated and queasy in equal measures. "January's half gone."

"January is what's open. Either the thirtieth or the thirty-first."

Leo peeked in on Promise, who gave him the thumbs-up. "Oh yeah!" he said and sealed her back in the basement. Of course, on the other side of the door, he started singing "Hello, Dolly!" to the children in a Louis Armstrong voice.

Promise was almost ready to sing. Really, January was just right. The baby was due at the end of March, and the timetable in the Castle memo had the museum closing in July. "Will you help me?" she asked, as if Emmy hadn't done enough already. "I mean, thank you for asking, for lining this up, but I'm not sure what I'm getting us into."

Emmy said, "It will be great. You'll be turning help away."

When Promise emerged from the basement, her family let out a cheer.

"Holder of the White Lotus," Leo said. "Presence, Wish-Fulfilling Gem."

"Ocean of Wisdom," Promise added to his list of the Dalai Lama's aliases.

The children thought they were speaking gibberish. Lydia made her head go wobbly on her neck as she joined her palms together in imitation of Indian dance, while Felix began singing, "Shake, shake, shake. Shake your Buddha!"

For a second, Promise saw the scene from her mother's perspective—strange rituals, these people—except that Peg wasn't looking askance. Slyly grinning, she was nodding her head in wonder or maybe appreciation of family joy.

————

Arriving at the Naval Hospital a few hours later, the Whittaker-Wellses saw a smiling doctor backing away from Joseph's bed. "We'll see, we'll see," he said. "I'll check in again at fourteen hundred hours. It's encouraging, to say the least."

Emmy did a little dance after he left, similar to the one Lydia had done at home. She seemed to exude healing. Promise was glad to have practiced opening her eyes wide in astonishment for Felix. She said, "I can't believe it."

"Quite a coup," Joseph agreed.

All three of them beamed at Emmy, who looked positively fashionable in a blue silk blouse and a large embroidered scarf over a broomstick skirt that twirled around her legs. "Thought I'd brighten up a bit—those nuns have quite a flair!"

Promise was beginning to think "convent gift shop" was a euphemism for Bloomingdale's.

"Who was that masked man who just left?" Leo asked.

"Head of the neurology team," Emmy explained. She detailed Joseph's problems rather jauntily. "There's unspecified nerve damage from the hypothermia and Joseph's head wounds—the cut, along with his earlier concussion. We'll know more in twenty to thirty days."

Joseph spoke up. "*Adam uttuz, Khuda toqquz.*"

They focused on the sick man, who elaborated, "That's Uygur for 'Man says thirty, God says nine.'"

Promise was relieved he was making sense. "Is that like 'Man proposes, God disposes'?"

"It is," he said simply. Joseph was wearing a knit shirt with the Navy insignia stitched on the left side, and he'd been given another, better shave. His left arm had been freed from tubes, which meant he'd finally made real progress. The biggest change appearance-wise was that they'd lifted off his helmet of bandages, leaving him with one stripe of dressing along the top of his head. Gray bristles of hair stood up on either side—short near the wound, longer elsewhere. His hair resembled Felix's craft project of nails poking up all over.

Promise and Leo had brought bagels, spreads, fruit, juice, and coffee, which the four friends enjoyed as comfortably as the circumstances allowed. Joseph ate nearly all the fruit.

"I'd forgotten what a melon could be," he said, licking the fingers of his left hand.

"You've forgotten most things," Emmy teased. "Don't ask him about anything before 1998. Except Steve McQueen's movies."

"I urge you not to count me out," he said.

It wasn't long before Promise had to excuse herself. Her absence gave Leo the opening he needed to relieve himself as well. He launched into an apologia for his role in the great bowl disaster, seeking absolution for unknowingly inspiring Talbot.

Promise flipped off the light and fan in the bathroom; though she was rejoining the group after only a few minutes, the mood had changed. Joseph's eyes darted around the room, and he was tugging on his ear with his good hand; meanwhile, Emmy, who'd been solicitous of Joseph's every discomfort, gazed out the window as if his agitation were none of her business. Promise inferred what Leo had been saying from his posture—he was practically on his knees.

"Terrible, not wise," Joseph mumbled his disapproval. Here it comes, Promise thought, as a wet blanket of shame began smothering the morning's good spirits. Since the accident, she'd been expecting a serious reprimand, and Joseph was the likely choice to deliver her re-proof.

Newly attentive, Emmy brought her husband some juice, which he could now hold for himself. After a long shaky drink, he spoke: "Some would say a museum that destroys deserves to be closed." He held out his utilitarian cup, waxed paper with an innocuous flower motif. Had he the strength, he would have crushed it in his hand to demonstrate his frustration. Oh, but what was the use of that? A paper cup doesn't last long anyway. See beyond it, he coached himself, remembering Emmy's reaction to the news of the museum's fate: the cup is already broken.

Joseph's eyes registered his change of heart, from a hooded betrayal to deep-set loss to clear acceptance. He looked with kindness upon Promise, who was already sniffling, prepared to be scolded. "You know, I'm not in a position to judge." Thus, he lifted the shroud from her shoulders only to wrap himself in it. "One way or another, we all get our karmic comeuppance. I got mine."

Incredulous, Leo said, "You did not deserve what happened to you."

"Maybe not."

"You didn't," Emmy said with finality.

Promise wiped her nose on a rough napkin. "Should we get to work?" she asked squeakily, and all agreed. She trotted out stacks of clippings and the list of politicians, policy makers, academics, and re-ligious types they'd contacted since the bowl broke. In fact, Joseph had already seen the morning paper, and he complimented her on her choice of words. He followed along even as nurses came in to take his blood pressure and temperature and to bring him medication. In fact, he introduced and subsequently filled another category of person they needed to call, their wealthy donors. His astounding recall—an unfor-tunate consequence of overreliance, he said—got other memories flowing, and he reclaimed snippets of his last months at the museum. Carried along by the current were Cecil's scone falling to crumbs, Talbot eager to fire everyone, Zemzemal soothing the peacock keeper, Min emptying her museum accounts, Zemzemal suggesting that the entire senior staff resign alongside Joseph.

Emmy said, "Zemzemal tried to visit last week, but they wouldn't let him in. Turns out he has some ongoing visa trouble."

No one mentioned Talbot now. He'd apparently never made it to Joseph's bedside, and Promise hadn't called him this morning. She wasn't being very professional, but at the end of the day, she figured she could live with that.

After discussion, Promise settled on Monday, January 31, as their Dalai Lama date. While they needed a strong showing, she was frankly nervous about the size of a crowd a Sunday could attract. Besides, it behooved them to pick a day Congress was in session. The importance of museums to religious tolerance, preservation of cultures, and education were all possible links between them and the Dalai Lama. How blatant could they be in announcing their cause when their boss institution was the spoiler? Leo suggested a banner reading: WELCOME, DALAI LAMA—SAVE US FROM OURSELVES. The museum obviously couldn't spend any federal funds for this event, whatever it ended up being. This brought them full circle to Joseph's list of wealthy donors, at which point Promise felt a sharp cramp in her gut, either a false contraction or gas. It was an effort not to double over, and she held her breath for what felt like a minute. When the discomfort passed, she spoke quietly. "We should be heading out. Leo, give me a hand here."

Emmy took Promise's briefcase from her. "Oh, you don't look so good," she said.

"I'm tired," Promise answered.

"Me too," Joseph said, though he maintained he'd be up for a public appearance in two weeks. He held his bandaged hand to his stubbly head, speaking melodramatically, "A shadow of my former self." Sadly, that accurately described him. With a glimmer of his past friskiness, he volunteered to make some personal appeals. "Who could say no to me?"

Leo raced home through Rock Creek Park, the ground still glistening more than a week after the big snowfall. He peppered Promise with questions—was she in pain? was the baby moving around? was it like this last time? Not now, yes, she couldn't remember. It occurred to Promise that they'd just left a hospital, where presumably she could have been examined and hooked up to a fetal monitor, assuming they kept a fetal monitor around for soldiers. She released the car seat lever to recline, which helped the small of her back but lifted the baby practically on top of her lungs. She righted her seat, wondering if a call to her midwife could wait until morning.

"You're forty-three," Leo said. "We have to remember that this time."

"I know," she said. "My chart is labeled 'geriatric pregnancy.'"

Just out of the park, Promise spotted four deer high up on the hill of a research facility. A family circle, as Felix used to say: two youngsters, a doe, and a buck with modest antlers. Even in the twilight, they were easy to see against the snowy fields, trees bare of leaves. Promise started to point them out to Leo, who was licking his lips compulsively and leaning into the wheel, hell-bent on getting home. They'd been trying so very hard, the two of them, and she pushed out of her mind all the ways they could fail. Promise looked past her reflection in the window. She saw the buck raise his head at the sound of their approach and bound away from them, leading his charges back into the tangled woods.

————

Monday morning, Promise offered the car to Peg, who preferred walking Lydia and Felix to school. Once Peg got outside, the bitter wind and low winter sun stung her eyes, but what really disturbed her was seeing three homeless men and one woman along Connecticut Avenue—this was in Chevy Chase. The privilege on display in Washington was as unsettling as the troubles. Oklahoma City was less extreme on both ends. In Oklahoma City, it made a difference if you helped a family or taught a child to read. You could nearly always buy a sandwich for one drunk on the street; when they started showing up by the dozen and were undermedicated and violent to boot, a sandwich wouldn't do squat.

After dropping the children off, Peg rode a city bus up Connecticut Avenue, proud of her resourcefulness. Back at Promise's house, she managed to get all the doorknobs to stay on using only the contents of Leo's meager toolbox. Mostly she wedged in matchsticks, though she wasn't above trying a few drops of glue. While she was working on that project, a member of the Chevy Chase Historical Society called to ask if Promise and Leo's home could be on the Sears House tour in the spring. That tickled her, but she just took a message. Peg was surprised they considered a Sears House such an honor when they wouldn't even get the children's picture taken at Sears. After lunch she took her curtain fabric two blocks down to the community center, where the woman in charge was happy to let her use one of their sewing machines. She finished two curtains in the hour and a half before she had to head back to school for Lydia and Felix.

Promise's workday was just as productive. She'd called a staff meeting for ten o'clock in the auditorium. It looked empty despite the fact that most of the eighty staff members showed up. She'd only seen the auditorium filled for chamber music concerts, which must have been why the museum offered those performances. "Come on down," she urged them forward. "Publications, in the balcony, come down front, please." They filed out of their rows into the seats near the stage. Min, her paleness accentuated by the navy blue jacket she wore buttoned up to her chin, sat at one end of the second row. At the opposite end sat Arthur, relaxed and joking around with Sam and the other guys from Photo. Unlike Min, he was out of uniform, wearing a plain blue shirt without a coat and tie.

Leo sat front and center next to Talbot, who had also changed something. Different glasses? No. Shaved his mustache? Never had one. *His hair!* He'd had the long sides cut enough that they didn't fall forward, and it made him look less like the young prince and more like the heir apparent.

"That's a new look for you," Promise said noncommittally.

Talbot put his long hands over his ears. "Too much exposure," he said.

Promise stuck out her belly. "How do you think I feel?" She figured Leo had briefed him, but maybe he hadn't.

She mounted the steps to the stage with great care. "Good morning," she greeted them. "Thank you for coming." She was happy to update them on Joseph's improved condition, then moved on to familiar issues of funding and the visitor count. "What's new," she said, "is a patriotic concern that Asian art does not warrant such a prominent place on the National Mall."

"No," someone moaned, and others joined in. Promise was glad for the unrest, especially since Arthur had told her of people's mixed reactions to the memo. Because their museum had always suffered from an inferiority complex, being traded to the National Gallery confounded a few of them. Would their collections enjoy more prestige or less as part of the National Gallery?

She said, "Our horrible loss of the Jingdezhen bowl has brought us a great deal of notice—perhaps you've seen us in the paper." She'd pledged not to hint that any good had come from the accident, and so she simply moved on. "We believe that the Castle's plans are in flux, and we think that generating enough opposition will convince them of the folly and narrow-mindedness of their target. Some of you are uncomfortable with our defiance—"

"No we're not." "That's a big lie." "What the hell?" The crowd practically shouted in disagreement.

"Oh," Promise said, startled. She'd prepared a justification for their actions, which practically amounted to seceding from the Institution. She said, "Never mind," and the crowd laughed. "Well then, allow me to tell you that Emmy Lattimore has brought our cause to the attention of His Holiness, the Dalai Lama, who has agreed to be our guest here on Monday, January thirty-first."

As if she'd set off fireworks from the podium, the audience sighed admiringly. "Oooh, aaah." Even those staff with no ties to Buddhism had ended up asking for His Holiness's blessing the last time he'd visited.

Promise said, "Joseph is hopeful that he will also be able to join us. His devotion to Asian art, coupled with his nationality, made him a target, and he is eager to speak out on the museum's behalf. If we're lucky, the chief justice and the vice president will agree to have an audience with them. Otherwise, the Dalai Lama will help make our case to the gathered people and press."

Fatima Hakim stood up as the appreciative hooting and clapping subsided. She adjusted her chador. "I applaud your efforts. The Islamic community could provide many unfortunate examples of intolerance, if you see fit."

"Thank you, Fatima," Promise said. "Are there any examples of tolerance? Or even overcoming intolerance, because I want to include the Islamic community. I'm just worried that this will look like an Amnesty International event."

Leo rose from his front-row seat, waving to the assembled as if taking a bow.

Promise said, "Arthur? Did you want to say something?" He'd been waving his hand in the air like a second-grader flagging the teacher.

"First of all," he said, "I want to thank everyone for being so understanding since the accident. As a measure of contrition, I've been fomenting cooperation among my peers, and we've come up with a few ideas." He held up a notepad that everyone could see was filled. "I made a list," he said, which they appreciated on Promise's behalf.

"Well, it's about time," Promise said, beaming back at him. She didn't yet know all he was taking on, but it clearly suited him. For her part, it felt good to be on the same side as her old friend. "Could I have a chair up here, please?" She took a seat, eager to hear what the crew had come up with. The way she'd been feeling lately, she shouldn't be standing anyway.

———

On the morning of January 31, Promise Whittaker stood in front of the Museum of Asian Art and looked up into the Persian-blue sky, its color reminiscent of the enameled tiles on the Samarkand mosque. Did it ever sleet on the Dalai Lama, she wondered. Jet contrails fanned across the Mall, striping the airspace in fluffy bands of white. So close to the airport, the museum was nearly at the intersection of the vapor trails, and it looked like the spokes of a maypole or a carnival tent around her. It was unseasonably warm. Except for the Fourth of July, there were as many people as Promise had ever seen in this space. The Dalai Lama was, of course, a huge draw, as was Morty's bright idea, which had occupied the top slot on Arthur's list.

The crew of *What's It Worth to You?* was all over the south entrance; news brigades covering the Dalai Lama commanded the north. *What's It Worth* had never devoted an entire show to Asian antiques, though they had filmed in Washington before. Their eagerness to stage an episode at the museum with such short lead time was solely because Morty's ex-lover was the producer.

(Morty's current lover was on probation in both his personal and his professional life. Eager to rehabilitate himself, Arthur had presented the inspector general with a signed affidavit. He didn't want the museum defending itself against insurance fraud when the motivation was pure vanity. For his greater glory, he'd freed the bowl from its secure wire mount. Regardless of Leo's reckless remarks and Talbot's subsequent suggestions to him, Arthur should have known better. In fact, he should have known better than to go home with Talbot, but the point was that he was responsible. He'd dropped the bowl, made off with a chunk, then discarded said chunk. His case was pending.)

Appraisers from *What's It Worth* lined the south hallway and filled both the Chinese Painting gallery and the conference room. The show had die-hard fans of every demographic. Viewers recounted episodes where some know-nothing carted in an attic find, only to discover it was *museum quality* and therefore worth a chest of gold. What better location than the nation's attic, as some liked to call the Institution? People had lined up overnight—in January—for a chance to get their Asian doodads appraised. Ever since Promise had worked there, the museum had staged a monthly show-and-tell in the conference room with the curators, a popular enough feature but nothing like this.

On the other side of the building, within the giant rectangle that is the National Mall, were the Dalai Lama groupies. A throng had gathered near the large screen that would carry a feed to the auditorium. Every manner of Buddhist accessory was on sale, from Dalai Lama paraphernalia to prayer flags, beads to incense burners. Among the Buddha statues, you could choose between the meditative Buddha and the snarling Buddha adorned with a belt of skulls and an eye-poking trident.

Emmy's convent had set up a station to minister to the hungry or cold. A circle of monks and nuns were intoning their om-mani-padme-hum prayer. "Oh, the jewel in the lotus," they endeavored to repeat one hundred million times, until their blood thrummed in rhythm with the syllables—the point was to internalize the refrain until, rather than the body reciting the chant, the chant drove the body. Promise wondered how long it took to say the prayer one hundred million times. Thanks to Leo, the human rights community was out in full force. Demonstrators in support of Tibet were filling petitions with names, as were people worried about violations throughout the Middle East and Asia. There were clumps of music and a general feeling of well-being. How different walking among these groups was from walking through the galleries, where she'd felt one civilization sealed off from another.

Promise enjoyed seeing families come up out of the tunnel escalator into such a happening. Traffic for *What's It Worth to You?* continued to stream by, including an Asian grandmother hugging a quilt and a heavy black man, trailed by a three-year-old copy of himself, pushing a stroller whose passenger looked to be a bundled up vase.

For a team accustomed to spending five years preparing an exhibition, the museum staff had moved with phenomenal speed. Promise wasn't sure what in the last two weeks had surprised her most. Arthur showing up in jeans and work gloves, prepared to do some heavy lifting, was unexpected, though he was full of surprises. He helped the registrar and art handlers pack up parts of the collection for the storage facilities in Suitland: mainly the erotic portion and the bulky Chinese furniture, as well as shop inventory and files, files, files. The Design Department transformed the freed-up space with fabric and blown-glass lanterns, fashioning a Moroccan tearoom and vegetarian lunch counter (with a kids' menu). Then there was Nathan's proposal to invite a dozen guests each day for lunch in the staff room. Wouldn't an exclusive restaurant overlooking the courtyard be good exposure for possible donors?

That idea would take some time, as would suggestions for the courtyard, which ranged from café space to a small Asian habitat. Keep the peacocks, maybe add some red pandas—they couldn't fare any worse in the courtyard than their fallen comrades at the zoo. After-hours ideas for other spaces included kung fu movies and martial arts classes. English classes for Asian immigrants. Chinese, Korean, Vietnamese, or Laotian classes—everybody teach each other! Art classes and religious ceremonies. Asian comedians, karaoke, shadow puppet shows with gamelan orchestras performing nonstop from dusk to dawn. There was street parking and Metro access; the Founder never said the place had to close at five o'clock. Many of the ideas were purely commercial ventures; however, they enhanced the museum's mission. This was the difference between the Castle taking over and the museum inviting people in.

Promise made her way up the steps through the huge bronze doors. It smelled like paradise inside. Huge columns of flowers stood in the lobby like blooming pillars, an ephemeral gift from a mail-order billionaire and his wife. The art handlers had hauled the bronze Shiva statue into the lobby, and Promise had invited Hindus from a temple in Laurel to attend to him. She wanted every blessing they could lay their hands on. Having struggled with the issue of people handling the piece, she did request that they skip the milk bath. The Hindus wrapped Shiva in bright silk and strung him with garlands of carnations and jasmine blossoms. Many of the staff were also wearing leis, and the stony dampness of the lobby had been supplanted by fresh orange blossoms and honeysuckle. Lucy brought Promise a necklace of white orchids, which bloomed atop her flowing crimson dress.

Promise wished she felt better. Back spasms made it painful to walk—there was this nerve that traveled all the way down her left hip through her leg. She'd been having cramps as alarming as contractions; however, when Mahalia had examined her on Friday, her cervix hadn't started effacing or dilating. Blood pressure, protein traces, all checked out. Please, please take it easy, Mahalia had said to her. You've still got eight weeks to go. Lydia and Felix had both been full term, but Promise didn't think Edgar was going to make it that far. This morning, she'd been checking her watch with each spasm—they were running about twelve minutes apart.

"Miss Promise." Sergeant Becton approached her, walkie-talkie crackling. "Your guest is waiting for you in the greenroom." He made it sound like one of her kids' games—Miss Promise with the Dalai Lama in the Green Room.

Zemzemal and Talbot were both there to receive the Dalai Lama, who was swamped in attendants as well as museum types. Along the back wall, Nathan had set up a buffet, and it was beginning to look like a staff meeting in the large room. Zemzemal watched his colleagues fawn over the holy man, astonished that they could recognize his powers. Usually, few among them had time for God. Educated, wealthy by any standards other than their own, the professional staff was thin in believers. Zemzemal's experience was that people with all the advantages assumed they'd achieved their stature on their own; they gave themselves the credit and the glory. This was the reverse of what he'd been raised to believe, which was that while the bereft might deservedly feel abandoned by God, those who had been heaped with gift upon gift should have the intelligence and piety to recognize the higher source. For Zemzemal, five times a day of giving thanks was miserly. He had nothing against the Dalai Lama. It was just that on a day devoted to religious tolerance and cultural preservation, he wished the acting director had done a little more to include his religion.

Promise entered the huddle, wondering if she should shoo people out or not. His Holiness's face was visible above the group. Although his head was nearly shaved, there was evidence of a receding hairline: his bowl of stubble sat a ways back on his head. Oversized glasses stood flat in front of his eyes like a windshield, magnifying his unlined face. He obviously enjoyed laughing; in fact, his joy was making everyone almost irreverently informal. Each time he chuckled, his small eyebrows became part of a crease that stretched across his forehead, dipping down in the middle to resemble a bird in flight.

People stepped back, urging Promise forward. He smiled almost shyly at her as she approached, and they each bowed. "Your Holiness," Promise said. "I'm Promise Whittaker, the acting director of the museum. We are so grateful for your presence."

He placed both hands on her stomach, and for the first time she saw how natural, how compassionate a gesture it was. Edgar kicked with everything he had, connecting to those palms with elbow, fist, and foot. The Dalai Lama said, "The baby is due?"

Before Promise could respond, Emmy opened the anteroom door, and a cheer rose up as she escorted Joseph in from the hallway. Zemzemal, gracious Zemzemal, instantly had a chair for him. Joseph had been leaning on a cane; he tipped his weight back to fall into the chair. The Dalai Lama crossed the room as if it were empty, and the effect of his floor-length drapery was that His Holiness floated to Joseph's side. They clasped each other.

Joseph didn't look healthy, but with his prominent cheekbones and his large ears flat against the sides of his thinned face, he inspired memories of how he'd looked when Promise first attended his class. He may as well have worn a robe then, for the students wanted only to touch the hem of his garment. The college students were lucky if they spoke French or recognized Borobudur. This man could read and converse in a dozen languages; was familiar with the story of man as told by myths, shards, temples, and what passed as history. He knew a dozen forms that God took outside of Milwaukee, and he'd talk to you about it over a beer. Promise felt her belly drop even lower at the sight of him. Here was yet another surprise, that she was moved more by Joseph's presence than by the Dalai Lama's.

On his wounded hand he wore a leather glove, and his silver hair, evened out now, was trimmed close to his head. He and Emmy resembled each other, survivors made fragile by their ordeals. Promise had to remind herself that Emmy was just Leo's age.

Joseph was obviously thrilled to be back. He said a word or two in Tibetan, which the Dalai Lama's translator had to clarify, much to everyone's amusement. The inner circle was content to eavesdrop on their visit. "So many prayers for you," His Holiness said.

Maybe it was delight or maybe it was pain medication, but his first words in English to the Dalai Lama were "What did you say to the hot dog vendor?"

The gathered got a little nervous for Joseph's state of mind as the translator asked his question. In response, the Dalai Lama raised his puffy eyebrows, and the bird wrinkle took flight atop his forehead. "Make me one with everything!" He laughed again. "I like that so," he said, then turned to his translator.

The translator said, "His Holiness says that the joke is more Lao-tzu than Buddhist."

Promise couldn't believe Joseph had told His Holiness a joke, but then it seemed one more good reason to let the day wash over her.

Overflow crowds rushed the auditorium as Sergeant Becton and his astonished staff courteously turned them away. Up on the dais, Emmy sat between the two men in her life. Joseph had put on about ten pounds in the last month, although he needed a good thirty to fill out his features. Emmy had said that the slightest variation in temperature affected him—like the objects in the museum cases, Promise thought. In fact, she saw the museum's plight all over him. Extremists had taken Joseph hostage, and they'd weakened him, made him more vulnerable for the rest of his life. Likewise, even if the Museum of Asian Art survived, the fact that they'd been targeted made them forever at risk.

Emmy whispered something to the Dalai Lama, and he stroked her arm in response. He radiated pure understanding, as if his entire reason for being was to shine his countenance upon her. He could have been an Asia geek like any one of the museum workers, except for the impression that at any minute he was going to levitate right up over their heads.

Promise's pulse fluttered on the side of her neck, and when she pushed off from her chair to stand, her ankle almost gave way. Seeing her rise, the crowd hushed, which only intensified her jitters. How do you introduce someone of this stature? Even her mother had called him a great man, though she'd also pointed out that he hadn't gotten far in changing China's mind about Tibet. Promise was having her spasms again and decided to take the humblest path available. She gave silent thanks for the crimson dress she'd found for today's event.

"Ladies and gentlemen," she said. "Welcome." As succinctly as possible, she mentioned the struggles the museum was facing and entreated all who were listening to make their views known to those in the Castle. There was a surreal moment when a cheer from the crowd watching monitors on the Mall made its way into the auditorium. She smiled to hear their support. "Our guest today has had many names and perhaps even more honors bestowed upon him. In the cause of the Tibetan people, he has met history head-on. To Mao and to Nehru he described Tibet's plight, as well as to Popes Paul the Sixth and John Paul the Second. He received the 1989 Nobel Peace Prize and is revered by Buddhists around the world as an avatar of Avalokiteshvara, the Buddha of Compassion." A sharp twinge made Promise wince and required her to stop for breath. Reverently, the audience took a deep inhalation along with her and then slowly let it out. She said, "When people ask him about himself, he likes to say, 'I am just a simple Buddhist monk, no more, no less.' It is with profound gratitude that I present to you His Holiness, the fourteenth Dalai Lama."

As he walked to the podium, his feet poked out from beneath his robes. He was wearing sandals with socks, the way Leo liked to wear them. Promise's pain had passed, and after a slight bow, she sat down. She noted the time on her watch: ten-seventeen, only eight minutes since the last spasm. After His Holiness, she still had to introduce Joseph, and she was also scheduled to bat cleanup.

The monk bowed to his audience, who put palms together and dipped their heads. He said, "What an honor to be called here. On behalf of the past. The present and future." Then he shrugged. "How bad is my English, I apologize." He smiled, more self-conscious than you'd imagine. "Hard language." Laughter, forgiveness rolled toward the stage. They'd wait a day to hear a sentence. "I rely on my translator." He gestured toward the man who'd followed him to the podium.

He said, "My teachings are aimed at acceptance. And—"

He spoke to his translator, who said, "What better way to promote acceptance than through the cultural preservation we see in this American museum of Asian art?"

They were like a tag team, stepping in and out of the Dalai Lama's sentences.

"Such a nice museum," the Dalai Lama said, turning to Joseph, Emmy, and Promise, who folded their palms together. Promise felt her cheeks grow tight with smiling.

He addressed his translator, who said, "We tolerate what we understand."

"Yes," he said in English. "We *tolerate* people we appreciate. We *tolerate* the gods we revere. Revere—that is the word?" Everyone, including his translator, assured him that it was. "Your turn," he said to the translator and rattled off several sentences.

The translator said, "My good friend Joseph Lattimore has just endured a harrowing experience at the hands of those who would kill in the name of their god. I am relieved he has escaped, and I am honored with his presence today. Those who captured Joseph Lattimore seek to regain their homeland, a tragic problem I share. However, nothing good can come from putting others through such suffering and fear."

"Thank you," he said to his translator, who gave him a nod. He spoke directly to the audience. "I left my homeland. My culture, Tibetan culture, is in danger. We seek nonviolent ways to—"

"Negotiate."

"*Negotiate* with Chinese government." He swept his hand toward Joseph and Emmy. "See whom they might have harmed negotiating with human lives!"

His translator took over from there, the Dalai Lama talking softly by his side. The translator said, "Joseph Lattimore was almost killed for his devotion, for examining or honoring the past. So many of the great works in this institution were made to commemorate battles, conquest, bloodshed. Still, the creative act itself is not violent and, I believe, does not glorify the terrors that inspired it. Just as many works here are a testament to sheer creativity, and those we share for entertainment as well the appreciation of beauty."

His Holiness scanned the flock, smiling until his dimple bored deep into his right cheek. He spoke in Tibetan, knowing his translator would make up the difference: "It is important to laugh, to enjoy ourselves and our families, to remember, and to preserve, for who knows what terrors await us?" There was a long pause when the translator finished.

In English, the Dalai Lama said, "Your struggle touches my heart. May your leaders *negotiate* in good faith." He brought his palms together and stepped back from the podium so he could bow more deeply. He said, "I. Wish. You. Peace." And then he sat down.

After a respectable silence, Promise stood to introduce Joseph. She wasn't sure she was going to make it. She felt like she might throw up, and though she could hear herself breathing heavily, it seemed she couldn't get a breath. She had to resort to humor because just about all she could say was "Unlike our previous speaker, R. Joseph Lattimore needs no introduction." She mentioned his eighteen-year reign as director and his brave and cunning escape from the Al-Faran. At least she hoped she did. When she sat down, an earthquake shook the auditorium. No, it was applause, the sound of a thousand hands clapping. They were clapping for both Joseph and the Dalai Lama, she thought, though there was no doubt that the assembled wanted to give Joseph a rousing homecoming.

Joseph's walk to the podium made his desert trek all the more remarkable. He fumbled with a crutch, and people in the audience edged up off their seats, willing him to stand and walk. It was balance that was his problem, for his legs had not been injured. Strength, stamina, nerves—these were problems, too. He trailed a cord from a microphone that had been clipped to his jacket. He'd never needed a microphone before, not even in the cavernous auditorium.

"I am so glad to be here," he said, pausing at each word. He began by telling them how Promise had effusively thanked Emmy for bringing the Dalai Lama here and how his wife demurely said that all she did was make a phone call. Joseph said, "May you live your life so that when the time comes, you can make that call or, failing that, marry someone who can make that call."

As the audience laughed appreciatively, Leo saw an ugly grimace cross his wife's face. He looked around him for confirmation, but everyone else was staring raptly at Joseph. Promise exited the stage through a nearly invisible door to the waiting room, prompting Leo to push his way past knees and purses. Talbot was on the aisle a few rows up, and Leo had to overcome his own reticence to hand him the reins. "You're in charge," he whispered to Talbot before running toward the back of the auditorium.

Sergeant Becton was posted in the hallway outside the auditorium doors. "Officer," Leo called out. "We need the ambulance out there."

"Yes, sir. Dr. Lattimore's not holding up?"

Not holding up what? flashed through Leo's mind before he realized the ambulance must be in reserve for Joseph. "It's for Dr. Whittaker, Miss Promise. We need to go to Columbia Hospital for Women," he said, choking up a bit.

"You got it," the sergeant said and began talking into his radio.

Leo ran to Promise's aid in the greenroom, where she was doubled over a trash can. "Oh, Queenie." He held her hair back and kept her lei of orchids from falling forward.

"I don't feel well," she said. Snot dripped from the tip of her nose like a leaky faucet.

She had another, longer contraction in the ambulance, which wailed more rhythmically than she did and with better results, delivering her smoothly to the nearby hospital. Someone told her Mahalia was already there. Promise thought to worry about abandoning the museum until a sledgehammer hit her just behind the pelvis. The bunching up of her uterine wall was an intimate, gripping pain she recognized with a sick familiarity from her last two labor experiences. She tried to focus on the results—she'd be getting a baby out of this—but in the midst of the searing cramps, she could look neither back nor forward. There was no intellectualizing, no theorizing, just raw animal instinct. Thank God she didn't have to squat in a field.

Mahalia donned a robe as she greeted them. "So our boy couldn't wait for spring." Although she was accompanied by a doctor, the midwife showed no signs of letting him take over. Her demeanor slowed Promise's contractions down a bit, allowing her to catch her breath. The doctor concurred with Mahalia that there was no stopping this labor and that everything seemed in order. "He'll be skinny," Mahalia surmised. "They get nice and fat at the end."

"Normal, low-risk pregnancy," Promise grunted before an especially

hard spasm walloped her. She broke out in a cold sweat. The anesthe-
siologist arrived and pronounced her too far along for his assistance.
"Don't go," she begged him. Leo brought a towel to her back; though
he'd held it under the hottest water, it didn't pack the punch of an
epidural.

This third time around, Leo was a pro. "Do you want to go away or
be in the moment?" he asked, and when she could tell him what she
wanted, he obliged, talking her out into the middle of a warm lake
where she floated effortlessly in the sunshine. Or he took her inside
her own pelvis to witness each muscular contraction, though it
squeezed her like a vise, pushing the baby farther out of her uterus and
closer to them. Then he took her to the movies. Her eyes were red
from crying, and when her teeth began chattering, he told her she was
beautiful and brave.

Surely she would not survive this. She was so cold and shaky, and
her right leg trembled. Mahalia had filled her head with stories of
third babies who slipped right out, but with the baby crowning, she
felt herself split open. "Go ahead and push," Mahalia coached. Promise was overwhelmed. "I can't," she yelled. "It's too much." Here was
life or death, and it didn't matter whether it was too much for her or
not. She was certain this seed would crack her in two and she would
be nothing but a broken vessel, irreparable, of no use to this baby or
the rest of her family. The pressure intensified until she screamed
again.

"We're minutes away from meeting Edgar," Leo said with forced op-
timism.

"That is such a vulgar name," Promise managed to say. Edgar,
Edgar, it sounded like the grunts she was making as she pushed.
Better, perhaps, to honor the one who had summoned him forth today.
Emmy referred to the Dalai Lama as Kundun, which meant "presence"
and nearly described where the baby was born, in his presence. There
were plenty of other names for him that meant Great Protector, Joy-
Fulfilling Jewel, Ocean of Wisdom. What do you call a child who was
conceived on the Fourth of July and touched by the Dalai Lama?
Lucky. Blessed. Anything you want.

Minutes turned into an hour, until at one o'clock on the thirty-first
of January in the year two thousand, Promise Whittaker and Leo Wells

welcomed their third child into the world. He cried out on his own, and he didn't need anyone to show him how to suckle a breast. Weighing all of four pounds, fifteen ounces, Thomas Joseph Whittaker-Wells was small but mighty, possessed of good instincts, much like his mother who bore him.

Picking Up the Pieces

March 23, 2000

It took four coats of Steamed-Rice White to cover the red walls in the director's office. Before painting, the contractors had pried Joseph's name plaque off the door and dismantled his ornate window treatment. The couch stayed put, as did the wing-back chairs trimmed in nailheads. His massive cherry desk in the northwest corner, however, was replaced by a colossal chestnut one. Unfurled across the front of this family heirloom was the Stars and Stripes, twenty-nine stars carved in the canton of the flag, and anchors aweighed from bundled ropes all along the sides. A daunting arrangement of military regalia filled the back wall, including sabers and some kind of military kimono. Where examples of Asian calligraphy had been displayed, the new tenant hung ukiyo-e prints of sumo and samurai masters. Although Talbot Perry was only acting director, he was working to make the office his.

The museum's crew had turned the tide that unruly day in January, when devotees of Joseph and the Dalai Lama joined forces with fans of a popular public television show to go up against the Castle—the day Promise Whittaker practically gave birth onstage. Whether the tide would return to swamp them wasn't clear. The announcement temporarily rescinding the food court decision was even more disembodied than the Castle's initial memo to Joseph. Again with the photocopied sheet, but this one was from the acting secretary to the acting director (and Talbot knew that some considered him the acting acting director). Adrift in uncertainty, Talbot decided he might as well set anchor.

Just now, he'd summoned Arthur Franklin to his office, and the curator was obviously surprised at the extent of Talbot's changes.

"Don't get too comfortable," Arthur advised.

"I'm keeping my knees bent," Talbot said. "But I'm also recruiting. If they appoint me director, I'd like you to be the ancillary director."

Arthur tore at his thumbnail for a moment, as if it were of more importance than Talbot's invitation. "Flattered, as always, by your attention. Unfortunately, I've been deemed ineligible."

"How long is your probation?" Talbot asked.

"Three years. Let's see, I'm frozen at my current position and salary level, I'm not allowed to handle the collection unsupervised, and I can essentially be terminated without cause. Meanwhile, you are promoted. That seems about right." Arthur lengthened his neck and, pointing his nose up, he lightly shook his head back, a habit from years of wearing shoulder-length hair. In fact, he'd shorn his long locks not too long after Talbot had. More dramatic than Talbot, of course, Arthur had chosen to leave only about an inch all around, scant more than a crew cut. Though no one could have mistaken him for military; in his fashionable getups, he could be diplomatic corps or even aging rock star. A bigger revelation was that chestnut had not been his natural color—clipped down to his roots, he'd come out as a brunet. Filaments of gray caught the light as well.

Arthur handed Talbot a set of galleys. "Here's the label copy that's up in the galleries."

"Thank you." Talbot tossed them into a deep drawer. "You've done a nice job with this exhibition."

"Thanks," Arthur said, "and thanks for the space." He'd appropriated three of the four Japanese galleries.

Arthur was the visionary behind "Picking Up the Pieces," a display of broken, nicked, burned, and otherwise compromised Asian art. That made him the curator of two concurrently running exhibitions. "All Fired Up!" had required five years of his time from start to finish, whereas he'd had ten weeks to pull together "Picking Up the Pieces." Another difference between the two shows was that in the new one everything was already damaged.

Talbot said, "I just heard that Super Glue is underwriting the openings."

Arthur let out a laugh. "That was Min Chen's doing. They only gave her two years' probation—you might want to consider her for ancillary director."

"She's lucky the Castle didn't make her hand over the baby," Talbot said.

Catty as Talbot was being, Arthur went with it. "Raised by bureaucratic apes in a Washington fortress—will he be able to live in polite society?"

"He?" Talbot asked.

"Will he or she be able to live in polite society?" Arthur amended. Before leaving, he planted his feet and, arms akimbo, took in the full measure of the room. "You've got some nerve—I'll give you that."

"Did I ever tell you about the time I bought the head of the Regents a drink?" Talbot asked.

"No," Arthur said. "Let me guess, you had a porterhouse back at your apartment."

"New York strip," Talbot said.

"Of course," Arthur said. "Listen, I'll see you at the opening." He wanted to hurry out of there, and he had a good excuse. This afternoon he had a spa appointment—deep tissue manipulation and the laying on of hot rocks—a present from Morty for working so hard. He swung Talbot's door shut and walked briskly past Nathan's restaurant, already attracting attention. Downstairs, he picked up his coat and keys, peeping through Promise's door. Technically she was on maternity leave, but she'd set up a portable crib in her old office as soon as Peg had returned to Oklahoma. It was all the room could hold, her desk and the netted cube of the folding crib; neither she nor the baby was in attendance. Arthur missed her company and good counsel. To his surprise, he missed Leo as well. The whole crew would be at tonight's event, an unprecedented party limited to staff and their guests.

As the curator, Arthur had invited every single person on staff to submit contenders for "Picking Up the Pieces," and he'd received permission to grant amnesty, if necessary, to those who came forward. Even Arthur was alarmed at things Security had seen, not to mention disasters the registrar had buried, just to name two departments. Each wound was accompanied by a wrenching story, sometimes of more interest than the object. Inspired by Arthur's inclusive approach to the exhibition, Talbot was the one who'd suggested two openings, the first for the staff and a second for the public.

Arthur imagined the stir his exhibition would cause among those inside and outside the museum's realm. His porcelain exhibition already filled the three prominent Chinese galleries on the north side of the museum, and he'd chosen to mount "Picking Up the Pieces" in the Japanese rooms, Talbot's territory. With the installation of this show, Arthur Franklin was responsible for what was on view in six of the museum's sixteen galleries. Probation or no probation, he believed it could be said that he'd made the big time.

————

Dry cleaner bags hung from the backs of office doors throughout the museum. For half the staff, this was their first formal opening. Word had spread that dark suits were fine, that no one need rent a tuxedo. There was no reason, really, that they couldn't show up in their work clothes—they were only going upstairs—except that they wanted to rise to the privilege of having been invited. Talbot, of all people, had declared the staff deserving of a party, making his appointment more popular than it might have been. He'd arranged to have the event catered so Nathan could enjoy the night without cooking; he'd hired guards from African Art to allow Sergeant Becton and his crew to come as guests.

When Lucy Yarmolinsky walked into the women's room to wash her face and put on some eyeliner, she found herself backstage at a pageant. Curling irons crossed cords with blow dryers along the crowded countertops. There were sequins and satin and *hats*. Vanessa, Promise Whittaker's assistant, was lining her lips next to Miss Grace from the maintenance staff, who expertly glued on false eyelashes. Lucy was as delighted by the fuss as she was by the exhibition. Damaged art was her favorite kind of art. Once she'd absorbed the shock that Arthur had tossed a piece of MAA1999.127 off the Key Bridge, she'd come up with plenty of objects for his consideration. "Scoot over, ladies," she said, happy to be in a crowd for once.

Promise and Leo brought their family in through the Independence Avenue side. Once you had three kids, you needed a staging area, so they went downstairs to Promise's office to off-load the diaper bag and everyone's coats. Promise had dressed Thomas in a tuxedo jumpsuit, and Lydia had bought a miniature fez for him in a pet shop. Atop his bald head, the tasseled hat was held in place by an elastic band stretched beneath his triple chin. He looked as jaunty as a wobbly two-month-old could. Felix and Lydia both had new clothes for the occasion. Promise, however, wore the crimson dress that had taken her from the auditorium stage to the hospital maternity ward on Thomas's birthday. Much to her annoyance, the dress still fit.

The Whittaker-Wells clan moved upstairs and headed around the western half of the ground floor so they could see the show from the beginning. Along the way, staff members in high spirits greeted them, making a to-do over Lydia and Felix as well as the baby, whom people had taken to calling T.J. Promise wished she'd thought of inviting the staff to the "All Fired Up!" opening, the only one held during her short reign, but she'd been preoccupied with the museum's survival. The librarian, literally beaming with pride, introduced her husband to Promise, who had to shift T.J. over so she could shake his hand. Promise had an uncharacteristically cynical notion that Talbot was gathering intelligence on his staff. For example, who knew Nathan's sous-chef was a single mother of two? Who expected Officer Jackson to be gay, his partner unabashedly holding his hand? The officer seemed pleased to catch Promise off guard.

As she passed the director's office, a hot flash came over Promise, despite the fact that she neither wanted the job nor could have been performing it these last two months. Still, it galled her to think that they'd rewarded Talbot and that he'd turned Joseph's scholarly lair into a militarized zone.

Having come around to the front of the museum, Lydia and Felix pressed their noses to the courtyard glass to search for peacocks. They were joined by Sally Chen, who'd bravely left her parents' side. Meanwhile, Leo and Promise (holding T.J.) froze in place, a diorama unto themselves. Topping the stairs was the notorious vitrine, the very glass box that had previously displayed Arthur's prized porcelain. In fact, it still displayed Arthur's porcelain. Lit from within were two bowls of equal size. The vessel on the left was a clear glass bowl filled with the crumbs that had constituted the magpie-and-plum masterpiece. Within the bowl, the remains made a mound of ragged shards.

Next to that catastrophe was a blue-and-white bowl that looked to be fine. Promise couldn't read the label for the tears in her eyes, and she pulled Leo away with her free hand.

"First a glass of wine," she said.

Leo said, "I'm sorry, Queenie. All they seem to have is champagne."

On her way to a drink, Promise spotted Emmy and Joseph in a mob of well-wishers. Emmy simply reached out her arms, and Promise handed off the baby to her. Although Joseph was standing a few inches taller than he had in January, he hadn't put on much more weight. He adjusted the baby's fez without losing his train of thought; Promise heard him say, "We have here as many examples of despotism as beauty, some in the same piece of art."

T.J. had seemed content enough to be with someone else; however, two sips into her champagne, Promise heard his cry. Her breasts responded first, and she had to fold her arms across her chest. She bore down on her nipples to keep from leaking through her nursing pads, then, having stemmed the milk flow, she hustled over to the baby. Emmy was swaying side to side, doing the mother's standing rock, as if her boys had been infants this morning.

T.J.'s cries had brought his siblings running, too. Leo reclaimed the baby and escorted his family into the exhibition, Sally tagging along. Felix, who had done some fast maturing as a big brother, was on his best behavior, but it was also the case that this exhibition of damaged goods was sobering. Usually the art was pristine, well-protected from his antics. These cracked and dented choices were rife with vulnerability. A little unnerved, Felix stayed close to his parents, hands well in pockets.

There were pieces that had endured ritual damage, such as the Near Eastern bust whose nose had been hacked off in a ceremonial gouging circa 2500 B.C. From the Islamic collection that Fatima oversaw was the Koran folio that had been split and rejoined, courtesy of Ross Perot and a Persian bookseller. This was the same folio whose scribe had been killed for depicting the Prophet's shadow, a good example of what Joseph had been talking about when he'd said despotism and beauty might coincide in one piece of art. There were lacquer, jewelry, and scrolls that had chipped, melted, and ripped. Arthur had included a Mughal album—open to a page of Rumi—charred in an eighteenth-century fire. There were some seventy pieces in all, including objects the Founder had acquired under circumstances that seemed an awful lot like stealing. For example, who had the authority to sell him a portion of the world's oldest manuscript out of the Dunhuang caves? And there were objects whose presence had damaged the cause of archaeology. Min's Chinese *ding* fit that description. Although scholars would be pleased at having access to the three-legged bronze, its context had been lost for good.

Blooming inside Promise's flowered maternity dress, Min Chen stood next to the *ding*. When Sally saw her and Douglas, she ran to get between her parents. They were visiting with Sergeant Becton and his wife.

"Are you having a boy or a girl?" Sergeant Becton's wife innocently asked.

"We've requested that they not tell us," Douglas answered.

"You want to be surprised," the wife assumed. "Jerry wanted that, but I said, What color are we going to paint the baby's room—yellow? I like being prepared."

Min and Douglas exchanged a nervous smile just over Sally's head. Lady, you don't know the half of it. Douglas had suggested that ignorance could be bliss in this situation. Hadn't Will Rogers said that? No, he hadn't, though the western sage had said, "When you get into trouble five thousand miles from home, you've got to have been looking for it."

The inspector general had accepted Min's apology for her personal use of museum funds; he'd meted out only two years of probation and rejected the proposal of Min traveling to China to return the *ding*. This child she carried, Min knew, had inspired his leniency. She was so caught between superstition and science, between mercy and desire, that she prohibited Dr. Fan from revealing the baby's gender. She was still hoping for a boy, but she also thought she might welcome the chance to show love for another baby girl.

"Boy or girl," Douglas said when he and Min were alone, "as long as it's not born in prison." She and Douglas thought they might move their family to China after she'd served out her probationary period.

At one point, Promise broke off from Leo and the kids because T.J. needed a fresh diaper. She carted him down to her office, where she took the opportunity to relieve him of his goofy fez as well. She and the baby returned to the exhibition entrance to see Morty and Joseph on the landing together, the crowd having devoted themselves to the art of crab puffs and tempura. This time, when Promise approached the pedestal and saw the two bowls side by side, she couldn't help but think of breasts. Now she was ready to read the story of the second bowl Arthur had placed in the vitrine.

Morty was staring at the mound of crumbs. He kissed Promise on the cheek, then returned to his brooding. Joseph stood in quiet companionship by his side.

Morty said, "It reminds me of an owl pellet—you know what that is?"

"Yes," Joseph replied, "those cocoons they cough up."

"Right, with the leftover bits of bone and teeth from their prey." Morty pointed to a spot in the vitrine. "There's a beak, and over here are two claws."

"I don't see any indications of trauma on the blue-and-white one," Joseph said. "But my doctor says it may be time for glasses." He was thinking about the bowl of salty broth Coconut Head had brought into the yurt twice a day and the bowl of stars above his and Kanraku's heads out in the desert. There had been no indication of trauma in those bowls either.

The label revealed Arthur's wisdom. Morty and Joseph and Promise silently read the text, which explained that the Yuan dynasty bowl had been one of a pair, the two of them painted with a ribbon-tied bouquet of lotuses in bud, blossom, and seedpod. Early in the Ming dynasty, this bowl's identical twin had broken, diminishing the value of the remaining bowl by more than half. Nonetheless, its owners had packed the unharmed bowl away for protection, and it had survived, if that was the right word for something that never saw the light of day.

Arthur approached his three favorite people, and they convened there on the landing of his favorite museum. Joseph stepped forward to give him an anemic clap on the back, which meant a great deal.

"Moving exhibition, Arthur," he said. "First-rate."

Morty asked, "How you doing, Joseph?"

"I'm fading. Could I ask you to help me find Emmy in this throng?"

All three of them volunteered, but Morty insisted. Promise was glad he did.

Arthur offered her his silk handkerchief.

"Thanks," she said. "I've never been in an exhibition that made me cry." It was hard to blow her nose while holding T.J. In fact, she might have used the baby as an excuse for her ready tears—hormones and tender feelings certainly abounded in her—but she didn't want to take credit away from Arthur. "Consider it a compliment," she said, sniffling.

"This probably sounds melodramatic," Arthur said, "but I imagine I could be in a vitrine all my own." He pretended to lift his tuxedo shirt. "See this scar? It still hurts, and here is a swatch of my hair before it started being replaced by gray wires and I eventually decided to cut it off."

Promise was struck by how profound that was, especially coming from someone she'd once deemed superficial. Really, any one of them could be on display, though it might take the accompanying catalog to describe the damage. What she'd mostly lost was her innocence about, or maybe it was dependence on, Joseph and the Institution. Though she also bore the nicks of friendships broken and mended, the stress fractures of marriage, guilt over the children's care, stretch marks to accommodate new lives.

"You're priceless," she said to him.

"No, my dear. You are."

"Arthur," Sam and Zemzemal called out to him. "Come on over here." They wanted to offer a toast to the exhibition and its curator.

He held out his hand, which Promise squeezed, an odd re-creation of their podium dance on the day the bowl fell. When Arthur let go, she reached around T.J. to clasp her elbow beneath his rump, so that he sat in the sling of her arms.

"Go ahead," Promise told Arthur.

She wanted to bear witness to those two bowls for a while longer. Broken and intact. Priceless and worthless. Pushed close together in a box built for one, the two circles made a figure eight, symbol of eternity. "What seems to be keeping you from joy may be what leads you to joy," Rumi wrote. Meanwhile, there was every possibility that their days were numbered here at the Museum of Asian Art. What had the Dalai Lama said—"Who knows what terrors await us?"

Nothing had been guaranteed them. The Castle was between Secretaries, and the powers that be had merely granted them an extension. Promise knew that from here on out they'd always be on probation. Once such an idea was on the table, someone was bound to pick it up again. She held T.J. asleep against her heart and looked again at the bowl of shards, glinting white glaze amid dull white edges, exposed by their undoing. Arthur had chosen to put the pieces in a clear bowl about the same size as the one that broke; however, he'd mounded the shards within like a cone of sifted flour, prepared to start a new recipe. A person could be demoralized in the face of such destruction, and yet, Promise thought, here was everything she'd gleaned from her brief, formidable reign: Admit there is loss, and all can be treasured.

ACKNOWLEDGMENTS

I am deeply grateful for the support I received during the protracted writing of this book. Decades of loving thanks to my husband, Gary Zizka, who bought me a map of Asia at the onset. Jonathan Galassi's faith sustained me. Sarah Burnes is a wonder of the world. Deborah Galyan provided keen insight and camaraderie, as did Catherine Batza, Theresa Ganley, Karen Sagstetter, and Annie Wedekind. Millie and Phil Zuravleff gave help and encouragement. For the bounteous gifts of the Virginia Center for the Creative Arts, I give thanks, and praise be to the good people of Jocelyn Street, many of whom opened their homes to me.

All mistakes are mine. Even so, I benefited from the guidance of Massumeh Farhad, Sarah Ridley, and Jan Stuart, along with just about every department of the Smithsonian's Freer and Sackler Galleries. I am beholden to Kate Blackwell, Maxine Clair, Kathleen Currie, Ann McLaughlin, C. M. Mayo, and Leslie Pietrzyk for reading murky drafts of this work.

Among the sources I relied on, Walter Kaufmann's *Religions in Four Dimensions* offered a luminous understanding of Asia's religions. My dear friend David Cooper called with weekly pep talks and led me to Tim Ward's *The Great Dragon's Fleas*, an odyssey primarily devoted to Buddhism. Jonah Blank's *Arrow of the Blue-Skinned God: Retracing the Ramayana Through India* was crucial, and it is the source of the *Ramayana* quote in chapter 19. Milo Cleveland Beach's *The Adventures of Rama* supplied the gravy. The lovely Michelle Lara made me a gift of Peter Hopkirk's *Foreign Devils on the Silk Road*, and *The Mummies of Ürümchi* by Elizabeth Wayland Barber augmented my Niya and Taklamakan research. Descriptions of that region were inspired by Li Xiguang and Michael Browning's articles for *The Washington Post* and Jonathan Tucker's for *Cloudband* magazine. All Rumi quotes are taken from Coleman Barks's ecstatic translations, primarily in *The Essential Rumi*.

Louise Cort and Jan Stuart's treatment of Chinese porcelain in *Joined Colors: Decoration and Meaning in Chinese Porcelain* was instrumental. The *Padshahnama* is given its due in *King of the World: A Mughal Manuscript from the Royal Library, Windsor Castle*, by Milo Cleveland Beach and Ebba Koch, translations by Wheeler Thackston (the source of the *Padshahnama* quote in chapter 19). These two books accompanied exhibitions at the Smithsonian Institution's Freer and Sackler Galleries of Art, which, dear reader, you should visit while you have the chance.

A NOTE ON THE AUTHOR

Mary Kay Zuravleff is also the author of *The Frequency of Souls* which won the Rosenthal Award from the American Academy of Arts and Letters and the James Jones First Novel Award. A former editor of books and exhibition texts for the Smithsonian Institution, she lives in Washington, DC, and teaches writing at George Mason University.

Camilla Noli lives in Australia with her husband and children. She is a graduate of the Varuna Writing Program in Sydney's Blue Mountains. *The Mother's Tale* is her first novel.

THE
MOTHER'S
TALE

CAMILLA NOLI

An Orion paperback

First published in Great Britain in 2009
by Orion
This paperback edition published in 2010
by Orion Books Ltd,
Orion House, 5 Upper St Martin's Lane,
London WC2H 9EA

An Hachette UK company

1 3 5 7 9 10 8 6 4 2

A CIP catalogue record for this book is available
from the British Library.

ISBN 978-1-4091-0242-7

Printed and bound in Great Britain by
Clays Ltd, St Ives plc

The Orion Publishing Group's policy is to use papers
that are natural, renewable and recyclable products and
made from wood grown in sustainable forests. The logging
and manufacturing processes are expected to conform to
the environmental regulations of the country of origin.

www.orionbooks.co.uk

For my husband and children,
without whom nothing else would matter.

ONE

*I*t is early evening. I am suckling my infant son. We sit on the rocking chair in the nursery. Gently I rock backwards and forwards, pushing up and down with my toes. The lamp casts a golden glow over us. We are picture perfect, 'Madonna and Child in the Candlelight', a study for the old masters.

I look down at my son, at Zach. The small dimple on his temple works in and out with his efforts at drawing the milk from my body. His eyes are almost closed. I cradle my hand around his head; it is covered with a fuzz of hair, almost not human in its softness. I run my fingers over the dents in his skull, pleasantly concave to my touch. I press gently. They yield, a little.

I have always been fascinated by these unfinished areas on a baby's head. It is where they are most vulnerable, where the hard bone of childhood is yet to form. It is one of the reasons human infants must be tended so carefully and nurtured for so long.

What would happen if I press too hard, I wonder. What would happen if I took a skewer and broke the skin of his fontanelle, if I pushed it further until it met the soft resistance of my child's brain? If I continued pushing, would the steel cleave a pathway of immediate destruction and death, or would the results of its passage be more benign? Would the wound heal? Perhaps there would never be any obvious effect, or perhaps Zach would continue to grow for a time, until one day a mass of scar tissue pierced the trajectory of his development, keeping him forever looped in eternal childhood.

Even as I protect my baby so carefully, these are questions upon which I cannot help but ponder. It is the creative destructiveness of my motherhood; the alternating tide with which I wrestle.

Now Zach is almost sated. His sucking has slowed, but he is unwilling to relinquish the comfort of my breast. I insert my little finger between his lips and my nipple, carefully breaking the suction of his mouth. He pulls at the air in a desperate attempt to regain contact with my body, but then his head falls back. He is asleep. Breast milk, warmth and gentle rocking are powerful opiates.

I cradle Zach firmly to my body, rise to my feet and slip to the cot. Leaning over, I lie him gently on his side. One little fist rests on the sheet, the other is relaxed against his head. His skin is amber in the lamplight. I press my lips to his cheek, feeling the firm softness of very young flesh. In his sleep my child is archetypal, as am I, his mother and protector.

Tiptoeing, I move silently from the room. Closing the door behind me, I hold my breath and listen to the sounds of the house. From Cassie's room there is silence, from Zach's not a noise. Both children are asleep. I breathe again.

Remaining there a moment, I allow my pent-up energies to begin their dissipation. Sometimes at this hour I feel I might collapse, as if only the fast-forward movement of the day has kept me upright for so long. Now that I have an interval before the duties of the night begin, I am heavy and inert, a rag doll stuffed with lead.

I look at the clock in the hallway; it is seven-thirty, half an hour until Daniel arrives home from work. What will I do with this precious time? I decide to read. I made it to the library last week. 'A small victory for mothers everywhere,' I'd joked to Daniel.

But I ignore the books, piled so hopefully near the sofa. Instead I pick up the newspaper. When you are as tired as I am it is easier to focus on things in small bursts.

I try to turn the pages of the paper without rustling them. Rustling papers wake Cassie. There is a competition between the child and the written word for my attention. During the day I read standing at the kitchen bench. I turn the pages stealthily; occasionally I turn on the tap as though I am washing up. Then my daughter can't be sure what I am doing. In these small things, at least, I maintain some control, some power.

Tonight, I scan local politics and run my eye over the world news. All this is perfunctory, a prelude to the letters. I have always enjoyed the letters page. Once I was a frequent contributor. I enjoyed seeing my name in print; I could argue esoteric points with the best of them. Now I am an armchair intellectual; I observe from the sidelines as the regulars carry on their debates and trade their witty observations without me.

There's a discussion on child care being conducted in the letters page at the moment. Isn't there always? Those who have the time and energy, those without children, argue back and forth, quoting studies that invariably contradict each other.

We, Daniel and I, solved our domestic debate simply. I quit work. 'It won't be forever,' Daniel assured me, 'just until the children start school.' I agreed because I was too tired to argue. I have been too tired ever since. My views, my desires, my wishes have been silenced by exhaustion. I wear fatigue like a mantle; sometimes it settles over my head so tightly that I cannot think. Often I cannot finish sentences. My neurones stop mid-leap and I am left voiceless. My children have taken away my ability to speak. Thankfully they, my children, are sufficiently distracting that my lapses are rarely noticed.

Those with whom I now socialise are unlikely to care anyway. Those with whom I mix can be summed up with one word: 'mothers'. Once I knew no mothers, except my own desultory example of one. Once, if I met a full-time, stay-at-home mother I would not have known what to say to her. I would have devised an excuse to leave, to drink with someone else who was able to speak my kind of language. In those days my girlfriends and I were women who did things; who had fabulous jobs, successful businesses, rich boyfriends. We were witty and indestructible, a force with which to be reckoned. We worked, we exercised, we socialised – but most of all we had enough sleep to be able to function as rational human beings.

Now my regular social circle is a group of women who were herded together by the local early-childhood clinic for one reason only: our success at procreation. We cling together like jetsam thrown from a sinking ship. Perhaps I cling harder than most because the group provides the yardstick by which I can measure my behaviour. I am sometimes terribly afraid that without the group I would have no idea of how to be a mother at all.

The mothers' group met at my house today; there were five of us. That meant five toddlers, two babies, two pregnant mums and Rachael. Rachael is the one member of the group I do not like. She is a redhead, short and built hard, like a coiled spring. Her eyes penetrate; they see too much. Beneath her gaze I fumble; I am unsure. I dislike Rachael for the way she makes me feel, but deep down my reaction to her gaze makes me dislike myself more.

The group of mothers tries hard to be like larger society. We air-kiss, sometimes we discuss politics, we swap recipes. Often there are undercurrents of personality conflict, battles that nearly erupt and have to be smoothed over. There is much gossip and, apart from Rachael, a certain amount of mutual support. After all, most of us had no idea what we were taking on when we embarked on this motherhood business. Members of the group have even assumed roles of sorts: there is the organiser, the cook, the pessimist, the financial controller. We are a soap opera in miniature.

But always, in the midst of the intrigue and socialising, we are looking out for our children, to ensure they are safe, to ensure they will not be the child to first gouge out the eye of another. Our conversations are disjointed, our attention spans short: most of us are operating under conditions of extreme sleep deprivation. Not all of the mutterings make much sense. What a social study we would be!

'I've been trying to get Christopher off the dummy.'

'He's only one and a bit, Michael still has his. When he goes to bed anyway.'

'Yeah, I wouldn't mind that, but Christopher uses his all the time.'

'Yeah, Charlotte too. It's getting embarrassing. She's getting *big*.'

'Shit! Simon is into the CDs.'

Mad scuffling as a vain attempt is made to save the CD tower. Several minutes are spent collecting the CDs and removing them to my bedroom.

'Mind if I make another cup of tea?'

'Did you see the horrible accident last night, where the car was run over by the truck?'

'A truck! How many were killed? Charlotte, get away from that plant! No! Naughty girl!'

'Hey Odette, how come Jo couldn't make it?'

'Tamara's sick.'

'I saw them yesterday. She's bought a bike seat for Tamara and they go riding a lot. Jo's lost a heap of weight.'

'Really? It's ages since I've seen her.'

'Is it okay if I open the door for them to go outside?'

'Is she getting over her man... What's his name?'

'Gavin?'

'Yeah, Gavin.'

'I think so, but it was a huge shock. Apparently he'd been having the affair all through her pregnancy.'

'Bastard!'

'I'd cut his dick off.'

'No way. I'd never allow myself to get that close to it again.'

'Get away from those rose bushes. You'll get scratched.'

'Who's for coffee and who wants tea? Jessica, can you pass me those cups?'

'I need another cup of coffee. I'm so tired I can barely keep my eyes open.'

'Tell you what, our sex life's been a shocker lately. It's like Simon knows when we want to do it and wakes up!'

'At least you feel like doing it. I don't have the energy anymore.'

'Me neither.'

'Sam bought me a black negligee thingy for my birthday. What a joke! It was two sizes too small. I told him to keep his fantasies to himself.'

'Hey, have you begun toilet training yet? Mum says I was done by now.'

And so it went on. I think I may have fallen asleep at one point. My head hit hard against the back of the sofa. It was lucky I didn't drop Zach.

Sometimes I yearn for an unbroken conversation: a conversation that is not centred around babies or husbands, or how tired we all are; a conversation that progresses somewhere in linear time instead of weaving and ducking around snotty kids; a conversation that has a purpose and an outcome. Now we talk to fill time, not to solve problems. We are people thrown together, who try desperately to have something in common besides our children.

Tonight I will attempt to complete a crossword. Once I was good at word puzzles, cryptic ones in particular. I always had a flair for language: an ability to make my point; a capacity for being noticed. My Year 6 teacher said I would go far. What is far, I wonder. Is this it?

TWO

A cry resonates down the corridor. It's Cassie. I look at the clock. She's been asleep exactly fifty minutes, one sleep cycle.

I hear Daniel's key scraping in the lock. I stand up, closing the paper as I do so, and open the door for him. A gust of chilly wind enters the house and in the glow of the outside light I can see spots of rain being blown around. Daniel pushes the door shut behind him and I reach up to give him a kiss. His clothes are cold, his face warm and slightly prickly.

'Will you try please?' I say.

'Okay.' He knows what I am asking.

I head to the toilet, but I am simply buying time. I am the only one Cassie will allow to settle her. It has been that way since she was born. Yet Daniel adores her and she him. On the weekends they spend hours playing together. Since Cassie's discovered the power of her legs she loves to run. Daniel chases and catches her and then tickles her tummy and her feet. Cassie relishes the attention from her father, but when it comes to sleep I am the only person she will allow near her. I know that it is simply part of her need to control me, but it doesn't make my lack of sleep and her constant demands any easier to cope with. It doesn't lessen the despair of what I have become.

As Daniel enters her room Cassie screams with all the power of her fourteen-month-old lungs. I hear Daniel's voice, low and controlled, trying to soothe her. He rarely loses his temper.

Cassie is still screaming as I wash my hands. I walk down the corridor to her room and tap Daniel on the shoulder. 'You go and warm up dinner. I'll be quick.'

Cassie's screams subside to a sob as I cuddle her. I squeeze, perhaps unnecessarily hard, and she gasps. I laugh quietly, 'Now you know Mummy's here.' I remember when I was young and had baby chicks to look after. I loved them so much that sometimes I wanted to squeeze them hard just to show them how much I *really* loved them. I worried about them excessively; sometimes I had dreams that I was too rough and broke their legs. They were such a responsibility, just like children.

Cassie kicks. She is not happy with my grip, not happy to go back to sleep, perhaps not happy at being asleep in the first place. Who knows? She needs to make her point. Her legs do it for her usually. They are expressive, powerful legs. They kick when she is happy or annoyed. They run when she wants her own way: to you or away from you. It all depends on what suits Cassie.

I remember the day Cassie first saw Zach in the hospital after I had given birth to him. She had not liked him – not the way he sucked at me, nor how I looked at him, nor how Daniel held him. The day that we brought Zach home from hospital, I put him on my bed to change him. I turned away for a moment and as I turned back Cassie's foot was coming down on his face. I wasn't quick enough. It was lucky, I think, that his bones had not yet hardened. Cassie received her first smack that day.

It was hard. Red welts rose between the fingermarks. I was sorry that I had to hit her, but it was the right thing to do. Now Zach was my responsibility as well, not just her.

Cassie grows heavy in my arms and her breathing deepens. Is it deep enough to put her down? Maybe. Sometimes we dance. I put her down, she screams. I pick her up again. It can go on for a while. Thankfully not tonight. I cover her and she rolls towards the wall with her arm around Scruffy. Her back is relaxed in the torpor of sleep.

I enter the kitchen; Daniel is heating dinner in the microwave. He has changed out of his work clothes and wears black track-pants and a white T-shirt. He is still nice-looking, I think. Still thin and tall. He jogs sometimes during his lunch-hour. I envy him the freedom of that time. I have no time to exercise and five baby-kilos cling to my hips and legs. Daniel says that they balance out my milk-laden breasts. I hate those as well.

We sit and begin to eat. Daniel chews slowly and carefully. He has always done this, no matter how hungry he may be. He is always the last at the table to complete his meal. I have seen waiters remove his plate, sure that he must be finished.

Sometimes, at dinner with other people, they've grown tired of waiting and ordered dessert before Daniel has finished his main course. He has never suffered from indigestion.

'Good?' I ask. I care what he thinks of my cooking now. Once I didn't. Once he was a better cook than I. Now I think he's forgotten how.

'Mmmmm, very nice.' Daniel nods and swallows. He knows my need. There are a lot of things about me that Daniel knows.

'How was your day?' he asks.

'Well, you know I had the marauding hordes. It was okay, but the house was a pigsty when they left. It took me nearly two hours to clean everything up. Luckily Cassie watched TV and Zach was so tired that he passed out.'

I need Daniel to know that I work hard while he is away. Sometimes I list the housework I have done: three loads of washing, cleaned the bath, scrubbed the toilet with my toothbrush. It is pathetic, I know. Daniel never seems to think so. He enjoys it when I talk. He enjoys talking as well.

I ask about his day. I do genuinely care. It is important that he is happy. Then I can be as well.

Office gossip is good from a distance. Daniel tells me the news from a recent sales conference.

'Samantha, you know Dirk's personal assistant, well she got together with one of the southern sales reps.'

'You mean slept together?' I ask. Daniel often speaks in euphemisms. I need clarity.

'Well, originally, yeah, but also just got together. She's leaving her husband.'

I search my mind for what I know about Samantha. 'Doesn't she have two kids?'

Daniel swallows. I see his Adam's apple working. 'Three.'

Three. That means stretch marks, flabby boobs, the works. I am amazed at her courage. It reflects the level of her desperation.

'So what about the kids?' I ask.

'I don't know. John didn't go into any details about them. I'm sure the kids are all right.'

Of course, I'm not really concerned about the children; what I want to know is if Samantha has made good her escape. I am sure that what Samantha has attempted is the effortless soar of an untethered bird. But I wonder, does she just have the new lover, or does she have the new lover and the old children?

Has the affair meant the beginning of a new life or the continuation of the same dreary old one, albeit with a different man?

'Find out for me, will you?'

Daniel nods, yes.

I can barely remember my own distant working life. I did it well though. I was one of the top account directors for my age in a major advertising agency. I had built and maintained an impressive client list – corporations that always insisted I be the one responsible for their new advertising campaigns. I thought I was unstoppable. That was until a missed period, a positive pregnancy test and a husband who was desperate for a child.

Now I have turned my efforts to being a perfect wife and mother, a gourmet cook, a spotless cleaner. I could chronicle what I am good at, write duty lists to show you what I can do. I know how important my work is. I know that without my labour the house would disintegrate, be buried under the weight of dirty laundry, the filth of unchanged nappies, the stench of accumulated garbage. This knowledge doesn't take away the tedium though, doesn't blur the frustrations.

On the days when I can laugh about it I invent new job descriptions for myself: 'defender against the chaos'; 'keeper of the order'. I once filled in the blank on a government form requesting my occupation with the description 'ordermaker'. Some data-entry person replaced it with 'homemaker'; the government has no sense of humour.

After Daniel has thoroughly masticated his last mouthful, we clean up. Daniel washes. I dry the dishes. There is companionship in this ritual. We have always done the washing-up together, from the first time I ever prepared dinner for him. It is one of the few things that has not been changed by marriage and children. I wanted to buy a dishwasher once, but Daniel said, 'No, leave it to me, leave it all until I come home. I'll do it for you.' And so I do leave it.

Following the washing-up we move to the couch to watch television. I lean against Daniel and he gently strokes my hand. He is very comfortable. I hear the thump of his heart under my ear. It is a calm heart, and strong. His chin brushes the top of my head.

After a while Daniel's hand slips to my breast. He works his fingers between the buttons of my top and gently pinches my nipples. I try not to push his hand away. My breasts are numb from Zach's tongue. They are functional attachments; they are not an erogenous zone.

Now Daniel leans over to kiss me, prising my lips apart with his tongue. I attempt to understand his desire. I know that he is not touched all day, not constantly pulled by the earthy demands of children who cannot have enough human contact.

Daniel flicks off the television and leads me down the hall. I know that he needs me, and through my fatigue I can clearly remember when I used to need him as well. Sometimes, after a good night's sleep, I can sense the longing again. And it is this longing that I miss the most, the breathless anticipation that sharpens and transforms the act which follows.

Daniel turns on his bedside light and I lie down, removing my clothes under the covers. I do not like my body anymore. Like an over-full bathtub it spills and tumbles wherever gravity is able to exert force. Two babies in just over twelve months have taken their toll.

A naked Daniel lies beside me and pulls down the covers. He rubs one hand against me, from my collarbone to my knee, from my knee to my collarbone. His fingers barely touch my skin; he resists touching my breasts or pubis. He is a musician tuning a fine instrument. After a while he turns me over and strokes my back in the same way. Small goosebumps of pleasure rise as his fingers travel smoothly up and down my bare flesh. There is a pause as he reaches into the cupboard for some oil. He drizzles it down my back and legs. I feel some trickle into the space between my buttocks and despite my tiredness I feel the wetness glide like a stealthy traitor between my legs.

Daniel refuses to hurry. He massages my shoulders, my spine, the back of my legs and knees. I feel lighter and longer as my muscles release. The fleeting desire has left me and now I simply enjoy the sensuous feel of his touch. I wonder if I will fall asleep like this, lulled by the warmth of his hands.

And then, Daniel runs one well-oiled finger down my spine, down my bottom and between my thighs. He slips it into me and the wonderful, the unexpected, desire returns, it frissons down my spine and I raise myself to meet his ministrations. As he continues to stroke, Daniel presses his penis against me. It is hot and hard like a rock that has lain in the midday sun. I am pleased that he wants me so strongly and the aphrodisiac of his desire builds my own. Very quickly, more quickly than I dared to hope, I am ready to come. Reading my body Daniel turns me over and pushes into me hard. He has timed his movements perfectly. He comes and in a few moments I follow. In the great rush of oxytocin that follows, milk spurts from my left breast, a white fountain of celebration that sprays Daniel and myself in its exuberance. I still haven't become used to my body bursting and leaking in ways beyond my control and I try to stem the renegade flow with my right hand. Daniel laughs at me and bends down to lick up the trickle that escapes from under my fingers before he collapses on top of me.

I laugh too. 'Holy shit! That was good.' I am being conservative. It was the best I have had for months, perhaps since the children were born. I feel as if I have been granted an unexpected, beautiful gift.

Daniel nods. 'It was good for me too. I love to see you like that.'

I roll from underneath him and kiss his forehead.

'Thanks. I love you so much, you know that?'

He nods. 'I know. I love you too. You know that?'

I nod. I wonder what I ever did to deserve this man.

THREE

We lie together. I am near oblivion. I am entitled to sleep tonight. Today, I have been a good mother, a good host, a good wife and a good fuck. What more could the world ask of me?

I begin to drift into the hazed world of sleep when Cassie screams. Daniel is snoring, so I ease myself out of bed. We tried letting Cassie cry once; it went on for nearly two hours. Daniel said never again, and I agreed. She likes to sleep with us and I used to let her, but now I often fall asleep with Zach in the bed and I worry about Cassie smothering him. I don't sleep very well in those circumstances. It is easier to attend to her.

Cassie is sitting up. Her face is red and blotchy. She is so distraught that she is having trouble breathing properly. She draws air in great quivery lungfuls and exhales in spurts broken up by her sobbing. Her hair sticks in tendrils to her forehead. I give her a cuddle. This time I am gentle. I don't have the strength to even attempt to assert my superiority. The sleep torture routine, which the children subject me to, is very effective in determining dominance.

It is a long time before Cassie can get her breathing back under control. I bring her a drink of water in a bottle and she sucks on it lying down as I push the hair from her still-flushed face. Her curls have begun to dry and I separate them with my fingers. The movement of my hand calms her and soon her eyes are following the up and down motion as I stroke her forehead. Her eyelids flutter and she loses the battle to keep them open.

I wonder what it was that caused Cassie to wake in such a state. Maybe she has had a bad dream. What nightmares do children her age have? Being left alone in the dark; becoming lost; travelling down the birth canal? Maybe it is the latter. Cassie's birth was long and hard. I remember it well, too well. I remember the pain, the unremitting pain. I remember how it tore, and thudded, it pulled and pushed, it pummelled. There was no part of my body that did not pulse with pain. There were cramps in my legs, spasms in my back, hammers in my head, a pulsating rock in my belly.

I remember how the pain stirred and swelled, heaved and peaked and then sucked back, taking parts of me as it went. I remember how the world, the building, the room, had shrunk to my pain. How its walls were as solid as brick; how I no longer had the energy to push through them or even against them. I remember the lack of control; there was me and pain and nothing else.

But even in the midst of this pain I knew that I had been betrayed. Nobody had warned me to expect this. Nobody had warned me that my mind and body would be sacrificed to a primitive hormonal force beyond my experience. Nobody had warned me that I would have no more control than a sick animal that lies panting in the mud.

I remember shivering in the shower that was now colder than the green bile which rose from my stomach and flowed around my toes.

I remember the nurse whispering to Daniel, 'I think we need to get her out of there.'

And Daniel asking, 'Can we give her something that will help?'

And the nurse replying, 'Gas, maybe, that's about it. She's close, too close for anything else. It might harm the baby.'

And then I can remember being angry. The *baby*, I thought! The baby was all right; I was protecting it with my body, it was encircled in the warm folds of my skin and tissue. For nine months I had been a human incubator while the parasite within fed from my blood, breathed from my air, sucked calcium from my bones and teeth, stole my mobility, my comfort, my identity. And now I was being told that the baby still needed to be protected while I was forced to bear this pain, this constant, dehumanising, unbearable pain.

I remember the need to push; my body being ripped in two; tissues tearing; a tic in my eye that wouldn't stop; my legs that shook with the force of supporting myself. I remember pushing and pushing again. I remember the unstoppable wave, the fundamental power.

I remember the tearing, hot pain of the head. The drop of shoulders and then the relief as another body slithered out of my own. It – *she*, I realised – slid into the hands of my husband, the arms of my husband. I remember the eyes of my husband examining this body, this creature to whom I had given birth. I remember him cuddling her, talking to her, warming her with his body. I remember that his eyes never left her.

I remember being alone on the bed, suddenly pain-free, shivering and bleeding. There was blood, so much blood. I remember the blood pooling on the floor down my leg. I remember my toes resting in it. I pictured a sponge being squeezed of its moisture until it was empty and shrivelled.

The nurse threw a blanket over my shoulders.

'There's so much blood,' I said.

'Yes dear, there always is. It's perfectly normal.'

Yes, I thought, *yes, there is always blood when something has been taken from you, when a sacrifice has been made. There is always blood when you've lost something.* I remember looking over at Daniel with our daughter. He still hadn't looked at me, and that was when the fear began to set in.

~

When, finally, Cassie was handed to me, I saw an ugly creature with a sloping forehead and flat nose and thought, *This could not possibly have come out of me*. I remember wanting someone to take her from me so that Daniel and I could go home together, so that we could forget that this had ever happened. I remember wanting to scream, *This is a mistake, a terrible horrible mistake that I never meant to happen*. But there were no screams, no one heard me and no one took her away.

When I had Cassie alone, I tested her reflexes. Her grip was surprisingly strong. Babies are like apes when they are born. Their hands are powerful enough to hold tight to a hairy underbelly. Their arms startle when they are dropped or scared, as if to cling to a tree branch.

I practised saying her name. 'Cassie, Cassie.' It sounded odd after months of referring to her as 'baby' or 'it'. The nurses were much more comfortable with it than I was. 'And how is little Cassie today?' 'Has Cassie had a bowel movement yet?' 'Cassie looks just like your husband.' I stared at her after this last comment. *No she doesn't. She resembles nothing more than a wrinkled prune.*

Cassie's face was slightly bruised; she had a small graze on her right cheek, caused by the pressure of her already long fingernails as she journeyed down the birth canal. She looked like a boxer who had been trounced. For a moment I felt sorry for her. Then she opened one eye and looked at me. *Look out*, that eye said, *for you will never be ready for what I am*. And you know what? I never have been.

In hospital I learned the mechanics of being a new mum. I learned how to change a nappy. I learned to bathe Cassie. I learned to hold my breath as my child's steel gums latched around my grazed nipples. But nothing had ever prepared me, nothing *could* ever prepare me for the mind-numbing tedium of it all, the torturing slowness of those first few days and weeks and months, the body and mind-sapping tiredness that meant I would sometimes fall asleep in the bath. Things have become easier since then, but I have never really become used to this new life.

I try hard not to reveal the extent of my anxiety. I am an actress playing a part for which everyone else knows the script except me. I search desperately for role models. Heaven knows my own mother never provided me with one. I follow Daniel's lead in parenting. I reference my actions to the members of my mothers' group. I believe that I am skilful in my deceptions. It is only myself whom I am unable to fool; only myself who understands the deep well of my fear.

FOUR

I stroke Cassie's forehead for a few more minutes before I decide she is fast enough asleep for me to be able to slip out. I enter the kitchen and make myself a cup of tea. I rest my head on my arm against the cup. The warmth of the tea is comforting.

I wake with a start fifteen minutes later. Zach is crying for a feed. Is it that time already? I feed him then wander to the lounge-room. Perhaps I shouldn't bother sleeping tonight. Once I suggested to Daniel that I move a mattress into Cassie's room so that she would settle when she saw me. He wouldn't hear of it. But he is not woken several times a night.

I am now too alert, too tense to be able to return to sleep easily, so I choose a novel from the pile near the sofa. It is *Love in the Time of Cholera* by Gabriel Garcia Márquez. I first read it when I was a student, but now my books are packed up. Our small house no longer has room for bookshelves. Zach's birth made sure of that.

Márquez's dense description fills the room. I have always loved the way he writes. In his books even the most mundane events become romantic. I wonder, if I could view my life from another angle, would it echo with the resonance of possibility and the capriciousness of fate, rather than with the dull thud of reality? Would I be able to view this time of child-rearing as simply a phase, simply another colourful weft in the tapestry of my days?

There have certainly been times when my life could have been fodder for fiction. Before I was a mother, *I lived*! I was a woman others envied and desired to emulate. I was influential in my work-life; successful in my personal relationships. I was a siren, able to lure men to my rocky shores.

Let me tell you how Daniel and I met. There are not many people who know the truth of it. It was at a gathering – someone's birthday, I think. I had come to the party alone, let down by a friend who had pulled out at the last minute. Apart from the host, I knew no one. Daniel was there with a woman. I can't remember her name. He was the centre of a group that I approached. I remember noticing how his hair flopped over his eyes and he kept having to push it back. I remember how he stood with his back to the sun and how, as he raised his head from his drink, his grey eyes met mine and I found myself caught in them, a small insect in an orbed web.

Daniel welcomed me into the circle. I glanced up and sideways at him. I could see that he was strong and steady. He looked as if he would be able to handle all that I am. I remembered my father; sometimes he had looked at me in the same way as Daniel had, as if I was the only creature in the world who truly mattered – supremely special. Daniel was the first man I had met since my father died who made me feel that way.

Later in the day, when Daniel's girlfriend was not around, I approached him again. He was sitting on a stone wall. I sat next to him. I found myself leaning towards him. I was a small metal filing experiencing the pull of the North Pole.

'Where is she?' I asked. It was a test: if he asked whom I meant there was no point in my going on.

'She went home with a headache,' he replied.

'Leaving you here at the mercy of all these women.' I was trying to be light, but my mouth was dry. I knew that I had a chance with him.

He laughed. 'Yes. It was brave of her.'

'Very,' I said.

He looked at me for a while, but I refused to look away. I knew what he didn't. When I want something, very little can stand in my way. And there was no doubt that I wanted this man.

I reached out one hand and ran it down the fuzz on his arm. He trembled, but didn't draw away.

'Perhaps I didn't realise just how brave she was being,' he said.

'Perhaps she knows how strong you are,' I replied.

'Strong.' He was not asking a question. He needed to fill the silence.

Gently I ran my fingertips between the webs of his fingers. Few people realise how sensitive these spots are.

He pushed down hard on the wall. The skin of his hand grew white.

'That's nice. No one's ever touched me there before.'

I laughed. 'You'll enjoy it more if you relax.'

'I can't relax here. Too many people know me, and her.'

I knew that I had him. I experienced a leap of triumphant power. I had tempted him away from another woman.

'My place isn't far away,' I whispered. I hadn't stopped rubbing and his body had begun to sway slightly.

He nodded.

We left the party separately, but rarely have we been separated since. It was as if we were never meant to be apart.

The night after Daniel and I decided to marry he presented me with a box.

'What's inside?' I asked.

'Open it,' he replied.

Slowly I opened the lid. The interior was lined with maroon velvet and inside was something that resembled a twisted figure of eight. I picked it up and turned it over. I could see that it had been made by joining together two pieces of broad, stiff tape. The tape had been given a half twist and linked so that it formed a unified structure. I had never seen anything like it.

'What is it?' I asked.

'It's a Möbius strip. Run your finger over the edge.'

Intrigued I did as he asked. The band had only one edge; I could run my finger over it for eternity.

'It has only one edge and one surface,' Daniel explained to me. 'That's what we are now, two people joined together to form one entity with a single purpose. I want you to keep it and to remember that's what we are now.'

Tears welled in my eyes. I had never been given anything so wonderful. 'Thank you,' I said. 'Thank you, thank you, thank you.'

As I moved over him that night I knew that no woman other than me would ever have him again.

I reckoned without Cassie, of course.

FIVE

oday is Saturday. I wake with Zach beside me, lying over my right arm. I don't remember bringing him into bed with us. Perhaps Daniel collected him at some stage.

Zach is dreaming. His mouth moves in and out, his eyelids flutter, his nose twitches. I watch him for a while. Babies' faces are endlessly fascinating.

As I try to ease my arm out from underneath him, Zach wakes. His face screws up, ready to call for attention. Both my children usually wake angry, enraged that some of their living time has been stolen from them. I've heard stories of babies who wake happy, content to lie or play in their cots while their parents exit sleep at their leisure. I am not convinced that such creatures exist.

Zach sees me and stops mid-bellow. His face contorts from a howl to a smile. He has forgotten that he was annoyed; now he gurgles and lifts his legs. His smile and eyes are flirtatious and warm. I tickle his toes, enjoying this moment of peace with my son.

I can hear Daniel in the kitchen with Cassie. They are making breakfast. Cassie is helping to mix the eggs. 'Round and round,' says Daniel. 'Faster, faster.' Daniel and Cassie are good friends.

While they finish cooking, I feed Zach. His red cheeks glow with stored fat. He is an eating machine. I will have to be careful when I start him on solid food. I don't intend for him to be a fat toddler.

When Zach and I enter the kitchen, Cassie is sitting in her highchair. Daniel puts a plate with small pieces of soft egg in front of her. He starts to feed her. Cassie doesn't much like her egg. Her legs twitch.

'Eat it, Cassie,' I say. 'Daddy cooked it for you specially. Yum, yum.'

Cassie pushes the first piece out with her tongue. Daniel inserts another morsel. This time Cassie's reaction is more dramatic. She spits it all over Daniel.

'Cassie!' I scream. 'That's not the right thing to do.' I feel myself turning red with anger. Cassie has always been extremely fussy with her food. It is another of her power plays.

Laughing, Daniel places one hand on my arm. 'Don't worry about it, sweetheart. She can just wait until she gets her next meal. Then she'll eat what's put in front of her. Won't you, Cassie?'

Cassie laughs at him lovingly. She has no idea what he is saying, of course, but Daniel is the centre of her universe.

While Daniel unstraps Cassie from her chair I put Zach in the baby rocker and sit at the table. Daniel has my coffee waiting, hot and milky the way I like it. I love the weekend. It is such a luxury to have someone else around to make breakfast and placate one of the children. My anxiety levels reduce dramatically.

Daniel leans over and gives me a kiss. He looks as if he slept well.

While he reads the paper I sip my coffee and eat the egg that Cassie rejected. She is fixedly watching television. As least she is not destroying anything.

After breakfast we dress the kids. Lots of layers, it's nearly winter. Then we head down to the park by the lake. We will have an early lunch while we're there, feed the ducks, push Cassie on the swing. Perhaps she will wear herself out and we will have a peaceful afternoon.

It is quiet at this hour. Fog-wraiths rise from the lake and dance for a moment before being burned off by the sun. Swatches of brown leaves cling stubbornly to spindly branches. The smell of wood-smoke tickles my nose, reminding me of a long-ago year in Europe when I rose early each morning to kindle the enormous fires of the hotel where I worked. Ducks on the lake move in slow motion until they see us, then their legs churn impatiently under the water to reach the lake's edge.

Cassie and Daniel scatter bread crusts, collected all week and carefully stored. Suddenly, man and infant are surrounded by ducks and moorhens. Zach and I are pushed outside the circle of hungry birds, but he has a good view from his position strapped to my chest and he squeals with delight at the raucous noise and movement. I squat, and Zach comes to rest against my legs, removing the pressure from my back. He is so happy that he begins to hiccup, especially when a curious duck comes over to see if we have anything to offer.

Two swans saunter out of the lake to join the melee. As if in the presence of Hollywood royalty, the duck crowd parts to let the swans through and they stand haughtily in front of my husband and daughter, demanding food. The swans' graceful necks rise over Cassie's head. She's had no experience with such massive creatures and she loops one arm through Daniel's legs. Tentatively, she offers a skerrick of dry crust to the biggest bird, but is too slow in the offer of another. The swan rears his head and hisses at her. The violent sound is harsh in the morning quiet. Cassie starts to cry and Zach's hiccuping stops with his sharp intake of breath. Daniel lets out a whoop of anger and surprise. I stifle my laughter.

Daniel reacts quickly to the swan's abuse. He scoops Cassie up, cradling her to his chest and shooing the birds away with his free hand. 'It's okay, honey,' he half sings to her. 'It's okay, they're gone.'

Daniel looks at me. 'Damn birds. Did you hear that?'

I nod. I wonder what it would be like to have a creature that size hiss at me: horrible, I imagine, but it was funny to see Cassie over-awed.

'Have you had enough feeding the ducks?' I ask Cassie. I have learned the hard way that distraction is the key to dealing with her. 'Let's go for a walk,' I suggest as I stand up.

Suddenly Cassie is okay. She wriggles out of Daniel's arms and runs ahead, kicking leaves and waving her arms at the ducks in imitation of Daniel.

'Do you want me to take Zach?' Daniel asks.

'No it's okay.' I am enjoying his solid weight against my chest and maybe carrying him will help burn a few extra calories.

Daniel and I link hands; his is warm and soft, mine cold and hard.

We walk fast. Cassie has trotted ahead and we are anxious to keep her in sight.

'Slow down,' I call. As usual she ignores me. She is bent on her own adventure; parents are an encumbrance.

As we round a garden bed I nearly collide with a woman. She is dressed in a dark grey leather coat and red scarf.

'Sorry,' I say. I am in a hurry to pass. I step left and she moves with me. I step right and she follows.

'It's you,' she says.

I look at her face. It is vaguely familiar.

'Don't you remember me? It's Maureen, Maureen O'Dowd. We went to school together at Cumberland.'

Daniel has moved ahead. He waves at me and indicates that he will chase Cassie. I motion him on. Now I have no excuse not to stop and talk to this woman who is demanding my attention.

I take one of her hands in mine. 'Of course I remember. You were captain of the hockey team. And the 100-metre record holder.' *Not much chance of that now*, I think to myself. She is quite fat.

'And you were a debating champion; your team won the state titles, didn't it? Do you keep in touch with any of them?'

I laugh. 'Oh no, there's a lot of water under that bridge. What about you?'

'Oh yes, I still have contact with quite a few people from school. It's good to have old friends, people that you shared things with growing up.'

I am still holding her hand. 'Well, it's certainly nice to see you again. What are you doing with yourself? I didn't even know you lived around here.'

'I haven't been here long, only a couple of months. I moved back here with my children. I'm recently divorced.'

'Oh Maureen,' I murmur. I give her hand a gentle squeeze. 'I'm sorry to hear that.' I can see now that she has been crying. Her eyes are red-rimmed and puffy.

'Do you need a tissue?' I pull a crumpled ball from my pocket and pass it to her. It gives me the excuse I need to let go of her hand. 'It's clean.'

'Thanks.' Maureen sniffs into the paper. 'But don't be too sorry. He was a real pig,' she sobs in earnest, 'but I don't know if that makes it better or worse.' Tears stream down her cheeks.

Oh God. I will have to hug her. I lean over and give her small butterfly pats on the back. The movement is very awkward with Zach between us and thankfully he soon begins to squirm. We pull apart.

'Thanks,' says Maureen. 'I needed that. And who's this?' She pulls at Zach's toes.

'Zach,' I reply. 'He's a bit over two months now.'

'He's adorable. Mine are with their father, every second weekend. With him and his new woman.'

She pulls out her wallet and shows me a photo of three rather ugly children ranging from about two to six. I mutter the appropriate compliments.

'I'm going back to school,' she says. 'I'm going to study accounting. As soon as Danni's at school

I'll get myself a good job. I'll show him I don't need him.'

I nod approvingly. 'Good on you. Never let the bastards get you down.' We both laugh. *Good luck*, I think to myself. Maureen is thirty-three, fat and unattractive, with three children. It is unlikely any man will want her again. She will have to raise three children alone. She will barely be able to keep them in order, let alone go to school herself.

'I'd love to catch up with you some time,' says Maureen. 'Can I get your number? And I'll give you mine.'

'Sure,' I say. 'Do you have a pen?'

Maureen rummages in her bag and produces a chewed pen and a torn envelope. She scribbles down her phone number and then hands the pen and paper to me.

'I really appreciate this,' she says. 'It will make such a difference to me to have a friend in the area. Especially someone like you.'

I finish writing and hand Maureen my phone number. It is fake, of course. I do not want Maureen crying on my doorstep when the grief and loneliness really set in.

By this time Zach has begun to kick impatiently. I use his agitation as an excuse to keep moving.

'It's been so lovely seeing you,' I say, 'but the natives are getting restless and I'd better go catch up with the other two. I didn't even have a chance to introduce you to them. Next time.' I lean forward and kiss her cheek. She smells of peaches.

'Bye,' Maureen calls. 'I'll keep in touch.'

I trot gently after Daniel. He and Cassie are crouching on the wooden bridge watching leaves sail downstream.

'Who was that?' he asks when I reach them.

'Just someone I went to school with,' I reply. 'Maureen O'Dowel or something.'

'Were you close at school?' he asks.

I try to remember. It is possible, yes. I remember sending notes to her once. I remember fancying her boyfriend in Year 10. I don't think he lasted long with her.

Daniel and Cassie drop some twigs in the water and then we walk again. The sun warms us. Zach's head comes to rest against my chest. The rhythm of my movement has put him to sleep. We stroll a little further and then turn around. If we go too far Cassie will need to be carried all the way back.

Our daughter is not happy at this about-turn. She pulls determinedly on Daniel's hand. 'More, more.' She learned that word very quickly.

Daniel hunkers down to her level. 'Time to go back, honey.'

'No! More!' Cassie pulls against Daniel with such force that her back is almost parallel with the ground.

'No.' Daniel is firm. 'It's time to go back.'

Cassie, too, is firm. 'No! More!'

'No, Cassie. What about the swings? Don't you want a go on the swings?'

Cassie relents for a second. The word 'swing' has resonated with her. She will consider this.

'No!' she decides. 'No! More!'

Daniel stands and sweeps Cassie into his arms. 'No more arguments. We're going back now.'

Cassie draws in her breath. This is the calm. The eruption will come. Her face reddens as she yells. She arches her back and kicks her legs. Daniel does not bother talking to her. It is all he can do to hold on. I start to walk. I don't want Zach to be woken by the din.

Daniel waits until Cassie realises that no matter how much she howls he will not release her and then he starts after me. I stop until they near. Cassie's bottom lip is heavy and her face blotched from crying. I am relieved that Daniel won the battle with her. Otherwise the next time would be even worse.

By the time we reach the playground Zach has become heavy and I ask Daniel to take him. I unstrap the pack and Zach wakes. He has on a red peaked cap that sits above his ears. He looks like a pixie. His eyes are grey, like Daniel's, not like mine. Neither of the children look like me. Lucky I gave birth to them, or I might be suspicious of their origin.

Cassie uses my freedom as an opportunity to pull me to the swings. I strap her in and push, higher and higher. I see her legs silhouetted against the sky. She looks as if she is catching white clouds with her feet. I wish I were able to swing again. I used to love going so high that I imagined I would swing right over the bar.

Suddenly, Cassie screams. I wonder what is wrong and then I realise that Daniel is calling to me.

'Too high, you're pushing her too high. Slow her down a bit.'

I reach for the chains and check the movement of the swing. I do it carefully, so that there is no jerk and Cassie will slow gradually.

'Sorry,' I murmur. I'm not sure to whom I'm apologising. Perhaps to the universe for the fact that I have failed to remember the extreme youthfulness of my child. Her personality is so strong that it is easy for me to forget that she is only fourteen months old.

Once Cassie has come to a stop I lean over and unstrap her. She reaches up to me; her face is wet with tears. She buries her head into the side of my neck where it is bare and she sobs quietly. It is unpleasant to have her cold, wet nose pressed so hard against me and it takes all of my resolve not to push her away.

Daniel pulls Cassie's toes. It is the distraction she needs. She wriggles to get down, and the three of them run. Zach bounces in Daniel's arms. His cap falls off and his fine hair lifts up and down in the air currents. Cassie giggles as Daniel tries to catch her and misses again and again.

I decide to begin the barbecue. Soon the sausages are sizzling and the onions are browning. Waves of heat rise from the plate. I breathe in the smell. It reminds me of a time before the children were born. Daniel brought me down here after I had won an important new client. The resulting international advertising campaign would bring millions of dollars of revenue to my firm. Daniel cooked sausages and opened champagne. I knew that he was proud of my work, of what I did and how I did it.

We also came to this park the afternoon I found out I was pregnant with Cassie. We sat on the water's edge eating fish and chips. That was before the nausea kicked in and I was unable to eat any food that had been cooked in oil.

We sat there for so long that day that the sun began to set. It was the end of the day and I felt as if it was the end of my life. Daniel, by contrast, was barely able to contain his exuberance. He had wanted children since we were married and ostensibly we had been trying to conceive for six months. But I had been secretly taking the contraceptive pill. As far as I was concerned Cassie was definitely not planned. If Daniel hadn't kept such a sharp eye on my cycles it is unlikely I would have gone through with the pregnancy. Cassie would not be here and I would not be what I am.

Today I look at the three of them running. Daniel was a good husband – *is* a good husband – only I share him now with two other people. On that fateful day at the lake we had agreed that once the baby was born I could do what I wanted – work or stay home. But after Cassie was born, Daniel made it clear that his real preference was for me to be at home. I did it for him, but, as I keep telling myself, this is only a phase in my life and phases don't last forever.

That night I have a dream.

I am in a pine forest. The fresh coldness of the air stings my nose and my feet slide on the needles. I am climbing – there is something or someone I must get to at the top – but I have a pack on my back and it is heavy, so heavy. I can't get the straps undone so I cut them with a knife. The pack rolls back down the slope and it begins to moan. Now it is a small black and white dog and it will fall off the mountain unless I save it. I lie down flat and try to reach it, but can't. I stand and inch downhill towards it. My feet slip from under me. I try to crawl but the dog slides further. I turn away from it. The dog moans more loudly, but I now know that it is him or me and the call of the mountain top has begun to drown out his cries.

SIX

One Wednesday night a few weeks later Daniel returns home from work very late. I have fallen asleep in the lounge-room waiting for him and I am woken by the feel of his lips on my cheek.

'Hello Sleeping Beauty.'

I wipe the tiredness from my eyes. I don't feel very beautiful. 'Hi, what time is it?'

'Nearly ten-thirty.'

'Oh God. It'll be time for Zach's feed soon. How come you're so late? You were strange on the phone when you told me not to wait up.'

'I've got some great news to tell you...but first, I have something for you.'

He reaches around into the hallway and hands me an arrangement of roses in a vase. It is an expensive vase, Wedgwood maybe.

'It's for being so beautiful, for being such a good mother, because I love you so much.'

'They're beautiful. Thanks, Daniel.' I reach up to give him a kiss. It is a nice surprise. He does not often bestow flowers upon me. Although I do wonder if he should have spent so much on the vase.

I put the flowers on the coffee table and we sit on the couch, clutching hands like lovesick teenagers.

'I'm glad you're up,' he says. 'I've got some great news. I don't think I could have waited until morning to tell you.'

'What?' I wonder what it could be. I have not seen him this excited for a long time.

'Well, you know how Ken's leaving?' I nod. Ken is the sales manager, a rather obnoxious man I've always thought. He was retiring, to tend his gardens or something equally ridiculous.

'Les has asked me to take his position.'

I let out a gasp. I know how much Daniel wanted this, but in our wildest dreams neither of us ever believed it would happen. Daniel's company rarely promotes internally at management level. We often joked that if Daniel wanted the sales manager's position he would have to leave the company first.

Daniel's hand is gripping mine so hard I can feel the pulse drumming in my fingertips.

'Do you know what this means, sweetheart?' he asks. 'More money, more responsibility. It means the company thinks a lot of my work, more than I ever expected. Les told me that they never wanted to lose me and that by promoting me they would be sure that I'd stay.'

'Oh, that's wonderful. They *should* want to keep you. I just never thought they'd be smart enough to realise it.' I rub his shoulder. 'I'm so proud of you.'

My words are right. I know that they are, but my head has begun to pound. I cannot stop the tears. Daniel wipes them away with his free hand.

'I knew that you'd be happy for me, for us. This will take so much pressure off us. We'll be able to pay off the mortgage much faster...you won't have to go back to work. We've both put a lot of effort into my career. It's finally beginning to pay off.'

Daniel is right: we have put effort, and money, into his career. He has recently completed a graduate diploma in business; it was a sacrifice of time, of money. And now he is successful. He will have more responsibility, more travel, more time away from home.

I look at the flowers he has given me and now I see them for what they really are – a present to his success, a present to his power and freedom. I begin to cry again. I am happy for him, I know that I am. But I also feel strangely empty as if something has gone from me. Or perhaps it never truly was a part of me.

SEVEN

*I*t is as I feared.

Over the next five weeks Daniel takes up his new duties in earnest. It is a busy time of the year, he tells me; it will not always be this hectic. But he is rarely home before eight o'clock and he leaves the house before six each morning. Some days he does not see the children at all. When he is home he is tired. He falls asleep in front of the television. I grow weary of reminding him to take out the garbage, to mow the lawn, and begin to do these chores myself. I am now a single mother with three people to care for. The knife-edge on which I walk is perilously sharp.

During these early weeks of Daniel's new responsibilities, Cassie senses my vulnerability. Her
behaviour, already difficult, worsens. She acts as if
everything I request of her is an imposition. For
Daniel, however, she simpers and bows. If she is
awake when he comes home he is greeted at the
door like a conquering hero.

I now cannot dress Cassie without holding her
down with one hand while pulling on her clothes
with the other. She has discovered how to take off
her nappies and she does so, often. While I am
feeding Zach she will undress and urinate on the
lounge-room floor. She is only sixteen months old,
but she has complete bowel and bladder control,
when it suits her. One morning she wakes, strips off
and shits on her pillow. Daniel has gone to work
when I find it, and her. She has climbed over the
side of the cot, which we now keep lowered for her,
and she is playing with some blocks as I follow my
nose to the stench. It has obliterated most of the
pink fairies that adorn her pillow slip. It has slithered
down the back of the mattress and dripped on the
floor. I am aghast and angry. I pick Cassie up and
without thinking I rub her face into the mess. She
gasps, gulps, inhales and bellows. For the first time

in over three weeks I feel like laughing. She has no idea how small she is, how vulnerable. It is good to remind her.

Daniel tells me that he has to go away for three days. I can see that he is uneasy. He has never liked leaving us for any period of time. At his news I feel a chasm open at my feet. At the bottom are the monsters of insecurity, of fatigue and desperate boredom. I want to scream at him not to leave me. I want to bury my face in his chest and reveal that I will be unable to cope in his absence. I am shaking slightly as I give him a kiss.

'We'll miss you, but we'll manage,' I reassure him. Daniel appears to relax, his shoulders drop a little. If only it were that easy for me.

I write a list. We will keep very, very busy while Daniel is away. We will attend story time at the library on Monday, playgroup on Tuesday and visit friends on Wednesday. I will be so tired that by the dreaded dark of night I will fall into bed exhausted. I will keep the monsters away by the sheer force of my will and energy.

Monday comes and goes. I cope. I manage to get a few hours sleep that night. It is not enough, I know that, but it will have to do. It is all I have.

Early on Tuesday morning, before either of the children are awake, I make the mistake of looking at myself in the mirror. Was it three months ago I had that colour put in my hair? The regrowth is terrible. My eyes are puffy, with deep dark circles and crow's feet that run from their corners. I can't remember when I last put on make-up. I will do so today, I decide. It will lift my spirits. The ritual of mask-making will enable me to cope with the world.

I drag out my black make-up bag from the back corner of the vanity. I open the case. It is like looking at a lost world. Most of the products date from the days when I still worked, when I wore a different lipstick depending on my mood, the season, the colour of my hair. I have twenty shades of eyeshadow; my favourites are almost worn through to the metal canister below. I sift through the bag. I find some bronzing powder. I remember the exact occasion for which it was bought. It was a night cruise on the harbour. I dusted it over my – is décolletage the right word? – and over my shoulders. It was summer and the colour brought out my tan. I looked as if I had been touched by fairy dust. I knew that I was beautiful and so did Daniel. He couldn't keep his hands off me that night. I remember him rubbing against me as we danced. I pressed back; my nipples were hard with desire.

On the way home Daniel had unexpectedly turned down a side road and driven along it until it became dirt. There was almost no moon that night and when he had stopped the car and turned off the headlights the stars were liquid crystal pouring through the thick mantle of the night sky. The air was humid and redolent with the smell of the summer forest; it moved through my lungs as if I were breathing thick, sweet honey.

Without speaking Daniel moved round to my door, opened it and scooped me out in one movement. I rested one hand on his bicep. It was tight with the effort of lifting me. The back of my knees rested against his other arm. I was a current arced between his limbs.

Daniel placed me against a huge old tree. My feet were buried within its roots; my back rested against its trunk. I could feel the roughness of its bark through the flimsy material of my dress. My body resonated; it pulsed in rhythm with the earth. I stood before Daniel, an ancient sacrifice to the gods of the forest. His was the power, mine was the offering. But even as I stood compliantly before him I knew what I wanted. Never before had I desired a man so much.

Assuming the right of the victor, Daniel dispensed with preliminaries. He lifted my dress to my waist and pulled apart the lace of my underwear. I was exposed before him. He pressed his finger into me, up into my yielding flesh. And then he entered me. He was harder than I had ever felt him. 'Do you know that every man there tonight wanted you,' he whispered into my ear. 'And I'm the one who's got you.' He pushed into me again. 'You're mine.'

I reached backwards and held tightly to the tree for support. The heavens moved above me. The earth lived beneath my feet. As my gaze rested on the blue-black branches of the tree stretched out above us, Daniel came with a shudder of body and spirit that left him almost unable to stand. Quietly I laughed to myself. I know with great certainty that it is in the webs of desire that the real woman binds her man. Daniel might have thought that I was his, but that night I knew that he was mine.

Today, back in the dismal present, a cry echoes down the corridor. It is Cassie. She is awake and obviously not in a good mood. I put the bronzing powder back into the case. When was the last time men have desired me like that? Tears form in my eyes. I close the bag. I won't be bothering with make-up today after all.

Cassie lies listlessly in her bed and doesn't even raise herself to a sitting position as I enter. She is flushed and red blotches cover both cheeks. I feel her forehead. She is hot. As I bend over her, she coughs. It is a hollow cough that comes from the bottom of her lungs. *Shit!* The idea of spending the day at home with two children, one of them sick, is unbearable.

If I can reduce her temperature, then perhaps we will still be able to go to playgroup. I turn the heating down, wet a facecloth and place it on her forehead. I measure the appropriate dosage of paracetamol and, using a syringe, I shoot it down the back of her throat before she has time to protest. Cassie is not keen on taking medicine, although today she barely manages a murmur.

Now Zach bellows for me. I go and feed him and when I return to Cassie she is sitting up and taking more of an interest in the world. I feel her forehead again. She is a bit cooler. Will playgroup be okay or not? I prevaricate. Cassie is prone to exaggeration; she's probably not very sick at all. But then I wonder, what if she is really ill and something happens and I have done the wrong thing by taking her out?

I am shaky with the effort of thinking. Once I made decisions about contracts worth millions of dollars; now I do not know what to do with a sick child.

The phone rings. As I run to answer it Zach protests at being left alone for so long; I snatch him up as I go.

It is Daniel. He is calling us from breakfast. I can hear the genteel clinking of cutlery in the hotel dining room. He sips his coffee as he talks to me. He had a successful day yesterday. It's very warm there. He might be able to get home a bit earlier tomorrow.

I respond to him as best I can, but my mind is still on Cassie. Should I ask Daniel's advice? I want to and I hate that I feel like this. I hate that I can't make decisions about my children without feeling that I need to seek someone else's counsel.

Cassie toddles into the kitchen and wipes her nose against the back of my leg. Zach is trying to grab the telephone cord. I pull it as far from his reach as I can. Thwarted in his efforts he lurches for my hair instead and holds on with the desperation of a drowning sailor.

'Hang on, Daniel, will you?'

I forcibly remove Zach's hand from my tortured tresses, grab a tissue from the top of the microwave and wipe Cassie's nose. As I do so I notice that we are out of bread. Fuck! Two over-ripe bananas nestle forlornly in the fruit bowl. I know that we have no cereal. Looks as if breakfast will be a non-event.

When I return to Daniel he has begun on his toast. My stomach rumbles. I have two children to take care of and he is having his breakfast hand-fed to him. I will not ask Daniel what to do about Cassie. I will make this decision alone. We will go to playgroup and Cassie will bloody well enjoy it.

Playgroup is a disaster. The first person I see when I walk in is Rachael, from my mothers' group. She's never been to this playgroup before, so what the hell is she doing here now? She has come to spy on me, to make her snide comments, her rude remarks, to try to reveal my inadequacies as a mother. She is sitting on the floor playing with her child, and she nods to me, smiling, revealing her perfect white canine teeth. I murmur hello, but do not walk over to where she is sitting. I do not want her here, and I realise that if she continues to come I will have to find another playgroup. Fuck, another irritant in an already awful day.

No one is able to play outside. A cold easterly wind has begun to blow and it looks as if it might even snow. For most of the time Cassie sits listlessly on my lap. Her breathing is ragged and she only rouses herself occasionally in order to cough that same echoey cough. Zach is also restless and I try to rock his pram with one free hand. My coffee grows cold in front of me until someone takes it away to wash up. I still haven't had breakfast and my stomach cramps in protest.

Towards the end of the session, Cassie begins to burn up. Rachael walks over and places her hand on Cassie's forehead. She points to a rash on the side of Cassie's neck. 'You need to take her to a doctor,' she says. 'One of the signs of meningococcal disease is a rash like that. I can take care of Zach for a while if it makes it easier for you.'

I resist the temptation to pull Cassie away from Rachael's assured hand. 'No, thank you,' I reply. 'I can cope perfectly well.'

By this stage I am fuming. How dare Rachael, or anybody else for that matter, tell me what I should do. I am the girl's mother, after all. I will decide what is best for her. I attempt to shoot another dose of paracetamol down her throat. She spits it all over me. *You little bitch*, I think to myself. Cassie is determined to ruin my day and I am just as determined that she will not.

After playgroup I decide to call in to the shops and get some bread. I need at least that in order to get through the rest of today and tomorrow. When we arrive at the shops, however, both Zach and Cassie have fallen asleep in the back of the car. They have done it to spite me. A rage starts to burn.

I cannot leave the children in the car. This car park is patrolled by police and the fine for leaving children unattended in a car is high. I need this fucking bread. I will have to wake them and take them with me.

I wake Cassie first. She looks shocking, her eyes are bright and her face is even more flushed than before. I tell her to stand on the footpath and wait for me. Gently I ease the straps away from Zach's shoulders. If I am careful I might be able to carry him into the shop without waking him. I move his arms through the straps. He is still asleep. It is only as I lift him to my shoulder that he wakes and raises his head. I push his head down against my shoulder. If I can get him to keep it there maybe he will fall asleep again.

I take Cassie's hand; she pulls it away. I grab it again; she rips her hand out of mine and puts it behind her back. Being ill has not made her any less defiant. I grit my teeth and squat down to her level. 'Take my hand.' The words spit out of my mouth.

'No,' she says.

I hesitate, and we both know that she has won. A tiny child, flushed with fever, has got the better of me. Zach's head is bobbing around; he is well and truly awake. He starts a gentle keening. I turn my back on Cassie and enter the shop; she trails about ten paces behind. She is too short to set off the sensor that opens the door and she looks as if she will be crushed in its metal mouth. I take a step back to reopen the door and she moves backwards as well, still outside. If this weren't happening to me it could perhaps be funny.

'Cassie, come inside darling. The door will close on you otherwise.' I use the voice I save for when I am with my children around other people. It is the voice of a strong, calm, reasoned adult who expects her word to be obeyed. I move away again. I will not look at her. I won't. If I look she has won, again. As I move with bridal slowness down the aisle, I imagine her running into the car park and being squashed by a reversing car. I imagine a man walking past, putting her under his arm and running. But I will not look, or I will never be able to get this bread.

Cassie screams; the door is closing on her. It will open as soon as it touches her, of course, but she doesn't know this. I hurry back to her; Zach bobs around and dribbles down the back of my shirt. His keening becomes louder. The checkout ladies are looking at me. I am sure that the one with the steel-grey perm clicks her tongue. *Tsk, tsk, what a terrible mother, can't even control her own children.* I grab Cassie's hand; she has lost her opportunity for gentleness from me. She comes, pulling slightly, like a sail caught in a mild breeze.

The bread is at the back of the shop. We drift past some lollipops; a tactical mistake. The mild breeze becomes a gale. Zach and I are caught in the force of Cassie's longing. She has not eaten all day, but now she has seen what she wants. 'Lolly, lolly.' I reach over and get a red one. Her feet stamp. I put the red one back, get a green one and rip it open with my teeth. I will pay for it later; now I just want to be free to get the bloody bread.

I hear a sharp intake of breath as I hand Cassie the sweet. Belatedly I realise that she wanted to open it herself. But I have had enough. I leave her there to bellow, to drop the lollipop in protest. I trot to the bread stand, grab a couple of loaves and trot back to Cassie. I put the bread under my arm and seize her hand, half-dragging and half-carrying her to the checkout at the front of the shop.

Letting go of Cassie's hand I plonk the armpit-squashed bread on the counter. 'And there is a lollipop on the floor. I'm afraid I opened it and my daughter didn't want it. I'll pay for it, of course, but I wanted to let you know that it's there.'

Steel-grey perm shakes her head. 'Which aisle?'

'I don't know. The lollipop aisle?' Humour attempted.

Steel-grey perm shakes her head again. Humour rejected.

Cassie has collapsed in a dramatic heap on the floor, her head is under the counter and she is bellowing for all she is worth. Zach wails in harmony with her. Suddenly Cassie stops. I breathe a sigh of relief – one down. And then I wonder what Cassie has found. I can imagine her scraping up some forgotten chewing gum and ingesting it. I try not to gag.

The bread is bagged. This ordeal is nearly over – or so I dare to hope. 'Come on Cassie, time to go.' The little feet with their red shoes and frilly socks do not move.

I step over her. 'Come on.' I attempt my reasoned, not to be argued with voice, but the quaver at the end belies my assumed confidence. I reach down and pull her out; using her bottom as a pivot I spin her around to face me and pull her up by one arm.

It is quick; she is too shocked to protest. I have the bread bag dangling from the hand with which I am holding Zach. My bicep feels as if it will burst. I drag Cassie towards the door. Steel-grey perm turns to the other shop assistant. 'When my children were that age I never went shopping with them.' I swallow my vitriol. She is hardly worth it, but I will not be shopping here again.

I deposit Zach in the car. His face is blotchy from crying, but he likes the car and I know that he will soon settle. Cassie arches her back as I try to strap her in, and she starts screaming. I have had as much as I can take. Quickly I look around to check that no one is watching. Then I give Cassie a hard slap on the face. By now her cheeks are so red from fever and crying that my fingermarks cannot even be seen.

EIGHT

When we arrive at the top of the steep driveway of our house I see that the garage door is open and Daniel's car is parked inside. As I pull up behind him I feel relief wash over me. I am glad now that I made the decision to stop and buy the bread. Daniel likes to have bread with his meals.

Both of the children are asleep again and I leave them in the car as I greet Daniel, who has come out to see me. We hug for several heartbeats and then he pushes me back to face him, kissing my mouth, my nose, my eyes. I laugh. His lips tickle, his breath is coffee-laden. I burrow my head in between his jacket and his armpit. I can smell his sweat; it is sweet and cloying, like a tropical carnivorous flower.

'How come you're back so early?' I ask.

'Things were cancelled. Not long after I spoke to you. There was nothing to keep me there so I caught the first available plane. I tried to call you a few times but there was no answer.'

'We were at playgroup. It was dreadful. Cassie whinged and whined the whole time. I didn't get to drink my coffee and I haven't had breakfast yet, let alone lunch.'

'Come on then. Let's get the kids into the house and we can make something to eat.'

Daniel walks around to Cassie's side of the car and as he lifts her from her seat he exclaims, 'My God, she's burning up. Has she been like this for long?'

'She was warm this morning,' I reply. 'But I got some paracetamol into her and she seemed all right. She spat the last dose out so I suppose that's why she's a bit warm now.'

'A bit warm! She feels as if she's on fire. You went out with her like this, in this weather?' He sees the bread. 'And you went shopping?'

I nod. 'Yes, but she wasn't this bad when I left home and I needed bread.'

I can see that Daniel is reluctant to say any more, but of course he has said enough. I have been judged and found wanting.

'Don't take Zach out of the car,' he says. 'I think we should take her to the doctor. Did you see this?' Gently he lifts Cassie's chin. Underneath, the rash is now burning bright red. 'One of the symptoms of meningococcal disease is a rash.'

And Daniel, like Rachael, obviously believes that I have failed to notice a rash on my own daughter. Do they both think that I am completely incompetent?

We get into the car and head to the 24-hour medical centre, which is unusually quiet; we are led through to a doctor in record time. Perhaps the fact that Cassie is lying listlessly in Daniel's arms helps.

The doctor examines Cassie carefully.

'How long has she been like this?' she asks.

'She was a bit warm when she woke this morning,' I reply. 'But she only really started to burn up around lunchtime.' That was my story and I was sticking to it.

'It's lucky that you brought her in,' says the doctor. 'I know that you've been focusing on the rash, but that's not actually what I'm worried about. Your daughter has fluid on the lungs, a lot of fluid in fact. I think she has bacterial pneumonia. Another day without treatment and she may have required hospitalisation.'

Daniel looks at me. I know that I have failed.

'So what now, Doctor?' Daniel asks.

'I'm going to prescribe some antibiotics. It's important that you keep her warm and maintain her fluids. It's also probably better if you don't take her out anywhere, particularly in this weather. I'll need to see her again in a few days to check that the antibiotics have kicked in. But you should bring her in earlier if she takes a turn for the worse.'

With our instructions and our antibiotics we return home. It is almost two-thirty and I still have not had anything to eat.

Daniel carries Cassie inside. He lies her on the couch while he makes up a mattress in front of the television. Then they lie down together watching a children's program. Daniel strokes her hair in an almost absentminded way.

'Don't worry baby, Daddy's here now. You'll be all right now.'

Baby snuggles in against Daddy's chest. I can see the tops of their heads, but I have been excluded from the circle of their mutual affection. I turn away. I will continue with the task of settling Zach. At least he will be happy to be with me. For a second I allow myself the thought that maybe it was a pity Daniel returned home early.

NINE

Cassie bounces back with a vengeance in the weeks following her pneumonia. It is as if the antibiotics have given her even more stamina and greater defiance. She runs me ragged. Daniel frequently comes home from work a little earlier now, but I do not flatter myself that it is because of me. It is Cassie whom he kisses first, Cassie for whom he buys little gifts. Now I wait in line to see if there is any affection left over. Sometimes there is, sometimes there is not.

I am beyond exhaustion. I am beyond expectation. I am beyond hope. I can see nothing but my own fear and fatigue and self-loathing stretching before me for a lifetime. I feel as if there is nothing left.

Tonight Cassie is calling for water. As usual Daniel snores through the noise. His greater solicitude towards his daughter has done nothing to cure his nocturnal deafness. I am still the one woken by the children several times a night. I am the zombie who cooks their meals; I am the maid who cleans their shit.

Now Cassie is screaming. I fill a bottle and take it in to her. She sucks at it lying down; her eyes are still closed, eyes that look nothing like mine. Her eyelids are purplish; I can almost see the blood moving within them. She looks so small and vulnerable, but I know the strength of her will. It frightens me; perhaps I will always be a slave to that will, to the power of her kicking legs.

I see a future where Cassie and I continually clash – and Daniel may not choose to take my side. I see a future where I will be excluded from their favour, from Daniel's favour. I see a future where this period of my life is not a phase and will not pass.

Cassie finishes her drink and lets the bottle fall to the floor. I pick it up and put it on the night stand. She rolls around and grumbles about something. She wriggles and squirms as if she cannot become comfortable. Her breathing is growing heavy, but she is having trouble settling.

'Shhh, Cassie, shhhh,' I whisper. 'Time to go back to sleep.'

Cassie grumbles a bit more. She has never liked to do as I ask.

I pull a pillow from the rocking chair. It might make things more comfortable for her. It is a small pillow, not much bigger than her face. I put it close to her in order to better compare its size. I see that the pillow covers her whole head. I hold it against her face gently and then more firmly. Her legs begin to kick. She fights against me as if she expects me to give in to her as I usually do. But this time I don't.

After she has been still for some time I take the pillow away and replace it on the rocking chair. Cassie's mouth is open a little. No breath comes out.

I have told her many times that she must listen to me.

I return to bed. I hope that Zach sleeps through the rest of the night.

TEN

*D*aniel's screaming wakes me. He is surprisingly loud. *What is he doing?* I wonder; *he will wake Zach.* Then I remember.

I rise from bed and put on a dressing-gown. By this stage Daniel is almost hysterical.

'Call an ambulance, Cassie's not breathing.'

I hurry down the corridor to her room. I see Daniel's back. He has placed Cassie on the floor and is crouching over her, breathing into her lungs. *Exhale, turn head, inhale.* I remember learning the action at Girl Guides. With a child as young as Cassie there is no need to hold the nose when blowing into the lungs. An adult's mouth is large enough to place over both the nasal and mouth cavities. This is what Daniel is doing now.

I move into the room and step around Daniel. Cassie looks so tiny lying there on the floor. I reach down and touch her toe. It is very cold.

'Will you call an ambulance!' yells Daniel. I jump at the urgency in his voice. As I leave the room, Daniel starts CPR.

I reach the phone and dial 000.

'Ambulance. We have a child, seventeen months, not breathing.' I pause. 'She is very cold.'

The voice on the other end is detached and professional. It asks my address.

'Tyson Avenue. Number fifteen.'

The voice gives instructions on emergency measures to try before the ambulance arrives. I reply that Daniel is already giving Cassie CPR, but that she is cold, very cold.

The voice tells me that the ambulance will be there in a matter of minutes, that I can hang up now, but to stay calm, help is on its way.

Zach has been crying for some time. I enter his room. He greets me with a smile. I pick him up. He is so warm. I feel his breath against my cheek. I hold him to me. There is nothing I can do to help Daniel and I am enjoying the warmth of Zach's young body.

There is a sharp rap on the front door. It is the paramedics. They were quick, I think, as I open the door. It is a man and a woman, both dressed in black pants and white jumpers, like penguins. I direct them to Cassie's room. The woman enters first. She touches Daniel's shoulder and asks him to move away from Cassie's body. Daniel doesn't want to give her up to them. He hovers and circles, like a search plane. I can see that Daniel is in the way of the paramedics so I go up to him and pull him out of the room, away from Cassie, into the corridor with Zach and me.

I cradle Daniel in one arm and Zach in the other while the ambulance officers look after Cassie. It is a relief to have her in professional hands. Daniel and I cry. I join him in his rhythm. Only Zach is happy. He dribbles on my hand.

Daniel travels in the ambulance with the body of our daughter. The paramedics do not bother with the siren. It is obvious to everyone that it is too late for heroics and last-minute dashes.

Zach and I follow the ambulance to the hospital. The two previous times I have taken this trip at this hour I was in labour. The small bodies of my children were ready to begin life on their own. Now I am following the lifeless body of my daughter. It is the cycle of things, I tell myself. It is not what I would have expected – to lose a child before myself – but there it is.

By the time I find a parking spot at the hospital Daniel has disappeared with the paramedics and Cassie. I want to follow, but Zach is overdue for a feed and my breasts are aching with their load. I take myself to a small waiting room, sit in a quiet corner and close my eyes while Zach eats. Suck, suck, swallow. It is the rhythm of motherhood, the rhythm of my life.

Finally, Daniel joins me.

'She's gone,' he says. 'There's nothing anyone can do for her. Cassie's dead.'

I reach out one of my hands and clasp one of his. A terrible silence settles over us. It is broken only by the steady dripping of Daniel's tears.

We are led to the room where Cassie is lying. We are encouraged to pick her up, to hold her. I give Zach to Daniel in order to free my arms, but it is all I can do to run my fingers through Cassie's hair. It was washed last night and it slips through my fingers like quicksilver. I lift her hand and it falls back. My eyes feel as if the lids are coated in sand. I blink and tears form. Daniel takes my hand. Zach gurgles. He does not know the enormity of it all. I think that I am beginning to.

We are asked to wait in a large room clad almost entirely in linoleum; the material covers the floor and runs halfway up the walls. It is a dirty grey colour. The room is dreary and smells of antiseptic and old age. After a few minutes, a figure in a white coat enters the room. He shakes hands with Daniel, then me.

'My name is Doctor Hadid,' he says. 'I am terribly sorry for the tragedy which has befallen your family.'

He is softly spoken. Or perhaps he is simply respecting our need for quiet at a time like this.

Daniel chokes back a sob.

'We will all do everything we can to help you through this period. The hospital can put you in touch with grief counsellors, support groups.'

Daniel and I both nod. We know that everything will be inadequate, of course, but we can't refuse their offer of help.

As Doctor Hadid is talking a nurse enters and stands silently by the door.

The doctor continues. 'Right now we want to try to understand what may have happened to your daughter.' He motions us over to a small table in the corner of the room.

'We hope you will not mind answering a few questions. We understand it may be difficult, but it is important that we do this quickly while your memories are clear. You see, sudden, unexplained, infant death is not as common as people think, and at your daughter's age it is very unusual. What we are hoping is that you may be able to give us some clue as to why she died.'

'Yes,' says Daniel. 'Of course we will do everything we can to help.'

I concur quietly. I realise that what we are finding ourselves up against is a system that has to be seen to cross its t's and dot its i's. In the darkness of last night I had not paused to consider what might happen next. I now understand that things have not ended with Cassie's death. It seems as if they might be just beginning. My instinct has carried me this far, but I will need more than that to get me through this. I will need to be clear-headed and very, very careful.

We sit at the table and Doctor Hadid begins.

'Was Cassie her usual self last night when you put her to bed?'

Daniel looks at me. I nod. 'Yes. She always liked me to be the one to put her to sleep. She went down fairly easily last night.'

'She hadn't appeared sick...no temperature, no cough, no complaining of aches or pains?'

'Well,' I reply, 'she was only seventeen months old.' Doctor Hadid makes a note on his paper. 'She couldn't really tell me in detail if anything was wrong.'

'She had pneumonia a month or so ago.' Daniel breaks in. 'But she was prescribed antibiotics and was given a clean bill of health.'

Doctor Hadid is scribbling on his paper again. 'Really? How serious was the pneumonia?'

'Serious enough,' says Daniel. 'It developed extremely quickly, and the doctor told us that if we'd waited another twenty-four hours there was a good chance she would have had to be admitted to hospital.'

'Oh God, Doctor,' I say, 'you don't think that had anything to do with her death, do you?'

Doctor Hadid shakes his head. 'It's unlikely unless the symptoms recurred, and you say that she appeared well last night – not grizzly or off-colour at all?'

'Not that I noticed,' I say.

'I got home around eight o'clock and checked on Cassie then,' adds Daniel. 'She was asleep, but seemed absolutely fine.'

Doctor Hadid makes another note. 'Was Cassie in the habit of waking during the night?'

Daniel nods. 'Yes, she was becoming better at sleeping through, but most nights she still woke, she...wasn't a very good sleeper.' His voice wavers on the edge of tears.

'What about last night?'

'I didn't hear her,' says Daniel. 'But I was pretty tired.' He looks at me. 'What about you, sweetheart?'

'No, I have to admit I didn't hear her either. I did get up to Zach at about midnight. I didn't go into Cassie's room, because I didn't want to run the risk of waking her.'

'Did it worry you this morning that she hadn't woken?' Doctor Hadid looks at Daniel. 'I understand that you were the one who found her?'

'Yes, I was. This morning I really only checked her out of habit. As I said, she was beginning to sleep through the night and even if she did wake I didn't always hear her. But when I looked in on her this morning she wasn't breathing.' Daniel begins to cry again.

'Yes, I see,' says Doctor Hadid. His gaze rests on Daniel a little longer than seems necessary and I notice that the nurse hasn't moved. She has been quietly noting our reactions to Doctor Hadid's questions. *My God*, I think, *could it be that they suspect Daniel of having something to do with Cassie's death?* The thought seems ridiculous; I know that Daniel is an exemplary father, but of course these people know nothing about us, nothing at all.

Doctor Hadid turns to me. 'And how have you been since the birth of your children? Two babies born in such quick succession can be very taxing on the body, and the mind.'

How dare he! 'I have been perfectly well,' I reply. 'Tired, of course, but perfectly well.'

'I can vouch for that,' says Daniel. 'My wife has handled the birth and raising of our two children very...' he stops as he searches for the right word, 'well... As she handles all things.'

There are a few more questions from Doctor Hadid. And then, a statement. 'We would like your permission to perform an autopsy.' He looks at each of us in turn.

'It's standard procedure in cases like this, I'm afraid. From the information you have just given me, the cause of Cassie's death is not readily apparent and cannot be ascertained without an autopsy. Requesting your permission is a formality really.'

'So why ask us?' I am horrified, caught off-guard by the doctor's request. I realise now that it was stupid of me, but I never expected this. 'I mean surely it's clear what Cassie died of, Sudden Infant Death Syndrome! It's always in the news. Surely that's what she died of! What else could it be?' I am nearly hysterical by the last word.

Daniel grips my hand. We'll get through this, he seems to be saying.

'My wife is upset. Naturally the thought of our daughter being...interfered with in such a way is distasteful to us both, but, as you point out, we can do nothing but agree.'

'Thank you,' says Doctor Hadid. 'I know that this is terribly upsetting. Hopefully an autopsy will give us some indication as to what may have caused Cassie's death,' Doctor Hadid turns to face me, 'but, I would still like your blessing on this.'

What can I say? I utter the only words available to me. 'Yes, of course. If you think it is necessary. We will do everything we can to help.' I hope that I sound convincing. 'Can you tell us how long it will take?'

'About four days I expect. We will do everything we can to speed it up. We understand you will want to make funeral arrangements as soon as possible.'

Four days. I have four days in which I can do nothing, four days to wait while others decide my future. Only four days. They will be an eternity.

ELEVEN

We, the three of us, all that remains of our family, return home. Daniel drives as I am too overcome with emotion to handle the car. I sob uncontrollably into a handkerchief. To the world outside my head I am shattered-grief personified. But what only I know is that I cry for myself, I cry to cover my fear, for I am very afraid. I am afraid of what the doctors with their sharp scalpels and inquiring minds will find. I am afraid that they will have no respect for the family that Cassie's death has left behind. I am afraid that they will uncover what should be left hidden.

Daniel speaks. 'I hated leaving her there. I hated leaving her on that cold table surrounded by people she doesn't know.'

That is an understatement. I had to drag Daniel out of the hospital. Hadn't he been able to see that Cassie was dead? There was nothing, nothing either of us could do for her. Now it is time to get on with the lives of the three of us who remain.

I begin to sob even harder.

Daniel reaches out with his spare hand. He doesn't speak. I don't think that he trusts himself to.

When we arrive home I am shocked to see a police car parked out the front.

'What are they doing here?' I ask Daniel. I expect him to reply that he doesn't know. Instead his answer surprises me.

'It seems that a death-scene investigation, as well as an autopsy, is par for the course in a situation like this,' he says dryly. Obviously he also is not impressed with the level of bureaucracy that's slammed into our lives as a result of the death of our daughter. 'I gave them the key while we were at the hospital. Apparently they need to do it as soon as possible. I wanted to get it over and done with. I hope you don't mind.'

I shake my head as fear runs through me. I know that Daniel has done the right thing, that in his shoes I would have acted as he did, but I feel betrayed by his actions. The problem is that in the cold, numb emotion of last night I had not considered scenes such as these. I am unprepared. I cannot be sure that everything in the house is as it should be.

A uniformed female police officer comes out to greet us as I am taking Zach from the baby capsule. She introduces herself as Senior Constable Coombs.

'I'm so very sorry about what happened here this morning,' she says. She succeeds in sounding genuine in her concern even though this is simply another job for her. 'Thanks for being so good about letting us in. Families find things like this really hard, but it helps everyone if we can get in and get it all over with.'

'Have you finished yet?' Daniel asks. He is using his professional voice. I know that he is trying hard not to crumble.

'Almost, sir. We just have a few questions. If you both wouldn't mind…?'

'No!' Daniel almost barks. With difficulty he manages to modulate his voice. 'No, we don't mind. Let's get this over with.'

Senior Constable Coombs shows us into our own lounge-room. We make ourselves comfortable, but the scene is all wrong. I could never have imagined that my life, our life, would come to this.

Another officer enters the room and Coombs clears her throat. 'Ummm, I'm sorry, but it's standard procedure in a case like this for us to speak to the parents separately.' She gestures towards Daniel. 'Sir, could I ask you to accompany Constable Stanley? He will speak to you in the kitchen.'

'No,' says Daniel. 'No! I'm not happy about this. Can't you see the state my wife is in? She's absolutely distraught. We've been through so much already today.'

'I understand how difficult this is, sir,' replies Coombs, 'but these are only routine questions that must be asked. There is nothing to be alarmed about. It will all be over in a few moments. Please, sir, if you would accompany Constable Stanley we will be out of here in less than half an hour.'

Daniel hesitates. He looks at me. I nod slightly. It is better, I think, if we get this over with. I will gather my reserves. I will answer their questions. Since when has some half-educated policewoman been any match for someone like me?

As soon as Daniel leaves the room with Zach Coombs begins her questioning. They are what I imagine to be largely standard. What time did Cassie go to bed last night? What did she eat? Did she wake? Was she well? Who was in the habit of putting her to bed? You've watched enough police dramas to know the score.

I really can't remember all the questions. The to-ing and fro-ing is strangely melodic. Some of my fear has begun to abate and I have almost slipped into a trance when Coombs unwittingly drops a bombshell. 'We noticed there was an empty water bottle near Cassie's cot. Can you tell me who put that there and when?'

The water bottle! I had forgotten about it. Why hadn't I got rid of the fucking thing! A cold sliver of fear slices my heart.

I begin to cry, silently at first and then with more vigour as I succeed in working myself up. All the time I am wondering what the right reply might be. I can handle this, I know I can. This policewoman will not get the better of me. There is, after all, no need for anyone to know when the water bottle found its way to Cassie's bedside table.

Before I can speak, however, Coombs continues, 'Do you think perhaps that your husband was woken by Cassie during the night and he left it there for her? Was that something he was in the habit of doing?'

Is this where their thinking is bringing them as well – to Daniel? Do they really believe that men are more likely to murder their children than women? How absurd! After all, what do the men care about domestic life! They are never there. They are too busy conquering the world to have any idea what really goes on between a mother and her children. They are not confronted every day with the dreadful tedium of child-minding. They do not comprehend that personality conflicts can exist between a mother and a very young child, daily creating deep wounds of aggravation. They do not understand the shifts of power within a home that can be seismic in their implication. The obvious direction of Coombs's questioning is so bizarre that I feel laughter may soon replace my tears.

I manage not to laugh, however, and the part of my brain that cares desperately about survival files away the useful piece of information this woman has presented to me. The police are looking for something – and someone – to blame. How easy it would be for me to give it to them. How vulnerable Daniel is in the face of their prejudice. I will remember this. There may be a time when the natural instincts of people such as these will come in handy, very handy.

My thoughts are broken as Daniel and Zach re-enter the room. I manage a smile in their direction and then, wiping my eyes with a tissue, I answer Coombs's question.

'I'm sorry, Constable, it's just that I brought her the water bottle and it was the last time I saw her. When I put her to bed, she asked for water and I brought it to her. It wasn't unusual.' Again I sob wholeheartedly.

Daniel sits on the couch beside me and rubs my back. There is silence as Coombs scribbles in her notebook. Obviously she has no more questions. I just wish that she and her colleague would get the hell out of my house.

'If that is all…?' Daniel has read my thoughts.

'It is, sir,' replies Senior Constable Coombs as she closes her notebook. 'Again, please accept our condolences at this very sad time.'

Coombs and Stanley exit and Daniel, Zach and I are left alone in a Cassie-less house. It is a situation which I have fantasised about for months.

TWELVE

I have learned that, with grief, life is lived in lumps of time. There's not much yesterday and very little tomorrow; there is only a pain-filled *now*. Anything else is too much to cope with.

In the *now* that is our first evening without Cassie, Daniel is dealing with his grief through activity. When I enter Zach's room to collect a clean nappy, I find Daniel dismantling Zach's cot. Tears are dripping off his nose. I wonder how he can see properly.

'What are you up to?' I ask.

'This won't fit through the door unless I take it apart.'

'Yes, but why do you want it to fit through the door?'

'Zach's coming in with us. He'll sleep in our room from now on. I want to be able to keep an eye on him. A better eye than I kept on Cassie.'

In with us! We have a three-bedroom home inhabited by three people and we are all supposed to squeeze into one room? Life without Cassie was meant to be easier. I was supposed to be able to sleep. What the hell does Daniel think he is doing?

'I want to be able to monitor his breathing.' He looks at me. 'I was sure you wouldn't mind. I want to be near him. You don't mind, do you?'

Of course I fucking mind, is what I want to scream. 'Of course not,' is what I say.

That first night without Cassie is strangely lonely. Zach, exhausted by the day, falls asleep early. Daniel and I sit on the couch. Sometimes I hear a noise and go to get up, as if I am being called to attend to Cassie. I realise that it will take some time to become accustomed to the fact that I will never have to respond to her demands again. Despite the fear of the impending autopsy, my soul is light; a heavy burden has been forever removed.

We have the receiver of the baby monitor on a table near the couch. It is turned up to its highest setting. The transmitter is near Zach and we can hear his baby breaths as if through a megaphone. At times there are gaps in his breathing and both Daniel and I stare at the monitor, willing the amplified inhalation to begin again. As it does, each time.

I look at the curtains that cover the floor-to-ceiling windows in the dining room. Cassie used to hide behind them. Giggling, she would clutch the edges with her grubby fingers and wait for me to find her. I imagine that I can make out her form behind the greeny blue material. I half expect her to step from behind the curtains and begin to run, looking back at me and laughing and inviting me to follow her. I will miss her games, I think; perhaps I will even miss the strength of her personality. But it is too late for such nostalgia, I tell myself, far too late.

Will her spirit return to haunt me, I wonder. It is easy to believe that her body has been vanquished, but her spirit was so strong.

Daniel speaks. 'She had so much to offer, so fucking much. Even at her age everybody could see that. It seems incredible that someone with as much life as Cassie had, could just go, like that.' He clicks his fingers. 'It can't be as easy as simply turning out a light. It can't be. It can't be that one minute she's here and another minute she isn't. I can't believe that it would fucking end like this. I thought that one day she would be holding my hand as I lay dying. Never, *never* did I think that we would see her go like this.'

'Oh God, Daniel. I agree.' I focus on how cold Cassie felt when we found her and I am able to cry. 'I can imagine her there at the hospital, cold. I was always so careful to make sure that she was never cold. I want to have her here again, so I can keep her warm.'

I rest my head against his shoulder and for a time we are lost in our thoughts. After a while I speak.

'I'll make us both a hot drink.'

I am in the kitchen for some time. When I come out with two cups of steaming tea, Daniel is sitting on the floor with his back against the dining-room wall. He is crying and in his hand he is holding a small plastic hammer. It was one of Cassie's favourite toys. Daniel must have found it behind the curtain.

He has his head resting on his free hand and his shoulders are shaking with his weeping.

A spasm of pain rockets through me. I hate that I have hurt this man. After all, he is the one who replaced my father; the one in whose eyes I am truly special. I remember the Möbius strip. I look to the box on the mantlepiece where it has been kept ever since we moved into this house. I remember how I felt when Daniel gave me that special gift. For the first time ever I felt as if I belonged to someone, as if someone cared about me and me alone.

I feel what I think may be real guilt. Did I do the right thing in the ill-prepared, little more than instinctive action that I performed last night? Was I right to assume the role of the earth goddess in deciding whether or not someone – my daughter, his daughter – would live or die? For in the process I have exposed Daniel to a lifetime of sorrow. It is the same sorrow that I felt when my father died and I know well its full incarnations. I know its sharp edges and blunt jabs, I know its ability to thrust and parry just when one has the gall to believe that the joust has been won. Mastering grief is an unpleasant game in a world that is already too cruel.

But then, what I have done is not so unusual, I tell myself. For centuries unwanted children have been killed, exposed on hillsides, sacrificed to gods and bricked into the foundations of bridges, forts and castles to guarantee the strength of the edifices. Children have been beaten, made to work in mines, bent over looms and bowed under with hard labour. What I have done is simply to build on an ancient tradition where children had no rights and adults determined whether they would be allowed to live or to die.

These days, it is different. Now, such actions are not publicly condoned; as a result of Cassie's death our lives will be rummaged through and dissected. Secrets will be difficult to keep, motivations will not be understood. If the truth is ever revealed what everybody will fail to understand is that what I have done will be for the best. Daniel himself cannot see it yet, but soon things will be more like they were before. He and I will be able to spend more time together. Zach is an easier baby than Cassie. I will organise a regular babysitter. Daniel and I will be able to go out to dinner, to the movies. Things will be as they were in the past. We will be a couple again, instead of simply a mother and father who share the same sleeping space.

I carry the cups of tea over to where Daniel is sitting and place them against the wall. I bend down and take him in my arms. We rock together a little, just the two of us, locked in a grief-laden embrace.

Later that night I conduct a careful search of the house. I collect every one of Cassie's toys and put them in her room. I close the door. I do not want the entire house littered with physical signs of her presence. I don't want Daniel to be hurt again the way he was tonight. I will protect him as much as I am able. After all, I tell myself, it was for him that I did what I did. I have been strong up until now, and I will continue to be strong, until the results of the autopsy are known, until I know whether or not I am really free.

THIRTEEN

*T*he day after Cassie's death, the visitors descend.

They are my third trial, these visitors, and yet another for which I am woefully unprepared. I have had to deal with the doctors, the police, and now comes perhaps my greatest challenge: maintaining my role as grieving mother in front of others, those who expect nothing less than a display of deepest anguish.

The visitors are like vultures, they pick over my shredded emotions, digging deep with their pointed beaks. They bring offerings in exchange for their feasting, of course. There are the obvious gifts: flowers and food, sometimes full meals. But they also bring their own stories of sorrow. Now I am a magnet for other people's tragedies. I'm not sure who are worse: the people who think that their stories give them the insight to know what I am experiencing or those who are desperate to outdo me with the scale of their misfortune. Until now I had not realised what a pathetically tragic world it is. How do people bear the weight of all this personal sorrow?

In the constant presence of these visitors, the necessity for me to play a role is greater than it has ever been, and I wonder that nobody can see me for what I really am. So intense are the projections of what I have done, I feel as if I have the words 'Child Murderer' stamped on my forehead. I am in a state of ceaseless anxiety about the results of the autopsy, but I am obviously unable to share this with anyone. Instead I am forced to talk about my grief, about how much I miss Cassie, about how precious she was. Because what I am feeling is not grief, but fear, my reactions – to my own eyes at least – frequently seem inappropriate. I am not sure when to cry, when to stay silent, how to hold myself, how to deal with Zach in front of other people. The skills of social interaction and appropriate emotional reaction, which I have had to learn over time – those skills which are obviously second nature to other people – desert me. I am in a situation without precedent in my life, and I am adrift in a sea of other people's emotion.

The worst of the visitors are Daniel's parents. They have driven for eight hours, without a break, in their desire to be near us. While they have the good sense not to stay with us, they visit every day, with their endless tears and their memories. We spend one afternoon going through the baby photos, cooing over how beautiful Cassie was. It is so fucking morbid.

Daniel's mother is a big woman, tall and strong and well covered in flesh. She has five children, all of them still alive. She is used to nurturing, used to providing comfort. She closes her arms around me and I feel subsumed by a maternal power I have never before allowed myself to experience.

'You poor dear,' she moans. 'You poor, poor dear. What a dreadful thing to happen to you. You poor dear.'

For a moment I feel as if I may sink into her grief. It is difficult to fight myself free, but when I do, I want nothing more than to scream at her.

Leave me alone, is what I want to cry out. *Just leave me alone, go home to your perfect family and your balanced life and stop feeding off my family and my emotions.*

Above all, I want to be able to live these days in private, to close the door on all my visitors, to be able to do nothing but crawl into a big bed and sleep until I find out the results of the autopsy. I don't want to be an emotional window display for people and their needs.

On the afternoon of the third day Daniel and his father take a walk. I am left alone in the house with his mother. For the first time I become aware of her scrutiny. Her gaze contains the expected sympathy, but in the unusual silence of the house I have the opportunity to see that there is something more to it. Suspicion perhaps? Is it possible, could this woman, this simple, naïve woman, be suspicious of me?

She has never taken to me, I know. I have never been good enough for her youngest son. Daniel was her baby and I took him from her. He is no longer hers; now he is *my* lover, *my* husband.

I tried with this woman when Daniel and I first met. We used to go shopping together sometimes. I would pick out dresses that suited her, that would have looked better on her than the shapeless bags she prefers. A few times she bought the clothes I suggested, but I never saw her wear them. After a while I gave up.

Daniel and I moved soon after we married, back to my home city. I was relieved; Daniel wanted to spend far too much time with his parents for my liking. Now we only have to put up with them a couple of times a year. Probably Daniel's mother has never really liked me. But she has never looked at me quite this way before.

That afternoon I conduct experiments. I carry Zach to the bedroom to change him; she follows. I prepare some baby food – Zach has recently started solids – she watches my every move. I allow her to bathe him and I see her minutely checking his little body. Does she think I am that stupid, I wonder. Still, I cannot help but feel afraid.

That same afternoon Maureen visits. Somehow she has heard about Cassie's death and, despite the false phone number, has managed to track me down.

As soon as I have shown Maureen through to the lounge-room she puts her arms around my back and pulls me to her. She is a squid whose sucker-encrusted tentacles make escape impossible. I am captured, prey to the black ink of her emotion.

'I'm so sorry, so very sorry,' she slobbers. Fat tears roll down her cheeks. Her mascara has smudged.

I shake my head; there is nothing I can say to this woman. Maureen's grief is surreal in its intensity and its focus; after all, I am the one who has lost a child. I feel disgusted by Maureen's overt display of raw emotion, and I want nothing more than to push this woman away from me. I have experienced too many self-centred exhibitions such as this. I have fucking had enough.

'I lost a baby, you know,' Maureen manages through her tears. 'It was when I was pregnant.

I was only two and a half months, but I can understand what you are going through.'

My body grows rigid in anger at Maureen's confession and I breathe deeply in an attempt to control myself. How can the loss of her unformed foetus be likened to my loss? Compared to me she has no idea what tragedy is; she is a charlatan, an impostor.

'Cassie looked like such a beautiful girl,' says Maureen. 'An adorable child.'

My anger with Maureen, with everyone, pushes me off-guard and for a terrible moment I come close to revealing myself.

'Really!' I say. 'In that case it's obvious that you didn't know her.' All my frustration at what Cassie had already succeeded in taking away from me, all the pent-up anxiety over what the autopsy will reveal, all my anger at the visitors who will not leave us alone, and the fear I have over the suspicions of Daniel's mother come out in that sentence. I am careless.

Maureen looks at me. I see her fat white forehead wrinkle as she tries to work out what I mean.

I am horrified at my indiscretion, and I search desperately for an escape from my loose words.

'What I mean,' I say, 'is that since it's obvious you didn't know her, I appreciate it all the more that you've made the effort to visit today.'

Is it enough? Maureen's brow unfurrows a little, but I am unsure if she has accepted the renegotiation of my original meaning.

I wait, and between the two of us there is an awkward silence. I, who have been so careful to act appropriately over the past few days, may have made a trap for myself. *Not now*, I want to scream, *not now, not here, not in front of this woman.*

Suddenly, I hear footsteps. Daniel and his father have returned from their walk and Daniel has come to see who I am talking to.

I carry out the necessary introductions.

'Daniel, this is Maureen, we used to go to school together. Maureen, Daniel, my husband.'

Daniel and Maureen shake hands. Her podgy one inside his.

'Yes, I remember.' Daniel is nodding, his smile warm and sincere. 'That day in the park; we didn't have the chance to be introduced. It's lovely to meet you.'

'And you.' Maureen is nodding and smiling also. Smiling does not suit her; it emphasises the awful lines at the corners of her eyes. 'But I'm sorry, the circumstances are so sad. I can remember Cassie that day in the park. I remember her running. She was so alive. What an awful thing to happen to her, to you all.'

'Yes,' says Daniel – he is struggling to keep his composure – 'I wouldn't wish this grief on anyone, but it's good that you've come. We've been overwhelmed by the visitors we've had. Even people who didn't know Cassie have come.'

'Like me,' says Maureen. 'I've already been thanked for that.'

She has chosen to let my comment pass! I gulp, a turtle coming up for air. I had not realised that I'd been holding my breath.

As I escape the room on the pretext of making some tea I can hear Daniel repeating to Maureen, 'It's so good that you've come.'

I am shaking at the thought of what I have almost revealed.

FOURTEEN

That night I sleep badly. I swim in the world of the dead. It is a world where my daughter reaches out to me endlessly in a silent scream, where floating, faceless eyes watch my every move, my every reaction, where strong arms hold me hard. In my dream I am fighting for my freedom, for my life, for my right to be what I need to be. In my dream fingers proclaiming guilt point at me.

Afterwards, I cannot sleep because I cannot allow those images to claim me.

I rise and slip into my dressing-gown. I make myself a cup of tea. There are too many hours between now and dawn. Too many hours for me to fill, and I cannot – will not – return to my tortured sleep.

Holding my cup, I wander from room to room. The dining room is unswept and empty, the lounge cold and dark with its curtains drawn. I walk down the hall to Zach's room. A mobile still hangs from the ceiling. Decorations remain on the walls, but the room looks purposeless with the cot and occupant removed.

I move further down the corridor. I cannot help myself. The door to Cassie's room is closed. It has remained closed over the last few days. Daniel will allow no one in there. One day he will have to confront its emptiness, but not yet.

I open the door; the hinges squeak. I had been meaning to oil them before Cassie died. My heart pounds. I am almost afraid to enter this room that has become a shrine to our daughter. A sliver of moonlight through the curtains shows me the way across the room to the night-light. I flick it on. Its shade is decorated with fairies and it casts a pink glow over the room. I lean over Cassie's cot, its quilt covered in fairy fabric. I trace my finger over a fairy wing. We had given Cassie pink fairy wings for her first birthday. They were covered in glitter. She had worn them the day before she died. I am still sweeping glitter from the kitchen floor.

I did love my daughter, I think defiantly, *I did love her*. But of course I had not loved her enough. I had not loved her enough to allow her to take everything that was mine, and I certainly had not loved her enough to allow her death to ruin me. And now I am afraid. I am afraid that what I have done may not be sufficient to earn me the freedom I need.

I think about Doctor Hadid and Senior Constable Coombs. I think about their suspicions and prejudices. I think about things that might have happened. I think about alternatives and possibilities.

If I close my eyes I can hear Cassie calling out the night she died. I can hear both Daniel and myself turning over in our sleep, neither of us wanting to be the one who will have to respond to her. But then I can feel the mattress lift a little as Daniel swings his legs to the floor and rises from the bed. I hear the light switch being turned on in the kitchen. I hear the sound of Daniel removing a water bottle from the cupboard, the sound of it being filled with water and the top being screwed on; I hear the sound of the kitchen light being turned off, and perhaps, if I listen carefully enough, I can hear Daniel's footsteps on the carpet as he tiptoes past our room, past Zach's room and down to Cassie's. I can hear the small squeak as her door is pushed open, and the sound of Cassie grumbling as she reaches for the bottle and lifts it to her mouth. And then, if I were to be honest, I would have to admit that perhaps I dozed and heard nothing more...well, nothing more until the small squeak as Cassie's door was swung closed and my husband returned to the bed, now cold on his side.

These are the things I might be able to remember if I am pushed, if I am threatened. And if pushed more I might remember the strain Daniel had been under at work and how it impacted on his patience and ability to deal with the children; how he had been complaining that the children were still waking us at night. I might be able to recall some incidents when he had been unreasonably angry, with us all, but with Cassie in particular. I might remember all these things and many more. It's amazing what one is capable of remembering when placed under sufficient pressure.

I think that I will write down what I have remembered. It is important that things are written down.
People believe what they see on paper. I will feel
better after I have done that, safer. I will be able to
return to bed; I may even be able to sleep.

FIFTEEN

On the morning of the fifth day the phone rings. Daniel answers it. I hover in the background, trying to work out to whom he is speaking. It is Doctor Hadid. My heart hammers. I strain to overhear what Daniel is saying, but the conversation is over almost as soon as it has begun.

I am standing virtually on top of Daniel as he puts down the receiver.

'What did he want?' My desperate excitement has made me breathless. 'What did he say? What news does he have?'

Daniel puts out his hand and grabs my arm as if to steady me, or maybe it is himself he is concerned about.

'They have the report.'

'The autopsy report! What does it say? Have they found out what happened?'

'Doctor Hadid hasn't told me yet. We both agreed that it was better for him to explain things face to face. I made a time for us to go down to the hospital this afternoon.'

This afternoon! I have waited four days to discover what my future will be. I don't know if I can wait any longer. I feel as if I might scream.

'He says it should only take half an hour or so.'

That little, I think.

'Did he give you any idea?' I ask.

Daniel shakes his head. 'No, and I didn't ask. I thought it would be easier if we were there together. Maybe he can explain things to us that we would have trouble understanding otherwise.'

Yes, that is true, I think, especially if they have found out what really killed Cassie. There are not many people who could understand it, who could understand the forces that drove me to kill my daughter. Even if people had been privy to my deepest, driving emotions they would have trouble understanding it.

Perhaps there are some things which are not meant to be understood, merely accepted.

By the time we arrive at the front desk of the hospital my nerves are stretched tight. There is a slight humming in my ears, the sound of a distant jet engine or a persistent fly. I am a tuning fork resonating at an extreme pitch.

Doctor Hadid is here to greet us. He is still in his white coat. This time, however, we are shown into his office. It is extremely small and messy. Piles of papers ring the floor. The shelves are full of books; some lie horizontally over others. I balance Zach on my lap. There is no space for him anywhere else. The room smells of old dust and half-drunk coffee. It is so stuffy I can barely breathe.

The doctor, the good doctor on whom my future rests, picks up a folder and clears his throat. 'Well, as you know, I received the autopsy report this morning and I considered it best for us to talk through it together.'

I am squeezing Zach's arms so tightly that he squirms in protest. *Surely*, I am thinking, *it must be okay, they couldn't have found anything wrong or we wouldn't be sitting here like this.* Or is this a set-up? Will armed police leap from behind the filing cabinets as soon as Doctor Hadid has revealed the findings of the report? I am not sane at the moment.

'Please,' says Daniel, 'we are both anxious to know what the report has found. We are both desperate to know what happened to Cassie.'

I nod; incapable of speech.

'Well,' says Doctor Hadid, 'I'm afraid that the findings will come as somewhat of a disappointment in that regard. The official cause of death has been given as undetermined.'

'Undetermined,' Daniel and I sing in unison. I am genuinely surprised. I had hoped Cassie's death would be put down to SIDS; I had not expected to encounter this nebulous 'undetermined' finding. I am suspicious it could morph into something sinister, something that might turn around and bite me. I am not sure whether I can relax yet.

Doctor Hadid nods. 'Yes, I am afraid that on the face of it a finding like this doesn't seem to tell us a lot, but from a medical point of view it *is* quite informative. It tells us that Cassie didn't die from an unexpected asthma attack; that she didn't die as a result of a severe allergic reaction to something; that she wasn't poisoned, or interfered with in any way...as far as we can tell. A finding of death from undetermined causes eliminates most things, but unfortunately for me as a doctor and for you, as Cassie's parents, it doesn't tell us what *did* cause her death.'

Daniel nods, 'That's right, it doesn't.'

I manage to speak. 'But what about SIDS? I thought that if a young child like Cassie died unexpectedly then it was usually due to SIDS.'

'Well,' says Doctor Hadid. 'The generally recognised definition of SIDS is of a sudden, unexplained death occurring in an infant under the age of twelve months. That doesn't mean, of course, that children of Cassie's age don't die suddenly and inexplicably. It's just that their deaths are not normally recorded as SIDS, but rather as death due to undetermined or unexplained causes.' Doctor Hadid spreads his hands in a gesture of futility. 'Not that the distinction is important for you, of course. Unfortunately the finding simply means what it says; we just don't know what Cassie died from.'

Daniel leans forward, his elbows on Doctor Hadid's desk. 'So, Doctor, does that mean that we have to be extra careful with Zach? Is it possible that he could be more susceptible to something like this happening?'

'Actually no,' replies Doctor Hadid. 'Most large studies on infants and children who have died suddenly and inexplicably, indicate no increase of unexplained death in subsequent siblings. In fact, the prevailing wisdom now is that if more than one child in a family dies from what appears to be undetermined causes, then the real cause of death is more likely to be something else.'

'Such as?' asks Daniel.

'Such as homicide, usually by one of the parents.'

I feel Daniel shudder beside me. I begin to sob. Is this a warning? I think not, but there is not very much about which I can be sure right now.

Doctor Hadid's warm, brown eyes meet mine. 'I understand that the very notion is abhorrent to most people, but such events do occur and, unfortunately, unless there are obvious signs of trauma, they can be very difficult to pick up in young children.' He turns his attention back to Daniel. 'So, to answer your question, sir, I can say with near certainty that your son will not die from sudden, unexplained causes. Zach is as likely as any of us to live to one hundred and one.'

There is silence as Daniel and I allow that to sink in.

Finally, Daniel speaks. 'Well, I'm pleased that we don't need to have any particular worry for Zach. We've both been very concerned about him. But, Doctor, what I wanted, what we both need, I think, is some explanation for Cassie's death. Death from undetermined causes tells us nothing. We're left with no answers, no reason, no way in which we can understand this dreadful tragedy.'

Doctor Hadid nods and clears his throat again. He looks uncomfortable. 'I understand. I really wish I could tell you more. I am never happy with a finding such as this. For me, it asks more questions than it answers.' He looks at each of us in turn. His eyes are gentle, but probing. They are eyes which are not satisfied by unanswered questions. 'Unfortunately, however,' Doctor Hadid continues, 'the finding means what it says. We have no way of telling what Cassie died from. Sometimes things like this happen, even to the healthiest of infants and children. It is inexplicable, it is terrible, but I'm afraid that I can tell you no more.'

I begin to cry again. I have been doing it a lot lately. I am becoming really rather good at it, but this time neither of the two men in the room could guess the real cause of my tears. I am crying with relief.

Doctor Hadid picks up a piece of paper from his desk.

'Here are the contact details of the local parents' bereavement support group. The hospital also has a counsellor on staff; I have written her name and contact details on the bottom of the paper. Please remember, these people are here for you. Sometimes the strain of a loss such as this can manifest itself in unexpected ways. I urge you not to feel that you must deal with things alone.'

It is Daniel's and my turn to nod. We agree that we will probably take up the offer of the counsellor. With that, our interview is at an end and we are free to leave this stifling room, free to face the sun, free to farewell our daughter and to continue with the rest of our lives. I'm not stupid; I realise, of course, that Doctor Hadid may be suspicious, but I have outplayed better people than him in my life. He may have his suspicions, but I am free, free and Cassie-less. I am giddy with the wonder of it all.

SIXTEEN

We decide to cremate our precious child. Neither Daniel nor I can bear the thought of her in the cold dark ground. Cassie will remain in an urn on a special shelf in the living room. She will never be cold. She will always be with us, where I can see her, where she will be within my ultimate control.

The ceremony is held on a bright early spring day; the world has taken on crystal hues. The unusual light makes everything seem brittle, hard but somehow unstable. The trees on the hill overlooking the crematorium appear to be etched against the sky. There is a very slight breeze blowing. A lightness fills my body and soul. I am so ridiculously free and unencumbered that I feel I may float into the sparse air.

As we approach the stone chapel, the gravel pathway crunches beneath our feet. I recall a medieval carving I once saw where crusaders marched their way over the bones of hundreds of children. There are many sacrifices that have to be made in the fight for true freedom, the carving was saying. My personal experience has now told me how true that is.

I clutch Daniel's arm with my left hand and hold Zach with my right. Daniel and I are dressed in black. Zach is in dark blue. We look appropriately dignified, a family in deep mourning. As, of course, we are. Except for Zach who still finds the world a joke, sister or no sister. He has handfuls of my hair and is pulling with all the power of his six-kilogram body.

My dress is new, bought especially for the occasion. It is fitted and extremely flattering. My skin is pale from winter and the stress of the past week. I have added chestnut highlights to my hair. It glows in the mid-morning sunlight. I know how good I look.

It seems as if hundreds of people have chosen to attend the service. I make eye contact with a few of them; I nod and smile and murmur thank yous to those who have come out today to witness our deepest sorrow. I am determined to play well the tragic figure, the strong but suffering mother. After all, I know the importance of rituals such as this in shaping people's perceptions.

We enter the chapel and make our way to the front row of seats, just behind the coffin. Daniel chose it. It is very small, and pink. Cassie would have approved. I chose the dress she is wearing. It is green, her best one. It has been worn only once before. I remember the occasion well. It was the birthday party of a little friend. Cassie had danced in the dress, its full skirt flaring out as she had spun around. Daniel said that she looked like a fairy princess. He loved her in that dress. He cried when I told him it was the one I picked for her to wear today.

Once Daniel, Zach and I have settled ourselves in the chapel others follow. Sounds and smells wash into the enclosed space. There is coughing and clearing of throats, an occasional blown nose. I hear someone whisper my name. Perfumes and aftershaves clash in their fight for dominance. In my imagination the individual mourners meld together, as if a great grey beast with many tentacles lies at my back. Its presence is almost overpowering.

A thickset man stands up and approaches the microphone. He is the chaplain we have chosen. He has an extremely melodious voice. He talks about Cassie as if he knew her. But, of course, he didn't. He didn't know her will; he didn't know her determination; he didn't know what she was capable of.

When it is time I hand Zach to Daniel and make my way to the microphone. Now the quiet rustling, which had accompanied even the chaplain's words, is subdued. People lean forward to better hear what I have to say. I know they must be intrigued. It is unusual for a mother to speak at the funeral of her infant daughter. There is awe that I am standing here, and wonder at what I will say. I had forgotten how satisfying it is to have an audience, a collection of people hanging off my every word. I will enjoy this. I clear my throat.

'Cassie was with us for such a painfully short time, but it was a time which changed the lives of our family and indeed the lives of all who had the privilege of knowing her. Cassie impressed everyone with her vigour and spirit: she was a flame in a room of darkness; a breath of fresh air on a still day; a ray of sunshine breaking the gloom. Her body and her awesome will might no longer be with us, but her memory and the joy which she brought to us all during her short life always will be.'

Daniel's mother, that most annoying of women, sobs so violently that she drowns out my words. I lean closer to the microphone, raise my voice and continue. 'I have a poem which I would like to share with you. It's called "The Water-Lily" and it was written by Henry Lawson in 1890.

'A lonely young wife
In her dreaming discerns
A lily-decked pool
With a border of ferns,
And a beautiful child,
With butterfly wings,
Trips down to the edge of the water and sings:
"Come, mamma! come!
Quick! follow me–
Step out on the leaves of the water-lily!"

And the lonely young wife,
Her heart beating wild,

Cries, "Wait till I come,
Till I reach you, my child!"
But the beautiful child
With butterfly wings
Steps out on the leaves of the lily and sings:
"Come, mamma! come!
Quick! follow me!
And step on the leaves of the water-lily!"

And the wife in her dreaming
Steps out on the stream,
But the lily leaves sink
And she wakes from her dream.
Ah, the waking is sad,
For the tears that it brings,
And she knows 'tis her dead baby's spirit that sings:
"Come, mamma! come!
Quick! follow me!
Step out on the leaves of the water-lily!"'

By the time I have finished the poem the chapel is filled with the sound of weeping. I have not lost the ability to influence people with my oratory. A cold surge of power tears through me. I am overcome with emotion. I press my handkerchief to my eyes.

It is all I can do to make my way back to my seat and reclaim Zach.

Now it is Daniel's turn to take the floor. He speaks of his joy in having known Cassie and how he refuses to mourn too much because, no matter how short a time she was with us, it was a privilege to have been her parents. I sob uncontrollably. Someone puts an arm around me and someone else takes Zach away.

I am not the only one crying. People cry for us, they cry for Cassie, but generally they cry for themselves. I know this most of all: people are fundamentally selfish. It is not only for the soul of Cassie that people cry. It is for the soul of others who have died and others who may die. There are many present who will hug their loved ones a bit harder this evening. The grief of our family has simply been a catalyst for theirs.

The service has ended and once more we step into the brittle outside world. Streams of people come up to offer me their condolences; the whispered messages are endless, repetitive, unimaginative. Someone has taken Zach from me again and I have no shield against the barrage of sorrow everyone directs towards me. I shake hands, kiss cheeks, blink back tears. It is all terribly difficult. Daniel and I are separated for a time and I panic. We have shared our sorrow for the past week. I don't know if I can do it without him. I feel as if my grief-mask may crack.

A bit longer, I tell myself, *just a bit longer; you are nearly there. The river has almost been forded; you are nearly at the other side.*

With relief I see a blond head above the crowd. It is Daniel. As I am pushing people out of the way to reach him, someone calls my name and I hesitate for a second. It is Maureen. Hasn't she intruded on our grief enough? At least this time I am prepared for her. As she lurches towards me I step back so that she is unable to hug me.

Maureen trawls through her handbag until she finds a tissue. 'That was a beautiful ceremony,' she sniffles. 'And your speech, I don't know how you had the strength to do it.'

'Thank you,' I say, 'it wasn't easy.' I wave madly at Daniel. Thankfully he sees me and makes his way over.

'Maureen,' he says, 'it's so nice to see you again. I'm so glad you could come today. It's wonderful to have your support.'

'Yes, isn't it,' I nod. My tone is dismissive and at the same time I begin to move away from Maureen, towards the car. I expect Daniel to follow, but, I see to my horror that his eyes have filled with tears, his shoulders have collapsed forward as if he must protect his heart. He has not cried all day and I am not prepared for his tears now. I pause for a moment and a moment is all it takes for Maureen to step into my gap. She has her tissue, which she is pressing into his hand, she has one arm around him pulling him to her, she has her head on his shoulder next to his head, she is whispering something to him. I cannot hear, I cannot hear what she is saying. Her mouth is so close to his ear that I think perhaps he would be able to feel the small drops of water vapour that are expelled as she speaks. Daniel leans into her. I imagine her soft, large breasts pressed against his chest. I imagine their hearts beating in unison, left heart to right breast, right breast to left heart. I am appalled at the liberties she is taking; I am aghast that Daniel is allowing himself to become so close to another woman in my presence. I am standing by myself in the crowd of people drifting around me. Only Maureen and Daniel are anchored, only Maureen and Daniel are comforted. I am alone.

I am so dreadfully alone. They are making a spectacle of themselves; they are making a spectacle of me!

I picture myself stepping between them, pushing them apart. It would be like opening the jaws of an oyster shell. I would expose its grey glutinous heart. I would spear it with a stick. I would expose it to the sun, to wither and die slowly. I would take pleasure in my actions.

And then they, Maureen and Daniel, step apart. Together they look at me and I wonder what it is that they see. I wonder.

The crowd has thinned enough for us to make our way to the car. There will be some family at a small wake, but not too many people. I reclaim Zach and he seems to wink at me. It is a long slow wink that obscures one grey eye – an eye that is not at all like mine.

SEVENTEEN

My mother has decided to grace Cassie's wake with her presence. She has turned up for the occasions in my life she has deemed suitably important – my birth, the death of my father, my marriage, the days after the birth of my children. At other times she has been mercifully absent: sometimes metaphorically, sometimes literally.

My mother insisted on organising the catering for the wake and so we have food that is completely unsuited to mourning. There is too much finger food, light and tangy with no depth of taste or sustenance. I had never considered it before, but as I bite into a caviar-laden rice biscuit, I realise that some foods are appropriate to grief: warm potato chips, chicken soup which has simmered for hours, bread heavily smeared with butter. But my mother wouldn't understand the importance of that kind of food; she has been starving herself for the whole of her adult life.

Zach is with my mother now. She is whispering into his ear. Her hair is ridiculously spiky and red, her skirt too short, her skinny knees too knobbly. She resembles an expensively dressed street urchin – one of her guises; it has fooled many intelligent people before now. Zach is cooing at her. The secret is obviously a good one. I will never be privy to it, of course. My mother has never included me among her initiates.

Daniel moves over to them and tickles Zach's feet. He has been doing the rounds. 'Thank you for coming,' he has murmured over and over again. I can see that fatigue and grief have reduced him to a robot. 'Thank you for coming, thank you for coming, thank you for coming.' I can imagine him doing it in a Dalek-type voice. Now Zach giggles in delight at Daniel's attention and my mother joins in. Her ridiculously white false teeth flash at Daniel. I am almost nauseated to see that he smiles back.

I have been drinking all afternoon; Mother has provided sherry for our guests. At least she had the sense to refrain from the champagne that she normally prefers. I will ask Daniel to give Zach a bottle tonight instead of me feeding him. I don't want to give the boy alcohol poisoning. Suddenly the idea of that seems horribly funny. I realise that I am drunk.

One of my long-lost cousins appears in front of me, blocking my view of the happy threesome.

'How're you going?' He speaks with a slight drawl. I think he is a carpenter.

'I'm okay,' I reply. I have plumbed the depths of grief far too often today to offer him anything more than this.

'She's a funny old bird.'

'Who?' I genuinely have no idea whom he is talking about.

'Your mum.'

'Oh yes, her.'

'Haven't seen her in a while.'

Lucky you, I think. Aloud I say, 'Me neither.'

'She still looks good.'

'Yes.' *If you like chicken legs.*

'Remember how she chased us when we were kids, that time we pinched her undies off the line? Rob put them on, remember; they were purple.'

'Lilac,' I correct him. I do remember the time. My mother was terribly embarrassed, as she should have been. The pants were brief and the bra padded. I thought them completely unsuitable for a woman her age, although at the time she was not much older than I am now.

My cousin looks over at my mother. 'I think I had a thing for her when I was young. She was kind of exotic, you know.'

I nearly choke. The masturbatory longing of my cousin for my mother is not something I feel like discussing now.

My cousin examines me searchingly. He was the first person with whom I shared a cigarette. He knows me pretty well, even though we haven't seen each other for a while. After all, it is only at times like this that I allow my family to force themselves upon me.

'You look like her,' he says.

I purse my lips as if I have tasted acid.

'You've never liked her, have you?' he continues.

I don't bother to respond to this statement of genius. She, my mother, is looking over at us. I raise my glass in a half salute. The last thing I want to do is encourage her to come over.

My cousin is still talking. 'She's not so bad, you know. She helped me a lot with my schoolwork after Mum died and she did a lot of cooking for us. Do you remember?'

No, I certainly don't remember that. I remember my cousin living next door and I remember his mother, my aunt, my mother's sister, dying. She was knocked down by a bus and died in hospital a few days later. My cousin was almost fifteen. I was thirteen. All I can remember from that year is my mother being terribly absent, absent at a time when I needed her, at a time when we might have been able to forge the friendship, the mutual regard, which has always eluded us. I have never forgiven her for that.

And now I am talking with my mother. She has one hand above my elbow and she is squeezing. She surveys the room. It is almost empty. Despite the lack of comfort in her food, most of it has been consumed. She is pleased by this. She has provided; I am in her debt.

'I don't usually go to funerals,' she confides. It is spoken breezily, as if she has just proclaimed that she doesn't 'do lunch', or can't wear yellow.

'No,' I reply. I also cannot imagine her at funerals – not enough colour, too many tears.

'Your father's death ruined them for me.' Another dreadful thing which my father has done to her. My mother blames, has always blamed, my father for as much as she can. She blames him for the estrangement with her family, for her wrinkles, for the fact that she and I do not get on.

But I also have been thinking of my father today. He died when I was eleven, nearly twelve. Our family has been unlucky with accidents. My father had woken in the night and gone into the kitchen to get a glass of water. It was unusual for him to do this; it was usually Mother who had problems sleeping. What was also unusual that night was that, somehow, a bottle of oil had leaked over the floor. He slipped and hit his head against my mother's prized granite benchtop. My mother found him the next morning. Later she told me that it looked as if he had bled oil all over the floor. There was no actual blood –

the wound itself was very small, just enough to have killed him. A freak accident, the police called it.

The day after his funeral my periods began for the first time. I was lying with my feet up on the couch, watching television. My mother entered the room…perhaps 'waltzed' is the correct word. It was the day after my father's funeral and she began to talk to me about clothes, fucking clothes. I could barely see the television, my eyes were so swollen from crying, and she wanted to discuss fashion. She knew we would get some insurance money as a result of my father's death and she was planning how to spend it.

'I can buy a new summer wardrobe. You'll need some new things too, darling. Pink's in this year, I see. You look good in pink; everybody looks good in pink. We can paint the house. Tom and I have been wanting to do that for years. Poor dear Tom! We can only do these things now that he's gone.' From the depths of her bosom she withdrew a handkerchief, part of the previous day's funeral attire. It was black with a dainty lace border, also black – my mother always was the queen of accessorising. She dabbed daintily at her eyes with it.

'Poor Tom. Your poor daddy.'

It was too much for me.

'It's your fault!' I screamed at her. 'You've taken him away from me. You should be happy. *He* shouldn't have died. It's your fault he died.'

My mother looked at me. I couldn't tell what was going on behind those black-rimmed eyes.

'You never loved him properly, and you hated it that we got on so well together.' I was almost sobbing now; my fists were clenched. Never had I hated anyone as much as I hated my mother then.

My mother began to shake slightly. I could see that she was controlling her own temper with difficulty. I didn't care. I was surfing on pure emotion, a bit more only added to the surge.

She exhaled heavily; her breath was sour and old. It clashed with her sweet, awful, chemist-brand perfume. I thought I might throw up.

She leaned over as if to give me a hug, but I pushed her away and swung my legs off the couch so I was sitting upright. I felt as if her perfume would suffocate me.

'Don't touch me you bitch,' I yelled. She recoiled at the use of that word. I had never sworn in front of her before, but I was angry.

'Daddy told me what you said. Two days before he died. He told me that you thought I was spoilt; that you said he was going to ruin me by giving in to me too much. I know that you always hated it that he treated me as if I was special. And now you're happy, happy that he died. YOU BITCH.'

My mother slapped me on the face.

In my imagination the sound of that slap echoed around the room. It has certainly echoed through both our lives.

For a moment neither of us moved. I could feel where each of my mother's fingers had connected with my face. I knew that I would never forgive her. My mother sat firm and rigid as the adrenaline of her anger washed through her. And then, she slumped.

'You're tired,' she said. 'Having your period for the first time is difficult. I'll forget what you just said to me, and I think you should too. I'll tell you what I hope. I hope that you and I can be friends. I hope that if anything positive comes out of your father's death, it is that we become friends.'

As usual my mother was too optimistic. She and I never did become friends.

The night after the fight with my mother, I crept to my father's wardrobe and took out one of his shirts, the one that smelled most strongly of him. That night, and for many after, I slept with it beside me. When it lost the smell of my father I ironed it. The heat brought out the aroma of his sweat and deodorant. I have always been very olfactory.

Cassie's wake is finished. Finally Daniel and I are able to crawl into bed. We are exhausted. He has deep purple circles under his eyes.

'Thank God that's over,' he says.

Perhaps he is thinking what I am. Now we can get on with our lives.

I roll over towards him. As usual he is naked. He is smooth-skinned and slightly downy, like a young deer. I begin to play with his nipples, they harden under my fingers and suddenly I am so hungry for him that my mouth goes dry. I want this man. I want him like I wanted a pink bicycle when I was a child, like I wanted my mother to tell me how much she loved me, like I wanted that blue dress that hung in Casey's window. He is the amalgam of all my yearnings.

I lick his purple eyes. They are salty with dried tears. His lashes gum together with my saliva and I separate them with my fingertips, gentle, oh so gentle. He used to give me butterfly kisses when we first met. He would be so close that I could feel the wet feather of his breath.

Daniel is hard now, but his eyes are still closed. I hold him first with my hands and then with my lips. I feel the hard beneath the soft. It is everything I have always loved about him; he is steel beneath fairy floss, but it was always the strength I needed.

He joins my movements. I know that he needs me more than ever and now his body knows it also. I have always been good at this game, good at opening the trap of flesh that makes men want more and more. For a while it has been forgotten. But I know that I will reclaim the power that is mine.

Later Daniel cries as he lies beside me.

'Poor baby,' I whisper. 'Poor baby.'

EIGHTEEN

*I*n the weeks following the funeral we learn to live without our eldest child. Daniel has started tentatively back at work. Often he lasts for only half a day. When he returns home he slumps in an armchair. He doesn't do anything, just slumps. For long periods of time he barely speaks, or eats, or sleeps. Grief has made him inert. He looks pitiful, as if he has shrunk. His cheeks are sucked in; he is stooped; he shaves badly or not at all.

I caution myself to be patient with this lassitude of Daniel's. I have read about the stages of grief; I know that they take time to live through. But I want so desperately for Daniel to be happy again, as I am. I want so desperately for us to be able to move on with our lives that sometimes I make mistakes; sometimes I stumble; sometimes I reveal the depth of my impatience.

One Friday night I prepare a special dinner. I light candles. I burn aromatic oils. I greet Daniel at the door with a kiss. Tonight I am determined that we will sit across the table from each other and talk about something other than Cassie. Tonight I want to shake Daniel out of his lethargy and guilt. I want him to see things as I do, to recognise that this event, terrible as it may have been, opens up all sorts of possibilities for us. I want to show him that this is not the end, that it is in fact a beginning of sorts, a time to make up for the mistakes of the past eighteen months or so, a time when we can pull together as a couple again. Tonight I am impatient.

Dinner is a success. Daniel appreciates my effort. He comments on each course. It looks as if the night will be everything I hoped.

After a while we move to the couch. I have bought Daniel's favourite dessert wine; we sip it while nibbling on a cheese platter.

I rest one hand on Daniel's thigh.

'I have a surprise,' I announce.

'Another one?' Daniel is almost laughing. I can tell that tonight has done him good. 'What is it?'

'I've hired a babysitter for tomorrow night. I thought that you and I could go out, have dinner or see a movie. We haven't done that in so long. We can have Zach asleep before she comes. He won't even know that we've gone.'

'No!' Daniel's reply is instant.

'No?' I am not sure if I have heard correctly.

'No. I won't leave Zach in the care of anyone outside the family. First of all he's too young, and after what happened to Cassie, I don't trust anyone else to take care of him.'

'But you heard what Doctor Hadid said,' I reply. 'There is virtually no chance that Zach will die unexpectedly. Nothing will happen to him whether we are here with him or not.'

Daniel is shaking his head. 'No, I don't want to do it. I *can't* do it. I think about Cassie all the time. I feel there must have been something we could have done or shouldn't have done that might have saved her.'

For fuck's sake! I feel as if I will scream. *When are you going to fucking move on? When are we going to be able to get on with our fucking lives without sitting around playing funeral dirges and tiptoeing around the shrine of guilt that our daughter's memory has become?*

Outwardly I say, 'I understand, Daniel. But we have to think about moving on, getting on with our lives, filling our lives.'

'Don't you feel that?' Daniel continues. He has not heard anything I have said. He has me captured in the intensity of his gaze, and like a transfixed animal I am forced to reply to his original statement.

I sigh. 'Daniel, I don't know. Maybe. Maybe there was something we could have done. That was what we hoped the autopsy would tell us, I suppose. But we'll never know.'

'I just can't help thinking... If she'd eaten lamb instead of beef that night; if she'd had a different quilt cover; if she'd worn different pyjamas – would any of it have made a difference? If we'd kept the baby monitor in her room; if she'd been sleeping in the same room as Zach – would *that* have made a difference?' His voice is raised. 'If the room was cleaner; if the window was open; if she hadn't had pneumonia a few weeks earlier – would any of these things have made a difference?' He is shouting now. He is angry and grief-stricken and confused all at once. He is shaking his fist at fate, demanding answers from the gods, insisting that he *know*. His profile is upraised, his skin tight, his eyes shine with near madness. He is magnificent.

And then he collapses. His head drops forward; his shoulders slump. He is crying great sobs of anger and denial. I put both my arms around him and hold him close to me. It will not be enough, I know, but it is required that I at least make an attempt to comfort him.

'I just wish I knew,' he keens. I am reminded of women in war-torn countries whom I have heard on the television news crying for their dead sons. Their lament is as old as the world. 'I just wish I knew.'

Suddenly Daniel's head snaps up, looking at me, eyes so close to mine. 'Did you hear anything that night?' he demands. I am unprepared for this near accusation. My head jerks back as if to protect myself from his words but as I see the tears continue to well in his eyes I realise that all he wants is the reassurance that I couldn't have done anything; that neither of us is responsible for Cassie's death.

'Nothing,' I whisper. 'This has tortured me too, Daniel. Don't think I haven't gone through all this. I wonder if she made any noise before she stopped breathing, and perhaps if I'd been able to hear it, I might have been able to change things... But you know what, Daniel? I've come to the conclusion that there is absolutely nothing either of us could have done. Cassie's death was as inevitable as her birth; it was woven into a pattern of fate that nothing and nobody could have prevented.'

Daniel is looking intently at me. For an uneasy moment I wonder if he has seen through my carefully chosen words.

Finally he says, 'You've always been a fatalist, haven't you? I wish I could share your easy acceptance that some things are preordained.'

'Oh Daniel, all I'm trying to say is that you must stop torturing yourself about this. There was *nothing* we could have done to have prevented it.'

Daniel rests his head against my shoulder. I run my fingers through his hair. I am afraid that he will begin to cry, but his breathing remains regular. Maybe, I dare hope, maybe if I can make Daniel see some of the opportunities which Cassie's death has brought, then maybe this will be a turning point in his grieving. Maybe, just maybe, I will be able to reclaim my husband.

'Have you thought,' I begin, 'of what we can do with Cassie's room? I was thinking we could turn it into a study. I've got a nice paint colour picked out...'

I feel Daniel stiffen. He sits upright and for a few moments he stares at me. Then he rises from the couch and puts on his shoes. The door is slammed hard behind him.

NINETEEN

*N*early six weeks after Cassie's funeral I decide the time is right to return to my mothers' group.

The host for the get-together today is May. She is the oldest member of the group. She has one child, a boy, James. He was born after several attempts at IVF, and May dotes on him. He is spoilt rotten and very, very naughty. Despite her son, everyone likes May and everyone enjoys going to her house. She has old-fashioned armchairs and a coffee table made for putting one's feet up on. Her garden is semi-wild and the older toddlers disappear into it, emerging only when it is time to go home. May is the wise woman of the group. If anyone has a problem, she knows about it; if anyone needs help, she offers it. I will feel comfortable at May's.

The get-together goes something like this.

Silence as Zach and I enter the room and then, too quickly, renewed conversation. May comes over and hugs me. I've never been hugged by so many people as I have over the weeks since Cassie's death. I have always protected my personal space; I don't like people to touch me too often or with familiarity. No one rubbed my stomach when I was pregnant. Today, however, leaning awkwardly over Zach, who is on the floor at my feet, I am forced to hug May back. Our cheeks connect. May is wearing sandal-wood perfume. It reminds me of a necklace I bought in Asia. It was carved from sandalwood and for years its fragrance scented my jewellery box.

Thankfully May doesn't say anything. Should I pull away? I never know when to end these things. I think that May is waiting for me to release her and so we hug until Zach screams for my attention.

I pick him up and gradually the other mothers come over to pay their respects at the altar of great sorrow.

'If there's anything I can do.'

'Call any time.'

'I'll be here if you ever need me.'

They are uttering platitudes. We all know it.

Only Rachael does not come over to me. She is sitting on the couch and I try to catch her eye so that she can offer at least a nod in recognition of my situation. But no, she will not give me even that.

After a time I make my way over to her.

'I suppose you heard of my loss?' I say.

Rachael nods, lowers her eyes and sips her tea. 'Yes, it must have been terrible for you.'

How right she is. *Yes, it was terrible for me.* No one else has seemed to understand this. Losing a child is not only sorrowful, it is also difficult and inconvenient. One is on constant public display. One has to be solicitous of other people and their emotions. There are so many things to organise, so many personas to play.

But then Rachael adds, 'It must have been terrible for you because I know how concerned you were for Cassie's well-being, always.' She looks up at me and will not look away.

I, in turn, regard this woman, and suddenly I think, *She understands me, she understands me as nobody before ever has.* For a moment I have a terrible urge; an urge to open myself to her. Never before have I felt the pressing desire to share my innermost thoughts. I almost shudder. I have searched for a person to understand me for a long time. Once, a person like Rachael might have made a difference to me and to the life I have chosen. Someone like Rachael could have been my sounding-board, could perhaps have held me back from the dangerous currents of my impetuousness.

Now, of course, it is too late. This woman is dangerous; perhaps the most dangerous person I know. She understands me too well. I don't go near Rachael for the rest of the morning, but sometimes I catch her looking at me sideways, out of lowered lids. I realise that I will have to act, today.

I bide my time until I see Rachael packing up to leave and then I approach Odette. I am as hypnotic as a snake: one warm hand is placed on her arm, my eyes lock with hers. I am wide-eyed, upset and appalled. 'Odette, something has happened and I don't know if I should tell May or not.'

Odette leans forward, she cannot help herself, she is mesmerised by the potential for poison gossip. 'What is it?' She is heavily pregnant and we are so close that her stomach presses into me. I can feel the bulge of her belly button like a warm slug; I steel myself not to pull away from her.

'I was just in the garden and I saw Rachael...' I shake my head and Odette's moves with me. 'Oh look, perhaps I shouldn't say anything...' I lower my hand from Odette's arm.

'No! Tell me... What happened?' Odette is leaning further forward as I sway slightly back. Her eyes do not leave mine.

'It's only that she hit James, hard. It's left quite a red mark.'

Odette brings one ring-encrusted hand to her mouth, leans back slightly. 'How dreadful!'

'Well, I suppose she had cause... James had just pushed Tamara.'

'Was Tamara hurt?' Odette leans forward again, we are doing the dance of the cobra.

'No,' I reply, 'she didn't seem to be, but still, James shouldn't have pushed her.'

'I know, but Rachael had no right to hit James. That's terrible.' Odette is shaking her head in disbelief. Her body sways with indignation. 'I mean, no one has the right to hit someone else's child.'

I avert my eyes. 'Well… James is pretty naughty.'

'No,' Odette is quite convinced, 'it doesn't matter. Rachael shouldn't have hit him. She should have told May, not hit him.'

'Mmmm, maybe you're right, Odette. Rachael can be a bit quick sometimes.'

Now Odette is nodding righteously. 'Exactly, I agree. She lost her temper with Chris once. He did some little thing. She *has* got a bad temper, you know.'

'Oh yes, I know,' I agree – must agree. She is, after all, saying the things I want her to say.

'Look,' I lean forward as if to whisper. 'I think it's best if we don't tell May. It'll only upset her.'

'No, I don't agree.' Enthralled and empowered by her knowledge, Odette is decisive. 'I think that May should be told. If you don't want to do it, I will. I don't mind.'

'Oh I don't know, Odette, I feel a bit bad about this.'

'I won't tell her who told me, okay?' I nod, yes. Odette's proposal is really more than okay.

Odette glances around the room. 'I'll just wait until Rachael leaves before I say anything.' Odette is not, after all, completely stupid.

As I prepare to leave I notice that there is a lot of whispering going on. Across the room I see May sitting on the couch with Odette. She looks pale and shocked; on her lap is James. High on his thigh the outline of a red hand mark can still be seen.

I smile to myself. Rachael's act of betrayal will not go unpunished. There will not be any direct confrontation, of course. That would be too upsetting for all involved. No, ostracism will be sufficient for these women; after all, why give Rachael the chance to defend herself? Gradually she will be excluded. Soon enough she will get the hint. She will find other activities with which to fill her life, activities outside my social orbit. It has been a good morning's work, I think to myself. That'll teach Rachael to cross me; that'll teach *anyone* to cross me.

It is only when I am halfway home that I allow myself to laugh. *I enjoyed that*, I think. I'm not sure which was more satisfying: hitting that little shit

James, or so cleverly manipulating Odette to achieve what I wanted. Who would have thought such a silly trick would have worked so effectively?

What I have done is so funny that my eyes stream with tears of laughter. I can see Zach in the rear-vision mirror. He is looking at me as if I have gone mad. That idea makes me laugh even more. He has no way of knowing what his mother has become: first a murderer and now a liar. It all seems so terribly funny.

TWENTY

*I*t is a long, hot summer. I take Zach to the park often. It is down a steep hill. Zach rides in a baby carrier on my back. He sits straight-backed stretching high; he is desperate to see as much as he can. Zach loves it when we run down the hill to the park. He giggles and throws his hands around. His wispy blond hair floats up and down in the puffs of air.

The walking does me good. I lose weight. Old clothes fit. I change my hairstyle. It is very short and black. Daniel likes it. He runs his hands over my scalp until my hair stands up in spikes. We both laugh. It is good to hear him laugh again.

I meet new people in the park, people who do not know that I was ever mother to a daughter named Cassie, a daughter who did not like to sleep and who threw her legs around in anger.

Now I have only one child to wake me at night, and Daniel has agreed to move Zach out of our room, provided the baby monitor is turned up to full volume. Finally the cloud of fatigue which I have worn for months does not lie as heavily. I can think again. Daniel and I have begun to have regular sex and one night towards the end of summer he says to me, 'I think we should have another one.'

In my post-orgasmic glow I am not sure what he is talking about. Another what, another session? I don't answer, so he clarifies: 'Another child.'

I am horrified, too horrified to speak. Does he not realise that my life is just settling down again, that for the first time in months I can read a few pages of a book without my mind wandering, that toys no longer litter the hallway, that we are having sex again? For God's sake, does he want to jeopardise all of this?

I find my tongue. 'It's too soon, Daniel. I can't do it, not just yet.'

'But you seem to be coping so well. It seems to me as if this might be the next step that we both need.'

'Appearances aren't everything,' I reply cautiously. 'I'm scared, Daniel. I'm just very scared to have another baby.'

Daniel persists. 'Maybe there's someone you could talk to about this. I know you don't want to see a counsellor, but what about an old friend? Someone like Maureen? She might be good for you. You know, someone you can talk to, open up to. It was very nice of her to come to the funeral and she seems to be someone who can... I don't know...give comfort or something.'

Daniel's tone is casual, too casual; I have not forgotten the funeral clinch.

So, I think, *you suppose Maureen would be good for me, good to convince me to have more children, good to convince me that I'm happy in the suburbs, that it's okay to become what she has become, it's all right to turn into everything I despise. But if you think I am about to let that happen then you are sadly mistaken.*

'So,' I say, 'you were thinking that Maureen, with her sympathetic ear, might be able to convince me that rushing out and having another child is the right thing to do.'

'No, not that.' Daniel sounds exasperated. 'I was thinking she might be able to help you. She's very emotionally honest. You might enjoy spending time with someone like that.'

'No, Daniel, I wouldn't. There are things I would like to do, but spending time with Maureen is not one of them. Maybe you're the one who's really keen to spend time with Maureen and her precious "emotional honesty".'

'Be reasonable, sweetheart. All I want is for you and Zach to be all right and for us to have another child. We're not getting any younger, you know.'

He's right. We aren't. My body is older; it wouldn't recover as well. Zach is almost walking; he is becoming more independent. I would have to begin again. My heart hammers. I clench my fists in agitation. Heat spots rise in my face. I turn away from Daniel. I don't want him to read my betraying body.

Daniel misunderstands the movement. It is better that he does. He drags his finger down my spine and rests it in one of the dimples above my bottom.

'We know that the odds of something like Cassie's death happening again are so low as to be almost nonexistent.'

He sounds like a textbook, but I know he is desperate for me to agree with him. He is desperate to return us to what we were – a perfect nuclear family. Can he not see how dangerous that would be? It would be dangerous for us, dangerous for Zach, dangerous for any new child.

I reach around and grab his hand, pulling him closer to me. I am beginning to calm my renegade body. The control is returning.

'Oh Daniel, I love you. You know that I do, but I can't do it again...' I choose to leave the door open a little, '...just yet.'

Daniel is crying. 'I loved her so much. And we live with her death every day. It's not only what she was, it's what she would have become. It's the useless waste of her death that I hate so much.'

I cuddle him hard and say, 'Remember what you said at the funeral – we were lucky to have her as long as we did. Some things aren't meant to last.'

Daniel grunts. 'You're always telling me to move on. Well, that's what I'm *trying* to do, move on.'

'I'm not ready to move on to another baby,' I say. I will not continue down that path any further. Daniel hears it in my voice and understands. It makes him angry.

'Fuck it! Why will you never discuss this properly? You close the fucking shutters and that's it, end of conversation, nobody home.'

'Don't ever speak to me in that way,' I say. 'Don't ever take it out on me. You're not the only one hurt by this.'

'By what?' He is almost shouting. 'By what? Why will you never say it? By the senseless, useless death of our beautiful daughter, our Cassie. Why can you never refer directly to her death?'

Again I turn away from Daniel. I will not respond to his anger and he realises that. The fact that he is angry now is a sign of his desperation, but I will not let him know that I understand. It is important that I maintain some power.

I close my eyes. The conversation is over. Daniel picks up his pillow. He will spend the night on the sofa.

I am awake for a long time that night. It is difficult for me to control my breathing. *Nothing has changed*, I am thinking. *Everything that I have done for Daniel so that he and I could begin to live again has come to nothing. I'm still a mother, he a father. True, I am not as tired as when Cassie was alive, but we still don't go out together; we still haven't learned to live again. Now Daniel wants to drag me back to what I was, a barely functioning machine, a mother who dwelt only in the half light of other people's needs.*

It is unfair of Daniel to put such pressure upon me. Not only do I understand the danger of what he is asking, but I understand more than that. I know, even if Daniel is unwilling or unable to acknowledge it, I know that I have barely begun to live.

TWENTY-ONE

*T*he next week I find an advertisement in the paper:

ADVERTISING

We are an award-winning, full-service, boutique design and advertising agency.

We provide our clients with high-quality solutions ranging from marketing communications and brand advertising to direct marketing and design.

We have a dynamic culture in which the team works hard, achieves results and has fun.

You will have a solid background at Account Director level in a mid to large-sized agency.

You will possess energy, initiative and a burning
    desire to add value to your clients' businesses.
You will work closely with the creative team to
    develop innovative advertising and media
    solutions which are sensitive to your clients'
    needs.

I have heard of the company: it is only a few years old with a reputation for being progressive. I know that it has already won a couple of awards, including a Cannes Cyber Lion for online advertising.

While the pay level is slightly below what I was on before leaving work to have Cassie, what interests me most about the position is the scope it might present. In small, dynamic companies, power bases are constantly shifting, new opportunities arise all the time. I am particularly excited by the fact I would be working closely with the creative team. I have a very strong creative streak which was not allowed expression in my previous workplace with its rigid, old-fashioned division between the account and creative sides of the business.

I decide to send in an application.

For the next few days I am busy. From the back of the filing cabinet I pull out my old résumés and letters. I buy a book on job application and interview techniques. I search the internet for tips on securing a job. I have been out of the workforce for over two years; I know how quickly things can change. It is important that my application is up-to-date and relevant. I will *not* make a fool of myself.

When I am ready to write I put away everything I have read and sit before the blank screen of the computer. I have thought carefully about how I wish to present myself. I am ready to become the person for which the company is searching. For the next three nights, in the time between Zach going to bed and Daniel coming home, I create and re-create, buff and polish. In lines of text I represent myself as a competent, dedicated employee able to work to direction and tight deadlines, capable of building and maintaining strong client relationships, but with a creative flair which can be called upon if necessary. It is myself as I am capable of being – if I get the job, of course.

Finally I am finished. All my effort has resulted in two flimsy pieces of printed paper upon which my future rests. For as I have created, the yearning within me has grown. I know that I want this job. Not only is it a connection to my old life, but it will hold at bay Daniel and his demands for another child.

I send in the application.

Ten days later I am on my way to the interview. I have enough warning to arrange care for Zach and to have my hair trimmed and recoloured. I do not have enough time to buy a new outfit. An old, almost fashionable black suit, that was squeezed, forgotten, into my side of the wardrobe, has to do.

The firm's offices are on the edge of the city. For many years this area was a slum. Now it is revitalised. Red brick buildings with iron grids on the windows have been replaced by reflective high rises with fancy names and heavy-set doormen. Slick women with expensive blunt-cut hairstyles and designer shoes cruise the sidewalk. The men are groomed and exercised. They look as if they have stepped out of the pages of a glossy magazine. There is a vibe in the air. This is where it is all happening. Suddenly I feel hungry for it. Hungry for the artifice and pretence, hungry for the energy that is bouncing from person to person, hungry for the feeling that this is the centre. God, how I have missed this, trapped in my suburban haven; God, how I have missed the power of it all.

I wriggle in my uncomfortable suit. I look around my car, at the greasy fingermarks on my back window, at the half-chewed rusks that have been thrown on the floor. I know with certainty that this is not what I want.

Suddenly I hear my mother's voice. It comes at me from the depth of a nightmare. *'Stay in your room until I call you. I don't want to see your face until then.' Next, a male voice. 'Where's your daughter?' And my mother replying. 'At a friend's place. We have the night to ourselves, just you and me.' That night I am too afraid to leave the room. I pee in a cup I have near the bed and pour it silently out the window. I don't leave the room until morning when my mother greets me and cooks a breakfast that I am unable to eat.* It's not my fault, I tell myself; the women in my family have never been good mothers. Why has Daniel failed to see this? Why is he so desperate for me to be something I am not?

Today I am lucky with parking, pulling up right outside the address I have been given. It is a post-modern building that, from the street, looks unstable.

Like one of Escher's drawings, I imagine it to be full of impossible spaces and infinitely looping stairs – leading to nowhere except themselves. I wonder if, once inside, I will ever be able to find my way out again.

Inside, the building is so new that I can smell the fresh paint, the glue rising from the carpet. Signs are still being erected. Everything is clean and untainted. Many of the offices are unoccupied. They stand open and expectant at the promise of what they may become.

The firm I seek occupies one of the uppermost floors of the building. As I make my way there I realise I am not nervous. I feel like a thoroughbred whose best race is still to come. Adrenaline is a powerful beast which I have long ago learned to tame and ride. It will carry me through today. Of that I have no doubt.

The interviewer and company principal, Mr Drake, sits behind a huge desk, rising to shake my hand as I enter. He directs me to a seat near a small table in the corner of the room and, picking up a pad and pen, joins me.

There is no preamble; Drake moves right to the point. 'Your credentials certainly look good.

A Bachelor of Communications, several years in a large advertising firm at the same level as that advertised.' He looks up. The world is reflected in his glasses. I see myself, hands clasped and resting on the table, face suitably alert and agreeable. I see the door behind me and, at an angle, distorted, I can glimpse the next-door office tower. 'But you've been out of the industry for a couple of years.'

He stops for a moment. I refuse to step into the silence just yet; let him finish what he has to say, let him fully expose his concerns. 'So what makes you think you can do this? We have younger people applying for this job, people with more recent degrees, more relevant job experience.'

I had not expected him to be quite so direct, but I know that I can answer his concerns.

I uncross my legs and lean forward. 'I know what I want, Mr Drake. I'm hungry for this type of work. I can guarantee that none of the other applicants will have my hunger. On top of that I am eminently qualified. I graduated at the top of my class in over seventy per cent of the subjects I studied at university. During my years in the industry I brought millions of dollars worth of advertising revenue to the companies I worked for. I captured

clients whose advertising campaigns gained international recognition. I can give you a list of referees
to contact. I am thorough, meticulous and disciplined with an unerring eye for detail. I assure you,
no one else of my calibre will apply for this job.'

I can see that he is taken aback by my response.
I know that not all I have told him is reflected in
my résumé. I learned this trick many years ago. The
application should contain merely enough information to get you to an interview, nothing more;
you leave something up your sleeve for later.
Something to surprise people, to put them on the
back foot. Then you have won…and with Drake's
next words I know I have.

'Why are you interested in working for this
company then, why us? Why not try for a job
with the organisations you have worked for in the
past?'

'You're new on the scene,' I reply, 'with a reputation for being progressive and dynamic. I'm no
longer interested in working for large companies
that provide no flexibility. I realise that I'll be starting
at a lower pay level than when I left the industry.
But you'll get value for money out of me. I promise
you that.'

I am not surprised when Drake rings the next day to offer me the job. He would like me to start in two weeks. I am cautiously excited. After all, I still have Daniel to deal with.

TWENTY-TWO

That night, Daniel and I are washing up when I begin. I am so casual that you would never believe my heart is racing.

'Daniel, I've been giving some thought to the things you suggested – you know, about talking to someone and having another baby. I'm sorry, darling, but I'm just not ready for another child yet. I'm just not. And as much as I like Maureen, and I know that you do too, she's part of my past. I need more than that. I need something to take me into the future. You have your work. You're out there every day. You have people and things that give you something else to think about. I have nothing. I'm here every day with Zach and the memories.' My eyes are downcast; it appears as if I may be about to cry.

Daniel places his soapy hands on my shoulders. I feel the wet seep through my shirt. He pulls me to him. 'I know how hard this is. That's why I think you need to talk to someone about it, about what's happened to us. Anybody, it doesn't have to be Maureen. Anybody you can trust.'

I burrow my head into Daniel's chest. 'Oh Daniel. I know. I know that you only want what's best for us, but I don't think that just talking to someone is going to help.'

'Come on, come over here.' Daniel shepherds me to the couch. 'The washing-up can wait. It's really important that we talk about this. I've been wanting to have a conversation like this for weeks.' He settles a cushion behind my back. 'So what is there,' he asks, 'what is there that you think would help? I would do anything to help us move on.'

'Well...' I hesitate as if afraid to proceed.

'Yes,' says Daniel. He uses the voice he usually reserves for Zach. Soft and low. 'Yes, tell me. I really, truly want to know.'

'Well, I had a phone call yesterday. An ex-work colleague heard about this job that was going and she thought I might be interested so she passed my contact details on and a...' I hesitate a moment as if unable to remember the details, '...a Mr Drake rang. He's looking at expanding his advertising agency. He's on the search for good people...and he thought I might be interested.'

'You?' Daniel sounds dumbfounded. Obviously, this conversation is not proceeding as he'd envisaged. I almost laugh. Some things are too easy.

'Oh Daniel,' I chide, 'is that so hard to believe? I was good, you know. People still remember me. This isn't the first job offer I've had.'

'It isn't?'

'No, it's not. I just haven't told you before, that's all, because I haven't been interested. But Daniel, I really feel as if this is the right thing for me. I'm stuck you see. I'm in a loop. I can't go back and I'm too scared to go forward. I just *can't* contemplate having another child while I'm in this state.'

'No, I can see that,' says Daniel. There is old sadness in his voice. 'I just can't see, can't believe, that you going back to work is the right thing for us.'

It's always 'us', I think, *always us*. It's never enough for Daniel that sometimes it should be 'me'.

Ever since the children were born I have not been a 'me', I have been an 'us'. I am so sick of it.

'But Daniel, I want this. I need this.'

'So what are you suggesting? That you go back to work full-time?' Daniel is shaking his head, 'Because I can't, I simply can't agree to that.'

'Oh Daniel,' I wipe my eyes. 'You know what advertising agencies are like, they need me there full-time.'

'No.' Daniel places his hand on my shoulder. 'I'm sorry sweetheart, but if this... Drake person won't let you work part-time, then you will have to find somewhere that will.' He is shaking his head, a small frown on his face.

I see that Daniel will not budge on this point. But he *has* implicitly agreed to my return to work; at least I have that to build on.

'And what about Zach?' Daniel asks now.

I am ready for this one. 'I've thought about that,' I reply. 'Apparently a new child-care centre has opened down near the park. They still have some vacancies. They're supposed to be very good...maybe I could ring them tomorrow, arrange a time for us to go and have a look... What do you think?'

Daniel nods slowly, reluctantly, '*If* this child-care centre is any good, and *if* you can get part-time work...maybe we can look at this a bit more seriously.'

And then Daniel is hugging me, pulling me towards him. I know that my returning to work is not what he wants, but he has told me that he would do anything to help me move on, *anything*. 'Are you sure,' he asks – his mouth buried in my hair, 'are you really sure that this will help us pull together as a family again?'

I nod as much as I am able. 'I'm sure, Daniel; I'm really, really sure.'

TWENTY-THREE

I start work. I love it from the moment I walk in. The vibe is back. I have on new clothes. I have even pulled out my old make-up bag and used one of my twenty eyeshadow colours. *Watch out world*, I want to scream. *Watch out, I'm back.*

The first couple of days I set up meetings with some corporations that were former clients of mine. I know that winning their work for Drake's agency will be a real coup for me. I am excited about the prospects which this job has given me.

Drake has agreed to me working part-time for the first few weeks. *To ease myself back into the workforce*, I tell him. I have, of course, not told Daniel that this part-time arrangement is only temporary. I hope that when he sees how much happier I am at work he will understand that working full-time will be a far better arrangement for me.

The centre where Zach is in care rings me at eleven. He has not stopped crying since I left. The staff are concerned that he may be coming down with something. I tell them I will pick him up as soon as possible.

At five-thirty I arrive at the centre. Zach's eyes are puffy and when he sees me he clings to me as if he never wants to let go. That night he wakes up five times; each time he is screaming for me and I am the only one who can comfort him and rock him back to sleep. By the next morning I am exhausted, but desperate to go to work. Daniel offers to drop Zach off at the centre and to pick him up. Thankfully, I agree.

At lunchtime the phone rings. It is Daniel. 'I'm home with Zach. He couldn't settle. They told me it happened yesterday as well and that you didn't pick him up until late afternoon.'

'Look Daniel,' I reply, 'I picked Zach up as quickly as I could. There were just things that had to be done.'

That night Zach has a fever. I put him to bed and come out to the cold stare of Daniel.

'He's sick. You left him in a child-care centre when he was clearly upset and now he's sick.'

'Children get sick all the time,' I reply. 'Especially when they've just been exposed to a whole new set of kids.' I will not bear the brunt of Daniel's anger. My mother used to get angry with me when I was a child. No one is allowed to talk to me that way anymore.

'Look,' says Daniel, 'I understand that you feel you need to work and I understand that in the first few weeks things can be difficult – you're on trial, you need to work hard – but I think it's important that Zach is picked up from the child-care centre by five at the latest.'

I snort. 'There's no way I can get away from work every afternoon by four-thirty, especially since I'm only working three days a week anyway, you know that.'

'Yes,' says Daniel, 'I do know that so I'm not asking you to. What I am suggesting is that we share the job. One afternoon a week you pick him up early and I'll do it the other two afternoons. The next week we alternate.'

'Yeah right,' I say. 'As if your company will let you get home that early.'

'They have no choice. They'll have to agree to it, or I'll leave.'

I roll my eyes heavenward. I have never heard Daniel be more ridiculous.

'How could we afford that? We wouldn't be able to make the repayments on the house if you did something that stupid.'

'I don't think you understand.' Daniel is tense and stiff; he is barely breathing. 'My family comes before anything. Zach is the only child I have left. The company will let me do this; they will have to let me do this. I'll do some work from home in the evenings if necessary, but they will agree to this. Now you need to find out if your company will agree as well.'

I shake my head. 'For God's sake, Daniel. Zach will get used to child care. There are numerous studies showing high-quality child care is actually good for children. Most kids just take a bit of time to settle in.'

'He's not "most kids" he's our kid. I don't want him in child care any longer than is absolutely necessary. We need to try this. I insist that we try this.'

I am speechless at Daniel's request. Even if his company lets him knock off early one or two afternoons a week, what about me? I have just started work again. I haven't yet proved myself. I am working on a part-time basis which Drake expects me to up to full-time sooner rather than later, and I cannot imagine a request to leave early on a regular basis being met favourably at all. But I know Daniel. He is easygoing to a point. And once that point is reached he is a prize bull. I know he will not back down on this.

'Okay,' I nod. 'I'll ask. I'll see what I can do.' Already I am beginning to plan how I can manage the situation.

Daniel decides to take the last three days of the following week off to care for Zach while I work. To give me time to settle in, he says; to give me time to request some early afternoons.

Each night over those few days I arrive home to find Daniel and Zach playing together in the lounge.

One night it is trains, another it is puzzles. Daniel dotes on Zach now. There is no other word for it. When they are together Zach giggles like a breathless steam engine. So engrossed are they in each other that it can take some time for them even to realise that I am home, standing, watching them.

On Friday night Zach staggers over to me and buries his head in my knees. Daniel gives me a brush on the cheek. He has barely touched me all week.

I find myself speaking. 'I talked to Drake; he understands that I'll have to leave early one or two afternoons a week. He says he can live with it.'

Daniel nods. 'Okay, it should be fine from my end as well. Les's not happy about it, but we agreed to give it a trial for a few weeks and see how it pans out. So long as my work doesn't suffer it should be okay.'

Daniel leans over and kisses me properly. 'Thank you for all you've done in this. I know how much work means to you.'

He really has no idea.

For two weeks we go about our arrangements. I work long days when I don't have to pick Zach up, and slip out from work early – without telling anyone – on the days that I do have to. With the slightly shorter time in child care, Zach seems to have settled in quite well. I am hoping that in a couple of weeks – with a happier Zach to dangle in front of Daniel – he will agree to me working my full required hours *and* increasing my days at work; Drake is growing impatient for me to move to a full-time basis as promised. *Maybe I can make this succeed*, I think, *maybe*.

It's a Wednesday. It was Daniel's day for picking up Zach; I have come home late to a dark, seemingly empty house. Where is Daniel? Even the television isn't on. I discard my bag and shoes and make my way to the lounge-room. Daniel has dragged a chair to the window overlooking the back garden. His back is to me. All I can see clearly is his head silhouetted against the last of the light.

'Hello,' I say.

'When were you going to tell me?' he asks.

I stop mid-inhalation. My breath is frozen, an icicle inside my throat.

'Tell you what?' I play for time; I have some inkling of what may be coming, but I am not sure.

'I called your office about twenty minutes ago. I wanted to catch you before you left work. I only wanted you to pick up a loaf of bread on the way home. That's all, just a loaf of bread.'

I am quite sure that the dark house and Daniel's back are due to more than a loaf of bread. I am silent until he continues.

'Drake answered the phone. He said you'd just left. I thanked him, like a fool I thanked him for agreeing to you going part-time and for letting you come home early one or two afternoons a week. Guess what he said?'

Still I remain silent.

'He said that he'd never agreed to any such thing; that you'd never come to him with a request for shorter afternoons and that you promised him you'd up your hours to full-time gradually over the next few weeks. And Drake told me one more thing, one more very interesting thing.' Daniel still hasn't turned to face me.

'What was it Daniel?'

'He told me that at your interview he spelled out very clearly that you would be expected to work long hours. That they were a small, boutique company, that they couldn't afford to employ anyone who would fail to pull their weight.'

Now Daniel turns to look at me and I wish that he hadn't. His eyes are vacant. He has not been crying, I can tell that, but I have no idea what is going on in his head. It is the first time this has happened. 'You lied to me when you agreed to go back to work on a part-time basis *and* you lied to me even before that: you very specifically told me that you were offered that job on the basis of your work history, that you hadn't even had to go through a job interview, that you hadn't had to write a job application. Well, look what I found on the computer.' He holds up two pieces of paper, my job application.

It is the written word held up to condemn me. Anything else I might have been able to deny, but not that. I blurt out the first stupid words that come to mind: 'How did you get hold of that? I deleted it.'

Daniel snorts, 'You're not as clever as you think, are you? The recycle bin hadn't been emptied. A simple, stupid mistake.' There is silence as he breathes, as I breathe, the same air, but a galaxy apart.

'You know,' says Daniel, 'all I wanted was for you to be happy, for Zach to be happy, for us to be a real family again. And all I've got from you are lies – lies and deception. You've disregarded all the things that are really, truly important to me. You've torn them up like tissue paper and held them to the breeze.'

'Oh Daniel.' I sink down beside his chair. 'Oh Daniel. I'm sorry, so sorry. I didn't tell you about the interview because I was scared you'd be angry if you knew I'd gone looking for a job. And I kept quiet about Drake's preference that I build my hours up to a full-time basis because I was afraid that you wouldn't agree to me working. But really Daniel I did it all for the family. I looked for a good job so I could put Cassie's death behind me, so I could be a good wife again, a good mother again.'

'How can you say that? You've hurt the family, you've hurt me, you've hurt Zach. He's the one you really need to apologise to, not me. How long did you think you could keep all this going, all this lying?'

'Oh Daniel, I knew that Drake wouldn't take me on if I couldn't work full-time. And then I was sure if I almost immediately asked for early after-noons once or twice a week it would mean the end of my job there. I *need* that job, Daniel. I need it, to get better, to be able to move on. I thought, maybe, maybe this week I'd talk to Drake about the possibility of staying on as a part-time employee on an indefinite basis. Drake knows my work now, he likes it; I think that he'll agree to my requests. I just needed some time to prove myself.'

'Prove yourself! At the expense of everything. At the expense of telling the truth to me. At the expense of being there for your son. That's not good enough and you know it!' Daniel is angry, intractable.

I am so desperate to cling to my hard-won freedom that I start to cry. I have never tried this with Daniel before, but I have seen it work for other people. I dissolve in a heart-wrenching heap on the floor. The tears flow effortlessly.

Daniel cries as well. I move over to him and sink my head onto his lap. We cry in harmony. Finally, he speaks.

'Look, just tell me what you want. You want to work full-time and for me to stay home? Fine, I'll do that, but please don't punish Zach for your desire to work.'

Daniel's suggestion takes me by surprise. Surely he is bluffing. We could never keep the house on my salary alone. His real agenda is obviously to force me to stop work. It has been his agenda from the start. Daniel has never appreciated all that I have done for him. He is selfish and ungrateful. I wonder why I have not previously seen this.

Daniel speaks again. 'Anyway, we can talk about it this weekend, I've asked your mother to come over and care for Zach.'

'My mother?'

'I've booked a couple of nights in the mountains. We need time to talk, to sort this thing out, and I don't want to do it here. There are too many memories in this house. I want us to get away. I don't expect the weekend to be a pleasant or easy one. But it's something we need to do. It's something I need to do.'

'And you're willing to leave my mother to care for Zach while we go away?'

'I am. This is important and your mother loves Zach. She's part of the family. I trust her. She'll take good care of him.'

I allow all this to sink in. A couple of nights in the mountains would be nice. Even if I have to see my mother to be able to do it. How typical, I am able to think, that my mother should have the opportunity to view another important moment in my life, headlined something like 'The year my marriage reached crisis point'. I try not to laugh out loud because it is, of course, inappropriate to share this thought with Daniel at this point, so I don't.

TWENTY-FOUR

My mother arrives fashionably late at six-thirty when Daniel had asked her to be at our place at six. She is, if at all possible, skinnier than ever, as her ludicrously short skirt reveals only too clearly. She air-kisses me as she minces through the door followed by a cloud of perfume which will no doubt make Zach gag when she bathes and feeds him.

I show my mother Zach's carefully arranged food in the fridge, enough for every meal while we are away. I also show her a selection of frozen meals for herself. She nods absently at this. They won't be eaten, I know, but I have done my duty as a host. She waits until the end of the tour to rub it in.

'You know, darling, how delighted I am to be able to help you out like this. I know how independent you and Daniel like to be, but, really, who better to call on in this time of need than your own mother.'

Yes, my mother. The woman who, when I was three, locked me in my bedroom so that I wouldn't wake her at night; who put me on my first diet at seven; and who, when I was fifteen, tried to steal my first boyfriend. I know how desperate Daniel is for us to have this weekend away together, so I will not allow myself to be antagonised by her. Instead, I nod sweetly. Daniel has obviously told her too much.

My mother and Zach stand outside to farewell us as we drive away. Zach has one little fist raised and he is clenching and unclenching it in his version of waving. He is teary. His bottom lip quivers, and his nose starts to twitch, but I'm sure that he'll be okay. Children are amazingly resilient. We wave and blow kisses until we are at the bottom of the driveway and then we are away.

This is the first time that Daniel and I have gone away together since Cassie was born. It'll be the first time since the children were born that I will sleep under a roof which doesn't shelter at least one of them. Such freedom! Despite the issues that remain to be resolved between Daniel and myself, I know that I will enjoy this weekend. Finally we are doing something for ourselves. I am so happy to be leaving the house, that I'm sure I'll be able to face anything Daniel might throw at me. After all, he can't exactly forbid me to work. And I know that the further we move away from suburbia and my role of 'mother', the more power I will have over him.

Daniel has told me that we are going to the mountains, but he has not told me where we are staying. This omission makes the trip even more exciting. We spent the first few days of our honeymoon up here. It was winter; at one stage it snowed. Flakes of shaved ice piled against our door, tumbling over the threshold when we dared to venture out. It was a wonderland. I had never seen anything more beautiful.

It is after ten when we begin to descend a long driveway to our mountain hideaway. I lost my bearings nearly an hour ago. We are further into the mountains than I have ever been. We are driving over gravel now and the sound of the crunching echoes around the car, too loud for conversation. It doesn't matter anyway, we have not spoken much during this trip. It's the way we both want it. The ride here has given us a chance to shed our skins, to become once more the people we were, before I gave up my career, before we had children, before one of those children died. I can feel my old self, my old confidence reasserting itself.

The headlights of the car suddenly illuminate a sign showing the name of our destination, *Mountain View*. I have heard of this place, have read about it in lifestyle magazines. It is expensive and exclusive. I am impressed that Daniel was able to book here on such short notice; I am impressed that he feels we can afford to stay here; I am impressed because his choice of accommodation reflects the obvious importance he attaches to saving our marriage, to bridging our impasse.

As if reading my mind, Daniel breaks the silence that the halting of the car has brought.

'They had a vacancy. We were lucky. And I thought that anything less than somewhere like this would be a compromise.' He turns to face me and takes one of my hands in his. 'I'm determined to work our way through this. I'm determined to reach an outcome with which we can all live.'

His words are solemn. Daniel has always taken things seriously. He approaches any problem, even personal ones, as if it is a puzzle needing a solution.

'We will, darling, we will,' I reply. I lean over to kiss him. He smells tired and slightly sick. It is evidence of what these last eight months have taken out of him.

Our room is beautifully appointed, the spa-bath deep, the bed exquisitely comfortable. I sleep the sleep of the dead, or the innocent. I do not dream. I wake before Daniel and observe him while he sleeps. He is restless. His eyelids flicker. His hands clench and unclench. He seems to be running a marathon in his sleep and when he finally wakes, there are deep black circles under his eyes.

Daniel has planned a hike for the morning. The hotel has packed a picnic lunch and Daniel puts it in his backpack. This walk will not be anything too strenuous. We will make our way over a small rise known as the Devil's Hump, and then along the valley floor before making a steep, but short ascent of the other side to a viewing platform which, according to the guidebook, promises 'a panoramic view of the five pillars'.

It is overcast and the sun hangs low in a beaten pewter sky as we set out. We have not yet spoken about the issues which we have come here to resolve. I have determined that I will not be the one to raise them. There is power in knowing your enemy, but not being the first to strike. I am languid and relaxed, a lioness in her prime. It will take a lot to defeat me.

As the path narrows I am content to follow Daniel, keeping up with his steady, insistent pace. I count my footsteps, five hundred and nine, five hundred and ten, five hundred and eleven. My mind echoes with the beat, nothing more. By ten-thirty, flies have settled on the slight dampness of Daniel's shoulders. We are about three-quarters of the way along the valley floor when Daniel calls a halt. We find a spot, a grotto, perhaps. The rocks are damp as if perpetually watered by a hidden spring. We perch: me on one rock; Daniel on another. Daniel swings his pack to the ground and passes me a water bottle. I drink deeply, counting my gulps. The water tastes like canvas. It reminds me of a camping trip

I took with my parents before my father died. It was winter and there were no showers, only a river, which flowed so slowly that it was covered in lily-pads. We didn't bathe in three days. My mother declared that she 'would never do that again'. My father and I laughed at her discomfort.

When I stop drinking I find that Daniel is looking at me.

'Good?'

I nod. It is good. Good to drink, good to be here with him, good not to have to worry about changing nappies or preparing baby food.

'Are you happy?' I ask him suddenly.

'Happy?' He rolls the question around in his mouth. 'Happy to be here with you. But everything I do now echoes with her.'

I don't ask who 'her' is. I know: my daughter, our daughter. My forever rival for his affections.

I wipe the sweat from my forehead. 'Yes, I know how it is for you.' My reply is too short and sounds too much of accusation. I realise it as soon as the words are out of my mouth.

His grey eyes look steadily at me. 'But not for you.' Is it a question? I'm not sure, but I will treat it as such.

'Of course it is for me. Of course I miss her. Of course I think about her all the time.' Even to my ears it sounds like a well-rehearsed litany.

Daniel leans towards me. 'Do you? I wonder. I wonder. I've been wondering a lot over the last few days.' His voice trails off and he looks into the middle distance.

My heart has grown cold. What is he getting at?

Daniel continues. 'I've done a lot of reading about infant death recently. As Doctor Hadid told us, the chance of a child Cassie's age dying from an unexplained cause is very small.'

My hand has begun to move without my control. I realise that I am tearing at the moss that covers most of my rock, ripping it from its mooring. With difficulty I gain some control. Daniel is being unfair. This line of discussion is not what I had expected.

'Yes, of course I know that,' I reply. 'I've read about it as well. That's why it's so dreadfully difficult to believe that it happened to our family.'

'So you've been reading? I thought you'd dealt with it all by putting everything behind you. That's what I told Cindy.'

'Cindy?' He is taking me down pathways for which I am unprepared.

'Mmmmm, Cindy.'

'Who's Cindy?' If he is seeking my attention, he now has it. My hands are firmly in my lap.

'Cindy's the counsellor from the hospital, the one you would never agree to talk to.'

Shit! Cindy. I remember now. She'd rung me several times in the weeks after Cassie's death. I'd never responded to her and finally she'd seemed to realise that I didn't welcome her attentions.

'I spoke to Cindy on Thursday. I wanted to know what a normal grieving process for a mother might be. I was hoping even now to find some way to help you, to help us. Cindy said there was really no normal pattern, but that it was usually the mother who – externally at least – took these things the hardest, who often blamed herself for the death of her child. She said that sadness and guilt could manifest in many different ways – maybe a morbid fear for your other children; maybe an intense sense of culpability, such as blaming yourself and questioning your actions in the lead-up to the child's death. What Cindy said got me thinking and I realised that you've never exhibited any of the classic signs of grief. Maybe someone who didn't know you well wouldn't have realised, but I know you well, very well. You haven't changed, you haven't reacted. You haven't wanted to talk to anybody, to confide in anybody – not me, not Cindy, not Maureen, nobody. You've carried on your life exactly as if Cassie had never existed.'

There is silence. In the distance I hear the cry of a solitary crow.

'What do you think all this means?' Daniel looks directly at me. Unfortunately this is a question for which he requires a real answer.

'Daniel, I don't handle things like other people, you know that. You said it was one of the reasons you loved me, one of the reasons you asked me to marry you. Why should I exhibit these classic signs of grief? They're classic because that's what the majority of people do. Why should I be the same as everybody else? Surely you're not going to punish me for not mourning like an automaton!'

'Not an automaton,' he fires back. 'Like a human. Like a mother. Like someone who cared about whether our daughter lived or died. I know that you don't always handle things like other people and that's why I've been so patient. I was sure that one day the dam wall would break and you would finally reveal the full extent of your grief. But it hasn't happened. And you know what? Now that I've learned how easy you find it to lie to me, now that I've discovered how easy you find it to turn your back on Zach, I've been wondering…'

Fuck, fuck, fuck. I can barely breathe.

'Wondering what?' I manage to croak out.

'Wondering who or what you really are. And then, I remembered.'

'Remembered what?' The words almost don't make it past my lips.

'I remembered that the night Cassie died, when I came home from work and checked on her, there was no water bottle beside her bed. I realised then that you lied about when you brought her the water bottle, which means that at some stage during the night you spent some time in Cassie's room and for some reason you wanted no one to know about it.'

I sob silently. Huge salt drops fall onto my clenched hands. For the first time that I can remember, my tears are real. I am crying for lost opportunities, for things I might have done, people I might have been. I am crying for the fact that for the first time ever I have been fully revealed. I am crying because my husband has constructed a prison for me. It is a prison built on knowledge and power. It is a prison that may be strong enough to contain even me.

Daniel walks over to me and places one arm around my shoulders. It is a magnanimous gesture, that of a conquering hero showing his captive some kindness.

'Do you want to know what I've decided?'

I nod. It is impossible for me to speak.

'I thought about what is important to me, about what might be able to be saved out of all this, and I decided that the only thing I can really do is to make sure that my family is not destroyed any further. It's the only thing I have left to cling to. I expect Zach to be raised in a way that is the best for him. I will have nothing denied to my only surviving child, *our* son. Do you understand what I'm asking of you?'

Of course I understand. I am to subjugate myself to the needs of the family; I am to return to the role of being Zach's mother, Daniel's wife. Daniel's knowledge has granted him the right to demand this of me and I do the only thing I am capable of: I nod again.

Daniel removes his arm. 'Come on, let's keep walking.'

He swings the pack up onto his shoulders and sets off. I follow, even though I am unable to control the shaking in my knees. Bile rises in my throat and I must swallow constantly to keep from vomiting. All my negotiating power has been removed and we both know it. For the first time ever, someone, Daniel, understands me, fully and completely. My future has been defined, decided, limited. I have been stripped bare, pegged and laid out in the sun to dry.

Daniel's pace is quicker than it was before. I struggle to keep up. The clouds have broken; sun slants into the valley. The flies become heavier, the heat more oppressive. I move as if through a thick fog.

Soon we begin our ascent to the viewing platform. Loose stones, dislodged by Daniel's feet, sometimes roll onto my head and hands. Once, a rock comes off in my hand and in the cool, red earth beneath I see a centipede. Its glossy back shines iridescent in the sunlight. Carefully I replace the rock.

At a particularly steep point Daniel turns back and offers me his hand. I take it gratefully. His steadiness emphasises the trembling in my own limbs.

We reach the summit and, as promised, a semi-circle of flat earth about ten metres long and six metres deep constitutes the viewing platform. Daniel and I stand for a few moments, the silence broken only by the sound of our breathing.

Ahead of us are the five pillars, splendid in the noon sunlight, rising defiantly from the valley floor far below. They look like carefully arranged layers of loose shale, as if some giant child has constructed a play city. But their almost fragile appearance belies the fact that they are the only remains of the material that once stood all around them. They alone have been able to withstand millions of years of weathering. Far below, at the base of the pillars, is the forest: green in their shadow, shimmering blue-green in the distance. It is as if we are the only creatures alive up here; it is as if we own the Earth. I know why the devil chose a hilltop upon which to offer Jesus his greatest temptation.

I am standing as close to the edge as I comfortably can. Heights have never been my strong point, but even from where I am, I can see that the viewing platform is actually a ledge. We are suspended in a gravity-defying time and space. One day this ledge will break away and tumble into the valley below. I picture it, somersaulting over and over until it crashes against the trees and pulverises into a cloud of lung-choking dust.

Daniel has walked past me, beyond me; he stops only when he is standing on the very edge of the world.

I look at Daniel, his silhouette superimposed on the almost impenetrable bush that stretches below and beyond us for kilometres. If someone fell from this ledge his or her body would probably never be found. I wonder for a moment what Daniel is doing. Is he challenging me? Or is he offering himself to me? He has just uttered the words that will circumscribe my life, and yet he is standing before me as if he is unknowing, as if he is deliberately offering me what is now perhaps *my* greatest temptation.

And then, with a great rush of clarity, I realise the truth. Daniel doesn't know me at all. He has no inkling of what I am capable. Oh, he may think he does, but the truth he has grasped hold of is merely a shadow truth, merely a small glimpse of the power and ruthlessness that live at my centre.

Daniel is guileless, a simpleton, offering himself to me in that way. I feel almost giddy with the thought of the endless possibilities opening before me, and the enormous temptation that he is presenting to me. I move closer. The dry dirt crunches under my feet.

Daniel turns his head to look at me. In his grey eyes I see myself reflected, reflected as I have always been. It was this way when we first met. I had believed then that it was the stillness of his gaze that would grant me my uniqueness, now I knew better.

I stop in my forward movement and regard him. I realise that I will go no further. It would be too easy. This is not, after all, how I want it to be. There will be other edges, other times. There is strength in knowing your power and yet holding back.

And then, the moment is lost; Daniel moves away from the edge and we begin the downhill trek.

That night Daniel is a man whose shackles have been removed. He is gayer than I have seen him in a long time. His shoulders have straightened and his steps have lightened. He believes he has played his trump card and won.

If he expects me to be morose, however, then he is mistaken. I act the woman who has surrendered gracefully to her fate. I act the compliant wife, the demure mother. My demeanour is the unruffled sheet that covers the writhing nest of vipers.

Later we fuck.

Every pore in my body is hot and Daniel meets me with his own fire. I seek out every way I know of amplifying my own pleasure and Daniel seems happy to acquiesce. He believes, after all, that he has won. Why shouldn't he satisfy me in this at least. He works hard and yet I hold myself back. It is only when his head is firmly buried between my wet thighs that I allow myself to come in a great shuddering gasp that shakes the room with its assumed surrender.

TWENTY-FIVE

We are home. It has been a long trip, much of it travelled in silence. I drove while Daniel slept. I didn't mind; after all, I don't have to work tomorrow. Anyway, I didn't need Daniel's conversation to keep me awake; I was surging on adrenaline. I found a radio station playing dance music. It pounded out a rhythm that thumped in time with my heart. I pumped the accelerator to the beat. I felt good. As we entered the city it began to rain. I kept the windscreen wipers on high and opened the window a sliver. The fresh blast of cooling afternoon air did me good. I felt as if I could go on forever.

Now, at home, I am making a final cup of coffee for Mother before her departure when I realise there is no milk in the fridge. Daniel says he will go out and buy some as I have done most of the driving today. It is a simple offer by him, one which in the past I would have accepted without a second thought. Once I acted instinctively, out of habit, or indifference or desperation. But now I have changed. Now I know – every action has a reaction and in every offer there is an opportunity. And so, I agree to Daniel's suggestion and at the same time ask if he will take my car and check the tyre pressure. It's a bit of a nuisance for him as he will have to move his car from where it's parked behind mine in the garage, but it's a job I don't like to do and one that he normally does for me.

When Daniel leaves I make my way down the hallway to begin unpacking. As I pass the internal entrance to the garage I notice that, as I have expected, Daniel has left the garage door open. He often does this when he slips out for a short while, and today in particular, he would not want to get out of the car in the rain to open the garage door when he returns. Our house sits on a slight rise; you cannot see into the garage until you are right at its entrance.

Zach is pushing his pedal-less trike around the house. It was a gift from Daniel's parents for his first birthday. He has only recently started to use it and his feet barely touch the ground. After a short time I can't stand the noise of Zach pushing up and down the corridor. It is still raining and I suggest to Mother that she take Zach into the garage. He has plenty of space to ride in there and she can supervise him while I unpack. If nothing else, it will kill two birds with the one stone: remove the need to talk to my mother and deal with Zach's noise.

I return to my unpacking. In the new silence of the house I begin to hum. It is a tune of my own creation, rising and falling, speeding up and slowing down with complete unpredictability. It pleases me, this unfettered melody that needs to satisfy no one but myself.

When I have finished unpacking, I head down the corridor towards the garage in order to store the suitcase. It is then that I hear the sound of my car, driven by Daniel, beginning to accelerate up the drive. He knows that the garage door is open, waiting for him, and he drives quickly to avoid the bother of changing gears. It is how he usually drives up the rise to our house. I have told him before that he comes much too fast up the hill.

I can see my mother's back as she sits on the floor by the internal door to the garage. She is leaning against the door jamb nonchalantly flicking through a magazine. She is as predictable in her habits as Daniel, and as usual she is not watching Zach properly. I have warned Daniel many times that my mother cannot be trusted. I have told him how much I despise her. Perhaps after this people will listen more closely to what I have to say.

I am not far enough along the corridor to see directly into the garage, but as I hear Daniel speed to the top of the drive, I can imagine Zach caught like a startled rabbit in the glare of his headlights. I know that in such a situation split-second reactions mean the difference between life and death. I know that in my car the pedals are further apart and higher up than they are in Daniel's. Daniel does not often drive my car, and I wonder: will he be able to find the brake in time?

It is only now that I allow myself to picture a scene in the future. Senior Constable Coombs has re-entered our lives. This time she is questioning Daniel. He sits on the couch with his arms pulled tight over his chest. He looks like a man whose soul has been removed. I imagine that his eyes have sunk into his face. They have lost their reflective quality. Perhaps they have even changed colour. He looks at me and I know that, finally, he understands me. But now I am strong enough that I no longer care.

In my imaginings I also respond to police inquiries. This time, however, I am not afraid of what they may ask; I am not concerned that my reactions will be inappropriate. I have had practice, you see; I am better at this than ever before. This time I will be prepared to help the police. I will honestly answer the questions they ask me about Daniel. I will show them the note I wrote all those months ago, the written word which proves how Cassie really died.

But for now I wait, I wait to see. Will Daniel find the brake in time or won't he?

EPILOGUE

There are very few things I have taken with me. Even most of the memories have been discarded. Memories are burdensome things, almost as bad as names, and if you think I care at all about what happened to those I left behind, then you are mistaken.

There is, however, one possession from that time which I cherish, one which I keep with me. It is the twisted Möbius strip, which lies nestled and safe in its velvet-lined box. It is not for sentimental reasons that I maintain this one possession. True, it was given to me by a man I once thought I loved; a man who regarded the gift as a symbol of two entities becoming one. For a time I had believed him, but now, after all that I have survived, I know better. Now I know that *I* am the Möbius strip. *I* am the self-contained entity needing no one and nothing to make myself complete. This is the only knowledge I will ever need. And it is the Möbius strip which serves to remind me.

And now perhaps you wonder, where am I, what has become of me? And I laugh at that wondering, because in that question I sense some fear. Does it trouble you that one day I may reappear, perhaps as your neighbour, your lover, your friend?

Anything, of course, is possible. And you may have good cause for fear...

ACKNOWLEDGEMENTS

When I first started writing *The Mother's Tale* – in small amounts of private, stolen time – I had no idea how collaborative its path to publication would ultimately become.

I didn't know that I, and my book, would need the help of people of all sorts: those to believe in us and cheer us along; those to provide an opportunity when some doors seemed to be firmly closed; those whose skills in editing, or promotion or marketing, no good book or author can be without.

There is first and foremost my husband. My one-man cheer squad, who believes I can do absolutely anything I set my mind to. There are so many things he did, but just as important are the things he didn't do. He didn't push me to get a real job when our youngest child started school, he didn't complain when beds weren't made, floors not swept, windows not cleaned (even when I had been at home all day and appeared to have done nothing at all with my time). He didn't complain when for many weeks, he acted as a single dad while I wrote. *The Mother's Tale* would not be without him – so to my husband with all my love, thank you.

And then there are my children, my great levellers, who also put up with all of the above but who, if I became too stressed about something, would bring me down to earth with statements like 'But Mum it's only a book'. Not nearly as important as when dinner was going to be served and how the arrangements for their birthday parties were progressing, and nor should it be! Thank you my children, you are my reality; solid and unbelievably wonderful.

To my extended family and friends who gave me support every step of the way (including child-minding, dog walking and dinners for my family when I was away). It is a tribute to them all that I can think of no negative comment I have *ever* received about the path I was pursuing. And believe me that is no small thing, when the journey often seems so long and the outcome so uncertain! Thank you all for your love and encouragement.

Taking *The Mother's Tale* beyond my tight network of family and friends was a big step. And I have no doubt that its path to publication would have been much, much harder without the help of one amazing person and one completely unique foundation. I am talking about Peter Bishop, the creative director of Varuna – the Writers' House – administered by the Eleanor Dark Foundation (Varuna was gifted to the foundation by Eleanor's son, Mr Michael Dark). Peter and Varuna are unique in Australia (and possibly the world). They provide a link between writing as a solitary pursuit and writing which is part of a wider community of fellow practitioners, publishers and readers.

Peter was the first 'outside' reader of *The Mother's Tale* and his insightful comments, ongoing support and enthusiasm, combined with a couple of residencies at Varuna, resulted in a work which I felt confident in taking to the broader world of publishers and agents. To Peter and Varuna, I don't think you will ever know how eternally grateful I am.

A big, heartfelt thank you to Pippa Masson, my agent, who believed in *The Mother's Tale* from the very early days – still evolving as it then was. Every writer needs a good agent and Pippa is one of the best. Enthusiastic, responsive and professional!

To my publisher: the full-spirited, amazing Vanessa Radnidge at Hachette Livre. Not only does she have an eye for a good book, but she is so wonderfully up-beat, highly intelligent and a pleasure to work with. Vanessa saw *The Mother's Tale* at a reasonably early stage of its development and believed in it from the start. Thanks for everything Vanessa!

Thank you also to Amanda O'Connell and Deonie Fiford, who did the final editing fine-tune (which resulted in improvements to *The Mother's Tale* even at the eleventh hour!). I cannot express what a relief it was for me to have the two of you to help hone some of the finer points of my novel.

Now to the Orion marketing and publicity teams led by Sandy Weir and Emma Noble. What a professional group of people! Again it is your capability and enthusiasm which shines through. I feel so lucky to have had *The Mother's Tale* in your talented hands for the final stages of its development.

Camilla Noli, 2008

The
Mother's Tale

CAMILLA NOLI

Introduction to *The Mother's Tale*

What lies beneath . . .

Hidden fears, intimate secrets, dark motivations.

From the warm light of her sleeping baby's nursery, the curve of her husband's arm, the soft embrace of an old friend, the anonymous narrator of *The Mother's Tale* whispers to you her private fears, her deepest held desires.

Mesmerising, confronting, revealing, her hidden secrets are a distorted echo of the emotions of everywoman: mother, lover, friend, daughter.

From its softly lit beginning to its explosive, emotional conclusion *The Mother's Tale* takes the reader on a journey to the dark recesses of one woman's heart and mind; within are the truths that are not spoken, the realities that are not written about.

The Mother's Tale is a taut, beautifully constructed book which, once begun, cannot be put down, told by a narrator who will not be forgotten easily. It engages and confronts; it provokes.

About the author

Camilla Noli lives on the Central Coast of New South Wales with her husband and two children. *The Mother's Tale* is her first novel. She is currently working on her next book.

If you visit Camilla's iLounge (www.camilla noli.com) you will find links to her discussion board with online debate, a range of her short stories, news and information about Camilla, and some useful information and links for readers and writers.

Camilla Noli on writing

I have been a writer for a very long time – long before I was published in any form whatsoever.

I never gave up my dream of being a published author, but along the way I completed two degrees [BA (Hons) in Literature and an MBA], I travelled, worked, got married, worked a bit more, and gave birth to two wonderful children. During this time I never stopped writing.

In the very early days, writing was my way of working out the world. As a child I would write down those things that worried me, moved me, disturbed me. Often these writings were in narrative form, sometimes they were fictionalised. I vividly recall writing one piece from the point of view of a foetus who was just about to be aborted. Not long before, I had seen a picture of Edvard Munch's classic painting *The Scream* and I remember that his work was very firmly in my mind as I wrote.

Another short story that I wrote in primary school was entitled *The Girl Who Loved Apples*. The protagonist of this story, a primary school girl, loved apples so much that she would do anything to find the perfect source of her favourite fruit. One day in the park, she met a kindred soul, an old man who possessed the source of the perfect apple – a tree in the garden surrounding his ramshackle house. The story ended with the girl going to live with the man so that she could have constant access to the tree. In my story the two of them, young girl and old man, were perfectly happy with the arrangement. Following her desires seemed to me to be a much more interesting story than if the girl had given them up in order to be a 'good daughter'.

Exploration of the concept that Jung called the 'shadow', or what could simply be called our dark side – those repressed desires and impulses that most of us work so hard to hide and which are actually so important in understanding our motivations – is a large part of what has driven my work to date.

Writing is still my method for working out the world and for fully developing and exploring ideas. It's just that now some of the things I want to explore are more serious and complicated than they once were. The other difference, of course, is that now I am published I can look forward to other people reading and discussing some of the ideas that fascinate me.

The background to *The Mother's Tale*

In 2001, I began writing the book that would become *The Mother's Tale*. From the very first, it was the intriguing character of the narrator that captured me. My anonymous narrator carried me along and the majority of the book was written very quickly. By 2002 I had a book which I knew was nearly, but not quite, right.

In 2003 I was lucky enough to be chosen to attend a manuscript development program run by Peter Bishop at Varuna – the Writers' House in the

Blue Mountains. With Peter's insightful reading and comment on the novel, it developed further – to the extent that in 2004 I was the recipient of a Varuna/HarperCollins Award for manuscript development. This was a 10-day residential program where I, and four other writers, were given the opportunity to work with an editor from HarperCollins who had chosen our manuscript as being a work which they wanted to help develop further.

What an amazing experience that was! It was the first time I had been exposed to the workings of the publishing world and doing so in the environs of a place like Varuna, with an editor who truly loved my work, was surreal. *The Mother's Tale* developed further under that editorial direction.

Towards the end of 2004 I began my second novel. This book also benefited from the reading and feedback it received from Peter Bishop. In mid-2006, with two as yet unpublished novels under my belt, I was lucky enough to have Pippa Masson at Curtis Brown Literary Agents agree to represent me as my agent. Early in 2007 I learnt that *The Mother's Tale* would be published in 2008 by Hachette Livre, with another novel to follow in 2009.

Q&A with Camilla Noli

Q: How did you come up with the idea for *The Mother's Tale*?

The Mother's Tale is a book which is driven entirely by its strong central character and first person narrator. The personality of this character presented itself to me almost fully formed one night and from the very beginning she fascinated me.

What would it be like to be inside the mind of someone like her, I wondered? More importantly, what would happen if someone like her had responsibility for very young, vulnerable children, and if she were placed in situations which for her were increasingly stressful? It didn't take long for both this character and these scenarios to absorb my thinking, and so *The Mother's Tale* was born. In a sense I felt as if I *had* to create a story for this person.

People who have read the book have told me that the narrator's character is one which they also find difficult to get out of their mind. Mothers have told me that, often to their horror, they realise they have moments in their lives when they find themselves thinking and acting (in small ways!) as she does. The truth is that we all have times in our lives when we 'act' things out, when there is a disconnection between what we think and what we say. But the narrator of *The Mother's Tale* is a full-time performer – all her life is an act, and so she becomes an increasingly fascinating person as we almost, but not quite, come to understand her.

This fascination with strong, often unpleasant, unusual or unhappy characters is something that recurs in my work. One of my short stories – which you can find if you visit my iLounge – is called *Groom or no Groom*. Once again this story grew from a dream of a very intriguing main character, who practically demanded that a story be written for her.

In fact, in my opinion the best stories all have very strong, unforgettable characters at their centre.

Q: **Many people find the idea behind *The Mother's Tale* quite disturbing. Did you ever find it difficult to write?**

The ideas at the centre of *The Mother's Tale* are disturbing. But I do believe that they are ideas that need to be talked about, and highlighting certain issues within a fictional context is a perfect way for opening debate on them.

Interestingly, the most disturbing parts of *The Mother's Tale* were written very quickly, driven by very powerful emotion – a kind of suspended horror – at what the words were saying. I suspect that it was necessary for me to construct these scenes in a rush or they wouldn't, or couldn't, be written at all.

In fact those more disturbing parts of *The Mother's Tale*, written in a burst of emotion, are the ones which have changed least over my many years of working on the novel. I have found this both before and since with my writing. Scenes written with a very strong emotional content seem to flow, as if every word knows where it needs to be.

And as disturbing as some of the ideas and scenes within *The Mother's Tale* are, they are absolutely central to understanding the personality of the main character and for exploring the issues which are at the heart of the novel.

Q: What kind of response do you hope readers will have to *The Mother's Tale*?

Well, of course I hope that readers will love it! And I hope that it makes people think. I hope that it provokes debate.

I think that all the best books are capable of generating a conversation around themselves; they have a life beyond their covers. These are books which you just have to talk about with your partner, or your best friend, or the person sitting beside you on the train. This 'desire to discuss' is what the best books do and I hope that *The Mother's Tale* does that as well.

Already, different people have had vastly different responses to *The Mother's Tale*, often depending on their own experiences and background. And that's a good thing! I hope that people do want to discuss *The Mother's Tale* and its issues. If the book achieves that then it will have done as much as I could have hoped for.

Q: What research did you do for the book?
The Mother's Tale reflects preoccupations I have had for many years and in this sense, much of the 'research', particularly with regard to the personality of the main character, was carried out prior to writing the novel. Because the novel takes such an intensely personal point of view, once the character of the narrator was firmly established, large slabs of the book were written with me simply making sure that I stayed fully inside her head.

I did, however, carry out specific research with regard to some of the more technical aspects of the book. And I don't really want to say more than that, in case you are reading this before having read the book!

Q: What do you think of reading groups?
Books shouldn't exist in isolation, they should be shared and the best of them should be capable of acting as springboards to a whole range of emotions, and topics for discussion. I believe that a good reading group provides a purpose-built mechanism for that to happen.

Personally, as well as being a writer I am also an avid reader and a member of a number of formal and informal book clubs. I love receiving book recommendations from friends and I love having the opportunity to discuss thought provoking books with other like-minded readers. It is truly one of the great joys of my life!

Q: Who are some of your favourite writers?
I read widely and voraciously and it is very difficultfor me to pick out only a few favourite writers

as I enjoy a wide variety for different reasons – but I will try!

I have spent many years enjoying the South American magic realist writers such as Gabriel Garcia Márquez, Jorge Borges and Isabel Allende. I also love the metafictional works of people like Umberto Eco.

As a child I enjoyed Agatha Christie. Her ability to show the dark side of seemingly idyllic English villages and lives, still fascinates me. At his best, Stephen King has a similar ability – the exploration of seemingly normal lives pulled apart by sinister events or dark impulses.

I still enjoy good detective fiction – writers such as Gabrielle Lord, Ian Rankin, Lisa Gardner and many others.

At university I studied a range of Australian authors with my Honour's thesis being written on Peter Carey's *Illywhacker*. At the time I found his work to be a breath of fresh air and I have continued reading many Australian authors including Kate Grenville, Tim Winton, Helen Garner, Gail Jones, Patrick White and Janette Turner Hospital (whose writing I truly admire), to name a few. We have an enormous depth of talent in Australia and my shortlist has merely scratched the surface.

It is always a delight to discover fiction which is truly imaginative. Books which fall into this category for me include *Life of Pi* (Yann Martel), *Perfume* (Patrick Suskind), *The Raw Shark Texts* (Steven Hall) and anything by Haruki Murakami.

There are also books which I have enjoyed for the sheer beauty of their writing. Novels such as Shirley Hazzard's *The Great Fire*, Ian McEwan's *Atonement* and Cormac McCarthy's *The Road* can be savoured for almost their every word.

Finally, my list would not have even scratched the surface without mentioning: A.S. Byatt, John Fowles, John Irving and Margaret Atwood.

And believe me that is just the beginning!

Q: You've just finished writing your second book, how did the experience compare to the first?
Unfortunately it doesn't become any easier!

I believe there are two truly amazing points when writing a novel. The first comes when you are visited by the original idea. It is an idea which seems entirely unique and which must be explored. It is an idea which you believe can sustain your interest as a writer (and your readers' interest).

Reading group questions for *The Mother's Tale*

The Mother's Tale is a provoking, unconventional novel daring to explore one of society's last great taboos – the idea that there are some women who are quite simply neither naturally maternal nor nurturing. Below are some questions which could be used as starting points for your reading group's discussion of some of the topical issues raised by *The Mother's Tale*.

1. The narrator of *The Mother's Tale* remains unnamed throughout the novel. Why do you think the author has chosen to do this? Do you think it is a successful device and if so, how and why?

2. *The Mother's Tale* breaks from convention in the fact that its narrator is not an immediately warm or likeable woman. At any stage during the reading of *The Mother's Tale* did you find yourself feeling sympathetic towards its narrator? If so, when did you lose sympathy for her? Did your sympathy return at any point?

3. The narrator provides the reader with a graphic description of the birth of her first child and its aftermath, where she had trouble bonding with the baby. In your opinion do you think this failure to bond can be seen as explaining any of her subsequent actions? Do you believe that the narrator's behaviour could be attributable to postpartum depression? Why or why not?

4. Do you think the hospital should or could have been more vigilant in picking up and addressing the narrator's ambivalence towards Cassie at the time of her birth? Do you think this would have made any difference to her subsequent actions?
   - What is your experience of, and views on, the postnatal care provided by hospitals and child-health clinics?
   - What is your experience of, and views on, the support provided in our society to families in general?

5. The narrator's husband, Daniel, is an important character in *The Mother's Tale*. To what extent do you think his actions can be seen as being either a contributing or driving factor behind the

narrator's actions and responses throughout the novel?

- Do you think Daniel should bear any of the responsibility for what happens in the novel?

6. The narrator claims that her relationship with Daniel is similar to that between herself and her father. Do you see similarities in the relationships, particularly when taking the roles of the narrator's mother and daughter into account? Do you see differences?

7. The narrator partly blames her mother for the lack of confidence which she experiences in her own mothering abilities. Do you think this is true?

- Do you believe that the mothering instinct is innate, or do you think it has to be learned?

8. One of the images used in *The Mother's Tale* is of a Möbius strip. In what way do you see the

---

* A Möbius strip is a mathematical construct which can be made by taking a flat band of material, giving it a half twist and then joining it. The resulting structure has only one side and one surface. Sometimes known as the 'eternity symbol', the Möbius strip has fascinated artists and writers since its discovery in 1858. M.C. Escher, amongst others, has used it as the basis for a number of his etched images.

image of the Möbius strip as being important to the novel? You may wish to consider this question with regard to both the nature of the narrator and the structure of the book.

9. *The Mother's Tale* is a self-contained novel told from the point of view of the narrator and main character. To what extent do you think her story can be fully believed? Are there any points in the novel where you feel the narrator's authority as storyteller, and ultimate source of truth for the novel, is undermined? How would any such undermining affect your reading of the novel?

10. What do you think has become of the narrator by the end of *The Mother's Tale*? Do you think it is important that the reader knows from where the narrator last speaks?

11. One of the books which the author says influenced the writing of *The Mother's Tale* is Dr Robert Hare's book *Without Conscience: The Disturbing World of the Psychopaths Among Us*. In this book Dr Hare describes a psychopath as: someone who is capable of 'using their charm

and chameleon-like abilities to cut a wide swath through society and leaving a wake of ruined lives behind them'. A person 'lacking in empathy and the ability to form warm emotional relationships with others . . . who functions without conscience'. To what extent do you view the narrator of *The Mother's Tale* as exhibiting psychopathiclike qualities? To what extent do you think she is simply highly narcissistic?